About the Author

I came into writing by way of a challenge and not one that I took on with any alacrity, but once I had given one opinion too many, it was presented to me that if I could do better then get to it. In carrying out any task that I am to put my name to it has to be to the best of my ability. I will never stop learning.

Dedication

I would like to dedicate this book to my mother and my sister Joan, and to Betty Valentine who threw down the challenge to write something different. Though they have all passed on, they are still remembered.

George Garner

THE SCORPION AND THE KNIGHT

AUSTIN MACAULEY
PUBLISHERS LTD.

ISBN 978 178455 738 6 (Paperback)
ISBN 978 1 78455 740 9 (Hardback)

www.austinmacauley.com

First Published (2015)
Austin Macauley Publishers Ltd.
25 Canada Square
Canary Wharf
London
E14 5LB

Printed and bound in Great Britain

Acknowledgments

I would like to thank Mary Bool; a friend, who in her time was a school teacher. Though she did not read all of the book due to technical faults with my computer and printer, she avidly read what she could and was quick to point out the failings in my grammar in the gentlest of ways to an ordinary lad that was trying his best.

Reflections

It was the time of the Kamsin, the curse of the poison wind; or the red wind as it was sometimes known. The days of the desert's heat seemed long and sticky when the hot sandy wind blew across the land like a bad breath, turning the vast, flat, arid low land soil into a sea of hot flaming sand; killing and swallowing all growth and men like an unstoppable monster that it was. This wind was born screaming; and like a petulant child would have its way. From its birthplace in the emptiness of the great African desert it moved relentlessly until it finally exhausted itself somewhere in the area of the Levant; where the mountains rose like a wall from the flat plain to arrest its progress.

Apart from its suffocating hotness in its passing; it inflicted on those unfortunate people caught within its realm with nought but wretched torment. Sometimes the cursed wind would blow for days; its confounded grit managed to get everywhere like an invasive canker.

As for travellers that chose to cross the emptiness of the waste lands; there was a need to show vigilance and be prepared for the signs of sudden heavy dark storm clouds that loomed malevolently across the distant horizon. Like a sagging curtain the cloud would hang lazily; threatening to cancel the sun's presence in what was once a clear blue sky; offering only a fearful warning of its arrival. The sand-filled wind roamed freely without a will to steer a course; stories have it told that the spirit carried harpies of the devil to hover like mad creatures on the wing in waiting to spy a victim. Without notice of its approach; sounds like the devil's horn blew wild with warning of its intention; whilst the jaws of death opened for the fools that refused to heed its warning. For the vanguard of death was not particular with its victims, the last sound a man would hear was the madding din of the wailing song of the devil's messenger. After the swirling grit silenced the traveller's screams; escape became futile; in passing; the hot violent wind wilfully sucked at the souls of men to claim it from their bodies. Just as quickly as the screaming slaves from hell feasted on their prey, they moved on in continuance to satisfy their insatiable appetite of unsuspecting souls.

As a witness to what had passed; a solitary sentinel watched from the high ridges overlooking the desert's plain; Robert Simmonwood had seen these storms pass by many times. Having the good sense and experience; he fled the omniscience of his lofty eerie to seek shelter of a cavern lower down the hill and out of harm's way.

He was a quiet, courageous man; who had had his fill of the warring service to his king; on the day of his leaving for his home in England; he was duped to remain giving up his longing expectations of cool winds and snowy winters that he had long missed, which now were almost lost in a fog of passing memory.

During his time of the Crusade he had faced many dangers, this was a land cursed with wasted blood and death, how long he would remain on the high hill top he did not know; but by recent order of his superiors; his mission was to wait where he was until a messenger sought him out. Simmonwood was an individual who mostly worked alone, happy in that undertaking; most men were, he believed, untrustworthy, tending to serve their own instincts and greed above duty. Yes, he thought, too many times he had placed his trust in others and too many times he found himself innocently tangled and helplessly bound up in the thick of other people's conspiracies. Power struggles of greater Lords whose service he was once bound to were thick on the ground; it made for a difficult and dangerous life. In war, Lords come and go; men die on the field of battle or by sinister means; he knew very few that died in their own bed peacefully. But his serving continued as if bound by the will of steel, of loyal obligation and by word of his given oath. Duty was what he was about; he was born to it; and the life of military service because of it. Back in his homeland; his father held lands in the county of Rutland in England; given to him by the Lord he then served; which in turn for was to be repaid in time of war when the King so demanded the service of those men to whom he had once given that favour.

In thinking of that service, he chuckled aloud; here he was in the King's service in the Levant being occupied as a lookout in the middle of no man's land, lodged in a small hollow with a shelter lower down in the hillside that he shared with his horse. At least they were loyal to each other having been together for so long.

Once the howling wind had subsided, blue skies followed; the sun immediately shone just as relentlessly as it had before the arrival of the storm; it was a time of interlude for nature to rid itself of bad its humours. During the time of the wind's duration, in his seclusion, Robert could only spread his blanket, keep low and wait for the storm's passing; idly, his time was spent talking and rationalising his theories to his horse; in truth, the mare was a good listener and there was little else he could do while the wind howled ferociously.

With the passing of the storm, he was conscientious enough to be scurrying back to his chosen position taking up his vigil of scanning the open space of the vast emptiness before him. The new outlying view from his rocky prominence was one that had changed the landscape dramatically; not a soul could be seen nor a mark on the untouched surface of the newly-blown settled sand that created new features to the shifting dunes. It was too soon after the winds passing to expect anybody to be seen; the desert was a place of burial, but he would not dare return to face his masters with weak excuses of failing to see or meet their messenger's arrival.

That was Robert's purpose at this God forsaken point on the edge of civilisation overlooking a great emptiness of the sandy waste land.

He was to make contact with a stranger whom he had never before met; and whoever he was; Robert was strictly instructed that the message being carried was of no concern of his. Woken from his sleep and dispatched in the dead of night so that no one would be aware of his leaving; he had saddled his mount and entered into the cold of the dark night; but not before swearing a vow of silence; shivering in a state of drowsiness in a cold empty chamber being not fully awake. Bound by secret orders that were explicit; no questions were to be demanded other than a password; and he was to regard this messenger with the highest of importance and shown respect. Who this mysterious rider was; he did not know; only that it was of the greatest importance that he protect the messenger, with his life if necessary, and to safely bring him to Acre.

Politics of the Court at this time were turbulent if nothing else, too many people were thirsty for war on both sides. In such situations, no one was trusted; the prizes to be gained were imaginary; in the belief that war could fill empty coffers and inflate the standing of avaricious men amidst other leaders; and followers were many.

To avoid any deception at the point of meeting with the messenger; and in the interest of good security; Robert was to receive something to validate his being the true messenger. A remnant of material would be presented bearing a Rosy Cross to signify his being of who he was supposed to be.

In his past days of patient waiting; it sometimes amazed him to discover that the traffic across the desert was sometimes not as infrequent as he had first thought it might be. Some days went by when there was no movement at all, though when he did see riders; he had no idea of whether they were hostile or not. So long as he kept his head down and was not seen or threatened; he remained safe in his appointed place.

Apart from the storm just passed; there were other dangers out on the sand; what manner of a man, he wondered, would take such a risk with his life? He showed courage crossing the sands alone; probably a traitor leaving before being discovered; if he carried his master's plans he would be truly valuable. That was not his concern; but then he thought; men change their colours every day on both sides; driven by grudges against those they served.

He stretched his neck to give relief from the sweat and stubble that caught on the scarf around his neck; the sun had climbed high and he was losing moisture as if it were running through a sieve.

Out here life is hard; which makes for hard men who care little for anything, including God or Allah. For this was certainly bandit country and for him it was far safer to remain hidden to avoid attracting attention to their kind, though he was aware it was in the land to his rear that housed those greater dangers. Though poor and on the edge of the desert; this scrubland offered a possibility to hunt; that meant men who were keen of eye and quick to strike were about. Thinking on that subject unsettled him; all the more reason, he thought, for his caution; away from the eyes of others.

3

His mind slipped back to the time of his shelter from the passing sand storm, God help him, he told his horse, if his man is out there looking for us; he wished him luck; perhaps his God watched over him to guide him safely to us. He told his horse that with supplies running low; he had better be quick about it; because we can't stay here forever.

For the last six days he had fixed his war-weary, broad frame, statuesque like, half way into a hole and inconspicuously wedged between the rugged rocks on the sky line of the hills that gave him his view across this part of the open desert.

In the later morning, after the shadows gave up the protected places to the ferocity of the sun; Robert remained in his hollow in the ground, stuck under the cover of his dark heavy blanket. Planted in the hollow was the only comfortable position to watch through the gaps in the rocks and kept him concealed from view; as well as his only relief from the sun's searing rays.

On the lone high hills; scorpions and sand lizards were his companions; his eyes were as vigilant towards the rocky crevices as they were towards the far reaches of the desert. He endured the discomfort of the sweltering heat as part of his function; he was realistic to accept the conditions he had trained for, this duty was, he believed, no different than killing a man if required. Taking orders for tasks that others would find difficult; it was a duty he was prepared for and ready to run with, such were the risks of his work; if discovered, the penalty was severe resulting in painfully being tortured for being where he was.

His once pale western complexion had long gone; browned from the sun so much so that these days he was easily taken as a native; except to those that knew him well. His head was a thick curly mass of dark hair and sported equally a bearded chin; it was little wonder why he confused the guards when dressed in tribal style clothing. He was popular with women and loved their company; he took great care to ensure that they were not promised to any other man; tangled in such love games was a dangerous pastime; especially in this country.

During the cold nights that he spent lying with his horse for added warmth in the cave below; there was little comfort wrapped in his single blanket, sometimes the night's cold air set his teeth to chattering and sleep was difficult in such low temperatures. By morning he was more cramped than when he was crouched after a day's watching from his pit above. It was a long way from sharing the comfort of a bed with the whore from Acre alongside him; she knew how to raise a pleasing sweat on him to deflect his mind from thinking of anything other than her company; never mind the cold nights here. To make life more disagreeable through those cold nights; he was forced for his safety to forego the simple comforts of a camp fire, any sign of light from a dancing flickering flame in these high hills would easily be noticed; and once having raised the curiosity to other watchful eyes; they would soon know the place of its making. Such foolish action he knew would put vigilant hostiles on his trail and place his life and mission in utmost danger. Better that he complete his mission than suffer the unwanted experience of having to fight off the fierce tribesmen of these hills. These tribesmen had a wry sense of humour with their captives; he would rather not experience their form of entertainment. Besides; dropping his hand sympathetically to his genitals; he knew they were suitably content where they were without the need for any readjustments to their position.

It was difficult being a sentinel; enduring the waiting under the sun's intense heat; looking out into the emptiness has some drawbacks; it can make a man go mad; he needs a diversion; if only to think aloud of all manner of things as he often did. To pass his time through the empty gaps of the long hot day; Robert's mind had taken him down many avenues of enquiry. Curiosity had him straining his mind as for the messenger's reasons for taking what no doubt was a very great risk to his person. Though what this valuable information was to his peoples gain; he could not help but try to grasp at the justifiable reason.

Other than gauging the manner of men; he queried this messenger's intent; spy or traitor; or is he just selling information? If he was a traitor it struck him as a distasteful act that would leave little trust between them on their return journey. He posed the questions who; what; and why. A man is driven to turn against his own for many reasons, jealousy, a bad master a woman or revenge. Life is a little like a wind that turns against any man he mused; one moment you're risking all for your leader, the next you're faithful service is being swamped away like water in a drain. Life doesn't seem fair at times; but that's what happens when you're close to the centre of events; there's always someone or something going on behind your back; and when you're not aware; then look out; the world and all its weight has a knack of crashing down on you.

The rocks up here were hot enough to bake bread on; no wonder the lizards didn't stay on them for long; understanding their predicament he also felt that he too could be moving on.

Between the daydreams; his eyes continually scanned the expanse of land beyond the rocks that concealed him; he reached out to pick up a small pebble; Robert puckered his cheeks and popped the pebble into his mouth to draw moisture; it was an old trick; and it worked. Christ it was hot; what little moisture he drew onto his tongue was welcome. If it wasn't for the blanket covering his head; the sun's rays would be drawing on the fluid of his brain and likely making him dizzy. When he chose his place of watching; it was important to dig out a deep hollow in an effort to keep cool. Now in his makeshift tent under the protective blanket, his mind had absently lulled back to a time when he once acted as a messenger.

Yes, he mused raising a wry smile; human nature was no different wherever he had been. He had witnessed grievances on his own side to twist a man to extremes. The question shot back into his mind; could he trust this person on the journey back to Acre?

In many ways, this land of mixed peoples was ruled by men of a similar ilk to that of his own; there was always a pecking order in the line of supremacy as there was in each level of importance in the peerage. Though they were intelligent men; even greatly respectful to their religion; they were not beneath scheming to murder. In his observations, he included that of his own family as being no different; he was the youngest of his brood and had no means of inheritance to see him through life when his father died. Robert, like his other brother, had no other choice than to take up the crusade if he was to gain wealth and land to establish a position and a lineage for himself; that he had to earn for himself. He shrugged his shoulders as he thought about it; yes, that was the way life was.

Beyond the borders of humanity in the realm of the animals; it was there too. Life in the jungle held similar terrors for the weak and strong alike; unless they first moved against their siblings or natural enemies in their rush for supremacy and continuity. The similarity was clearly seen by him; though the only difference in his lot he believed; was that he was out here freezing his cods off in the cold of night. Suffering without water during the heat of day; doing his master's work as a sentinel for something that was no business of his. Sliding his tongue across his lips, his tongue rose against the dried skin; he became concerned about how long his water ration would last. By the Christ, did God in his wisdom choose for men their place in life; setting them against each other for His own amusement to see if they could raise themselves above such difficulties? It's a hell of a way to live life; but who are we to question Him?

Robert's mind was often in turmoil when he was without company; the things that went through his head even surprised him; but no matter how seditious or frivolous the subjects were; duty always brought him back in the direction to those that he served.

So here he was in this hellish place scratching his sweating arse feeling for irritating grains of sand that had him twisting himself to find comfort; left wondering when this messenger would arrive; if ever. Sweat prickled his brow; he rubbed at its running wetness with his sandy sleeve; only to wince as it touched and dragged against his raw tender skin. For six days he had been doing the same thing until the coarseness of his peasant like coat had made his skin eventually tender to the touch. "Damn" he winced; retracting his arm, damn this heat, he cursed.

Life was full of curses of one kind or other; bloody fool he was to be talked into such a role; cut off from his friends, hmph; what friends?, he reflected; contradicting himself sarcastically. His friends; or the friends he used to have were dead; his only remaining close friends he didn't and couldn't see very often because of the way they also lived. They were those that shared the same role in servitude as he did. His brother was one of those friends, he loved him dearly; yet it struck him that they never seemed to worry for each other; or not knowingly; believing that no harm would ever visit them.

Recalling a time he was summoned before the King on the afternoon of his preparations to depart the Levant; it was then that his service, like his leaving plans were long overdue; coming as an expected relief to his present way of life. He was fraught with suspicion after living on his nerves, riding the most dangerous of patrols for so long. More than most other men, someone he believed, though he knew not who; placed him at the forefront of the most savage areas away from civilisation to patrol. It had become an unpleasant joke to some around him; and not a very good one. Well, his allotted time was up and that afternoon he was leaving for the coast; it was almost too good to be true, but he was going. When the vent of his tent was noiselessly opened; causing him to react by turning quickly on his heels; almost knifing the king's messenger as he chose foolishly to test the knight on his ability to be aware of his presence. A row erupted for the foolhardiness of the man; and after he had explained the secrecy of his news; Robert's heart dropped. He had been summoned; it was unexpected and unusual; the King and he were not known to each other. That summons filled him with dread, death happens that way when you least expect it. When the mild affray blew over and all had settled down, he obeyed the command and visited the King. He struggled not to laugh at the memory of himself; how simple he must have appeared to be taken in so easily with words and promises. The audience was alone except for another that he knew not then; he was being praised for his courage; his ability noted; and his talents to speak the enemy's tongue was noted as remarkable. Robert that afternoon was enlisted into a secret unit of men solely doing the King's bidding in his time of great need; there would; he promised be rewards forthcoming. The young knight foolishly supposed that he could be excused for his lack of worldliness then; after all he was a willing subject. A straightforward but honourable knight unused to being in such auspicious company; how could he deny his lord? He would do anything for his King; the King was smart enough to play him as expertly as a musician's finger when passing over the strings of his lute; his guile knew that a refusal would not be forthcoming. Oh, he recalled how embarrassingly easy it was done, and he was soon to learn and understand just how slick a King could be with his grand words, encompassing arm and promises of riches.

In truth, looking back it was not a choice he was asked to make; having no say in the matter he had been caught in a trap to extend his service; he was not foolish enough to refuse the offer; which was, as it turned out, to be somewhat of a fait accompli; for a man to remain healthy and free; he could not have refused outright the offer from his king. Had he done so, the King would have been a bitterly disappointed; most probably for Robert it would have led to his never seeing his home again; and the remainder of his time in this land would have been inconspicuously confined to a darkened four walls of a cell and fed bread and water once a day if he was lucky. Now he was trapped and resented the feeling; not only for his ineptitude of mind but his inability to do little about his situation.

Much he was to learn of the politics of ruling; it came to his way of thinking that in reality; his time out here in Outremer had been spent sleep walking through brief moments of war and peace. As a faithful and diligent servant to duty; he presently realised events were not quite as straight forward as the intelligence that lay before him. During his training he began to wake up to the fact that not only was there a war fighting an enemy he recognised as the Muslim; but another of sorts that was raging behind the scenes between Church and crown and the unworthy subjects of the King. Seeing behind the veil of realisation; the truth of events had dawned on him; he began clearly to see the dangers that lay in waiting for him at Court should he have made the error to correct his superiors that lacked his insight. It was a close-run thing between ego and common sense; this new company offered a man illusions for improvement and advancement. Knowing other people's secrets became a burden and a danger; for why should men that had not bothered to recognise him before, suddenly need to converse with him; using him for the intention of trespassing on the King's confidences. It suddenly became imperative to his own safety that he was learning too much too quickly; with a sober mind he perceived that life would be more profitable for his health to distance himself from as much court contact as was possible.

His enlistment into the new nucleus of events was reasonably straightforward; some of the work excited him; it was certainly different from patrolling the desolate hills where tribesmen stalked him; or sitting around suffering the ennui waiting for something to happen.

These new methods of training were alarming to him; his objective in the field was to win no matter what the cost; honour and fairness even justness became obstacles that stood in his way. The weapons he had so painfully endured to practice with over the years to reach proficiency in were no longer of use. The battle line had changed; it surprised him to learn that he was under the tutelage of men that served the Holy Father; though they wore no uniform they were an arm of the Templer establishment. They were severe and demanding; stooping to all manner of devious methods that were acceptable to serve the prize of victory. For his own safety and welfare; he cared not to question anything that he was told nor questioned orders he was given or knowingly do anything that would serve him no good.

Though he dare not say it aloud; the King had not been very kind to him; with his new intelligence he deduced also that he was at times very sparing with the truth; and all that what was promised remained in wanting and in great need of fulfilment. In truth, the reward of gold did come occasionally; though at times it seemed small and in a trickle and not regularly enough for the risks he took; and the promised rewards of land and position could not be counted on. Too many high born nobles coveted the rewards of land; the King's need for armies weighed against the suppositions of intelligence. One day perhaps; such a reward would fall into his lap; Kings like Christ it seemed moved in mysterious ways. It became sensible and prudent for a man in his situation to lift whatever riches he could during service in the field as a compensation; better that or find himself starving to rely on the empty promises of his master.

A lizard sat nearby on a rock absorbing the heat from the sun; whilst Robert sought shelter under a blanket in the shade. It did not move from the sunlight; remarkably Robert watched its stationary body pulsating in enjoyment of its reverie. He looked away; not to see if his messenger was nearby; but to allow the creature his moment of peace. Peace he thought; when will he have peace, could there ever be peace in this land of turmoil? Whilst men do such covert work to kill as he; his enemies have likewise sworn the same deeds for their masters, for God and for peace.

An odd aspect to his new way of life; which he found great difficulty in maintaining was against everything he had been raised to respect. Learn to walk in shadows; never confront an enemy unless you have to. Run away and save your skin to save the information you have gathered; killing people was easy, he was told; killing himself, he was told, was better than being captured for the manner of horrors that were to await him should he be so unfortunate. That belief never sat right with him for a long time; it went against everything an honourable man would do, so what the hell was he doing here, he mused.

Since he was a boy, from an early age he had practised his skills of war alongside his elder brothers with sword and bow; in time he further developed new skills with horse and lance. The practice for war and the tourney became everything he would work towards; it made a man strong, he was told; and so it did. It not only brought honour among his contemporaries; but made him better off to boot. In his dreams it thrilled him to think that one day he would be alongside his father in battle, whom he respected and loved greatly. Nothing could have pleased him more than an opportunity to display his skills to his father; to underline the benefit of his effort in all the work. Robert Simmonwood was a winner; though he suffered for it having to bear injuries for some time, but winners don't moan nor do they show suffering. He was young then and full of spirit with not a thought in his head; other than becoming the victor in all he took on. In his age class, he proved himself to have the potential of a future champion and men approached his father to signify that they were looking for men just like him. In some circles he became the toast of the company, swelling his young head; though I doubt that his mother would have been so happy. She knew the truth; and it would have hurt her deeply to believe that men of high birth would have willingly trespassed on her need to steal him away. If anyone was pleased it was his father and his brother Edward, they were close. Edward was more of a scholar than a soldier; Robert knew well that when backed into a corner and the feathers were flying, it was wise to be at his brother's side; for once he was riled, he was more than a handful to overcome.

As for his father, well he was filled with pride; for he had sired the best young knights in the county. He was overcome with satisfaction and found it difficult not to be composed when the wine was flowing in his son's honour. Though Robert was his youngest; he was certain that he had the ability to rise above the others. Robert squinted across the openness; breaking a smile; more of irony than of amusement; for this is where it all landed him; here in a dirt hole at the edge of the earth on the brink of insanity and loneliness. With head bowed and resting on his open palm, Robert had entered into a storm of the past and present. All that he believed in seemed lost, and yet in this new life of the shadows he had learned so much of the world; in the company of those that would shape the destiny of ordinary men. He had become disillusioned; but had grown to grasp its terror and use it to strengthen himself further against the world at large. He never did get to ride alongside his father; one winter the old man went down with an ague; and in less time than he imagined a fever came and took away his life. Christ, Robert thought, he had seen more fevers and poxes take away the lives of so many good men in this land, friends too; he never expected illness to be so hungry for souls, but then life was cruel and unfeeling at times.

Doubts and Suspicion

In Jaffa, the King paced the floor of his royal quarters anxious for news. His recent attempt to take the holy city had been thwarted by bad conditions and dwindling supplies and near starvation of his troops; at the time he had believed that his chances of success had reduced drastically and decided to give up the cause. Strategically, it may have been the right decision to make; but despite his belief, it only fostered dissent within the army who were willing to foolishly wait and chance the outcome. However, that was in the past; and he knew he had to look forward in spite of his continued concerned of thoughts of right and wrong and how they were to play on his mind. To add to his troubled thoughts, he had received bad news from the North which concerned him. He had hoped that security and sanctuary for the safety of his army would have by this time become obvious to those under his command; proving that his decision to retreat was the right one. They had had enough time to have realised his reasons; Sweet Jesus, he justified; the winter was no longer biting at them and the clothes that were rotting on their hungry shivering backs had now been replaced with the comfort of new fine attire and they were comforted in a new warmer environment. He could have crushed the cup he held with the anger that surged though his being; they, his trusted leaders, were ungrateful for his forethought. Good men turned by a dream and hungry for a victory that could never become a reality; if only they had the sense to see reason. In the new season; perhaps he could return and renew his efforts; but for now he was relieved; the people were quiet; at least he was thankful for that. Though at times he sensed it was unusual and that made him suspicious, why could his followers not see that also?

In the games of kings; this unseasoned quietness brought nought but anxiety which led to unfounded rumours; there was not a word that was spoken to him that had him doubting the integrity of the speaker; even though he knew many of those around him were friends. It seemed this turning situation had a way of eating into his troubled mind, creating doubt that all was far from being as it should be. He slouched into the comfort of a favoured chair, looking about him as though he was able to draw something tangible from his gaze. This seasonable peace; the King knew was frail; he had no guide to knowing its reason; and because of it he trusted no one. Everything about him seemed to be waiting for his next move, haunting his thoughts and weighing his decisions. The war and the humour of those close to him made him into a sick man; but far from helpless; all he had to go on was a constant churning of his gut feelings; he counted his enemies and those that would be disloyal to him; watching them constantly; waiting like a lion to pounce to force the truth of their souls out into the living world. This time there were no obvious indications as to who held the strongest grievance against him; for there were many; he knew too well that he had enemies that coveted the throne and were willing to go to extreme lengths to achieve their aims. Therefore, it proved a prudent and diligent cause in the use of the chosen men he relied on for information; sending them far and wide to seek out grounds for his suspicions; but as yet there was nothing fruitful to report.

Being a wise King, he needed to be prepared; he was alone in a sea of hostility; not knowing who his real enemy was. He could not openly increase his military numbers for fear of the showing the Muslim the hand of distrust; and that he was using this time of peace to rearm and strengthen his army. This impotent situation was eating into him like some rotten disease; as if he was not ill enough already. Though he was thankful that what peace was abroad held; stability to the economy was providing a general prosperity; and he could not rail against that. The people were at ease in the towns; taverns were full and even farmers were content. As for his own people; they were learning that all Muslims weren't the enemy; it was a lesson that took some time to get through to them. So many times in the past; during the arrival of new groups of the militia; their ignorance failed to grasp that important fact; believing that all Muslims were the infidel and unworthy to be walking the streets of their newly conquered towns and cities. This lack of respect and disunity gave men a self-belief of superior arrogance that could only lead to provocation; resistance and to war. A situation that had taken a long time to overcome, yet there were those that nursed those feelings still. It was true that trade had improved; so who and why; asked the King of himself, would want to destabilise the peace. To ascertain a basis to his reason; he first asked; who was it that would gain most should such an outcome develop? The Muslim, of course, was the natural enemy, having been defeated and lost their lands; but they had made a pact and no matter how much it appeared that it was possible, he refused to yield to the idea that they would break with their agreement. In the North, a rumour was born that Antioch was moving towards greater cooperation with its warlike neighbours; under normal circumstances it was a move to embrace; but he knew Guy too well and he was one of that number that could not be trusted. He was ambitious and there was no secret abroad that he coveted the throne. He had already spoken to his master of spies who acted accordingly; his agents had been dispatched with little more than a thread of a story in the hope that they may yield a plausible answer. What the King needed was a reason to act; should word reach the ears of his enemy of any suspicion; it could lead to open incitement and further unrest. This anticipation of past error or misjudgement was resting on a future meeting with one of his agents; it was hoped that vital information to this end would enlighten the King's direction to right the hostility. Though he knew little of the timing of meeting; he stood optimistic that all would be clearer when he returned to Acre. Yet doubts ruined his optimism; in spite of the ability of the man who was dispatched, the place of their meeting was where he could not be protected; and success might give way to chance that was born on hope. A crop of peace can never be gathered in when watered by rumour and doubt; for it will yield suspicious weeds that can never agree to satisfaction or unity. By dispatching his man to wait in the thick of hostile territory for a messenger who had chosen the desert passage to reach him was a lot to put faith in. In his reasoning; he envisioned this as a way his enemies might work; to test him by reducing his intelligence in the field; in so doing, sever a vital requirement should he need to plan a future campaign. Agents, he believed, were vital; though good ones took time and money to educate; but should they perish in their duty, it was regrettable. Usually their loss indicated a reason for such action; being indicative of their enemy's designs or movement; but never to be taken strictly; for the game of spies can be confounding. Whilst he anxiously paced the floor, the King pondered; believing that the chosen agent was reliable; and such men he could ill afford to lose. His anxiety troubled his thoughts; he wanted to act decisively, but against who? The waiting game was not good for him, creating a tension that his body could well do without. Clutching at straws would only play into the hands of his enemies; and it seemed he had plenty of them. Power was a wild animal that was not so easily tamed; if screaming and lashing out would help overcome his frustration with this beast, he would willingly do it; but he was aware that it was a useless premise and one that would display a loss of control. It was the waiting of course that pushed one's frustration into action; if only he had an inkling of news. Everything, it seemed, was hanging on a thread of incredibility with the mission seeming desperately futile; like a drowning man, he would need to take deep breaths until the hoped for correct information arrived.

The Waiting

An unexpected wind hesitantly blew the blanket of Robert's shelter; the coolness it brought was welcome; it took him back into the depth of his memories, when his life appeared to be going so well. His mother's heavenly face, whose complexion was of spring apple blossom, appeared to mind, sharp and perceptive as any master spy caught the edge of his thoughts. Though he could not then foresee the shape of what was to happen; she could see far deeper into events; it took her to brooding over what she feared were to be churning times proving to be an ominous omen, a passing of dark clouds over the family's future; and all fell into place the instant the mother laid eyes on a visiting Bishop. Depressingly, her feminine intuition warned her of storm clouds that lay ahead; not only for her sons but for herself as well. His visit heralded the taking away of her boys.

She railed passionately at the Bishop, "Was it not enough for this King who once proudly stated that he was guardian and father of all his people; would he not be satisfied until he tore the heart out of every mother in the land?" The news that her boys were to leave broke her heart, though she held herself proud. Inside, fear gripped her; her eyes held back a dam of tears that she would shed only when alone.

The following morning the Bishop left, taking Edward and Robert with him; the boys, thinking it was a new adventure, were silently happy, unable to feel and see the worry in their mother. Taken with exuberance and alacrity of joining the army; escaping from the boredom of life and estate management, her boys betrayed her by the show of their eagerness to follow the Bishop. Robert closed his eyes recalling the scene that morning and wished for it to happen all over again so that he could change the heartbreak his mother suffered. In the great hall he discerned their mother lecturing him and Edward on their duties to the King; and honour to the family name, knowing how proud she was; it was the only way she had to withhold herself from breaking down. She was a stoical woman who refused to show what her gentle heart really wanted to say in such situations. The leaving was very moving; they left with long embraces and quiet words that didn't say enough of what they truly meant or felt; but that was down to a young man's heart and the willingness not to show signs of weakness of character; especially before a King's messenger. On thinking back, he would have drowned his mother with affectionate kisses and have reassured her that there was little or nothing to worry about. But most of all, he would have assured her that he loved her without a need to shed the tears that did finally break her heart in two. Though both her sons served the King and faced the enemy many times; they both remained well and wrote to her making sure that fact was known. It must have been little compensation for her to read those letters; knowing that in his mind he saw her constantly viewing them in anticipation that the next piece of news would not be so acceptable. Though he had no way of knowing, she read those letters as if she enjoyed the heartache which was unknown to the boys; and how her tear drops fell for the long days ahead. For Robert and Edward; they did not really understand what a mother's love was all about, but time and events were changing that supposition.

Never in a two lifetimes would they have dreamt of the terrors of war and the suffering inflicted on people that were caught up along with it, but only being there and living the carnage and death and all the twisted symptoms of madness that goes with such a conflict does any man relate to history of how suffering affected them. For those men that served it was the way of life; it was thrilling and heroic and he had lived it all; still less than twenty six years of age, he sometimes felt very old at night. All in the name of righteousness and their King; if he was to live out his life to an old age, he would never know the numbers that gave up their lives for similar reasons. That's what being a Knight in a King's army is all about, he thought with a huff of resentment, what a crazy world.

Robert stretched his cramped body trying to become a little more comfortable in the pit he called his resting place; he was being cynical and knew it; though his turn of mind had it that if his messenger failed to show before sunrise the following day then he would have to leave without him. He had grown used to the stink of the sweat of his unwashed body, being half ashamed that at times the smell had him turning his head for fresh air; even some of the creatures seemed to give him a wide birth.

Robert had proved himself a good soldier, but what really got him noticed was his ability to communicate and mix with the local people who, understanding his efforts to speak with them, encouraged him all the more. Having proved himself to have gained this knack, he began to act, on occasion, as go-between for his friends in trading and communicating with women. He was popular and at the time it was a game; he was showing off and he enjoyed it. His ability, it seemed, turned against him, being the root cause for his being where he was today. A lesson learned, though too late for him; he could not go back because he had been tested by Templar agents and because of his hidden talent, he was condemned, as he saw it, to being driven as a student of further dialects whenever he was at home, that was in Acre. It was quite devious the way he was manipulated; they were the men that convinced him that rewards were forthcoming should he improve his talent. They placed him with a tutor; she was a whore who was in the pay of the Temple. He never knew that at the time, and she could be good for him and also very demanding. Knowingly she could not falter in her work; being off the street depended on Robert's growing command of the languages she taught him. The Templer teachers may have been religious, but they were harsh and very strict in their word; quick to deliver on their threats to whoever was under their control. Always they would send for Robert and put him through tests that they had devised, if he failed any of them the woman would be warned that they would replace her; and her fear was, she suspected that their idea of replacement would costly to her, being the price of her freedom or worse.

In these new ways of life survival, Robert was instructed not to run any unnecessary risk and he was always under scrutiny; the Temple had invested an interest in him and were careful not to see it wasted. That seemed difficult for him to swallow. Worst of all, and he shook his head in memory of disbelief of some of the methods he was taught to adopt, and whilst he accepted some, he dismissed others, resorting to his own way of doing things. These days his life was forever hanging by the thread of life and death; not knowing how or where or when death may come from. To be a spy master was no easy task; a man of his kind had only a moment to think and assess how best he could infiltrate his enemy or escape him; the situations he found himself in never gave his type the luxury of time to leisurely make up his mind.

His mind gave way to a long drawn out yawn of tiredness, it made him realise that the memory of those days seemed so long ago.

Robert's vigilance depended on keeping himself aware of what was going on about him, though the desert held his main interest; it was a credit to his skill that others could not see his movements or trace his position. For this reason he was often carefully moving his position, checking out for hunters or small bands of tribesmen that may pass by before returning to his chosen site.

He could never be lax about his security; though sunrise was a time of excitement; whilst it remained dark he always made his return to his hide away before sun up.

They were long days; planted like some withered tree straining for life; whilst he remained patiently huddled between two ancient rocks waiting for someone particular to appear.

It was not so unusual for a soldier sick of killing to turn his face to God; no man could tell him about death or survival. He had given and taken life without blinking; because of it, he had dwelt in the depths of his mind's damnation of conscience. Killing has a way of tearing at the soul; a man has to have the strength of heart to survive it or else give in to it and lose his soul. He ran his hand through his matted hair rubbing his scalp hard and thinking how fortunate that he had spared the world that outcome and those close to him to have escaped such a misfortune to befall them. Christ in his wisdom and despair of such a confused acolyte must have guided his mind into abandoning such thoughts for his own sake as well as those around him. Because of it, he somehow believed that he would not be condemned for the whores that he had lain with; or the killing that he had committed on the behalf of the Holy Fathers. Considering the few merciful acts he had performed, he hoped that his judgement day should stand well for him; at least he felt he was suited to being pardoned.

"God," he silently exclaimed; it was boring trawling his mind's memories; how long am I to wait here? His restlessness was a symptom of viewing this waste land; offering nothing to feed his intellect, only haunting memories. Not even a new smell to think on, the idle waiting was beginning to prompt him into believing that his being here was futile. Spies were everywhere; could they have been the cause of his being here as a lure; he should know, no one could be trusted, perhaps the stranger he was meeting had it in his mind to lay false plans. Screwing his face in opposition to his orders; he knew it was a puzzle that was of no concern, finding it hard to accept, but patience, he hoped, would be its own reward and his anxiety was, he hoped, unfounded.

The Old Man of the Mountain

It was late when the word went out from eagle's nest in Alemut; the home of the Old Man of the Mountain. Like an answer to a prayer; a chance opportunity had arisen from the strangest of meetings. From it, his devious mind had nurtured the seed of a plan, and who would have thought that another holy man from across the sea could yield hope for the Old Man of the Mountain to seize it as an opportunity to be rid of his enemies. It gave the Old Man great pleasure in choosing his best agent; the one he named the scorpion for the instruction of its delivery.

High in the windy mountains of another country; the waiting agent regularly checked the pigeon lofts in readiness for such a message to arrive; ready to act whenever any such order was sent.

The Old Man of the Mountain was not one to ignore any opportunity that he would benefit by; especially one that could free him from the bond of an agreement he was once coerced into accepting. Although a holy man; he was also a man of immense culture and intelligence; deeply taken by the sciences of the day. Hassan Ibn al Sabbah was already a legend; whose name had fearfully crossed the lips of every individual in the land. He was a Shi'i fundamentalist whose life ambition was to put to rights all the wrongs his faith had suffered from others. Being a religious fanatic, he would not rest until he rid the world of those that opposed his will; especially those Seljuks and western invaders that had once beaten him. Time would be his ally; his enemies would pay dearly and publicly; knowing that one day death had come to them via the hands of his devotees. So determined was he, that he chose his moments to strike when his enemy least expected it; for maximum effect the tools that delivered the final blow would strike whenever the chosen place was at its busiest. His enemies were not the only ones capable of a little duplicity and connivance in their plans. Allah; praise his name; had delivered such good fortune to him; his faithful servant; from a westerner greedy for power and seeking his help. It was indeed a fortuitous day; one that would herald the demise of those enemies he so detested. The plan was simple, cunning and true in most part; it amused him that the westerners, in his eyes, were falling apart in their unity like cracking eggs. Once the plot was in place; doubt and uncertainty he presumed would accelerate the process of his plan. His most faithful servant, the scorpion, was resourceful and capable to deliver this information to the Franj; if on delivery of this vital news; doubt were to invade the mind of the Temple's Grand Master; his agent possessed such persuasive skills to convince him otherwise.

True to the master's demands; the emissary would without question set out immediately; travelling mainly at night as was ordered. Though the journey held many hazards; the agent was equipped to deal with most dangers; it was not a new experience to escort danger in his pursuits; for the Old Man of the Mountain was not a fool in his choice of emissaries. Death and persuasion; was this emissary's stock in trade; but he knew that the emissary would not countenance such a need as violence.

The hazards of the journey would be overcome; the desert's tribesmen knew better than to endanger themselves once the emissary made it known who was represented. Though the tribes were mainly hostile to strangers, they were fully aware that the power of the Old Man of the Mountain was absolute. Long ago; his devastating shadow had fallen across the desert encampments and caused him to demonstrate the strength of his word and punishment to those that had stood against him. That was a day women wailed the death chants of their men's passing; children also suffered a similar fate. The tale is never told openly; for it carried the weight of the suffering of villages and encampments that were affected. The males were rounded up; the women whipped and made to watch as their husbands and sons were buried alive. Only the sand carried the evidence of their deed; such horror could never be forgotten and ever since no matter how deep the resentment was, no one has dared stand in the way of the Old Man; such was the dread of his vengeance. When the soldiers of the Old Man returned; the tribes were quick to swear never to oppose him or that no emissary of his would ever be harmed or approached in the future. Bad news travels fast in the desert; and to this day it has remained that way. Only foolish men harbour revenge against such an antagonist; beneath their outward belligerent ways they remained bound together by faith; they all bowed to the East each day and to lie on their word was nothing less than to lie in the face of their God. This was no guarantee of a safe passage for the messenger; but it went a long way to ensuring that if challenged, acknowledgment of safe passage was sufficient to show respect to his emissary and the Old Man of the Mountain.

The nights were indeed cold and the days as hot as hell's fire, but the emissary would not desist; within the breast of the emissary was the knowledge that failure was not a recognisable trait of the hashashin. Travelling on horseback would be a drawback; camels would have been the better choice; for horses would find difficulty in surviving the desert's waste. After the desert came the mountains and plains; out there the Old Man's reputation did not stand for much; and being with a Franj would not be an option for safe passage to their destination. It was then that they needed to rely on the speed of horse; for that reason the emissary would set out with an extra steed to ensure the completion of the journey. Once into the desert it would not be long before the strain of the crossing would prove too much for the beast; it was expendable and necessary for its purpose.

The news that the emissary carried would prove vital to the Franj; their gratitude, the Old Man anticipated, would be enthusiastic. Anxiously the Old Man prayed for success during the travelling period of his agent; as for the demons that called themselves the warriors monks of the temple; who had in the past laid heavy losses to the Old Man of the Mountain's fighting men; their time was coming. He recalled the humiliation he suffered then; but rather than surrender to the victors, which would have been below his station, he had devised a pact of peace with them; offering to throw in his lot; acting as eyes and ears in the corridors of those countries that the franj was not be able to travel. He also had to pay for the Temple's protection; such as it was, but the payment of money was not a worry, only a consequence of dealing with these barbarian invaders. They had been spurned from the devil; to curse the people of the desert lands; the title barbarian described them adequately. That is what they amounted to in his eyes; they were coarse in their ways, unclean and without culture. Their brutality had no bounds, but they were the most disciplined body of fighting men that had ever been seen. It took a great deal of time and lost lives before the Muslim armies learnt how to bring their enemy to a halt; it was a difficult task and never complete.

The emissary had achieved good timing knowing that if all went well the arrival would be accurately timed.

Hell's Window

Robert sweated like a pig in this heat and scratched at himself knowing also that he smelt vile. In his time in this land he had learned to take a bath more regularly than he might if he were home, although abhorred by some of his so called betters; he had adopted the custom and grew to enjoy it; washing every day. He itched from his coarse clothing; yearning to be in something light and breathable; fresh and clean and alongside his whore in Acre. She was good for him, and she made him laugh and forget the work he was involved in. Christ, this life he felt could be hard on him; he was becoming irritable with his impatience; life was nagging at him to come to terms with what was going on around him.

Ironically; there once was a time when he believed everything in what he had been told, he was an honest man with brains of shit then; of that he was certain; learning that wisdom comes always after the fight. He now believed that he was lured to this country under a pretence; being told that the Muslim had broken his word he had once solemnly given to the Holy Father before God. Christendom was denied any further right of pilgrimage to Jerusalem, that poor travelling pilgrims had been cut down defencelessly on the roads; suffering vile tortures unnecessarily at the hands of the demons of Outremer. Pastor John, he thought, was driven by his own agenda and was very convincing when it came to the rabble. He was an outrageous fellow and grew strong because he was accepted by the mass of unintelligent people. But he was later to learn his mistakes and the army marched onward without him.

Robert was nobody's fool now; but it is fair to say that men who are not fully enlightened with the necessary information at hand are easily misled, being only able to form an opinion on what they are told. That, he acknowledged, was acceptable and of no fault of their own; but he, with his new learning and perspective of what he encountered, could see himself turning into a maker of mischief at times. It was not in him to be argumentative but he could see easily the way that his liege bent men's will; like the willows in the wind.

Payment for such experience came at a price as high as a man's life; whilst his present judgement came from his own mind and from what he was able to see with his own eyes. Once; he would not dream of challenging his leaders, no matter how he looked at politics; but as true as the sun rose in the east; he knew in his heart where the unrest from liars lay; after all he was a go-between;

carrying messages; experiencing what was likely to occur before any decision had been implemented. Man on both sides was driven by greedy eyes that rested on lands that were not theirs; looking to the heavens he could not believe that this ridiculous turmoil of life was meant to be.

More sand lizards skipped jerkily across the hot rocks; catching his attention; stopping momentarily to catch the heat before speeding on to the cover of the shade beneath the rocky ridge.

There was no doubt in his mind that those that lived under this searing heat on the Devil's arse must by nature have had a short temper; for the heat in this land was reason enough to turn any man short-tempered.

Though this land was shaped from the furnace, he somehow felt there was purpose to the hard and cruel outcome of life. Was it a punishment from God he wondered; well, that he could not tell; but one thing he did feel in spite of the way things were, was a strange allure in the beauty here that even pulled on his heart. Something he could not explain in words; though he knew that one day he would leave; yet in his innermost being the land would cling to his memory like a sickness that would either kill him or force him back.

He clawed at the fuzzy itching growth around his face, "Shit," he exclaimed; under the cover of his blanket he could hardly see the flies that were buzzing excitedly around him; he knew by their bites that they were feasting on him. If it wasn't an aching back that made him fidget from the grit and stones that he had slept on, it was the cold; "Jesus," he complained, a bed would be something to enjoy and with a note of yearning believed it would be even better with a woman in it too. "What the hell was I thinking of!" If only he was able to freely walk around and stretch his legs. Annoyed that boredom changed his temperament; his head was a jumble of thoughts; he clawed hard at it wanting the jumble to leave him be; it seemed a waste of time to dwell on such subjects. He closed his eyes as a searing hot breeze blew in through a gap in the rocks washing over his face; how he longed for coolness? He thought of the sea; its gentle drifting wind that would ease and refresh a man from the summer sun, mm, he mused before opening his eyes onto the vastness of an empty shimmering desert. He could remember it, but he was careful not to lay awake at night pining for the green meadows of his home in England, dreams such as those could pull on a man's heart and drive him to a sickness in the head. Birth places held so many ties, not only of his kin and friends that he had missed, or almost forgotten after so many years. Such memories proved to be heavy baggage that a fighting man could well do without. Memories, he shook his head as if attempting to empty it of those thoughts; no sooner had he tried to put them aside, they popped back into the mind with an annoying insistence, he could not help fear for those he suddenly remembered; were they alive, and did they ever have a thought of him. The war had been a curse on so many good men just like him; he looked away trying to shield his thoughts from the personal losses of good friends whose lives had been wasted. Why, he posed, was it God's reason to wrench families and countries apart, was it for the sheer pleasure or punishment or the making of His own amusement; what confounded game was He playing with us?

He dropped his head; it was time to move; get a change of scenery and time to alter the rhythm of his mind. He was unable to stand erect for fear that he would be seen, therefore he had to scurry around from place to place to check that he could see all without being seen himself.

Time here seemed to draw out; home, the word came out slowly and with an attachment that was dreamy and far away; just as was his day dream. It was a distraction he once remembered; telling his mentor of the difficulties of not day dreaming and in reply it was suggested that he should try praying. He almost laughed aloud in his face thinking of it.

To him the image of home lingered less and less in his mind these days though it never buried itself permanently; somehow he felt strangely aware that it was not going to be there anymore. A premonition that he once had prompted a feeling that he would die here; though not in battle; more that he was caught up somehow in a way that he could not explain.

Time made all manner of things turn inward when not occupied in his work, curses, he felt grit in his teeth, when will this stranger appear, and damn him for who he was and keeping him here?

A man, he mused, no he remembered the phrase; he was informed that a rider would come out of the desert. He thought on that a moment; so, it could be either a man or woman or youth. He dismissed the thought partly; for no woman could travel this desert alone. He had thought on this subject yesterday and the day before. Communications were directly with the Marshall or so it seemed; a wry smile broke on his crusted face, if it was a woman he wondered if the old Templar was bedding her himself; Templers were men of God and didn't debase themselves so, no; he should be ashamed to think that way. In truth there were Templers; and in war; they are men first before they think of their sacred duties. Rotten apples turn up in the barrels all the time.

Thoughts filled his head to stop the flow of the rubbish that his mind was trawling through, and he didn't like what he was thinking much. He was back onto the messenger, strange he thought how the mind suddenly throws up a rotten apple; no; it couldn't be.

His sole duty was that once they had met; it became his prime objective to get that person safely to Acre and the Marshall. If needs be, in times of danger he would defend the said messenger with his life to save that person from harm or falling foul to any forced admissions. He rolled this odd command over in his mind, he felt uncomfortable that somehow in the wording of his orders was a clue to his suspicions; that his messenger was likely or could be of royal patronage. To show respect for a traitor would not come easy, even though the Temple was making good on it, spying was one thing; but turning against one's own, well a man like that could not be trusted. Whatever the information was; it would save a great many men from death; though he felt it still did not cut cleanly with him. The more he dwelt on the matter the more he began to dislike and mistrust the messenger he was ordered to show respect to. Why risk his life for a worthless turd that turns away from his own, it was asking a lot of him. His own safety he felt was being casually overlooked, without men like him they would temporarily be hamstrung. He believed he held the right to measure his own security, and test the rider, courier man or woman; damnation, gritting his teeth as these thoughts put his blood to boiling, emissaries, couriers, messengers whatever they called themselves, painfully he learnt to mistrust them all; be it of high or low birth. So be it, no matter how much that he huffed and puffed; he was a servant to the King and believed sometimes that he did not always know best. He had been amongst those that used the darkness long enough to know if a trust was to be held between them the moment he was to set eyes on his man. Orders were not always so easy to go along with, no by God they weren't; and exhaling a heavy breath he believed that these missions were leaving him more and more exasperated.

It was probably the loneliness; life he felt was passing him by, he had been on these shores now quite some years that many he had almost forgotten, time and events passed by so quickly.

After such extended times of thinking; he was not so keen to view his own image, believing that he must have aged somewhat; rubbing a hand roughly over his face he felt the tousled untrimmed beard and felt dirty. Presently he probably looked like a turd; he certainly felt like one. Though he was in no hurry to be back at Acre, he was aware of the commands of court. He had gained an intelligent understanding of the King's cunning and dared not show it; for being too clever amounted to being too healthy for one's own good. The court was a nest of vipers; and it did not take him so long to learn about the shallowness of his so-called bickering betters. Caught in the middle of truth and non-truth within the intrigues of power; he no longer knew what was truly right from wrong, and the world of rumour seemed to rule and sometimes men, good men, met with accidental deaths that could not be fully explained. He had experienced this much; that what appeared right in his topsy-turvy world may not always turn out how things first appeared. Politics and events within his occupation had corrupted his mind somewhat, and importantly he had learnt only how to survive for himself. Behind his back he sensed men used him as the butt of their humour at the manner of his dress and at times they even openly sneered at him. But for his own kind and rank, well that was a different matter altogether. He had few friends; he enjoyed money when it came his way like any man would; but he didn't scheme and covet it to achieve more. Nor did he flaunt it; for that was a shortcut to ending up in a dark alley with one's throat cut.

Huddled under the blanket listening to the whooshing of the hot low driven wind around him; he gave out a short almost manic laugh over his naivety and high ideals; he could go mad with his brooding; but that was the way he was and he knew no way to change it. When others spoke of high ideals, he thought little of it, rather studying the character that spoke was much more revealing. Robert no doubt had become the ultimate cynic in himself and in the eyes of others.

A sudden light puff of air lifted the corner of his protective blanket bringing him back from his theorizing state to the present, he knew that he should at all times be alert and not let his mind wander under these conditions.

Wind flicked at the blanket again; this time bringing with it windblown grit catching his eye, he winced at being caught off guard and cursed. The blast could leave his eyes smarting for a day and he knew better than to rub it, shit he exclaimed; it was now possible he could miss his expected visitor. In anger he blurted out through his teeth, "Where the hell could he be?" He could not stay in his high look out position indefinitely; this was going to have to be his last night in the barren rocky look out; he had named as hell's window.

He needed to piss and stretch his legs; sitting in this cramped hole makes a man stiff. In his thoughts of disappointment that his expected messenger was not showing tumbled around his head, resigning himself to failure and possible explanations later; he may have been followed and fallen foul of brigands along the way. Sundown was to be his deadline, he would not wait any longer, his supplies were already desperately getting short; with barely enough to get him back to civilisation.

The Meeting

As the thought of that outcome of leaving dawned on Robert, something resembling a moving shape on the shimmering horizon formed to catch his attention. He screwed his eyes up tight in concentration, believing he had caught a darkened shape in his squinting vision; a tear streamed off his cheek as he strained to notice that there really was something moving out there. No need to get all excited, he told himself, it may not yet be my man; and it would be quite some time before he could be sure it was him. In his need to see better; he rubbed his hands together to rid them of any traces of grit before reaching for the edge of his shirt. Lifting a corner to wipe away any grit; he inspected it to ensure its cleanliness; before coming in contact with the rough material; as the material caught the eye he gave a startled jump; it became irritated causing the eye to glisten with a wetness. Immediately his lid closed making him wipe the area of the eye again, he cursed his luck; holding the eye closed he let the natural fluid flood. Though the irritation remained, the flooding fluid helped to clear away grit that had settled there; he failed to open his eye peering for the rider, Christ; the stinging persisted, the irritation was fading and his vision seemed glassy. He shied away from the light trying again; with one hand cupped across his brow to shield the glare; whilst his other hand held open his eye refusing to avert his gaze from the dark shapeless specks advance. Attentively, he watched the shapeless form slowly growing to become more discernible as it approached, blurred by the sun; he had the time to wait until his vision returned. He moved his gaze pausing to rest his vision; squinting, he found it better; the distorted speck took better shape. "Christ's bones," he exclaimed in an audible excited tone; raising his heartbeat in expectation; this could be him. I don't believe it he muttered; he has done well this man; conceding he was all balls and no brains. The figure held its course and Robert felt relieved; convinced that this was his man. Although the rider remained distant; he noted that he was travelling at a steady casual rate and with certain intent towards the pass and his direction. His wet eye was drying up; which came as some relief. Well, he mused, so far, it seems that he is alone; let's hope it stays that way. Watching the stranger's progress he scanned all directions making sure that no other specks appeared beyond the rider on the horizon. His thoughts were erratic though cautious; better err on the side of caution and not make any moves, it matters not how long he waits below for me to make certain no one has followed him.

On arrival at the appointed place in the mouth of the pass, the horse's pace slowed to cautious advancement over the last two hundred yards; like a hawk Robert watched closely his every movement; finding it difficult to view his features.

If this was his man, then he would proceed further into the pass, he might not like being left in the open but Robert dared not take any risks. The rider urged his horse on showing a caution of his own, he liked that; it showed he knew his business; he also watched as the rider carefully scanned the higher ground; but Robert remained concealed not moving a muscle. The messenger was as cautious as Robert; for almost nothing escaped their scouring eyes; standing in his stirrups as if for a better view; the fellow scanned the rocks about; but still no sign of the guide was to be had. He showed more sense than to call out but proceeded to pull out a scrap parchment from his clothing to check his directions. His movements were short and measured; it was if he was making himself be seen; giving Robert a better view that he was openly showing himself. At least there was nothing suspicious that took Robert's attention; the messenger was ordinarily dressed like any Arab in black galabia and shiwal. That meant little to him; under those robes Robert knew that he could be discreetly armed. He must have sensed that he was being watched and displayed his willingness to wait by dismounting; he patted his horse's head to probably reassure him before the stranger led him away towards the shade of a rock. Showing himself further to be in no hurry or to ride on; he cleverly and more importantly sought refuge; using his place of resting for a defensive position. Robert grew satisfied and could plainly see it as a statement of his arrival; and an invitation to his watcher that he was waiting for his guide to examine him.

Caution; always caution; he was not about to turn his back on the knowledge he had absorbed in his training; and continued a while longer watching hawk-like every movement. Robert was not prepared to be so easily convinced; the rider was not careless enough to be a spectacle for all to see. On the contrary, he was good and confident; knowing his business; allowing the one that watched a while longer to settle his mind. There was respect here; Robert took one last look for any further detail of the rider who may not appear right in his hesitant mind; a simple clue may betray something of his true identity behind the tightly wound scarf around his face.

The road that led into the pass was open and exposed; catching the sun's brightness that bounced off the rocks; it was hard on the eye; the stranger was the vulnerable one in open hostile surrounding; barren without shade; this was not a good place to be caught alone. Hidden from view, Robert was finally satisfied that this was his man; then giving one final scan over the horizon to ensure no one had followed; he scampered down to his horse and mounted up to meet his man down below. Thankfully there were no other figures in the distance; giving Robert peace of mind from any unexpected company.

It was moving scree off the slope that alerted the stranger to Robert's approach; and he noticed the slight attentive jerk of the stranger's head to the disturbed sound; at least it showed he was alert. There was no sway of attention away from the stranger; nor the penetrating gaze and untrusting eyes behind the scarf. Watching Robert closely as he made his way down the track; the stranger's horse was soothed from its nervousness, the man reacted as Robert expected; he had quickly mounted and cautiously made ready to meet his guide.

Robert's eyes likewise stayed on the stranger taking in all the details; most important were the arms he carried, strange it seemed; there were none to be seen; though Robert knew well that no man would cross the desert unarmed; whoever he was; would soon be revealed to him. The two riders scrutinised each other from a short distance apart, there was little or no trust between them; in this line of work it could cost a man his life being casual. Robert noticed through the folds of this messenger's scarf, the depth of his scanning eyes and his squinting flicker; it centred at the long straight sword at Robert's side and to the bow and quiver strung around his body; the stranger's eyes moved just enough to show a certain surprise that the Franj mounted soldier carried such a weapon. It would have come as a greater surprise to learn that Robert could ride and use his bow as good as any Turkomen archer. During the time of their coming together they both sat erect in their saddles, silently; a short distance apart; though fractional in the time, the silence seemed long. Their eyes were fixed assessing each other's worth; with still not a word spoken.

Robert raised a hand hailing a salutation; "As-salaam-alaikum"; a reply came though; "wa-alaikum-as-salaam"; it was hardly audible, the mouth that spoke from behind the cover of the scarf. At first it appeared to Robert that the rider really was unarmed; though a nervous movement revealed a concealed glint from a dagger hilt in his sash. Each watched the others heaving chests; they knew how it was between fighting men; the silence of suspicion and evaluation; but not a further movement; time passed; each remained in judgement of the other waiting expectantly for one or the other to break the silence. Surprise must have shown in Robert's eyes, from where he sat in the saddle, this stranger he suspected was either a boy or a young male; short in height and slight in build, there was no way of truly telling his size and age; but he was sure that he was young; though well-trained. The rider made no attempt to adjust his scarf and when he finally spoke up; his words remained muffled as before; being almost incomprehensible to Robert's ears with the sound of the breeze rushing around his head. He's doing this on purpose to disguise the fact that he's a youth, thought Robert. It seemed an obvious caution; the silence between the two horsemen lasted a little longer, the hand of the stranger slowly disappeared into his clothing; it caused Robert to stiffen slightly; his sword hand dropped slightly from the reins, but not enough to startle the stranger. When the hand was revealed; it resembled a fist; edging his horse forward; a ragged scrap of dirty cloth was revealed what passed as part of a Christian cross; it was offered to plain view in his open hand. That, Robert presumed, was probably taken from the uniform of a dead Templar; but never the less, it was what Robert was told to expect as proof of the strangers validity. The boy must have guessed that the sound of his voice could betray the age of his years; remaining silent, only nodding his head in recognition of the evidence that convinced Robert that he was the one expected. Alarmingly,

Robert did notice the unprotected hand that extended beyond the sleeve of the galabaya; it was small and slender, and that agitated him.

"I have been waiting for many days for your arrival," he said, "was there trouble?" a shaking of the head was the only gesture he received in return. From then on there seemed no point in making conversation; for it became obvious that the messenger's guarded reluctance might betray something further of his identity.

Robert was concerned and it only heightened his suspicions that he had fostered earlier; did he know something of this person, he wondered. Then as if thunder struck with a hammer; it came to him; Christ's Bones, Robert realised; it could be a woman!

Christ, it came as a silent roar of disapproval; I'll wager all I have on it.

He knew that something had struck him as odd when they met; it presently dawned on him how the hands had remained hidden; which most certainly would have been a giveaway. Urging forward his horse to come alongside the messenger, he stared hard, straining as much as he could to view what he could of the person; he wasn't sure, but was prepared to wait and see. He nodded but any effort to make casual conversation proved futile; the response was cool, almost a rebuff, he soon got that message and remained silent.

"We've a long way to go so let's keep moving"; that was more of a command than a friendly suggestion. With his suspicions raised, there grew an annoyance within him; one, for being sent on this mission and also the risks he had taken. It was insulting having to wet nurse a woman or a youth, alas he sighed, that's what it's come to. She must be a sour-faced bitch of a wife from the harem that had fallen out of favour; or perhaps about to become one. Oh yes, he surmised, now he was sure that he could most certainly expect trouble.

Many thoughts raced through his mind; what use was she? I'll wager, she'd overheard plans being discussed and made it her opportunity to escape her fate of the harem. Whatever she's got, it must be damned important and she has risked everything to get here. Sure in his mind that he was escorting a woman, he took to assessing her worth. She's fled for some reason, or perhaps she's a princess who is being forced to marry another man, come to that, she's even more of a threat now once these plans get aired; death, he felt, could be close on the wind. He became angry at his being here, and halted his horse wanting to give her a piece of what he thought; turning towards the rider he prevaricated; changing his mind.

It was here, through the lands of Trans Jordan, that held the key to the major caravan routes bringing great wealth to the traders and those that deemed it their right to place a tariff on those passing through. Along with the caravans came all manner of peoples and their troubles. They attracted bandits like a turd attracted flies; that's probably why she skirted her route, clever little bitch; and she has guts to make a desert crossing alone.

Most men wouldn't do it; that worried him also; whoever heard of a woman crossing the desert alone? No, that did not sit well for him; was it likely that she had an escort until she was within miles of their meeting place? He would have to be watchful and alert; careful that her friends didn't catch up to them.

The land hereabouts was also a constant worry and threat to those that presently held the peace of this area, for whenever a siege of a southern city was imminent, these arterial routes were used as a back door to move bands of men without any signs of them ever being seen. This back door was a troublesome factor to the military outposts; this was a huge land and difficult to scout without knowing what was going on behind your back; it was not always possible or safe to have scouts out at the times most needed.

Having accepted the rider as almost the genuine messenger, Robert steered his mount in closer alongside her; there was no easy way to say it and he had to make his position clear; better let her know now than allow her to think me a fool.

"They never told me to expect a woman"; the tone of his voice told her everything she wanted to know of her escort. His words fell on her like a collapsing wall; though she was trained well enough not to allow him to detect any sign of surprise.

So this franj was observant and no fool; but he was arrogant like the rest of his kind and smelt like a shit hole in a brothel. It was no more than she expected; they told me that the franj had manners; well, she had been talking to the wrong people when they made that assessment. He has shown me no courtesy and was rude to the point of provoking her into a retort beneath her station. She huffed under her scarf; he was probably like all the rest; coarse and without manners; now she suspected that he was going to need watching. Barbarian was a good name for the Franj she thought; and she decided it would not be worthy of her to enter into any battle of words with him later; but it would be sensible to warn him to keep away from her.

His dark staring eyes did not take kindly to what he looked upon; she was trouble; he sensed from the start and he was far from happy. From what he had seen from her eyes earlier told him that she was a cold one, empty and dispassionate; displaying the emptiness of the company he had gained; well, Jesus Christ, he asked himself; what does she know of anything? It was as good as an insult for him to judge her so; though she did not let on that she understood his tongue and his cause for bad manners; rage filled her.

With the sound of the wailing wind and sand swirling around them; Robert realised that there was no point in trying to make conversation; he gestured that the rider should keep up close to him. Although he felt no threat from the youthful female, he did feel uneasy. He had already noticed the concealed daggers in her sash and wondered how useful the female was with them? But if that was to be the case he would like to know who sent her; whoever they posed to be, foolishly they did not know this knight.

To exercise his caution of not being followed, Robert had to risk keeping to the higher hilly trails to give him a constant vision across the flat low lands below and the slopes before and behind him; if there was anyone following he would certainly see them and treat his young friend with a different kind of courtesy she required. He did not give a damn or show a care in making it obvious that trust did not travel deeply between the two riders. There are times in every warrior's life when apprehension would form knots within the gut from unease and mistrust of his company; that feeling was with him now.

She sensed his feeling wanting to tell him that she was not followed; she also knew the risk they were running being on the high ground and in open sight. Wanting to tell him of his foolish exposure where he allowed himself to be seen, she decided otherwise; he was a headstrong and untrusting fool; she hated this Franj. Along their silent trek, Robert offered no information, neither did he try to make small talk as a gesture of friendship. As ordered, he did not even probe into the reasons behind this clandestine meeting; he would carry out his duty and escort the silent rider to his master and be done with her.

He said all this to himself, yet there were a hundred questions he wanted to pose to this female; if only in the interest to know how secure his own position was. Throughout the day they rode without stopping; it was hot and occasionally a cooling breeze blew that was welcome; it also brought with it grit that clung to the sweat on his face and irritated the skin. They were both to travel far and silence would be their companion along the way. Silence would not be a hardship between them as far as he was concerned; after all he spent most of his time alone. He was more company with himself and assured of his safety whilst concentrating, searching the wind-swept plain and looking out to avoid trouble.

Whilst she kept up to the guides pace she cursed his back for his lack of respect as an emissary; she was risking her life to deliver this information, yet this arrogant Franj thought nothing of it; only that she was a woman. She sneered behind the scarf that he was unworthy of his race to ride alongside one such as she; given her way she believed he deserved a flogging; she would make it known to his superiors once they arrived in Acre. Along the exposed higher ground that bordered precipices, Robert picked his way along stony winding trails where patches of seared grasses and wild flowers struggled to survive. There was little of any soil at their height to create fertile growth; what soil existed was hard-baked and made up of grit, sand and small stones underfoot; little room for grasses to flourish; but game that was about grazing on wild herbs and the scrub; though anything green was hard to see.

He travelled without haste; needing constantly to be vigilant, not wanting to be seen, but that was a risk he could not help; sooner or later he knew trouble would eventually cross his path. His guts tightened with his exposure on these trails; he knew there were dangers from man traps such as rock falls or hidden archers. Being no stranger to these hills; in his passing he had cause to leave behind casualties that nursed not only old wounds but bitter grievances.

It had been a long, monotonous and silent day; the late afternoon light was beginning to fade; Robert announced that they would be making camp, they had reduced their elevation and reached a convenient depression in the hills that would afford them sufficient cover from open view. He plainly stressed there would be no fire, thinking that she would give argument; but none came only a silent nod. They both spent time with the horses rubbing them down; Robert talked to his, sharing his thoughts; the horse didn't seem to mind and it eased the nervous tension in the camp. With only an occasional grunt serving as communication, the two bedded down; though it was hard for them both to relax; trust was scarce and the night was cold and uncomfortable; sunrise couldn't come soon enough.

When sunrise broke, Robert took time to view the way ahead; though the hills far behind assured him of their progress; the terrain ahead offered no comfort, appearing to change back to hill country. First they would reach lower open country and dried river beds where the game was more plentiful; it gave Robert a bad feeling that the chances of coming across a hunting party could grow appreciably. In an attempt to nudge his travelling companion awake, he was surprised that his foot received a gentle block as an outstretched arm quickly prevented him from his action of contacting with her body." We've got to move"; was all that was said, surprised at her reaction. It was unusual, he mused, to expect such a rapid reaction; she was quick and to be alert so early in the day by someone who had led the soft life; walking away, he thought little more about it. It was not long before they were in the saddle and riding; nothing had changed between them; the silence that had prevailed the previous day seemed to be exercised further.

It was later in the morning when they were crossing between open hills that they realised they had been spotted by a group of mounted tribesmen. "Friends of yours?" he turned to ask the female; receiving a clear and definite shake of the head; followed by a definite angered muffled "no" from behind the scarf that concealed the face.

There must have been six or more; "Do we run and lose them?" she asked.

Being a soldier that knew the terrain; he replied telling her that there was a canyon up ahead; "I suspect they'll wait and try to steer us into it; they know it to be a dead end and that's where I'd guess that they will want to make their move against us."

"Then why should we allow ourselves to be manoeuvred that way?" she replied in a sarcastic tone, "Is it not foolish to put ourselves at their mercy?"

Oh, suddenly he realised she spoke his tongue; crafty bitch; maybe she was not so dumb after all; and she had opinions as well. "It suits me," he answered without explanation, "these foolish people will never learn that I am not so easily dealt with; Lord knows I don't want to make more widows." He turned to look at her and winked; she adjusted her scarf at his action; "Stay up close and don't fall behind. We are safe while they think we are doing what they want; let them believe that we are falling for their plan; they will regret their error before the day is up."

Having the female with him was a problem and a burden; he did think of running, for her sake, but he felt that he could handle the situation; his orders echoed in his mind reminding him that the information was vital and best kept intact. Two more riders came into view on the opposite ridge and curses ran off his tongue; he could take four with ease but six or more would need some thinking about to assure his mission being successful; besides, there was nothing he could do to alter his plans now. Their pace had increased and they were nearing the blind canyon where Robert guessed was to be their place of confrontation. He looked towards the woman telling her to increase her speed and keep up with him, a sound came from her direction but he could not comprehend; nor did he care as long as she obeyed his order.

Quickly he looked for an option of advantage; "We're going to ride hard along this hill into a blind canyon," he shouted loudly; "that way they will not be able to surround us. At the end of the canyon there is a steep climb out up to the top, though you will have to dismount to reach it. Take it and save yourself and then head northwards until you reach the first village, then due west," he leaned across the gap between them thrusting a small pouch into her hand, "there's enough silver to buy yourself another horse to complete your journey, I'll catch up if I can. If luck is on our side, we'll beat the tribesmen into the canyon; allowing them to imagine they've got us boxed in; and that's where it is going to turn into a fight. Instead of playing with me, they are going to wish they had taken me in the open."

The pouch he had offered was pushed away by her small hand and then reached to the scarf around her face. The words that issued forth from her were loud and clear as well as angered and without mistake. "I will stand with you, Franj, I will not run, what do you take me for?"

Robert shook his head in disbelief at the clarity of her voice; there was no misunderstanding in her reply and it gave Robert quite a surprise for such a small person as she. All of a sudden, she had spunk, he gave her that; but he feared that she would be better off finding safety or staying behind him and out of his way. Before he could say another word, the female had started off for the canyon ahead of him; Robert reached out to snatch at the horses bridle to take control but she was away.

Meanwhile, the tribesmen were beginning to cut across him to shorten his path, waving their swords wildly above their heads; Robert wasn't going to allow them to set their trap as they wanted it. He made a sudden dash for cover through the opening into the rocky trail that was little wider than the space for two horsemen. Onward he rode towards the end of the narrow canyon following the female where he would turn to meet his aggressors before they could stop him. His eyes were everywhere as he rode on, looking at all aspects of the terrain for somewhere advantageous to make his stand, and he saw it.

"This is bad, Franj," she shouted as they came to a stop and turned, "There's not much room to fight in this narrowness."

"Quiet," he demanded, watching as his enemy slowed taking up their positions at the mouth; boxing him in.

"We both can't ride forwards," she told him; he turned looking at her with fire in his eyes.

"I do not need your help and until I ask for it remain silent and watch, and please make your way to safer ground." His order was for her own good; but he could see that she was not used to taking orders; in fact, he thought that he saw hostility at his words. In reality he was quite alarmed at her attitude towards joining the fight; having had the feeling that she might just take a stupid chance just to show her ability as a fighter. He cared not what she thought; repeating for her to stay back and do nothing at all; to make matters worse, he told her that she may get in the way and cause herself harm and that almost made her feel as if sparks would fly from her.

The tribesmen gathered in a group at the opposite end of the canyon, believing that the strangers were at their mercy. Their number was eight of them; all seemed happily disposed at their advantageous position. Robert still believed he would win the day, knowing that they could not come at him all together. Taking his bow from around his body; he unslung his quiver of arrows and tied it to his saddle. His first arrow was knocked ready and held at his side whilst his other hand held the horse's reins. He wanted to appear a little awkward as he rode forwards to meet his foe to let them believe in their own sense of superiority. He moved forwards as if to take up the challenge to his enemy; hoping that they would laugh and mock his approach. There was now about three hundred yards between them as he came to a stop; he waited as if baiting them.

A leader shouted across the gap between them; telling him how they knew that he had ridden their lands freely many times and without permission to do so; as if he was its owner. "You disregard our right and presence here; causing harm to our brothers; for that you shall pay a high price."

"Leave me in peace," Robert cried back, "I do not wish to make any more widows in your people; I mean you no harm; but as a man, if you insist, I will defend myself."

A scream issued forth and two warriors came forwards at a charge. "And so it begins," Robert muttered under his breath and rode out to meet their challenge.

He quickly transferred the horse's reins between his teeth and kicked the horse's flank. The two warriors rode out singing a death song and waving swords high above their heads in active threat to their adversary. Guiding his mount with his knees and reins held in his mouth, they quickly neared each other; the tribesmen had shields covering their upper bodies and swords raised aloft in readiness to strike; Robert could see plenty of exposed areas in which to shoot at.

With the narrowing of the canyon passage there was not enough room for both tribesmen to meet Robert in their fight and it was too late to amend their believed advantage. Yelling in rage the leading tribesman urged forward his mount into the narrowness of the path; at the same time he had to take care to keep to his course on the path. Momentarily, his eyes dropped to better view the safety of the path; it was then that he raised his guard slightly to shield his face; it was what Robert expected of him and saw his target. Without seeing his fate, an arrow struck the tribesman in the abdomen; with a reddening of his shirt and a scream before falling from his mount wide-eyed and open-mouthed in disbelief. He fell from his saddle into the path of the second rider; enough for the man to lose his concentration on his intention in saving himself from being thrown. It was enough to allow Robert a clear shot at his second opponent, who received an arrow in the throat and fell before Robert had reached him. By this time, two other riders followed screaming their death wish at Robert. The leading tribesman's horse caught the next arrow causing it to stumble throwing its rider whilst the other could do no more than stumble headlong into the other. Both riders had gone down with such force onto the path's rocky edge causing them to suffer unconsciousness with the force of the impact.

Robert manoeuvred around the fallen mounts and moved closer into range of the waiting band; he had had the time to draw a further arrow and knock it ready on his bow. The action had occurred too quickly for them to realise their situation. As Robert continued onwards towards them, they watched helpless as if in a suspension of time as he loosed his arrow at the group wounding one in the shoulder; stopping and turning, he swung around in his saddle in retreat and prepared for another shot which hit another in the thigh, though not seriously, and before he lost his range, fired a further shot wounding yet another. There was one among them that was not prepared to live down the insult and rode out to meet and finish Robert. On seeing this, Robert thought it would serve his attackers best by finishing the lesson. Drawing the attacker further away from his friends into the canyon he quickly turned his horse and drew his sword and rode forwards to meet the tribesman. The two men met in a clash of swords; steel clanged out the sound of meeting steel; and in passing Robert's force of his clashing sword had pushed the rider to a sideways defensive position allowing Robert to return his sword in a backwards swipe into the nape of his neck. A contacting scream filled the air and a red stripe appeared immediately where sharpened steel had struck his would be assailant. The rider slowed and howled long; it was a killing wound; the rider had no more fight in him; he would soon be a dead man and he knew it; if only he could speak a prayer before his breath ran out.

It was over; Robert pulled his horse to a halt and trotted towards the surviving two. "It is over, you have fought and lost," he told them, "and cost your brothers dearly for your foolishness. This day let it be known that I have looked mercifully upon you, collect your wounded and take them home and let there be no more hostility between us." His words were met with reluctant agreement and embarrassment, though the survivors knew it to be true and in that short moment Robert could see that the fight had also gone from their eyes. Though they were young men, they knew that they had been outmatched by this single man, whoever he was, and even with their ardour broken, their thoughts remained sour and resentful; no doubt threatening; but they were not foolish enough to chance their luck against this man. "Our people recognise you, Franj," they said, "by what name do you go by so that we can pray for strength and guidance to meet you next time."

"Hear me now," said Robert, "for I will speak only once on this matter, do not seek me out for I am death in many forms; as for my name; it does not matter. I move with the direction of the wind and bear no man any harm unless he becomes a threat to me. Should you come at me again, I will not be so merciful; I bid you; tell your people this, for I bear no man any harm or malice." He begged them to put those thoughts of a revengeful death to one side and go in peace; and may Allah be with you. With that, he turned his horse aside to allow the others to pass him before signalling to the waiting woman to join him.

He waited while he watched the two able riders collect the bodies of their wounded and dead companions before riding off.

When he was joined by the woman he saw no need to speak, but turned and led her out of the canyon; no words were spoken, but she had changed her mind about the ability of the man who was escorting her.

Their journey was to take them in the direction of the North West that led them to Acre. He cared not of how anyone viewed him; other than those he served, it was as he had spoken to the tribesmen that he bore no man any malice. Though at times he was apt to be more wary of some of his own kind, whom he had discovered were trouble makers and two-faced, even before their King. It concerned him not that he had killed other men unnecessarily; but they had shown rashness and were foolhardy and were never really a threat. Neither did he wish to make a name for himself as the slayer of ordinary men; that is why he held back his name. That last point could help him; for there was little honour in boasting about the death of a man that bore no name. It was enough that he was able to pass safely through their lands unnoticed and unharmed; at the same time enjoying their distant respect. No sooner had he mused of the passing event; than he had moved on back to the business at hand.

When the task of delivering the stranger to the Grand Prior's secretary was concluded, both parted without a word, it was as if a package had been deposited. Robert was not sorry to rid himself of the company quick enough. Though he had born a mistrust, he held no bitterness towards her. He never mentioned his run-in with an enemy rather he announced his withdrawal and where he could be reached. Thankfully, his duty over; there was no point in attempting to show that he was eager to see more of the female; besides, he knew of one who would be waiting for him with open arms. Glad to be free of his silent companion, he did not ever expect to see that person again, but he was mistaken in that assumption, for little did he know what events were to bring them back together; sooner than he expected...

Luca's story

On an early bright September morning, a gentle breeze was blowing across the expanse of the still, languid lagoon, the glare of the morning sun on the shimmering waters exaggerated vivid reflections from the multi-coloured painted houses and the grand visage that was the island city in the lagoon. Venice was an intense pastiche of colour in the early light, highlighting the armada of ships that lay at rest at the quayside; and whose decks were ever swelling with people waiting to be transported to far off shores.

This was the busiest port in the republic; daily, ships busily sailed to and from the harbour with all manner of trade goods; that made this city one of the richest in the land. Apart from its expanding trade and wealth, the state raised fearful armies under the auspices of the Doge that supported and gave rise to the growth and splendour of its City and state.

A visitor to these shores would have been excused into believing that a festival may have been in the making, had they been guided by their ears. But their eyes would have given a different explanation; by the sight of so many ships carrying armed men that had patiently lined the dockside; enthusiastically ready to carry them to lands abroad. Within its magnificence, the city was not just the jewel of the Adriatic Sea, but a city that was a vibrant centre of modern living; its trade and culture was an example to the rest of Europe in its architectural grandeur, modern ideas and wealth. The sounds of milling voices that travelled outwards suggesting this pageant was stimulating activity for the holy cause and the glory of war, and it was bubbling and building like driven spume on a sand bank.

Throughout this tumult rising from the excited throng; to what at first appeared a happy time from those cheering voices in the city and about him, Luca Rici walked silently beside his grandson like a condemned man, down in spirit and doomed to being the unhappiest of men. Yet through it all, he wore a fixed smile that pained his heart much, but for the sake of his grandson he could have screamed his true feelings to the crowds around him.

The reason for Luca's heaviness of heart lay as far away from any excited crowd as one could imagine; the revelry that was building was, in his opinion, misconstrued for those that were about to leave. Since the appeal by the Holy Father the Pope, there was a war waiting to be fought in the Levant; now small armies of men at arms had gathered, choking the port in their eagerness to embark on their mission with ideas of becoming land grabbers and wealthy victors of a just war. Full of their own imaginings, they believed that they were going to destroy the Muslim infidel; but first they had to cross the world to achieve that goal.

These were ordinary men driven by a belief that the Holy City of Jerusalem that was in dire need to be relieved of the rule of the Muslim. For those brave enough to embark on this journey that would result undoubtedly in crimes of murder, rape and wanton destruction; the Holy Father assured them they would be absolved and cleansed of all their past sins and be born again; ready to be received into the hands of God in Heaven; should they perish in the process of war. For most men who had been in the ranks of the mercenaries it was an opportunity to grow rich; whilst divorced from the mundane life of a hand to mouth existence. For the simple, unworldly man, the inner thrill and ability to kill at liberty was a new sensation; reality would in time dawn on him; but if he wasn't expended in the first wave of battle, he would experience sleepless nights and a longing wish that he had not had made so foolish a decision to be where he found himself. Whilst the mighty among them with their hired men had practiced much in the art of battle; the rest of the army being mostly fools and criminals with a fool's imagination of hope had their uses; being little more than objects and numbers to be cast wastefully before their sworn enemy.

As if it wasn't enough to be reminded of a previous loss that Luca had secretly born over the years; another was at his side and already in the making. He could not bear to talk or think back to that time; a deep wound had been inflicted and one that had been created by his own folly.

That memory stung him to anger and clung heavily about him whenever he was reminded of it, the loss of a son through his own fault of selfish neglect was hard enough for any man to bear. Now, fate once again had drawn this lot for him, Luca had failed his only son some years back; and now it seemed he was going to lose his grandson as well. Like a father and grandfather, he had tried his utmost to dissuade the boy to change his mind; but instead of uniting them, they fell into deep argument; and for once Luca had to yield or suffer the outcome of losing the most treasured thing he loved. Educated to a higher degree than most men; when the news of the plight of pilgrims in the Holy Land came to the young man's attention, he was quick to retaliate with the most honourable of intentions. To further qualify his intent, he was inspired by the words of appeal by the Holy Father and the mould of action had been set. It mattered nothing that Luca was the richest man in Venice; he dared not hold back his beloved grandson from a mission he had so passionately set his heart on achieving. His one and only grandson that he cherished and loved like no other; Luca was a slow learner when it came to family values and love of his fellow man. The present situation did not sit well with him at all; but under the circumstances he feared for what his vindictive senseless heart was telling him to do.

Dogs ran wild, in the crowded mass of people the excited animals were yelping and barking loudly and jumping up on passers by; people made their way to the harbour; the air filled with nervous laughter at those that stumbled drunkenly in their path; but not so for the dogs that received a swift kick for their yapping presence. Dogs, Luca felt, were like children at getting in the way at the wrong time; and he had little time for them; many people also; his face twisted into a grimace in his thoughts.

The public face of Luca was one of an upright citizen; a fine gentleman; being among the most beneficent of men around to the world at large; it was a role he worked diligently in portraying to the well-bred society of the city.

The truth was that he was far from it; he was secretly viscous to the core and concealed his secrets well, though in his later years, behind his wealth and aura of respectability, he remained hard, being far more active in the shadows of his maritime empire. Luca was a charmer; he had worked hard perfecting his mask; just as he did with his business. Though these days he preferred to sit behind his desk; cruelly manipulating his minions within his empire doing his bidding; and woe betide them should anyone fail him. Having such power and wealth gave him the ability to have his way, and he would have it no matter what cost; fair or foul. His cruelty served him pleasurably in sweeping aside adversaries, maiming and murder might depend on the degree of stubbornness of those that opposed him. Though on this day, he was powerless to do much in his usual activity; banished, was the sour faced antagonist that he was. His mind hurt because he could not secure a way to cajole his grandson into changing his mind; however, he was resigned to the fact that it was too late in the day having ceded to his wishes. Time had long passed that expectancy; though it was in Luca to try to press gold into the palm of the Duke himself to reconsider the enlistment of his grandson. Alas that too failed; it was rudely pointed out in a rather disdainful manner that his grandson had chosen the way of his honour; something that Luca knew nothing about. It reflected on Luca quite badly; and into the bargain it openly displayed the Duke's distaste of what he and others of higher birth really thought of him; and it hurt Luca to learn that others of high rank thought likewise of him. One thing became quite clear; the Duke had not done himself any favour in so plainly speaking his mind. Luca left with his tail between his legs; it meant only one other option lay open to him; though he was powerless at present, he would solve that problem in his own way before he embarked to wreck the life of this Duke, who had been more frank than he should have.

It was difficult enough for Luca, trying to smile his worries away; being well aware that this moment was not a time for examining what had passed; though the sin of losing anything weighed heavily on his mind. Luca was only used to winning; though for the time being, he had to let go; it was not the cup of success he was forced to take, but one of bitterness; and it was an unpleasant experience.

There was lively gossip, plenty of it as they walked; friends had joined them, though Luca had no stomach for his Grandson's supporters, he thought it best that he nod occasionally and remain silent whilst smiling a lot. With head held high, he walked his grandson closer towards the waiting ship; Luca was doing his best to desperately hold onto his emotions whilst he endured the masquerade of being happy. His mind was whirling. Madness, it was all madness, as far as he was concerned; the boy had no idea what dangers he was placing himself in; he had told him so a thousand times until it became a point of their falling out. His head lolled backwards and forwards in silent consternation; at such a young age, what could the boy possibly know about war or about life? Luca wanted to strike himself for being so foolish for cosseting the boy over the years, but he had had his say many times in his efforts to dissuade him in changing his mind, but alas he now had to give way.

This young man, one day, was about to inherit the wealth of the richest man in the whole of Venetian world, he simply had only to snap his fingers and whatever he wanted was his.

Whilst everybody else seemed to be out on the street, so were the whores, enticing those single young men to have a last fling before embarking on the long voyage to the Holy Land. Luca knew them all, though he did not want to be recognised at present. It seemed the women from the whole of the Venice had turned out to see off their men folk, and Luca could not understand this almost carnival like atmosphere.

Despite his animosity, he would not let the boy leave under a cloud of discontent; by making this his supportive duty he would see it through; even though it be a sham.

Seagulls filled the sky, screeching out their shrill notes as the old man's mind raced; were they an omen? He hated seagulls, at least their incessant noise, they sounded like shrieking sirens as if they had raised their piercing voices just to annoy him. Somewhere deep, deep inside Luca remained the vestige of a soft spot; it had never been displayed to anyone before but it was there; dormant. It took his grandson's leaving to reach that secret spot and as hard to as he tried to smother it; tears welled in his eyes and a sickness churned in his gut; his mind suffered most, conjuring drastic images of the boy's possible fate. He looked away to wipe his eye of a tear; feigning recognition of someone in the crowd. Worst of all was the waiting for that sound of the last haunting goodbye and he knew he could not prevent it. Through the inward pain in his ageing heart; and in the fog of his memory when he bid the lad goodbye, he would capture and hold what he believed was likely to be the last image of his beloved grandson and that would painfully become a haunting image for the rest of time.

Behind all the upset and argument between the two men, Aldo's passion for justice for his fellow man became his sacred cause; it had built like a tidal wave filling his young heart. He knew it was too late to defend the rights of the defenceless pilgrims who lay dead along the way; what tortures they had suffered; the butchery of the Saracen in God's own holy country had to be stopped. After all; what harm could innocent pilgrims do?

Words from the Holy Father in Rome had told them of the numerous years of the violation of their agreement; it could not and would no longer be tolerated, the Church's refusal to preserve a servile passiveness was long past trying to find a peaceful solution. After constant pleas to the Muslim to desist in their persecution of pilgrims, emissaries were turned away; all talks had broken down, the Holy Father in his conscience had waited long enough; feeling compelled to put this wrong to right. So to the four corners of the Holy

Roman Empire the call went out for a holy crusade and for Princes and Kings alike to unite and prepare their armies to amass and move forwards against those devils across the great sea. The passive voice of Rome called on Christians to march on the Holy city, where Our Lord himself shed his sacred blood for all of Christian mankind; people lifted up their eyes to swear their revenge while quiet voices became a roar of command.

Grandfather and grandson walked side by side, the younger proud and in awe at the jubilation and excitement that was generated in support of the cause. Passage through the streets was difficult; thronging with soldiers from places abroad of varied tongues, sporting their colourful raiment and banners of the royal houses that they were enlisted to; but none of it moved the aging Luca one bit. He could not help but see what he had seen many times before, tearful women with children hanging on to their husbands and fathers as if they too knew some terrible secret, as they kissed and wished their loved ones well before leaving. With a contemptuous eye, Luca looked upon all of what was happening about him with disinterested sarcasm and disgust. Whilst the mind of young Aldo was actively absorbing the whole event around him, Luca's was the opposite, his feelings were inward and contriving only for a way to have his foolhardy and zealous grandson safely back by his side.

The moment that Luca was recognised, whores lewdly hung out of windows calling to him. He was well-known along these streets; in fact, he kept most of these females in employment, but today their calls fell on deaf ears; his mood was distant and his ardour for pleasure non-existent.

Eventually they had arrived at the quayside where the clamouring crowds had gathered to say their last farewell. It was as though the population of the entire city had amassed at this one point. Aldo had never seen so many people, nor had he seen such a harbour that was bursting with so many ships. Many of those ships belonged to the Rici line, it was a trial for the boarders to push their way forwards. Children were held high above the shoulders of the milling crowds as they waved to their father's on board ship with tear-filled eyes, until becoming unnoticed as they passed from view. The warm, balmy air became filled with the potent aromas of drifting incense; when a procession of priests with an entourage of altar boys appeared swinging their unctuous smoking urns.

Copious amounts of holy water was being flicked over the heads of the crowd onto the timber hulls of waiting timber ships that creaked with every rise and fall of the swelling sea; as a blessing for a safe voyage to their place of destination was given. The advancing holy procession, performing its blessings ritual, continued along the quay ceremoniously to the sounds of unending religious chants. To allow the procession to perform its religious ceremony unhindered, the swelling crowd mimicked a breathing monster that moved in rhythm to the priests passing as if it was inhaling and exhaling to move in order to find space wherever there appeared to be space where there was previously none before.

On bustling gangplanks men boarded, as one by one they filled the decks; orders called from each heaving ship when ready to cast off its holding ropes and let the ebb tide carry them away from the wall, once clear sails were dropped as ships turned away seawards to the cheers of the waving crowds.

The ships had set their course for the far horizon and as each loaded vessel became distant from the shore; so the jubilant waving crowds became smaller and quieter; drifting back to their homes in the city.

Now that the crowds were fewer in number, leaving only the ship that Aldo was to sail on. Those of Aldo's young friends that had walked with him to the quay now flocked around him for their last farewell. Luca stood back wearing a plaintive smile; he should have been an actor. It gave him respite from one of his pretentious roles, for all he wanted for his grandson was to see other happy smiling faces. He was lonely standing on the quayside among the friends of his grandson, there was a life time of difference between them, and for a brief moment he became quite oblivious to the activities going on around him. Above the shouts of the crowds the scene was mixed with the shrieking sounds of crying gulls, and seawater lapping noisily against the ships hulls and against the quay wall, Luca felt somehow out of place.

The mask of Luca's good side remained smiling and happy, but inside he so much wanted one last chance to keep the boy from leaving. After his friends had wished him well and the congratulatory handshakes and farewell wishes ceased from all the admiring young ladies, it left the young man quite saddened and overawed, finally leaving only the two of them facing each other.

A warm westerly wind was blowing from the land as Aldo walked forwards and gripped his grandfather's bony frame, hugging him lovingly and almost hurting him with his youthful strength. Whilst in their embrace, Aldo whispered in Luca's ear, "I will miss you grandfather, there is no one in the world quite like you, I want you to take special care of yourself while I am gone, for I will be home sooner than you think." Luca looked at him curiously with a smile on his face; little did he know just how soon it would be should he have his way. With a pride that was overflowing, the young man told the ageing grandparent that he would not forget to write to him. When a call was raised to board, he took a backward pace; he held his grandfather at arm's length, and with a smiling youthful face said in his thrilled boyish voice, "It won't be long grandfather; I'll be home in no time at all," and hugged the weakened frame of the old man. Aldo looked upwards to the sky, his face catching the breeze, full of self-assuredness; his body bristled with excitement of embarking on the adventure that lay ahead of him. He took in a deep breath letting the air fill his lungs.

"Feel that wind," he said, "now there's a good start, mark my words that same wind will soon be carrying me swiftly back to you."

With one arm hugging his grandfather's shoulder, he jokingly said, "just think of the stories I will be able to tell you on my return," and opening the gap between the two he added, "I must go now, remember; I love you grandfather." Luca remained silent and smiling, Aldo's parting words were like a dagger piercing the old man's ageing heart; but the words of the boy's affection broke him and it was all he could do to save himself from breaking down. They embraced once more, Luca clung to the boy whilst holding on to his emotions trying not to show his true feelings and the spectacle of being overcome. The doting Luca mustered his final reserve of grit to withstand his true sentiment and feeling, bade his grandson a fond and safe farewell in a hoarse voice. Aldo smiled, turned and walked toward the gangplank, stopping before embarking he turned around,

"It really won't be long, take good care of yourself grandfather," and giving one final smile he gave a wave, moved onto the gang plank that heaved up and down with the motion of the waiting ship on the swell of the waiting sea.

Luca felt his emotions tearing at his inner body, he wanted to collapse in his distress but his determination to appear normal for the sake of his grandson was crumbling in his weakness of unusual yet genuine emotion.

The ship was eventually freed from its moorings and with its top sails raised, allowed the ship to gently slip away from the quayside. The space between the ship and the ageing man on the quay grew ever greater. Luca stood waving to Aldo who was having difficulty keeping a place at the side of the ship with so many aboard her shouting their goodbyes, but Luca remained; waving for as long as he could be seen after all others on the quay had gone. When the ship faded on the horizon, Luca was still standing alone and statuesque; smiling a fixed smile; waving and staring out to an empty sea. The warmth of the late morning air went unnoticed by him; a passing cloud masked the sunlight momentarily bringing with it coolness and a slight breeze, which engulfed the ageing man's body. There seemed a silence everywhere and for Luca it became quite chilly. Drawing his arms tightly around the inside of his cape, he clung tightly to himself to conserve what little warmth in his body remained. He felt somehow hollow; his fragile body imagined that the blood was draining from it, his teeth chattered nervously with the sickly concern for his grandson. The longer he stood the worse he felt, but he could not move. Against the wind he was transfixed; his old eyes were riveted to the horizon and his body racked with an inner sickness of worry. A fear began stalking him, gnawing at his old heart of a fear of the coming loneliness and of probable loss. The man suddenly became a shell, empty yet racked with antipathy. Luca had never been a weak man, but from disappointment rose a stirring of malice that filled him with bitterness and hatred.

Before he could move; the acidity of his bitterness was actively brewing into a storm that would soon be vented, it didn't matter to Luca how much he may hurt others; but no one was allowed to bring grief to him, it was unheard of. So whosoever puts my grandson at risk sets out to hurt me; and will live to regret it. Luca Rici was a survivor, and a man who had spent most of his time surviving whilst destroying others. A new anger built within his twisted psyche, bringing a swelling of rage towards those responsible for this stupid crusade. Thoughts of outrage ran through his head, the Holy Fathers will also pay for this. He disliked them and their kind; they were no different than he. He believed that all men have their own ways of seeking power; they were only masquerading in their belief of everlasting love and repatriation of souls with those closest to them after death. Hmph, what rubbish he felt; ha, they were already paying dearly for his ships and for this hurt they have brought me; will pay a lot more; when he was finished with them they will be on their knees. How dare they encourage my grandson away from me, secretive, like thieves in the night. Hatred was festering within this old man's heart like a growth, and his mind became an erupting force of destructive vindictiveness against the holy cause and the land they called the Levant and everything about it. He gave his last weakly wave to the diminishing speck at sea; as he turned to leave the quayside he staggered and reeled across a small case of cargo, losing his balance he stumbled to the ground. It was at that moment his true human feelings spilt forth, and like a child with fists held tightly, the man wept like a child for his grandson. It was not for long, for there may have been people nearby who may have seen him fall, but he had little to worry about; for they were at a distance away and did not hear the wails of the old man. He gathered himself together and brushed off his clothing with a shaking hand; the affluent and powerful Luca Rici could not be seen crying like a babe in public. He fought with himself to overcome any undignified appearance that may have been displayed. All that day and for the next he shut himself away as if in some hermitic cell; and like a bursting dam he wept real tears of loss. His mind refused to release him from a self-inflicted imaginary grief which had not yet occurred, his dreaded nightmarish thoughts refused to leave him and for a while he was lost as those imaginings grew into nightmarish proportions. Mental pictures of a battlefield death and a visitation from a cloaked messenger with a hollow sounding voice; told of his grandson's fatal demise, it was so painful that he had to hold his head in misery. His ageing face screwed into contortions and a relentless tide of tears stung and reddened his already swollen eyes each time he caught a glimpse of the parting dockside recollection.

In his present loss, anger was evoked in waves from his self-pitying grief on anyone that approached him, no servant in Luca's household chose to be idle or present near the master; it most certainly was not a time to be around him or spare a sympathetic word whilst he grieved.

How dare they do this to me, how dare they! He would bang his closed fists on the table or throw anything that came to hand, he even stabbed at himself; but it was without real intent. His rationalising did little to help him; nor did it come anywhere near soothing his twisted thoughts. In his wounded and miserable state, he began to imagine that society at large had ganged up on him to repay him for his wicked past; by playing this trick on him in revenge for his many past misdeeds. Past misdeeds indeed, he thought sneeringly; and he vowed that the last word would be his and he would not rest until he had his grandson back safely home and then he would rise again and show this city all about evil deeds.

As an incoming tide turns to the ebb, so too did Luca's tears subside, allowing him to emerge again back into the world of the living from his place of mental distress. Some days his manner was better than others; disturbed he certainly remained. Occasionally, whilst in the quiet of his dim lit office, his loneliness or despair for his grandson generated a small change to take place in him. Within this cruel stone-hearted man, something clicked; allowing recollections of the past to resurface from deep within his memory. His father, mother, old Venice, his youth and his rise to power began to return as if he was accounting for his past.

A Winding Path

Luca Rici had an affinity with the sea. He grew up in a small fishing community on the salt marshes that lay across the lagoon from Venice, his place of birth carried no place name; neither did it have a house of worship to unite the odd and distant people that resided there. The peculiar notoriety of the people being unfriendly and distant stemmed from being endowed with the same lot in life, abandoned by the society of the city and left in a state of dire poverty it bound them together as a close and tightly-knit community. Apart from general poverty and a daily struggle to survive, the ram-shackled community's location was situated conveniently for all the dross of the criminal world to pass through when in need of a hiding place from the authorities; or for gangs of raiders that occasionally passed through en route to pillage from the outer reaches of the affluent city. Because of such events they became outcasts; a bastard community in an area that decent people avoided. Outsiders recognised the place and dared only to point towards its direction calling it 'that place over there,' fearful of ever venturing within miles of the marshes.

Life for Luca as a young boy was spent either assisting others working in boats or repairing them. He never enjoyed the same enthusiasm as his tough, rugged father for fishing, but rather thought that his life held a different course to travel. Where, he did not know, but it did not stop the gaping of his eyes; or the strange longing in his heart. Hence his romancing over the distant sight of the city he saw daily; he could not help but wonder what was going on at the other side of the lagoon. It is not a sin to dream, for if it is, everyone is guilty of that sin; but this boy knew that one day he would be out there, but until that day and without knowing why, Luca's being would ache away. How his wistful thoughts carried him away during those early sunny days in play amid the sand dunes of his youthful years. He was presently a pirate, as he played on the edge of the dunes, and the small boats that had been beached for repair had become his armada to take into battle. He did not know his age, only that he was old enough to work in and on the boats when his father ordered him so. It was important to the family that he shared in the work load, being the eldest son. It was expected that he earn his keep, in the heart of his hard-hearted father there was no room for weakness; or weaklings. As young as he was, he was strong enough to haul the lengths of fishing nets around and help carry out the necessary repairs that were required. He had learnt a long time ago that not being able to complete a task had its disadvantages, with the memory of such

46

a recent disappointment Luca felt a twinge of pain from a fist that had caused his small arm to deaden at the touch.

He was not a handsome boy like some; his hair was a shaggy mass that grew wild with curls; his piercing eyes poised above a hawkish nose and his mouth was more like a slit in his face; not like other boys. He was inclined to be churlish, due probably to the treatment he received at home; the burden of work gave him an ageing that was before his time. Whenever he sat with the fishermen in his ragged make shift clothes working on the nets, he always wore a smile for he was happy; calling out cheekily to the other fishermen that were embroiled in their own net repairing duties. The precocious youngster bandied asides with those around him, always raising a smile from the others with an odd threat to turn his ears to glowing red whenever he stepped over the mark of respectful jesting.

In such times as those hot sunny afternoons when the men were together, he loved to listen to the old fishermen whose younger days were spent at sea. He became especially amused and enthralled when the old fishermen telling their yarns forgot their usual line of the tale that did not happen previously; Luca knew the reason for the break, for he had heard these stories so many times before and was aware of the changes each time that they had taken place. Disrespectfully, the cheeky boy would spit into the sand in unison with the story teller, although some never realised this; Luca was telling them that they had forgotten their own story line. Their other favourite ploy was to scratch at their matted beards whilst holding their audience waiting for the tale to continue, always the boy was ready to run as he would remind them that the story line was about to change again. At a distance he would shout and taunt them for their memory loss, but in truth and to his envy he more than realised they did have a yarn to tell. They had seen life, unlike himself who yearned so much for a tangible experience; it left him at odds with all who dared talk him down to restrain his imagined calling.

Lost in his thoughts, he often gazed out across the salt marshes, watching with a latent fascination at the tall masts of ships with their great canvassed sails. Had those sails, he wondered, been filled with the winds of the four corners of the world? Did their crew fight with sword and dagger to protect their captain on the high seas, and did those ships carry those aboard safely homewards into the lagoon of Venice with treasure from lands afar? Strangely, his gawking was filled with a curiosity; and imaginings of their strange and bizarre cargoes. One day, he believed he too would sail on a ship such as he watched; no longer would his dreams lead him to think where they had come from; and what new sights their crews had seen.

It was all a daydream and daydreaming had become a hazardous pastime for this young boy, too often he would receive a back handed swipe or the buckle on the thick leather belt across his back from his impatient and aggressive parent for not doing what was expected of him. His hand reached up to his face, pain shot across his eye as his hand touched on a large bruising of his cheek; that was another lesson. His caring mother had hardened due to the yoke of cruelty that she too had to bear from her arduous day-to-day existence; being too weak to oppose her man's brutish bullying ways and for the sake of the children, endured the harsh treatment of suffering at the hands of her uncaring husband. As head of the family, Marco, Luca's father, was an irresponsible and callous husband, who cared little for his family, more how he could best use them to suit his own interests and nobody was allowed to enjoy the simplicities and pleasantries of a normal upbringing when he was around. The fish markets that gave him his means of support lay across the lagoon, and all too often when Luca's father frequented it to sell his catch, there always followed a lame excuse to his mother about missing the tides for his delayed return. She knew that it was nothing more than a transparent lie; his corrupt and uncaring ways became all too common; his preference for women's company had degenerated to those that he chose to drink with and the whores that resided in the brothels across the lagoon.

So Luca's mother resigned herself to a lonely life with a selfish husband, and raised her four children the best she could. Considering her situation, it was understandable why his mother changed so; due to the troublesome burden that she silently bore. Fatigued and barely surviving herself at times, the strains arising from the difficulties in raising her discontented and recalcitrant children was constantly wearing her down. As hard as life was, her spirit and depth of strength, drawn from reserves that seemed boundless, enabled her to persevere. Where her children were concerned, the strata of motherly love beneath her hard outer skin remained tenderly soft; always very loving towards her brood in her own peculiar, guarded way.

Having suffered continuous maltreatment through his short existence of undeserved bullying and beatings from his intolerable sot of a father, Luca, having reached an age of self-confidence, had decided to run away from home. His father was again late returning home, and the moment was stirringly opportune for him. In the late afternoon, he finally built up the courage to leave; without a word he stole a boat and sailed across the lagoon towards the city's port. By the time he arrived at a ship that was lying off shore, darkness was closing in, he had climbed aboard easily; there were few mariners on deck and they were busily engaged in their chores so did not see him sneak into the fo'c'sle. He stayed concealed in the shadows until he felt it safer to move about; he didn't care much where this ship was bound for; anywhere away from the marshes was freedom.

It had been nearing spring when he had made his decision to flee his home, he was growing lean and scrawny; he wore a look on his face like so many others before him that had escaped such insecurity and coerced labour in their homes to seek a future at sea. He had become angry at the world and was ready to stand his chances, confronting it with all its dangers and adverse situations that he may find himself caught up in.

It had been raining hard the night that he was discovered hiding away under spare canvas in the storage area of the fo'c'sle. Droplets of rainwater from his sodden clothing had left a trail of water running across a dry deck to his place of hiding below decks; exposing his carelessness after his luckless attempt to steal a morsel of food to sustain his weakened famished being. He was hauled before the captain; trembling with fear and no matter how he struggled to free himself he could not escape the firm hold of a burly and uncouth grinning bearded seaman standing over him. He was terrified, much more so than anything that his father could do to him; the eventual outcome, he believed or imagined, was being flayed alive or hung from a yard arm. Little did Luca know that the iron fast grip of the hands that held his quaking struggling form so firmly, belonged to one that a lifetime ago also had shared the same sense of adventure when at a similar age as himself. He also had learnt the hard lessons of survival and proved to be strong enough to remain aboard the ship that he had grown up on; and presently called his home.

Believing his situation could get no worse, Luca finally stood firm before a stern faced captain, whose voice boomed and growled when he spoke. Luca could not avert his eyes from his bubbly red nose and a beard that covered most of his face, his eyes were deep and hard; it plainly appeared the men themselves were loath to disrespect him. In spite of Luca's youthful age, he quickly recognised that the growling voice and wild eyed face that looked upon him was soon sure to announce his fate. Stowaways were a regular occurrence in most ports, the captain had resigned himself to this distraction, that is not to say that he tolerated the practice; but on that evening when Luca stood before the captain he believed it was to be his last upon this earth. The captain ranted and raved before becoming silent, as if judgement was to be passed; eventually the captain rose and walked around the crewman and faced the prisoner his hands rising to rest on his hips before demanding why Luca had chosen his ship to board? The boy just shrugged his shoulders and remained silent; "You are a cargo I do not require," the captain growled at the boy, "do you know what I do if I do not want that extra weight on board?" Before Luca could reply, the captain told him that he would think nothing of tipping it over the side; and he continued, "it would be your own fault for choosing the wrong ship." Some would say that the captain was a hard man; the truth being that the sea was cruel and life was tough. It spared no man its terrors, and so it had shaped men like the captain to judge events plainly as he saw them, kindliness or sympathy were sentiments that HE could not afford to foster.

He was not always a patient man, fair perhaps, depending mainly on his mood; but if the mood was bad, so was the outcome for any poor wretch that had been hauled before him. "You know;" he said looking directly at the boy, "if you step out of line I will think nothing of giving you the lash. Do you know what that is boy?" His question came through quite harshly; his men knew and understood that they must obey his word for he was their natural compass once at sea. Argument at the wrong time could cost more lives; such decisions were tough; like throwing young boys overboard he added. He had to be hard, though in latter years he had softened somewhat and could never explain it. Sometimes boys were given a chance, but one thing was certain if they stayed; they had to fight to survive as there was no one to watch over them, life at sea only favoured those that were strong of body and will.

The resigned empty eyes of Luca stared widely defiant at the captain, watching him return to sit in his chair. Luca's innocence in his years was fully prepared to receive whatever fate befell him; he would not show weakness or defiance and he was not afraid of them. The captain's silent assessment of the boy was mixed with exasperation and disbelief of his choice; it was one thing to leave home, but why choose the sea as some sort of refuge? It was a question he had asked so many times. For him the situation was different, he was born from a dying mother and his father had little choice other than raise him aboard ship as soon as he was old enough.

Over the years he had had his successes with stowaways; why even the mate was one of them; his stubby gnarled fingers pulled and scratched searchingly at his stubbly bearded face whilst he contemplated knowing there was a tough future ahead for the lad. He wondered if he should say aye, there would be nowhere for him to skulk to for solace of any misdeed, and there would never be the comfort of a kindly voice to commiserate with his actions. For some time the captain deliberated in silent thought. Luca's empty passive eyes offered no warmth or presence of feeling, the captain caught sight of this as he sneaked a sideways glance at the boy. He thought the boy quite brave; for not once had he grovelled or cried, nor had he wet himself in fear of what treatment had to be meted out to him. He liked that truculence, it showed grit. It was in him to give certain brats a chance, should they fail through disobedience there would be no second opportunity. They would end up like the waste; overboard; he had already told him that his decision was always final.

In the poor light of the oil lamp that swung in rhythm with the heaving sea that cast silhouetted moving shadows about the cabin, the boy was admonished by the brusque, burly captain about the waste of his valuable time. "I cannot turn back to shore just for you," he ranted, "so what is it to be, hey?"

The burly mate that held him by his scruff of the neck grinned and nodded eagerly at the captain's suggestion; eager for sport with the lad to see what he was made of.

The captain was not totally as cruel as he purported himself to be, but he sometimes enjoyed the sounds of his own growling voice; if not to prove that it was still there and giving rise to his pretence. The more he eyed this forlorn, ragged and hungry individual that quaked in the grip of the mate, he pondered on making his decision of putting him in the crew's custody. With his decision to allow Luca to remain on board, the captain barked out his rules once again; he finished by pointing out that above all he would not tolerate weakness or whimpering, he gave the mate orders to put the lad to work in the galley immediately to earn his keep. The boy did not smile in gratitude or thank the captain, though he knew that he had been spared and Luca's life as a mariner was in the making.

Life was not as easy at sea as he first expected; the long hard days of work fetching and carrying made him tired out by evening, and resting his head before closing his eyes, the captain's words echoed in his ears like a warning mantra. Gone was the romance of the faraway places, time was no longer his now to day dream, what had he done? He had felt that his dash for freedom was little more than condemnation to slavery, but he would not allow himself to cry nor would he give way to the bullying crewmen. He had the courage to continue and the backbone to defy those that taunted him, and he had made up his mind to be a seaman and that was what he was about. Only his memories, such as they were, were his to keep, gone were the cheeky chats such as he had enjoyed with the fishermen at home; here life had become very different; the sustained daily dose of bullying and occasional knocks would persist until he had made his mark. Crew members were unwilling to tolerate the youth under their feet, especially a green whelp. What concerned him most and taunted his young mind was the occasional fearsome threatening promise that often hovered in his sleepless moments of his darkened corner of space that became his quarters; that one night he would be used to serve the pleasures of the crews sexual ends. He didn't understand what was meant at first; but when it was made clear to him he was terrified at the thought of what could happen. Between rough seas, bad men and hard work, Luca Rici quickly grew up developing a natural toughness that was always within him.

Alone in his office, Luca smiled at his reminiscence of the event, reliving the feeling that he as a young boy could not interpret those inner feelings of triumph. To the younger Luca, the thought that when he delivered a deserved fatal blow to a drunken seaman who had constantly threatened him, made him feel more at one with some of his rougher shipmates; and it made him proud of himself.

On a night many weeks out, when the sea was running a heavy swell and it was difficult to sleep, a drunken crewman once actively threatened to make Luca his bed warmer. In his drunken state, he chased the terrified young cabin boy around below decks and stalked him like a hunted animal until he cornered the shaking cowering boy. As luck would have it, the swell of the sea came to his rescue, the drunken crewman who was unable to maintain his feet firmly on the deck became unbalanced by the rolling sea. Finally falling down and awkwardly trapping his unfit hulk between the staircase and tangling himself in spare rigging ropes that had been stowed nearby. The seaman, in his dizzy and incapable state of restricted movement, prompted the terrified Luca into a defensive action. Seizing on a large discarded piece of splintered timber the frightened boy remorselessly rammed it into the drunken man's neck while the crewman lay on his back cursing abusively in his stupor. The need to survive came easily and would continue so on future occasions during his life. The trembling young boy stood rooted to the deck, his immature innocent eyes stared down, satisfied by his impassioned victory as he gazed fixedly at the sight of the helpless mariner. Blood oozed across the deck, the drunken sailor's clothing soaked up copious amounts of life-giving blood that flowed from the wound like an erupting volcano; leaving the bloody gurgling sot writhing in agony helplessly trying desperately to remove the stave that was taking his life. Luca watched him until the body stopped twitching and without sorrow or feeling for his dire youthful deed, turned in for a peaceful night's sleep. There was neither feeling nor fear of the possibility that his shipmates would seek any kind of retribution from his act; the mariner had gotten no more than his just desert.

In the silence of where he rested, he remained nervously elated, partly through his fear and partly through something deep within that he could not quite comprehend. For the first time in his life he felt like a conqueror, this was nothing like that of trapping a rabbit and ringing its neck; no, it was much deeper. This feeling of victory endured with its exhilarating rush of blood through his young veins; his body shook with fear and triumph over his dead crewmate, that feeling did not leave him and he liked it.

When the mariner's death was brought to the attention of the captain, he readily accepted the story offered by crew members as accidental, some remained silent but others suspected foul deeds, saying as much as good riddance. The following day the body was stitched into a canvas sheet and weighted so that it would sink into the depths of the sea. They gathered on deck standing around solemnly in a chill wind; they mostly felt the same; he was no great loss, yet they did their duty by saying their few words of departing over him. When he slipped off the plank to splash into the water Luca sneakily smiled to himself; he had somehow come of age and it made him feel like a man. Oddly enough, Luca gained a certain respect from the event and from that day onward neither was there any further bullying below decks. After serving the master for two years, he left the ship in the old Roman port of Marseilles in France, feeling confident of holding his own on any ship afloat.

By the time he was sixteen he returned to Venice, he was older and felt like a man, he had travelled to North Africa, France and Spain and countries he had no name for. One day, after docking his ship in the Venetian port, he looked across to that place across the bay that he had long ago called home and wondered. With nothing better to do but drink, he decided to return homewards and set out to cross the marshes to see his mother. The sun was high and hot and trudging along the lonely soft sandy track, he became uneasy; his ideas of reunion began to fade. With each step he grew very unsure of how he would be received, he thought it prudent to first spy for activity from a distance. When he came upon sight of the small thatched cottage he lay down among the tall tussocks of grass; there was little sign of life. He noticed that the boat had gone, so contented with the assumption that his father was absent and that he was out fishing, he began to make his way forwards. He knew the cottage had not been abandoned; he had earlier seen a faint wisp of smoke leave the chimney; standing erect he watched attentively as the smoke curled and twisted in the meagre breeze to make its escape skywards.

He drew cautiously closer and dropped into the warm sandy dunes, fearful of what he had started. Waiting and watching in the hope that his mother might appear, he almost wanted to prompt her out into the open. When he saw her he gasped; catching his breath to stop himself from calling out, he noticed that she was still of slim build and appeared leaving the coolness of the cottage with her arms filled; struggling with a bundle so large she could hardly see her way. With her heavy load she blundered awkwardly, bumping blindly against the doorway as she made her way outside to begin washing clothes in a tub alongside of the timber and sod house. Although he recalled that she was suppressed in feelings due to her husband's black moods, he smiled as he bent his head on the wind. When left alone to be free, she always reverted to her simple girlish ways, she loved to sing just as she was now doing whilst carrying out her washing as Luca watched and listened carefully, concealed from her view.

Two of his younger bare foot siblings came into view chasing the other wildly around her skirts, hampering her progress; they fled laughing as she scolded them threatening to further chastise them. He held in his hand a small pouch, which was a secret gift of money for her; perhaps it would help in a time of need. It grew sweaty in his hand as he gripped it, it was not much but it was a way he thought to make amends for his sudden and silent departure. His plan was to leave it as a surprise for her where she tended a small garden of flowers, but as the thought of his father came rushing into his head; he quickly thought better of it and changed his mind. His young eyes strained as he furtively viewed her busily washing and wondered if he should leave without making his presence known, but with a change of heart he cautiously began making his way toward the house trying not to draw any attention of his presence to the children. By this time, his mother was wringing out her washing over a large wooden tub, her hard working hands bore the signs of raw reddened skin. There was a smell too of newly washed clothes that drew him back in time. Unaware of her advancing son she began laying out the clothes on the top of scrub bushes scattered around the cottage garden; such as it was. When she turned around she could see him, recognising him instantly approaching the corner of the house. Startled at first, she was lost for words and fearful that her children would come running, her eyes looked over him; first as a mother who had lost her son, then questioningly of what he wanted of her. She knew he could not stay and could tell how he had changed, he was taller and more mature with a cocky air of toughness somehow, just like his father. She did not like that; it filled her with both anxiety and happiness to see her boy once more. No sooner had she moved forwards to greet him than she stopped herself and suddenly withdrew inwards in fear. As young as he was, Luca could read the conflict in her eyes that she had envisaged between her husband and her son should he ever discover his presence.

Luca approached hesitantly to within a distance of hearing, she raised her voice inquiring his reason for being here; her voice died, carried off in the breeze and there was no answer until he approached closer. She attacked him verbally for running off and leaving his younger brother to have to cope with his father. There was less than a small boat's length of space remaining between them, which made him feel uneasy and unwelcome. Looking downwards to the ground to hide his guilt, he apologised for the way things turned out for his younger brother; at the same time appealing to her that it was not his intention to argue, but that he needed to know if she was well. He gazed upon her seeing that life had not changed for her, there were lines beginning to form in her once pink-skinned face; probably, he thought, from the worry of his father. His eyes were full as he gazed upon her, but he dare not allow her to see his weakness and he turned away and mumbled something that was lost. After he had composed himself, he looked back and smiled and she returned the same; and although no words were spoken, he felt that with the passing of time she would have forgiven him for his absence. There was much left bottled up inside him and the words became lost, somehow it was the same with his mother; she wanted him to speak yet he knew she was fearful that friendliness could complicate their lives.

In spite of his years, Luca too sensed the difficulty of the situation guessing that little had changed at home for his mother. Another short silence occurred and he walked forwards towards her, reaching out for her hand, he placed a small bag of coins in her palm and closed it tightly. It was not a lot of money, but he was aware that it was more than she had ever held at any one time. He held her lovingly like a son, that short embrace cried out for forgiveness and understanding. He kissed her gently on the cheek and for a while gazed upon her one last time, then turned and left. Aware that he could not stay, nor could he cling to his mother, he was a man now and knowingly realised in his father's house he was not welcome. She stood rooted to the ground not knowing what to say or do. In her heart she wanted to chase after him and bring him back; but fear crossed her mind and bad thoughts of her husband came into her head; a vision of two men struggling with each other, which she could not abide to see. He was a good way down the old salt marsh track now out of calling distance and it was in her to shout her goodbye and wish him well. She took a pace or two and shouted realising that he could not hear her call, nor could he return, as her goodbye faded to a whisper and holding back a tear of loss she uttered under her breath.

"I will always love you my son." Then, with the surviving instincts of a mother, she turned and walked towards the blooms that sprang forth in a small patch in the garden and hid the pouch of money in her flower-bed; where Luca suspected she might, and in a melancholy mood returned to her washing. Luca never went back, nor did he ever see any of his family again from that day on.

The Core of a Man

After drinking for most of the evening, Luca needed to escape the sentimental stench of Venice. His next signing was to be his mistake of all mistakes; it took his life into an uncharted course of perilous waters which would lead to the shaping of the new man. Unknown to him, the merchantman that he had thought he had signed up with turned out to be a Venetian privateer. By this time the young Luca had considered himself a man; though on his next ship he was led and fashioned into becoming thoroughly corrupt. His new captain had seen something in Luca and had taken to the boy; slowly he gained his confidence and steered his progress downwards until he no longer recognised who he was. Within a short spell at sea he had learnt that survival by any means, fair or foul, was the rule of the day; on board ship, he who could steal and cheat and hold on to what he had, gaining the respect of the others aboard. In his short past, the exhilaration of the memorable time he killed the drunken mariner stayed with him; it became the key that opened the lock of Luca's dark inner being. He was a natural; only the wily captain had seen it; to him Luca's wickedness was a pearl that had dropped into his fortuitous hands from above.

They sailed the Adriatic coastline killing and stealing all they could get their thieving hands on; there was easy money and gold for the taking. In the middle-eastern waters, their favourite ploy was to feign helplessness of a stricken ship, luring other well-meaning souls to their assistance. The fate for those ships that foolishly came to their aid was a costly penalty for their humanitarian spirit, the ship would be taken, and in most cases the crew would be sold into slavery. Those who were not fit enough to earn their keep were sadly to lose their lives. What values Luca had placed on his clinging principles, he soon let loose; in truth, in those few years he graduated from a murderer to a wanton cut throat. Murder was more or less the order now given, and once he was through his pirate's pubescence there wasn't anyone more eager to fulfil evil deeds; it brought wealth, false respect and fear, and so his life tumbled along until he was eighteen.

After a long period of time of ravaging merchant ships, the news of these pirates was out and pressure grew on the Seljuk Sultans to rid the seas of this notorious human garbage. In answer to the outcry, the Sultan gave word to his naval fleet to hunt down the worthless pirates who were the scum of the sea, and a scourge to mankind that deserved all that was coming to them.

On a clear day and a calm sea, after many days of rain; eventually a lone naval scout sighted the privateer. Afraid to leave position to give the word of the sighting to other vessels of the fleet; they cautiously followed the ship at a safe distance to where the privateers weighed anchor in a lonely bay. Aware that there was no other ship to aid them in their task, the galley commander feared that to delay could cost him his prize; its captain took the only course of action open to him.

Whilst the pirates felt they were safe, they lay at anchor concealed in the small bay; its seclusion under the starlight canopy promised safety, and peace enveloped them in the night's cloak of darkness. Had it not been for their over confidence and negligence of carelessly leaving lanterns glowing on deck, marking their position for any other ship close by to see, a change of their fortunes soon came about; they now became the prey of the naval ship. Unaware that there was a predator out at sea that had been in pursuit all that day, they remained untroubled and relaxed, foolishly believing they were free from any threat of discovery. They were without concern, having taken a merchantman recently, and were living high on the new supply of wine; unaware that the naval battle galley was out on the open sea less than a nautical mile away and under the observation of the keen eyes of the galley captain having picked up on their position.

Excitedly and quietly, the captain issued his orders for silent ramming speed after sighting the ship's position; this time the privateers were not going to escape.

Slowly and silently, the oars of the war galley dipped into the salty waters causing each of the rowing crews determined action to build with speed as they neared their target, giving the greatest momentum to their final impact. The sounds of the oars could not be heard over the lapping waves of the sea; nor could ears affected by alcohol detect the stealth of approach. In fact, there were no watchful eyes to witness death's visitation emerging on its revengeful speeding course through the darkness. The galley's target neared quickly, the speed and the warriors aboard the galley had readied for their final assault; the intense slapping of the oars of the galley's blades ripped through the water to increase its ramming speed, building into a maddening crescendo. To the sleeping crew and those inebriated sailors that rolled the dice below decks, the sounds outside were inaudible whilst the incoherence of the external activities continued to be enjoyed. The parting waters marked the collision course; The Sultan's Galley directed its menacingly powerful armoured hull onwards to contact and a final bloody retribution. The oblivious crew could not have had time to save their miserable lives. Those that gambled could not cede the pull of the dice, neither could those full of drink find the energy or the nimbleness to draw themselves free from the comforting grip of their hammocks. The impacting contact with the pirate ship was with such violent force it almost heaved the anchored ship out of the water as the galley's speed and momentum carried it onwards, cleaving the pirate ship in two. The crashing impact was so effective it caused the sea to flood its broken sections, quickly sinking its remains and ejecting its crew helplessly as if sprinkled from a pepper pot into the murky waters of the night, leaving those few survivors there were floundering and dazed.

The heaving naval galley came to rest with a lurch over what was left of the floating remains of what once was a ship that caused such mayhem at sea. The Sultan's men were eager to seek out those struggling crewmen that failed to perish in the ramming; the galley's crew were ready dangling oil lamps over the side of the ship to aid the sporting archers and spearmen to deliver their piercing points of justice into the murderous floating bodies. Those that fought with their last gasping breath to remain alive did so for the benefit of the waiting archers, but for them their efforts of self-preservation were all in vain. The last few remaining survivors, who were seen splashing about helplessly in the shallower water, were to become the sport of the naval crew who taunted and hacked and slashed at the bobbing bodies mercilessly before leaving them for fish bait.

Only one man escaped that terrible slaughter in the water; Luca. He was on deck at the time of the ramming, talking with the watchman and looking landwards into the night, contemplating how he would spend his ill won gains, and on sudden contact with the galley was thrown clear on the point of impact. He didn't know what hit him, but being a born survivor, once he had hit the water he had the foresight to instinctively swim underwater to remain undetected when the slaughter commenced. Whilst the mayhem and death were in full play, he managed to drag himself out of the water and onto the darkened shore line, his panic stricken breathing was heavy and his heart raced faster than he had ever experienced in his effort to remain hidden from the eyes of those that sought him and others of his kind. The shocked and exhausted Luca, half drowned from the amount of water he had swallowed after his sudden projection to the sea, paused at a nearby tree to catch his breath and look back. His aching body retched, expelling the intake of salt water, and his sodden clothing ran off water like a cataract. Back in the torch lit darkness, his shipmates were screaming their heads off; butchery was the order wherever they were found.

Having the instincts of a rat to leave a sinking ship; Luca did not linger; there was definitely no time to rest. To escape the hunting parties that were bound to take place, he knew that to survive this night he must make for the cover of the denser undergrowth and move as quickly and as far inland as possible. With great effort and determination, he forced himself up the beach and out of view of searching eyes. Panting breathlessly as he took each painful step to search for a route inland and away from danger; all the time his body craved for rest. Echoing in his ears were the occasional screams from his persecuted fellow crewmen that were discovered alive and left in the water to fend for themselves. The cries behind ceased in number; he wasn't stopping to view the scene, guessing that the hunters would shortly be ashore looking for signs of any men that may have escaped them.

The weight of his saturated clothes on his tired body impeded his hasty retreat into the trees; terror filled his contorted mind and his heart pumped to bursting. Flashes of the event filled his racing mind as he imagined he could hear the oars dipping into the water as the merciless avenging Muslims began closing in. Without stopping, he pulled off his clothes to reduce the weight that slowed him down, although he was in a panicked state, his mind's instincts for survival told him sensibly to keep a good hold on them, for come daybreak his need would be for their protection from the searing sun. He ran for his life, to where he could not tell, only away from the carnage; the cold night air caught his body in a grip and in his exhausted state, weakened him even more. Almost naked and shivering, he had little choice but to press on. His advance at times had slowed a pace in the darkness, his aching and tired body screamed for rest but the need to sustain the distance between those he felt were pursuing him was impelling him frighteningly onwards.

Weakened efforts to wring out his wet clothes as he ran caused him to blindly stumble; snivelling along his miserable way proved awkward; he found difficulty watching his path to prevent stumbling and clearly occupy his thoughts at the same time. Occasionally, he was thwarted by outstretched branches of trees which tore at his skin and poked at him like accusing fingers as he forced a path through the gauntlet of prodding spears. He felt persecuted; overgrown thorn branches that strayed across his darkened path snagged at his flesh, as if reaching out to slash at him and impede his flight. In his fear he felt nothing; the single most important thought in his mind was to run for all his worth; to get away as fast as he could. Though the sounds of the dying screams of his shipmates were far behind, they remained echoing in his ears, causing him further blind panic. Feeling the forest was closing in on him, he could not help to save himself from franticly stumbling through clumps of darkened prickly undergrowth which so often occurred in his way. Alone and driven by fear, he broke down and cried; it was as if he was trying to draw attention and help, but from whom? No, Luca realised it wasn't going to happen; instead his instincts for fear turned into determination with a will to survive; he would not bend or yield. His prime concern was to find a place of shelter to hide and somehow warm his now bloodied, freezing and grazed body. The sheer compelling determination and strength of his spirit had driven his exhausted body and demented mind onwards, almost to the point of collapse. Tantrums of the mind wanted to scream out his temper and frustration. On higher ground, his exhaustion finally slowed his pace; spent of energy he could not subdue the loud sounds that came from his breathless and fatigued being. He fell, unable to continue his flight; it became quiet and all above him in the heavens was peace. His head fixed in a gazing position gasping loudly for air into the void whilst his body transfixed to the earth shook nervously; his brain told him that he could go no further.

Suddenly, without reason other than instinct, he became alarmed; he cocked his head so that he could listen more intently to the sounds in the night that had caught his attention. Fearful that his enemy was near, he dramatically held his body close to the earth; the scrubby undergrowth he believed would save him from searching eyes that may be out there looking for him. For some time he lay there quite still, shivering and riddled with terror; stricken and anxious of what was to happen to him, only the sound of his chattering teeth could be heard above his pulsating heartbeat. His crazed frightened mind cautioned him to place both hands over his mouth to prevent any sound escaping so that the searchers whoever they were could not detect his cringing body. The night sounds subsided into calm, he listened intently as normality returned; certain that he was safe he edged stealthily forwards cautiously listening for whatever it was he thought that he had sensed earlier. A sound definitely broke from ahead which startled him, there it was again; more sounds; but they seemed different, his tormented ears found difficulty distinguishing what was real and what he imagined. He was almost at the point of breaking, the helplessness and finality of life that he once inflicted on his past victims had returned to repay him. With his nerves stretched to the limits, his hand groped blindly for some kind of weapon to defend himself, refusing to give in to any man who may be out there. He began to talk aloud, whilst his cut and bleeding fingers caught onto a piece of dead wood, which he clutched firmly. In his effort to build a false sense of bravado within himself, he cautiously closed in on the sounds ahead. His nervous and frightened state made his sense of hearing more acute to the sounds in the night as he tentatively listened. Now a different fear grew as he realised that the undergrowth was thinning out, leading to open land, and he became fearful for the loss of tree cover to shield him.

Strained like a cornered animal and pushed to his limits, feelings of discovery rose, almost choking him; he paused now for the final time to gain his breath before having to chance at dashing out into the open darkness. Unlike his character, he knew not what fate awaited him; something akin to bravado stirred within; Luca Rici would not go down without a struggle. The noises came again and he stiffened in readiness to strike out with the stick he had previously stumbled on. The noise returned again; unsure of the numbers that awaited him, he began to question the sounds; his hand gripped the weapon harder as if to encourage himself forwards. His grip suddenly relaxed, confused with the sounds he was lost to do anything; his emotions gave way to little more than a helpless squeak of tearful relief, forcing its way out of Luca's throat like a kitten desperate for its mother. He fell to his knees crying and laughing; the noises in the darkness became louder and recognisable, relief flowed over his taut features; his tense strained body relaxed, the noises became plainly identifiable; they were goats.

Without any doubt, Luca was relieved, yet spent of energy and feeling safer, his divisive mind began building on a plan, and the thought of food and heat, which he was desperately in need of. A nagging sensation of caution in his mind told him to stay his action, realising that where there are goats, there was most likely to be a goatherd. Luca's progress through the undergrowth so far had been somewhat panicked and cumbersome, his scratched bruised and bloodied body was testament to his ordeal and his eyes still strained in his attempts to guide his path of frenzied escape through the night. Overhead low cloud had drifted in on the night winds offering little or no light from the twinkling stars as the curtain of darkness draped itself over the landscape, hampering his sense of sight. The cold of the night air forced him to wrap his wet clothes over his scrawny shivering body that was now beseeching him to seek a means of cover.

His heartbeat slowed; his sanity returned; assured that he had escaped the predators back at the beach. He set about concentrating his mind on the simple goatherds that must sooner or later come across him. Only for the odd glimmer of light from the twinkling stars of the firmament enabled him to spy a crouching shape; staring hard, he suspected its form to be the herd of goats. On the other hand it could possibly be a resting herdsman, the more his eyes searched the more he was sure of it in his mind. He paused, gripping the wooden branch that he had found and prepared himself for attack. Weak and spent of energy, Luca's mind worked at a rate; his active cowardly mind began to weigh the disadvantages of stealing forwards to kill the shepherd. Thinking it could lead to complications, he thought better of his plan. First, he felt that he must hide most of his clothes in the brush making it appear that he had earlier been waylaid. Fearfully cautious that there may be others about and though he was freezing, the agility and cunning of his mind calculated his chances like lightening. Slowly he moved forwards then quietly dropped on all fours and began moaning aloud. Lying outstretched on the ground, he took the role of a man in need of help and in deep distress, which he truly was, for no man could be more in need of aid than he. Shouting was heard and soon after two herders carrying lighted torches curiously approached in his direction as his helpless and lamented sounds of need had drifted to them through the night. Luca played his role with excellence, guiding the unsuspecting and innocent searchers to their discovery, probably his training as a privateer had proved most useful for this very ploy.

When the innocent shepherds came upon him; they were truly shocked at the sight of the distressed bleeding man lying naked before them; shocked and dismayed they immediately began to discuss how and why this poor man came to be here. This was not quite what Luca expected, the heat from the torches that the two goatherds carried were comforting; but it was not enough to stop him shivering from the cold. He felt like ordering them into action, he was freezing to death and the stupid rescuers were talking over him instead of attending to him. Luca moaned, hinting his needs as best as he could; it was all he could do to encourage the rescue to get under way. The inactivity lengthened whilst he supposed they were discussing his needs; it was a relief to hear the older voice rattle off what sounded like orders for help. The next thing he felt was the weight of what he imagined to be a hairy strong smelling pelt being thrown over his body, he had been close to worse smelling objects before and this one at least offered protection; at last.

Shivering with extreme coldness, the covering of his nakedness gave him some immediate relief from the night air. Jostled awkwardly for a moment, he was lifted and bundled over a shoulder like a piece of meat for the butcher's block; before being carried off most uncomfortably. He smugly suspected that his rescue was now underway and a feeling of relaxation entered him in the safety of the company of the simple Samaritans. Like a dangling sausage, he bounced on the shoulder of the lumbering oaf that carried him, Luca felt like complaining, he didn't have a grateful bone in his body. Like an inquisitive spy; he eyed everything that he could without being detected. When they reached the campsite, he noticed through his squinting sight a young man busily crouching over a fire, having built it up in readiness as previously ordered by the elderly man, probably his father. He was carefully placed down alongside the fire; his cover lifted away to allow the heat of the blazing fire to quickly reach him. Whilst the elderly man set about attempting to revive him by rubbing his arms and legs to encourage the blood to flow better through his body whilst the flame of the fire did the rest of the work. The rough hands of the goatherd did little to excite him with all the rubbing of his flesh, even in his famished state he felt like telling his Samaritan that a good woman would have saved him his energy. Before long, the shivering Luca slowly felt the warming heat of the fire reviving his chilled body, once warmed he became relaxed; free from fear of being hunted, and in his state of contentment did little more than draw the animal skin over his exhausted body and fall into a deep sleep.

The next morning he woke early, stiffened by the previous night's exhilaration and strain on his unused muscles, in his panicked efforts to escape from the night's slaughter he had overworked his muscles making him feel pained and impossible to rise. Watching his strained efforts to rise, the herdsman came to him with a skin bag. They spoke to him gently but he could not understand them; neither did he care. He hesitated as a skin bag was raised to his parched lips, apprehensive of the knowledge that he was unsure of what was to be drunk. The hand that gripped him was strong raising him forwards almost to a sitting position; the bag was placed to his mouth the burly bearded herdsman smiled at him gesturing that he drink, which he did so with a certain reluctance. It was milk and it tasted foul to his taste yet cooling as it passed down his gullet, soothing the rawness in his throat that had been caused by the copious amounts of seawater he had swallowed the previous night. It was far from what Luca was used to drinking and the taste of the offensive liquid caused him to break out into a fit of coughing; he stuck his tongue out and pulled a face. The attentive herdsman swiftly reacted patting his back and smiling whilst gently offering a word of comfort, though his words were wasted on Luca.

"Good," he said, Luca was baffled by the man's words. The herdsman repeated, "Good" in his language, this time Luca grasped his meaning without smiling repeating, "Good" in a gruff and hoarse voice. Holding the flask aloft, it was pushed forwards again for him to take one more long drink. There was no doubt he was the centre of attraction but there was not much activity between the herdsmen watching him. The warmth of the flaming fire that had been built up was for his benefit, it must have burned brightly most of the night to maintain the heat for Luca's comfort, it was their way to extend the courtesy of their camp to one in so much need. Another skin bag of liquid was offered which Luca took for more goats milk, he took it down unsuspecting and quickly he felt a fire grow in him causing the blood to surge through his veins and making him sit up quickly drawing in large amounts of air as was possible. Laughter ensued from the onlookers; the unsuspecting fiery liquid gave instantaneous life to his sickened limp body; in spite of the shock; the reason why they didn't give it to him last night for a quicker revival completely escaped him. With heavy breath, he believed that was more like what he was used to, instead of their repulsive loathsome milk. Sitting more comfortably, but still weak and aching, he sat upright and cross-legged, bent forwards over the fire absorbing the heat and staring blankly into the dancing flames. Although Luca appeared slightly numbed, his brain was only resting; he only wished that the great smelly patchwork of a goat skin wrap that covered his nakedness could be discarded.

In the safety of the camp, Luca enjoyed the luxury of having time to pass his mind over his new plans; first he congratulated himself on holding back from storming the camp, knowing now that he would not have stood a chance in an affray. He was not stupid enough to convince himself that in his weak state he was going anywhere; his flight from his attackers back at the beach had taken too much out of him. His eyes grew heavy and he did no more than pull the borrowed goat skin wrap tighter around himself, his body slid helplessly back to the ground and he laid his aching frame sideways in readiness for further sleep.

All eyes were watching him, and on the spur of the moment his naked arm reached out from inside the clothing offering his hand in thanks to the good Samaritans. They knew instantly the message was a gesture of thanks and it gratified them to see it, and to the simple herders it gave them a great sense of fulfilment to their moral code. Great smiles and sounds of consolation filled the camp as Luca's weakness gave way to sleep, his head snuggled down beneath the covering of the skin; a smug smile showed on his drawn features, if there was anything that delighted him most, it was the satisfaction of getting something over on gullible and unsuspecting folk.

Luca slept soundly that day and was awakened in the morning with a hot brew under his nose causing his mouth to fill with juices; he was famished and ready to eat a horse. After a second bowl of hot meat stew he felt so much better; considering what length of stay he may burden his hosts with. Then to his surprise, the answer lay at his feet. His cheeks filled with redness as he realised his game was up; his clothes had been collected and dried and placed close by. Hardened to the world as he was, his embarrassment was short lived as his mind passed fleetingly over the event, though he dearly hoped that he would not have to explain their being found so readily. Not so much to hint that his time had come to move on, but if he felt strong enough to dress, his clothes were ready for that purpose. He looked around for the first time; noticing that the herdsmen had chosen their camp well.

With a rocky outcrop to their back to shield them from the cool night breezes, scrub and woodland close by to provide them with sufficient kindling wood for their fires. Below them stretched a lowland plain, promising plenty of grazing on the slopes leading down to cultivated orchards of citrus fruits. He dressed and stretched his body, which was presently proving to be much stronger. Looking out across the plain he knew he had to leave, but where he knew not what direction to make for? His senses at this moment could not help him for he didn't have a clue as to where he was; nor where the nearest sea port could be found. Confusion over his location didn't help, in truth he had slept late; too late and missed the sun rise for any indication of where to start. The high points that stood before him in the distance he had never seen before, which left him guessing for a route to take. It seemed he wasn't much better off than before. Beyond the plain he did not know what to expect, there could be bandits or worse; perhaps some official body waiting to capture him and take him back to the nearest city to try him and cut off his head for his misdemeanours.

The herdsmen came to him with a small bundle containing food and a goatskin bag of water. Distracting his concentration he felt like ignoring them, he smiled openly to avoid any discourtesy. It was then that he decided to have one more try at communicating, to try to ascertain what his actual position was. He began very badly, there seemed to be no getting through to them, his hapless efforts almost made him short tempered in frustration.

One last try, he thought, and speaking the place name of Lattakia; it gave an immediate response from both herdsmen as they smiled gleefully repeating the name before pointing in its direction with knowing recognition. The elder looked around and found a branch, which he began to use; drawing in the sand a route that Luca should take. It seemed clear that his way was to take him across the plain and through a gorge in the distant mountains that would eventually lead him on to Lattakia. The herdsman ushered him forwards from the camp, not in any way to be rid of him, but to simply point him in the right direction. The clearing overlooking the valley was expansive; to enable Luca to see his way clearly, the elder of the two men positioned his body behind Luca. Extending his arms alongside of the head, he focused Luca's eyes in line with the direction for the way of his direction. Luca nodded and smiled as his eyes caught onto the shape of the mountain pass that the elder man had earlier drawn for him in the earth. With Luca's sign of understanding, the herdsmen appeared happy that they were able to help this unfortunate man. Whilst the men babbled on agreeably in their own language in a manner that conveyed some kind of pride of their achievement, excited with the new knowledge, Luca was at last content he was fixed on a point in the direction of his choosing. Unable to delay his journey any longer, he said his farewells leaving the herdsmen before their constant babbling sent him mad; they meant only to be helpful. Although the hand of kindness was extended to a stranger in distress, Luca found it difficult to understand their willingness to exercise such charity; and thought little more of it as a means of easy exploitation.

Settled that he had a course, Luca set out in a south westerly direction to the point he was shown on the horizon, crossing through the orchards and Olive groves he had seen earlier from the shepherd's camp. The plain opened to him, displaying the distant peaks that were to be his destination for this day's walking. It was pleasant passing through the groves that led on to the fresh dewy green meadows, where the grass cooled his bare feet as he trudged onwards with a carefree heart and a feeling of wellbeing. He felt lucky, he was free and making his way back to civilisation and who knows what opportunity he would find, once he had arrived at his destination.

Thinking back to his shipmates; he thought on his good fortune; at the same time his lip puckered as he imagined their fate. The memory of the terrible screams that fateful night soon became short lived, what really wounded him was thinking of his share of the treasures that presently lay on the sea bed amidst the shattered timbers of the ship.

It had been a good season and the wealth he had lost would have set him up for life.

By mid-morning he was feeling the heat, his brow was leaking an abundant amount of sweat and was continually being wiped with the cuff of his open shirt sleeve, which presently hung loosely on his wrist. The material had become stiff and abrasive in drying on the softened tissue of his brow; causing him some discomfort whenever he used it to soothe his reddened sunburnt forehead. The air was still and dry and the sun was climbing higher towards its peak; getting ever hotter and making his journey uncomfortable. His legs ached and his bare feet were getting sore; he wanted help but there was no one to appeal to, leaving Luca feeling very sorry for his situation.

Looking about his position, he suddenly became aware of the openness of the land before him; he had to keep going no matter what the terrain; it was useless snivelling. By the end of the morning his feet were becoming troublesome; he was a mariner and not cut out for this tramping around the land. The deck of a ship was what he was used to; it bore no similarity to the hot scrubby earth. Hard though it was, he put aside his aches and pains recognising the plain fact that if he was ever going to reach Lattakia he had to make some positive means to safeguard his aching feet, or else they would soon be raw and possibly bleeding, making his progress impossible and left to be marooned in this sea of emptiness. That was enough to concern him and spur his progress onward; for if he could not walk he would die here and that was the shocking realisation that would bring about his final end.

As a means of diverting his mind away from aches and pains, he became actively engaged in ways to utilise something as a protective covering for his ill-fated feet. His mind was shallow and unable to maintain concentration for long enough to solve his problem, which was constantly yielding to the pain in his feet, making his inability to come up with an answer to avert his feelings from his unhappy state. He admonished himself out aloud and wrestled to rid himself of his defeatist sense of destitution; "Luca," he shouted aloud, "it is useless feeling this way," and deep inside the message sank in because he knew it. Throughout his suffering bout and just as he was failure was to descend upon Luca, fate smiled upon him; hope stared him in the face as he spied a small group of palms coming into view up ahead, which he eagerly made for. Apart from the constant reminder of his troublesome feet, all he wanted was to drink and lay down for a while out of the heat of the day.

Relief came when he reached and stood beneath the shade of the overhanging branches, he threw out his arms in delight to welcome their coolness which had become his saving refuge. Although the air was hot, he was at least in shade, escaping the relentless burning rays of the sun. Flopping his body down into the shade of the leafy palms, he lay motionless for a short while, accepting the comfort of his present position. Now that he was saved, he struggled with the dilemma of remaining in the shade and resting up for a while, believing that he would be stronger the following day. Luck for him was the voice of reason; reflecting his time before being rescued, he recalled the coldness of the night air; would he be able to withstand that coldness or would it certainly see him off with the lack of suitable clothing or a fire to warm him. He was caught in a situation that gave him little choice, it was then he decided he would only stay long enough for a nap and something to eat. As weak-willed as he was to press on, his head ruled the day for the realisation of his survival should he delay. His attention was soon drawn to his shirt that was twisted into uncomfortable creases, it rubbed and clung to his sweating body. The sanctuary of the tree's cooling parasol seduced him to relax a little longer; doing so, he once again viewed his sore and aching feet from his lying position. They had become an angry red, bordering on raw, and did not look in too good a state; that became another problem to consider. He knew he had to continue his trek, or perish; Luca was a survivor. A solution to that problem was required, though hunger was his first priority; remembering the herdsman's gift of food, he reached over to the small parcel that he had been carrying inside his shirt. It had been pressed against his sweating body throughout his journey and had become quite wet and smelly; though by this time, his hunger was such that it would not deter his eating it. This was his first food of the day since leaving camp and he was eager to unwrap the lumpy cheese curd and set about greedily gorging on it. The messy contents within the skin wrapping was licked clean, there was a saltiness to the cheese's taste that kept his tongue busy moving around the edges of his parched lips. That wasn't as bad as he remembered it, his lips smacked at his enjoyment. Popping the small cork of his water skin bag he offered it up to his mouth; it was refreshing and cleansed the cloyingness of the cheese from his tongue and throat, giving him a new vigour to get on, feeling better and restored of energy for the rest of his journey. Laying sprawled in the shade, he casually viewed the two peaks that he had to keep in view, the distant mountains appeared much closer; but quite obviously still a fair walk away. It did not occur to him that he was not making the best use of the daylight period and that it would take the rest of the day to reach them, and the best part of the following day at least to reach the coast.

Under the coolness of the tree, his idle mind drifted back to his immediate problem of his sore feet. He pondered whether to rip his shirt to cover them by placing the long loose cuff of his sleeve over his foot for size. It did not take long before that considered opinion was rejected; realising that without the shirt to protect his back his body would be badly blistered before nightfall. There has to be another way, lingering on the subject further until a smile of intuition appeared on his face. Holding up his shirt, he set about ripping out the sleeves, he tore at the thick green leathery leaves that sheltered him until he had enough for his purpose. Then, folding them, set about placing them on the underside of the foot before binding them to his feet. He was sure that this would enable him to journey further; at least his feet felt cooler and better already. The hem line was next, tearing at his shirt, he carefully managed to draw off enough material to act as a tie band for his head. With the shirt draped lengthways and secured with his new creation, a band around his head allowed the shirt to fall covering his back. By crossing his arms across himself he gripped the edges of the shirt pulling in the sides to prevent the sun from attacking his back and partly exposed areas of his upper arms when walking. Although it was uncomfortable walking with his arms crossed, he felt a lot happier that he remained protected from the pitiless sun; this increased his confidence in his ability of crossing what was left of the plain by nightfall.

By mid-afternoon he had left all trace of any green scrub behind and was now crossing a hard-baked, totally barren, plain denude of growth of any kind.

Though the terrain had changed, he found himself following a well-trodden hard clay road that he did not at first realise he was on. It resembled an old scar that meandered across the landscape before heading upwards from the plain towards the mountains, and what's more, there were encouraging signs of fresh camel dung on the road. He was quick to notice that it was only sufficient dung for one camel, although his sharp eyes detected that there was more than one set of animal prints. Scanning the horizon in both directions, he covered his brow with his hand to see if there was any sign of travellers in view. Exhaling deeply at the absence of life anywhere to be seen, he hovered over the dung with thoughts that his expectations could be wrong. Studying the dung further, he poked at it with his uncovered toe. It was soft; to make sure, he rolled it around under his toe, gently squeezing it for moisture and warmth hoping for a hint of information. It was soft and definitely fresh, the warmth that he felt could possibly be from the heat of the day, and the look on Luca's face indicated that there was new hope for him. The fresh spongy feel of the dung was encouraging, had it have been there much longer it would surely have been crusty and dry. Less than a day and raising it to his nose; it proved to contain a newness of passing. His mind had become suddenly very active, giving rise to his theory that the travellers would probably camp in the hills that night.

Driven by the fact that he was without shelter and food for the evening gave rise to his hopeful heart; believing that if he found the camp, perhaps these travellers may extend their hospitality and shelter to him.

Convinced that he was on their track, his spirits were up but that was more than he could say for the state of his foot coverings, they were beginning to show signs of wear and further his feet were tiring and sore. He had to reach the mountains to survive and it was there that he hoped and expected help and sustenance from his would be Samaritans at their encampment.

By evening, after persevering against the harshness of the baked ground and searing sun, he had achieved part of his goal having crossed the hard barren plain and reaching the base of the mountains; the sun was falling and the heat was rapidly leaving the day. To his great disappointment the road surface had changed from hard baked clay to one of stone and grit; the trail was misleading. To Luca's despondent eyes they did not appear to be leading directly into the mountains; but appeared to skirt around them. There were no tracks to follow and, unexpectedly, he had lost any signs of his would be Samaritans. In his frustration and disappointment, his temper erupted into exasperation at the idea of having to continue onwards blindly with his search. To add to his feelings of discontent, his stomach began to rumble, prompting the awareness that he was without any food and in need of nourishment. It seemed that it had been long ago that he finished his water after believing that he, or they, the Samaritans, would be like their brother shepherds willing to give sustenance to a lone man wandering from off the desert. The saltiness of the cheese had long dried up his lips and mouth proving it a hard lesson to Luca to have wasted his ration of water.

When the sun came up the following day, if he survived, hunger and thirst would add to his troubles; he was desperate to seek out the camp site this very evening. He had surprised himself on his ability to walk the plain in the day; it gave him confidence to continue; after all he had endured, he was determined.

Luca continued on as far as was safe to go, dusk was falling and his empty stomach continued to audibly rumble, only now hunger was proving a painful reminder of his plight. His hand reached from below his thin shirt to rub the noisy erupting disturbances that emanated from his gut; his skin was cold and he gave a shudder with the sudden drop he was experiencing in the temperature. He tugged tighter at his thin shirt to hug his body, telling himself that he must maintain his strength and find cover to survive the night's chill. About him grew scrub and other vegetation; his eyes strained in the shadows of dusk, attempting to find a place where he could nestle for shelter from the cold night air that was descending upon him. Once again, he felt that lonely feeling about him; through the gloom there seemed no sign of life anywhere; he was totally alone; then his eye flickered fleetingly catching on what he thought was a momentary flicker of light from afar. Fumbling to hold on to the thin shirt around his body, he awkwardly rubbed his eyes with his fingers. That must be the camp he thought, I'm saved, oh how it changed his mood, then disappointingly there was nothing to see through the gloom. Shit, shit, shit, had he imagined it after his sudden rush of blood that made him forget his shivers; but despondency was with him and he was back to feeling alone again.

He could only stand and stare into the darkness disappointed and unsure whether it was some kind of trick of the shadow and light, he looked again but alas there was nothing. He was confused, his brow wrinkled with his doubts, he could have sworn he saw something; this sort of thing never happened to him before. Frustrated, he screamed out an abusive mix of foul language from out of the dryness of his parched mouth; running forwards in a desperate attempt to discover what he had seen; he realised he had lost that, which disappointed him so. Stumbling forwards, tripping on loose shale, he lost his balance and careered forwards destined for a fall, missing his footing and balance altogether. The ground began to rise, he could not fail in scraping the skin on his hands as they instinctively reached out to break the fall. His weakness of character, with the fall and the consequence of the bruising effect on him, gave rise to a further stream of obscenities. With tears of frustration forming in his tired eyes, he clutched his skinned, hurting hands tightly around his cold body, whinging and feeling sorry for himself. His view was becoming pointedly desperate with the darkness and his instincts of survival diminishing; he was rapidly weakening in spirit. Tormented by the need to reach cover and warmth, the evening chill struck him deeper, sending shivers through his quaking skeleton. Looking around for means of support to assist his rising, his eye once again caught that elusive flicker of light and instantly his heart leapt; now he knew that he wasn't imagining what he had previously seen. A sly grin showed onto his chilled face; for he had realised that the fleeting light to have been the glow of sparks dancing high above a healthy flaming fire; "yes," he whispered, giving rise to the hope that this night Luca Rici would sleep well. The dark side of Luca began to emerge, his mind raced with ideas and the craft and guile of his character began to take over, the villainous coward had to decide whether or not the camp ahead was friendly, for that; he would first have to sneak within sight of it. Removing the ties that held his shirt on his head, he now slipped it around his shivering body, with the freedom of his hands he set about to clamber the rocky slope.

The night sky was clouding over, promising the arrival of total darkness; there were few twinkling stars to be seen with only sparse light to give any hint of shape that loomed up ahead of him. The gloom limited his vision, but he could not be stopped; carefully and quietly he picked his way over the rocky slope like a night creature on the prowl across the rocky darkness of the hillside. Drawn as if he could not help himself, the glow became less elusive until he was able to clearly see the burning campfire, visible to his eye, it remained a distance away. Luca dared not make a noise; slowly he continued stalking the camp like a hungry cat until from a rocky ledge he could clearly see all within the camp site. Shivering and hungry he arched his body upward from the ground to improve his view, he became guarded with his sighting, puzzled that he clearly viewed only one person and three camels in the camp. Luca instantly looked right and left; he almost panicked; perhaps the missing man was out here looking for him; he could be armed and that worried him. He would wait and see if one returned from the shadows; his nerves were bristling, but the longer Luca waited, the colder he became.

On the brink of the ridge, Luca glared at the fire almost hungrily for the heat of the flame; the fire burned brightly spitting its sparks in all directions, while the man in the camp busied himself unconcerned to the activity about him. Standing with his back to Luca, it denied him any knowledge as to whether or not the traveller was armed. The lone character appeared to be preparing food, probably his supper, Luca drooled at the thought of food and his heart ached at the thought that he was out in the cold and not sharing this repast; it was not a sight that Luca wished to endure. His searching eyes darted everywhere, whilst his mind weighed the argument of entering the camp as a lost individual. The decision was otherwise; though if there had been another man he should have returned by now. With a mind filled with a riot of thought of multifarious reasons for delaying such action, flashes of warrants entered his mind. He could have been well-received and fed, only to be duped, to be later arrested in the villages ahead; a warning could have been posted to be on the lookout for any unwary travellers appearing in a distressed state seeking assistance.

With mixed feelings, his mind returned to the question of the chances of the man being armed, he could be an old warrior; he cared not for the chance of being left wounded, to die in the middle of nowhere. The thought of being hurt did not appeal to him either and his inaction only made him restless with further indecision. The groaning of his empty stomach bubbled away reminding him of the delay to act; he needed to sweep this fear aside and ignore the cowardice that had unsettled him, if he were going to eat he would wait; the safest way to share in this man's food was when he was asleep.

Time went by and there became little doubt that the traveller was alone, too much time had gone by for another to have just been absent; though Luca continued watching the traveller. The damned man was humming a tune and appearing in high spirits, Luca hated that, for he was shivering while this damned man was rejoicing. He watched him walk over to where he had hobbled his camels for the night; drawing a bag from the shadows, he dutifully poured each camel a small mound of grain onto the ground, which the beasts hungrily snaffled up. Impatience filled Luca to overflowing; silently urging the stranger to get on with his duties so that he could get on to resting. His resentful eyes did not miss a thing, every morsel of food that was shared around the animals was met with a groan of envy, and the careless traveller even spilt water on the ground. Luca's parched tongue edged from his mouth and over his lip as if to taste the spilt water and his head bent forwards with contemptuous disgust as he realised he could do little about the situation. Nothing escaped his covetous eyes that glared hard and longingly from the shadows; especially the movements of the traveller about the camp, how he held himself and how agile he was, Luca's eyes grew wide taking in his quarry's every movement.

With his chores complete, the traveller turned and returned to the warming fire, maintaining his content frame of mind whilst continuing to hum his song. Luca carefully eyed the stranger's appearance for the first time, clearly in his view, he could now see the stranger was an ageing man, well dressed but armed with a sizeable knife in the sash about his waist. It gave heart to Luca to learn that this man was likely travelling alone in the desert; he was certainly taking a risk or knew this country well to feel so safe.

From what he now was able to deduce, Luca felt much better; still apprehensive about his quarry being armed, he considered that it would be safer to wait, and it was his guess that the aged gentleman would soon prepare to rest and sleep soundly. The chilly night air gripped Luca's body, bringing with it a shiver, unable to warm himself he stared painfully at the fire as if to glean heat from its image. How long he could maintain his position he did not know, but the shivers that ran over his body now were much more frequent, causing his mouth to close tighter as his teeth chattered erratically. The aged man sat contentedly eating his supper, unaware of the jealous and enviable eyes of a hungry onlooker beyond the camp. When finished, he then proceeded to build up the fire and lay down beside it to go to sleep.

Luca desperately fought off the urge to rush forwards prematurely before the man was in his slumber; he nurtured a longing to smother his chilling body over the warmth of the flaming fire. But he would have to be patient and wait until the man was snoring and the fire was low before making his move.

Lying outside the camp for so long with the bitter night air assailing his body, Luca once more exercised his stiffening limbs with silent and sickening patience. He could feel a numbing in his extremities taking effect; he tightened his body by holding himself in as strong a grip as he could. It worked for a while, but he knew that he could not withstand the restraining torture of his waiting much longer. Betwixt his thoughts as to chance whether to creep stealthily past the old man or wide of him in making for the fire or towards his baggage for food, the rocks that he lay on were fast becoming as cold as he was. That made his mind up; he was colder than he had ever been in his life and, driven by his aching stiffening limbs, he cautiously made the first tentative movement towards the centre of the camp. The sounds of the sleeping stranger further encouraged Luca; in the camp his shivering body caught a wave of residual heat from the fire as he closed on it. The numbing of his fingers stretched out to receive the heat; it was good, so much so that he had to have more of it; he lingered to catch its heat. The fire may have been dying but Luca coveted its heat with his body; he was as close to it as he could bear, absorbing the needed heat with much appreciation. It was some time before Luca could leave the fire; driven by his other need to overcome his hunger, he was aware that the baggage and food lay near the animals. Warmed to a greater fitness to move, he was at the bags and impatient to find sustenance; he was oblivious of the noise he created, noisily searching for food. The sleeping man grew restless and began to stir. Making an effort to sit up, the old man in his sleepy state was curious to see the cause of the sounds about him, he uttered words of enquiry of who was there.

Well, Luca was scarred out of his wits, blood surged rapidly through his aching veins, and in a blind panic he reverted to doing the thing that came most naturally to him, he did no more than pick up the first hand sized rock he saw. Racing over to the old man with fearfully incredible speed, the assailant rained a series of frenzied and heavy fatal blows remorselessly down upon the ageing man's head. He was probably dead with the first blow, but excitement surged through Luca's veins, finding it difficult to stop his attack. Blood pumped wildly around his head, causing him to grow slightly dizzy from the spasm of mania that caught him; exhausted, he slowly and breathlessly returned to his senses; hauling himself over to the fire where he slumped before it panting in exhaustion. Luca's head throbbed from his actions; he was unaware that he was bending so closely to the fire, there was insufficient heat coming from it to burn him, but it was all he could do to return to his senses. He staggered to his feet, his legs were shaky, unable to walk the few steps required to the pile of kindling and dung that lay nearby; he stretched lazily, exhausted with the effort. The attack had weakened him so much he failed to grasp the kindling that had been stored for the morning fire. Slowly his fingers gained their feeling and reached onto the pile enabling him to grasp and drag the needed kindling over, placing the pile carefully over the embers he patiently waited for the flames to rise. Patience was no longer with him, heat was required and to boost its reviving heat, he gave the fire a blow to draw a flame. Waiting eyes opened wide with satisfaction as a flicker grew into a glowing flame; the fire rekindled itself afresh, which was so welcome to warm his frigid and aching body. Once the heat had taken effect, he could prop himself upright; nervously, he drew more of the heat of the flame but his body remained shivering from his foul deed. With enough dung nearby to keep the fire alive, he relaxed; weakness crept over him; he was tired and hungry and his body finally yielded to the warm ground. The flames grew ever higher; and in the moments he remained lucid; he knew that he was sapped of his energy; slowly fatigue had taken him into a state of unconsciousness.

Luca did not awaken until daybreak and then it was only because of his body shivering in the coolness of the early morning, his first reaction was to reach for the warmth of the fire. Luckily the ash was still warm and with care he realised he could easily blow life into it, as he did the night before. He crossed the camp, troubled and nervously shaking to where he found the few remaining scrub twigs he had missed the previous night. Eagerly, he carried them over to the remains of the fire, where he carefully placed them on the ashes. His face was close to the earth as he blew onto the ashes of the fire, his actions sent plumes of ash billowing upwards into clouds. He screamed when his eyes stung as fragments blew back into them; the blowing ceased, waiting for the ash to settle, he thought he felt a glimmer of heat shortly after. His head lay still in the soft earth, through the haze of his watering eyes, they focused on the rigid lifeless body of the old man who had died from Luca's frenzied onslaught across from where he was crouching. He had forgotten about him, and in the immediate seconds that followed, shock waves reverberated through his body; sickness numbed him, scared with discovery at the sight of the bloody mess that was his doing, he momentarily became rigid with guilt.

Accepting that the man was dead, his mind began to flick back with sordid images from the previous night; he closed his eyes to forget, but there was no forgetting. He rose and coolly walked over to the body, he didn't want to kill him then and it was not his intention, but the fool took him by surprise and what else could he do. Well, it's done, he thought; shrugging his shoulders with the reality of it all. It took only the blinking of an eye to overcome the fleetingly terrible feelings he had previously experienced, he began to relax as he looked down at the lifeless hulk, it made him feel better to think that he was old and probably didn't have much living left in him. Who is to say that this could have been his last journey; hmm, he smirked, it was his last journey. Well, that was for sure; with his foot, he pushed at the lifeless cadaver; just like he did with the camel dung to make sure that there was no longer any life in the old man. Shrugging his shoulders in acceptance of the fact, he sighed, his disposition had returned to normal; he looked back over his shoulder to the fire to see if it had taken new life, but it had not. Roughly, he removed the night covering from the stiffened body without care or reverence; unabashed, he drew it around himself and returned to sit by the smouldering fire. His empty stomach began rumbling, pleading for food; leisurely, Luca rose to his feet; awkwardly carrying his aches from the discomfort of the previous evening, he crossed over to the old man's bags. Rummaging around, through assorted little parcels of his supplies, discovering dried meat and other goods, he came upon a type of flat bread he had recognised. After smelling it, he immediately thrust the bread into his mouth, biting off much more than he could manage to chew. His hunger was so great he swallowed prematurely, almost choking, bread spewed everywhere from his congested mouth. He needed water and remembered seeing it over by the old man's body; he crossed the space holding bread in one hand and a ration of dried meat in his other hand, whilst clutching at his covering by pressing his arms tightly to his body. With a full mouth, he began coughing on his way across to the lifeless cadaver. The skin bag was there, only it was trapped beneath the body that appeared to be looking at him almost accusingly, he didn't want to touch his victim; but then he was dead. But, being Luca, he soon rid himself of any self-conscious feelings and coarsely rolled the body away from the water container, looking at it once more, snatched up the bag, popped the stopper and raised it to his parched lips and drank his fill.

By this time, the fire had begun to crackle into life and Luca took himself over to warm his body and to comfortably finish his meal. Lying outstretched on his side and lifting the covering to trap the warmth of the fire, he ate and drank in his own good time. Through the haze of the fire, he could not help but gaze upon the body of his victim; his mind was dormant; he was not moved to thinking anything of the old man or of anything in particular.

Though the sun had not long risen, there remained a chill in the air; Luca regained his wit from his day dream and shivered, the body across from him suddenly became an object of curiosity. In his reasoning, he first thought it odd that the old man had risked travelling across the desert alone; merchants are always in a caravan, unless, thinking aloud and climbing to his feet he did not want to draw attention to himself. Answering his own question, he stated a loud, "why?" He was up on his feet and in no time his form cast a shadow over the merchant; Luca bent stooping over the body, which had now relaxed from its stiffness of death, he had handled it before and was no longer nervous at its presence. Rolling it over and unafraid he began carefully stripping the victim. Piece by piece he removed each item of clothing. When he unfastened his shirt he beheld the sight of an oversized lumpy pouch hanging on long thongs resting on his paunch; also an ageing rolled up leather scroll fell from his clothing. The first item of interest to him was the oversized weighty pouch. His hand went to it grasping it at first touching it with a certain tenderness; oh it felt promising and his heart leapt as the lumpiness gave way to sounds of noises that he was familiar with. Money, he assumed, just what his greedy little mind hoped for. Slowly, he cut the thongs with the old man's knife, upending the bag. Surprised when the contents spilt out displaying an assortment of large cut gemstones into his awaiting hand from out of the bag. The sight that beheld him left him dumbstruck, all he could do was stare at the contents in his hand; a thousand thoughts filled his head at these newfound riches. It began to worry him that this man was not just any old traveller, he must have been a man of some esteem, and the scroll he held in his hand must be of some importance. Holding on to what he now possessed, he tied the bag around his waist securely; it was his now and he wasn't about to let go of his find for anything. He stripped the entire body of all its clothing but failed to find anything else. Interested in what else he could find, he crossed the camp over to where the camels were hobbled. Searching the panniers that the camels carried, he was delighted at his finds. Sure enough, the bags were stuffed with goods for trade in the market. There were bales of silks, perfumes spices and all manner of goods, a handsome haul, why there was more than enough to gain passage back to Venice for a host of people. Consumed with excitement of his new fortune, he began to dance around the fire in glee, eventually falling to the floor in his state of joyous delirium. It did not last for long; ever being the realist, he lay on his back facing the early morning sky, a sudden hesitation caused his jubilation to subside.

Luca needed to rethink his strategy regarding the merchant, a man does not travel alone with all his wealth about him for no reason; it was likely that there could be somebody awaiting the arrival of this man; his goods, he feared, meant that he could be important. Most likely he was; perhaps for Luca, too well known; now the question that begged was how powerful a man was he, for rich men have many friends, the type that Luca would not wish to know. Temporary panic set in, those friends could have a search party out at this very moment looking for him; after all, he was carrying a king's fortune in gemstones; somebody was expecting him. His attitude towards his situation became seriously prudent and deeply concerned about any early discovery of the body. This was no longer a time for dallying; he had already slipped capture and death from the navy and didn't need a reminder of the trouble he could find himself in. Motivated by the fear and concern that built in him, he quickly rose to his feet, busying himself around the camp by removing any trace of a second person. Removing his sandals quickly donned them himself before picking up the body of the old man, he dragged it away from the camp and carefully disposed of it in what appeared to be a natural depression, covering it over as quickly as he could with stones and dirt. Back in the camp he dressed in the old man's clothes, and after making certain adjustments, turned his attention to loading the camels in readiness to complete his journey.

It took him most of the day to reach the coastal town, but not on foot; this time he was uncomfortable, he now rode on in a sort of ease on the back of a camel and with the luxury to his feet wearing the old man's sandals. Now he was in no hurry, for he was fed, clothed properly and with transport.

The port town of Lattakia was a busy place, people of all colours and persuasions thronged in the busy streets; this was the sort of cover Luca was hoping for. There was nothing new to him in these places, where men fought in alleys for what they could hold on to. Yes, this was where he felt at home and Luca's first priority was to seek out a certain type of person that would not ask too many questions when it came to handling stolen goods, and the best place to find them would be lingering near to one of those shady alleys close to the dockside. He didn't have to look too hard nor wait long before he eyed up a suitable looking laggard lurking around the shadows; he was alone, keenly watching others pass by, like a predator casually eyeing up his prey. Luca observed him from a distance; the man had the keenness of a hunting hawk's eye, although he tried not to show it. He was lean in looks and filthy, Luca knew the type well; he was waiting with interest for a suitable victim to pass by to use his devious talents on. Luca hobbled his camels and furtively made his way close to him. He stopped alongside him and when his attention was focussed elsewhere, Luca slid up closer to the unwashed fellow; he did not speak directly to the anonymous character, but leaned against the wall and nonchalantly spoke as if he were idly spending the time of day talking to the street. The individual in the shadows remained nervously concealed as if not wanting to show himself.

To acquaint himself with the stranger, Luca spoke first, without much knowledge of the local dialect he remembered his old shipmate and friend Ali as a young man on his first ship. Ali was of the east, a quiet man to most and was kind to the young friendless Luca at a time when he most needed a friend. Ali was a hard worker and a good mariner, there was little that anyone could teach him about ships and the sea. His only problem was his difficulty with the language aboard the ship; a likeable fellow that Luca had decided to befriend, putting it to him that they could help each other by sharing their joint problem of language; a simple way of educating himself at the same time as working. It was difficult at first for Luca to make himself understood, but as confidences grew, their understanding became positive and although neither became fluent in each other's tongue, they managed to freely converse.

That experience stood well for the present with this stranger, the two men entered into a banter, asking many vague and various questions of each other, at the same time showing a highly suspicious regard. They spoke as if in innuendo, almost as if their tongue was of some coded language, not for any other to understand. When the man in the shadows was satisfied with the answers to his numerous questions, and not before, did he agree to Luca's request; but before he was willing to move, he reminded Luca that he did not run errands for free and that there was an expectation of a more tangible kind than a thank you for his services.

It satisfied Luca that he had chosen well, and to maintain his position of superiority, he casually tossed a coin onto the ground, which landed at the feet of the unsavoury-looking lascar. The coin that fell at his feet in the sandy street remained there for some moments, it was as if he was asking for more but there was none forthcoming. The lean body bent down stretching outwards showing himself; as the sunlight caught him, Luca was quick to notice that sometime past he had suffered badly in a fight, showing heavily marked scars standing out on his neck and back, though they were lost under his shirt, it was noted that he was lucky to be alive. Fellow pirates Luca had sailed with had suffered similar lesions; he was not the sort of person whom ordinary folk would choose to talk openly with, and when he showed his face fully, it proved that nature had not been too kind to him either.

Luca's voice was confident, "Inform your master that profitable business awaits him, and be swift about it," he ordered.

He was aware of the chances he was taking and without a sword he felt naked, but he still had his knife and wits to rely on. Using the thongs from the bags that had hobbled the camels at night, he wound them loosely around his waist; looking around him, he scanned the street before stooping to the ground and filling both hands with sand.

It wasn't long before two dubious characters came into view walking down the alley in his direction; he knew what to expect, he was a master at this type of deceit and treachery. His keen eyes were quick to notice that both men were armed with daggers that gleamed conspicuously under their thick leather belts. They confronted Luca, he was unworried that he could not cope with them, and they probably thought the same of him. One was fat and out of shape the other scrawny and sly, looking him over as they spoke, the fat man ordered him to follow them to their master in a broken western dialect. Luca did not move and neither did the scrawny fellow whom Luca believed would have delivered him a stunning tap to the head with the hilt of his dagger, or worse had he have followed as he was ordered. Instead, he stood his ground feigning ignorance that he did not understand very well, which seemed to try the man's patience. The villainous individual hated dealing with the Franj and their like; he consciously found it difficult to make himself understood, he took a breath and was about to repeat himself. Luca let fly with both handfuls of sand one in each of their unwashed faces whilst they were off guard; the attack gave him an instant advantage over the two burly men who were crying out aloud and bent double attempting to rub the sand from their faces. Now he had his chance, his hand reached out and drew the dagger from the belt of one of the disabled characters and mercilessly thrusted it into his side, wounding him severely, sufficiently to render him harmless. Whilst the second man was still bent over with his hands rubbing at his face struggling to regain his sight, Luca quickly took a leather thong from around his waist and wrapped it around the man's neck and held him in a chokehold. Once in his control, with his knife to the man's neck, he beckoned the wounded man to go back, but this time to bring his master.

A deep rich voice from behind took Luca by surprise; the voice was laughing and unhostile; it told him that his battle with the men was no longer necessary. Whoever he was he was a very big man and dressed finely, Luca was congratulated on his abilities to survive in this strange and hostile place. "I see you are resourceful and a useful man to know; and one who does not appear as he truly is." This extremely large, oily-looking man, weighing far more than was healthy for him, emerged from the shadows into the sunlight. He was huge from the over indulgence of food, he wore a little red fez on his overlarge balding head that also looked out of place. Beads of sweat hung heavily on his brow as well as the broadest of grins on his fat chubby face, which disturbed Luca somewhat. The observations of the big man did little to settle his nervousness. Luca was sure that he had won the match; as for the big man who presented himself, Luca knew he would not enter into any kind of a struggle. Observing the big man who had spoken, he believed that he was not the type to roll around fighting in the dirt of the street. The atmosphere became settled as the two men talked like distant friends for a while, until such a time as a bridge of recognition and respect had been formed between them. Remaining within his shirt, Luca protected the valuable gem stones that he had taken from the traveller, these were not for sale here. He knew well that they would fetch a handsome price elsewhere, far more than they would here; no, these he would keep to be sold in his own country. He left to bring the camels to the alley and joined the large dubious trader. Luca watched the big man closely and could tell that he had done this sort of trade many times before; he was not interested in asking questions regarding what he carried. It was enough to view the expression of avaricious interest on his fat face; the rising of his trimmed eyebrows spoke volumes. One thing was certain, experience told him that this new found friend's standard of credit was more than adequately acceptable. The glowing approval and an eager handshake gave more than an impression that they could do business, and unknown to both men, fate would bring them together in such a way that they would prosper in the years that followed.

The fat man was not disappointed at the sight of the goods, in fact, he was impressed and not wanting to know their origin. It was much more than Luca had admitted to, assuring Luca that he was able to handle the goods; though it left the fat trader aghast when he received the full inventory of their high quality that Luca brought. The big man was very impressed and stated as much that he was very fortunate to have met with Luca. This stranger, the fat man believed, was an interesting character; perhaps there was a business opportunity in the making. There were many questions he put to Luca, but he proved wily, and it somehow pleased the fat man for his caution.

As for the two thugs in his employ, they were a disappointment, but the fateful outcome of their employment was enough for the fat man to realise that they no longer were of use to him. Luca knew his type, understanding him for what he was, the big man laughed and placing his hand around Luca as if comforting an old friend he led his new friend away towards a dockside dwelling and the comfort of his place of business. Walking along, Luca had one thing in mind and that was his return; with this character he believed there was hope. During his journey into Lattakia, this new wealth had his mind working towards a new future; he had plans for his homeland and more before returning.

The Affluent Villain

In the ensuing years, Luca became very successful, for him business thrived. Venice had fostered a new ship owner to add to the number of budding entrepreneurs; only this one was different. Because of his past, he could not easily abandon what he truly was; a freebooting villain with an uneventful life of luxury and idleness. Luca, from the very start of his homeward journey, had plotted his future. With the right men, which were not too hard to find, he could take up where he left off; only this time he would direct the course of events under the guise of a respectable man, away from where any action was to take place. His ideas were dangerous to those of his men who committed Luca's plans into reality. Whilst Luca worked the eastern ports as a genuine trader, he carefully watched and took in what cargoes were aboard and the ships he fancied most; by befriending the captains and surreptitiously gleaning from them their next port of call. With that knowledge, he would send messengers to tip off his waiting crews at sea whilst he would sail away to be noted in some foreign port should his name ever come to the ears of any judiciary after the ship went missing. The captives fate hung in the balance of their worth depending on their ages and fitness before being put to death or sold into slavery. The African coast was where that dirty deed was accomplished; the flesh trade was a lucrative business and very few escaped their chains or the market place. Also, his prize, the ship, would be towed into a yard where it would be reconstructed; by the time it was ready to set sail to sea, it was unrecognisable.

In a short span of years, Luca became a shipping mogul; though he made sure that his exploits remained very secretive. His presence in the more affluent circles of Venice were not accepted, his birth line, like his outward presentation, was viewed with a certain disdain. There was a vulgar side to Luca that came out after drink and that was more readily and frequently exhibited to the horror of his new friends. Vulgar or not, he succeeded when others failed and there was little doubt that he had an uncanny knack in turning a gold piece. Success and wealth was his passport, and it was for this reason that he was eventually and reluctantly accepted by those in the inner circle of the trade society. Whilst Luca cleverly listened to their idle gossip, he gleaned much intelligence from it; at the same time he was aware that certain members were not slow in looking to him for pointers in his outlandish yet successful schemes in exchange for acceptance.

To have come from nothing to being top dog in their society appealed to Luca's sense of achievement; he was smug and he had plans knowing how to use these fools in society. After a time, trade from the Port of Venice fell under the unspoken management of Luca's influence.

Whilst nothing could be proved, Luca's surreptitious movements around the port always appeared natural for a man of his interests, but they were far from natural. Though it was never proved, a man was flogged openly within a stone's throw from the quayside; that action brought fear and silence to those that were made to stand and watch the punishment for not recognising Luca and refusing to carry out orders the man was given. Luca's unusual success created a natural line of enemies that were dealt with in his own amusing way; he was subtle with these powerful people, seeking grounds to bind them to him through their own stupid misdemeanours. To Luca it was no more than entertainment making him laugh at what these so-called honourable gentlemen deemed as a misdemeanour, when he openly whored most nights. For years Luca had built an intelligence against his enemies; by using blackmail, covering their gambling markers and paying household servants for evidence of sensitive deeds or acts of a dishonourable nature to confound them, should they ever be foolish enough to stand against him. Once in his grip, they were done for; Luca didn't care how they acted as long as they continued to expose their secret side to him and furnish him with the information he required. As long as Luca remained within the sphere of society, he was reasonably free to continue playing his games with those he used. Though there remained a hard core in their views, few stood against Luca that he could not break; and they believed that they would treat Luca as boldly as he did others. Evidence was what they needed; they believed the answer lay somewhere within his meteoric rise; and as rumour had it, they would quietly pursue their course of inquiry until he faltered or they were informed of the mystery of his past.

Luca entered into the mercantile world fully-fledged, aggressive and hungry for dominance; nobody knew from where he came, his background always remained a mystery and he wasn't saying anything. Prosperity and luck, it seemed, were always with him; but if the world had eyes to see, a very different Luca would appear. *Pescecane* was what he had been nicknamed by those that had been ravaged by his avaricious trickery, it became an apt and fitting name for this scavenger shark from Venice. Respectable traders lost more than their fortunes when entering into business transactions with Luca, some faced ruin, some were never seen again and, oddly, Luca was always the richer for their meeting, though nothing could ever be proved. Suspicion shrouded him like an old cloak, and without proof to the contrary of any disreputable dealings, the authorities could do little against him. He sneered and laughed at them. In his mind they were all fools for the taking, Luca was not a man that took foolish risks without first knowing what the powers that govern were planning.

He was without doubt a most unsavoury character, though he would not appear so to those that he dealt with. His driving force was business, leading to his great wealth; and his life was undoubtedly consumed with his work. Driven by a need to possess greater wealth, his weaknesses were women and drink; he carelessly and regretfully overlooked that which was closest to him and in consequence lost his only son to the same vices of the father.

The streets were not safe. Luca ruled a most unsavoury army of rogues and layabouts that served him in all manner of ways without ever being allowed to make their presence obvious to anybody. He was ruthless and cared little for those he tricked so cleverly, his charm overwhelming, his devious and cunning nature was cold and bitter as any frosty night.

During his rise to the summit of his success in those early years, Luca decided that it was time that he married; not that he desired a loving partner. He could have women any time of the day or night; half the whores in Venice sported his off springs with a likeness similar to his; he cared not what happened to any brood born from his wasted seed. His idea was to create an air of respectability and there was no shortage of suitors, as he had rapidly become the most talked about and richest man in the city, living alone in the big empty house that overlooked the lagoon. His decision to wed was not based on love, more an alliance of fortunes and he was presumptuous as to his own list of possible females that suited him best.

Married at the age of twenty six with more than enough money for a dozen grand affairs, the merriment and celebrations carried on for many days until he tired of them. Celebrations were a distraction to him running for so long a period; it made him irritable and eager to return to his real love, business. That held the real excitement for him; it wasn't long before he fell back into his old habits of spending more time at his business than at home. When his wife fell pregnant from his rough demands for daily satisfaction, it somehow came as a blessing when he was absent on occasions long into the night, returning home late. He was devoid of love and tenderness; his passion was no more than a reason for sex; he was rough and treated her like the whores he knew. In her belief that his drive for sex was little more than his immaturity, she never found a way to curb his excesses or to lessen his eagerness to make it over as quickly as possible. She never learnt of his past, but it was obvious whores was all that he had been with and he was used to passing from one to another as long as his ardour allowed him, when it was over he was miserable and ratty and still yearning for fulfilment.

His first setback occurred as his wife neared the ending of her difficult time of carrying and was due to give birth to his offspring. There was an outbreak of cholera in the city and regrettably she became tainted with the illness on the evening of the birth. The child was delivered perfectly healthy into the world; a boy with a good set of lungs to announce his arrival, but Luca was not there to witness the joyous occasion. He was back at his office drinking with a local whore who served his unquenchable demands for continual pleasure whilst his wife was vomiting up her innards as her malady plagued her whilst being so heavily pregnant. The result of the disease weakened and exhausted her so badly after giving birth to his son and heir, she unfortunately failed. Her illness had sapped all of her strength so that her body became wracked with fever and in the early hours of the morning before she had chance to watch the sun rise over the infant that lay beside her, she expired calling for her beloved Luca.

With the loss of his wife, Luca pursued his idealistic energies of ambition for the future. His bonny son, whom he named Renaldo, had everything that money could buy, gifts rained down upon the child like blessings, and the house was altered to suit the baby's every requirement. After two days of playing the doting father, he was tired of watching his son regurgitate his food on a regular basis and knew nothing of cleaning the child whenever his natural bodily movements required to be tended to. Escape was what he needed to be at, the chore of being father and nurse depressed the active Luca, he was not cut out for such menial chores and wondered why he did not think of a substitute mother earlier and immediately settled for that course of action. Once that task had been accomplished, he was again free, allowing himself to make for the sanctuary of his office away from the smells of the child's room.

That was how it was for him and over the ensuing years, children were uninteresting to his way of thinking and it was always easier to make preparations and show himself on occasion to the child. As the infant grew into a young boy, his life was only punctuated with passing visits and the child never really got to be close to his father. From the early teenage years the boy grew up without principle, and became a conceited dandy, expecting his father's attitude of generosity towards his son to be in everyone. As life was so easy for him, a snap of his fingers or a suggestion of his needs was all he had to voice and his will was catered for, but boredom soon took over; that is with other male friends, but flirtatious girls and bawdy drinking was quite something else.

It would be fair to say that Luca never allowed his son to want for anything and cosseted him in every way, yet failed miserably to be a father with a father's love. Unaware that his submissive deeds to satisfy his son's needs were moulding him into a more obnoxious character than himself. By the time he was fourteen, he had become the talk of Venice; forever in trouble, creating scandal upon scandal and a great disappointment to his father, but Luca, blinded by his own interests, was also blinded to the boy's developing nauseous character. On one occasion when he had been moderately over boisterous, more the worse for his over indulgence of wine, his excited exuberance led him to overstep the line of good manners by insulting a lady who was escorted by a middle-aged male of one of the oldest and respected families in Venice. The outcome of which almost ended in a duel over the lady's honour. Instinctively, like his father, he was cowardly in the face of adversity, when in his early days he too backed down at the thought of bearing any form of pain, not having the backbone to support his rude remarks. When the news was reported back to his father that his son had been threatened with personal violence should he dare to show his face in that particular venue again, Luca was livid.

Firstly, he attacked his son for his folly in running off at the mouth without a second thought of the outcome. To ensure that he would never belittle the Rici name again, he assigned a villainous bodyguard to ensure his son's protection, and make others apprehensive in taking objection to his son's weakness. This only caused the boy to exercise a latent bullying nature that had so far laid dormant in him, and with the ox of a bodyguard continually behind him, he became a match for anyone; thinking nothing of enjoying his bodyguard's brutal abilities to the full. His persistent use of this fellow caused many innocent people to fall beneath the thunderous blows of the oafish bodyguard; to which the sadistic son derived much pleasure; it was sickening to watch as he would urge the brute on further as the sight of blood and suffering stirred joyously within him. He was in so many ways the double of his father, as was Luca to his, but Luca would never give way to such an outlandish suggestion.

By the time he was aged seventeen, half the city refused to have anything to do with him and turned their backs on him making him a social outcaste. This was not what his father expected of him and regular and heated arguments broke out between them. There was little his father could do to change his son's ways, he knew that, and allowed him to continue enjoying the excesses of his youth. Further sagas of tales of misdeeds and indiscretions grew like an avalanche, until one evening he was taken aside by the Doge's secretary and told outright to do something about his son's behaviour or suffer being ostracised himself. That was a personal wound that he could do nothing about; for the Doge was a much more powerful man than he, being the ruler of the state in which he presided. Luca began to view his son differently; long gone were the days when he genuinely loved his boy and recalled the few times he bounced him on his knee whenever he had the time to be with him. Now he had become hateful and an embarrassment, there was only one course of action left, he had to leave Venice and make his way alone. Luca no longer wanted to see his obnoxious son any more, endowing him with sufficient funds he ostracised him for good.

There was much trouble to follow, that much he suspected, and sure enough it wasn't so far away. A young female that young Renaldo had consorted with for some time had fallen pregnant. The misleading goodwill and broken promises that he spoke of to have his lustful way with her all meant nothing to Renaldo but fun. When he was done with her, he forgot the promises that she reminded him of and looked to bed another equally eager to share his wealth and favour. There were the usual rumouring threats of a forced marriage by the girl's father but when news of the affair reached Luca's ears he was furious and would have none of it.

Vito Mollina was a baker, a very good baker and proud of his reputation. His premises were small yet barely sufficient for him to cope with, but it enabled him to earn an honest and good living selling his products. A man who was not driven with ambition, steadily and optimistically realised that a time was coming towards a move for expansion, for only recently he had reason to inspect new premises with high hopes of increasing his already flourishing business.

He was not a man who went out in life to be the biggest of anything; his dreams were reasonably moderate, and always encompassed the welfare of his loving family. The news of his daughter's situation brought with it a shame and a certain prolonged gloom, but unlike many fathers that might turn against their offspring, under these circumstances Vito believed otherwise. His belief in his simple way would be only right for this Rici boy to do the proper thing by his daughter and marry her, thus lifting the stigma from the family. When he had finished his chores for the day he had made up his mind to send word to meet with Luca, believing that it was time that he had it out with the boy's renowned and powerful father.

He stood amidst his flour bags in the store room of his bakery, after removing his apron, imagining that Luca would mediate towards a compromise. By hoping to make Luca force his son to see sense and take the respectable course of action was deluding, but then Vito was a simple and honourable man.

The candlelight in the upstairs office window indicated that Luca Ricci was working late; Vito anxiously paced the street in the piazza outside his office, deliberating how he should respectfully broach the subject of a wedding. Knowing that Luca was an important man and due courtesy of respect was required, he was certain that his plea for his daughter's wedding to Luca's son would be heard. His pacing continued for so long until at last he found the courage to face Luca, as the longer he dallied, the worse he felt. Eventually, he had settled his fears and plucked up enough courage to enter the office, with a nervous heart he feared Luca's domain and was surprised by the dimness within. This was not what he expected, the merchant he came to see was far richer than a thousand of his kind, yet he fails to burn sufficient candles to allow his visitors to see their way to the clerk at his writing desk. Approaching the clerk a lump formed in his throat and his mouth turned dry; the dark spectre that sat close to the far corner of the room hardly moved, yet he knew that he was there. Illuminated by the few stumps of burning candles, it reminded Vito that there was a similarity to a picture that hung in his church when viewed from a distance. Vito screwed up his eyes to see him clearly; the candles were way past their best and began to flicker nervously as the wicks faded into the last remains of waxy pools in the metal cups that held them. Not before the dying candle had flickered its last light, the clerk had reached out offering the taper of a new candle to brighten the gloom when light was finally descending to extinction.

Vito shook his head in silent criticism of Luca's careful approach at wasting his wealth; it did little to encourage him in the delicate matter that was on his mind. Moving cautiously towards the centre of the dimly lit office, Vito's attention was diverted away from his inquisitive gazing around the office when he was finally confronted by a sharply-spoken clerk whose appearance resembled someone looking down on this luck. Nervously, he outlined his need to see Luca, stating that his business was of a delicate and personal nature. The office clerk, who appeared more of a lackey in view of his shabby dress, eyed him for assessment; there had been many of his like here before and guessed it was to do with Renaldo. He had lost count of the number of fathers that had stood in Vito's position; though he did not know the cause, he guessed that it was another with scornful tales of Luca's son's disgusting behaviour. There was no love in the clerk's heart for Renaldo, the wastrel as he knew of him, but dared not say the like of what was in his mind. He was as cruel as his father in every way and it sickened him to the core to think that two could be so much alike.

On entering the premises Vito was told to wait in an unfriendly cynical sharpness of tone, it disturbed him and he became suspecting that now that he had entered the portal of Luca's office, sympathy would become a figment of the imagination. It was not until the clerk began to move from his desk to announce the stranger's arrival that Vito noticed that he had a serious limp and that his body was slightly twisted and guessed that sometime in his past he had suffered a serious accident resulting in his present condition, but could not guess the real reason for his pitiful state. There was no telling that this clerk had once been a steady and promising young business man who had once approached Luca for help, nor was he aware that once Luca had drawn him into his confidence. The poor man had met with a terrible accident and suffered severe injury that he could no longer carry on his business. It was suggested that he come and work with him; it was Luca's way of watching him and keeping his mouth shut; besides, it was a better offer than that of starving.

The man moved awkwardly past Vito, dragging his handicap towards the staircase that he himself also anticipated to climb in due course. The reluctance to face such a powerful man as Luca filled Vito's heart with a foreboding anxiety; he listened as the crippled man reached the top of the creaking staircase to knock on the office door and listened to the pained softness in the clerk's voice to announce Vito's presence below.

Vito would surely have felt better in himself had he been allowed to go straight up those stairs alone to face Luca and have done with the affair. He was not a hard-hearted man and would have willingly spared the clerk the awkwardness and pain of the climb. Unknown to him, kindness or sympathy was never shown to anyone that entered Luca Rici's office, least of all those in his employ. Luca took great pleasure in probing and observing another man's weakness, it gave him a sense of power and superiority and the ability to exercise his pathetic sadistic will over those who were unable to withstand the force of his aggressive personality. Luca sat behind his rather large desk, which was littered with scrolls, one being a deal that he was giving his consideration to or had completed. The upper office was far better illuminated by its numerous candles that surrounded the master, unlike him that had to strain his eyes under the meagre light that was allowed in the office below, a sore point to the clerk's way of thinking. He sat upright from his bent studying position when the clerk entered, placed down his quill and looked sternly at the clerk. Luca was well-dressed and smart in his velvet jacket of royal blue. His long hair showed signs of silver strands that glistened in the flickering light of the candle, presenting a distinguished look about him, and his ageing face was kindly-looking to the unsuspecting. Indeed, should one get close enough to see into his face they would detect the piercing cold in his calculating eyes, empty of any form of affection or warmth. In the false light of his office, there was no

83

immediate trace that his vacant eyes betrayed his character. Though they glistened in the candle light, there wasn't a sign of cruelty and acrimony within; when he looked down pitifully on the unfortunate, he doled out hard words that only added to their suffering and misery.

For reasons unknown to the stricken clerk, he was the example that jollied Luca's day; the master's sadistic pleasure was heightened from the dullness of the day's monotony, listening to this poor crippled employee's efforts as he struggled laboriously up and down the staircase at Luca's every call. A faint smile cracked the stern face below the large nose that dominated Luca's visage that resembled a killing hawk's beak. The clerk, short on his breath, bore his pain that was visible to Luca's piercing eye when he announced Vito's arrival, hinting for what he suspected was the nature of his business. Luca was silent, he breathed a deep breath as he leaned back comfortably waiting in his soft upholstered chair. "Another one," he silently sighed, he did not have time for such distractions and was about to order the man sent away when he suddenly changed his mind, suspecting that this must surely be the last. Stretching his lean body and thinking pensively as he viewed the crippled clerk, this could be amusing; how easy they succumbed once their will was broken. He stretched forward his wrinkled hand and toyed with an inkwell as if to make it appear to be out of place then looked up, slyly viewing his clerk before he spoke.

"Show him in, quickly," he snapped.

As Vito looked around the dimly-lit reception room below, he was in awe at the countless scrolls that filled the complete wall; he was amazed and impressed at the amount of trade Luca must have been involved in.

"The master will see you now," said the clerk in passing.

Vito knew his time was now, the announcement came like a judge's death sentence. Vito looked up at him, meeting the man's pained eyes and quickly looked away as not to embarrass him. The baker became uneasy, almost apprehensive; he stood upright as if being called to give an account of himself before the high judges of the city. The dimness that shrouded the staircase to the upper floor appeared to be the way into a black void that he would have to enter into and possibly not return. The baker swallowed hard before climbing the stairs; he was careful not to stumble as that would tell the waiting Luca a fool was approaching. Each tread of the stairs creaked so loudly under his weight that he imagined that spying angels would carry the news of a tormented Vito to Luca's ears. There was a nervous sweat on his body by the time he reached the door of Luca's office and his heart was thumping madly. He paused before entering into the bright candle light of the interior, remembering his manners he quickly snatched off his hat to show his respect and entered. Luca did not look up from his writing. He had already guessed the size of the man by his steady climb up the creaking stairs. It was a little trick he had acquired over the years, he had learnt how to gauge the size and weight of those that needed to see him, and was more often right. By the sound of the straining timbers creaking he could tell if a visitor was nervous or not by the speed of step in their ascent. Luca, it seemed, never missed a detail; it made so much difference to business to be at an advantage, and over the years it had proven itself so. Slyly, he peered at the man as he entered the room, his keen eyes quickly assessed his position but the only threatening attribute he picked up on was that he was quite well-made for a tradesman. Luca showed no fear of this big man; he had made it his business to find out all about the baker from the back streets ever since he had applied for his appointment. His clothes were mediocre in quality, clean but really quite tasteless in style. There was a small rip in his short cape which he exposed when his hand nervously dropped to his side; Luca's eyes were keen and did not miss much at all. The man respectfully made his salutations and nervously proceeded into his previously practised appeal for the wedding of his daughter ending with the appeal

"After all, your son had taken away her honour," he concluded.

"Yes, you're right," barked Luca, snappily in reply, "but if she had not been so forthright with her favours, she would not have been in her present position, would she?" he barked? Vito felt hurt at his words; he was not sharp enough to enter into the cut and thrust of argument, being an honest man he was taken aback, void of a smart reply allowed Luca's words to strike him with his daughter's guilt.

Luca sneered in disgust having to deal with this witless baker from the back streets. What did he care about the girl, and knew that this baker was no match for the likes of him, he had lost all sign of respect and shown his weakness when he presented himself at his office. A stronger man would have demanded an appointment or even stormed the stairs and he would have received a lot more respect from Luca. Vito was confused, he had believed he would have had a fair hearing, if nothing else in the interest his family honour. Tired and irritated by the baker's inability to express himself, Luca exhaled hard from the tedium of the present matter, angrily tossing down his pen into a tray before him. Vito was about to appeal but the merciless Luca held up his hand silencing any chance of Vito's appeal. Luca's approach to any problem was always business like, leaning back in his well-padded chair with his face growing less visible as he distanced himself from the candlelight.

"I am not an unreasonable man," he said, giving Vito a further rundown on his virtues. His eyes squinted as he peered at the well-made baker; he paused before teasing out his proposition. "First," he told him, there was no chance of his son marrying the girl, besides, he added, he had sent him away out of the city. Continuing in his domineering voice and outlandish manner Luca made his offer known. "If the girl gives birth to a boy, I will agree to take the child off your hands," without allowing Vito a chance to protest, he quickly carried on overriding any form of argument, "and settle with a reasonable sum for compensation". Vito had eased to a relaxing posture, but when Luca continued, "Should the child be a girl, then you can keep her, I will not be interested." The young girl's father was outraged by the proposal and warned Luca that this was unthinkable, and would not be the last of the affair; his anger was rising, never before had he heard of such a monstrous proposal. This simple baker was no match for Luca, who was quick to sense that the man was about to quickly burn his bridges by threatening Luca; it would have finished any deal between them for good. With a commanding sharpness in his voice, Luca cut him off as he severely and strenuously warned him to think before he regrettably buried himself with his own damning words. Luca snarled, leaning forwards, his twisted face emerging into the light.

As big as the baker was, Luca showed no fear.

"Be warned, you stand to lose everything you have, should you persist with your ludicrous ideas of your daughter marrying into my household. Preposterous!" Luca exclaimed, and looked down his nose as he spoke making Vito feel totally inferior; he further retorted loudly, embarrassing the baker as he stood nervously before him fiddling with his hat. The man stammered in protest, failing to get his words out, but Luca anticipated his intent and held his hand in the air, preventing him from committing himself to Luca's wrath.

There would be no quarter given; Luca almost growled his distaste.

"Remember this, push me too far and you will have wished that you had spoken to the devil, I am too powerful for you," he barked at the honest baker.

"I hold the deeds on your property and the power to destroy you and your family should I wish it. Now be gone, and less of this foolishness." The fury in Luca's voice undermined what little confidence Vito possessed. With his nerves frayed at the thought of the threat being carried out, the unsure and discouraged baker left the room feeling most dejected.

It was not until the child had been born that Luca saw Vito again, this time as always with visitors that he cared less for, it was late in the evening in his office. Vito stood before Luca, this time it was not his hat that he held nervously, but an infant.

The babe was quiet, content within the arms that held him. He held forth the child; Luca gently took the baby and placed it on his desk like a piece of merchandise to inspect it, opening the wrappings he had to ensure the baby was a boy; Luca Rici was not a man to accept anything on trust before agreeing to settle a bargain. The proof clearly portrayed itself; Luca nodded his head in acceptance; the agreement was demonstrated by a bag of gold being tossed across to the baker without bothering to look at him. It had been a long time since Luca had playfully taunted any child with a playful finger, the infant reached out, and clung onto his offending digit refusing to let go; this act of possession appeared to inject delight into the old man, who audibly and out of character laughed with a fondness in his sound. Simply amused by the baby's reaction, he was sure this boy was a survivor and as such was worthy to enter his household. The longer the child gripped his finger, the more convinced he was that he believed he was a true Rici.

Elated by the child's reactions, he became truly joyous and he began to make silly sounds to the baby; he even pushed his nose toward the child's, playfully rubbing them together. At the sight of all this, Vito, with feelings of regret and shame, was lost; his mind was in a confused swirling confusion, so many thoughts hurt him; lost for the right thing to do. He apprehensively reached for the bag of gold that lay on the desk. With this gold, Vito knew he could expand his business without worry, it lay there on the desk waiting to be taken. Shame, guilt and a sense of his wrongdoing suddenly filled Vito with second thoughts and he withdrew his hand from the gold that beckoned to be picked up. His actions had not gone unnoticed by the wily sly Luca. Beginning to speak, Vito's words stumbled out, appealing for an understanding of his mistake. Suddenly, as if courage had gripped him and with a strength of voice that came from his conscience, he claimed that he had changed his mind. Regretful and full of hurt feelings he walked over to take the child that Luca was playing with. His sturdy arms reached out across Luca's body to seize the baby but Luca's reaction was speedy, nobody dared to take or remove anything that he had paid for.

"Oh, no you don't," Luca shouted angrily as he turned his head just in time to view the baker's intention. "What do you think you are doing?" he shouted bringing his lean skinny body around to block the baker's attempt to move in on the child and take him from the desk.

"We agreed," Luca said childishly.

The look on the baker's face said all. "No bargain was made over this child, I cannot find it in my heart," said Vito, almost weeping as if he had committed a mortal sin. With his spirit rising, Vito straightened himself to his full height like a bear that was to defend itself.

Maintaining his curtesy towards Luca, he softly stated, "This child is not a chattel to be sold," guilt ridden and almost sobbing, Vito insisted that he knew this is not right. Taken aback by the change of heart and the size of the baker who was puffed up before him, Luca had no intention to let this child go. He knew he was no match in strength against the baker but Luca was cunning and knew the ways of a man's mind and decided to punish him; he likewise straightened himself upright like two bears preparing to fight. Enraged, and with a fury in his eyes, a tirade of vitriolic words spilled from his thin venomous lips. He looked the man squarely in the eyes with all the vehemence he could muster, "You will take the money and return to your family whilst you are still breathing, do you understand?" Luca's threat stopped Vito, as if thunderstruck he knew full well what was meant, especially coming from one whose dangerous reputation went before him. The man did not know what to say, he was a simple man at heart, not one giving to scrapping like a dog over a bone. He did not come to be in fear of his life, and deplored his own cowardly submissive actions; he had a family to think of and so he gave in.

The staring dead eyes of Luca Rici reflected his other side, and it shook the quaking agitated man, sending fear running through him like a cold sword penetrating his innards. He leant across the desk staring hard at Luca with the realisation of what he was almost mixed up with, being a realist he grabbed the bag, then hurriedly left the office without stopping or turning back.

Luca continued playing with the child as if there had been no fuss at all. Bending forward over the infant, he whispered something before straightening his back, telling the child that it was a promise, between you and I. When Luca was finished playing with the child, a catalogue of orders was given to his clerk for preparations to secure the child's comfort.

Leaning back in his chair, smiling on the child, Luca experienced the oddest feelings. His mind began to drift back to his childhood family, and to his surprise, he almost became emotional, discovering that he almost missed them. Although he had run away from them, it was not because he wanted to, but he believed he had to. His parents would now be dead, but what of his brothers, he thought. He did not ponder on that point as he realised that he would not know them at all. Things were different now, he welcomed his new grandson and looked forwards to playing with him any time he had the time too. He realised that he had made a mistake with his son and swore to himself that he would not repeat it ever again. The child had been bought from the family and the name of Molina was lost to his mind; he was not interested in suck folk nor did he ever think of them again. The mother bore no value to his son, so in Luca's eyes the baggage was offloaded. Luca Rici did not help people unless something was to be yielded in return; he was not a charity and would not appear to anyone to be soft at heart.

A change took place in Luca that night, he became a different man in some respects, but only where his grandson was concerned. He had the room next to his office properly transformed to accommodate a nurse for his grandson and all his needs, but if the child played in Luca's office, no other voice was allowed to intercede. This was Rici territory and only for the Rici's.

Luca's dream took a new direction in his lonely life; his grandson, he vowed, would one day sit in his chair and direct the trade of the whole Mediterranean; his empire. He was going to be above Kings, he was already richer than most.

Luca's love for his grandson became an obsession with him, throughout the years the graft and deals the grandfather had contrived now had meaning. It was all for his little Aldo that Luca's empire would pass. With the passing of time, Luca fell into his old ways and remained working late in his office with the whores that he had long ago drifted away from. He never purposely overlooked the young boy, but felt that he should catch up with the little pleasures he had missed having. Luca watched Aldo growing into a strong youth from a distance, but never neglected to rain on him the needs to educate and the means to please the young man's ego.

As the years passed by, Aldo became a young gentleman and a credit to his loving grandfather, but dark days were to overshadow Luca's happiness.

Aldo grew into a strong-headed young man, he was not unlike his grandfather in many ways; he was determined and high spirited. There was no reasoning with Aldo; if he had made up his mind to do something, the subject would be closed and no amount of persuasion could deter the young man's intent. He was athletic and fit in body, his passion was for sword play and had for many years been tutored by some of the best sword masters in Italy; he became very accomplished and great in skill. He could ride from an early age and had also been cultivated in the genteel arts of court. His friends and associates were those of other wealthy and powerful families, and for once, in his case, the name he bore was carried honourably.

The day that Aldo arrived home sporting the raiment and crest of the Duke du Cavelli was not a day for celebration but one of anger and crass stupidity as far as Luca was concerned. "Isn't it wonderful," he gestured as he coquettishly displayed himself, in a blue and white quartered vestment before he excitedly announced that he was soon to join the coming Crusade to fight the Saracen in the east across the great sea in the Levant.

Unlike his own son, whose ungoverned childhood made him into a wastrel, Aldo was educated, cultured and moralising. The news was both shocking and unreal; it came as a thunderbolt from the blue to his grandfather, how damned stupid he thought, almost being moved to temper knowing that the boy knew nothing of danger, least of all war. This, Luca knew, was of his own doing; although he was proud of the boy, he had tried hard to guide him into a safe and secure life of business. Rebuking himself for being so soft hearted, especially after his past experiences with his own son, his folly this time was that of loving and his error was that he had failed to learn from the past. The past weakness he suffered was the indulgence that his grandson to have everything as was his right as a Rici. Regrettably, Luca's own inaction and prudence as a guiding guardian was settling on Luca like a dust cloud of depression.

Dread drifted into Luca's mind, the Levant, he knew, was no place for a romantic. Should anything happen to him, well the thought was quickly dismissed as unthinkable, and he set about ways of conniving to have his grandson back, safely within his control.

Pious Temptation

Darkness cloaked the great Roman city; nothing stirred, the alehouses and brothels had long closed, scavenging dogs no longer roamed in search of scraps dropped by night revellers, leaving a quietness to descend all around. While night owls hooted their presence, hungry bats created waves of buzzing ripples in the still languid air, darting here and there flapping their busy wings flying haphazardly through the still darkness.

The chanting canticles of benediction and late night prayers had long ceased, leaving only the natural rhythms of the night for any listener. Traces of trapped burnt incense odours and the previously ignited candles hanging in stifling closed rooms of the chapel bore witness to recent activity.

Night, therefore, in offering its cloak to those scurrying creatures with nervous intent were free from identification in their need to operate their covert movements in its silence. Here, there was immunity from discovery; that too was the similarity for those who spent their time in the nether world of covert political affairs who, like the creatures of the night, survived in lengthened shadows with the need for silence when plotting in their odious activities. These men, faceless and free of discovery during the daylight, were the manipulators of civilised mankind. They were the chess players of life in the Latin sphere, the politically-hungry and interfering who held sway over the many; they who cared not of the masses, so long as their cause was advanced.

High in a third floor office overlooking the Gardens of the Innocents, so named after the victims of the Children's Crusade, there was a stirring. Not of restlessness caused by the stifling summer night's atmosphere or of any foraging creatures, but of a small group of monks who found it safer to meet at this ungodly time in the dead of night to discuss their politics and policies, to further enhance their dominance into the reshaping of the recently-gained territory of the near-eastern world.

In this city within a city, in the meagre dimness of candlelight that illuminated their chosen place of meeting, long, haunting shadows outlining silhouettes of monkish figures seated around a large table central to the room were depicted. These were not the kindly, merciful monks that moved about the poor and needy carrying out their tasks of humanity that were known to the populace at large. More the grey in character type, the politicos, the less sensitive to charitable works, more the diplomatic type, weavers of the tapestry of their changing world. Unused to the day time hours, they were secretive by nature, easily lost in a crowd and loathe to communicating with anyone of lesser intellect, unless they were to be used in their design in the so called games of life.

In the dim world of their influences, they worked surreptitiously, not by direct orders from above, more by action of innuendo and suggestion; even by a knowing nod of silent consent. Ideas that clandestinely passed forwards by veiled whispers to others. Who they were seemed irrelevant to outsiders, yet they worked successfully within the corridors of power, living quietly and innocently in a back drop of plush apartments and offices, whilst deploying the most furtive of methods of their work. For the appointed head of their obscure committee, the use of ideas no matter how bizarre, or their rhetoric wild and perhaps at times amusing, though it could be, it was their objective to define and refine such responses put forward. All suggestions passed along this chain of indifferent silence, proceeding to another level where the information would be reprocessed in the same unusual manner that it had been collected. Strange as it may seem, remarkable results in the past had borne great rewards from the odd methods used by these faceless caucuses who were not, as it appeared, allied to any one order, but were used as an airing point for many an odd proposition.

The gathered cadre were handpicked for their intellect and insight into the established workings of the committee, they were not from any one place or order but widespread, having one aspect in common; their scholastic abilities.

The flow of their conversation this evening related to the Levant, and the recent deplorable state of the treasury from the said cause, and their slipping control on general eastern events. Power was uppermost, and a greater grip on the land conquered in their name by others in far off countries for their benefit. To sustain their grip on what they already gained; also how to continue to generate more wealth from its source, after all this was the medium that kept the wheels of their organisation turning and growing ever stronger.

Their meeting had not yet started; their leader being late gave those around time to sound out their own opinions. The core subject of this conclave amidst the candle lit room was based on the disappointing relationship between the Lords, Princes and the Templers. Matters of diplomacy had degenerated to an outlandish abuse from the feudal lords, their establishment of private estates and a growing and intolerable lack of respect for their mother church thus far.

Now, unfortunately, after such a long period of conflict, others appeared to be prospering at the Church's expense, giving rise to an obvious and disquieting imbalance of gains that needed correction. Greed was everywhere; the Pisan, Genoese and Venetian militia and merchants alike were eating into the gained prizes like a canker. With grasping fingers, they could not wait to prize concessions from the church for their past services. They had forgotten that we remembered, how they used us when the platform of war raged out of hand and the church was in desperate need for assistance. That was a time of opportunity for them; how their fleets and private militia were dangled like carrots before the donkey of Rome; they forced Mother Church to pay their price to transport their army, and she did in order to relieve those that needed that vital help in the Holy Crusade. By giving way to their needs of help, they snatched at the opportunities they sought; and to make matters worse, when after all this help they became victorious, they changed their stance to one of concerted blackmail talking of war losses and rebuilding costs and a need to invest in them to build up the trade in order to repay part of the money advanced to them. That was their thanks

The leaders acted quickly by taking control of various ports and the trade routes, but that was not enough? Although trade was never within the sphere of Mother Church's control, there were usually recognised ways of drawing a levy from an indirect source for her favours, softening the direct losses of monies flowing out from the Church's coffers.

"The princes and the Templars had done very well," growled one surly voice, whose responsibilities lay in the collection of levies.

Another brother with a husky voice entered into the discourse, and leaning forwards in his seat, cast the shadow of his great bulk across the table as if to attract the others around to draw closer, he commenced to inform his attentive audience.

"It is a shameful act indeed; the new inroads into Transjordan and Syria had been established; trade was good, once again he begged the question, why have we been forgotten?" There was an agreed consent that money should have been flowing back to the treasury in Rome; " That remains lacking, in truth, it was a bad business that the Church was being overlooked and as for time", the monk stated, "it has been in their favour.;" using a stiffened finger, a monk waved it to stress his point before tapping it on the highly polished table top as he spoke in his hushed but strong voice. "Realise this," he stressed, "that the inroads to this new wealth has been gained initially with our financial backing." his starring and penetrating eyes fell upon all around him. Silence suggested that the point was being digested; there was pique in the sound of his now whining voice as he continued.

Leaning back casually on his chair, another member of the group spoke up, interrupting the speaker.

"They came to us for support and now it would appear that the Templar Brotherhood and our new found Princes are going it alone, whilst the Church is left deprived. Where, I ask, is their moral responsibility? When gains were made, it was always the established custom to compensate Mother Church for the benefit of maintaining her wealth; the guidance received for future good fortune, after all," he blustered, "we have never refused them absolution for any of their misdeeds."

Amidst the mutters a voice spoke up. "No, you are quite right, I see your point, brother," came a voice of concerned agreement from across the table. "It had become apparent that a new course had to be devised, to tip the scales of advantage back to the Holy Sea. The City of Jerusalem was the prize that the Princes had gained, truly, that was their objective, thanks be to God. Now we have regained control and maintain the road to the Holy City; the pilgrims can safely travel to the shrines and the sacred places that our Saviour Jesus Christ once frequented."

"If I can just point out something that you seem to have overlooked," said another, to stress his point he continued, "most of the campaign was self-financed and there were great costs in war to consider, and the need to extend to the army its rewards is the only sure way of ascertaining its loyalty.

"No one will fight if there are no monies forthcoming; at the end of the day we have to give way. That is why these aspects of the war are proving to be a little disappointing and the expectation of land gain also does not meet our anticipation."

Suddenly, with the sound of that like a woodcutter's axe cleaving a tree, two open handed slaps to the face of the heavy waxed oak table brought all to a silence. Each turned their head to face the end of the table to where their leader, a hooded figure, sat. He had entered the chamber silently, listening and taking in as many of the varied points of argument he could stand. He apologised to the gathering, it was obvious that they had no idea of what they were supposed to discuss; the meeting was called hurriedly with no notice of its purpose. He welcomed them all and admitted that he had eavesdropped a while, "Whilst everything you said has a basis," he told them, "there have been other revelations that are disturbing, but first." With a nod from a silent monk at the head of the table, a great gold-edged embellished copper-covered tome was opened and reading of general costs and losses from its accounting pages began. As it was, the lack of money was not entirely the only topic to be discussed, but it was more of an entrée to the cause of the meeting; something had happened that was not generally known of, and as yet had not surfaced into the discussion. After a while, the monotonous voice of the myopic monk delivering his singsong critique broke into a croaking voice, which gave an opportunity to another, to voice his opinion. The new speaker, a rather rotund character had a more deep and resonant voice, which he used to embellish his concept for the failings of the subject. He had hardly spoken when a sour faced monk that had been nodding his head throughout the negative discussion spoke over him.

"It would appear our brothers made an error of judgement by electing Godfrey as King when Jerusalem fell."

"Correction, brother," interrupted the reader, "in all fairness he was honest and honourable enough to have refused that title and accepted one of Protector."

"No, no; you miss the point," spoke the rotund monk abruptly, "brother, it was our mistake, we, none of us and he indicated with a sweeping hand, were there to guide our clerics at the council. This man was a great warrior; no one would dispute that fact, but unfortunately he had a weakness; and dare I say it was his piety."

Realising that he may have been a little indelicate with his choice of phrase, he quickly stood and waving a finger in the air he cautioned, "Do not misunderstand me, this was a good man, but I ask you," he said with appealing resignation, "whoever heard of such a warrior who grew calluses on his knees through his piety, and who dare not make a decision to march before the need for extensive prayer was exercised? No brethren, what we needed was a destroyer, not an advocate for prayer; that is why he could easily sway or override secular council's guidance and direction. After all, how can a secular council overcome the aims of such a devout leader?" He paused, allowing his shoulders to rise engulfing his neck as he presented the question.

"We should have driven this campaign and taken double the land whilst we could, destroying all the enemy whilst he was in rout." Rattling on, he refused to give way for anyone to speak, he continued, "I believe we had the strength to have taken Egypt."

"Hearty words, brother," another interjected, "but armies have to rest and recover, there are such things as logistics and, furthermore, Godfrey did yield much to us".

Waving a hand in the air in rejection of the last comment, the agitated monk cried, "Bah, the prize was so great; they should have run themselves into the face of death itself."

"Is it not our army," came an objector to the last speaker, "do they not fly our banner of the Holy Father?" the monk retaliated. "Well, I think that we should point out to the army just who is in charge of their souls; if it wasn't for our prayers and absolution of their sins they would all be rotting in hell by now." Having had his say, he felt a little ruffled and sat down with a rather reddish complexion. "Had we looked to Raymond, who was," he stressed, pointing his finger across the table at the reader, "the right man, he would have seen to it that victory was imperative; he would have dutifully seen to it that the Church was not overlooked in any prize that was forth coming." Stressing his point, endeavouring to promote Raymond of Nantes; a distant relative to the notice of his master, the harangue continued. "Had we have had control, another army could have been in waiting to become the vanguard of a further onslaught and the victory over Egypt, the richest prize in all our world would have certainly followed." The room fell into an uproar as the debate lost its way; one side openly challenged fine points of strategy while the other fell back into the history of past mistakes.

The smell of the burning candle wax burdened the already stuffy air in the room with a heavy sickly smell. The candles having reduced somewhat in their size, gave off a light less bright than earlier, adding to the pungency of its blackening smoke to the stifling air in the stuffy room causing irritation to the eyes and, in some cases, tears to form.

The head of the group was not tall or large in stature like some of his colleagues; though he did not command a striking appearance, he was not a person to be taken lightly. Indeed, many had in the past unexpectedly fallen because they had underestimated this man's ability.

Father Bernard was an extension of the austere brothers of the monastery from which he had been brought up. Rumour had it that he was the bastard son of a nobleman whose alarmed reactions at the sight of the child at birth gave the father cause to snuff out the life that lay innocently besides its mother. Manifested before him, and for the world to view, was nothing less than an embarrassment; had God in heaven played a cruel joke on him. Such was his rage that he threatened to throw the babe out of the castle window into the night. The stain of such a sin on the mother was unthinkable; it was her child and bore no reflection on the love that husband and wife bore for each other. No, she sobbed; he must not die; God has seen fit to give him life; there was mercy in her impassioned heart; she pleaded endlessly with her husband to see through the error of his judgement. Knowing she was unable to keep him, her final suggestion was for the child to be placed in the care of the monastery, avoiding any stigma on his family name. Rather than such a heinous sin stain their souls for all eternity and mar their future happiness, it was preferable to allow the infant live than bear the burden for its death. After much thought, the alternative began to ease him; he was not a bad man, but the sight of the child's misshapen form had him fearing that enemies might make mischief for his safety, citing that there was something evil in his make-up to spawn such a child.

This was a hard time in the land; his King had many enemies; in his weakness he thought only of himself and what others might say; looking at his wife, he saw the goodness in her.

So, it was arranged that a weighty purse of gold be conveyed for his keep and education, and at all costs the father's name be kept a secret. Bernard grew up never knowing of his parentage, nor did he ever consider enquiring the nature of his arrival in the monastery. He grew up a well-educated and responsible member of the monastery, always thinking towards his own betterment and achieving a name for those that he served. Eventually, due to his cleverness and astuteness of mind, he fell under the eye of the bishop who decided to take him under his tutelage and in later years he eventually aspired to the position that he presently held.

He was not to be taken lightly; being strong in character he was considered a cunning and dangerous little fox. Clad in a rough brown robe that he proudly wore, his voice screeched out, cutting through the silent void in the room. "Come back to the present, brethren; I beseech you. I've listened to your points of interest but must remind the assembly that this is about recent events and not the King of Jerusalem.

"In order to clarify the point I will take the younger brethren back in time before asking for your valuable propositions." Talking in a steady and sombre voice with a knowledgeable air, he first cleared his throat of the fumes that had caused a thickening in his gullet; sitting well back in his chair in a nonchalant pose, he began with the history lesson. Pointing his finger downwards to the table top, he continued. "When the word was sent out across Europe for all to join in a great Crusade, it came from within the very font of Christianity, here. Because of the need for protection for our persecuted brothers and sisters against the Saracen, who had previously taken it upon himself to ignore the agreed treaty he himself had signed, offering freedom and protection to pilgrims visiting the holy city?" Alas the damage is done, the decision to decline the treaty does not really matter anymore. The important point was all Christians suffered the risk of being put to the sword and all roads were closed to Jerusalem. This denial," he said, shifting his position in his chair, "became not only a political insult but also a physical insult by the many numbers of the dead pilgrims that lay along the roadside.

"Of those pilgrims that escaped the cruelty of the Saracen by managing to escape that land, they eventually found sanctuary in the bosom of our Mother Church, recounting the beastly treatment from the Saracen, that the Holy Father be resolute in avenging the wrong done to them. The cries of tormented pilgrims who suffered," the speaker paused bowing his head in sympathy and momentary silence, he continued, "could not go unheard." With his attentive audience hanging on the next word, the lecture continued. "What was our Holy Father to do but appeal to the princes, and nobles and all others who would follow in a Holy War of attrition against this enemy?

"To do this, we agreed that the lands that were conquered by the army would be their own in exchange for the advancement of Christianity, also a promise of absolution of all their sins committed in the ensuing conflicts.

"At that time, there was only one route by land open to reach the required destination, that was by passing Constantinople. We owned it once, but with the passing of time, it had become independent of our rule. Messengers were sent and returned suggesting that they remained friendly, agreeing to furnish us with supplies to see us onwards on our journey to Outremer. After many months of the army's travelling, suffering the privations of hunger and thirst, the affliction of disease bit hard at the army. If that wasn't enough, they suffered severely from the scorching heat which was relentlessly their constant companion. Human nature being what it is, a great impatience brewed among the leaders. This march was proving to have a disheartening effect on its followers before they had reached their destination. Disputes broke out within the ranks and in spite of all attempts to keep together, further disputes between the leaders erupted as to who actually was in charge of the army. That was only the start; within the dissention came a need to vent the feelings of certain leaders; they needed a diversion to quell the ranks and divert their minds away from the present problems; blood and action was the recipe required. Throughout these foreign lands, they had observed the passing of fine cities and great palaces. These people were not their enemy, they relied on them for supplies; but in their hostility and envy they saw only a means to satisfy what they had travelled so far to achieve. They lay siege and eventually sacked the cities; carried out the usual atrocities; but worst of all, they left their victims hanging from the city walls after they had satisfied their need. Discipline became a word that drifted on the wind; enemies rose like corn in the field for revenge against them and bloody battles then ensued along the way. The campaign suffered great losses and won few victories, and had yet to reach the Levant. Supplies seemed to be a word that hungry men could not grasp; foraging parties became raids; knights and their princes could not wait to fill their caravans with looted gold. People died by the thousands, all for the lack of discipline; the barbarism that followed ignited deep feelings of hatred from the Muslim and Christian alike; they grew like the fires of Hell. The Cilician gate being their only route through the Taurus Mountains for our army to reach their destination, proved to be one that was to pose a high price for its use. The vengeful Muslims waited for their chance, which was just a matter of time; once into the forests and mountains they were constantly harried by the Muslim archers in their thousands. When they fled to open ground, cavalry was waiting for them and were very effective in their harrowing strikes, before retreating to safety. Water or the lack of it tore at the throats of men, not a man was spared the experience of its wrath. The ravages of the heat took its toll, good men fell to the diseases of the heat and thirst, their armour and weapons of war become a burden to them, proving too heavy to bear and soon fell to the wayside as their condition weakened and extreme fatigue took a hold on their wasting bodies. If that was not enough to cause their numbers to dwindle, they were soon to approach the highest point in the mountains and the Cilician gate, where for their want of protective cover fell further to the armies of archers that lay in wait in the towering rocks they had to pass by. There was no alternate route and ambushes created losses that were high, so much so that those lucky enough to have survived thus far were forced to near starvation as they continued on. Only God knows how they managed to come through it all; but whilst waiting for another part of the army to catch them up, they decided on a last ditch attack when they confronted the face of the enemy. Inconceivably, it was a victory that enabled them to continue towards their objective and to eventually take them onwards to Antioch." Shaking his head, he admitted that that journey had cost thousands of lives, too many for it to continue that way again as new campaigns were in the planning. It finally appeared that the sea route offered the greatest hopes for an army to safely reach the Holy Land in greater numbers.

"Nobody liked the idea of a sea voyage, there were risks of course, but at least there would only be one enemy present, the sea, and there were no other forms of distraction to cause an army to splinter and fall into disarray." The brothers sat in awe as they listened to their master, Brother Bernard, delivering his knowledgeable account; no one dared to interrupt him whilst he spoke. "At the rate our armies were shrinking, for stupid senseless reasons, we had no other choice than to seek that route which was less precarious and open to distraction. Therefore it was agreed, whilst the army could not afford to pay for transportation and deliver a land campaign, Mother Church agreed to forward the sea costs. This venture was too important to linger over; the wealth of Mother Church was to be made available to seek out ship owners and builders alike to see our purpose through. Our plans were on course until we fell into the clutches of a son of Satan; it appeared that he controlled the hiring of the fleets throughout the land. Appearing to be eager to assist the Church with the transportation for the troops, the ship owners drove hard bargains which we had no choice but to yield to under the pressing circumstances. This son of Satan was a man named Luca Rici; why he particularly targeted the Mother Church as an opportunity to wring every last gold piece he could from us is a mystery.

"The war, it was hoped, would be little more than an incursion; it has now become a burdening ongoing annual event. The Muslim has proved not so easy to defeat. Regretfully, the war is proving to be very expensive; it has shown to be a misconception and has caused an irregular balance to our expected wealth, our Holy Land is proving a costly prize to maintain. What is desperately required, it has been suggested, is a new approach; we need new ideas to temper the defiance of those highly placed to cede to our will. The Templers, our chosen holy soldiers, appear to be squeezing us; it is our mission to subtly lever and prize away the grip that these princely brothers have on their holdings; whilst containing the political and general management of our affairs in a more balanced light." Now with a hint of optimism entering into the sound of his voice, he urged all around him for a unified effort to overcome this setback. Whilst there were no objections to the role of the army or their methods of rule, it was difficult at first to understand fully what was being asked of them. Suggestions were being put forwards but none complied with the ideas that were in the head of their leader. Leaning forwards over the table, he continued his appeal. "Come now my brothers, I was hoping for a little more than we have so far endeavoured to present, we have fertile minds here and have never been unable to present our special services to those that rely on the need." Introducing a note of optimism in his voice, the speaker called on one of his brother monks, "Father Dominic, I believe that you have been working on a method to alleviate this problem."

A tall thin friar who had remained silent throughout the earlier display of blustering further along the table rose to his feet. The good father displayed the faintest of smug smiles as he began to speak, reading from a manuscript of events. "In the recent months we have entered into secret exploratory talks with emissaries of the Sultans and Caliphs." The sound of those titles brought frowns to the monks around the table; where they not the enemy? "I am therefore optimistically able to outline an engagement of mutual interests in this report for the assembly."

A long drawn out speech followed, presenting an elaborate and intricate plan, revealing to the pensive audience to be a deviously dangerous and far-reaching plan in its conception. It was alarming, the look on the faces of those around the table showed its impact. Some felt that the plan in its unveiling made visible some favourable proposals of huge sums of cash to be paid annually as a fief from repatriated rulers for the return of their lost territories. This, it seemed, was a little over ambitious and dangerous for some of the father's to openly accept, it would result in nothing but a destabilising of the army and church. "If this is inaugurated," one brother stated, "it could be the end for us; it is nothing less than treachery." The council was divided; there were mumblings of dissention and Brother Bernard felt it so. The monk continued expressing that a guarantee could be given to protect the future safe passage of pilgrims whenever they came to the Holy City through their varying routes. With a shaking head a doubting brother asked "of what binding agreement could be entered into to enable the church maintain its possession of the Holy City and other cities and ports within the kingdom of Jerusalem.

But Jerusalem was not the nub of the dissension." there was a polite interruption as a question of the likelihood of acceptance by the military and the Royal houses already ensconced out there. "There would be an outcry, nay more like a rebellion to give up their gains; least of all, how would we account for those lost souls left behind on the field of battle in our name."

"There was no need to enter into talks with anybody," the voice that spoke came from Brother Bernard at the head of the table, "this is at present to be our affair. If put into effect; various significant and consequential events will begin to unfold; which we will allow to dominate the course of this episode in history." Although vague, many around the table understood his meaning; as one brother had already stated, "It would be nothing less than treachery for such a plan to take effect. Worse of all what would happen when the Muslim turned on those he had agreed to protect; the situation would be right back where it started. Change could take place, perhaps certain calamities could be enacted which will ease the scheme into reality. As you are all aware, the Templar power is growing and they are gaining strength and influence each day, indeed 'we' are now borrowing money from them." The words were snorted out with contempt; his vehemence for the Templars could not be disguised. The truth of his feelings brought frostiness into the warm, sickly atmosphere of the room. If there was any discomfort in his audience from creased clothing or awkward seating positions, then it was now overlooked as the mood of the meeting veered towards the nub of this dire subject.

Control was what the Council had lost and it was proving a very bitter potion to swallow. The Templar Knights in truth had gained too much power; they now worked outside the Church's agenda, being driven by their own enterprise. Combined with the clammy conditions within the room, the speaker's agitation caused great beads of sweat to hang on his brow and through clenched teeth and anger hanging on his every word, they spewed forth like a torrent of curses.

"I told you earlier," Father Bernard hotly stated, "that there were other reasons for discussion. They, the Tempers, have shown their evil forces brethren; they have outgrown our control and now there is rumour of necromancy hanging over them." There was a gasp of horror as the news of such practice was revealed. "Yes, brethren, news has reached my ears that they are communing with the forces of Hell in their dark practices and raising the soul of one called Baphomet. What their purpose is we do not yet know, but I will seek to overturn this Baphomet and destroy the very existence of this demon until he is no more. If this rumour is true, the Templers will pay dearly; their leaders will burn for their heresy and those that followed them will be made to renew their vows to the church before riding back into the jaws of battle against our enemies. Should they survive their period of penance, then perhaps we will allow them to live; but shackled to our service and in the name of the one true Son of God, Our Lord Jesus Christ." Reaching for his crucifix, he drew it aloft in reverence in both hands, his long sleeves slid back exposing two white spindly arms showing outlines of puce coloured veins travelling their length from the lack of exposure to the light of day. A momentary pause gave birth to a pregnant silence for the awaiting council. Then with purpose once more in his voice, he asserted, "This is a situation I will not allow this convocation to lose grip of."

In the excitement of his tirade of the Templars, his hood slid back, exposing a larger than normal head and his full bearded face. The disfigurement of his scull had seldom been seen, never to most who were his subordinates, as it was considered a personal disfigurement and embarrassment. With glaring eyes, he continued his onslaught of the Templars. "Those dogs are strengthening, almost controlling the master, and as for the royal houses, pressure is required in the right place." The sweat of his fervency grew apparent, displaying a straining clenched fist around his outstretched crucifix, "We will bring them back under our control," he vowed.

Signs of a sudden exhaustion manifested, brought on by his manic dislike for anything opposed to the Church. He relaxed, his breathing slowly becoming regulated; his nerves regained control almost metamorphosing to a completely different personality, finally quietly uttering, "Father Dominic, your plan may have much to offer, but a little more work on the tapestry is needed, yes," he affirmed, "I can see great possibilities there. Of course, if accepted, we will have to assist in creating a little extra colour whilst unravelling the chain of command out there." Meaning that his superiors would have the final decision; now, he cheerfully unfurled his arms with a flourish gathering their attention once more. "I will need a role of those who are indebted to us for positions gained, including those merchants under contract as well as those whose purses we could further massage, and a complete reappraisal of our intelligence for weaknesses within the ruling families." He proceeded, quite satisfactory, and by the end of his extensive request to his subservient brethren, closed the business at hand with a prayer. Father Bernard concluded by slapping the flat of his hand once more on the waxed-topped table declaring that the meeting was over. With his arms outstretched, he spoke once more. "We will now pray once more for further guidance in this matter".

Early the following day, in the dimness of his office, Father Bernard was sorting through the parchments left hither and thither on his desk. His mood had become quite morose over the previous evenings outcome, fuelling him with anger toward his clerk, who had not made the slightest effort to compile the documents as he was ordered. The office was starved of daylight offered from the single narrow lancet window, where a meagre shaft of sunlight hardly wider than an arrow slit struggled to allow light into the room. He was a worker, diligent and loyal to his position and the high ideals of the Holy Father. "What possible hope was there of bringing a successful conclusion to such a dangerous and delicate task if I am unable to first study my documents, I'll never find them in this wretched light," he whimpered. Disappointed that his own pleas for an office with better light for study had not born any sign of acknowledgement hurt his feeling. Offering a new candle to ignite from an already flaming light to further his search, his disgruntled mind continued in its disaffected mood. After all, it was in the interest for the Holy Father to encourage those of us whose faithful and assiduous endeavours bring reward and results to this holy household. His was a secret and secure office that must remain so; nor was he one to allow others to wander in and out, seeking previews of his agenda. His place and affairs were in the background of events, never to come to the notice of the other brethren, or the world at large. Great store was put by for the reasons given by his superior when he was elevated to his position to always closely guard that which he worked on.

With little more than a sigh of reserved acceptance of the order from his superior, and an almost ungrateful comment that he work a little harder on the schemes completion, he had humbly raised the question once again if only he could make use of a place that offered better light to work by.

Patience was the reply, and it was snappy; it was added that he be tolerant, in the due course of time he would be amply rewarded, but for now he must remain where he was and continue being a faceless person. He stood alone in that office with reasoned understanding and reluctance, an aggrieved disciple. Unsatisfactory; a thoughtful but not active rebellion in his dumb silence was all he could muster, yet every time he thought of that reply it was like having to bear the discomfort of a splinter of wood being thrust down his finger nail, piously to bear its pain as its reminder. His wounded feelings brought the return of anger and rejection back to the disgruntled monk. In his mind he began to fume like a smoking volcano, looking for a vent of release, perhaps by the shortcomings of his clerk. The expectation of walking into his office and picking up the waiting document for study did not seem to him to be too much of a difficult task to set anyone to. Thoughts of a replacement soon ran through his mind but not before chastisement; yes, definitely a release of the unwanted tension; he would enjoy that. He suddenly visualised the superior doling out the appropriate punishment, that idea lessened the dark depression that had clouded his mind, a wry sadistic smile twitched at the corner of his slit of a mouth. At last, after scattering at least half a dozen important documents around, he placed his hand on the lost document.

The room was already full with candles emitting a heavy waxy pungency into an already stuffy air-starved room. Father Bernard sat at his desk toiling over the plans put forward by Father Dominic; in his indulgence, he was sat on an old loose rickety upright stool swinging his short legs and bared feet to and fro under his desk. His sandals beneath him had long since dropped from his feet and fallen onto the bare stone floor. Now in deep concentration, he became suspicious of the document before him, the proposals revealed that the Sultans would be more agreeable not just to return, but to regain full control of the Northern provinces in exchange for certain very large annual payments to the Church for the release of these strategic areas. The idea of such large sums appealed; it was little short of a King's ransom, his carrot to steer the donkey he thought, but he would not be taken in so easily with the generosity of such an annual tithe payment, even over a long period. He was not very happy with what he could not see, which proved difficult in the light of the flickering candles. Growing more frustrated and irritated by the inadequacy of his dim office light, he angrily hauled himself from his chair.

He crossed the room bare foot in the direction of the door, over a cool flagged floor, offering the only relief to his body in the repressive warmth of the room. Being a lean man and carrying little weight, on reaching the door he down-heartedly discovered that it had jammed; it was in him to kick the door. His temper, prompted not only his disappointment but the lack of fresh air getting to him; being practical and of prudent disposition, he overcame his frustration, realising that panicking might possibly make matters worse for himself. Cupping his sweating head in his hands, he thought better of hurting himself in some half-baked reaction. He pulled at the door three or four times but on each occasion it proved to be caught in the jamb at the top edge. He called loudly numerous times for his cleric on the other side of the door, who alas had moved away unable to hear the desperate tones from the air-starved chamber, leaving a distressed superior suffering a frustrating fit of annoyance.

Once the situation was known, the cleric returned within a short time with an army of assistants, soon to be united in a concerted engagement of pushing on the door to release it from its jammed frame. When it finally gave way, the host of clerics clamoured around father Bernard fussing the now almost faint and self-conscious father. His frustration had turned to open embarrassment, which quickly transcended into anger. So upset was he by this time, that he indignantly ordered them all out at the top of his voice. There were no thanks for the release from his temporary confinement. The air that rushed into the room filled his lungs, renewing his determination to bestow on the responsible individual his feelings for deserting his master in his time of need." Not you," Father Bernard scowled at the young cleric; who thoughtfully had a flask of water for the relief of the suffering senior brother. The young cleric became crestfallen at the lack of recognition for his concern, walking towards the open door considering his immediate fate. Unfortunately for him, this poor boy was to receive a lesson in humility experiencing the vengeance of the lord, which was to prove to be the ruin of this young cleric's day.

With the office now adequately illuminated with extra candles and an unwanted increase in temperature, the door of the office remained firmly fixed in an open position. Fully recovered and feeling better after exercising his exasperations, Father Bernard resumed to perusing the Eastern emissary's reply. It was further proposed that all the lands from Tripoli in the north to Montreal in the south across to Ascalon on the coast could all be maintained under the Kingdom of Jerusalem. There was also the provision that all Muslims would have rights of access to pray in their holy places within that territory. On the face of it we were offered a hugely handsome rent in return for nothing of any great value, this bothered him, it was too good an agreement. Deciding to study it further with the thoughts of the Muslim in mind; on the contrary it meant we gave up the northern territories for nothing, but he recalled, wars and the Holy Land are forever in a state of flux and expensive.

The reader was well aware that he had to evaluate the cost of trade loss, military expenditure for times of unrest and weigh them against the newly-proposed payment of a fiefdom. There was of course a nagging danger, which kept returning to him. By turning over the northern territories, the Muslim of the north and the Persians at the east was risky; the brother's words the previous evening resounded in his ears. Could they be trusted if they were given an open road? Should they ever break the treaty and flood into our kingdom with their armies? Resistance would be useless once passed Eddessa and Antioch. This raised a serious worry in the presiding father's mind; it required some lasting and binding guarantee, a piece of paper saying as much might not be worthwhile to the enemy. Perhaps it may be that a sea voyage is required to speak to these people face to face. In the meantime, he would give all his thoughts to perfecting this plan.

The Route Northwards

The interior of the apartment of Grand Prior of Acre appeared sparsely furnished yet neat, reflecting a meticulous order that Robert of Simonwood never had the time or luxury to adopt. To the small group of knights who stood waiting for their commander in the coolness of his high office chamber, the thick walls of which must have measured the depth of two standing men, . Looking about the sturdiness of its construction offered some reassurance to anyone within, with knowledge that one could stand his ground in this most substantial fortification. To the wandering eye, it could not help be noticed that the interior seemed to lack a certain luxury that would have been expected of such an important military leader in the Levant.

Of the unusual group of knights that had been gathered together, Robert Simonwood was the youngest, and their leader. Yes, he was a young, though not immature, and a fearless knight at that; his ability to see a mission through was exemplary. He was dashing; in the eyes of many women he was considered handsome and a fair prize to be had; he enjoyed their company but would not be swayed by their allure. Unfortunately for them, his way of life did not permit the luxuries of a lasting engagement; relationships for him had to be fleeting.

He had arrived with his older brother at the darkest time of night, and by clandestine means, so as to keep their presence unnoticed. So too were the others that had also joined them in the chamber, but much later; companions all had journeyed from afar and different directions to be at this meeting. This little band rarely came together; all knew and trusted each other, having worked together in some time past. The nature of their work was always dangerous and secret, sworn to secrecy, even to death, especially to those of the Court that were above them in rank. Although most nobles were not aware of their function, many were highly suspicious of them, even to the point of asking the King why he favoured these men. Their questions got them nowhere; they soon backed away when they saw the mood of the King turn against them should they persist their enquiry.

These handpicked men were unique because of their special abilities in the field, of which, one was their ability to have mastered many languages, and another was their ability of ease to blend in and pass amongst the local populace. That took time and a great deal of study; one had to generally act, walk and take on all manner of aspects of the populace. It was not an easy task, but they had all trained under selected tutors within the enlistment of the

Templers whose rigorous training required nothing less than perfection. The King's demands were many; it was imperative that he was constantly abridged for the need of knowledge of his enemies, just as the enemy's eyes were always turned to them. Therefore, disguise and daring made the difference to any mission; also to life and death, and death, if one was caught, came always at the hands of the torturer to seek out what had been learnt. Ability was a highly valued asset, discipline essential; coupled with intellect, their act became more of an art in their ways of gathering intelligence; above all, dedication and propriety was their protector.

They were, in the main, an odd bunch that had suffered their own particular type of scars; and they had seen good men sour. They were young when they arrived in this land and been in a state of war ever since, fighting hard. Age came upon them before their time, leaving them battle worn; they had witnessed too many sights of weeping widows holding dead husbands close with crying children at their side; blood was spilt and for what reason, it seemed to be lost in the madness of it all. They knew of their Holy Father's desire to hold Jerusalem, but the cost kept rising; they too, like everybody else, watched their friends die, women raped and what it was to lose their past friends of long ago. Out of it came a loneliness that led to nowhere; there was in them all a need to find a new path whilst always maintaining loyalty to the sovereign, in short they chose to be loners, almost outcasts of their own society, but not lacking in rank or without influential connections.

Their talents being used solely for the King, in a display of necessity of their particular line of work he conferred on them a special rank of office with direct responsibility to the Royal Council and through the Grand Prior of Acre.

The lands of the Levant for this small group held inspiration in its culture, here they saw learning of a different kind to theirs; mathematics, philosophy, astronomy and science. Though they were fighting men, life did not disbar them from thinking. Sometimes their thoughts could lead them to the edge of argument; a dangerous place to tread for anyone in their occupation. They enjoyed the country's mystic charm, at the same time appreciated its people, mixing freely with all groups that made up the assorted races of those surrounding countries interesting and challenging.

As individuals, Robert's little group had been through much to make this sacrifice in the Holy Land. Many times they had thought deeply of where and what their loved ones were at. War changes men; one thing they all seemed to depend on was their partners whoever that turned out to be. They were the nearest they had to family, not knowing whenever they parted if they would ever see them again; that was why reunions were so joyous. Their secret lives brought with it a heightening of feeling with the dangerous situations they entered into.

When the fighting ceased, or in the season of resting when the rains came or peace pacts were enacted, a non-fighting knight became redundant. He had a duty to make good use of the suspension, by taking stock of his weapons and armour, his livestock and his men. For those that looked after themselves, life could develop into boredom with little more to do than waste time; becoming a drinker, a gambler or debaucher, anything was better than the hum drum life of waiting the season out or servile military service. It suited many, but not Robert and his associates, during that period life gave rise to interesting observations of his fellow soldiers; it was the same for both sides, but spies cannot afford to lay back and wait for conditions to change. Just because an army can't be turned out under adverse conditions doesn't mean that preparations cannot be followed up for the coming season. Here on the outer reaches of a limitless frontier, where life was feverishly unstable and men such as themselves had to be sharp, they plied their trade just the same. Of course, they did not always move in the size of group that they had been called on for this such occasion, it was mostly in ones or two's that they operated, being able to drift from one place to another with impassive immunity to whatever was happening about them.

When the Grand Prior entered his office, he was apologetic and almost breathless. Excusing his lateness because of his other prolonged duties, he raised an arm in casual salute, greeting them all cordially before setting about outlining the need for their abilities. The purpose of their recall, he informed them slumping into a wooden chair tired from his many duties of office, was extremely delicate. It pained him to believe what he knew; before he could make his knowledge public, he needed the aid of the group to secure a basis for any such announcement or action. Disturbing information, he told them, had reached his person, of a destabilising force at work in the north. Somebody, it appeared, was stirring up the enemy against the various leading Christian families that ruled the Northern provinces. He was genuinely appalled by it and still found it difficult to believe; within one of those provinces that gave peace to the land by their vigilance and fortitude on the borders, there was a traitor. Relentlessly, these valiant men maintained their strength of control over warlike tribes that threw its armies continuously and senselessly at its Frankish enemy, like rats at sacks of grain. One day, the enemy vowed, with hope and prayer, and Allah's grace and love for the faithful, they would eventually burst through the protective coating that protected their prize.

Quietly, he explained that their task was to uncover any pieces of information to that end; "Believe me," he added, "this land and peace is so fragile." Who or what this force represented was to be the object of the group's mission. Holding back on his suspicions he told them that there was no other indication other than a source of discontent and rumour, which his secret sources indicated lay at their own door. This was a cause of great concern and distress at the very thought that the army or one of its leaders could treacherously turn inwards to unsettle all that they have fought for. Annoying and disbelieving as it was, he first needed to discover a definite motive for such a move; he reasoned that no one man could rule such a territory alone; he would need an army of tens of thousands, but a rumour as serious as this had to be investigated. It came as some relief to be aware that there were no Templar Knights involved in this conspiracy, as they had nothing personally to gain monetarily. Before joining, they generously relinquished all their wealth to the

Order. Their purpose in life was to forward the purpose of the order and the word of the true cross.

The strong sea breezes that occasionally enveloped the high stone façade of the fortress walls blew wafts of refreshing salty air in through the stone lined room, leaving as quickly as it arrived by rushing through an adjacent lancet window like a great cleansing draft, relieving the discomforting heat that stagnated and stifled the air for those that occupied the room, particularly the old Prior. Fearing the ruination of relations between his old enemy, he became bitterly disappointed, especially after making peaceful and profitable trading agreements with many foreign rulers, that gave rise to a more congenial and responsive understanding of each other. With matters so surreptitious as those which had been recently reported arising to inject doubts; if not settled, it could pose to destabilise the newfound fragile peace. There were those that did not want peace; tribal hatred and distrust of the European invader would not cease, nor would those leaders rest until the franj was forcibly ejected from the land to which they had no right. The Templar, along with the Royal families, had won it and had settled, they were growing very influential and powerful as they reached out to their enemy with a charitable hand. Whether they be enduring hostilities or at peace, in many cases the Templars felt that they could contribute substantially to the welfare of the ordinary people, by filling a gap in society in their dire need for hospitals. By treating those that had unfortunately been touched with the hand of leprosy and other disabling illnesses, hospitals were built and for the first time there was a caring refuge for these unfortunate people. This hand of mercy and compassion did not go unnoticed by the Sultans and Caliphs. If anything, the Templars' character became somewhat ambiguous, conquerors and barbarians on the one hand and Samaritans on the other. Of course there was much more to their presence than that, they were also viewed as tax collectors for the Church, as well as traders, scoundrels and rapists, indeed whatever manner of misfortunes befell the people of the Levant, the blame inevitably fell to the franj.

In spite of the conflict, the relationship grew; the Templars took every advantage, extensively trading with their Islamic allies building up a control of certain goods, which made its way to Europe and in turn enabled them to truly bond with their old Islamic enemy and in some cases created friendships that were to prove lasting.

The old Grand Prior was a solid character and warm in his sincerity to anything relating to his belief. His service record was exemplary; he had in many ways been a strong sword arm for the brotherhood and was well-liked by all, it was without doubt the reason for his rapid rise in the order; his honourable standing was well deserved. The limp he had borne these many years gave him little pain these days, until he left the environs of the summer heat. He dreaded having to sail to Europe to submit a biannual report to the council in Rome. It would be there that his pain would return in the cold days of the Roman winter, reminding him of a day when he had been carried off the field seriously wounded after a furious battle. He was lucky, so he was told, that his leg would be saved, but for his armour, he would have lost it. That was a long time ago, yet these little trips abroad were his reminder of the pain he once suffered.

Whatever was on his mind made him irascible as he paced the stone floor of his chambers; the news that he departed of the impending alleged action was sketchy, expressing to his audience the depth of his concern. Since this rumour had reached his ears, he had hardly slept; its conception had come from a source that he dare not impart to his men. To add to the Prior's already disgruntled mood, it had not given him any pleasure to have repeated his dire news openly. So far, the information revealed had only been circulated to those in the highest of positions of command, he had no need to further warn them of loose tongues. They had worked with the Prior long enough for him to know their silence was above all others.

Sighing heavily, as he spelt out the news; the worried Prior nervously admitted that this plot must never be allowed to come to fruition; there was no telling what would happen; war, he said, was or seemed inevitable.

The old Prior sniffed the early morning air in huge breaths to release the pressure that he had borne; half turning, he uttered stressfully the need for swift results if the situation was to be contained. His plan was to dispatch the six agents before him into the northern territories reporting in at Antioch; digressing, he added that he did not know the captain, but he was sure he was a good man. From that base they were to fan out and gather as much information as was possible, and hopefully meet up to discuss their findings, and make a decision on the course of action that they would adopt. Before any action, the Prior stressed, Robert was to send news by a carrier pigeon with an outline of his intended plan.

"Do not go off on your own. I need to be aware of your every action, because of the delicacy of this mission I do not want to wait in a prolonged silence. Is that clear, my friend?"

The bristles of his white moustache fairly bristled as he stressed the order, as they always did when he was agitated. Robert reassured the Prior that he would at all times keep him up to date on all matters relating, but needed the freedom to act on instinct whichever way he thought best without having to outline his reasons for doing so to anyone outside their group. This prompted a silence of thought from the Prior. Viewing the men he had chosen, he once more regarded them with a dubious eye; in a doubting voice and with a wagging finger he warned them,

"I know where your loyalty lies, you have proved it too often, but," and changing his tone, he almost angrily warned them also not to go quiet on him, "too many times in the past you have left me hanging and guessing your actions, do not be tempted this time to repeat that mistake."

His manner and tone eased as he returned to a general ruling of his orders. More at ease, he altered his commanding tone and continued pacing the floor as he spoke.

"Bear in mind all courtesies wherever you station yourselves, remember that you are to liaise with the resident captain, alert him if necessary, if ever the need to arm or arrest anyone attempting to usurp the balance of rule in the region." Like a tutor, he reiterated their duties and responsibilities. "Remember always acting in the best interests of maintaining the continued stability of the King, the Temple and your resident host."

The Grand Prior had been in service in the Levant for many years, the climate, he always attested, was good for his aches and other complaints that come with age. With a spring in his step, he turned sharply as if he were a much younger man and came to face Robert, "The time for talk is over, now go and do what I ask of you." As they rose and turned to leave the Prior's chambers, he called on them to stop. "Stop by my secretary," he called, "and pick up the documents that I have prepared for you, but hurry now a ship awaits you in the harbour." As the old Prior scribbled his signature to another document, Robert arched his neck, peering in admiration at the flowing script of the Prior's ageing hand. His flowing handwriting was somewhat artistic, Robert's keenness of eye could not help noticing the date, 12th day of March, how the time has passed.

For a moment, Robert's mind wandered as he tried first to recall the year; though thinking hard on it, he had difficulty in recalling the length of time that he had spent in this land, how his time in it had passed so quickly. Although his posture remained in all appearances attentive, he simply lost interest in the Prior's writing with his own thoughts. Finishing the order of release, the Prior reached for a long reddened stick of wax and a burning candle. After melting sufficient red wax that had dripped copious blobs onto the parchment of written orders, he pressed his ring into the congealing mass to reveal the embossed Templer Knights seal of two knights sharing the same horse. Robert was jolted back to the present as the Prior stood up sharply to hand him the document and with a slap of good luck across his shoulder, he was warmly bid good luck and a wish of a safe return.

The men left the building at haste without a need to say farewell to anyone, they changed their guise and packed what few supplies they needed.

The secretary was serious and diligent in his work ethic; conscientious as he was, outside of his post he was not a man to relax and unwind with the lower ranks. That is not to say that he was unkind or unhelpful, but being a part of the high office of the Grand Prior made him aware of his high station and importance.

On their return for their documents, they approached the secretary; as always he was busy, with a lack of recognition of the interlopers into his official domain, he immediately barked at the strangers, telling them to get out of his office, as this was no place for any merchant to be. It raised a smile to Robert's face and he could not help but play his part and act dumb to the secretary's command. It was only when the official dropped his hand to reach for his dagger; Robert quickly realised that his prank had gone too far; for his own safety, he immediately spoke in English giving him some consolation that his present disguise was good enough to fool the secretary then he probably would get along in the crowds. Realising that he had been duped, the secretary, was flustered with embarrassment and failed to see the amusing side to Roberts jest, but slowly changed his attitude as he realised the effectiveness and importance of his colleague's disguise.

"Here," he handed Robert his orders for himself and an introduction to the visiting Prior in Antioch. Again he stared disbelievingly at Robert, reaching across the desk to retrieve his orders. The fact that he had been duped still laid heavily on him, so much so that his mood was running close to black. He took a deep breath to lose what anger he had harboured, thrust out his hand offering his wishes of good luck for Robert's mission ahead. He did not envy the young man, aware that he could not do the same, but he could and would request the offer to fight in battle if given the chance.

The old Prior walked to the lancet window and peered out towards the gate; there was a gentle cooling effect from the breeze. Watching Robert cross the parade yard, he looked down with amusement, wondering where this mission would eventually take him and what dangers would befall this young man and his associates. In a spy's way of life, events could change at any moment, taking him and his brave little group this way or that, like leaves blowing on the wind to who knows where.

Their business now was to find and board the waiting vessel which was to carry them onwards to their new objective so that they could be transported across north easterly waters to a region that was adjacent to the known heartland of the enemy.

Waiting for the mid-morning tide on a hot morning, the triple-masted merchantman left port, the wind was fair and the ships rounded hull bobbed up and down on the lapping water, leaving behind its spume like signature of passing in its wake. Sailing northwards towards a bright sun-filled cloudless blue horizon, the vessel cut its watery path across the waves en route for St Symeon. The port that was their destination for disembarkation lay in the northern principality of Antioch. From that port, there was only one road out to the great splendid city, which in good seasons had remained a road of uncertain safety. The caravans that arrived at the port for the great city of Antioch had become the crossroads of passage for most traders from the East, listing not only traders but emissaries and spies travelling to and from the Muslim nations.

The six western knights on the voyage were devoid of their military dress, their preference of choice was of silken eastern garb such as would be worn by merchants of the region. The softness and comfort of their new clothing gave them an air of comfort and confidence in their new pretentious façade; they flaunted themselves and quietly taunted each other with deriding laughing innuendo. For those who were slim and muscular, that was five of the six, had to increase their size of waistline by padding out an undergarment to display the impression of weight. Whoever heard of a muscular trader; this aspect they believed was essential. Their brief bout of self-mockery and laughter on their way to the ship about their appearance was good for them; it briefly lifted their spirits. The intelligence source that was not discussed made them wonder where it had come from, it was surely a very serious matter for its conception to be born from their own kind; it could and would have very serious repercussions to the strategic defences of their new found land. With similar thoughts, they questioned who had most to gain; why go to such extremes? One thing was certain, the Prior's intentions to send good men abroad on a whimsical rumour could not be discounted.

It was unimportant to Robert to raise the question of the identity of the source, but the Grand Prior was not giving that information over. He no doubt had his reasons, but Robert felt it must be of the most extreme delicacy not to have revealed it. He and his little company were sailing into the unknown with not an inkling of an idea where to look, it was like blind man's bluff, he thought, to carry out his orders and substantiate or disprove the rumour; on their word rested the alert of all military detachments. No doubt, as he pondered over the task ahead, he was sure that his Grand Prior was discreetly doing almost the same thing.

Earlier when they had found their ship and met with the captain, they had taken an immediate dislike to him, having the looks of a man that was not to be trusted. The first thing they were told was that they would have to take passage on deck. He refused to argue the point, insisting that they could be reimbursed should they press for accommodation; it was up to them to decide. It was impossible to make it appear that they had to discuss the matter and took the passage and the discomfort of deck without too much fuss. Merchants were known to be fussy, but even more careful with their gold. With a nonchalant air, they sat around openly talking of business as was the want of travelling merchants; the crew, it had been noted, dallied as they worked close to their gathering. That much was obvious, whether it be on the water or on land, information was always a means to a meal or a gold piece, if it were considered important enough. Later, when it was safer, they had gathered themselves into a small conversational huddle near the forward end of the vessel as to be less easily overheard by any of the crew-members, who by that time had decided that their conversations were of no profit to them and continued with their work.

Occasionally, one or two of the group would casually break away, traversing the deck taking in the duties of the crew. To do as others would by leaning over the side looking for something of interest in their act to appear ordinary citizens, or eagerly peering northwards into the spray as the ship heaved its way on the swelling sea. As always, once out on the great expanse of the sea, destinations always seemed afar; especially if one was not a good sailor, but hope was always present in this mystical land of changing horizons and tumultuous divisions of its peoples.

Inconspicuous as they thought they were, little did they know that their appearance and behaviour in their attempts to make themselves appear little more than inconspicuous traders had not gone unseen; secreted behind wooden bulkheads were dark eyes watching their every movement from within the hidden shadows of the accommodations.

With the coming of another day, the sun was climbing ever higher in the cloudless blue sky, promising another oppressively hot day, although the breeze from off the sea compensated for the sun's ever present relentless heat. Acre had become little more than a distant speck on a hazy horizon as the ship headed out to deep sea; behind, somewhere in the far distance, sat the walled fortress city they had left. It was built long before the arrival of the Franks to these shores to withstand any siege and probably had the best natural deep water port on their side of the Mediterranean. Being the focal point of trade on the coast or inland, it was filled with insidious Muslim spies and their treachery. After its fall, it settled under Frankish rule; the enemy remained deeply agitated and prayed daily for Allah to deliver their city back from the hands of the hated Christian pigs to those of the faithful.

The agents of the Fatimids of Egypt and the Seljuks to the North seemed to be secreted everywhere, in spite of a recent peace agreement; the Muslim was at peace yet their outlook in disarray; there was, it seemed, no secured lasting peace between the varying Muslim factions or the Frankish princes. It was a strange state of affairs in some respects; the want of cohesiveness that peace brings lacked any belief in unity between the ruling families, giving the Franks a break from any sporadic fighting that might break out. The peace was frail, but rotten apples in the barrel of Frankish nobles was not going to prevent the odd roguish knight from breaking ranks to exploit any opportunity to plunder their old enemy. This incessant greed for wealth by plundering Muslim families who were at odds with their neighbours was a grave act of recklessness, the King was horrified and threatened to put a price on the heads of those belligerent knights whose seditious acts almost tipped the balance of peace back to war, jeopardising all that he had worked towards between the parties. His efforts were barely enough to hold the peace; having to send out emissaries to explain the failings of your own kind was embarrassing, and Kings do not take kindly to such embarrassment.

In times such as this, normal life seemed unreal; whether working the land or managing affairs, without having to keep a sword in one hand was a new experience. Certain nobles that lived in their bitterness with a lust for action also found life unorthodox, finding it difficult to give way to the new peace; any interest to inspire confidence or trust within the ranks of the Moslem just wasn't there. Had it not been for the united and determined stand of the Templars, the peace would likely have long fallen into disarray.

As an insight into those times, Hubert now walked with a slight limp and Edward narrowly missed losing his arm after they had found themselves in tight corners; those type of scars were hard to carry and remain unaffected whilst keeping trust in others.

Alone in the vast openness of the sea's expanse and far from land, the small ship bobbed in the rhythm with the active sea; the wind was kind reducing the effects of the scorching suns heat but for one of the group it was not going to be a pleasant voyage. Hubert leaned his broad back against the centre mast steadying his large frame, Godwin was alongside him. They were good friends, almost always working together, becoming as close as brothers. Hubert was the first to speak. "Better watch this lot," he said out of the side of his mouth. Godwin smiled, knowing Hubert's first words were always the same, "Hubert," he replied jesting, "what's got into you? They are no different than anyone on land. Why these look like hard working men to me," he admonished Hubert for thinking less of his fellow man. "Well, I don't," retorted Hubert, "they all look shifty to me." He received a short dig of Godwin's elbow in his side, and his friend turned to him appealing for him to relax a little; it was not like Hubert; Godwin came round to thinking that something was not quite right with his friend.

Alas, in spite of Roberts earlier deception with the Priors secretary, the expectation that five merchants and one extra-large one travelling together on a ship seemed most unlikely, giving little credence to their supposed deception clearly ran short of that mark of belief.

Together the friends talked of their journey quietly, taking care not to allow any active words slip out by careless intent. In three or four days, if all went well on their voyage, they would arrive at St Simion where they would dock and collect horses to take them on to Antioch. It was in Antioch that they would first report, hand over their orders from Acre and hopefully receive their final briefing, if any.

The sun at this time had reached its pinnacle in the sky, and the company set about preparing an awning on the deck to shelter from the ever-present raging ball of heat in the sky that incessantly blazed down on them.

Since the recent peace pact, the military were allowed to relax their need from wearing their usual heavy military mail at all times, though for those that were in the knightly ranks they were encouraged to exchange their military garb for one displaying that they were less hostile and in a constant state of battle readiness. Of course, this change of dress offered advantages to which they had taken to quite easily, and for once it enabled knights to merge into the populace without a need for those sideways looks; it was a blessing and an added relief in the heat of the day to parade freely in silks and lightweight cotton, for which the opportunity had never risen before. But for the ordinary service man, although he had cast off his mail frock, the heavy leather garment remained.

The little group knew the northern regions, having their own contacts and friends that were not European; they had consorted freely with Armenians and Jews as well as some Muslims, but in the main worked alone.

The small group of Knights consisted of du Bray; a fierce, dark-looking Frenchman who quite oddly was never called by his first name; stranger still, his first name had never been known to any of them, though it was of no importance, nor indeed would it be asked of him to explain his reasons. Privacy ruled, curiosity remained; but respect for the individual prevented a need to trespass further. That way, they were left to their own peace to carry their secret burdens privately. Edward Simmonwood, Robert's elder brother, who had been exceptionally helpful during the time of the truce as an interpreter, was likely to be the quietest of them all. He had seen much and travelled most; he preferred most emphatically not to talk of his past to his local commander or anyone other than his priest; like all the others, whatever burden he carried he kept hidden to himself. To outsiders he was a strange fish, but others knew him as a patient and kindly man. He too had been blinded by the sport of conquest;

he had been born to it and though he never rebelled against it, his reservations eventually caught up with him. Luckily, by that time he had become a part of the new unit of men enlisted to the King's needs. He was not running away from the killing; he had only changed company and clothes, leaving the thrill of the butchery behind for those most suited to it. These days he was a free agent and like the others was poorly paid for his troubles; to survive he remained true to an unwritten rule, that when safe to grab at as much as he could to keep body and soul together; he did. Edward never ceased to fight; either on the field or in his head; and when pushed into corners, killing seemed not to have any meaning to him. Edward was a rising star and had soon gained a certain respected standing in the inner councils. He was not a happy man, for he was constantly drawn into webs of intrigue within the circles of high office. He learnt, as others, that the court was a dangerous place for a man's safety; to escape his position, he approached the King to suggest that he may offer himself to be better used out in the field.

He had later learnt that his younger brother was serving not less than three days away from him, all this time he had felt an undercurrent of despondency, thinking that Robert had been long lost to him. It was a joyous occasion when the two brothers met and it did not take long in discovering his younger brother was already at work learning the same trade as he after all. It was a great opportunity, he felt, that he could at last keep an eye on his brother and keep him out of trouble.

There was Godwin and Hubert, who also were a couple of loners that had come together and somehow grown to each other's company and were almost inseparable. Hubert, because of his love of food, had searched and discovered the best cuisine in the Levant. The desire to eat had been the fuel for his need to speak the dialects of the Northern markets, which he had managed and taken to like a fish to water. Hubert's size was never a disadvantage; he could wield a sword from the saddle in any given situation as good as any man. When enlisted, Hubert was soon introduced to Godwin, who was born of good humour with a gift to make men laugh in the face of adversity; the two came together as friends of many years. Guy Goodwin was often the dry and light-hearted member of the group, whilst Hubert Pryce, the most robust of them all, ate considerably to support his large stature. Both were intelligent, loyal and in general, quiet thinking men; they were not like any of their brothers in arms, for once they did not enjoy the excesses like some of their counterparts that revelled and made names for themselves as lecherous and debauched invaders. Godwin, in his early days, had been posted close to the Armenian border and was also gifted to speak the tongues of the area, this, to the Temple was a wonderful find. By splitting up, they were then able to gather a general consensus of the feelings of both the tribes and the cities; Edwards's group was beginning to prove its worth. There was in them a willingness to see their role played quietly and with purpose, serving their King faithfully in his chosen goal. Finally, there was the young Aldo Ricci, close friend of Robert; they had forged an extremely close friendship whilst fighting alongside each other in the border battles against the enemy. Some believed that Aldo looked to Robert as some kind of figurehead that he admired and copied himself on. He was without doubt the youngest man of the group; alas Robert once feared that he had fallen to the warrior's sickness of not feeling well unless he was fighting. The sickness fell indiscriminately upon young and older warriors, no one knew its cause but everyone recognised the effects. When Robert looked back on his own past, he shuddered to feel that he too could also have fallen to it, only for his elder brother rescuing him in time. Seeing these symptoms in Aldo, Robert felt that he could save the young man from a fated wasteful suicide. Unintentionally, soldiers affected by battle fever sometimes became swept up with fervency, believing themselves invincible; in their acts of recklessness they endangered the security of their own and other lives. It appeared that this was the fate lying in wait for this brave young man; Robert had watched him, observing this weakness working on him; if he kept him close like a fostered brother, he believed that he could save this boy from an early death. As for the sixth member of the group, du Bray, he was their man of mystery, quiet, intelligent and fearless when faced with danger. He was a closed book, nobody seemed to know anything of him or his past or were exactly he had come from. It was believed that he had been garrisoned in the South, but as discussions of origin were left unspoken, he melded into the group; no man within this company had not been scarred in some way or other. This was not uncommon, when battles raged; men were hewn like corn under the sword and scattered. He had drifted back into camp one day not knowing who he was, but since that day he has repaired and appears as normal as any man. Sometimes even a victorious army of thousands could be reduced to hundreds, and those left standing could be strangers to each other. Rumour, it was said, believed him to have suffered the sickness of battle, others say he had taken a tribeswoman as his wife and later watched her succumb to a fatal illness, to die a slow and painful death. His loss broke his heart, and in his grief he took on scouting the most dangerous areas of the borders in a bid that in death he would be reunited with his bride. That's how they stumbled across him, riding alone in the wilderness, and from that day he had been with them; the malady that haunted him it was hoped had diminished to little more than a distant echo. Though events may paint a picture of damaged men, the wind blows change; together the men became different from what befell them long ago. Hubert feared dying for the food he had not yet eaten, Godwin always laughed in the face of danger, which if anything was good for moral. Du Bray liked to be alone, that was his preference and no one said otherwise. Robert had split his partnership with Edward whilst Edward paired with du Bray; it seemed a sensible decision at the time. For a while the partnerships were fragile; as each became better acquainted with the other, all seemed to go well. For Robert there were odd and worrying occasions; Aldo's zeal took longer to adjust to the quieter life of living in the shadows than the battlefield. His young impetuous nature sometimes took a hold of him, causing Robert to have to beat a retreat from what could have developed into awkward situations. The young Aldo had no compelling reason to be in the Levant, being driven not from servitude but by his high moral principle. Along with the impassioned appeal from the Holy

Father, duty to his fellow man was the impetus. Whenever he thought back on that time, his grandfather's arguments came into mind; he didn't want Aldo to leave. Being the grandson of the richest and most talked about ship owner in all of Italy was a secret that he preferred to keep to himself.

Alert at all times, living on the edge of the blade but loyal to each other to the last; life was quite a trial to these men. For reasons best known, they had accepted their role with the risk of all the dangerous details that were presented to them; it was as if they had become addicted to the life of activity behind the enemy, which obviously excited them in a different way.

Sitting under their canvas awning, shielded from the sun's rays, they chattered away quietly; to some degree nervous for the time ahead, not one of them knew where they might be led or what this mission held in store.

It was bad luck and very unusual to have to accept the discomfort of the deck, denied the use of accommodations would, they knew, lead to a discomforting passage. They had no choice but to accept; a little fuss over accommodation was acceptable, too much may have raised a suspicion. Though the captain's words were short, he too, he too was enjoined to share with the crew. In other words, he was telling them that what he had to suffer was likewise good enough for others should they want to come aboard.

So, it appeared there were other passengers; it had become a topic of interest discussing those that had been able to move the captain from the comfort of his cabin. Who ever heard of passengers who preferred to remain unknown, shutting themselves away from others; they were indeed a mystery, who could they be? As odd as it seemed, those occupants weren't walking the decks; that also became a point of further discussion. Life in the accommodations could sometimes become a little claustrophobic, and it was hoped that sooner or later they would show themselves; it would be interesting to converse with others and reduce the boredom of the voyage; if nothing else it would satisfy the inquisitive group on deck. The aloof captain patrolled his deck ignoring their presence; so long as these merchants caused no trouble, he did not see them, nor did he want to. Only once did they express a casual enquiry regarding the identity of their mysterious co-travellers. The captain tried to ignore them at first, pretending to view the horizon as though he had detected something else of interest. When pressed for an answer, he preferred to change the subject, though it was written on the group's faces that they would keep pressing him for an answer if he ignored them so. Suddenly, in a protective manner, he informed the inquirers quite firmly that the passengers would not be showing themselves on deck or be conversing with their likes at any time throughout the voyage. Now that he had clearly stated the position, the captain strode away leaving the group to think on his last statement. But the captain's slip exposed the fact that there were two or more travellers, high bred and rich.

The morning passed into afternoon and the evening came upon them, bringing with it a chilling air and darkness to the horizon after a glorious sunset. They spent an uneventful night on deck, apart from the discomfort that their awakening brought with it disturbing sensations for one of their number. The conditions were changing, though not too dramatically, but the ship was beginning to ride on a swelling sea.

By the morning, the sky had turned to grey; heavy nimbus clouds hung lifeless overhead, suspended ominously in an array of colour from blue grey and almost black, threatening a heavy rainstorm coming their way. Shivering from the coldness of the previous night, they did their best to shake off the early morning chill; once one was awake, they were all awake. Each in turn did what came naturally to us all; once settled, the chatter of low voices was to be heard and the company began to think of eating; rummaging through their travelling bags, some in search of extra clothing, dried meat, bread and wine.

Hubert sat quietly; his pallor slightly grey, hands clasped about his drawn up knees that closed tightly to the body; oddly he preferred not to eat, the effect of the sea was beginning to affect him and he complained of a slight malady. He yearned for landfall, to escape the incessant rolling and rising of the ship and to feel solid ground beneath his feet. On the deck there was no way he could help himself, he felt alone and the increasing grey background made him feel more anxious and apprehensive of a long protracted voyage. His uncertainty showed more and more on his face; with his colour changing from different tones of ashen grey to shades of deathly white. He was irritable and the agitation within him surfaced when Robert slapped him on the back, telling him to cheer up and drink a swallow of wine from his flask. His reaction was unbecoming, and his friends realised the reason for his behaviour. He reacted immediately, lashing out in retaliation to Robert; his action immediately had him raising an apology, for which Robert nodded his acceptance; Hubert reciprocated with the same. That action had cast a sudden silence over the group with looks that spoke volumes; it was an unusual reaction, which was not characteristic of the man. Hubert was aware that he had acted out of character and felt guilty because of it. In all the time that they had worked together he had never remarked offensively towards his friends on anything, nor had he reacted discourteously, such was the disaffection of his condition; he had to explain.

"It's this confounded up and down. Up and down," Hubert exclaimed, repeatedly. "Give me some time to myself and I'll be alright." Not a word was said, leaving the matter to fade away; they accepted his word. It was not uncommon to see men stricken and turn this way whilst at sea, after all they were soldiers and not mariners used to this unpleasant experience; many men gave in to it and died. When his mood seemed to ease, it gave way to conversation, and his comrades believed that he was winning over his malady.

"I tell you," said Hubert with shivering lips, breaking the discord that had previously passed, "I was once strapped to a donkey for twenty miles over rough terrain and it didn't make me feel as bad as this." Then Hubert was taken again, bent over clutching his sides and his complexion turning greyer as time passed, and it was noticed that he had somehow tightened his grip on himself in his efforts to repress the sound of his chattering teeth.

Edward gestured to the others to leave Hubert alone, realising what was troubling him; the pallid face became more dreadful looking, the reason for his behaviour had been revealed. Hubert was a land man and soldier, the sea had definitely affected him, although the company quieted there was no doubt that their thoughts and sympathy was directed at their ailing friend; following the silent pause, du Bray leaned over to Robert announcing, "It is Mal de mer, I'm afraid," du Bray added in a whisper, "We will have to keep an eye on him, I fear it will most likely get worse."

A member of the crew walked by and Hubert called to him, asking, "When will we reach Symeon?"

"It will be some time yet, perhaps in two days." Pulling up his shoulders in a nonchalant manner smiling, he could tell Hubert's situation was not good; he had seen these symptoms in others many times. His answer was without thought or care, replying that, "First we are in for ride on the waves," he gestured with his hand rising up and down in a waving motion, and walked away singing a mariners song. Robert wanted to give the mariner something to sing about, but had to restrain his emotions for fear of giving away his disguise. Hubert was not pleased by the answer he received, he dreaded another day or more on board the bobbing ship; feeling sick inside with the very thought of it all. Robert and du Bray attempted to console Hubert, whose face by this time had rapidly lost all traces of colour. "Come along, Hubert," du Bray said coaxingly, "we haven't seen the enemy yet and you're turning grey."

"Just leave me be," he retorted sharply, "I know I'll be alright." Hubert rose and walked the lurching deck to try and steady his nerves and stomach. They all knew that there was nothing any of them could do, so they heeded his request and let him be, and carried on with their early morning meal.

It was quite some time later when Hubert returned, all were gladdened to see him noticing that he appeared to have put on a brave face. Still pale, he was encouraged to take a place within the circle of his friends; being hospitable they offered him a drink, which surprisingly he took, swallowing a considerable amount. They starred in amazement, though remained silent; his present recovery baffled them; intrigued, they asked how he had managed the feat of overcoming his mal de mer. Hubert sat smugly, turning his head away looking into space as if to catch the remnants of a distant memory, he began to explain. "It's a long story," they smiled and he added, "it all happened some time ago, I was caught up in the desert on the run after giving the slip to a band of blood-thirsty Muslim brigands that were on my trail. Only to come across three men robbing an old sage, they were nothing but a few desert rats. I made short work of them," he gestured nonchalantly. "The old man was very grateful for being rescued, and he accompanied me on my journey. I didn't mind at all; it was for his safety. One evening, I grew ill with heat exhaustion and he pulled me through it."

Nobody was aware of this episode in Hubert's past and listened intently, focusing on his every word in anticipation that some jewel of knowledge would be imparted to them from his story.

Continuing his tale he explained, "It turned out that he was a wandering holy man, the wealth of riches meant nothing to him; as for my part, I felt deeply indebted to him for the service that he had done me. By serving his need and my word of thanks was reward enough for a man of his position could ask for. Why, you yourself told me of your common duty in saving me, the old sage reasoned affably, let us talk no more about debts. Well, we talked; for a further day he continued helping me through my sickness of the sweats. That evening before our fire after sharing my meagre supplies with him, he imparted to me a lesson for the mind in the powers of concentration, which I will never forget. This old man of the far eastern lands, had travelled much; as for me, well, I came away a much wiser and healthier man." With a wry smile, the touching of his nose and a nod of his head to signify the use of the past information imparted to him, he told his audience of attentive friends; that knowledge had served him many times; stating proudly that he could not have wished for a greater reward. "Used it today," he said almost boasting with his superior knowledge, "I walked out to the prow of the ship, I stood before the wind, my legs shaking and my guts in a state of upheaval, I closed my mind and allowed the sickness to flee my weakened body," young Aldo smiled and it did not go unnoticed by Hubert. "I tell you true, my friends; do not doubt me, for who better than yourselves have encountered such mysteries in these lands."

"What?" exclaimed young Aldo with a prankish smile on his face.

Hubert, with eyes closed displayed a very thoughtful and serious look upon his placid face, as though the grace of his God had befallen him. Pausing, the silence urged the spellbound group to prompt Hubert to complete his story, which he explained, "I breathed deeply until my body was light enough to almost float, concentrating deeply on what was before me," he said, picking up a lamb bone and chewing on its remains. Aldo retorted with a smile, "But there is nothing out there." This gave rise to some laughter and Hubert, beginning to realise that Aldo could be poking fun at him, became a little huffy. Deciding to say no more except that it would be a waste of time to explain the mysteries of the East to such a young and empty brain as Aldo's, he turned his head away, indicating that their discussion was over. The company merrily laughed again. Not long after Hubert rose, all eyes watched his movement, his wobbly legs walked smartly to the side of the ship were he grabbed a hold of the gunwale and deposited the remains of his meal over the side into the sea. Robert stopped them all from laughing at Hubert, allowing him the chance to escape his embarrassment. Aldo could not contain himself fully and whispered, "Perhaps he's concentrating on one thing or learning more of the mysteries of the East." All with hand over mouth, they laughed into their palms; all rose and turned away except du Bray who went over to Hubert to console him.

The day passed slowly and quietly, the jesting at Hubert's expense was now far behind and although little was said, all carried sympathy for the knight who spent most of his time that long day beneath a blanket or bent over the side of the ship heaving his innards into the swelling sea.

Although the group's day was sombre, the only activity apart from the sea was the scurrying to and fro of the crew. In the late afternoon the voyage was beginning to be interesting, watching the activity of certain crewmen coming and going into the accommodation area. The little group began making wagers with each other as speculation and further interest in the passengers grew.

Robert guessed they had to be one or two women at least, and probably of high rank; perhaps royalty. Indeed, many times the captain of the ship left his station to cater to the varying requests from his mysterious occupants.

At one stage, Robert ventured over towards the forward cabins, but no sooner had he got within ten feet an armed guard filled the cabin doorway. Rubbing his bearded cheek in bewilderment, he thought better not to push his way through; his orders were very clear not to draw attention to himself endangering his plans so far. What those plans were, he knew were as clear as murky pond water, but all he hoped for would be revealed in time. A mariner crossed the ship's deck passing Robert; his arm was suddenly caught in a firm grip, the guests in the cabin, who were they Robert asked? The shock of the seaman had him quaking but not as much as the fear he showed by his unwillingness to answer the question. He begged to be let go; fearfully, he replied that should he be seen talking, it could cost him a flogging; "For the love of Allah," he pleaded, "release me." Taken aback by the sailor's answer, Robert couldn't help but press for more information; nothing but curses issued from the mariners mouth. "If I was to open my mouth," said the mariner, "it might probably be my death." He released the man, thinking it most odd that such a simple question could evoke such fearsome reaction in a man. Robert turned and walked away pensively to his friends as if nothing had happened; the reaction of the crewman soon became the topic of more speculative discussion within his company.

The remains of the day passed by and nightfall settled upon them. Hubert was laying under a blanket caught up in a shaking fit; to relieve his suffering all had contributed their blankets to him, but there was no cessation to the shaking of his condition. He had fallen into a very sorry state; they were all very concerned for him. The talk of men's suffering in such situations does not always prepare one for times when such illnesses visits the company you share; and the sickness that Hubert suffered they feared could lead to his death, and with him being so close to them made them feel even more helpless. Unaware to the companions, Hubert's condition of illness had not gone unnoticed from other eyes. Within the enclosure of the cabin, the secreted occupants had monitored Hubert's decline in health throughout the day; these sinister eyes not only demanded knowledge of all activities on board ship but held sway of life and death over every member of the crew.

Unknown to the passengers, the two women within were emissaries of the most feared individual within the desert lands; the Old Man of the Mountain. Considered by the westerners as a scurrilous bunch of religious maniacs, but to the ordinary man whether on board ship or on land he was not a man to take lightly. A great respect grew whenever people learnt those emissaries were nearby, for they were known to squander the power of life and death over such poor ordinary people. Not one single action they conceived was embarked on without reason; sometime, somewhere, assistance could be a means to draw an individual into a web of intrigue, used for the utmost satisfaction of their employer. Unknown to anyone, they had been cleverly devising a potion in preparation for the sick man; it would be a means they believed for these clever and devious women to manipulate these men at some time in the future.

Night fell, and as the moon peered through the intermittent breaks in the passing clouds overhead, it cast glimpses of light across the flickering eyes of Robert's face. In his restless state, it caused him annoyance as he failed to manage sleep, his objective proved difficult in his attempts to wrestle with the orders that preyed on his mind. There was something, he felt, they had not been told; it was not the usual way to send men out blindly ferreting for something that had no basis on which to work from; information on anything suspicious, as far as he was concerned everything in the Levant was suspicious. One comment of the old Prior haunted him regarding the Church's activity; its path of forwardness is not as straight as one might suppose. It was not part of the order but more of a slip of the tongue. Monks travel sometimes more than they should for their own good. The old Prior remained vague in his statement, appearing not wanting to dwell on the subject; after a pause it was as if he dismissed the idea and continued on with the orders. Well, he pondered over that suggestion, were they acting as couriers between the families that might make a claim for the throne? With spring's approach, so came a build-up of aggressive sorties into Templar territory. Cynically, he could have laughed at the amount of times he had discovered that his mission was not what it was supposed to be; the church, he thought, was not the only one whose path was not as direct as it should have been. Once again, he was being dangled as a lure for unknown reasons; he knew that something had been withheld; was he that expendable?

Squeaking metal of the cabin doors corroded hinges broke the silence of his reverie; a door was slowly opening alerting Robert's sharpened senses of hearing, there was not another distinctive sound apart from the sound of the lapping sea breaking on the creaking hull that could be heard. The riding ship rose and dropped on the swollen sea; Robert waited, his senses alerted; something was about to happen. The dodging moonlight dipped in and out of the broken clouds, exposing a silent slender shadow making its way over in the direction of Robert's sick friend Hubert. It was not a man, for he could define clearly a lithe and nimbleness of the movement; the shape was definitely sylph-like and female. Memories from somewhere in his past caused Robert to stiffen with fear; once, he too encountered a situation where he was lured to the bed and mercy of a female, whose murderous intent was to administer him poison. As true as there was a god in the heavens, he thought, he would not allow any harm to befall his defenceless friend.

Without a sound, he was up and behind the stranger, grasping both her arms and drawing them behind her into a defenceless position. Her lithe slender body tensed defensively as she sharply drew in her breath with the shock of his intervention; she was not about to expend her energy uselessly when she was so outmatched. Remaining calm, she did not struggle or scream as Robert's strength of grip restricted her movements. She was strong, there was muscle beneath her diaphanous clothing; he could feel the tautness of every sinew stiffen in his powerful hands. But she was caught in a trap from which she could not spring. Holding her arms, Robert held his head aside hers, perfume from her hair wafted over him in a disarming manner, the fragrance flooded his nostrils filling them with the scent of rose petals; in a flash of passing time, he was somewhere else. There were other fragrances also which left him stunned with their headiness; unprepared, he drew them into his breath. Her soft, deep voice spoke, gripping Robert with its intensity of meaning

"It is not what you think, good sir, believe me," her voice was not apologetic, rather candid and cordial. "My mistress," she purred, "has prepared a potion for your sick friend. I am here to administer it. We wish no harm; only for the quieting of the sickness of the sea and the bringing of relief to your friend."

This was not what he expected to hear; with his alertness dulled by the rush of mixed fragrances, her words briefly confused Robert; he put it to her that she could have sent the potion out for him to administer instead of sneaking out like an assassin in the dead of night.

In an attempt to break the deadlock between them, she admitted, "Your hands are strong on me, Franj. If it is your wish to do me harm, then so be it; I am only a servile woman, unable to resist your strength of hand." It was true that his grip held her steadfast; Robert became unsure of himself and could not reply to her statement right away. As if she grew impatient with Robert's silence, she retaliated with temerity and impatience.

"Are we to stand here all night while you decide your action? My fate is in your hands, Franj. Kill me if you wish, but I warn you, do not cause me to destroy what I hold in my hand; the power to heal your sick friend. Perhaps you can cause me to spill it upon the deck should you decide to squeeze harder and break my body, the choice is yours." Although there was little trust in the woman, there was no doubt in Robert's mind she was speaking true, but could he believe her intention?

The softness of her voice was disarming and the tone persuasive, he did not enjoy the calculated threat she spoke of; spilling a potion, especially that of which Hubert could be in dire need of. The strength of his hostile grip subsided, allowing her body to relax, no longer feeling defenceless against his intemperate attitude towards her. She was no match for the strength of the overwhelming knight but she knew her wiles carried equal potency as the mellifluous sounds of her soft, convincing voice filled the night air like a nightingale in the spring, seducing his subconscious spirit. Her voice resonated through Robert's head like an echo rendering him insensate, it was surely potent. The soft, sensuous voice continued, its dulcet tones were as disarming as a blade of steel that pierced the stupefied knight's mind. Within the blink of an eye, he had realised, had she have been a man, there could have been blood on the ship's deck now, his. This woman's ability confused and dulled his readiness to remain alert, her voice had penetrated his senses leaving him distracted; for him time was standing still. How did she do this?

His natural instincts as a collator of information demanded that he detect as much about her as possible; efforts to concentrate on the sound of her voice for some clue of her origins were useless, as the hushed whispering droll of her voice blurred his concentration. "Who are you? Why do you wish to save my friend, who is nothing to you?" It was true she answered, but it was not her intention to enter into a debate at that moment in time. With one last effort to convince the man that held her so strongly, she purred,

"My mistress is revered in these lands and did not want to make contact with anyone for her own private reasons. It was considered a better plan that the potion was taken without witness so that your friend's recovery appeared natural, concealing any interference from any other person."

They stood transfixed to the ship's deck in unison, which rose and fell in its relative motion with the swell of the sea. Together they stood as two statues, whilst the hair on his neck bristled with each word that she spoke, filling him with feelings of doubt and indecision to which he was unused. The rankled knight, having suddenly discovered a weakness in his own armour, cast aside caution, assured that she was no match for him. It was pointless to wake the others; they were fast asleep and curled up close to each other for warmth against the cold night air. His firmness of grip lessened more until he had finally released her. Turning her around to confront him, he was unable to gaze upon her face fully, being covered by a diaphanous silvered gauze yashmak. It was attached to her head veil; and expertly embroidered with small decorative silver and gold spangles, and though he had no way of knowing; in the moonlight's fleeting brightness, he sensed that the face beneath the veil was one of much beauty.

The motion of the heaving sea caused the ship to rise with rolling reciprocating movements; the regular surge of the ship on the coursing sea brought their faces closer to confront each other's. That brief encounter brought the two adversaries momentarily together, holding the gaze of their eyes in the search for clues as to which of the other would yield in the dominance of their present situation. Moonlight danced across her face, revealing a further portion of her beauty, the depth of her searching dark eyes locked upon him for but a brief moment. Robert was transfixed, he stood there mesmerised and speechless, for what seemed like an eternity, far too long for a soldier to pause, gazing into her deep brown staring eyes such as he had done, somehow enchanted by the effects of the silver spangles dancing in the moonlight's ray. He had never been bothered by any woman's alluring eyes before, and instantly he knew just how dangerous they were. Not only were they alluring and soft, she had much in her arsenal of distractions that invited to snare his concentration. Coupled with her fragrances and a Goddess's aid of the moon's enchanting twinkling rays that caught its glow in the bejewelled veil, he was truly stunned and moved by its effect.

Never before had he been short on words, it was in him to say so much but something had definitely caught hold of his tongue; for the first time he was unable to speak coherently. The stunning pause broke, he felt he had to regain the air of command to maintain a superior position; after all she was still a prisoner to him. His first words to her where those of a caution; on releasing his hold on her, he continued to show his dominance by warning her against any foolish attempts she might conceal in any endeavour to harm his friend.

His mood towards her, he promised, would change to one of a more violent nature, an unnecessary threat, which he regretted saying as soon as the words left his tongue, leaving him feeling stupid and immature. Having once more assured this knight of her true purpose, she cheekily chastised him, insisting he also act in accordance. Silhouetted in the darkness against the light of the moon as it bounced off the bobbing deck of the ship, were the shadows of two adults standing in debate over the sick man at their feet.

Standing toe to toe as if in combat, the confronting energies of their own forceful characters were locked in a trial of leadership over who knew what was best, and Robert stubbornly refused to give way to any woman. She was his equal in strength of character and likewise refused to give way. Her manner suggested that she was a woman of some position and always in control; certainly not used to being ordered about. Within these fleeting moments, the mistrust and apprehension suddenly gave way to a pact; she reached out to Robert, gripping his arms and fixing her gaze on his, defiantly uttering softly yet firmly, "You can trust me, Franj." She appealed to him, stating what was obvious; that she had no escape. If he refrained from further delay his friend would surely feel much better when he awoke.

Following her persuasive logic came a sharp warning, that once this potion was administered and he was roused, you must not allow him to eat or partake of strong wine, insisting that he must only drink water. Her tone was strong and firm, yet soothing, gentle and sensible. So convincing was the sound of her firm, soft rounded voice coupled with the touching of her outstretched hand making contact with his, did he readily become relaxed, and was quite perplexed as to how he could became so readily obedient. That move was a coup de grace; his body came alive with her touch; how did she do that? Their silent agreement brought with it unison of purpose; they knelt bending over his feverish friend, whose sweat laden brow and violently shivering spasms easily made one believe that he had been in the cold waters of the night. In her passive controlling manner, she gestured to Robert to raise Hubert's head. Gently sliding his hand around Hubert's nape, Robert raised his head forwards to enable an easy passage for the potion to pass without causing any choking. The two figures were bent over the sickly knight, the woman reached into her cape; her action had not escaped Robert's notice; his hand fell to a dagger that hung at his side and froze waiting anxiously to see what was to be drawn forth. His first reaction was to drop his hold on Hubert's neck and strike out at this conniving woman, but his fears were allayed as she drew forth a carved silver vial; "This," she added, "will bind the body back to the soul and mix with the curative already administered." Holding it firmly, she carefully removed its silver engraved cap, and poured it into the small container she had in her hand. She shook the mixture while Robert thought that she was clever enough to mislead him earlier. He would watch her every move from then on; her eyes flicked up to suggest to Robert that she was ready to administer the potion to his quaking friend.

With great care, she offered the potion to the sick man's lips, allowing the fluid gently to gently pass down his throat without cause for coughing; the comatose Hubert took it all like a babe whilst in his disturbed state. When the vial had emptied itself of its healing potion, she placed her hand over Robert's whilst assisting him in gently laying Hubert's head back. Her soft, almost caressing touch sent a myriad of feelings through Robert's body; the type that he could well do without at this moment. Robert's body felt a piercing in his every nerve in a most wonderful way. Her sensual touch caused him great excitement but he would not betray any flush of pleasure that aroused him. She rose, and Robert straightened himself likewise. Before speaking, he looked across to her quite intently as if to detect an extra quality that he had overlooked previously, but alas his mind had been distracted by her physical aspects and her mysterious air.

Betrayed by his own fascination for her, he snapped himself back to the present, quickly clearing his throat. Hoping above all, she did not notice the pause or his intense gaze upon her, the awareness of such a lapse of concentration with an enemy could cost him dearly. It bothered him much that so many other questions began to fill his mind and it was most likely that this female was far too sharp to allow anything to pass her by.

Their administrations over, he changed from protective aggressor into a man showing humility and gratitude. "Dear Lady, if this works I will be indebted to you for the relief of my friend's illness."

In a sort of chiding manner, she confidently assured him in her reply that the treatment would work. Brushing aside any doubt that he may harbour, he should have faith and pray to Allah for his kindness in prompting her mistress to create the potion that she herself, unworthy as she was, was deemed only to administer it and being no more than the tool of her mistress's errand. Robert took in her words expressing that God was great. Driven with curiosity as to the other mysterious female on board, he looked for a way in which to present himself to her to learn more of both the women.

"Then I feel that I should talk with your mistress," he suggested, "she appears to be a very knowledgeable and caring woman"

With a defensive step back, she begged he change his mind, "No sir," the young woman cooed, raising her hands with palms towards Robert as if to push him backwards in protest,

"That would not be wise nor appropriate, no one is allowed to see her," for a moment she hesitated looking for a plausible answer, "it is a religious thing, you understand. It would," she hesitated to further her converse; then apologising, "to be in the presence of any man would deem her disloyal to her beliefs," adding, "it would be unforgivable."

Aware of the different and strange customs of this land, Robert refrained from insisting any further. Now that all tensions between them had been overcome, Robert's interest was now directed towards her. He probed further, asking all manner of questions, but she too was very clever in the art of evasion, leaving him tantalised without any answers that may quench his curiosity. Before he would allow her to leave, his final question was if he would see her again. Her head fell downwards as if in thought, she held his arm tenderly at length, and was long in answering. He did not mind, the feel of her small light hand on his arm was pleasurable; the pause was clever and inventive for what was about to come next; she looked up to meet his staring probing eyes, then she spoke again with a depth of feeling in that haunting huskiness of her voice leaving the listener hopelessly baited.

"Not all things are within our power, but I have a very strong feeling our paths will cross again soon." With this short mystical phrase, she dropped her hand and then turned, almost running the short distance to the cabin door without looking back. Robert was left alone, transfixed to the deck; he watched her vanish into the shadow of the cabin and almost longingly called to her the words of his unspoken converse that remained hanging on his tongue. Left bemused at what had just happened; for one such as he, considered by others a tough and tenacious character and his own man, to be left standing without a plan to further his action. My, he thought, she was good; how very easily she handled me. No, he decided she was fascinating, yet in the back of his mind there was much to be wary of, he knew there was more to this eastern woman than met the eye. As he stood fixedly to the rising deck; much went through his mind about the woman. She was definitely no serving woman, he never met one that could wear dresses like a lady and her English was spoken with such clarity that he thought at first she was an educated Frankish woman, and how was she so sure that we would meet again?

Not noticing the chill on the night air until she was safely within the cabin, she demonstrated the completion of her task and her feelings by the clasping of her hands.

With nonchalance, she shrugged off a shiver from the freshness of the night as she entered the cabin, thinking that it went unnoticed. From hidden, dark shadows, her older companion and mistress studied her carefully and suspiciously. With the cabin door safely closed, the young woman pressed her back against it as if to act as a buttress; her thoughts of the man she had confronted remained with her and she could not help but raise a small secret smug smile at the events just passed. From within the shadows of the cabins shadows, a hollow crackling aged voice cut through the silent pause, it was sharp like a knife and severe in its intent. The voice was so authoritative, it sent shivers of fear down the young woman's spine and its direction was hollow and unfeeling; caring little of the delight of her young companions little game that had just occurred. The voice was only concerned whether the execution of her plan was successful, and it demanded conformation if all went well before it sternly questioned her delay in returning. "Quickly," like a whiplash the voice demanded. "What have you to tell little one," the shape that carried the piercing demands of the questioning voice emerged from the darkened corner, dressed in black silken robes. She was a much older woman, tall and lean; the robes she wore concealed the more mature lines of her ageing figure, presenting a neatly form, but her face was hawkish and lined. Her piercing eyes missed nothing, yet there was no doubt that once she had been a beauty. The outline of her eyes were painted to enlarge their appearance and the lids were of a bluish tinge; all of this could only change the impression, but failed to mask the age that she vainly attempted to conceal. Approaching her younger companion like a spider that welcomes its prey, she held forth a welcoming arm holding a wrap in her free hand, whilst the other was employed holding a black rod that maintained balance in her, keeping her long frame supported.

Not all her deceptions had been successful. Once, and once only, she failed her master in his bidding, and being young and vainly attractive made her master wait when he had urgent business for her to complete. When he discovered the reason for her delay, he became very vexed and filled with anger, so much so that he decided teach her a severe lesson for her temerity. When she finally presented herself before her master, she foolishly betrayed herself with more lies. To teach her a lesson in humility and obedience, the Old Man ordered her to be held down whilst one of his men first indulged himself with the use of her body for her vanity and lies, then on his master's orders with diligence and expert precision, smashed her leg with an iron rod. In the days that followed after her healing, the stick that aided her became a grim reminder of her punishment. It was a wicked lesson to teach, but the Old Man would not suffer liars or those that disobeyed him. She became wiser and a more slavish servant than ever before, and although vengeance dwelt in her heart for a long time after, she never had the nerve to disobey her master ever again. Her cruelty grew and her pain extended to other unfortunates that crossed her path. The stick that presently aided her movement now served as an extension of her arm, and many times it had been used to beat the younger woman for her insolent outbursts of self-confidence and defiance. Uma was her mistress's name, and if ever there was a servant to evil, she portrayed it with an alacrity that was unbending.

Hassan, her brother, was likewise as efficient and zealous in his duties to the Master and was duly rewarded by his appointment to spreading the word and fear that his master's cloak could encompass. Hassan, like his Master, was highly intelligent and a follower of the sciences; he also had grown into being a religious fanatic and became second in command, and Uma was superior to all under her brother's rule of terror. Her record of success, cruelty and guile was equal in every way to her brother's; Uma excelled in her methods of planning and was at present engaged in a plan that promised to set the Muslim world in fear of the very name of the Hashashin.

In spite of carrying a limp, she briskly hobbled forwards, bearing a stately poise towards her young associate; her frail, wrinkled hand quickly draped the wrap that she had carried single handed around her young associate's chilled form, as would a caring mother to her daughter. There was no warmth in her welcome; her hand remained high around her young companion's slender neck and insisted almost threateningly whilst smiling for an explanation involving the retelling all events for her prolonged absence. The young woman was not afraid, only suspicious of her mistress's manner, for she could stand her ground with most men and win the day but her mistress was menacing, knowing that there was a binding advantage that she had over her. The account was given almost like the confession. Similar to that to the way Christians do to unload the onus of guilt from their burdened conscience.

Uma remained rigid, her hand gripping the scarf tightly whilst standing listening intently to every word that the girl spoke, with her other arm remaining upon her shoulder menacingly without any relaxation as if waiting to strike should she have hinted at failure in her given task. It was obvious that her recount of the event was pleasing to her mistress, proving her to be absolved of any negligence in her duty. Upon the long, scrawny-fingered hand of her mistress that was settled threateningly on the girls shoulder, was a ring of gold with large sharp quartz-like crystals built upon its mounting; in such a way that it could be used as a vicious weapon. Aware of its use, the younger woman had been concerned as she eyed the ring anxiously as she gave her report, she had witnessed its effect when used on others. When struck by its numerous facets, it left deep lacerations causing copious amounts of blood to ooze from the jagged wound that resulted from her mistress's angered assault. The young woman watched carefully as Uma's hand slipped away snake-like from her shoulders; after listening intently to her explanation, Uma was satisfied; she turned her back on the younger woman and walked away.

Uma's trickery and slyness was known, and the younger woman was ready for her next sudden move should she endeavour to make one; surprised that there was none, she relaxed, only to stiffen and shudder as Uma's stick was suddenly and menacingly in her face. In a whispering and threatened tone, the voice demanded sharply if this knight swallowed the bait set for him. In a defiant voice, the girl replied that he had been awake; the squeaking of the door was not needed to awaken him and yes, he was a willing subject once he had discovered the use for the potion. "Good," Uma replied, but she would not take her eyes away from the young woman; quickly she snapped, would he become a future distraction to their objective. The answer also was a negative one, and it was delivered instantly, proving that she did not need time to think out her answer. This satisfied the crone, for she was loath to anything less than success. The crackling voice further enquired if she had discovered anything further to their mission from speaking with the foreigner. "He has a weakness," came the knowledgeable reply, "and I have found it." The older woman smiled, she was aware of the unspoken meaning; it was the weakness of men.

Uma hated everybody, but most of all she hated men, for men were the cause that betrayed her vanity and her playful attraction of them, causing her to suffer the punishment that became the source of her daily pain. That was a subject that the student was not allowed to pry into. Uma was aware that her young accomplice had used the wiles of her gender to weaken the Franj play actor, that is how she saw him, and she smiled as she heard the words spoken that he would be of no threat. When Uma walked away, the young woman noticed that shoulders of her mistress, that had been tense and ready to retaliate should she have been dissatisfied, had relaxed, signifying that she was safe and that she had done well. The younger woman leaned against the cabin door, relieved; her mind flitted back to the knight on deck. He had changed, she idly mused; he was brave and caring, though flawed; he was strong and a warrior but not as good as she, but he was different and the play in the future could be interesting. A smile broke once more over her ponderous face; smugly she remembered his attitude toward her. She admired his defiance and the high regard for his protective stance for his companion, but she was confident that she had his measure. In her musing, she recalled his strong arms around her body; it was true that he could have snapped her bones like a brittle branch had he have had the will. She also admired his caution, for he would have betrayed his guise had he done so, proving beyond doubt that he was no trader. Their meeting had become a challenge and that also thrilled her; he would not give any ground in spite of her allure, and out of it all, she enjoyed the feeling of contention; a smile broke through the wrinkled, calculating frown on her pretty forehead as she returned to the reality of her game. The Franj was nothing less than her enemy, and in spite of this fact, she felt that there was no harm in toying with him for a little longer for her own amusement, as would a cat with a little mouse.

Robert paced the rolling deck with a mind to barge in on the mysterious women to ascertain their identity, but backtracked his intention after remembering the help he had received from them both. His curiosity of these two females led him to suppose that their meeting was not wholly a coincidence, but he failed in his reasoning to establish the reason for their presence on the same day as they were travelling. He didn't like coincidences; he never trusted accidents that he felt were contrived. He paced the pitching deck as if he were a mariner losing all sensation of the sea's movement; his mind totally concentrating on the women. Her knowledge affected his sense of pride in his disguise; on many occasions he could recall that he had successfully passed himself off as a merchant, yet she saw through it all and knew him for what he was. She was aware that he was Frankish and it made him feel naked, that was uncomfortable; she also gave the impression that she had peered through the curtain of his subterfuge and spied all that there was to know about him, leaving him with an uncomfortable feeling by her words of meeting again; could it be that they heading in the same direction? That began to irritate him; her sources of information appeared up to date and that disturbed him somewhat, especially when his mission was supposed to be secret. How could it be that she was going the same way?

Hmm, he shrugged, aware that there were no such things as a secret in this land, but she had wounded him by her keen observation. He went over his appearance for outward flaws. He could find none in his dress and finally decided that he must at some time soon reach the nub of this mystery. It was the middle of the night, his mind was growing weary, causing him to become irritable. He appealed to the heavens to grant him rest, in his efforts to rest he tried propping himself against a bulkhead, but could not maintain any comfort to settle.

Flashes of his encounter with the woman whipped his mind into activity every time he felt drowsy, denying him ability to find rest or sleep, deeming it not to be possible. His imaginative memory of her provoked nothing other than a destabilising effect. It had been some time since he had been with a woman; rejecting those sinful girls that he had lain with recently as real women. They were in every town he would pass through; to him they were mere distractions.

No, he believed the type of women that he referred to was a type he would want to get to know and spend time with. This one, he felt, was a wild cat; with all the wiles that he had once dreamed of, he had agonised over the potency of her exotic perfume which had penetrated his senses deeply. The eyes, he recalled, were mystical and deep; when he starred into them they peered penetratingly back over her veil, they burnt into his mind. Were they gazing at him now, those dark brown eyes; for they had mirrored themselves so hauntingly in his head. He was tired; his fingers rubbed at his eyes as if he could press them into sleep and needed rest. He was disturbed to the point of a restlessness and agitation; becoming infatuated and not even realising it. Although he did not see her face, he guessed that the shape of it, from her eyes, she might have been part Greek.

Saving his best impression until last, he inhaled deeply, imagining her beside him; he knew that there was nothing to compare to the smell of a woman close up. It was provocative and sexual, and it set him trembling with apprehension by her ability to turn his mind away from his true charge. The task of caring for Hubert was over; it pleased him much that another was able to offer such help; she was gone, but the impression of her image would not leave him. Robert's agitation had him up on his feet; first he walked to one side of the ship, then the other; if he yawned once. He did so a dozen times. His balance was good considering the ordeal he was experiencing, then she was back again in his head and he suddenly had to throw out his arms to grab a hold of the rigging to steady himself.

The ship was still pitching and rolling, but not as much as the woman in his mind. Looking up into the darkness he could detect the star-studded sky between the breaks in the clouds; moonbeams filtered through brightening up the darkness, but always his mind returned to the haunting image of the woman. She had large beautiful brown eyes; he thought her body lithe and almost athletic. He recalled that she moved nimble-like, and had it not been for the squeaking of the cabin door, his eyes would never have been alerted to her silent shadow darting by him. He asked himself, could she know something that he was not privy to? It sounded as though she was very sure of herself; and difficult though it was for him, he reasoned in his muddled mind how she was distracting him in so many ways. He must get rest as the night's chill was coming over him and close to putting him beyond reason. He moved from where he was and sat huddled into a corner of the deck close to his friends. He snuggled down against the bulk head, pulling the corner of a course woven blanket over him; his pack was used to support his back by wedging it into a section of the wooden ribbing of the hull offering him a sheltered but uncomfortable position. His head rolled from right to left indecisively before finally resting his chin close to his shoulder in anticipation of sleep. In the dullness of his semi-conscious position, his mind relaxed and wandered; she wasn't small; he guessed dreamily that she would be about this high, gesturing with his hand just below his chin.

Realising the absurdity of his thoughts, he grew exasperated and argued demonstratively with himself, swishing his hand through the air in a dismissive action. Sweet Jesus, have I got a problem, his thoughts were running amok. I've had women before, enough of them to know their ways, so why should this one be any different, he asked himself. He held his head in his hands despairingly; with his eyes closed tight he struggled hard to clear his distressful mind. Drifting falsely into a fanciful state, his mind wandered; something in him wanted to lose the battle, from deep within his inner self he yearned to recall the soft mournful sounds of her persuasive utterances. The thoughts of the female's touch and her sensual voice aroused him; she was too deeply embedded into his mind. He tossed and rolled and grew impatient and inside his mood turned ratty, but still he could not gain any comfort. Being very unsettled for some time after, he came to the conclusion that this woman was beginning to haunt him, am I bewitched he sighed as if in resignation? Shall I yell loudly to dispel her from my mind? That's it, he exclaimed suddenly, she had woven a spell whilst he was off his guard. Still in his torment of trying to scratch an itch that couldn't be reached, a compelling urge came over him, deciding that if he was right and she was some kind of witch, he would be better killing her before he could be plagued by further damage from this person.

So confused had he become in doing the right thing, the spark of prudence provoked a change to his plan. Anticipating the possible dangers to his friend, he decided to wait until morning until his possible recovery, then he would kill her, in which case he realised they would never meet her again. No sooner was he up and stretching than something else passed through his mind; she was laden with gold jewellery on her wrists and about herself, now a servant couldn't wear that, he asserted. Damn it, he exclaimed, she was back into his thoughts once more. That's it, he declared, his hand dropped down to his side where a dagger had been secreted in the sash around his waist; I'll be damned if she's not an impostor to boot, he thought. Attempting to fit her role into some semblance more convincing than the one she purported to have himself believe, more urgent needs overcame his actions.

His bodily functions were demanding to be served, his irrational behaviour had side tracked his attention in restraining his bladder, which was now extended to bursting. Standing at the side of the ship relieving himself into the sea, a terrible thought flashed through his mind. What if she walks onto the deck now and sees me like this, she would fill the mouths of all around with laughter. He remained alone, for which he was thankful for, giving him an opportunity to settle himself down; his body ached with tiredness and this time he finally slumped and submitted to his body's need for sleep, which did eventually come, but all he enjoyed was little more than a short nap.

As the curtain of night was drawn back to make way for the morning light, the brightness of day gently flooded into bringing forth a golden horizon promising better sailing than the previous day had offered. It was not long before the group on the deck began to stir; the pangs of hunger began nipping at their appetite giving rise for the need to eat and drink, they chewed strips of dried meat which they had collected specially from a widow on the outskirts of Acre before leaving; she had a way of drying the meat and somehow treated it with honey giving it a sweetness that married into the spicing during the drying, making it quite unique and always in demand. One by one, they walked the deck to stretch and loosen up their stiffened joints, swinging their arms as they went, and relieving themselves as the need took its hold. They lost their look of being traders; to those that spied them with secret eyes, there was more to these men than it seemed.

All were awake except Hubert, whose breathing appeared shallow and almost lifeless. Sitting a little away from him and still in a half conscious daze from the lack of sleep after the night's events, Robert rubbed his tired face with his hands trying to bring himself into awareness; his mouth opened wide in an everlasting yawn. His eyes half open, he longed to fall back into his sleep, they felt so heavy; it was not in him to want to see this new day so soon. Voices around him prompted a greater effort; he rolled his body with little enthusiasm in a half-hearted way to arouse himself from his torpor. His head lolled down wards to the deck, with thoughts of his companions jostling around him, there would be little chance for further relaxation. In an effort to move himself into consciousness, he began to roll his head from side to side to loosen up the strained tired muscles of his aching neck. His eyes did not want to greet the brightness of the dawn and flickered to catch the dawn's bright light fragmentarily in his need to arouse himself. Without any thought to his actions, through his bleary vision he noticed Hubert lying without any visible sign of life. Moved into action by the shock; all of the previous night's events came rushing back, life suddenly surged through his lethargy, raising a deep concern for his friend. The stiffness in his body would not allow him to react as he needed too, but it did not prevent him moving forwards towards the sleeping body of his friend; many thoughts filled his mind, guilt filled his heart, which gave rise to anger. At the sight of Robert's attempts to massage life into his companion, Aldo was soon at Hubert's other side, shaking him tapping his face gently with his open hand; he cried for Hubert to wake up, but there was not a murmur. It was clear that Hubert was not quite dead; his life signs were weak and Robert feared dreadfully that he had been foolish by letting the woman trick him with her sorcery. Whilst the two men were busy in their efforts to revive their friend, Aldo could not help but overhear Robert's anguished words muttering his regrets in a low whispering tone of how he could never forgive himself for allowing that witch to trick him.

His anxiety to shake Hubert awake had almost reached a panic; his actions were almost quite violent whilst talking through his teeth, "Come on, you old dog, wake up." Aldo, amazed at Robert's actions looked up at the others questionably as they assembled in concern around their comatose friend. All must have heard Robert's words, and like Aldo were completely mystified to his meaning.

Aldo was fearful of what he heard, not only for Hubert's condition but also for words that came from his mentors lips.

"What did you say, Robert?" There was much concern in Aldo's voice, the 'what!' Robert was silent, he sullenly looked down at his friend, drained and unable to rouse his friend and quite blankly did not know what to say. He was half cradling Hubert in his arms, his mind was muddled and his heart was blackened by betrayal. He was just about to relate the events of the evening when Hubert showed signs of stirring from his great sleep. Groaning at his awakening; "At last," sighed Robert under his breath, and all enquired to Hubert if he was well. He could not have been better;

"I need a drink," he said. All eagerly offered their wine flasks but Robert shouted holding up his hands in panic shouting, "No!" There was a mysterious insistence that he had only to drink water and that he must also fast until mid-morning. "And who's idea is that?" croaked up Hubert.

"Give the man his food! Have you ever known Hubert to fast when there is not the need, nay, give the man sustenance." Robert could have killed them all for their goading; now he was forced to tell of all the nights events; heaven help any man that thinks I will be taken to jesting. "Oh, and why should that be?" asked Edward surprisingly looking down to Robert who began to rise to his feet.

"It is not good for him after the sickness," Robert stammered, nervously.

"Well now Hubert, it's good to see you in such fine spirits," Edward said with jubilance in his voice, "tell us, how did you manage this turnaround of your condition?"

"Was I bad?" Hubert enquired. "You were very close to the end, we feared," Edmond spoke with a rueful tone creeping into his voice as he helped Hubert to sit upright. "Well I remember going to sleep and concentrating on one thing." It was a slip of the tongue, poor Hubert didn't realise what he had said, but it had an uplifting effect. Those words had the company erupting with laughter remembering the last time he spoke of the experience; Hubert grinned, he screwed his face up unable to give a clear explanation for his condition. "Well, perhaps somebody must have been watching over me, what else?" he exclaimed, as another big smile appeared on his face, Robert muttered, "Or you had a visit from an angel."

"What's that about an angel?" Aldo enquired picking up on Robert's comment. "I thought you remarked of a witch earlier."

Clearly embarrassed, he reluctantly and sharply blurted out, "I'll tell you all later," and he rose to his feet, "but remember," shaking a finger at Hubert, "you must not eat; nor drink nought but water." Red-faced but now smirking, he was relieved at his friend's recovery, he walked away leaving all totally puzzled by his reply. At a quiet place, he leaned on the rail at the side of the ship and looked long out to sea. As expansive as it was, he did not see it, his mind was consumed by the events of the previous night. So this beauty, she spoke the truth, Robert thought, I will watch for her; and intrigue of the future meeting grew in his mind.

Never before had any female made such a mysterious impression on him in such a short time. Dubiously, he decided to comply with her request not to engage in seeking out her mistress to express his gratitude for Hubert's rapid recovery.

As time passed, Robert gathered his thoughts alone at the prow of the ship, realising that he had spent too much time there searching the sea and his mind, he decided it was high time he returned to his friends to convey the mysterious deed of the previous night that caused them to question him earlier.

When he sat among them, a bag of victuals was thrown over to him. "Come on Robert, eat your fill and tell me all about the angel that came to visit me in the night," Hubert joked, nudging Robert with his elbow, and grinning to the friends. Time had come to divulge the facts of the night's events. Holding his hands up in submission, he agreed, and went on to tell his story. There were hollow whistles at the end of the tale and Hubert spoke first, thanking Robert for his vigilance whilst he was unable to protect himself. Robert's hand rested on Hubert's shoulder, knowing full well the compliment would be returned a hundred times over should their roles ever be reversed.

Questions were now being raised from the group, mainly about the woman. Du Bray chirped in, "My interest is with the mistress, I think we should wait for her after we dock to see if she is up to any mischief." He too guessed that there was more to these women than what may appear to be. Robert was the first to agree with him and yet, he felt a disturbance stirring within that he had exposed the woman to further scrutiny. It comes as quite a surprise that most interest had been roused at the end of the voyage and the topic created great speculation amongst the group, which occupied their minds thereafter up to the sighting of land.

The Road to Antioch

St Symeon did not appear as large a port as they first imagined, not one of them had ever been here before; the port being known for its importance for serving Antioch had raised their expectations to being much bigger. Set in a small horseshoe shaped bay, the harbour was overlooked by mountains with steep precipitous cliffs to its sides, whilst its natural deep water berthing allowed all manner of vessels to visit the port. So much so was the port's importance, that the incoming cargo to this region served as a hub for all foreign trade to fan out taking its routes overland and throughout the Middle East. Its only drawback was it had only one exit road; that road had proved most fortuitous to the citadel of Antioch which was Symeon's protector in times of strife; also St Simeon's misfortune in lacking any land for further growth was in fact to Antioch's huge advantage. That single road out of St. Simeon exited at the rear of the town; its hazardous route to Antioch was on poorly-maintained tracks on a high coastal path which was funnelled at one point into a deep narrow pass. In times of upheaval, the route was ideal for the brigands of the day to pick off any caravan that was desirable to them.

When the western armies arrived; there were those amongst them who perceived the potential in keeping this track clear. The crusading army quickly took control over the land, ridding it of brigands; bringing this area under their control made it safe for travellers and merchants alike, ensuring safe passage and the ability to draw the prize of trade and the payment of tariffs firmly into their grasp. With the added support from Antioch's powerful fortress nearby, the military presence stemmed any such attacks. The leader of the conquering crusading army was quick to seize on the further lucrative potential of the revenues arising from the protection of merchant caravans, making certain that it was garrisoned and secured by their soldiers along its strategic length. During the time of war, the enemies of the West regarded that road as a strategic arterial route for supplies and troops; garrisons were constantly under attack leading to a degeneration of road conditions. For now a time of peace came to the region, but the track to Antioch remained in need of repair. Cargoes from the East and Egypt as well as Europe crammed the wharfs and the warehouses full of all manner of goods. Fragrant spices from the Indies, perfumes from the Far East as well as fine silks, slaves from the land of Africa and of the west were included in cargoes that could send a traders head spinning in anticipation of the profits to be made. Much of these cargoes of essential riches and other such finery travelled beyond the boundaries of the borders of the western armies control in all directions across the Arabian lands, making it difficult to stem the flow of infiltrators into the western held cities.

The ship carrying the small company was carefully guided, by the expert knowledge of its captain, safely toward the quayside as a mother would deposit her baby to its cradle. This captain was a man whose orders were not to be disobeyed, for on his orders the crew knew to come alive; canvas had been trimmed and neatly stowed and tied, allowing the ship to drift lazily on the lapping waves that smacked gently against the quay wall; the echoing sounds were like clapping hands to a performance of a job well done as the crew eased the ship home steadily to its new berthing. More orders were hailed; the crew threw ropes ashore to men waiting to make fast the ship firmly to the quayside and once secured, the lady of the sea would come to rest as if expelling the last breath needed to complete her voyage. Resting safe and restrained from wandering on the inward tide until the master's will deemed it ready to sail off into the distant horizon; the berthing would not be a long one; she would stand an obedient skeleton devoid of sail and unable to feel free to venture seawards to the four winds until she was divested of her cargo, reloaded and taken on provisions for the time of her release. For the meantime, the vessel would bump and groan at her station and noisily protest against her ties that restrained her hull fast against the quay wall. With a gang plank set in position, her passengers took the opportunity to disembark; on most occasions they did not stand on ceremony but were happy to make a speedy departing for the need to reassure themselves that they were free from the sea that had held them fatalistically in its control for long enough. Whilst her crew busily set about preparing to unload her cargo, the captain dealt with his business ashore on the quay. His firm commands had left the crew scurrying around obediently and busily carrying out their duties; this was the time that every sailor cherished, the task of unloading their cargo came with a certain amount of zeal and eagerly took aboard new cargo; once that task was complete they would lift their pay and seek the advantages of shore leave. With the promise of new money in their pocket, their spirits were lifted with thoughts of enjoying their fill of wild women in the brothels or to fill themselves with drink and forget the toils of their recent travels and all that they had endured during their past sailing.

Hubert at least was relieved that the voyage was at its end and could not wait until his feet felt the firmness of dry land; as a measure of his satisfaction he began humming a tune he had heard from somewhere. Gladdened by his deliverance it was only at this time that he was able to feel at one with himself; and although there had been no further sign of his sickness returning, he was nevertheless looking forwards to being off the ship and away from the cause of his past malady. Curiously, he felt it odd that he did not meet his watchful benefactors, he would have liked to have given his thanks to those that had provided him with the healing potion and thus kept him alive; but knowing that they had no inclination to appear to him or his companions, he passed that need, feeling not too perturbed.

Interested in the docking, Robert also watched for signs of the females; he too had watched the ship tie off; he glanced across expectantly towards the accommodations in hope to finally acquaint himself with the women before departing the ship. His disappointment showed, no matter how he tried to carry a casual air to avoid his face betraying his feelings. Eventually, he realised that she too must have suspected that their game had, for a while, played itself out between them. During those pensive moments, little did Robert realise that the brown eyes he had looked into the previous evening spied his every move through the cracked planking of the cabins bulkhead, moving the older female to anger for this man's weakness of waiting.

"This knight of the Franj who plays at being a spy is going to be persistent," murmured the crone, "you told me you carried out my orders, he is either a fool or he suspects something, did you overlook to tell me anything?" Uma snapped at the younger woman, who returned her reply; "He is just a fool; there is no need to think other than I told you." The young woman stared disrespectfully at her mistress in disbelief of her accusation and with a mind driven with hatred. "Can you not see how the franj is? It is not my fault that he has swallowed more than the bait." Although the women were far too shrewd to play his game of being embroiled in his politics, they did not want him and his friends in anyway watching them. They had their own orders to follow and could not deviate from their objective for one moment in matters of personal amusement; for they served an impatient and cruel master who would not suffer any knowledge of his own plans being known to outsiders.

Meanwhile, Robert remained waiting on deck in the rising heat of the sun; suspecting that he may have been jumping to conclusions about the women, but somehow he doubted that, the situation of recent events had undoubtedly presented them outside his understanding. He harboured an unhappy feeling that outsiders, that is, his mysterious female, seemed to know something more of events this far, having him wrestling in indecision. It certainly played havoc with his confused thoughts of them, aware that his gut feeling was rarely incorrect and would be foolish to ignore their presence as merely two ordinary women. He realised that this woman he had encountered had taken him by surprise with the knack of making him feel unsettled; women can be like that, they turn a man's mind away from what's important. Destabilised more like it, he nodded in agreement with his thoughts; he knew that he could not afford such distractions, but this was different, somehow deeper; she plagued his rationale that she was much more than she purported to be. His feelings were agitated enough; she had upset the balance of his world inside and out; being a serious man, he was frivolous about nothing that passed under his suspicious eye. By not being able to think clearly, his mind had lost its centre, she had proved to be a distraction that caused his curiosity in her to be intriguingly brimming over.

The voyage was over; the relieved look on the passengers' faces was unmistakcable; where there was once tension from the seas ordeal, smiles of relief and joy presently manifested their being. They had sustained the days of the rocking and rolling of the sickening sea for as long as they had to, allowing new thoughts of expectation and future events only to settle in their minds. Besides, they were in port and the activity on the quayside became a diversion in itself. Even at this early time of the day, the wharf was a jumble of people busy at their work; shifting all manner of cargoes from here to there, leaving little to see of the men they expected. Traders were busy energetically setting out their street stalls and displaying their wares in readiness for business in this busy little port town. Lines of slaves carried all manner of cargo from and towards the waiting ships. The air hung heavy with the smell of charcoal street fires burning; traders were about, the street abounded with sounds of banter as men haggled over prices and the cost of the early food presentations that the wily traders used to entice customers. Aromas of spiced savoury cakes were already on the breeze and the smell of roasting spiced delicacies from the cooking fires hung heavily and pinched at the eyes of those that that hastily blew on the embers in their efforts to have a good start with the day's trade. Not all the airborne aromas were of such a pleasant nature; gully's that ran from behind buildings towards the quay were full of shit and stale piss, its unpleasant odours abounded merging with the strong salty air of the sea drifting across the streets in all directions to taunt noses of the unsuspecting passers-by.

Hubert, being one of them holding his nose, after the sickness he was in need of refreshment to bolster his weakened state, and there was food to be had; he had caught the odours that turned his head, but had overcame the distraction being drawn almost spell bound by the taunting aromas. His churning wind-filled belly constantly created noises that told him that he must feast upon these enticing delicacies after the sparse diet that his friends so cautiously advised him to follow after his illness. He could hardly see himself as the man he used to be, but any excuse to be so easily lured towards the delicacies drew him onwards.

Before departing the ship, the two knights, du Bray and Robert, had approached the captain; in a courteous and pleasant manner they explained briefly the previous evening's act of mercy toward their friend from his passengers. "Would you introduce us to them, we wish to personally convey our thanks to those ladies responsible before moving onwards," they told him. The captain's reaction was alarming, his eyes almost popped for a moment, he must have been caught off guard and short on breath as he blustered for something to say; when he did, he almost screamed that was impossible. Revealing his fear to the two knights, he nervously tried to explain that these ladies were of high birth, and apart from the honour they did him by sailing on his ship, he had sworn to uphold a condition of strict privacy to be adhered to. When taking their money, he had assured them that he would live up to his promise, going out of his way to ensure that they would not be disturbed by anyone. Besides, he informed the knights that they would not be disembarking at this stop as they were on route to another destination. But no matter how they entreated the captain, he was adamant and would not give way to their request. "These women," explained Robert in his appeal, "through their own goodness helped to save our friend from his malady and probably death." Whether the captain was being facetious they could not say, but it was their duty to humanity to at least extend their deepest thanks. The answer again was as equally forceful as the previous reply to their plea; this captain was as tenacious as a ferret with his kill, they could not see any way to move him. In the haughtiest of replies he told them, "If you want to show gratitude, then get down on your knees and thank Allah; for it was his divine guidance that put the idea into the hearts of the women." His statement prompted him to look about; for he would never dare to address the female passengers so disrespectfully as 'the women' and he made that point to both of them. "Thank him and be grateful," he walked away from the ship muttering that he had other business to do, but in reality he swallowed hard in the hope that he was not overheard. Robert knew his answer was no more than an evasion, and it did not sit right with him, even though he was the captain. Aye, he fancied the little captain also showed more than a normal measure of indignation, more like fear and that interested Robert. Both men thought similar thoughts in conjunction, showing a wry knowing smile at the answers they received; they faced each other making it plain that the captain's reaction was no more than a front for something else; what, they could not yet tell but they would both think deeper on it, for there truly was a mystery in the air. Robert laughed, "Christ he was scared, did you notice his bulging bead like eyes? Why his face turned to puce, I thought he'd shit himself." When his tone became highly vociferous during their insistence, they had questioned too many liars in the past noting them all to be alike. "It may be none of our business, but this situation stinks; and our attention always comes back to the women. Now, who are these women who strike such fear into the hearts of men." too many questions suddenly came to mind but none that yielded a satisfactory answer. In These were strange days; he knew about fear and its uses and how easily a man could be broken or pressured, emotional pressure was an old and popular tool and he could not deny that it worked.

The two men walked closely on the flexing gangplank, debating the situation; du Bray, tenacious as ever, pressed in his persistence for the intention to catch up with the captain to have one more and try again, but he realised this was not the time or the place. Robert closed up to du Bray, muttering that it may be better to wait and watch, allowing their suspicions to be proved positive by the women's actions and that their really might be more to this puzzle. "Who knows, we may just get lucky and learn something that we were not meant to see." Du Bray was hot with a need to have the truth. "Why would they wait for us to leave, doesn't that strike you as odd that they're not showing?" There was a moment of thoughtful pause before the two men walked off to join the others who had taken up a comfortable position waiting nearby cargo that had been deposited on the quayside for collection.

The busy quayside was full of ships unloading their cargoes; the clamour from the working wharf gangs was noisy, so much so that they did not need to reduce their talk to a whisper as people were everywhere, not just confined to the quay but were beginning to well thickly within the side streets as well.

The early morning charcoal odours of the street sellers had snared Hubert, who was busy stuffing himself with all manner of spice-filled meat patties and other delights. It seemed an age since they had eaten proper food; and driven by the hungry juices rumbling in their bellies, he was unwilling to resist the aromas that drew him onward into the streets. They inhaled the gentle wind off the sea as it buffeted the cliffs; and was drawn downwards to encircling the port; it fell upon the harbour and circulated the small town like an angels breath until it caught a certain area of the quay; it cooled the heat of the morning, lessening the smell from sweating bodies working around them. It was short-lived, as the wind direction swirled and changed the around the water's edge blowing up a foul stench of sewage that was soon to put an end to anybody's hunger; prompting a willingness to move on from this section of the quay. Whilst they were together, Robert had told them of their plan; by waiting, they would soon discover if anything was amiss with their mysterious women. Also, it would be better if they did not group and draw attention to themselves.

Even at this early time, there were plenty of affluent traders dealing on the quay; purses changed hands, orders were shouted and slaves were quick to hump the purchases to their destinations at the crack of the whip.

Breaking through the hubbub of the street noise, there rose a noted disturbance somewhere beyond the crowd. Protesting cries drew the attention as mounted horsemen whipped at bystanders yelling for them to clear the way to those that obstructed their passage. To local people they were nothing less than barbarian invaders, people spat in their path in protest and the braver men shouted their dissent to receive a lashing for their variance of words. When they came into clear view, they were clad in mail, some armed with drawn sword in hand ready for action. Forcing the people to scamper to safety, the snorting horses were not stopping as they cleaved a passage through the masses of people before them; the frightened beasts were driven by the tempers of their riders; it was a far from friendly sight with the horses almost rearing, threatening to trample those before them underfoot. The rider's intolerance drove tempers high, pressing their mares to increase their pace to a cantor, no matter what price innocent bystander had to pay for their dalliance. Robert's eyes closed in disgust, who on earth issued the order to come here to meet men on a secret mission this way. In one action, these senseless idiots were ruining their plans; he became speechless knowing that bad news travelled very fast. A sergeant at arms led his small column of four, with another rider trailing at the rear towing behind six vacant mounts and a pack animal.

From their position near the cargo, the group watched in disbelief at the rider's audacious approach, and hailing audibly that they could not see the men they intended to meet. "Here is our secret escort gentlemen," du Bray, with an air of frustration, shook his head in disbelief; the others immediately came to his side to view the spectacle, casually they turned away as if unconcerned and alarmed and wary of what could happen next.

Meanwhile, the watchful captain strolled the quay, lazily taking his time talking with an agent whilst watching his cargo being unloaded, taking no care of events on the quayside as if he had other matters on his mind to concern himself. Robert quickly ordered his companions to merge into the crowd whilst he dealt with this sergeant and his would-be secret escort. With his temper fraying by the moment with the sergeant's display, he had to stop this pea-brained approach. The Sergeant at Arms neared; Robert stepped forwards, placing himself across his path to catch the rider's attention. The apprehensive sergeant had no time to waste his day, bellowing to the merchant; reluctant to stop to banter with this civilian, he called for him to get out of his way. Before the rider could react, Robert was alongside and threatening him in a low but controlled manner; telling him politely that if he didn't want to be busted back to the ranks, he had better listen carefully and rapidly. There was a look of shock on his face by being affronted by what sounded like an English speaking merchant; fortunately, the sergeant was quick enough to understand something was amiss. In a desperate need to make this conversation appear normal to the watching public, Robert quickly convinced the sergeant of the business at hand. Not to do so would convey to any watchers that there was something more to this meeting; from then on he fancied his enemy would be aware of his every movement. "Grab me," he ordered, "and gently push me towards the cargo as if you're threatening me; and do it now and damn quickly." Through clenched teeth, he called the rider a bloody fool, "If you have ruined all our work to keep our entry into this port a secret then you and your superiors will pay the price." Though the sergeant was taken unawares, he was driven on by his angered reaction; the threat grabbed his attention making him fearful of his position should he fail not to do as he was ordered. In the blink of an eye and from his mounted position and red faced, he eyed Robert suspiciously, but instinctively knew what to do for the best. Grabbing Robert, he spoke through a closed mouth asking, "Where are the others?" Adding, "There were supposed to be more of you?"

"God damn you and your stupid actions, we had to disperse quickly or else you would have told this crowd that you knew who we were." The bumbling sergeant was flustered; too much was racing through his head; to say the least at discovering his blunder but knew nothing of any secret manoeuvring; he wanted to apologise yet was stunned into blubbering at the mouth. "If you are who you say you are, I want a password," he demanded; out of the chaos of his action, he was at least appearing to be in a threatening posture; eyes were upon them even some voices in dissent were raised. Fortunately, he pushed Robert against a stack of cotton. "If you and your lot don't move yourself to a place away from here sharpish, you'll be wishing your mother ever gave birth to you." Robert gave over what was wanted to quieten any fear that the sergeant had not done his duty. "Move man to the edge of town," he hissed, "we will find you," and he added, "somewhere out of the way of prying eyes." Before allowing the sergeant to leave, and it grieved Robert to suggest such an action, he ordered the man to make this meeting appear normal. "Before you break away, you've got to make this look good; but don't get over zealous or you'll be having to explain yourself later." The Sergeant didn't need that any clearer and he pushed Robert aside in a fit of frustrated anger at being accosted and lashed him as he did so. The yelling certainly had the crowd's attention; the sergeant cursed Robert in the little Arabic that he had learnt. Those angry words made the confrontation appear normal; he was treating Robert like any other rogue that would dare approach him on the street, lashing out at him with his foot he knocked Robert sideways on to the ground. When those that had been watching saw their countryman being so maltreated, they reacted loudly; but fear kept their protest hidden from view. Their sympathetic reaction to his treatment told Robert that he had succeeded in his plan; though they dared not approach the soldier as they too many times had seen their countrymen trodden underfoot and left in a very sorry state by the barbarian horsemen. The sergeant had drawn his sword, as did the others in his company readying for action, although it was his intention to dupe the crowd; he was not about to take any chances to his own personal security. He rode away from the watching crowd, who rushed to help Robert to his feet; threats of retaliation bravely flew but they changed their mood when Robert announced that he was not hurt. It took some time before he could escape the attention of those that aided him, but not before giving his thanks. His eye caught that of his friend du Bray and with a sly wink indicated that he was to follow after him. The others, seeing the same, did likewise. With many words of dissent still filling the air, some men around Robert aired a view that one day the people will rise and this land would be rid of them all; "Inshallah," Robert replied, God willing. It was good that they had reacted that way and walked on; though the sergeant actions were pure folly, he felt like cutting the balls of his superior for his rank stupidity. Once he was free of the melee, he entered through the doors of a brothel house; the crowd realised that he was alright and like any man confronting the barbarian needed a glass of wine to steady his nerve or a good woman, both of which were in easy reach.

Meanwhile, du Bray was searching for his friend in vain, unable to see him anywhere; as much as he wanted to find him, he was not going to call out and draw attention to himself, knowing that he would find him soon enough. A few enquiries had led him into the whorehouse nearby; inside, he saw him talking to a woman; a smile was on his face. It was a good way to lose any interest that may earlier have been drawn to him. Du Bray brushed up against him to catch his attention; moments later they left discretely, discussing their escape from what could have ended up a nasty situation.

Outside, Robert was still showing an interest in the ship and the women. "Forget her," du Bray urged, "there are plenty like her in Acre." Robert shrugged off his friend's remark, showing a grin; telling him that he was mistaken in his reasoning. "You misunderstand me," retorted Robert, "I suspect something is afoot here, and I have an idea." They walked through the streets away from the quay; explaining that he had told the escort that they would meet up outside town and more discreetly this time.

They saw the waiting group and this time they were in a place best suited and out of site, Robert was still preoccupied and in a mood with his thoughts; not so much that he did not refrain from giving the sergeant a good dressing down for the incompetence shown down at the quayside. Robert's friends had arrived at near the same time and within a short time were mounted up, readying themselves for the road ahead, but something delayed their moving on; Robert had a further thought; his hand reached out and lightly gripped the sergeant's arm. "Do you know this port well?" he asked; the sergeant's moustache bristled with suspicion that he was going to be in trouble again. With a slight hesitation and a long exhalation of breath, he replied that for a while he was once leader of the escorts to Antioch. "If it's not too late," asked Robert, "is there a place we could view the quay from before we leave, in such a way that those on board could not see our position?"

"Of course, Lord," the sergeant replied, "there is a storage yard we have used in the past for the very same purpose." At the end of the harbour he pointed, he wasn't aware of the knight's reason for his request; his duty had been a disaster so far and knew better than to question his reasons. "We can wait there and watch the ship; are you just curious the sergeant asked trying to be helpful. We have the authority to board the ship and question anyone we like." Robert threw a black look to the sergeant. "Just obey the orders and take us to the yard," snapped Robert. The Sergeant noted Robert's terseness and felt a little dejected at the sound of the rebuke; he suddenly realised it was healthier to remain quiet. The sergeant felt he'd been treated unfairly for the reprimand he had received earlier, especially in front of his men; and now after only offering a suggestion. Christ, how am I supposed to know what's in this smart arse's mind; 'I'm trying to help,' he thought bitterly, but he was only a sergeant and kept his mouth shut. In observance to his superior's request, he turned his horse and made his way bypassing from the crowded waterfront streets. In a less than happier mood, the others followed behind.

It was as the sergeant said, a good observation point but rather cool in the shade of the building, it was also caught by a cool breeze that blew harder from the sea through the open yard. With little protection from the wind in such an exposed point, their thin silken robes offered little warmth against the winds forceful chill. They needed to wait for something to happen, something of which they had no idea of, but they all hoped it would be soon. Men with lesser persistence would have quit, but not Robert; but so far there were no signs that the women would leave the ship. The discomfort was worth the wait for the benefit of the intelligence; nothing happened; Robert's thoughts were yielding some problems with his decision, though he felt that he would rather not discuss them openly. He was reluctant to condemn the woman outright; he had suspicions, amounting to very little, but they held insufficient basis to act against; at the same time chided his belief for thinking the worst against one who helped his friend.

As Hubert drew up alongside Robert, he enquired "What irks you, my friend, surely not the woman?"

"Yes," came Robert's reply, "the woman does bother me but not quite the way you may infer."

Grouped together in the observation yard, Robert turned slightly to address the sergeant and his men, enquiring if the ship was a regular visitor here and might they have any idea where the ship was bound for when it left this port. There was a short silence as the mounted cavalrymen stared back with blank faces; only the sergeant offered any information. In the hope that he was not going to be balled out again, he spoke up, indicating that as he mentioned earlier, he used to escort the merchants into Antioch; during that time it was in his orders to discover much about what went on here. That ship was a regular visitor here, sailing out of Tripoli for Acre and back here again. When garrisoned at Tripoli some years ago, he also patrolled that port and had recognised the ship and the captain, but the vessel seems to be different somehow.

Du Bray almost read Robert's mind as he offered the question, "Then for what reason do they need to remain on board that ship just to return from whence they came? Perhaps they are waiting for someone to arrive and pass them something that they do not wish other eyes to view, or perhaps escort them somewhere," added du Bray.

"So at a guess, they know we are here and watching them, so they too will wait for us to tire of our game and clear the area," stated Robert, speaking his thoughts aloud whilst eyeing the ship at the same time. "For that we shall wait and see, and furthermore," he said looking towards his friend, "where could these women possibly go, but back to Acre? There are no other roads leading anywhere or dropping off points nearby. "So," looking at Hubert directly as he spoke, "that is why this lady interests me, Hubert."

His reply seemed to come a little curtly, "Very well, Robert," said Hubert, "I did not mean to ruffle your feathers or embarrass you," a smile showed on Robert's face.

"Of that I am sure," he replied, "but remember our orders where to look for anything out of the ordinary, and their actions so far certainly have me looking for other reasons for their support."

The more he thought of it, it concerned him greatly that she may after all be a messenger, but for why and from whom? They were questions that required an answer. Aware of her obvious attraction, honesty to himself and care to his mission regarding her was linked; a gut feeling it may have been, but tantamount to his own safety and that of his men. Should he find himself tangled up in any of her deceits in the future, he would require a clear and open mind. Should she turn out to be some kind of agent, well, he thought regretfully, that would probably require a decision of some finality. Sentimentality was a luxury he had to be without; only the coldness of logic and experience would guide his sword hand to enable him to stay alive. His mind pondered on that eventuality, before returning to the present; they had waited a long time and grew impatient with inactivity. The wind that blew from the sea in their unsheltered place eventually set their teeth chattering and goose pimples formed like boils under their fine lightweight clothes.

Hubert spoke out, "We have been here that long, I wouldn't be surprised if the tide would turn soon."

No sooner had he uttered the words than they observed the crewmen begin to draw up the gangplank as preparations were being made to cast off.

"Well, it looks as though your right, Hubert, and we are wrong," said du Bray, "but our captain appears to be over eager to leave." As the ship dropped half her sails, it began to awkwardly turn outwards in a seawards direction out into the bay, Hubert noticed the ship was struggling to make headway against the tide.

"I see what you mean, that captain is running a risk moving out before the tide has changed, I wonder why he is in so much of a hurry to leave?" They watched momentarily as the bobbing ship left the quayside with a fair degree of difficulty and they were very sure that the two females were still on board. With the suspense over, and the need for action no longer looming over them, the group of horsemen gave up their wait; turning their mounts they began to make their way towards the road that was to lead them to their destination, the citadel of Antioch.

It was a relief to be back in the heat, away from that exposed draughty and shady place, with the sun on their backs, they soon felt revived.

The road they travelled was coarse and broken; it had degraded in its condition and fallen into a state of decay; pot holes were deep and if no one did something about it soon, there would be no road to travel on. This was the main thoroughfare to Antioch, but considering that a state of war had recently been lifted then it was only understandable that its state of repair had not yet been undertaken. Supply trains to Antioch needed much care on these roads; it posed a question as to why was the Prince of Antioch was being lax in his duty in overlooking this main route; surely the merchants took a chance to reach the citadel this way? In places, the road was covered by several falls of scree that had slipped during the winter rain storms from higher up the steep slope and spread across the old pathway. It had filled in some of the depressions making the road appear reasonably sound, but in fact it was a risky passage being loose underfoot where the dangers to the traveller were not obvious.

To the riders it appeared too easy a way to lame a horse by picking up a loose stone. "If only we could try another route," Hubert complained, but he knew too well that there was no other road; the holes that might once have been infrequent were appearing consolidated and building into small craters.

Whilst the group continued their way lazily along the winding stony road that was to lead up onto the high ground, their curiosity of recent events had them generally quizzing the sergeant regarding the activity of the Muslim factions in the principality in an effort to gain an insight into the areas internal activity. "There is a peace now," the sergeant told them blithely, without any thought of a return to the discord that once was the norm. "Since that time of agreement, the roads have been overlooked but as long as the tribal families are peaceful then perhaps something can be done about the roads."

Robert listened but remained quiet and pensive in the saddle, whilst others with nothing better to say taunted him with asides and harmlessly poking fun at him with having to leave the ship without seeing the unseen beauty once more.

They were making casual progress up the hill road towards a dense pine ridge that bordered the fringe of the rise en route for the pass, when Robert kicked his mount and burst into life yelling for the column of friends to follow him as he galloped forward. Racing past du Bray, he pointed to an area up ahead, shouting that more could be seen above; arriving at the set point, he reeled his horse around in the opening in his attempts to view the seascape below. "Ha ha," he laughed, coming to a sudden halt; at the same time eagerly and excitedly pointed a finger out towards the bay before him.

"There, look," Robert shouted excitedly as if he was trying to prove himself right. The others were not far behind him and as they gathered in the same clearing; from their advantageous position they were able to view all below them. Robert could hardly contain himself, his beaming face explained his reasons for his past concern; excitedly, he began to convey his thoughts as they gathered at their assembly point.

"Hubert was right, I knew it, no captain would normally imperil his ship and the lives of his crew by leaving a port before the tide has changed. I expect that the women are behind all this, diverting our interest in them, damned dangerous if you ask me. Another thing what finally struck me in my slowness to gather all the facts was – what captain sails into a port without bothering to take on board a cargo before leaving?"

"Well done, Robert," Edward slapped his brother on his back, "don't chide yourself for being slow to notice that particular point when we all of us failed to observe it. "From what has transpired, I would suspect that it was us that was being watched on the quayside."

There was intrigue as others pointed out to sea, beyond the bay that spread out before them, Aldo commented laughingly, "These ladies are slippery fish if ever I came across their kind, they had that captain playing a dangerous game. They must be working together."

The feeling of being easily duped by two women dawned on them all, with the knowledge of their cunning settled on them all. They watched the ship below rounding on its position to return back to the quay; the deceiving captain's act to thwart their suspicious onlookers had failed, though he was not aware of it; in his cleverness, he was laughing. "Now, my friends," said Robert, "we will wait and have our reunion to see what these conniving females are made of."

When the other mounted soldiers caught up with them, Robert suggested that they continue on to wait in a more comfortable location. "If it is as I suspect, they too are travelling to Antioch; we may as well let the ladies come to us. After all, this is the only road out of Symeon so where else can they go?" A lookout was posted to wait and report on the traffic passing along this road; whilst an advance scout was sent ahead to view the road beyond the pass; meanwhile, they would wait somewhere in between to be joined by the two ladies who had been clever in their attempt to outfox them.

The sergeant and his men where much relieved by the news that they were to stop; after all, they had just ridden from Antioch and now were returning without any proper rest or refreshment they had expected at the port town.

The high terrain above was hard and unforgiving, yet held a beauty that was both refreshing and rugged. The coastal pathway ran high above the town on the open mountainside, holding the traveller to the mercy of the elements on that exposed road when gale-force winds blew from the sea; it blasted travellers threatening to push them sideways across the road and dangerously close to the cliff edge. The coarse road remained unchanged with its dangerous gullies wearing ever deeper; the rains had progressively carried their payload of running water across the track to spew out over the edges of the cliffs. The track at this point, so they were told, was also notorious, sometimes giving way to worn edges and had been lethal to many a traveller who was less than alert. Yet unbelievingly, caravans still used the route regularly to and from Antioch.

The group picked their way along the high ground; here they were able to see for themselves why others were intimidated with that route. Startling was the almost sheer and scarred craggy slopes ending by the sight of the pounding waves on the rocks below that withstood the daily nemesis of the sea's moods; and the relentless unending changes that carried its payload of eroding weather. Sharpened edges below the exposed rock faces looked upwards to the wary eyes that spied them as a warning of what could befall the careless traveller. Morning mists cloaked the cliffs near-nakedness, giving rise to clusters of sparse vegetation supporting little more than scrawny tree growth and small tussocks of grass that had probably been deposited there by the wildlife. Its only inhabitants were numerous nesting sea birds, their splattered droppings daubed the rock face like a huge painting standing as testament to their presence. In spite of its harsh appearance at first sight, the closer one cared to view it; the more it unfolded its hidden wild beauty. Salt filled the air making the tongue grow dry and almost soapy; Hubert guzzled at his water skin to relieve the thickness of his mouth.

Goat herders could be seen on the far hills, prompting du Bray to thinking that they must be mad to live and work in these inhospitable mountains. Poor people don't have the luxury of choice in such matters; here in the high hills only a chance to survive, he was told; at least they could hunt and forage on the wild herbs and other plants to keep body and soul together.

The sergeant's words bore truth to the eye when they eventually came upon the most precarious section of the cliff track, displaying the remnants of what once was a decent road. It was barely wide enough for the caravans to pass safely; it offered nothing less than a harsh warning for the greatest of care to be taken; looking at the crumbling edges, care had to be exercised. Where the edges appeared broken, it was obvious that sections had slipped into the sea; though there was some encouragement to proceed, with the track beginning to take on a better shape further on; there, the track steadily dropped downwards slightly in elevation. Travelling onwards, they were relieved to find the coastal track winding inwards away from the steep cliffs where it entered the fringe of the pine forest, where the strong smelling resinous barks blanked the previous salty air.

A good way into the forest they came to a halt, deciding that this chosen spot was a good place to rest. They were hardly off their mounts when the sound of galloping hooves could be heard approaching them. The sergeant recognised the rider as the scout that they had placed at the rear of the column. He came to a panicked halt before his sergeant, dismounted and in his eagerness began conscientiously spilling his information. It was a bad mistake for the young inexperienced scout and it caused the sergeant some embarrassment; angrily, he interrupted the scout to correct him for not recognising his new superiors. Robert hurried towards them for the news, taking in a deep breath of frustration for what he anticipated was to be another disciplining for the experienced sergeant in not giving proper instructions to the now confused young scout.

"What's happening?" cried Robert.

On reaching the scout, the sergeant broke in apologising for not giving his report directly. "Never mind that now," came the sharp retort, turning to the scout he ordered, "Tell me all that you have seen."

Realising his error, the young man apologised and spluttered forth his observations with shortened breath. "There's a caravan making its way towards us."

"How many armed men?" snapped Robert.

"I did not see any," reported the scout, "they are about twenty in number and they all appear to be merchants with others who appear to be serving men."

"Merchants are predictable," the sergeant intervened off-handed, "as soon as the hostilities relax they'll return to their old habits of refusing to pay for an armed escort."

By this time, du Bray and Edward had joined Robert, who turned to them exclaiming that the female's talents as a schemer were remarkable; surprised at her trickery of concealing themselves amid a caravan.

"I tell you, my friends, if she were a man, she would be a most able opponent and decidedly tricky to keep up with on the field, a compliment is deserved for her ingenuity."

They laughed and agreed together at her wit, turning once more to the scout he impatiently asked, "How soon did he think they would arrive here?" The scout replied that the caravan was travelling slowly and it had only just begun its ascent of the mountain road and he could only guess about noon. Robert walked away from the two men and suddenly wheeled around sharply directing one more question at the scout,

"Are you sure there were no armed men?"

"I did not see any soldiers or armed slaves in the caravan," he replied, "but they could be carrying concealed weapons," he added. "Don't you concern yourself about such decisions, I will support that information," said Robert. The sergeant was ordered to dispatch another rider to keep watch on the caravan's progress along the mountain road; "Make sure he reports back in plenty of time and to me this time." Before he was dismissed, Robert checked the scout for his lack of intelligence in recognising his duty by not directly reporting to him; as well as being told that he would do well to listen to his sergeant's belated advice in future. Once Roberts back was turned, faces became twisted in annoyance but none dared say a word.

"We may as well make ourselves comfortable," said Robert addressing the party, "until they catch us up, then perhaps we'll see what they are made of."

On hearing all of that, Hubert and Aldo began searching one of the packhorses pulling off their travelling bags with their supplies and rummaging around for whatever scraps of dried victuals they could find. Beneath the tall pine trees the other men set about taking their rest.

It was some time later when the second scout returned; to the relief of the sergeant, he remembered to report directly to Robert, repeating similar observations that there were no armed men in the party of merchants. They continued resting and eating, knowing that the caravan would have a tricky passage just before arriving to their camped position. It would be in view soon enough and if he was right he would hear them slowly lumbering their way along the perilous mountainside track. Guessing its progress from their resting place whilst they patiently waited its arrival, du Bray stood in pleasant but practical converse with the sergeant, who had been a little on edge not knowing the company he was sharing. There was never any hint of suspicion, but a dread of having to suffer further the length of his superior's tongue, which the perceptive du Bray sensed, and to divert the sergeant from his dismal state, casually enquired if the pack animals carried any weapons, to which there came an affirmative response that his master had made provision for such a request.

"There were swords, knives, weapons enough, I believe," delighted at the news, du Bray called his friends around him to inform them, advising that they dress properly just in case there was any surprised hostility. The baggage animals, poor creatures, must also have been relieved when the ropes holding their bundle was cut, releasing the weight of the weapons to fall from their backs. Hubert tenderly rubbed the donkey's head affectionately and blew gently up its nostrils as an act of friendliness, at the same time whispering in the beast's ear that he would no longer be required to carry his burden any further.

When the bags were cut open they were surprised to see what weapons tumbled out; they were old and had all been from previous battles.

"They're all Turkish," said Hubert.

"Sabres," exclaimed Guy, at his feet lay six sabres amid an assortment of daggers. The swords had a long narrow blade with a slight curve of the eastern sabre indicating that the weapons were most likely to have been Seljuk in origin. "They're old or haven't been used in a while," Hubert commented, swinging the sword to get the feel slicing through the air.

"The steel is good," exclaimed Goodwin. "Good," exclaimed Hubert, "it's more than good, it's the best he'd ever come across. I've heard it said that the smiths who make these blades use a process of folding the raw iron over three hundred times at the forge before they are ready, and this appearance of water marking he pointed at on the blade is a sign of their secret. Eastern steel from Damascus is the best," he chortled, "well worked, beautiful." As he spoke he cut the air with his sword getting the feel of its weight and ability to slash through his enemy's imagined armour; adding that they just were in need of cleaning and honing.

Edward hailed Robert, tossing a sword in its scabbard over to him, which he caught in out stretched arms as he walked towards his mount.

"They'll do, after all we are not expecting any real trouble."

All armed and mounted, the group of soldiers waited patiently.

They watched the caravan amble carefree along the high steep mountain road, not expecting trouble on such a short jaunt to the capital; that is until they came upon the group of mounted soldiers that barred their way. Spread out across the road menacingly, and with a raised arm, the sergeant cried to them to hold, whilst the group of knights moved slowly down the column, carefully eyeing each loaded animal and its keeper as they passed by. There were the usual suspicious darting eyes toward the passing riders; quickly heads dropped looking down when the rider's eyes met. Although there was no threat to the caravan from the barbarian westerners, there had been times when for such simple matters they had ended up losing more than expected. A short, fat, shabby man leading the caravan protested at the unnecessary delay by the soldiers; it was an unusual occurrence to be stopped when they carried nothing of any great value, and on this road to the capital.

In a happy mood, Robert and du Bray chatted as they neared the end of the line of the caravan. "I like these women," he said turning to his friend, "a caravan normally requests an escort should they be carrying goods of intrinsic value; merchants are predictable, they love the weight of gold in their purses. Here, there is no escort, only two women, who I wager will have paid handsomely to have had themselves included to avoid discovery from what would normally be of no interest to anyone."

The scout had reported correctly, there were no armed men, but there was great trepidation from one of the leaders of the caravan who was engaged in furious argument with the sergeant. Robert shouted a command back to Goodwin to slay the leader should his belligerence continue; startled by the command and his lack of understanding to their situation, the caravan leader took heed of the warning and shrank back, taking the order seriously. From past rulers to present day conquerors, changing conditions in this land rapidly taught men lessons of respect for their survival; for those that cherished life quickly learnt the difference between submission and death. The Sergeant at Arms continued his duty whilst the others passed along the caravan casually inspecting the loaded camels, but their interest lay not in baggage of that kind; towards the end they finally came upon a covered litter. The carriers quickly moved aside; they as slaves recognised the menacing sight of armed men with a purpose. Reigning in his horse, Robert felt that his day of confrontation had finally arrived.

"I fear we have found what we expected," he said. Drawing up alongside Edward, it was du Bray that was eager for sport, and with a prankish smile on his face reined his horse away from Robert. Crossing to the opposite side of the litter, he poked his drawn sword between the dark green silken covers that had afforded privacy for the occupants. Feeling the need at this stage not to be too intrusive he called aloud,

"I would ask the lady inside if she would show herself to me."

A short silence followed before a voice from beyond the curtain demanded that they show some respect; a sharpness and age in the voice declared that his request was impossible, "Can you not see that we travel in a closed litter? Leave us, my mistress is in mourning.

Robert's head jerked forward straining attentively, listening to the sound of the voice that spoke; he shook his head invalidating the sound of the older voice. The look on his face was blank and his head gestured that it was not the voice he expected to hear; Robert prompted du Bray to continue and try once again. Du Bray sat smugly in his saddle with a half-smile on his face, he had not had so much fun for as long he could remember.

"Madam," du Bray sternly raised his voice indicating his anger, being certain its effect was not going to make any difference. "We ask you with due respect to show yourselves, and I warn you I am not a patient man. You will show yourself now or remain in this place for good."

A soft gentle yet firm voice equally subjective in its purpose to defy; cried out a vitriolic harangue. "Have you no compassion? You have been told that my mistress is in mourning, are you so short of a gentleman's honour that you would invade a poor woman's suffering? You, who are not of these lands, are lacking in the understanding of our customs; you are barbaric and heartless," and the voice stressed further without a care for their safety. "You walk this land in your arrogance as conqueror and defile all that we hold true. How dare you, be off and show respect for a woman's grief, be on your way I say."

Robert grinned and giving a nod of confirmation and delight to du Bray, that was undoubtedly the voice he expected to hear. The listeners were in awe, being without any doubt that the voice carried such command and strength in its smoothness of delivery that it was actually disarming. This was no ordinary woman; her voice was cultured and worthy of rank, commanding a measure of respect being undoubtedly a weapon in its own right that even du Bray straightened himself as if ready to make amends for his intrusion. The woman's ability to question his action from behind the curtain of her litter had left its mark; du Bray was unsure that his chance for amusement was going to turn against him. He was without doubt a ladies' man that felt it necessary to uphold the delicacy and courtesy of the moment. His expectation of this meeting was not to display any unpleasantness as to indicate the subtleties of a gentleman's conduct, leaving him somewhat dumbfounded to the point that inclined him to be prepared to make his apologies. The mood was brought back to normality as Robert watching the situation change; chirped in,

"Now didn't I tell you she was good," Robert called to du Bray with a smile on his face. He ceased fussing himself, feeling rather foolish at being so easily led, "I must admit she is powerful, she could talk any man into submission."

With a swipe of his blade, Robert cut the curtain along its top fastenings, causing the silken drape to drop and droop only to be held by those fastenings at its corners of the litter; exposing two women huddled together, but not helpless, and sitting on a luxuriant, embroidered, silken mattress, laden with rose petals and other aromatics. One was elderly and the other younger but there was no showing of fear, and their faces were covered, but they could not disguise the look in their eyes; only rage showed in them from being exposed in such a high-handed way. Robert's hawkish eyes caught all that he needed to see in a glance, at the sight of the women he remarked huffily, "mourning, my foot," he exclaimed at the sight of their dress. She was a sight to behold, dressed in her finery, it was nothing less than an exposure of her lying character. He could have swiped at her after the way she had played on his mind; here they were, mistress and attendant, both found out, but their true game was yet to be discovered. As their eyes met, the visual truth revealed the look on his face; yet her strength of character held by not flustering and yielding to him. Brazen as she was, he could not help but admire her pluck; inside he felt a good slap was a worthy punishment for her deceit; he withheld his action allowing her beauty to restrain such behaviour in spite of the trouble she had caused. The hard staring eyes behind her veil were venomous, full of mischievous, intent and full of defiance; he somehow knew that beneath the act there was a secret smile hidden within her unbending will; he guessed his feelings in her game was becoming of interest to her.

The others were waiting and watching Robert with interest whilst he held the gaze of her deep dark penetrating eyes over her veiled alluring face. There was no mistaking the coldness of her eyes, it was as bleak as an English winter in their stare; it almost made him shudder as he looked away. The older woman was dressed in clothing made of the finest material, less colourful but very respectable, and like her companion, portrayed the similar cold, lifeless stare in her eyes. He held her gaze, discovering a difference in her look; apart from the coldness of her eyes, he felt cruelty churned within them which caused him to twitch at the thought of being at her mercy. Unlikely, though it was the lady less finely dressed who was the mistress; the younger woman had spoken of her whilst on board ship; she wore dark blue with a matching decorated head veil, it generated a hardness in her scornful featureless face. He almost felt uncomfortable as her observant eyes ran over him with some disdain; disinterested, he gave a shrug of disbelief at the thought of her story of being in mourning, at a glance he had gathered that she was beyond such an emotion.

His gaze shifted back to the younger woman. Robert tried hard not to stare leeringly at her, though his eyes could not help feasting on her beauty. It was the first time that he had seen her in daylight and although her face was still covered, he imagined every facet and every curve upon her rosy cheeks. She was indeed a fine sight, wearing a green silken dress with silver and gold threads running through the material, a semi-transparent head veil with the similar silver and gold flecks that raised every enquiry of her hidden loveliness, and upon her forehead she wore a golden pendant headpiece studded with gemstones. Hesitant of his secret blasphemous opinion, he believed her to have more beauty than the Madonna herself. Her body, arms and fingers were also covered with jewellery worth a king's ransom. Robert was speechless at the wealth that she displayed. She snapped at Robert like a spitting cobra for his rudeness of staring, du Bray and the others looking through the drawn curtain were also guilty of staring at the show of indecent wealth; they remained agog, straining to see the face behind the veil.

"Well, ladies," although Robert addressed them both, he was talking directly to the younger woman bedecked in jewellery, "at last we meet and this time," he said sternly, "there is no cabin to run and hide in."

Apologising for the intrusion on her privacy, Robert went on to thank her mistress for her show of compassion towards their friend Hubert whilst on board ship. The elderly woman replied sternly, her voice crackled in age, yet it was strong of voice unlike her eye; being empty and devoid of feeling, her words when spoken were clipped and carefully measured.

"Perhaps it was the will of Allah. I am no more than a tool, my actions are always positive and I find it unnecessary to account for my reasons to you. Thanks are not needed for my actions." Her words came out cold and candid. She spoke of the thanks as an afterthought, it rankled Robert that she was indeed off-handed, insensitive and very canny. He took a long look at her; much ran through his mind; her words settled on him like a blanket of evasion; behind that rich facade there stared the eyes of a most odd and calculating woman, never believing a word she spoke.

So she retorted with a tone of temerity, "Might I ask you why you have been equally false in your guise, was it not in your mind to have others think of you as you otherwise showed yourself?"

"I warn you now," Robert snapped, sharply, "my business is of no concern of yours, and I will remind you that it is I who will put forward the questions." There was anger in the older woman's face for Robert's attempt at slapping her down and humiliating her; he was keen to watch as her eyes narrowed with disdain.

Turning to the younger woman, Robert probed again,

"You play a strange game, you and your mistress. Tell me, why did you have the captain endanger his ship to avoid us?"

"I..." the voice quickly hesitated and then corrected.

"We needed to travel alone, unnoticed without hindrance from those that might have it in their mind to serve their own ends. We did not wish to attract attention to ourselves." The words tripped out with aplomb, but in Robert's mind the guilt of their past actions gave little credence to her explanation.

Neither did he like the insinuation in her passing remark. Robert noticed that it provoked a smile on the faces of the others around; remaining calm, he sought to find a different approach in the examination and thankfully was saved by du Bray.

"Madam, you made an oversight in your scheme," stated du Bray. "We were in your debt for saving our friends life, had you allowed us to thank you whilst aboard the ship, we would not be standing here talking now. I think you have over played your role. I assure you, so many questions were raised by your mysterious nature."

The younger of the two retorted in a defensive manner.

"The captain was well paid for his little ruse; I repeat, we did not require an escort nor did we want to be noticed," was the curt reply.

She proceeded after a short pause as if making up a story as she spoke. Turning to Robert the soft voice that delivered her words were like a fog enveloping him, "I was afraid, you made your intentions so obvious at the harbour, I cannot afford to have men attaching their feelings to me just to fulfil their desires."

There was open laughter at the audacity of her statement from the others. Robert instantly disliked her for the remark; yes, he was taken in by her beauty and manner, but he knew that her reply was heartless and a most unworthy statement to make; it served only to demean him in front of his men. His reaction was less jovial, "Madam, your mouth knows no caution; if you were a man I would cut you down for speaking such blatant words."

"My God," exclaimed du Bray in an effort to remove Robert's heated feelings, "her tongue knows no bounds, you do more harm than an enemy's sword. Madam, indeed you have a natural ability to wound people more than they deserve." Demanding that she explain herself truthfully instead of feeding them her concocted stories, so, "The truth is to be out at last, just tell us your destination," du Bray asked. After a short silence, the soft voice penetrated du Bray's attack.

"You did not take the road out of town immediately as you should have, were your intentions on leaving later or were you spying on us? I think it was the latter," she said pointedly denying Robert to have his say. He would not be interrupted nor would he be put off. "Enough of this lying game," he replied harshly, "your words are wasted; we thought you more intelligent, telling us stories; seeking only to hide your intent, or you would not have been watching us."

Du Bray was amazed at her cuteness and wit as she cut and parried in the swordplay of words and pointless explanations. She swallowed at being found out, though it did little to change her drive to confound Robert; it was obvious she was lying, or maybe she knows other tricks as well, he thought. "No, madam," he answered sharply, "I will not accept that."

Their attention was diverted as noises of a disturbance could be heard from some jostling at the front of the caravan, a chance to relieve the tension that was beginning to build. At the front of the line, the sergeant became irksome, the camel leaders grew dilatory to obey his commands; becoming difficult in their recalcitrant attitude, it was clear that someone was going to suffer. The sergeant was shouting orders to get the caravan over to one side, and at the same time threatening all who would disobey him. One foolish individual attempted to cheekily poke his staff into the sergeant's horse's neck to make him rear up and unseat its rider. A jest that was gutsy but foolish, in his trick to show his comrades these barbarians were not so tough as they seemed, and that they were not so clever if they were not to remain alert to leave themselves exposed. It was a foolish act and carried with it a disastrous reaction. To the smiles of the wilful watchers, the horse reared up nervously; it caused the sergeant to struggle in maintaining his position in his saddle. As soon as the horse had settled, the angered sergeant rode it at the foolish man with hurtful intent for causing him such embarrassment.

The spectacle that unfolded was not so amusing, the provocateur paid dearly for his act by being forcefully struck; the animal urged on by the unsettled rider collided with the man throwing him violently through the air. This caused the individual to impact and bounce off a nearby tree, falling crumpled on the ground like a broken toy and severely injured. A silence suddenly befell the playful crowd, it was instantly clear that the sergeant was not taking any nonsense from any of them; distressed by the outcome, they ruefully clamoured around their injured friend to care for him; he was hurt badly; the need now was set about carrying him to a safer and more comfortable place to nurse his injuries. The incoherent protest and jabbering between the miscreants ceased, silence fell upon them with that act of authority; everybody knew where best they stood and immediately obeyed the sergeant. Only the sound of wheezing camels being herded off the road was to in the air. With the distraction behind them growing quieter, Du Bray turned to the women putting it to them one more time; issuing a warning that if they refused to render a sensible and truthful answer, he would have them bound and tethered to be forced to walk or dragged along if necessary behind their horses to Antioch. "There you can languish in a cell until you decide to co-operate." There was silence from the two women but the air between the parties was filled with enmity. Dark eyes stared coldly at du Bray and though he cared not, he felt rather uncomfortable waiting for her response.

Like a spitting serpent the younger woman reacted like a cornered creature, "franj," she hissed, "I said before that you are no friend of ours; you do not belong here nor do you have any love for us, we helped your friend, how dare you speak to my mistress like that; after all, we have been careful not to cause you or your friends harm."

In reaction to her words, surprise was met with raised eyebrows at her temerity. "Do my ears hear correctly?" Robert said to his companions. "Now that's more like it," said du Bray, as the reality of their feelings was manifested. Turning to the older woman, he asked why she had been using the younger woman as some kind of decoy when all she had to do was speak truly of her intentions, "Your methods mystify me, madam."

"It was not my wish to reveal my reasons for travel; but you have placed us both in an awkward situation with your persistence. You will of course excuse the girl for her outburst, unfortunately I am not at liberty to divulge my name or the purpose of our journey, but, we do travel to Antioch to be with your commander the Prince himself." She produced a scroll, "Read this if you will, but you must explain your reasons to the Prince of Antioch for the breaking of the King's seal." Without the need to closely examine the seal's crest, he could see enough to dismiss the need to proceed further.

"I might have guessed," said Robert throwing his head back in disgust.

He thought by allowing du Bray to provoke the women, he would gain the answers he was searching for, but alas the woman's last comment proved beyond doubt that she had only been toying with them.

"Madam, your intelligence is to be admired, who supports you?" The woman with the bejewelled fingers contemptuously answered,

"I have given you sufficient to withhold your action; it was not my intention to draw attention to ourselves. By all means," then she succumbed, "be our escort."

She did no more than rest her back against the cushions, then with a sterner note in her voice she added,

"I warn you to be alert; my reason for taking this journey is of the greatest importance to the King of Jerusalem."

He had no need to implement his own Master's wrath for impeding his business, knowing that he had pushed a little harder than he should. "Bastards," retorted du Bray, "I'd like to know what's going on." As his discomfort crept over him, they conceded by being thwarted and especially with the King's name being used, this did not help them either.

"Very well, my lady," he replied. "Whether you want it or not you are now in our protection."

On the knights word, the column gathered itself together and the merchants were happy enough to have a free escort; as for the baggage train masters, who remained disgruntled by the treatment, they meted out to their foolish friend.

Robert and du Bray rode forwards, they bitterly complained to each other of their misfortune and embarrassment, being saddled with these women who had outwitted their every move and left without any clue as to what was their initial intention. The silence of the women was more than they expected, having confronted them in such fashion, hoping that their insolence, brusque attitude and discourtesy may frighten them into later telling of their purpose for travelling. Events were now dictating that they were not to be taken for granted, nor were they weak individuals who would easily break down under a firm approach. In the knight's frustrated and wounded indignation, a certain respect for the women had been born.

They followed the meandering, narrow mountain trails ever upwards to where the road would eventually take them, with the sea at one side, and to their left a sheer cliff wall constantly reminding them of its dangers. The breeze up here was heavenly and mixed with the strength of the fragrance of the tall pines proved stimulating to the slightly jaded travellers. Along this stretch of the road the pines grew out of the road's narrow edges causing further irregularities along the tracks stony surface. Natural water-courses seeping down the mountainside crossed the track inducing it to be slippery in part, difficult to the foot and impossible at times for a rider. At this point, all riders dismounted for their own safety, the trail ahead remained narrow and dangerous.

The track at its extreme height was coarse and rocky, being denude of trees and shade. The ground was hard-baked and gave way to the unpleasantness of the intense exposure of the sun's rays, and dust filled the air.

They were now approaching the high narrow pass, which always gave rise for concern. It was a natural place for an ambush; here travellers were forced to thread themselves singularly through the narrowness of its neck in the rocks, which meant that the ladies were temporarily better off out of their litter, having to walk the distance through the narrow arched gap. They complained much over the heat of the day, though away from the comfort of their litter they were well used to harder times.

The pass's perilous aperture gave rise to great anxiety, for it was long enough in length to be penned in its rocky length and be struck down from an archer's arrow, it had been the promise that work would start to make alterations to it to be broadened but due to the past unrest; that task was still wanting. The twisting road was turning away from the sea; towards the end of the nervous passage came hope and the road that would take them inland. Tension was in all eyes as they constantly scanned the rocks above for any threat to their safe passage. Once through, there was relief and talk among the merchants that the Gods had smiled on them for their safe passing. Although it was half expected to be so, they feared for their lives just the same; for too many stories had left their mark and blood spilt on that ground. With the threat of danger passed, the road at the high hill top widened out, giving a panoramic view of lush green rolling distant hills and a richly-wooded valley and a clear road ahead that led to their destination.

The bright sun dazzled, making the view awesome, the richness of the green valley below against an endless bright blue sky above; they grouped like a bunch of children to admire the splendour before them. In that open space the heat prickled their skin reminding them of the time of day; the sun, reaching its meridian, caused sweat to ooze profusely from every pore.

It was from here that the road slowly dropped downward, winding as it went through lower hills finally disappearing into the thick wooded valley below. A small dust cloud spiralled in the distance, giving rise to their curiosity. "Somebody is in a hurry," Hubert remarked, pointing at a trace of rising dust across the valley, "let's hope it's not trouble." They watched as the cloud grew in size and intensity; their scout was in some great haste. In his approach, it brought nervous tension that something was amiss; the scout must have seen their gathering making no attempt to slow his horse's pace. Exhausted by his hard ride, the scout made directly for Robert, rearing his mount in his sudden effort to stop; he had a report to make and he was wasting no time in delivering his news.

"Sir," the rider gasped for breath, a water bag was thrown to him taking him by surprise, which he grabbed at with waving arms.

"Catch your breath, man, before you faint and keep me from waiting any longer," said the experienced leader.

A short pause and a pull at the leather flask to slake his thirst was enough to enable the rider to speak. "Three or four," he gasped for breath, "miles back there are at least twenty men. I cannot be certain but they appeared to be Knights of some kind, he stumbled with his words before explaining that he had not been in this land long enough to be able to identify all the dress of the various knights or orders or their allies. "They were donned in white surcoats sporting a black cross, well-armed and I admit," he said apologetically, "that I have never witnessed their presence at the castle. I know not from which direction they had travelled. Seeing them and their uniform, "he gasped, "is new to me." Looking for an excuse to support his ignorance, the young trooper stumbled out his report. Fearing that he had made a hash of it and filled with embarrassment, he repeated his findings over again, attempting not to show his ignorance too readily and hoping that his comrades further back would not hear to laugh at his fumbling effort to report.

Robert held up his hand calling for silence, which made the young scout feel awkward and inadequate. The report was accepted, but for the apologies and the excuses of the scout almost having Robert telling him to shut up. He was aware of the young man's ignorance but to be sure of the news he had to ask him to repeat himself again and was questioned further over the uniforms. Showing great interest in the news had Robert puzzled; rubbing his unshaven chin he appeared to fall into a numbness of deep concentration whilst those all around him were as eager to hear more.

Realising that he had announced news that sparked an interest to the leader, the scout spoke once more with confidence, "I came upon them accidentally and I'm unsure whether they saw me. They looked like our troops," he chirped up, and then fell silent, hesitating once more.

Although Robert spoke, his mind was on deeper matters. "Good man, well done." Robert's words of thanks for a job well done proved so rewarding to the scout that his chest puffed out with pride. Drawing himself up in his saddle, he did not dismiss himself back to the ranks but remained in his position, he was clearly not finished.

"No, sir," he spoke out, "something was wrong."

His words fell confusingly on Robert's ears.

"Finish your report," coaxed du Bray.

Yet, before he could finish his report another voice broke the air.

"If they wore black and white, I have a good idea who they are," Guy Goodwin, leaning forward in his saddle continued, "but it doesn't make sense." They are the colours of the Teutonic Order and they are with us no more," he sternly stressed.

"What are you saying Guy?" asked Robert.

"I would hazard a guess that they are uniforms of slain comrades."

"Well, if that's the way it is, it looks as though we are in for some excitement, although there is no reason for us to expect trouble."

"Hold on, we are no threat as yet, nor is this caravan," there was a pause from du Bray then he added, "unless, and it is only a guess, but maybe their interest is in the women."

Raising his head, Robert brought his eyes back to the scout, addressing him once more with urgency in his tone, there was something else.

Not making himself wanting to look foolish and concerned at the speed that Robert had snapped his question, the young scout mumbled shaking his head, "It's just that they," he stopped not wanting to appear stupid; now he was doubtful of offering a further opinion; for what he was about to say may destroy the effect of the previous praise.

"Come on, man." urged Robert impatiently.

"Well, sir, I'm not sure you understand, but they didn't act much like knights to me when I saw them. They 'was..." he stuttered, "It was unusual to see them on their knees. I know they are Holy brothers in arms and that the need to pray to our Lord who is in us all in times of war, but they was bent over double they was. It's just that they did not compose themselves like knights when I saw them."

The smile that slowly broke through Robert's serious frowning face soon built into a broad smile, encouraging the light of understanding to fill his eyes with certainty from the report that the unknowing scout had submitted.

"My young friend," said the knight, "the sun is high signifying noon; you have much to learn about these people, but you have done well in your observations. When you saw them, you had observed Muslims at prayer. Now go to your sergeant and ready yourself for action whilst we prepare to find ground suitable to defend ourselves when we confront them."

Whilst Robert shouted orders for fighting, he was blatantly aware that something here was not right; the soldiers ahead could not risk a conflict unless there was war and he had certainly not heard anything to the contrary. No these men, he fancied, were tied up with the women; but for the life of him he could not reason it out. There was a mystery within the reasoning for the enemy to go to such lengths to dress up in Teutonic clothing, to kill the women and leave witnesses to tell their tale would be harmful. Could it be that simple? Obviously the message of slain soldiers would be damning later; if it was our own what motivated them to action, could this be leading us to what we are here for?

The group of Knights were herding the merchants into the brush in their efforts to clear the road whilst Robert remained with his problem; the activity brought him back to the present.

"Get the women out of the litter and tell them to conceal themselves in the rocks," came an order from du Bray, "and tell them it's for the sake of their own safety, and to be careful not to show themselves when their friends arrive."

The plan was that the caravan would wait on the high ground and only move as the enemy approached. Though it was hardly likely, should they fall foul of the enemy then the women may have a chance to make it on their own to Antioch. Robert rode back to the litter dismissing the soldier who was finding life difficult in argument with the women in his attempt to carry out du Bray's order. Robert dismounted and sighed hard; these women were beginning to be troublesome. He would have no contest of wills; he told them do as they were told or he would kick their arses personally all the way into cover. Ready or not, he said, he was not waiting for an answer; there was danger ahead; he looked the older woman in the eye telling her that twenty armed men are coming for her and I'll want some answers after this business is over. "They have no business with us," the hag hissed," it is for you they come and your secret little band. It is you," she hissed, who have the answers to give; that you are keeping to yourself."

"Will you not tell me," pleaded Robert, "your purpose here. Men will die here this day; do you not care to stop this bloodshed; these men are soldiers, armed and coming to see your end. One thing is certain, they are not here to plunder a worthless caravan, nor are they aware of our presence."

With a dire note of concern in his voice, he repeated, "death will visit many this day because of you," his finger pointing at her, "think again, I appeal to you; speak and save them from their certain death."

The hollow voice that emitted from behind the veiled face uttered, "You are confident Franj; that is good. Whatever happens this day is the will of Allah."

Pondering over her insensitive reply, Robert could not afford to be thinking of this woman; he was resigned to the oncoming battle and held his outstretched hand impatiently for one of them to be assisted out of the litter. "Then come quickly," he encouraged, "there is no need to make matters easy for those that have greater need of your blood."

"It is my wish, no," he corrected himself, "it is my order that you transfer yourselves to that place pointing the place with his outstretched arm, and remain hidden within the cover of yonder rocks until this confrontation has past." Impatience was with him, yet he did not wish to be discourteous to a person of her rank on the King's business.

It was the older woman who made the first move toward Robert; she held forth her limp lifeless hand for his assistance. The gold on the fingers of her hand dazzled the eyes in the blazing sunlight; he held her carefully as if she were his mother, though there had been no sense of urgency from her movement. With all due respect he aided her descent from the litter. Escorting her over to the rocks he ensured she was in a place of safety and reasonably secreted in the brush before returning to the litter to help down the younger female. She too was waiting with sport in her eyes, but it was not the time or the place. Holding forth her arm, she grasped Robert's hand nervously or so she wanted it to appear, but he was aware of the game she was playing with him. As hard as it was to conceal his excitement inside, the thought of open contact with her had his heart racing; she too perceived his feelings. It was difficult to hide; in this time of urgency she played at the awkward and helpless woman. Once in the grip of his arms she was well aware of Robert's bashfulness. "I am not going to bite you, my franj," she said tauntingly whilst feeling his nervousness. He held her tightly for a moment and could not help but feel the form of her body against his and once more the fragrances about her rushed into his nostrils almost intoxicating him. She was testing him, probing his weaknesses. "Damn you," he said aloud. She laughed, mocking him, "Careful, you will break me, I swear, my franj," she said softly looking up into his face and seeing the knight flushed with embarrassment at the joy of the feel of her body against his. He protested, telling her that this was not the time or place for such antics. He disliked his feelings being put on display by her, she was too clever for him and her probing caused him to look away, losing concentration that he almost dropped her.

"Do you treat all your women so roughly?" she said looking into his face.

"Please, my lady," he protested once more.

Robert replied, "Do not mock me," and began to apologise for his awkwardness.

"Did I not tell you we would meet again?" she purred teasingly, her arms about his neck.

Robert could do without this display of playfulness as he carried the younger female to her mistress. Once safely ensconced amid the undergrowth, he again instructed both ladies that they would be safe where they were, providing that they were not seen.

He turned and walked towards his horse, mounted and ordered the litter bearers to close up to the column. Robert turned in the saddle looking back to the hidden women, a voice issued forth, "May Allah be with you and strengthen your sword arm," cried the teasing veiled female.

From their place of hiding, they watched the caravan move slowly forwards. A little further on, the road broadened giving them sight of the enemy as they came into view. Robert had had time to explain what he required from his men and called to his friends to take up the formation previously planned.

It wasn't long before the sound of approaching horsemen could be heard; the troop of would be Teutonic knights slowed their pace before coming to a halt before Robert and his men. The two leaders rode towards each other keeping a short distance apart; there was an exchange of polite salutations from the two leaders.

The Teuton raised his hand in salutation; Robert saw the moment they came into view that they were undisciplined for knights. "We have orders to escort the two females in your party to the citadel," ordered the Muslim leader, he spoke clearly and in very good English.

"Well, now," replied Robert leaning back in his saddle with a relaxed air about himself, "good day to you," and with a tone of apology in his voice, "two women, you say."

"Regrettably, captain, your journey was in vain. If you want to escort them you will have to go all the way to St. Symeon to see them."

The smile on the captain's face tightened into a frown, he was expecting a more direct answer, "And how is that?" he asked.

"One of them was sick after their voyage so they decided to rest until tomorrow, we of course could not wait; our business is urgent."

"I may need to take a look inside the litter," the captain demanded. In his thoughts, Robert was taken aback and alarmed that this fool cares nought for diplomacy and calls me a liar to boot.

It was better to allow the man to satisfy himself and not have the group spread out along their flank, this he knew would spoil his plan and lead to the chances of casualties to his own men. In typical Muslim form, the enemy had spread themselves out across the road in front, barring the way of the oncoming caravan instead of keeping rank. This is what Robert half expected and had brought his men forward to form a wedge at the front of the caravan in anticipation, whilst the others were positioned along the caravan to enhance the size of the wedge and further reduce any of the oncoming numbers. The leader, who was no better disguised than his troop of men, moved forwards closer to Robert widening the gap from his own group to further parley. After certain further niceties were exchanged, Robert entered into innocent but boring small talk to put his adversary at ease.

"It is good to see that our Teutonic brothers have come to meet us; we were tiring of escorting this caravan in this confounded heat. Tell me," said Robert, "have you been stationed in these parts long? We have just arrived."

Robert noticed the nervousness of the cavalryman, to his eye he deduced that they wanted to do their job but was hesitant for the lack of opportunity to take the initiative. Beads of sweat began to form on the leader's face and a definite nervous tic was noticeable at the corner of his left eye. The enemy leader's horse was very excitable and showed that he had difficulty in controlling it from snorting and pawing the ground with its hoof. After much effort to display a relaxed front, he finally calmed his steed. A broad smile beamed upon the impersonator's face. He did not believe Robert's story about the women and was unsure of just how to start his battle. Casually he entered into a prearranged story, hoping to set Robert's men at ease before striking down the unwary company. Unfortunately for the Muslim cavalryman, Robert was much too wise to be taken in so easily, and seized the opportunity to implement his own plan whilst his enemy was in full flow. It was obvious that both parties were of the same mind and making the same ploy; the time to act was now, roaring at the top of his voice Robert gave the command, "Attack!"

He spurred his men forwards. The Muslim impostors were taken by surprise. Swords were drawn from their scabbards with urgency of surprise; an unsheathing whine filled the air as the sound of singing steel rang out like wild banshees in search of their victims, spreading confusion as they forcefully surged forwards. Daylight metamorphosed into a haze of dazzling flashes as the glinting of the raised naked steel swords in the noon sun prepared to fill their promise to the unguarded. Like avenging angels, Robert and his men advanced cutting and slashing. Before the enemy leader's smile broke into a fatal realisation of the threatening situation, a slashing sword, thirsty for the taste of blood had found its mark across his unguarded face. His defective eye with the nervous tic suddenly dropped out onto his bloodied cheek leaving the recipient useless for further battle. Screaming loudly, his hands clutched at his face to guard his unsecured eye ball, with the on rush of riders he fell forwards off his mount and onto the ground only to be trampled on by the advancing horsemen. His pain was short lived; the next rider in the wedge cut him down in the surge forward in their onward movement into the undisciplined ranks of the Muslim horsemen. The plan worked beautifully; hacking and slashing, the wedge proceeded forwards mercilessly cutting down all before them. The knight's steel did not stop hacking until the entire enemy had been killed or wounded. The effectiveness of the wedge was conclusive; twice that number could not sustain the surprising force within the manoeuvre.

When they turned to regroup and charge, the sight through the rising dust cloud from the sudden surge that was left in their wake, when the cloud lifted it exposed a scene of carnage and suffering, which was testament to their frenzied efficiency. Dead men were strewn across the killing ground; some with severed limbs lay about them moaning and praying their wounds would take them quickly to paradise; blood soaked, the sandy earth held the smell of death and it grew in the heat as did the sound of flies buzzing around, drawn by the smell of fresh meat. The second charge did not occur, the onlookers from the caravan that had stood well back in view of the affray were dumbstruck and agog, sick with fear at the sight that they beheld. The efficiency and ferocity of how the fighting knights set about their task of removing their enemy left them in awe of their ruthlessness. These were the men who so foolishly denied their co-operation; when suspicions rose about their paid passengers who were travelling in their train was brought into question. Greed lay at the root of their reluctance to speak out, and foolishly they thought it better to create their obstruction and show defiance. Not anymore, another lesson had been taught this day and from this moment on respect and obedience was rapidly forthcoming.

The victors casually rode through the fallen mess of bodies before dismounting. The air reverted to stillness once more, bringing with it the return of the stifling heat. They were wet with their sweat and it had not been caused by the heat of the day, but by the rise of their excited blood surging through their arteries by a throbbing excited heart that pumped away at fever pitch, urged onward by the heat of battle.

Answers were required as to who was responsible for the attempted ambush and why they had been chosen; it wasn't long before a suitable but unfortunate wounded man was found to question. Whilst the soldiers of the lower ranks busied themselves on the battlefield slitting the throats of the seriously wounded, and of course looking for anything of value on the person of their victims, an unfortunate survivor selected for questioning had been found. He had suffered a serious leg wound with a severed artery that was pumping blood profusely. The knights approached him; gathering around surveying the severity of his wound, their forms cast a shadow of imminent death across the conscious, wounded cavalryman. Seeing them gathered around him like vultures, he begged for mercy, but today there was no mercy forthcoming, only answers. Prodding his sword into the open wound had the wounded man screaming and writhing with the pain; du Bray knew his business and demanded the name of his master. The immediate pain sent a hopeless scream of suffering across the silent battlefield. There was nothing more obvious to the victim than the knowledge that he was to die a terrible painful death; he would say anything to quicken his departing from this world if he could, but he knew that at this moment there was little he could do to hasten its coming. His only option was to try to pretend that he did not understand what was being asked of him.

Knowing that pain was a great means of loosening a victim's tongue, du Bray provoked the helpless man by tantalisingly poking the tip of his sword about the man's open bloody wound again, and speaking in the soldier's own tongue as the question was repeated. The reaction was expected, the victim could do no more than vent the pain he was suffering by expelling the hurt he was undergoing with a further scream. More screams followed by more pain; it was unmerciful but necessary in the eyes of those men that needed the answers to their questions and they would not desist until the poor victim had expired or yielded to their demands. With impatience in his voice, du Bray went on to inform the injured man that he was waiting for an answer and he warned that it would not be providential to play games with him. Anxious for a response, the helpless man's pain heightened when du Bray's boot pressed down on the prisoners wound; sobbing screams rang out once more, shattering the quietness of the valley as a further spurt of blood gushed from the wound, but the man held his tongue. "We can keep you in this pain for days," he told the man, "speak up and save yourself the agony; you have fought well and deserve to die a soldier's death; no man can hold you to cowardice." The soldier struggled weakly to lean forwards, pleading for mercy as he tried to stem the pain in his leg by holding his thigh tightly; but his hand was swiftly rebutted with a swishing sharpened edge of a sword, causing more agony and blood to be drawn from the man. "Come on, man," du Bray demanded once more, "the name of the master you serve, tell me and I will save you from this pain."

With a fear far greater than that of betrayal of his master, the wounded man prepared himself for death. In an effort to draw himself up to rest on his elbows, the man struggled tirelessly with his pain, managing almost a sitting position. With sweat running from him, he grasped for breath and some relief from his immediate pain; words proved difficult for the man, he mumbled something inaudible. The group of knights stood around him half-heartedly allowing the prisoner to better position himself in readiness to expose the information they required. Du Bray was talking with Robert, only partly aware of the injured man's struggle to sit erect. Taking every advantage of the knight's inattentive stance, the prisoner seized on his chance to feign a response.

Aware that he would not have another chance to free himself from his captors' pleasures, the man muttered, "I serve," struggling further to reach his final position. The knights, appearing weary, nonchalantly stood awaiting the answer to roll off the wounded man's tongue and continued in their discourse. It was now time for the wounded man to act; whispering the words of a prayer, he reached out and seized at du Bray's sword bringing it downwards towards his own throat. "Allah Akbar," was all that he managed to speak as he tugged du Bray forwards off his balance. With this act, du Bray had lunged forwards of balance and unintentionally caused his death; it was over with an upward spurt of blood as the sword penetrated the wounded man's throat, severing his windpipe with ease. Cursing as he almost fell head over heels, du Bray's angry outburst filled the air, causing those who were still in the undergrowth to cautiously remain there silent until the knight's anger had cooled sufficiently for them to consider it safe to walk among them. "That's it," du Bray complained bitterly, angry at his own carelessness. "Damn, we should have learnt from this prisoner."

"It doesn't matter," a light slap on the back by his companion brought him back from his self-chastisement, "I suppose we had better finish clearing the road before we fetch the women." Attempting to cover his shortcomings with the prisoner, he broached off-handed his observation by remarking, "Quite easy that, didn't you think?" turning to Hubert. Hubert, still feeling high on the effects of the excitement, nodding his head saying, "Sending boys to do a man's job, they must have been green."

"Well, they're certainly red now," laughed du Bray, and he playfully nudged Hubert. They walked off laughing together and commenced their chore of clearing the bodies off the road; they stripped the uniforms from the bodies of the dead and collected them for a safe return for the captain's attention at Antioch. Meanwhile, the victorious soldiers from the garrison of Antioch were in high spirits as they worked; two at least had never encountered the enemy before, and they could not stop talking about the affray and the thrill of killing their first Muslim bandit. There would be a different conversation in their barrack room tonight; their sergeant looked thoughtful, allowing them their high spirits, for he knew not how long they would survive in this hostile country. Robert rose from his thoughtful posture and straightened himself, turning around to see the two women viewing the scene carefully. They had ignored his order and proceeded more closely to scrutinise the foray. "Christ," Robert cursed; if ever he was in a similar situation, he would have to bind these women to make them obey his commands; this sort of thing made him down right moody; though he altered his mood as he approached them to escort them to their litter; he found it odd when a compliment was forthcoming.

"I see you are a formidable force and not a man to play with when heated," said the elderly female through the gold-flecked veil. He had no liking for what he had just accomplished, it was his work, good or bad, and he had saved the caravan and company at the cost of these men's lives and he was not overly proud of the killing. Robert had no liking for the hag, a name that he had branded her in his mind, she was far too calculating for his liking; what went on in her mind he could not tell, nor what lay behind her probing eyes that he disliked so intensely; she never seemed to miss a detail. She continued talking, Robert somehow had lost his voice somewhere after the start of her congratulations; almost spellbound, he found difficulty in taking his eyes off the younger woman who held his gaze with equal interest. He got more than a feeling that they had watched the fight; more like they judged his actions and somehow made him feel that they enjoyed the abhorrent brutality of it all. With a pointing finger directed to the older woman, he told her that she could have prevented this bloodshed, but he was unable to see any life or remorse for the dead as she stared away. "It was the will of Allah," she responded; her excited voice spoke cackling excitedly as if she had been entertained.

In a smug sickening way she mentioned, "You remind me of another I know."

That statement allowed Robert to quickly ask who that person might be, but she declined to answer and skirted the question; Robert did not wish to give up on his enquiry. "I should know that person then," he stated, "I have met many of your leaders on and off the battlefield, so tell me, madam, do not keep me guessing who my competition is."

"You are quick, franj and I like a quick mind," she said, but she would not be drawn on her slip. "I will keep that name from you, franj, for that is one name you certainly do not want to know."

"But," she added, "I have learnt much about you this day, franj, and assure you this minor battle will be remembered, and I thank you for a chance to view your tactics and skill at first hand." She beckoned the younger woman to follow and the two females walked off towards the litter; the older guiding the younger as if she was reluctant to want to leave.

Robert sensed that the old bitch was laughing behind her veil, and it had displeased him that they had watched the affray; it further irked him to think that this clever female had gleaned some form of knowledge from his tactics that he had used and let slip.

Who she was, he did not know, but he was going to make it his business to find out, for if anything, they were to be considered unusual and suspicious; with a humph he believed they were certainly that.

With the imminent dangers of the affray behind them, the two mysterious females were ensconced once more in their litter, carefree of whatever the day might deliver to them.

The party continued to eventually emerge from the tree-lined slopes of hills onto the lush green of the valley floor; before them lay the dirt road from ages past that ran zigzagged across the gentle rolling plain that was to lead them to their destination, Antioch.

Approaching the citadel from a distance, they stopped to view the spectacle; they were in awe of this beautiful walled city, it lay beyond them standing in the distance across mount Silpus and it was colossal. It was truly huge, a welcome spectacle to the tired eyes to the travellers in the caravan. It appeared to cover the entire hillside of the mount with its great many towers along its walls, believed to be three hundred and sixty in all. They sprang every hundred yards or so, and one part of it sat along the edge of a deep ravine making it impregnable at that point. Within its walls, high above on the top of Mount Silpus, stood the fortress that made this fortification almost impossible to take. The fortress watched over the expanse of its citizens in the citadel of Antioch like a Protective eagle on its nest. Its fortifications protected the whole city below; should the enemy breach the lower walls and spill into the town, it still remained a problem, and it had been tried more than once to unseat this obstacle that remained safe to hit and run back to safety when under siege. It looked impregnable; they were later to discover that there were accommodated pastures for livestock to graze on should they ever come under siege. The stronghold was the seat of the Prince of Antioch, and the main garrison in that part of the County. There was a keep to the lower wall and a barracks which housed hundreds of troops; their duty was taken up patrolling the walls and ensuring the citadel was safe.

Sitting aloft in their saddles, they could not help but be fixed in awe at the magnificent spectacle that they beheld, truly they had never seen the like of its size ever before.

"There lies our destination," said du Bray pointing forwards, with his words there was a creeping excitement in their eagerness to reach the city and see it close up.

The Deal

The turbulent sea would normally have caused a problem to travellers on general sailing ships in its approach to the port of Tripoli, which had proved itself one of the strongest fortress towns on the Levantine coast that was in Templar hands. The bay was wide and had many cross currents causing most small ships that attempted to lie off port at anchor until the tide had changed; it was on most occasions the safest method of approach for general small shipping into the port. Little ships anchored their vessels to wait out the changing tide, during which they would roll aimlessly this way or that, striking terror into the hearts of misfortunate waiting mariners. In times of bad weather, some ships were forced sometimes to divert to another port or wait far off shore until the stormy turbulence subsided and which, on occasion, proved to be a more hazardous option.

The illustrious passenger of this particular ship had little need for any such concern for his wellbeing; he had chosen his mode of transport well. When Luca Rici travelled anywhere, his influence and power preceded him. People went out of their way to accommodate him, treating him like a royal personage, clamouring for the smallest of favours. He was well aware of his influence and wealth; the merchant took every advantage and used his persuasive powers like a weapon.

Presently, he was lying in the captain's cabin on the newest completed war galley in the Templar fleet; it had ploughed through the swollen sea without any difficulty or danger to its structure, manned by no less than a hundred and fifty oarsmen. There was little to compare it with trading vessels, being sturdy and as devastating as a cavalry force on land, it cut through the turbulent swell of the raging cross-tides with relative ease. Luca was very impressed at the ship's performance, wondering if there was a need for such vessels in his own fleet. He thought on the matter and dismissed the idea, thinking why and for what need he would require a warship, though the idea tickled his imagination. Laying back, he fell into a more relaxed mood in the pleasant isolation of his cabin, his merchant fleet was more in-keeping with his future plans. Relaxed in his iniquitous machinations, he amused himself feeding from the bowl of fruit at his side; he thought back smugly on how little his wealth and influence took to gain passage aboard this ship, his mouth curled exposing a sneer of a smile twitching into the corner of his conceited mouth at his thought to the secret purpose of his visit.

It had been just over a year since he had last heard from his beloved grandson; each passing day his absence proved more painful for the ageing Luca, who by this time had conceived a plan that was worthy of his scheming character. His whimsical, though serious, trance-like state became interrupted as he heard orders for docking being called out on the deck above, he had thought of going on deck to watch the activity; the captain was young and ingratiating. Better that he remain languishing comfortably a little longer on the cushions that bedecked the cabin, until the activity was over. There was a knock on the door, whoever it was Luca was certain that no crewman would be sent down to rouse such an important guest as he; his agile mind deduced that it was no lesser man than the young captain himself. Once more the knock was heard, this time a little harder and the door was opened inquisitively and gently so as not to disturb the guest within.

The captain, a young fair haired man with bright eager eyes, arched his neck carefully around the half open door of the cabin before entering; he was probably not much older than twenty and five years. Young for a captain, but for those high born sons of the leaders of the nobility whose wealth and position enabled their sons to be projected to positions of rank long before other men of lesser birth, here stood one such man. It was his intention to inform Luca that the ship was being safely tied up and he was able to disembark whenever it suited him.

"Come in," cried the elderly merchant weakly, the bequest was drawn out with a kindly expressiveness of his ageing tone.

"Captain," he exclaimed in a long drawn welcoming gesture, but did not rise to his feet to welcome him; the man took a stride forwards standing in the opening doorway, smiling as though he was happy to just be in Luca's company.

"Come," he beckoned, "I must talk with you." During the course of the journey, Luca had plenty of time to study the captain; he was young and ambitious but disgustingly naive. He eyed the captain as he stood in the doorway, his clear, young, open face disturbed Luca, his youthful zealousness to duty and diligence to please his masters by completing his crossing ahead of time left little room in him for selfish frivolities with his guest. Through their many night time discussions, Luca learned of the man's eagerness to please as well as his ambition to rise in the Templer ranks. The voyage, though quick, was boring; Luca would have been pleased to be ashore and about his own business. He remembered his own youthful years an age ago; life was hard and men were tough when he made his own way in the world. There were no advantages for him, not being high born with family influence to project his career forwards; no, he had to earn everything, kill and scheme, but he made it and was proud of every act of selfishness along the way. That was the way people on the lower spokes of the wheel of life survived, by the sharpness of their mind and the will to come out on top. He had to gain his advancement out of a hungered rawness and a need to pull through in a sea of humanity that fought each other like barracudas over their daily frenzied survival. His lip curled in the form of a sneer with the comparisons of the new breeds' backgrounds. No, this puppy dog was not worth the company of one such as Luca; and he was careful not to allow the captain to perceive his feelings or read the look on his face.

The captain, early in years, was a good mariner and eager to promote his ambition, studying hard for his captaincy he held an admiration from others around him. Advancement at his age was a difficult task for one such as he, hence his move to the 'caravans.' These caravans were so-called and were tours of duty patrolling the sea in search for enemy convoys that threatened their naval supplies and other vessels for the purpose of doing battle. Though his ambition drove his expectations high, he was not foolish enough to fall into a fool's trap; neither was he short of courage, for he knew that if luck was with him and success on his side, there would have a greater chance of promotion, of running a command or even a priory back home. His ship was one of seven or eight in the fleet, being small for a ship of battle, but fast, sail assisted, with an armoured bow for ramming and powered by huge oars pulled by slaves.

For those that follow duty, whose purpose in life is serving a cause, proved difficult for the influential Luca to handle. Their nauseous unbending ways of discipline became hard work for manipulation, and their conscience often got the better of them all too easily, that was their weakness.

Luca stretched out his hand to the captain, who in turn thought he was gesturing for assistance in rising. The captain rushed forwards to assist Luca's outstretched arm, Luca cunningly and deftly placed into the captains open hand a jewel the size of a small pigeon's egg. The captain was taken aback, turning his hand to view its content; with an open mouth at the sight of such a large gem, the like of which he had never before seen in his life. He could not compare it with anything; with bright eyes he looked upon it, viewing the gemstones temptation; it was in him to close his hand on the jewel in the palm of his hand. Something in him almost changed with this sight, the jewel's beauty almost burned its enticement; for a moment he almost yielded, feeling his fingers tickle with temptation to keep it.

"What is this?" exclaimed the captain embarrassingly.

"It's just a little bauble, a thank you in recognition of your help and service to me." Luca spoke now as if innocent of any corrupt act; at the same time he enjoyed his act of pernicious temptation.

The captain stared hard at the jewel that sat in the palm of his hand, truly it was beautiful; he openly admitted to Luca that he had never seen it's like before; it would have been simple to pop it into the small purse at his side which represented a small fortune, but he could not.

"Oh no, sir," the captain said graciously, refusing the gift that was offered, and returning it to its donor, with a tinge of regret in his voice, which the tricky merchant smugly bore witness to.

"I could not accept such a gift; it is far too great a prize to receive for such little service." He continued, "Consider my lasting thanks and admiration for all that you have said to my commander, I cannot accept it as reward, since you put it that way."

The old man was on his feet without assistance, deciding that there was no sport to be had with this innocent dullard, surprising the captain, who imagined that Luca needed help to rise.

"Once again, captain," Luca squawked, "you have been very kind and I do not forget those that show me such courtesies." This time he held his empty, limp, sinewy hand forwards as a mark of appreciation, which the captain gladly grasped and shook with alacrity. Full of smiles, the captain suddenly remembered why he came to the cabin. Before Luca could turn away, he spoke out. "I came down to tell you, sir, that as well as docking, a litter awaits you on the quayside."

"Ah", Luca said, with his finger pointing upwards in the air indicating his expectation and time for departure. In a mocking tone that was a veiled appeal to the captain, "Do you think you could arrange for one of your men to have my few belongings handed from your ship?" With nothing else to say, he marched out of the cabin aloof, leaving the captain behind answering to himself obediently, "Of course, sir."

On reaching the open deck, Luca was overcome with the old familiar smells and sounds that rushed upon him and took him like a spiralling eddy back in time.

The day was bright, the sea a turquoise blue and colour was everywhere impressing all the eye could view. The sun dazzled even at this early hour; breathing deep, he stood firmly fixed to the swaying deck and within the hubbub of the ship's activity, his villainous past flooded back before the elderly man's squinting imaginative eyes. The breeze unsettled the harmony of the moment, blowing the ageing silver strands of Luca's hair about his wizened face, encouraging him to poke it defiantly upwards into the wind, taking one more nostalgic long intake of air to fill his flaring nostrils.

Although it had been many years since he last set foot in the port town, the past would never die and would soon rush back to remind him of his earlier days. He smiled knowing how when he was a young and daring man, these ports were considered dangerous territory, that raised a memorable smile; how, he wondered, would our young captain fare here then? There was a snort of disdain, not long for his type; it takes a man with guile, ability and an iron will to know that no one would be allowed to oppose him and live. That's when Luca had been viscous and determined, not one that served others, that was what made him as powerful as he was today and would use every means he could to continue being so.

Sea ports or their dock side havens were known to be dangerous places where the lower dregs of civilisation gathered. It was a world apart from the present, but to someone such as Luca, it was a Kingdom that he once ruled and where he had harvested the crews and villains that aided the building of his maritime empire.

Luca secretly touched on the concealed jewelled dagger that he had beneath his silken jacket; he had grown older, but remained alert, as dangerous as he ever was. Even to such a lucky and slippery individual as he, out there remained many dangers for him; in this town he had crossed and cheated too many men;

170

they had long memories and to their kind grievances and old wounds were hard to heal. Luca's nerves tingled at the dangers ahead; his visit this time was of the utmost importance to him; it was to be brief and with a minimal risk, therefore he would set aside such likelihood of mere grievances in order to complete his task, in that he was not prepared to fail.

Luca had few friends but an army of old enemies, and his passage through the crowded streets could not pass quick enough for him. Apart from his enemies, there were those officials that he had once been able to buy favour from; they may have grown older and changed. Luca was a master of the human character; with a smile, he knowingly suspected that a villain remained a villain whoever ruled here. Perhaps they now served his enemy; that was a good enough reason to have his business done quickly so that he could return to the safety of his own havens in Venice. Although times and his shape and appearance had changed, the fact that he was visiting his old comrade in crime was no assurance. Criminals watch other criminals and employ spies to do their work; because Luca was not a fool, he would not chance such a happening and had sent word of his coming to have the streets cleared of any possible threats to his visit. It was, to him, a simple way of revealing his vulnerability, but believing that he had little choice, he preferred to make such arrangements as he thought fitting. An escort of a dozen riders would secure his safe passage; only the most foolhardy, he believed, would dare attempt to have him waylaid or chance incarceration to be left to rot in some dark filthy dungeon. Life in the cells or even the galleys hadn't changed and in some quarters of the high office of ruler, prisoners were expensive to maintain; shunting them off to the galleys at least turned a coin for those in office. Any attempt to waylay Luca would meet with his vengeance; fools such as those will never learn; he would set examples and flay alive those that opposed him; to complete his lesson he would mercilessly eradicate the family and all those known friends to that person. Mercy was not an attribute that Luca took to his heart, force and pain that led to a lingering death were the tools he employed and he wield them with a loving indulgence. He smiled smugly, almost jumping with glee at his recollections of his slippery past, and with an excited beating heart he eagerly looked forwards to be passing along those streets where he could recall those unscrupulous dealings; danger, coupled with the excitement of chancing his luck, once more elated him. Dirty fights were his line of thrills as well as a passion for thuggery. Once, he recalled, he came close to death in an alley, but with a memorable sigh he was saved by his comrades and later indulged in his other favourite pastime of drunkenness and spending frenzied nights with wild women.

Times had changed, with it the excitement of all that sort of life was long in his past; he was no longer the reckless adventurer he believed he once was. Now a sober and successful powerful merchant, why, he could tell the world he was doing business with the devil and no one would question him. His trading scope was so wide and varied that it took him into the oddest of places, rewarding him always with a certain profitable delight whilst dealing with the most dangerous of people. His raison d'être in life was about money and profit that would underpin his empire with ever strengthening stability. His grandson, he envisaged, would strengthen it even further, to carry the business forwards into another age so that the Rici name would live on. He cared not what people thought of him, but his secret dream was that his name would live forever. To achieve this great desire, he would trample ruthlessly over those that stood in his way and he would do it without a blinking of the eye. He understood fear only too well, it was a tool used as an extension to his business methods; but the cowardly streak in Luca made him step with trepidation with those that he was here to approach. It was his objective to appoint an old friend and partner in past crimes to make this contract. Luca was himself a dangerous man, but his core was weak and self-serving; this contract that carried so much importance for him was with the most feared of people in the whole of the known world of the East. They worked in mysterious ways with potions that he had no knowledge of; they walked unafraid through darkness and even walls, so he was told. No fires could burn bright enough to discourage them from their missions and no man strong enough to withstand their warnings that death awaited them; one thing he knew for certain was that they never failed in their work, a work he believed was mixed with devilry.

Luck, he suspected would play no part in the purpose of this operation, because they would desperately want what was within his possession. Luca held a prize that would prove to be irresistible, a prize that held an irreplaceable value in hearts of every Muslim. With this in mind, he knew those that he sought would zealously support him in the recovery of his grandson. Everything he craved and valued lay in his grandson's safe return; he cared not what it would cost or how many of their kind were to lose their lives in its achievement; their loss of blood to achieve this end would be the price of their success.

Power that called the tune that men danced to is a powerful attribute to wield; he knew well of this possession, it turned the mind of one such as this merchant; to know that he was superior, nothing would stop him from reaching out and taking all that what was within his covetous grasp.

A cutting wind whipped into him, bringing him back to the present, causing him to spread his feet for fear of being blown over as his lightweight silken coat caught the wind, billowing like the sail of a ship, threatening to force him off his balance, but he was steady. The subsiding forces of the wind brought back the searing heat, causing him to suddenly sweat as the sun's rays burnt onto the nape of his uncovered neck, warning him that it was time to escape the threat of the building, incessant heat. Just in time, the escort arrived to a clatter of hooves on the stony quaysides surface; Luca swiftly made his way to the comfort of the litter.

Once ensconced, he drew the curtain aside and gave the order to proceed to the home of his oldest trading acquaintance, Nazir the Persian, originally from Latakia; that was another of his accomplishments that kept him smiling. It was quite a joke between them of how Nazir was so named; he had never been anywhere near Persia, but for the sake of his own importance with strangers, it lent an air of respectability whenever he was introduced as such.

On their meeting, Luca had embraced his old colleague eagerly; there were many pleasantries to exchange after so long an absence of their friendship; they both gave way to retiring to discuss the old days and Luca's reasons for his brief return. Stepping back to view his friend's rotund abundance of size, he approved it had been built on his avaricious appetite for gastronomic extravagancies that most poor men could only dream to savour. Nazir's giggling laugh, Luca noted, had also remained; he was glad of that, for it somehow amused him, it always gave Luca a sense of easing whenever they had been successful in their roguery and dirty deals for keeping his wit as sharp as ever.

Nazir was reputed to be in close contact and, most importantly, in the favour with Alamut in north-western region of Khorassan, the stronghold of the dreaded Assassins; and it was this reason Luca told his friend for his being present.

It had been many long years since Nazir had occasion to take the long trip to visit the eagle's nest, after which the fortress had been named, but in recent years the sect had established a new stronghold just days away from his home since their influence and strength had increased. Whenever the trader, Nazir, had dealings with the sect, he did so through Hassan the priest, also named as the mad dog, one of his many cursed names. He made outrageous physical attacks on authority and ruling dignitaries under the orders of his master, The Old Man of the Mountain. Hassan was chosen by the Old Man of the Mountain and placed him in this part of the land because of his ability and loyalty. Deviousness in planning the political assassinations on behalf of his master was his speciality; his devotees carried out his orders under the influence of hashish, a tool devised by the Old Man to control those whose objective was to strike terror through the Moslem world and to build up the order against the Abbasid Caliphs of Baghdad.

His new stronghold was less than three days ride away; it was not Nazir's favourite place to visit; he was always fearful and never felt at ease anytime that he had to travel to Mas'yaf; although his transactions with Hassan were handsomely profitable, he was always relieved to conclude his business with him.

He was, Nazir believed, truly mad, though he dared not even disagree with him on any matter that would raise his temper. A trader to the last and with a silvery tongue, Nazir found great difficulty working with the madman. In truth, he was afraid of him and had good reason to be. Hassan was notorious for flaring into rages that would impose a forced hospitality on his visitors, spending the night in the cells of Mas'yaf. Nazir was clever and shrewd and one of the few that dared trade with Hassan; his money was too good to be ignored. He could not stand by and watch a contract go to a rival, and in cases of disagreement he would slither and slide like a snake, never grovelling, for Hassan would see through that. Nazir had learnt to use his methods of persuasion to glean a greater profit from the madman, having to avail the most outlandish arguments without upsetting Hassan to convince him of his point of view. He always came away sweating, wishing that there was some other way to do business without stepping into his lair; and besides, the money he wheedled from Hassan was hard won and duly deserved, so he thought. How, he asked himself many times, could a man relax in the presence of one who continually talked of the zombies that he created and their undying loyalty to him? Hassan's words were like veiled threats to the poor trader. It was his opinion whenever he was under Hassan's roof that no one in their right mind dared ever to be so stupid as to either trust him or to be talked into staying for longer than was necessary. Never would he tarry, for the madman, as far as Nazir believed, Hassan always hungered after new devotees into his order of drugged assassins. Fearful of his powers, he suspected that to be so foolish as to linger could result in the danger of never being seen again. Should Hassan ever stop to observe Nazir's mood for leaving, he would witness a man scared witless; but the trader was valuable to the madman, being one of the very few that would deliver those special things that he had a liking for.

The very name of Hassan made most people recoil as if they had been struck by a plague, and good reason there was too; 'Hassan the grave digger' was another of his names, after the amount of victims that had fallen to his assassin's ruthless and indiscriminate purposes. He had risen to becoming the most powerful man outside of Persia within the sect, second only to the Old Man of the Mountain himself.

He had stabilised his position in the wild rocky hills south of Tripoli in the fortress of Mas'yaf, more localised than that of Alamut. Links with Hassan had remained somewhat tenuous between the villains from Tripoli, although Alamut had given them aid, they were uncompromising in that they expected any gains he made to be favours to be returned. Those favours were always honoured and Luca sensibly acknowledged their value, though he kept his distance, for he was fearful of them and their activities. Business was good, but getting too cosy with a gang of madmen with political and religious ideals was not. Having indirectly assisted Luca in the killings on land and the high seas and in the taking of slaves, Alamut was content to turn its head away from their deceits and trickery. When Latakia became too hot for their dealings, Luca moved Nazir onwards and upwards in his seedy organisation to respectability in another port.

At the house of his friend he was entertained in fine style like a prodigal son; on their meeting Luca was respectfully welcomed and introduced into the comforts of Nazir's home, where they availed themselves into a most luxuriously decorated and comfortable room that overlooked a sunny vista on the sea and its endless horizon; when the winds were gentle such as at the present, they rested in the balmy atmosphere of Nazir's terrace, eating and drinking. Filled with mirth, they spent the morning gormandising on assorted dishes of fruits and savouries whilst drinking their fill, laughing at their past pursuits as younger men. Young women scantily dressed passed in and out of the room bringing the various dishes to them; Nazir could not help fondling each one that came to him, running his hand across their bodies and admiring their form making lewd suggestions, as they in turn attentively ministered to the comfort of their master. With women he was weak, Luca told him as much, but as long as he delivered in their sordid trade agreements, it mattered not how he indulged himself to Luca.

After they smoked and relaxed on expansive divans, Nazir offered Luca a woman of his household more than once as the completion to his desert, but this day Luca was not interested; declining meant that there was obviously something in need of discussion.

It was long after the eating that Luca believed the time for small talk was passed; beginning to unveil his scheme to his friend, he further surprised Nazir that on this occasion money was of no importance. It was Luca's intention to have a meeting arranged with a representative of the Shi'ite religious sect known as the hashashin. Nazir was taken by surprise and almost jumped off his divan in fright to silence Luca from speaking anything further until he was certain that his servants could not eavesdrop into their conversation. Although his house servants had been selected by his hand, he was uncertain if any of them might have had any link with that particular organisation. Where Hassan was concerned, Nazir was afraid, for all he knew his spies might very well be in his own house.

"Be careful my friend!" Nazir quickly looked around to see if any of the servants were about. He placed a finger across his thick lips and almost developed a sweat; in a warned whisper, he advised Luca against using the name of the sect openly; odd things can happen to a man that speaks their name without caution; he gestured further with his plump sweaty hands to keep his voice low. The heads of the two men dropped closer towards each other to maintain a strict state of secrecy, Nazir spoke of the Old Man of the Mountain almost with reverence and a quaking voice.

Sitting erect, Luca disappointedly burst out in a questioning tone loudly with surprise at his friend's reaction,

"We know these people, I thought you had strong links," said Luca, angered by what at first appeared to be a terrible mistake, he challenged Nazir loudly,
"Have you lied to me and brought me all this way for nothing?"
Once more, Nazir screwed his face up and gestured with his hands for quiet and they dropped once more into their cogitative huddle. He reassured Luca that he did have certain links with the hashashin, but for the reasons of his own personal security it had to remain secret. Wriggling his fat form uncomfortably from irritation, provoked by Luca's ignorance, he recalled the events of some years previous in another city. A leader of the assassins himself was duped into a meeting by a vizier that had been a so called protector of the sect. The vizier had sprung a trap for this feared individual and had the leader murdered and beheaded. His body was placed on display in a public place and in no time at all the word of his death had spread throughout the markets of the city. So relieved were the towns people to be rid of the evil power that suffocated their freedom that they frantically took up the sword and ran through the streets slaughtering many of the known followers of the sect. By night, there were hundreds lying dead in the streets, only the dogs were left to fight over their flesh. A shiver went down Nazir's back at the imagined scene and thought of

having his body left to the dogs to wrestle over, further insisting that was why his connections had to remain secret; also why those members within the sect were everywhere to ascertain that their presence was also safeguarded. Luca settled back in a slight pique from his position of agitated annoyance, relaxing again onto his cushion. "The Old Man," muttered Nazir reverentially, "is very dangerous, and he was guarded and fearful of any outcome of an unsuccessful visit to Masyaf."

"I have thought of that," Luca said with a twinkling eye filled with his own sense of inflated confidence. "What I offer will bind your friendship to him and reward you a thousand times over."

The sound of that caused Nazir's eyebrows to raise, bringing a gleam of light into the fat man's eyes.

The smile that filled Nazir's face spoke volumes but somehow Luca could tell he was not truly accepting his words. After power, which Hassan already had, "what else was there for him?" Luca asked. Nazir's face was blank, "He does not require money or riches and you cannot bribe a man such as he to your way, he already has power enough; I warn you Luca, my friend, do not trifle with this particular man, it could be your undoing."

A smile filled Luca's smug face while he drummed his hand on his chest; his company sat patiently waiting, suspecting something dark as Luca sat knowingly unafraid; something extra ordinary would be forthcoming. Inserting his hand inside his richly-coloured blue silken robes, he proceeded to draw from inside an aged old rolled leather scroll. Placing it between himself and his friend, he pushed it across the tiled space to where it came to rest at the divan to where his friend had seated himself. Luca instructed his friend to open the scroll, but with the greatest of care so as not to spoil its delicacy. Carefully and with the greatest of care, he did as Luca had ordered, half way open Nazir exclaimed almost blankly.

"It's a prayer scroll," he said staring at his friend. A faint smug smile broke on Luca's face as it became recognised and he nodded his head to continue.

"If you open it very carefully you may find a little more," he teased.

The stubby fat fingers of Nazir unrolled it with subdued eagerness; it revealed more characters of gold with colourful relief work around its decorous border. His friend's eyes began to bulge in awe, realising the treasure that had reverentially unfurled; reading it, he realised before him lay a treasure beyond his imagination. His drooling mouth lay open and became drier with the inrush of air signifying diffidence. He stared across to Luca, amazement in his eyes, he asked if this treasure was genuine, to which Luca smiled and nodded with smug omnipotent assent. Hesitant, with a deepening and worried frown, the smile had temporarily left the fat man's face as he questioned Luca to seriously consider not to trade with the Shi'ite assassins.

"I beseech you, Luca, if you have any doubt of its authenticity tell me now, for failure to do so will cost both of us our lives." Swallowing hard he continued, "It is one thing to play games with ordinary people, but to try and poke fun at hashashin is risking too much. You realise that this document will be studied meticulously each day for any fault; Hassan is a scientific man and will have many ways to test it"

"Let him," said Luca. Nervously jubilant, Nazir allowed his eyes to flick across the scroll and each time his eyes appeared more open. Betraying his avaricious thoughts to Luca, he found difficulty in containing his greed, suggesting in a near squeaking voice that had left him devoid of saliva, he began to speak.

"A genuine prize such as this could have a thousand men killed, why not just sell it?"

Luca leaned forwards delivering his order, "It has to go to Alamut or Mas'yaf," he stated sternly. "I need you to speak to him or his envoy."

His hand dipped into a hidden pocket inside his robe and produced from within an insignificant but, by its appearance, a weighty leather pouch, which he tossed casually before his friend Nazir.

"I believe that this will suffice your expenses," Luca added with a sly grin and an almost mocking growl in his voice.

The fat man nonchalantly took it, trying not to show his interest and continued his discourse, at the same time reticently weighing the bag in his hand. He could not help but loosen the tie that held its neck; he looked downwards to view its contents, which he had spilt into his other open soft hand. Nazir suddenly stopped talking, he was dumbfounded, and his opened mouth could no longer function at the surprising contents of pearls and rubies. Luca broke the silence.

"You have my request, old friend, believe me that as a bargaining lever it would ensure a successful conclusion to my request."

Before them, lay the open, sacred scroll written by the hand of the prophet Muhammad himself. Nazir tried once more to persuade Luca that he could sell it in Egypt or Damascus for a King's fortune.

"I know the right people for this type of very special sale," he said with an almost drooling mouth,

"I tell you Luca, you could buy your favour from Hassan with gold. I know how to get the best from such a sale; all the wealth of the Persian Empire could not purchase such a document, for it is truly holy writ." The day passed quickly and Luca had more business to conclude; now that his business with Nazir was completed to his satisfaction, Luca eased himself to his feet. Fighting back all the grunts and efforts that come with age in his rising, and full of his conceited ego, he stated that he really had to leave to prepare himself in readiness to dine with his most Royal Highness at the palace. The face on his friend dropped as he paused in astonishment at such a statement, then he laughed heartily saying "You are still a sly old fox, you have not lost the knack for having your feet in every camp, and I wish you well, my friend."

The two partners concluded their business and said their farewells with a hint of regret, this time their meeting was without the usual risk and excitement of those times long past. The reward came easy, the business swift and without the old satisfaction that made them wheeze with laughter, no one would hear the tale of this exploit. The bulge of the gem-filled bag in Nazir's hand made him hot with excitement and regret, knowing that he could not convince his friend to sell the scroll elsewhere; there was a reluctance to waste this prize; like a gambler who has to give up on a winning streak, his heart was heavy. Before their final parting, Luca's friend personally assured him that his request would reach the ears of those within the mountains in three days.

Antioch

It was a magnificent spectacle, even from a distance; the citadels defences were awesome. On reaching the city gate, the troop of men came to a halt, marvelling the city and its construction. The great biscuit-coloured walls towered above them reflecting its natural coloured stone in the bright sunlight, power and splendour reflecting in its image.

"This was surely one of our greatest victories; how on earth did we manage it?" prompted one in the company.

"With guile, I am told" said Edward.

"How's that?" enquired Hubert.

"I was once told that we never had a chance to take it by siege, but it wasn't without trying; in the end, one has to revert to using other methods such as bribing one of the guards, an Armenian I think it was turned by lust for the love of gold. . 'Gold my friends,' he said addressing them all, 'is a very powerful persuader.' One night the paid insider slipped a ladder down against the outside of the wall and a party of chosen men climbed up. Once inside, we slaughtered all before us until we were able to open the gates that had previously barred our entry. We won the city easily, but the fortress on yonder mount was another matter."

Passing through St George's gate, one of the great arched gateways of the outer wall, they found themselves on the busy market streets of the city. Thronging masses swarmed around stalls; traders haggled eagerly and noisily with their buyers over the cost of their wares. It was busy, typical of markets throughout the East carrying their familiar goods and smells of spices on hot fires on the air wherever one went; and the banter of everyday buyers was ever present, lively with a cacophony of sounds of different tongues and dialects. The crowd were busy tending to their own affairs; no one took any notice of the small troop until the riders had to force their way through, much to the complaints of those that were interrupted in their business. Those that gave resistance were pushed like toys into the stalls or other bystanders idly talking; curses followed but none dare look the riders in the eye. Robert became uncomfortable; he caught sight of an insolent bystander flicking his eyes suspiciously at the people he passed by; his kind were not liked and even distrusted. Robert had no illusions that his enemy watched with ever-mindful eyes their every movement, though presently he hoped that they were probably seen for what they were; westerners that were new arrivals. They were indeed new arrivals in a land that had seen much in its time; he had been told from his bible stories that this place had been like a melting pot for every civilisation who fought over it; if only it could talk back, what would it tell us and who knows who will follow us in time to come? Wars, Robert thought, he himself had known nothing else since he had donned his armour and followed the example of his father before him and here he was now in the middle of another in the making. The troop that followed were apart from Robert, making it appear that they were an escort for the ladies in the litter coming up behind. Robert mistrusted them, he twitched at the thought they could be connected to what he was sent to find out; calling to his men, he told them to be careful not to speak of their mission for being here to ensure that they gave little away.

His mind was on recent events as they passed along making their way up through the crowded streets and onto the main causeway that led up to the main castle where he expected to meet up with the captain to render his report. It still bothered him not knowing the importance of the females; who they were and on whose orders they acted was still eluding him. He could never have met the like of these women during his tours in the field; he wondered if they had come from beyond Syria; in this land, he mused, nothing was straight forward. Rubbing his dry hand across his sweating brow, he struggled to think out his problem; frustration filled him over what little intelligence he was able to grasp and then it was mainly based on conjecture. Too much coincidence and evasion of truth had passed; it also angered him that somewhere security was inadequate, making him suspect that all the intelligence leaked from his own people. Admittedly, the men that attacked them could have by passed the citadel without attention being drawn to their presence; hadn't those officers in command here heard about scouts and sentries to secure the valley? It seemed duty was a poor excuse for security; it was their own backs that they were supposed to be protecting as well as trade routes, did they not have a care? So many questions filled his head, it mystified him at the way this Prince went about their business of security; God in heaven, they must have their heads in the sand. Do these people think that because there is peace that they can forget what has passed? The Saracen warriors are like rabid dogs on a chain baying to be free to wreak havoc over the land.

Looking around, it eased him to see the sand-coloured mud houses, people at work and relaxed; peace, he thought it brought normality back into the land; for most, respect was the only tool necessary to winning the people over. There was no doubt this mystical land produced many strange scenes and events, the varying people who walked the streets were from every region and beyond bringing customs and habits from afar, truly it thrilled him to be here.

Reaching the castle they approached the guards at the inner gate, the company dismounted and stated their business was with the captain; once accepted, they walked through the inner castle wall and into the great yard, with his friends following behind. Across the great square, he could not help but be alarmed at the sight of Muslim soldiers actively presenting themselves as a guard, another small group were standing around acting as if they were in their own barrack, showing no fear to any of the western troops.

Whilst the women's personal future plans remained unknown to Robert, everything he took in was a picture built to the success of the Prince's rule. Regretful that the women had seen Robert's effectiveness in battle, they too had realised that it would be foolish to consider him as nothing less than a threat.

The sun never gave up its intensity in this land, even with their light clothing, sweat poured from the bodies of the knights, the thoughts of washing their bodies in cool water was a luxury that had to wait; other duties demanded attention, no matter how they had dreamt of bathing.

After tying up their horses, they stood in the shade of the stables. Christ, it was hot out there; Hubert dabbed his brow holding his sleeve against it as if to take away the heat. "I thought that no one was supposed to know anything about our being here," he said, trying to raise a debate. He continued, "how, or more to the point who, could have sent the soldiers."

"Robert," he called out, "when you see this captain tell him that the Muslims on the road wore the uniforms of the Teutonic knights. In truth there were a lot more answers required to other questions as well," Godwin angrily commented. It never ceased to amaze them all as to how information about all manner of things and events travelled so quickly out here; in their puzzlement and debate, they spent some time going over past events.

"What you have said is quite true," Robert added and it bothered him much. "I can only suggest there must have been leaked information of our route as well as our business in Antioch, with suspicions as to how the mysterious females just happened to dovetail into our mission." Hubert suggested that he would go to the pigeon lofts and get a message to Acre; in the meantime he would report in and he gestured to the others that they should try to eat and refresh themselves. Robert walked away mumbling to du Bray that these people in the north had a peculiarity to their dialect that he thought little of." I dislike the term 'Franj,' it shows no respect, and we seem to give little back," replied du Bray. It had caught on and was common place these days and the people soon learnt that the westerners didn't like the term either. That was their first slip exposing the females; could she have been of these parts, she also knowingly implied that they would meet again soon, she knew something that he did not; Christ knows how she was able to foretell that. Following the events, he could not fail to believe how they ended up protecting them.

Robert stopped as if something had hit him, and holding on to his friend du Bray's arm said, "I don't believe I'm thinking it, but the leak we seek could most likely be in Acre. We are here and so are these women," he stated, hopelessly. "Now I am beginning to believe it to be so." Robert rubbed his chin as though in thought, "My friend," he declared, "it seems we may have become a part of a greater scheme in future events; don't ask me to explain, it's a gut feeling that drives my belief. Somehow we are bound up with the women and where it will lead us and I hate to think about it."

Whilst the others stabled their horses and inquired as to the availability of accommodations, before leaving, Robert cautioned his friends to keep a watch out for anything unusual, especially those troops. They definitely were out of place, and forcing out a further breath added that they should reconnoitre the area as best they could. On the way over to the captain's chamber the heat of the day burnt into their backs, Robert and du Bray entered the building, it was instantly noticeably cooler; here he was to render his report on the events so far, as ordered by the Grand Prior of Acre.

Entering the outer room of the Keep, they expected to announce their arrival to the Sergeant at Arms for admission to speak with the Captain, only to find the office vacant of military personnel. At a desk scribbling away, a monk seemed to represent command; there was nobody else around; he, it seemed, was the Captain's scribe and when questioned as to the whereabouts of his master, he replied that there would be a short wait until the captain was to return.

Away from the heat of the sun, the room offered comfort; they were happy to avail themselves to a seat to be relieved by the chambers cooling effect. Du Bray, took the advantage of lounging on a bench, he was enjoying the relaxing temperature and viewing his surroundings, though he received objectionable looks from the monk scribbling away at the desk. Du Bray was taken by the strength of the fortresses structure; no wonder, he thought that this place was impregnable. After some considerable time had lapsed, Robert, having impatiently paced the floor long enough, believed he was likely to wear a groove in the stone slabs beneath his feet; it prompted a suspicion that this long a wait might have been a captain's ploy to usurp an interruption from strangers. He had experienced it on other occasions with lax commanders and their minions. Time was passing and there was still no sign of the Captain, they were growing fidgety and not used to such blatant discourtesy.

Du Bray, ever short on his patience when waiting, wanted to leave to find the others; he could not idly sit around wasting time doing nothing. Robert agreed and bade du Bray to go and let them know what the waiting around was about.

"Yes, go and help to see what accommodations we can expect to have," promising to join them all later on after he had submitted his report. To remove himself from indolent ears, he walked du Bray to the doorway, speaking confidentially to him as he went. The scribe at the desk slyly looked upwards trying to appear to take no notice yet leaning his head to one side straining to overhear their conversation. Reaching the large wooden door of the Keep, Robert drew it ajar to allow the sounds of the courtyard to filter through so as to deny the inquisitive clerk from clearly overhearing anything that may be said.

The dry summer heat rushed at him as the door was opened, which was not the only shock that they had. In the courtyard sat the litter; the women blatantly aware that their presence caused some embarrassment sat unconcerned as if was their right to sit in full view. They were waiting for someone or something; what, he could not tell. He could not help but stare at them; there was deceit in their eyes, at least that was what he imagined; as God was his judge, he believed there was nothing but treachery afoot but he was helpless to do anything about it. The temerity of their gaze maddened him, yet he could do nothing; they were guests of the Prince of Antioch and they knew well that they were disarmed in their need to render the truth from them.

"What the hell are they doing here?" he exclaimed angrily. "Keep an eye on them, du Bray, and see where and what they get up," and with a noise that came from the depths of his being he growled, "they bother me." Their watching eyes lifted as they heard sounds of soldiers approaching. Eight Muslim infantrymen appeared, running effortlessly at a jogging pace across the courtyard and stopped at each corner of the litter blocking the women for a moment from his sight as if they appeared to be receiving orders from the women. "Now tell me that I'm not imagining this, those soldiers are sporting the uniforms of the Caliph of Damascus. How is it they are here inside this citadel and taking orders from these women?"

"I'll bet my last gold piece that they are up to no damn good." The soldiers lifted the litter and carried it away to the other side of the rectangle, but to reach its point for their accommodations it had to go by Robert, and as it passed by the repaired green silk curtain drew aside slightly for Robert to receive a cheeky smile and a mocking wave. He could not help but return a half smile at the young woman's boldness; instead of abuse issuing forth from the litter, the veiled face that had haunted him briefly smiled, or so he fancied. He could not deny that this young woman had played a strong role in moving his emotions, and in truth he knew she still tormented him; his curiosity remained driven to see the face that remained concealed behind the speckled gauze, her eyes danced and her lips parted and mouthed a message in passing. Did he imagine the message in her words that came so invitingly from her sensuous lips?

"We will meet again, franj," though they were silent words, they seemed clear enough for him, and in passing, her head turned away and the curtain closed. She was goading him and he knew it; he would not withdraw from the game; that woman, he told himself, was in for a surprise; he believed the next time he was invited to her kind of banquet, he would not be denied the entree of his meal. Two could play those games and it will be no good protesting when he has his fork in his hand. He smirked, wondering who she really was; Robert could not help but feel that he was being sucked into the quagmire of his undisciplined emotions. Sadly that was a pathway that had no direction for him being a trained soldier; before he would afford such a trivial luxury of a soft body next to him; he must first concentrate on his mission, after all it was his duty. Curious of this activity, Robert stopped to ask the guard outside building the reason for all the bustle and fuss. "Things are changing," answered the guard, "I hear many rumours, sir, the origin of which I am not truly privy to, but if you ask me I think that my master has been in the sun for too long and is not thinking as he should. How's that?" Robert's curiosity was like his thirst and in need of quenching; more information about what was happening could only help him; sadly, the guard was reluctant to speak further of events or share any more tit bits with his enquirer. "All I will say is, now that we are at peace. My Lord has taken it upon himself to do great things, he's invited important and notable dignitaries from Damascus. I can tell you, sir, he tarries on dangerous ground. In my opinion, for all its worth, he's gone off his head, he has." Continuing, he informed Robert that a fine detachment of Muslim troops had arrived earlier the previous day. To his eye, they appeared to be seasoned soldiers and to his mind, unnecessary as escorts for the visitors, simply to assure all arrangements were properly prepared for the Amman.

Within a short time of Robert's retreat back into the coolness of the reception of the Captain's office, the thin weedy-looking cleric dressed in a brown monkish robe made of coarse, hairy material presented himself before him. Approaching Robert, he announced in a most obsequious manner that the Captain was unable to see him at present; he was entertaining the visiting Amman from Damascus. Intimating to Robert that in the waiting moments, patience and prayer could fill that period of anxiety; the Captain was a busy man and could not easily break away from the visiting dignitary. Should he wish it, the mealy mouthed individual continued, he would happily be his escort to the chapel were they could pray together until such time as his report could be rendered. Taking Robert by the arm, he attempted, in a gentle sort of way, to forcibly encourage him forwards. With such an off handed answer, Robert's anger rose; he wasn't having any of this; agitation bubbled at the neglect of the Captain to overlook the importance of a military visitor from Acre. With overflowing anger, he grabbed at the weedy little man lifting him into the air so that his sandals slipped from his feet to remain on the floor beneath his dangling digits. Hoisting him even higher, Robert threatened through clenched teeth that if he refrained from fetching the Captain he would seek him out and may soon find himself without an office to administer.

Suspended in the grip of his most violent visitor, the white-faced cleric quaked in fear; this stranger surely had no respect or fear of the mother church or its ecclesiastic classes. Speechless to concur when placed back on his feet, his only effort to react was to submissively nod his head vigorously in agreement. Never had this cleric been treated this way, it was unthinkable for any man to lay hands on a man of the cloth. A sneer showed on Robert's face; he cared not a jot for clerics, especially those types that obstructed his duty, the higher they were the worse he feared they were; he did not fear them and would whip them all to hell's gates if the cause merited such action. In a furious temper, he ordered the cleric to tell his master, "Sir Robert of Simmonwood, council to the King of Jerusalem and aide to the Grand Prior of Acre, does not like being treated as any ordinary messenger." Gently shaking him one more time to understand the necessity of the order, he looked into the eyes of the cleric and only when his ashen face appeared as though there was little blood left in his head did he see that the message was well understood. The monk, speechless at such brutal action, nodded his frightened head all the time he was held; fearful of this man standing before him, he couldn't wait to be liberated from the mighty grip of his tormentor. Robert released him so that he could refit his feet into his sandals before delivering his message.

"Right away, sir, my Lord, right away. I was not aware of your illustrious rank, you never told me who you were and please forgive me for any oversight towards your treatment."

He slunk from the chamber with his position of office sullied; slightly reduced to a sullen and subdued manner, in the passage he was heard to complain in a whimpering voice.

"It was not my fault, who was he to treat me this way?" before disappearing into the shadows.

Robert was glad to see the back of such an obnoxious and obsequious type; such as his kind left a bad taste in his mouth, sitting behind desks telling men of action what they can and cannot do. It was not his wish to have to expand on invention to the cleric or anyone, knowing that was the only way to have the captain leave his socialising and attend to the business of security. He paced the room anxiously until the officer finally showed himself.

The ageing captain presented himself in the doorway of his office chamber. Making his way toward Robert, his outstretched hand of greeting reached out as he crossed the cold stone floor, matching the sincerity of the sentiment of his words of greeting towards Robert with a similar cold disdain.

"My dear friend, I am so sorry to have kept you waiting," the mellifluous tones floated across the room with sickly intonation, not unlike his cleric. For a moment, Robert wanted to react violently at the unwarranted sincerity that reached his ears.

"I am surprised that you do not attend messengers from Acre with any urgency," said Robert frostily and with sarcasm in his voice.

The false smile of welcome on the Prior's face slipped away to a frowning seriousness.

"Now look here," the Captain replied defensively, "you simply do not understand. I have a duty to my Prince and my presence was requested."

This was a reply that infuriated Robert, who would not tolerate such convenience of sliding in the duties of high office, especially a laxness that put entertaining before security.

"Your duty is to the King, sir, and as I do not need to remind you, is paramount to your Prince's business."

With tempestuous forces in his voice, Robert lashed out at the Prior's inadequacy, his attention stressing the insecurity of his locality. In concluding his harangue, he added, "No doubt you are unaware that we had to do battle with no less than twenty or more Seljuk spies on the road to the citadel this very day," pointing to a bundle of uniforms left behind by du Bray, "here are the remains of their subterfuge as proof."

Without allowing the captain to answer he added, "Your county, it seems, is a place of unrest and insecurity to our own people as well as friendly traders and the like, do not tell me that you do not patrol it."

"I have to take my orders from my Prince," the old captain sputtered weakly. "I am sworn to him and," he added, "believe me, I am loyal to the cause and will always pay homage to the King before others."

The captain was a man of responsible position and Robert's accusatory words consumed his very being with guilt at his obvious laxity.

"As for the events of this day, I was not aware of this matter," he stuttered to regain his control whilst his whole body flushed with embarrassment. "For once there is a peace in the land. Yes, it is true that we have relaxed." The captain's explanation was swiftly stopped dead. Robert retaliated, "And you have the temerity to stand before me with excuses?"

On reflection, he knew he had served the King well on and off the field of battle even though he was younger then. His ageing, and in this time of peace, he allowed himself to forward a weak excuse; the peace and age it seemed was turning him soft, but having a younger man remind him of his duty irked him and inflamed his anger at such an abrupt exposure to the truth.

"How dare you speak to me in such a tone?" he barked, "I am still the captain here and don't you forget it."

Robert reached inside his tunic and drew from it a sealed parchment displaying the Templar seal. "I suggest you read this and speak with me in the morning. In the meantime," he added, "my men and I need somewhere to rest. There are six of us and we are in need of reasonable accommodation. Would you, in your high position of office, be able to give us shelter and food to sustain us for what is left of the day?" He did not enjoy sarcasm and regretted his outburst. The captain held up his hand in a gesture to stop; he did not speak, only nodded his assent.

Again, the ageing captain found it difficult to reply; embarrassment overtook him knowing that he was duty bound to do it. He looked down at the seal on the document which displayed the official Seal of the Temple, two Templar knights riding the same horse - indicating that what is mine is also my brothers'.

Mm, the sight of the seal sharpened his wit, understanding that this missive was carrying a weight of importance. "I might have some difficulty there," he stammered. Robert looked back in disbelief, which the old Captain caught sight of. "Give me a moment or two," he said, hesitating, feeling that his treatment of a King's councillor might not go unmentioned, "I'll see what I can do."

When the Captain left the room to make arrangements, he returned after a longer than normal absence with the cleric who Robert previously had encountered; showing himself again in an ingratiating manner, he asked Robert to follow him to join his friends so that they could be escorted to their lodgings. Along the way, he tactfully explained to Robert that he had sent a messenger on ahead to enquire of the very best lodgings available. Robert was in no mood to reply and continued in silence the rest of the way.

When the captain was left alone, he raged from having undergone such a confrontation with the younger knight. "Damn, damn and curse him!" he shouted, slamming his clenched hand down hard on the desk in his anger; the orders that Robert had given to him remained in his hand, which grew into a clenched fist as the upset surged through him again. He looked at the crumpled scroll and threw it onto the desk and to settle his feelings that he had deserved to return to the more temperate atmosphere of the function in the Prince's quarters.

The remainder of the group were waiting at the stable block, impatient and quite worked up about having to remain within such a smelly building and under guard; it had been most of the afternoon that they had been confined and tension was becoming awkward for any that approached them.

It was the time for the sun to begin to dip towards the horizon as dusk began to fall; just in time to keep tempers from flaring Robert appeared with his escort. Relieved on seeing their leader, the group became reassured of their anxieties for him and immediately began complaining about their treatment; anxious from such a time lapse, they issued forth a barrage of questions about their refreshment and lodgings. Strained by their wait Robert's escort became most uneasy and nervous; he feared a situation was brewing and anticipated that he might be drawn into it. Uneasily, he informed them as passively as possible that another brother was being sent to escort them; he found the task of informing them onerous after his own ordeal with the captain, Robert thanked the monk for his escort who informed the company that as a senior cleric he had other duties which forbade him to leave the safety of the castle enclosure. Reassuring them that another monk was due and would escort them into town where accommodations were being prepared. The waiting group became more heated and agitated at this statement about leaving the castle; it probably meant they were being farmed out here, there and everywhere. The place was in an uproar, this was a bad show of hospitality and something that they did not expect. Distressed with the present atmosphere of disappointment within the company of hostile fighting men, the Captain's clerk knew better to wait around, making haste in his retreat.

Finally, their escort entered the stable and, unknown to what had happened earlier with the senior cleric, announced calmly his duty; apologising for the delay, he assured the anxious company that they would soon be contented, fed and made welcome, as befitting men of their rank.

The sun was setting as they were led out of the inner castle and down the hill some way towards the town before entering a now shadowy almost deserted street; night beggars had taken up residence, some spent their time looking for scraps whilst others sat quietly rattling a cup for alms as the party strode past. Robert thought they were little more than spies paid to watch and report those that passed out of the gate; the crowds that earlier thronged in the street had long abated and had left for the comfort of their homes. Traders had mostly closed their stalls after the day's business; only the stragglers and those that dwelt within the shelter of their stalls remained.

Disgruntled though they were, the party of knights followed the monk; though far from being pacified by the clerics pointless and complacent chatter which failed to do little to abate their feelings of discontent. It had been early afternoon when they arrived at the citadel, having received no welcome other than being placed under guard and denied a morsel to eat. Hubert, concerned to where he was being taken, pulled up the short, fat monk who was leading them through the sandy streets, pointing out that they were heading away from the barracks.

"Yes, yes, the monk spoke almost fearing for his safety, I know, have faith," replied the monk fractiously, "you are having excellent accommodations, fit for a visiting nobleman, please be patient."

Hubert didn't care for the way he was told to be patient, it was like being scolded by his mother when he was a boy; the little fat fiend, the friar, carried a much larger form than his own, attesting that he fared well living in the citadel. Hubert ran his eye over the monk; he was in a mood that was becoming near to picking a fight, thinking that this monk had never had to exercise patience except when being seated before a table of food. In his unsettled mind, he began to compare the hardships that he and his companions had endured in the desert to maintain the peace, so that the likes of this oversized monk could sleep safely in his bed. Hubert's face flared beet red with rage; Aldo quickly noticed the signs of his friend's unsettled mood, catching him by the arm gesturing that tonight perhaps they could enjoy themselves relaxing after their long journey. Hubert, realising it had been a long day for all concerned; remarked that the rumbles of hunger from his stomach had got the better of him, needless to say the idea of teaching the monk a lesson in humility still remained strong in him. True to his word, it was not long before the monk led the group to the outside of a building on the edge of a square with high walls surrounding the property.

The doors were as tall as the walls being the height of two men, only rich men could barricade themselves away from the masses that filled the streets. Halting before two large wooden doors, the friar turned to address his party; a measured cough sounded as if to bring the attention of those with him to listen to his words.

"Gentlemen," squeaked the monk, "this is the house of the Prince's friend, Ibn al Assar, one of the wealthiest merchants in the city. You must consider yourselves very fortunate indeed, the dwelling that stands beyond these walls is I am sure of a luxury that you are not used to." It was not hard to detect the note of misjudged arrogance in his tone, "I repeat, this house is of the highest standard." He proceeded to look them over with a telling distaste; their dusty show of dress to his eyes touched on unworthiness.

Continuing, he told them, "It has been offered to you for the period of your stay. I am told by the Captain, who speaks for his Highness, that any disrespect shown to his most honourable friend's hospitality will be viewed as an insult." Speaking as if he had the Prince's authority, he cast his disapproving eye over them once more; there appeared to be a knowing sign of glee on the monks face in expectant anticipation of their inability to recognise the standard of accommodation they were being offered. In silence, the six men looked about each other like naughty boys being threatened with a reprimand before any event took place with a need to burst into laughter at the monk's announcement. With a slapping of his hand on the doors, he waited until he heard the sound of the wooden locking shaft being drawn aside on the other side of the door; he turned to them showing a smile of satisfaction, then with much effort the friar pushed the huge wooden doors forwards; there beyond the open gate lay a garden of beauty untold.

Inside the enclosed courtyard was a neatly tended garden displaying the most beautiful arrangement of exotic blooms. In the evenings dusk, it was difficult to distinguish fully the extent of the garden, though what they could see were interesting pots of palms and raised flower beds filled with blossoming flowers at eye level, alongside fragrant bushes which abounded with colourful flowers that seized at the senses with an overpowering fragrance of their blooms. Through the stillness of the evening, water sprang from various fountains singing out its gurgling song as it trickled and meandered its way throughout the garden, giving complete serenity to any occupant that spent time in meditation within this place of natural beauteous splendour. It was a paradise within the citadel and most obviously a rich man's home. Climbing an external winding staircase to its entrance, they were greeted at its summit by an elderly gentleman who was steward of the house. He was neatly dressed and showing a warm glowing smile; with outstretched welcoming arms he greeted the visitors to the hospitality of his master's humble home, begging them enter and take their pleasure. There was a bath house with warmed water to wash away the dust from their travels before feasting and taking their pleasures as they wished. An arched, open veranda appeared to go all the way around the house inviting the occupier to enjoy pleasant periods to sit and admire the garden whilst taking refreshment at leisure. Aldo added that a man would soon grow fat and lazy enjoying such delights, but Hubert wasn't so sure that he would agree. Palms and blossoms and bowls of fruit were everywhere; they seemed in every niche. A coolness away from sultry evening air greeted them; marbled floors as white as driven snow reflecting light and freshness and scented oil lamps burned illuminating the rooms and filling them with a fragrance throughout putting the men at ease. They followed their host towards the bath house, and through the rooms in which they passed, huge comfortable looking divans bedecked with the most colourful silk cushions and satins for lounging in were scattered around the floor, with silken drapes worth a king's ransom from the East hung everywhere.

The fragrance of Jasmine was intoxicating; it hung in the air, making the atmosphere pleasant to inhale the delicacy of its fragrance. Servants arrived to tend the weary travellers, taking away their clothes before they plunged into the refreshing warm waters of the bath house. Never in their wildest dreams did they expect to be languishing in such luxury, the monk was correct in his sarcasm when he referred to the luxury as above them, the luxury here was only what they could dream of. Once introduced to their steward host, the monk, satisfied his task was complete, leaving the group in the hands of the staff he hurriedly departed, not wanting to spend another moment in the presence of the rugged and outspoken barbarian soldiers from Acre. The men lost no time in stripping and displaying their nakedness, quick to take advantage to bathe and soothe their dusty bodies; they became quite vociferous and loud, laughing heartily at their luck. Refreshed after bathing and dressed in silks, they were ushered to a room in which to dine. Low tables abounded with fruits, and mezzes of assorted delicacies; meats and fowl and spiced goat and all manner of assortment of sweet meats fit for a king waited in readiness to be consumed. In the luxury that abounded their surroundings, their spirits were high; the nature of their good mood after their sumptuous feeding relaxed the fighting men. \it was not long before the excitement turned into tiredness which began to take its toll over them. Robert was restless and fought his weariness; he had much on his mind and his thoughts drifted back to the females who he knew deserved further investigation. He too had donned clean clothes from his host, and took a handful of figs to sustain his hunger; he left the house after bathing, making his way back to the main castle quarters.

Not long after their repast, all inside the house had retired and were soon asleep. Peace descended with the night's quietness, bringing with it long shadows that lengthened with the passing of the moon across the starlit sky. The moon was playing hide and seek with the shifting clouds above to wherever the restless winds cared to transport them. There were no movements that could be heard by the exhausted sleepers from outside, but shadows of a sinister nature moved furtively around the exterior of the house. The intruders knew of their accommodations, leaving them to wait until the time was best suited for their task; when they moved they did so stealthily as any night creature, with an aptitude that took many years of training. Quietly, they entered the house and visited each room of the sleepers, where they set about depositing their insidious gift. At the side of each sleeper was placed a small lamp, an incense tray held above the small flame on which the intruders sprinkled a small quantity of hashish was spread with an unknown additive, known only to themselves. Effectively, the heat from the flame was transferred onto the metal tray above, causing the mixture on the tray to give off very pungent and noxious vapours. As each stealthy visitor completed their task, they retired for a period of time allowing the vapours to render those within into a deeper state of unconsciousness.

Tragedy

For Robert the night was long; he had been invited to join in the festivities in the great hall but had declined the captain's half-hearted invitation. In truth, it came as some relief to the disturbed captain after their earlier meeting had begun on such a prickly footing, but that being passed, the two men somehow came to a nervous agreement over matters at hand and their relationship seemed to improve. It's not that Robert had been able to be on better terms with the captain, or that he did not want to join in the festivities. No, he needed time to spend alone in finding out as much as he could about the movements and the business of the women since he left them earlier. They too were presently enjoying themselves in the great Hall, as if nothing was amiss, being entertained by careless men that had thought little of infiltrators; no matter how long a peace treaty had been signed, he wondered what were they up to? Situations he had found made men such as he doubt many things he saw; events mainly came about through his recent education; it had set him that way and he had to follow his new improved instincts and discover the purpose of the women's real reason for being here; they were up to something and his time, he feared, was running out.

No matter how he tried, Robert had not been unsuccessful in his attempts at spying on the females though his efforts in evading notice to oneself was not easy; he could hide behind drapes that would shield him from view in the great hall. What he needed was to be close enough to eavesdrop, such as in and around their apartments where they were assured of privacy and would talk freely; but those apartments were within the visiting Amman's sector and outside his ability to reach. Wherever he went he had to be cautious not to show himself to them or intrude on their company, it would be a gross sign of disrespect to them whilst being under his host's protection. Frustration had got to him; his quarry remained privately protected behind closed doors, making him presently powerless to know their movements.

All night he exasperated the patience of the guard's, asking all manner of questions and cross examining them over and over about the women's movements and presence in the palace, as to who exactly they were, who they met with and so on, until he resigned himself to the fact that the women had outsmarted him once again. Distanced from him, they had succeeded in evading all attempts of their watcher and later left the castle without his knowing. Very little had escaped their attention for they, unknown to Robert, were far more experienced at this game than he.

That is how the evening ended for him; the game was lost; and it left a sour taste in his mouth; his persistence in the questioning of the palace guards grew embarrassing, almost making himself appear foolish. Not openly able to explain his reasons, the guards were becoming brazenly disrespectful to him and almost insulting, believing he was acting like a lovesick knight over a fresh Muslim wench.

Having lurked around the shadows literally without seeing anything untoward through most of the late evening, he turned his attention to those he sought next. The Prince's highly respected yet suspicious visiting nobles; did not escape his eye and stooped to spying on as many people as was possible through cracks in panelling and slightly parted curtains.

The women's departure, when the word had finally broken to him, had come as a depressing blow, making his suspicions of them even more circumspect. Disparaged he believed that there was something vital he had overlooked, it disturbed him deeply not to reach some inkling of what it was.

Filled with notions that he was as good as anyone at venturing out and mixing with the enemy undiscovered, these women had laid open the truth of his ability proving that they were superior in the art and much better at it than he. It peeved him to learn that truth; damn them, damn them, he protested. They've been here long enough just to pass a message and leave, with their dirty work done made him feel somehow easier. They posed no active threat having gone, but the question remained as to what they had left behind.

Realising that whilst he had been wrestling with words over the lax Captain in the afternoon, they must have completed their task, actively incubating their plans for who knows what; or when.

Tiredness that he could no longer resist finally reached out and touched him, his senses were numbing and his head was aching as he fought against his fatigue. Convinced that there would be little more open to discovery, his tiredness told him it was long past his time to retire, and decided to make his way to the stables for a bed in the hay to sleep off what was left of the night hours.

Activity in the palace the next morning was acute; the entire staff was busy preparing for the announcement and parade for their most illustrious guest, the Emissary from Damascus.

Guards had tirelessly scrubbed their mail coats and polished their armour with vinegar and sand over the previous days to look their best, in readiness to turn out smartly in full regalia, which in the heat of the day was a trial in itself.

The purpose for the Emissary's presence at the palace was twofold. The ruling Muslim families in the region had for too long been antagonistic towards each other; even when called together by the Caliph they were in need of control. This failing had been an advantage in the past, but was presently seen as an opportunity for the Prince, whose ambition drove him to believing that he was suited for much higher office. However, using the knowledge of the state of the families' belligerence towards each other, it seemed that whoever brought forward a pact for greater cooperation between the two ruling families could in a time of peace secure great rewards using the city of Antioch as neutral ground should any future hostilities be raised again. There had been much thought put by for such a giant step to take place; a westerner acting as arbitrator between the feuding families of this land became a novel idea. It was here, on this proposed neutral ground, that a young infant Princess was to be the offered prize as the tool in seeking the Prince's end. As a child, she had been snatched some years previously whilst away from her father, Abd al Rabwa, by one of the warring Seljuk chance raids; captured she was sold into slavery as a means to weaken him. This jewel of Damascus was a favourite grandchild. The Prince's idea was to seek out where she was to be traced and to successfully buy her back; and so she became the means to the Prince's end. Soon after, a messenger had been dispatched with the news of the girl's recovery to the Amman in Damascus.

So excited with the news of his granddaughter's freedom, the Amman had made it known to the world at large that he had misjudged the Franj and would send a peace emissary immediately to Antioch to receive his child and talk further of peace and a union between them. This act of mercy and kindness to an enemy showed that there was more to the westerners than they had once imagined. Now came the time to demonstrate that he too would put aside his attitude of open condemnation and aggression of the foreigners, and by their example learn to have a greater understanding of their culture and ways.

Antioch, being the centre ground between the Seljuks of the North and Syria, was the perfect place for the reunion. This act presented an historic opportunity for the Prince to show to his own people that he was truly a statesman as well as a fine ruler of his own province. The time had at last come for the Christian community also to introduce a lasting peace between two Muslim warring factions, and he was the one to implement it.

This act would make the council of Jerusalem sit up and take notice; in the past they had branded him as an avaricious war monger who had no place in the line of assent should the King fail in his health. Now, as if sent on the wings of a dove from heaven itself, a way had been found to usurp such beliefs. Only for his friend, the merchant Ibn al Assar, telling him of the child's abduction and steering him into seeing his chance to cement a new relationship of union mutually accepted peace for the future of all people, and not just of the opposing parties. A master stroke of brilliance; and the Prince seized on it as his own idea.

As for his friend, the merchant, he promised that if the plan was successful, he would be given great rewards over control of all the trade entering the city and beyond to the limits of his borders. It was a promise of a handsome reward, but his friend had other ideas and served a master far greater than the Prince. Antioch was destined to be favoured with a place in history that would last a thousand years; and he, Guy of Rouen, would be the one that held the key to its future.

There was a further prize behind all of this ceremony; the Prince was from one of the richest families in all of France, in spite of his wealth, added riches were not his prime objective on this occasion. The craven beast that lay dormant within his breast was power and it was now raising its head. In the south, the King was growing weak and losing his grip on Jerusalem and there was unrest and talk of another war brewing in the air from various suitors.

Bloodline alone was not enough for the Prince to secure the throne should anything untoward befall the King. Guy was aware that he had to use other means to convince the elected panel of church council to sway all others in his favour that might stand against him. An act of such unification would go far to show the wavering states his ability as a statesman, and this was his card to play in the political game to lift the crown of Jerusalem. Many times he had proved himself a leader in the field but never a ruler. Yet all was not laid open to the eye on the stage of politics, which was about to unfold many future surprises for the Prince. This new chance of peace between Damascus and Antioch gave further relief to the parties; the old arguments over land that was once the centre of disputes had never been fully agreed on, but it was not Guy's hand that had initiated the present peace, but that of the ailing King.

Robert rose early in another attempt to see the Captain before re -joining his friends. It was unthinkable for this Captain to ignore an officer reporting with military orders for some visiting noble; he would not believe that his rudeness and lack of duty could spill over to be repeated the following day. Foolish though it was to risk such an act, Robert knew that had he have shown such laxity in Acre, the Captain could have been slung in a dungeon as a reminder of who he served.

He dressed in a mood of expectancy and ate a breakfast of olives and bread washed down with a mouthful of wine, feeling suitably ready to exert his authority on the Captain. He set out across the palace courtyard in fine spirits to the Captain's office, taking note on the way of all the activity around him. There was expectation in the air; he knew of the Emissary's visit but he could not explain his reasons for such anxiety that bubbled within him, and he would not be surprised if it was somehow connected to those women.

There were two guards stationed ready to receive him with orders for him to wait yet again. It was too much, he fumed, isolated in the anti-room; after what had already passed the previous day, at least he was out of the heat; lost for words, his impatient temperament was not helping him much.

When he finally saw the Captain, he was received in a somewhat strange interrogating manner; many questions were put to him regarding his journey and his master the Grand Prior.

He was not a fool and would not be treated so, unable to hold back his anger, "Was there something wrong?" he asked inquisitively, with shortness in his tone, "Or a reason to doubt who I am?"

"Ah," the sigh of victory, Robert noted the sardonic look on the Prior's face.

"Now we are there," he remained baffled at the Captain's attitude, noticing the corner of the Captain's mouth twitch, unsure of the reason yet betraying a rye smirk of satisfaction. The old boy sat back stretching in his chair, another question followed, "You are acquainted with Sir Cecil de Neave?" he probed.

Robert concurred hotly, demanding to know what this was about; not wanting to remind the Captain of his business; he could not get a word in edge ways. "You are aware that I am here at the bequest of the Grand Prior," he said hotly injecting emphasis into his tone before presenting the question, "if you had read the communication?" His blood was beginning to rise, he could not understand the evasions, nor was he expecting games from the Captain. Robert's mind raced for clarity in the Captain's reasoning; it suddenly struck him that he had not observed his rank nor given him any credit for his experience. "I see," Robert said exhaling deeply and in a totally different tone as he thought he now realised the care the Captain was taking.

"Now I understand," with a sigh of relief, "that's good," he added, "you want proof of my person before any discourse." Relaxing his manner he became less guarded.

"I commend you," he began congratulating the Captain on his caution wanting to be sure of who he was, "if you send for Cecil we can continue with our business." Exploding like Greek fire, the Captain tore into Robert taking him momentarily off balance.

"Do you know the penalty we have for dealing with liars?" without giving Robert a chance to reply, the Captain continued his scathing onslaught, "their tongues are cut out and furthermore, Cecil informs me that you are no more the King's council than I am?" If there was a chill in the chamber earlier, it was certainly beginning to hot up now. Robert protested, unofficially so, before eventually giving way, apologising that he had slightly misled the captain, admitting that he did not totally or directly tell an untruth. He was of an advisory capacity that Cecil would not be aware of or privy to regarding the security of the council; or on matters relating to the stability and safety of the King; it was his position to report solely to the King or the Grand Prior of Acre. That still put him as your superior, but he did not care to stress that just then.

"I regretted having to say that, it's not information that I casually give out," declared Robert coolly, "besides, Cecil has his own agenda of which you would not be aware of," with this conflict of information the old Captain became confused and hit back like a striking snake.

With a deep reddening in his face, the Captain roared that he believed that he was aware of Robert's function, "I now know quite enough about you." Without listening to what Robert had said, "Furthermore," he bawled with an indignant temper, "you caused me some embarrassment the previous evening." Robert could see that they were getting nowhere in this confrontation and he regretted his behaviour, and without knowing when to give way, added, "with all due respects, as Captain you had shown laxness in your office towards a military intelligence officer, and a superior one at that." Robert failed to cede, but his position was becoming more precarious as he continued causing the Captain to almost strike him in temper. Being so used to having his own way, Robert, by this time, had failed to build the peace he had envisaged in his new relationship with the Captain as he continued to spike all efforts of reconciliation.

"I could have you thrown into jail," the Captain bellowed, "never to be seen again." With a thoughtless and insolent attitude to his remark, Robert pointed out that it would be a disastrous move on his part. Confidently reminding the Captain that it not only would be impractical, too many people would have to be silenced, including the King, and he did not believe any Captain of the Prince's garrison would take such indecent steps to silence a fellow brother in arms of the King's security. He was right of course; it was not the act of a Captain, but this Captain wanted to get a little of his own back, to tip the scales of redress back into balance a little for being so demoralised by this younger man. The two men stood across from each other almost eyeball to eyeball and neither wanted to yield to the others military position.

"Quiet," the word came forth like a cavalry order to charge the enemy, long and resounding ringing around the office and filling it with such ferocity that would make any man tremble; it was his only way to stop the opposing voice from correcting him every time he opened his mouth. In an attempt to control himself, the Captain walked away from the younger knight who now held the floor, somewhat victorious that the captain had lost his means to better him. The Captain's breath was hard and his heart raced; he realised that should he carry on; he could foolishly strip himself for any further advancement in the eyes of his Prince should word reach him from the King of his treatment to his agent. Realising that the officer before him held too many extremely powerful allies, bridges had to be repaired and he could not tell if this younger knight may have that ability in him. He needed a clear head in which to act; now was not the time. With his back to Robert, he issued an order in a more sober tone.

"You will consider yourself in my charge until I decide what to do. For the meantime, you will join your comrades but you will not make any move unless I have prior knowledge. "Is that understood?" His order sounded like a desperate last-ditch attempt at stressing what little authority remained. Robert was about to remind the Prior that he was his superior, but reluctantly under the circumstances, for the benefit of cordial relations, decided against that end. He decided it would be best to maintain a silence and to wait and see the lay of the land later in the day when he would return.

It was most unusual for the small group of knights staying at the apartments of the prince's friend to have slept so late. Du Bray was the first to rouse himself from his confused state by a tempestuous shouting and pounding on the outer yard gate. The sun's rays were threading through the cracks of the shutter and piercing du Bray's eyes like burning needles, he raised his hands to shield them but for some unknown reason had lost his coordination; it took some time for him to rub his eyes.

He was definitely weak and lethargic for no known reason to himself; his head was heavy and throbbing, and it was not helped by the thunderous thumping somewhere beyond his door. He looked around himself and through his distorted imaginings saw twisted colourful shapes that made no sense of anything; he was ill or felt as though the sun had got to him. The thumping noise from beyond angered him, so much so that he attempted to stand upright; the effort made wobble like a child taking its first steps, making him feel sick. It proved too much for him; helplessly he collapsed to the floor, his weakened legs had buckled under him unable to support his weight. As weak as he was, his will remained strong and resolved, if only the room would cease moving before him. He was trapped in a whirling place and feeling very nauseous, concentrating hard, he knew he had to gather his senses and focus on one thing; oddly, in his state of numbness, he giggled like a drunken man as he recalled the image of Hubert's amusing presentation telling his story on the ship. His giggle became a silly smile whilst he lay there on the floor, yet in his blurred unfocused manner he realised Hubert's message was right.

The air was unusually heavy; passing through the moving haze was so perplexing to his eyes; yes, he admitted, I need to focus on a specific object to fight the effects of his delusory state. The door became his minds direction of focus; with his arm outstretched, he pointed his way forward, concentrating hard to escape from his mental torpor. The door was large, seeming no more than a short distance across the room; this was worse than any battle that he had survived, yet if he was to succeed his ordeal he sensed he had to treat it as thus. Concentration would be his shield; and his inner strength would serve as his sword to determine his progress. So, with determined resolution, he proceeded to painstakingly haul himself across the floor; each inch of progress increased his resolve. Eventually, using all his concerted will power, he arrived at the door and struggled to lift the latch to make good his escape out from the whirling pit of obscurity that he had been trapped in. With the door open, it brought with it a rush of warm fresh air, its effect was not insignificant but did little to raise him to any clarity of mind, nor did it help to clear his dulled senses, though it was enough for him to escape the repugnant odours of the room in which he had been helplessly stifled and incarcerated.

His throat was dry and his voice weak, almost none existent; he believed that whatever he had drunk the previous night had left him tormented in his present state.

Surprisingly, there were no servants about to assist the knight who was plagued with the persistent banging and shouting at the great door of the yard. In the swirling fog that had snared his senses, he knew that he had to reach the door to cease his torment. Drowsily, he dragged himself down the winding staircase that he so easily stepped up the previous night. By the time he had reached the lower section of the stairs, his progress had proved most painful; rolling forwards he completed his descent by tumbling over and over finally collapsing to the sandy earth below, with a realisation that he was most uncomfortable. Sitting up, his head remained hurting; the throbbing sounds in his head beat in rhythm with the pounding and yelling of his name that came from the other side of the great yard doors that was the entrance that separated him from the world at large. He could not ignore the sound as it failed to weaken, if only he could stop it. It was not far to the sound but he was fearful that the door and walls of the garden would crumble as they could not stop from moving. Outstretched and aware he could fall no further, he felt it was safe to continue. Advancing on his belly for the short distance that lay before him, he laboriously crawled across the sandy yard towards the outer gate, passing the drooping roses that still held droplets of dew from the early morning on their fragrant petals.

The deep ruts in the soft sandy pathway to the great door portrayed lizard-like movements of his progress behind him until he had found the strength to rise to a standing position against the wooden locking bar of the great door. With each pounding noise the doors shook, bringing a new sensation to the struggling knight; whoever or whatever it was creating the awful noise had by this time made it quite clear that he wasn't going to leave until the doors were opened. With much effort the locking bar was slid back, the door pushed forcefully forwards against du Bray, whose weak body could not withstand the effects of the force against him fell into a heap. To make matters worse, his falling to the ground became an obstacle to the doors opening. The confused man lay holding his head; fortunately, the banging had ceased, though his head still throbbed incessantly; he swore to himself there must have been demons inside, sent to punish him for past misdemeanours.

The door was gradually forced open in jerking movements causing his body on the floor to be pushed painfully at each impatient shove at the door, its opening causing much discomfort to du Bray's limp body.

With the image of his friend looming before him, Robert sported a twisted and angry face to the sight at his feet. Shocked by the spectacle that presented itself, he exclaimed in a most disgusted and disparaging tone. "My God, look at you," he shouted, sneering at the collapsed du Bray lying in the dirt. He viewed his friend's dishevelled and undressed state, thinking he resembled something little better than a fallen scarecrow on a broken stick in some farmer's field, even a street beggar would have more self-respect.

Robert was ashamed and disgusted at how his friend's degenerate behaviour had sunk so low as to allow himself to become sodden by the effects of a long night's drinking. He screwed up his nose and drew his head back as he stood overlooking du Bray; he smelt like a compost heap and found it hard to believe what he had encountered. He pulled his head away sharply to escape the obnoxious smell that rushed upwards towards his open nostrils. Walking a few paces around the man that used to be so upright, he tried to escape the nauseous aroma, in disbelief he looked upon the heap that was his friend; he became aware that he had experienced that smell somewhere before. Turning his head away from the noxious odours, he entered into a tirade of insults for letting him down, rebuking him of his disloyalty at his unbelievable state. Sickened and angry at the sight that he beheld, he could not hold back his remarks.

In a disgusted tone, he vented his feelings, "I would not have believed it. I have only been away for one night!" Suddenly stuck for words, he began looking about for signs of external damage to the apartments it must have been some night of revelry and he could not understand what would have encouraged them to be so callous and so thoughtless. Although no external damage was noticeable, he continued in his tirade on his defenceless friend, "You mark my words, these apartments had better be in one piece."

Raising his hand weakly for assistance, du Bray could only croak to his commander, still doped beyond reason, and defenceless to his tongue, he had no choice but to accept the tirade that had been unleashed upon him. Robert with anger rising by the moment, threw up his arms exclaiming, "And what state are the others in?"

Ignoring his friend, who remained on the floor, his disgust with his men, especially du Bray, rendered him unable to speak further. Dread filled his thoughts; he imagined himself facing the Captain again having to explain away the imagined damage done to the property and the disrespectful conduct of his men.

Desperately reaching out to grasp Robert's clothing in an attempt explain his condition, du Bray's hand was roughly brushed aside; Robert stalked off, huffing as he went up the stairs into the apartments.

Du Bray's brain gradually became functional; struggling, he pulled himself to his knees to make his way on all fours to where he could hear and vaguely see water issuing from a cistern into a small pool that fed a series of minor canals that fed the rest of the garden.

The cool trickling stream of water flowed from the irrigation system into a pool; its bubbling, joyful sound reverberated like beating drums in the head of the drugged and dishevelled man. Lamely, he made his way on all fours towards the water and collapsed into it causing a splash; his head dropped uncontrollably into the soothing pool's cold water and submerged before flicking his saturated hair into the air, giving a groan of relief with its refreshing effect as he emerged back into sunlight. He knelt there, motionless, as if transfixed to the floor; the water was restorative but not enough to restore him to his senses quite as sharply as he would have liked. When an appealing shout rang in his ears for him to come quickly, he tried to rally but his limbs were still unable to respond. Making his best effort to assist, he stumbled awkwardly forward towards the apartment before reeling back to earth. Robert emerged from the interior coughing and gasping for fresh air; the hashish mixture from the rooms had got into his eyes leaving him partially groping; his tone had altered from one of anger to one of deep concern. Du Bray, a little stronger, careered with Robert in his eagerness to support his call reaching the staircase that led back up to the apartment. In his eagerness to support his weak friend, Robert held him at arm's length and with great sincerity begged forgiveness for the hasty misjudgement of his honourable character.

"I am so sorry that I misjudged you, my friend."

"What happened?" slurred du Bray, "did we get so drunk that we could not remember anything?"

Robert assured him that the condition of his head was not caused by any drinking but something had happened. "The stink of hashish is everywhere," rebuking himself for not having recognised the smell earlier. Supporting him, Robert's tone changed to one of care and reassurance.

"Do you know what happened? Try to think," he said as he held him at arm's length watching his face for any clue that may give him some idea of the events that led up to the present, "but first, if you are strong enough, help me get our friends out into the air."

Robert returned into the stinking quarters, leaving the weakened du Bray outside to gather his senses, realising that he was still unfit and incapable. In another room, he saw his brother slumped alongside the small incense burner undisturbed and unconscious under the narcotic's influence, probably still inhaling the residue that was once emitted from the ash on the smoking tray. Holding his hand across his mouth to avoid any of the noxious vapours, he grabbed at the limp form and dragged his brother Edward to the upper balcony overlooking the garden; then, without further thought of his brother's condition returned to open all the shutters allowing the stinking rooms to be rid of the obnoxious smell of hashish from within. Du Bray staggered lamely onto the balcony looking jaded and speechless, he slumped to the floor with his head in his hands, and he was exhausted as Robert could plainly see.

Stinging tears began to fall from Robert's eyes but there were others to bring out before he was done. His friend du Bray attempted to rise and was halted in his moving, being told to rest.

"I'll get them, you're not strong enough," said Robert and there was no reply of argument. Robert turned to re-enter the apartment; taking a deep breath he went forth, looking in all the rooms until he reached the rear of the house.

Robert became rigid at the sight he beheld, a fog of smoke hung in the room, smashing the window shutters into splinters with his boot to clear the air, half driven by survival and a maddening reaction and also by the need to breathe clean air.

With his hand holding his scarf around his face, he turned and looked downwards. His friend, Guy, lay dead where he slept, his throat has been cleanly cut and his blood had seeped everywhere, the floor was like a red pond, "Who did this?" groaned Robert. He had to get out of the room; his concern sprang to the thought for the others; frantically, he searched the rest of the house looking for them; but his friends were not to be seen anywhere. It was a relief not to find any other bodies, though it was a terrible and worrying shock that they were missing; it was not like the others to go off, unless they were in pursuit of Guy's murderer. Torn by grief at the sight he had witnessed, Robert returned to the room to view once more his dead companion. Leaning against the arch that was the entrance to the room, he viewed the body of his friend from a distance. Guy lay on the cold floor where he had slept; he was an appalling sight, his head was to one side and his clothing was saturated with his own blood. Robert approached the body disbelievingly; he knelt to pay his last sad tribute of respect to his friend of many years. On his cushioned bed of silk, he was laying at peace as if asleep, free from the tension of the world with the constant strain of needing to be alert from the dangers of his work. Robert was choked with a mixture of grief and hate, but only the sickness of revenge stirred in him. The disgusting act of killing a drugged man seemed an unnecessary message from the one that inflicted this terrible act.

Robert's head flooded with flashing images of places, laughter and past conversations; a hollow emptiness filled him and it hurt in his heart. In his passing impressions, he evoked recollections of a happier past when they had spoken of his home, hunting deer and watching the eagles fly across steep ravines. Alas, he was free now from this world's troubles; he would be missed by all, especially Hubert. In the humanity of the grieving warrior, Robert displayed his depth of feeling by touching his dead friend's hand, and bidding him a sentimental farewell on his journey to that place where brave men hoped they should all meet again someday.

After silent words, he rose slowly, deeply touched amid the stench that filled the room that brought his brave friend to his unjustifiable end. Viewing the bloodied body, he noticed that something was missing; his friend lay without his sword, which to a fighting man such as he, indicated that he was improperly dressed for the journey ahead. Reaching across Guy's body, Robert picked it up and returned to placing it lengthways on his lifeless form, placing his limp lifeless hand onto its hilt. A warrior deserves to enter the realms of the unknown prepared for any trial that his God will demand of him. He was the one that kept our spirits high with amusing quips when anger turned to frustration back into moments of unease. Before leaving him, he drew a silken cover across the blood stained body.

"Goodbye, my friend," he whispered with an affectionate lump in his throat, "We will all miss you." Halting in the doorway before leaving, he turned to view the body for the last time before sadly leaving the room.

Returning to du Bray and Edward on the veranda, he found it difficult to speak and tried with difficulty to regain his composure. He made several attempts to overcome the lump in his throat with efforts to cough loudly, but the tears of sadness that he fought to hold back began streaming down his tired face, making it more difficult to face his other companions.

Leaning on the balcony looking out onto the magnificent peaceful floral garden below, he drew in deep emotional breaths; he could not see the colours below him, a glistening teardrop formed filling his eyes to impair his vision. Drawing on another deep breath, struggling to control the emotions to settle his loss, he had momentarily forgotten about the others of his company who sat nearby in silence. With his grief controlled, he remained with his back to them, questions of how, why and when this all happened entered his head.

"Guy's dead," Robert murmured, "murdered whilst he slept." There was little response, the effects of the narcotic remained with them, numbing their reaction apart from the dropping of heads and further silence.

"As for the others," Robert enquired taking a long breath, "tell me they're out; or they went out last night and did not return."

"I do not know," du Bray choked on the fresh air as he softly replied.

"We bathed, you were there, Robert, for a time, refreshment was left for us and we ate our fill. After surviving on our rations for the journey, the opportunity to eat real food and drink a little wine was too good to let go by." There appeared guilt in his voice and Robert was quick to sympathise with his friend.

"I wasn't making anything out of your actions; I would have joined you only for my need to know what was happening at the palace. Thinking on it now, I suppose the food was all drugged, it seems so strange that we should all feel so tired at once; no one remembered anything with clarity." Robert let out at grunt of probability, agreeing with Edward. There was no doubt in his mind that there was a reason that they had been moved here; all of a sudden he and his group were in the way and he was going to make it his business to find out why.

Walking down the staircase to the bubbling waters of the fountain below, Robert set about filling two ewers of water, being careful not to spill a drop, he turned and climbed the stairs leading back onto the veranda where the two sat. He doused them both without a thought of how they would feel, they did not jump with shock as the water struck them into partial reality, nor did it cause them to stir with the shock of the water soaking them, but they remained slumped in a bemused and saddened state.

"We have got to be clear of what happened," Robert ordered his brother Edward to search the building for any signs left by the intruders. Gripping his brother, Robert held him at length and looked him in the eyes. "Edward I need you to remember everything if we are to make any kind of progress." Appealing to him sensitively, adding "No matter how small, when you are capable, search everywhere. Whoever carried out this vile act is going to pay with their blood, that I swear."

Ordering du Bray to his feet, Robert insisted that he go with him to the captain's office to corroborate the events of the previous night. Robert's mind was racing over his friend's death and the missing duo, his thoughts of seeing the captain would give them both an opportunity to discuss his own orders from Acre.

Satisfied that his two friends were almost in a reasonable state of mind Robert set off with du Bray to make their report.

Along the way he wrestled with himself for a reason for this act of the drugging and the murder of one of his friends, including the possibility of abducting two others, but he was unsure about the last act. In his mind it was obvious to Robert that a rat was in this scheme somewhere. What was the reason he asked himself for such an act of aggression, to confuse us or throw us off the track of something more devious? No matter how hard he tried, there was little clarity in his reasoning. Du Bray struggled as he tried to keep up with Robert, whose pace certainly had an impatient spring in it. Not quite back to his full strength and quickness of mind, he was left lagging behind struggling to keep on his feet due to his unsteady state.

Crowds were beginning to build in the narrow streets but it was of no consequence to Robert; he impatiently thrust his way through them with irritable intent. Leaving those unfortunates sprawling behind that he had brushed aside to call him all manner of insulting names to his back, his pace was so quick and his mind so occupied that those unfortunate to be in his way bounced off him to collide with the walls of buildings, leaving the weakened du Bray following in his wake to bear the brunt of their anger. The ailing knight, whose condition bothered him, coughed his way forwards, suffering the added aggravation from the smoking fires of so many open wood stoves cooking from all manner of spicy foods that caught in his parched throat irritating him by their offensive peppery pungency. Whilst Robert, whose thinking was about nothing but the problem at hand, believed that they had been set up in the house, he was furious that the Prince could be so easily manipulated and blind to everything other than his own political manoeuvrings. He was sure that the Prince's friend wasn't in the habit of extending the hospitality of his house and staff to strangers; he needed to be arrested and questioned as well as those of his staff.

Reaching the wall of the fortress he rounded its corner well away from the busy streets that led directly to the palace courtyard and barracks and the Captain's quarters. He turned to speak to du Bray only to discover that he was missing. In his present mood his mind was not on the living but filled with the concern for those missing and his dead friend. Du Bray; he knew would soon catch up and his waiting would help clear his thoughts; though he waited impatiently for longer than he should before wondering what could possibly have happened; and still his friend did not appear. With his concern growing, he back tracked his route for a number of streets until he came upon an accumulation of people at the end of the thoroughfare ahead of him.

Not wanting to get mixed up in an affray of shopkeepers, he walked wide of the confusion and glancing across at the mass of jabbering people, noticed du Bray in the centre of this melee. For some reason, he was caught in the middle of eight or nine of the mob that appeared to be taking advantage of his weakened state, he stood alone apologising, lost as to what was really happening about him and unaware that the mob were building with intent to using violence against the out of sorts knight, who was politely and weakly protesting at their behaviour. Robert could see that he was no more than a lame duck and easy meat for the gathering massing numbers; he was not putting up with, being already fired into a mood he immediately tore through the bustle of the mob hurling them aside as if he were coursing his way through a thicket with purpose and great force. It mattered not what injuries they may sustain derived from his anger, but they made the dreadful mistake of picking on his weakened friend and he cared not for their connivance. Furthermore, this was not the best of days, the death of a companion and his being greatly put out by having to return to an awkward Captain for help, as well as a delay in his plans in his need for revenge. It was not a difficult task to sort out the mobbing shopkeepers, du Bray, aware of his lack of wit to outsmart the store holders, attempted to thank Robert and apologise for the incursion; he was abruptly told to move on and keep up along with a series of complaints from Robert about having to watch him all the time. There was no malice in his words and du Bray knew it, realising what was on his mind was in all their interests now to solve their problem of the missing two friends.

When they entered the outer office of the Captain's chamber, the cleric was still busily scribbling on parchment at his desk; the admission of light into the dimly lit room as the door quietly opened alerted him to the entry. He was in no hurry to attend to any visitor before the completion of his task; casually raising his eyes he beheld the knights standing before him. The terrified reaction of recognition and a reminder of their last confrontation that had chilled his very being caused him to jump into action with such fear he almost fell off his chair in his attempt to appease the waiting knights. He was ordered to fetch his master right away and this time the tone in his voice indicated that he was in no mood for excuses; knowing that the cleric had already suffered a measure of Robert's anger, he knew better than to test him further, adding with a stern note of warning, that he would not accept any excuses. The poor man hastily disappeared out of the door and returned almost immediately, "The Captain will see you now," came the sullen reply.

Robert told du Bray to remain in the outer office until called for and not to sally off on some venture of wonderment. With a bowed head, the cleric ushered the knight into the Captain's office without once taking his eyes away from the floor.

The Prior was surprised at Robert's reappearance, not expecting to see Robert so soon after their previous skirmish; also having a feeling that he now held a stronger position, impatiently he asked the reason for being before him. After being told that his visit was neither social nor political, he began to inform the Captain of the seriousness of his visit, reporting the sad and alarming events that befell his company during the previous evening. Robert felt uneasy and sat in a chair; to some it may have appeared impolite having not been invited to do so, giving the Captain sufficient cause to feel indignant at this display of free rein. Unknown to Robert, who had kept talking, the officer grew speechless, taken aback by the forwardness of his act. So much so that he sat erect in his chair and to raised his eyebrows at the liberty of overlooking the courtesy of being asked and seating himself. Not wanting to explode and show further temper, the Captain tentatively remained calm, although he did blow air out from his puffed cheeks and gripped the edge of his desk. In his controlled attempt to dismiss any idea of chastisement from his mind, he awaited the explanation to what he was to be told.

Robert's face stiffened as he began to recount the events of the night as he saw them.

"It happened in the night whilst I was absent," he said in a sullen tone, "the men had been drugged and once the hashish lamps were in the place it was only a matter of waiting until they were unconscious. The rooms remained filled with the stench of the stuff; it was heavy and sickly in the air. I suppose it wasn't long after that the butchery took place," his voice died as he recalled the loss of his friends. "By God, I swear I'll have the bastard's balls on a spit when I catch up with the one that did this."

"I understand how you feel," replied the Captain, but warned Robert that he must not move against anyone until they are sure. Robert's eyebrows lifted at that suggestion; there wasn't any way that he would be stopped from doing what his mission intended. Moving from the absurd orders of the Captain, Robert added that he'd brought one of his men to be examined, should it be his wish. Robert explained du Bray's poor state of health, adding that he was without, awaiting his beckoning. The Captain raised a hand to suggest that was not necessary; his eyes fell in thought, lost to any reason for such an outrageous act to occur. Robert suddenly reacted banging the heavy topped desk with his fist adding that he should have expected something like this to occur, jolting the Captain back from the depth of his thoughts.

Both men were at a loss as what to suggest; with a change of subject he casually asked, "Was there anything in the orders that might indicate a reason for unrest?"

"Ah, the orders," said the Captain with hesitation, he had not opened them, and was reluctant to admit his oversight as he dithered trying to conceal the fact.

"There are parts I am not allowed to divulge to anyone," came the stupid reply. A reply of that nature indicated that the Captain had failed to treat the communication with any importance and had not bothered to even peruse them. Robert was well aware that there was a necessary provision in his orders, to whomever, to include the active intelligence officer in the field to any knowledge that may be deemed valuable to the situation at hand. With anger rising once more towards the lax Captain, he stood up sharply, causing the chair to fall onto his back.

Challenging him, he snapped, "Are you telling me that you have not read them yet?"

The Prior stood with equal indignity at the outrageous suggestion, his moustache bristled erratically in unison with his upper lip and his face betrayed his embarrassment.

"How dare you," said the Captain retaliating in reply and gasped as he almost failed to take in a breath; he was full of indignation and reddening in full embarrassment.

Robert had had enough of this Captain and stood square on to him as if they were about to exchange blows. "I dare because I am true to this cause; I am here to do the job that I was appointed to do." Angrily and at the top of his voice the rebuke thundered out. The sounds in the Captain's chamber resembled a battle royal between the two men, with the sounds of their fury resonating from the inner chamber to the outer office. The writing cleric cringed at the disturbance, lowering his head further into his writing as if he expected some form of blazing missile to be hurled at him from inside his captain's chamber. So much did the disturbance unnerve him that in his nervous state, the noise of the ranting voices caused him to lose his grip on his quill; dropping it fully charged, it blotted and spoilt his work. Du Bray sat back, thankful the torment of the rebuttal was not landing on him, at the same time smirking at the sounds from the two men going at each other without any immediate signs of either of them ceding to the other.

Back in the chamber, Robert would not let up. "I repeat my news to you, one of my company lay dead and two are missing, and furthermore, Captain, I have to remind you that I am your superior in this matter of field intelligence and I now demand an answer."

The Captain was beaten by the truth of the matter and like a dog with its tail between its legs stood silently. His ageing heart beat so fast it felt it could burst; leaning on the desk steadying himself with his head bowed, he struggled to find a reason for his laxness. Sitting down, his passion subdued he appealed to the younger man.

"You came in here last evening full of yourself, and I admit, perhaps I may not have been attending my office as I should have. You showed me no respect and I was aggrieved at your arrogance. Unfortunately, the air came hot between us and we both showed anger, and in my weakness and wrath I admit I overlooked the orders. Now that matters have worsened and come to a head, the truth is out," with embarrassment he acknowledged the accusations levelled before him. The ageing Prior laid out his guilt with Robert looking on feeling guilty himself; perhaps he thought his arrogance and lack of respect to the ageing Captain got the better of him; he was ill mannered and equally guilty of lacking simple sensibilities that came hard to except from one such as he who was active in the field. There was a brief silence as Robert took in the indictment, then with a dramatic change in his voice before he spoke and with sincerity

Holding his hand out first as a gesture of friendship, he asked if it was possible for them both to try again.

Surprised by the gesture, this was not what the Captain expected; it displayed a measure of the younger man's maturity and sincerity in his approach to rebuild a bridge of cooperation that had been damaged between them. The Captain grasped Robert's outstretched hand and agreed that it was most wise, regretting at the same time his actions. A new cordiality was immediately adopted and the two men made renewed effort not to stand on each other's toes.

"The orders," Robert reminded the Captain. "Yes of course," he replied, and went to a cabinet that contained his records; there, he opened a secret drawer from its side and drew out a scroll, the condition of which was noted causing no more than a wrinkled brow but not a criticism mentioned, the Captain sensing this breathed a sigh of relief. The book was full of varying codes used by the Temple; this code in particular was of the Atbash. Breaking the seal on the scroll, the Captain opened it and began to decode and read in a mumbling drone simultaneously. With the letter finally deciphered, he began to read aloud:

"Greetings and Salutations to the office of the Captain of the Citadel of Antioch. DISTURBING NEWS HAS REACHED US, WHICH WE SERIOUSLY CONSIDER TO ACCEPT THAT MOVES ARE AFOOT FROM FACTIONS UNKNOWN TO PROMOTE A SCHEME TO REDRESS THE BALANCE OF POWER IN THE LEVANT. THE RESTORATION OF VARIOUS SEATS OF POWER TO OTHERS OUTSIDE THAT OF THE PRESENT FAMILIES MAY WELL BE ASCERTAINED BY URGING THE ROYAL FAMILIES TO ENTER INTO BOGUS AGREEMENT RESULTING IN CONFLICT.

THE BEARER OF THIS LETTER IS TO BE TRUSTED COMPLETELY AND I CALL ON YOU TO AID HIM BY MAKING QUIET BUT VIGOROUS EFFORTS IN YOUR INVESTIGATION USING ALL OF YOUR SECRET SOURCES WITHIN YOUR AREA. REACH OUT REGARDING ANY MATTERS THAT MAY STRIKE YOU AS UNUSUAL AND YOU WILL BE BEST ADVISED TO CONSULT MY AGENT ON ALL MATTERS RELATING."

The letter was short and was signed by the Grand Prior of Acre. It read more like an order than a request and Robert noticed the Captain's eyebrows rise as he stared at the letter before him as he laid it down on his desk after reading it; it left little doubt that Robert's position was one of note and required respect which caused him further embarrassment after their previous confrontation.

"So," the Captain admitted, "you do have powerful friends. Heaven's above," he exclaimed as he leaned back in his chair, "there must be something really serious afoot, yet we have no indication that there is anything like this brewing." In his effort to make small talk, he stated that he was amazed at the letters content, "it ceases to amaze me how and where this information comes from."

"Do not underestimate our organisation, we have the finest network of information seekers in the East," said Robert with confidence in the knowledge, "well, that is until we met up with these damned women. It is quite possible that the recent events are a start; I cannot yet explain why or how but I feel it here," placing his hand to his stomach he stretched his neck and in open thought asked, "Captain, have you any reason to suspect or heard anything recently from your neighbours in Eddessa relating to new treaties or mysterious movements taking place?" With the image of the elusive females in his mind and reluctance in his voice, Robert conceded that he feared that it was bound to be as the letter stated. "My suspicions," he added, "are already taking me down a road I feared to travel," he said almost absent-minded. The Captain was at a loss with Robert's words, as he began to retell the tale of their journey to the Citadel. "The two women on board ship set us a merry dance, guests, they informed us, of your Prince. When we held them on the road they told us that they carried an important message of business from the King; they showed it to us, but since we did not break the seal, we had no way of disbelieving them; though I know that our King retains many messengers and they were convincing enough.

I saw them in the great hall last evening among the guests and they seemed at ease. Yet I still am no wiser what the content of what that message was about, only that I strongly feel that they are somehow bound up in this puzzle and all that has gone wrong with recent events, of that I am certain. I tell you, I fear their ability to create mayhem and what lies in store for us." The mention of the women created tension to grow in him, "God damn," he spat, "if only they were here now." With an understanding of the situation that had been figured out, the two men's attitudes became totally agreeable and at ease with each other whilst sitting in deep discourse until Robert had remembered his friends, who must by now be wondering what was going to happen to them.

Earlier, before the conclusion of their talks, the Captain sent word through his cleric to send people to the apartments to make the preparations for the collection of the knight's body and burial arrangement of Robert's dead friend. They both arose and walked to the door; Robert called du Bray forwards and introduced him to the Captain who was shocked at seeing his ashen appearance, "My God, man, you look as though you've come back from the dead." It wasn't exactly what he wanted to hear, especially when he was beginning to feel much better in himself. They parted, agreeing to meet later on to eat and discuss the matter together; as for the two females they didn't think that they would be far away, but before leaving the Captain promised he would send out men to seek them out, "Mark me well, before the sun sets we will learn just how important their official business really was." Robert felt that relations with the captain had improved and left the castle heading for the apartments in the town.

Ransom

Robert's determination to re-join his brother Edward was uppermost in his thoughts, and both men made their way back to the apartment as speedily as they could, causing them to force a path once more through the thronging busy streets that led directly through the market place. There were many times that he had caused upset with his brother knights for their inconsideration in their treatment of the ordinary street people when entering cities in a hostile manner for no good reason, yet in his urgent blindness of purpose he was as oblivious as those he had once criticised. Even now, nothing was going to slow him from re-joining his brother and hopefully to discover who was at the root of this diabolical upheaval. It was mid-morning and getting hot; sweat oozed from every pore covering his body, making his clothing pull on him in his urgency; the air had grown heavier with the usual intense street aromas; he sympathised with his friend as acrid fumes of wood smoke caught in his throat. Du Bray, although improving with every moment of his consciousness, still coughed suffering from the air filled with aromatic mixtures; his coughing slowed his progress for he was forced to stop at intervals to clear his head and throat and to gain support from corners of buildings that almost seemed conveniently spaced for him. He kicked at rats that scurried along the shadowy edges of buildings fiercely seizing scraps that had fallen or were dropped by passers-by; he couldn't abide them and was in two minds to skewer them on his sword point. Thinking better of it, he realised that drawing his sword may upset the nervous bystanders and only end up causing another confusion of minds and emotions in the simple folk. So the irritation that the rats caused could best be dealt with by kicking them from his path as he weakly progressed after his anxious friend.

Quickly, du Bray rushed on to catch up as they entered the town's basket making section; to his joy, the crowds eased and the air became more acceptable and clearer; it was easier to negotiate a freer pathway and he noticed it had a cooling condition on his friend, making him become calmer and easier than earlier.

Further ahead, Robert was nearing the apartment; by this time his temperament had eased, giving his mind a chance to clear and return to the mystifying events of the previous night. A chord of discontent in his thinking was the Prince's friend Ibn al Assar; he had shown himself to have been extremely clever to have hidden his true identity for so long a period, being able to gain the Prince's confidence and planting such a clever scheme in the Prince's mind. The Prince must have thought that he was secure with his wealthy confidant; thinking nothing of the security of his own people. Is he a fool that dreams of nought but his own empire, which won't last long if he is not careful. Ibn's ability to hold sway over certain decisions that the prince must have formed proved alarming. It was equally alarming that his friends and advisors failed to challenge the Prince's dalliance with Ibn, for fear of alienating his friendship with the wealthy merchant. His suspicions that Ibn al Assar's motive to house the outsiders in his apartment could only be for the purpose to restrict their movements away from the confines of the Palace, at the same time giving whoever it was the freedom of carrying out their dastardly deeds at the house.

If he was a pawn in the chain of command, then who was the one that held power over him? Who did Assar take his orders from and what deed was so important that would make him give up all he had gained just to frighten off this little band of men? It surely was not for fear of having an extra six swordsmen to support the Prince. He probed his memory, taking in all he could recall from the previous evening. Was there a face that he had missed? Or one that did not want to be recognised that was at work within the castle? This aroused Robert's suspicion but it led him nowhere, as if a bolt of lightning had struck him, he felt sure now that this track of thought had more probability. Something was going to happen; some devious scheme was already in motion; it was obvious; there was no doubt about the fact that the new arrivals were a troubling element, the more he pondered on the point the more it seemed to fit into this theatre of events. Then who would be aware of our presence and our ability to thwart a possible plot? There were too many probabilities; unfortunately there were no answers, well, none that yet made any sense. The high walls that surrounded the apartment were becoming ever closer as he neared the end of the busy street; perhaps, he thought, there was something here that would divert the many questions in his muddled mind; he turned to speak to du Bray but he was not there; again, looking around he shook his head in disbelief to see that he was still having difficulty in keeping up to his pace.

At least the doors of the courtyard would not be secured this time, which came as some relief to Robert. On entering the courtyard, Edward was nearby and ready to greet his brother; something smelled of bad news, for Robert could plainly see Edward's long mournful face. There could have been a flock of chirping birds about the garden and Robert would not have noticed; he somehow knew that there was news and it was all bad. If only there was something to be hopeful for anything, it would have shown in Edward's face; before anything could be said, Robert demanded the news. Somehow in all his hopes, he knew that Aldo and Hubert had not been overcome by drinking too much wine, nor were they the type to be lost in some strange place. The bad news that Edward reluctantly imparted descended on him like a depressing thunder cloud about to burst. Edward sheepishly handed a parchment to his brother explaining that he found it in the room where Guy lay. "It seems a bad day for news," Robert said as he began to mumble the message aloud.

It read – FRANJ, DO NOT TRY TO SEEK US OUT, WE HAVE YOUR FRIENDS AND THEY ARE SAFE. THEY WILL NOT BE HARMED, BUT A PRICE OF 500 GOLD BEZANTS WILL BE THE COST OF THEIR RELEASE. COME QUICKLY FOR THEIR RELIEF AS THEY WILL SUFFER SOME DISCOMFORT RESTRICTED TO THE CONFINES OF A CAMEL SKIN. IN FOUR DAYS, BE AT THE ENTRANCE OF THE CANYON OF THE SNAKE OR THEIR SITUATION MAY CHANGE FOR THE WORSE.

Robert could not believe his eyes as he read the note; instinctively he knew it was from her. She was the only one that addressed him openly with the term 'Franj.' His mind wandered a moment catching a glimpse of her dark alluring eyes staring back at him; he was sickened and terribly disappointed that it was her. Once again they had outsmarted him; there was no doubt of his vulnerability and the distraction that she had become; he cursed himself and her toying with his affection and being deviously clever as she did so. Once more, anger erupted inside Robert, as he was unable to contain his exasperation.

"Ahh!! By Satan's bollocks," he screamed loudly, "when I get my hands on her, I'll show that bitch who she is toying with," his anger was so great he issued a stream of threats not usually reserved for any woman. "I'll slit her throat, I'll cast her entrails into the shit pits of this city for the unnecessary pain she has caused, and make her rue the day she ever laid eyes on me." Du Bray, who was standing calmly behind Robert, looked to Edward who also stood back aghast at Robert's unusual outburst as he handed back the note.

With the content of the note's dire message striking home, the trio of men made haste their way back to the castle to turn in a further report to the Captain; Edward broke off to visit the pigeon lofts to send a message whilst Robert and du Bray continued on to the castle.

In the Captain's office the meeting was going well, they stood around openly discussing the situation close by a lancet window; it allowed sufficient air to enter the cooling shadows of the chamber, airing it from the repressive heat of the day. The heat never really reached to overbearing to the active men in the room, but no matter how disciplined they were, they could not prevent the burden of their bodies from sweating nor their clothes from sticking to them. Thankfully, the shade of the office acted as some form of salvation in its welcoming refuge. They deliberated over the note, reasoning the women's actions and sought to explain the previous night's events. They spoke in low friendly tones, also discussing the Prince's mischievous missing friend and where he may have gone to ground. Whoever he was, they suspected he must have been secreted in this place years ago, waiting to be used whenever it was most convenient to strike for whosoever it was that he served. Questions of who would have such a spy network with such a far-reaching plan for the future led him towards only one conclusion, but it seemed unreasonable for an ally to work against them. Their thoughts on the situation brought them to a silent pause; Robert had moved closer to the window in search of further relief for the lightest of breezes that may ease the stickiness that he endured.

The air was still; the courtyard outside showed little sign of life, not like the previous day when disturbingly foreign guards were everywhere to be seen. Robert's lonely form in the window presented an image to watchers on the outside that they had him where they wanted him, alone and isolated from the festivities in the great hall. He breathed a deep sigh and stifled a yawn; the searing heat outside proved a burden at this time of day, though he suffered no such burden as he languished within the coolness of the sanctuary of the Captain's office. The captain was speaking, though Robert heard only a subconscious drone; he had almost lost the train of the man's talk being lost in his own thoughts. He could not suppress the ideas in his head about the woman, when, without warning, he was suddenly brought back to the present with a jolt by a shattering blood-curdling scream, it cut through the quiet drone of the Captain's dialogue like a knife. Disbelievingly, their surprise showed dramatically as it was heard; each turned to the other as if to question the sound. Turning to the window opening, heads clamoured outwards to seek its direction to maybe ascertain the cause for such an ear-piercing, murderous scream. There was no sign of any unrest and no wiser were they to any deed of mischief, but not too late to see a falling body and a diaphanous drifting veil floating aimlessly downwards to the palace garden below the window of the great hall. "By the Christ in Heaven, what on earth is going on?" People in the palace building gathered, filling the space of an empty window where the person appeared to fall to their death; that must have been the cause for the alarm. The body that plummeted downwards into the garden area remained hidden by a wall that bordered its perimeter. Everything occurred so quickly, leaving them startled and inactive by the unusual event. Reality offered no explanation, but brought sudden stimulation urging the trio into action by dashing for the door in unison.

The Captain reached his door after the others had bolted passed and were on their way towards the main palace building; a wasted call that was the voice of authority from the ageing Captain calling out to remind them that they had no jurisdiction to intervene on any matter within the city's walls, but it was unheard in the moment. Realising it was to no avail, the Captain was not about to waste further breath and took up the pursuit behind them across the yard to discover the cause for himself.

Robert and du bray had ran swiftly toward the palace fleet of foot to discover what had happened pushing aside the guards that had turned inquisitively to do the same. To their right lay the walled garden just off the courtyard where they believed the unfortunate individual had fallen to his death, but first it was their intention to see what act could have occurred before the villain had plunged downwards to his death.

Silent and containing all the breath he could muster to maintain step with the defiant younger knights, the Captain vainly endeavoured to keep apace, but because of his years he was not as strong in breath or body like the others ahead of him, being powerless to maintain the same speed of stride. With undemanding effort, the two knights raced on negotiating two and three steps at a time as they sped on and up the spiral staircases leading to the reception room of the main hall; their rapid approach through the palace interior was unchallenged and any man that was in the way was handled roughly to be manoeuvred out of their path.

The old Captain slavishly followed behind hot on their heels, whilst they spurred onward superseding any courtesy of the Court that was normally demanded from outsiders. They stumbled forth into the main chamber at speed and were compelled to catch hold onto the stone frames of the doorways to prevent them launching themselves unprepared into the room. There was no doubt that they were stunningly struck and unprepared for the sight before them.

The Prince was surrounded by his guards and ready for action with their swords drawn, with the Emissary's guard likewise ready to defend their superiors. Thankfully, it was a muddled standoff, but for how long was going to depend what happened next. The sight presented itself with a distinct lack of order with the two opposing factions cursing the other out of anger and confusion, but there were a few dignitaries willing in their attempts to hold the peace and stay the imminent clash of arms.

The Prince it seemed had lost all heart, he appeared slumped on his throne, resigned, with his head in his hands lost for the need to positively act to contain the situation; clothed in all his finery and wearing his princely crown, he appeared no more a statesman that the cat that was arching its back at his feet at those around him. There he sat, firmly ensconced on his throne portraying himself an incapable pathetic figure; a drawn look of loss was on his face, it appeared almost near to sobbing. The dead Emissary's aids could only act verbally, accusingly pointing an attacking finger at the Prince and like baying dogs harried their protected victim, who was in safe refuge behind a wall of guards.

Before them on the pine laid floor, lay the blood-soaked body of the visiting Damascan emissary. There was no doubt about whether his condition held any prospect for revival, his throat lay uselessly gaping open; being lacerated by some terrible means such as a wild jungle cat that would have manically clawed unceasingly at his throat, he was a mass of deep cuts and his ageing fleshy skin was like nothing Robert had never seen before. A lake of blood had overflowed from the horrific wounds, the joints of the warped timbered planking sat like an open mouth drawing on the red flow that passed by; the gaps collected his life blood and acted as a conduit to carry its warm searching red force onwards, its flow reaching outwards before slowing into a congealing sticky mass.

In their accusing and confused melee, not one of the many ranting aids of the dead Emissary had the presence of mind to cover the body or offer any reverential respect toward the murdered man.

The knights were brought to a sudden halt when they entered, being stunned by the bloodied body lying before them; although a ghastly sight, dead men offered no surprise or horror to them, but this was most unexpected. They began viewing the body and were particularly drawn to the lacerations of the throat, never before had they witnessed such an amount of slashing cuts. His attacker had manically slashed wildly at his victim. "I've never seen anything

213

like this before," Robert added, "I wonder if this is another one of those messages from our ladies in question."

The ageing, breathless Captain bounded into the room, he could only stop himself bumping into his fellow knights who were deeply troubled at the unbelievable and harrowing sight of the visiting dignitary's body. The Captain appeared last in line of the pursuing number of arrivals; he was panting heavily and displaying the fact that he was not used to such energetic movement. Short on breath and attempting to disguise the obvious fact as best he could, he spoke slowly as if measuring every word he took; drawing on long steady breaths between his words, he told the knights to keep out of his way and not to interfere into his job unless asked to do so.

With an unexpected efficiency, he ignored the scene of the dead Emissary and proceeded to the crowd of babbling dignitaries, giving temporary relief to the Prince from their tormenting tongues. With dignity and controlled respect, he had the situation under his control in what seemed no time at all.

Robert did as he was asked and kept clear of the visitors, admiring the speed the Captain was able to control the tormented group of emissaries that had rallied around the Prince and continuing to harass him. . His only concern appeared that the plans that he had devised for so long had in such a brief moment of time collapsed into abject failure. Apart from the sudden and tragic death of his visitor, it was likely that the Prince's subdued state lay much deeper than sadness alone, but to those that stood outside his circle of confided influence were not to know his loss.

The sight of a mutilated body on the floor of his throne room held no horror for this man, it only reminded him that the image of the crown of kingship was slipping from his hands; it was that and that alone which weakened his spirit and lengthened his face. With a sympathetic note of consolation in his voice, the Captain asked the Prince for permission to take control of the proceedings and to remove the body. The request was a welcome relief to melee of voices that rattled outside his private thoughts.

As if he were a descending angel from heaven, the Captain presided to quickly restore a semblance of order into the somewhat disarrayed court by quickly taking command; all eyes patiently watched as the body was removed very reverently and with the utmost respect for those onlookers of his own people to see. Whilst the Emissary's aids looked on in conciliatory silence mimicking silent prayers in their reverence, the body was carefully handled before a calming audience to leave a restoring sombre stillness to fall over the chamber. It gave the Captain and the Prince an intermission from the once quarrelsome and menacing group that had gathered around him. Momentarily free from the accusations of trickery and deceit that had earlier been levelled against the Prince, the peace did not last for long; low voiced mutterings soon began to circulate again once the body of the Emissary had been removed. The air returned to one charged with anger that needed to be vented; the Emissary's aides had been duped, so it appeared, and if trickery could be proved, it could lead to a direct incitement to war.

The Captain's insistence to ask questions respectfully gave him room for conjecture. He insisted on a misunderstanding of what had taken place and that they must calmly speak to him remembering all that occurred; it was important, he stressed, that every detail be told by those present. The Emissary's aides instantly broke out into an impatient train of inadequacies regarding the security of the palace; the Captain did not say as much, only ignored the unimportant cant of the revengeful aides. Maintaining a firm hold on the interrogation as calmly and diplomatically as possible, the Captain turned to his Prince for his explanation of events.

In an almost weeping voice of self-pity, he exhaled, depressed by the recollection he stated despairingly that the girl had been brought from her chamber where she had spent the previous evening with her mistress.

"Was this servant an older person wearing a full face mask?" interjected Robert. The Prince looked quizzically upon him unable to recognise the face or voice of this stranger. The Captain intervened to vaguely explain his presence and that he was to be introduced later, but an answer to the question held great importance to the identity of the mistress in question. Robert intervened again without addressing the Prince through the Captain, which brought angered looks from the dark eyes of the ageing officer for his discourtesy.

"Who was she and what business did she have here?" Robert pursued without thought. His sudden interjection of the question left the prince bewildered, as he looked at the Captain to contest the question. Before the Prince could answer, the Captain elbowed Robert before humbly begging the question to be put aside for his own questions. The Prince looked at Robert then to his Captain adding, "Who is this stranger that is not known to me, and what business does he have here?" The Prince may have seemed to be off balance with his grasp as to what had taken place, but he certainly did not wish to discuss his reasons to the present gathering openly.

Robert silently corrected himself, believing that anything to do with this devil woman was his business; he knew in his heart that she was at the centre of all this trouble. Robert watched the Prince's nervousness as he continually tinkered with a long, slender chain that hung low to his belt as if he used its golden links like some kind of worry beads. There was more to come out, he knew it.

"Please, Sire," Robert insisted with an air of interested curiosity.

In his sorrowful state, the Prince was bewildered and further annoyed as his mood changed to anger as he pressed by Robert for an answer. He bluntly told Robert he would not answer any questions, the captain broke in suggesting it may help if he were to answer, a reluctance showed on the Prince's face yet he conceded.

"It started some months past during a banquet, I had many guests and somehow I suppose the good time had got the better of me; and unguardedly, I aired my views in an open manner about certain expectant forthcoming events." Robert immediately surmised that what the Prince failed to say in plain language was that he was drunk and blabbed his mouth off giving all around an insight into his planned future designs; as to where to start with his story, the Prince broke forth as if he suddenly remembered.

A visiting papal monk, of whose name he could not remember, introduced himself and explaining his interest in his ambitious plans and in a remarkable act of diplomacy, added that it was no accident that he arrived here unannounced at this time, for he was on his way to Jerusalem to meet with the ecumenical council and thus far his journey was more of a fact-finding mission on behalf of the Holy Father. " I take it" Robert asked "you were able to discover if he was genuine", "He carried with him a sealed papal letter of introduction, and he was," he confirmed, "who he was purported to be," answered the Prince almost snappily. "His purpose, he implied, was to secretly assess the Princes of the kingdom for those that may best be suited for future support to higher office before his intended stop-over en route for Jerusalem."

Robert was agog, he felt like laughing in the Prince's face at his over blown foolishness. There the Prince of Antioch sits in all his riches and finery and the power over armies of men to do whatever he beckons, yet with all that power and affluence he fails to use the sense that he was born with, believing in the first stranger that comes along with such a tall yarn? By God, will my fellow man never learn, he asked himself; but in spite of this folly, his thoughts led him to believe that at last he was on the trail of something of interest. Yes, this information assured Robert of a connection the old Prior in Acre had hinted at, could this be his mysterious papal connection?

The Prince's voice broke into Robert's train of thought; it transpired, he said, that the priest had a long-standing friendship with another dignitary whom he did not divulge by name, implying that he too considered his concerns for the future stability of the area an excellent idea. "When we eventually met later, it was plain that he was aware about my strategy and concerns for the future. It was most helpful that the Holy Sea had taken notice of his actions to consolidate the Northern Province intimating that they were in support of me. The monk was very helpful, offering all sorts of useful suggestions and hinting that upon his arrival in Jerusalem; he would actively give support to the ecumenical council in my favour. I did find him odd in appearance, misshapen to some degree, though a very amicable, intelligent man of the cloth; a likeable character with a great understanding of the conflict within the region." He added that their meeting ran for some considerable length time, for a whole afternoon and evening and into the following day.

"I recall him telling me that he had visited throughout Byzantium on his way this far to Jerusalem, a mission most confidential, telling me he had spoken to other dignified men of interest regarding a means of creating a new way to form a peaceful union with his Damascene adversary, the Amman.

The advancement of his effort should I ever need his support was reassuring; he even offered to act as a conciliator in returning the captured daughter of the Amman. Alas, the idea of not having him here for the reunion of the child came as a disappointment; it would, I felt, have offered itself as a great coup to the ears of the ecumenical council, but unfortunately, he was called away before today's event was to take place."

"Tell me about today," Robert asked eagerly, "what actually happened?"

The Prince thought, recalling the event carefully. "When the girl was summoned to be brought forwards to be introduced to the Emissary, it was a time a great excitement for him."

"My Prince," the captain added quietly," the facts sire." He didn't appear to take kindly to that comment of the captain's when he was in flow of his recollections. Robert's eyes rolled, believing that he believed the Prince was playing at theatre. It wasn't hard to see that there was much at stake here politically; he, the Prince, was milking the cow for all it was worth, and in a way, Robert supposed he couldn't blame the man for that. "The Emissary, poor man, had not laid eyes on the child for at least three years; he knew not what to expect. She entered the room dressed in a pink frock and coat over her long narrow trousers; she appeared innocent, making a delightful picture. She had a small angelic face and was adorned with long flowing black hair, which was bound together in a platted lacework mesh of fine silver and golden strands, a sweet thing," he remarked rather dreamily. "She was of average height for her age and veiled as was expected." The captain listened to the account, noticing a pain in the Prince's eyes before he spoke of what was to follow.

"Overcoming his nervousness, he did what almost anyone would do, he extended his open arms to express a loving greeting to welcome her to his bosom to show acceptance back into the family on her return. She bent before him in servile salutation; overcome by his joyful reunion, he naturally reached out to bid her to rise. It was then it all happened, the child that was born of yesterday's grace was suddenly turned into a screaming slashing demon from some deep horrible nightmare of hate and bent on death. We were stunned by the surprise of the act; it was over within a winking of the eye and when she was through with her demonic deed she ran to the window screaming some gibberish before flinging herself out."

Returning to his recollections, the Prince added blankly, "I cannot tell you exactly what she said, I was stunned and could not comprehend her words fully," he said falteringly. Searching for a way to describe her diatribe, he faltered in his thoughts giving somebody else an opening to speak. "Sire, I believe it was a religious slur," interrupted an aide.

Whilst the others were occupied in their argumentative discourse and believing that he had the gist of the story, Robert decided to walk to the window where he had fleetingly witnessed the woman leap to her death. In his mind, he could not believe that it was the same woman that teased and tested his wit during the past few days, why would she want to do this, why waste her life for such an imprudent cause? He was trying hard to put the pieces of the puzzle together in an effort to make sense of it all and where its destructive direction could be leading. It dawned on him that he was at the window; perhaps his question of the woman would be answered; he shook his head as if to awaken himself from his thoughts recalling his purpose for being there. Leaning forwards, he looked out across the greenery of the garden, its beauty was quite a delight; someone had spent much time tending the floral displays it beheld. Although he had no interest himself in the pursuits of the tending of gardens, he could not help but admire the trouble and time spent to maintain its beauty. Drawing himself across the depth of the sill and supporting his body's outstretched weight on the window mullions with his outstretched arms, he visualised the sight he expected to see. There was no forthcoming answer to explain this puzzle of the girl's fatal leap. His memory flooded with visions of dark eyes and beauty that he hardly expected to see; it could not be her, surely, he mused with a sigh issuing forth from deep within through regrettable anticipation. Below lay the twisted form of the assassin, sadly and he felt it could but there she lay, he had never met anyone quite like her; slippery as she was, he had accepted her as a worthy opponent.

Withdrawing from the window into the reminiscent sounds of the dissentient discourse within the room, a cold and unwelcome shiver of horror and waste surged through his being.

The sight of the body had not registered as anything different at first glance, then something suddenly dawned on him that there was something not quite right about the body below – he was uncertain but he suspected it was something to do with the clothing on the body. With a certain dread in his heart, he once again stepped back and peered out of the window to the sight below. Starring quite hard at the sprawled body in the garden, he suspected it really could be his mysterious woman he had encountered. Not so long ago, he had vowed to cut her throat as he would easily that of a Seljuk warrior; by heaven above, he swore that Satan himself must have spawned such a woman for her wickedness.

In his mind, there was not a living soul on the face of the earth that showed such a flair for cunning and artfulness as she. Although that crumpled body below was the remains of an enemy, his memory of her up to the point of the previous evening would had driven him to fancy a tryst with her in the future, it would be a delight of exploring further companionship with her, but then that was all in his mind. It was indeed a strange affair, a woman with a talent for murder and yet one, he imagined, carried all the wiles of a female that was fine and soft and perhaps in her own way gentle.

Fleeting thoughts filled Robert's mind of her suspected better side; no one could be all evil, but then a cloud formed of a sudden reminder of his missing friends and Guy, bringing a frown of repentance for his crass stupidity in his idle daydreaming.

This was the woman that was able to make him appear foolish with her wily ways. Changing his line of sight whilst in reflection of his condemnation of her, his head drooped downwards; his aimless gaze wandered across the patterned grain of the timbered floor. There, towards the wall of the chamber, he caught sight of a bloodstained scroll fixed with a small golden circlet, glistening as if to say 'pick me up.' It must have been purposely dropped at the point where the girl had committed her suicidal jump from the high window. This, it seemed, was beginning to appear a morning for notes, and whatever its message was, had to be another piece in his puzzled series of events.

Picking it up, he noticed the freckles of blood on the outside of the small vellum roll. He drew off the small insignificant ring off the rolled parchment, unfurled it and began reading.

He shook his head as he read in disbelief, knowing that this particular writer was involved in his intrigue. What he read was surely deepening the puzzle. Believing that matters couldn't get any worse, with this message he clearly saw who his enemy was and that events would promise to get rougher when they met up. Now, it seemed, fragments of the mystery were coming together.

Robert looked around searching for du Bray; he was listening intently for a direction that may point to a clear and decisive clue to the incident that had taken place. Managing to attract his attention, Robert beckoned him over to join him near the window. Explaining what he had found, Robert pointed out this was further evidence to explain the event. "You had better see for yourself," handing over the note, he beckoned du Bray to take a look downwards into the garden. With his head out of the window, du Bray viewed the sight of the body below; straightening himself, he half turned his head in the direction of Robert who showed an appearance of deep speculative expression on his face. With the question waiting to be asked, Robert instinctively guessed du Bray's thoughts and sighing nodded his head in confirmation that this could be the same girl.

"That's a waste of a fine looking woman," said du Bray, adding that although he never had the pleasure of seeing her full face, he imagined she was so, and having the most beautiful brown alluring eyes that he had ever seen, such he believed that could send a man crazy.

He did not mean to infer anything to add to the weight of any embarrassment that his friend may feel, though he instinctively looked at him.

"Let's get on with this," Robert scowled.

Du Bray protested, almost apologising, "I didn't mean..." Robert held up his hand cutting him off. Du Bray reread the parchment, "I can't believe we're dealing with him. What's written can't lie, it's from him but it's not addressed to us, that's not like him." He replaced the ring back onto the parchment it's for them, and more of a notification of the Emissary's death sentence put upon him by our own ally, the leader of murderous sect of assassins." It was from the Old Man of the Mountain to the Amman of Damascus.

YOU HAVE IGNORED THE TRUE RELIGIOUS PATH OF THE PROPHET, REFUSING TO ACKNOWLEDGE MY WARNING OF WHAT WAS TO FOLLOW. BY YOUR OWN FOOLISH ACTIONS, YOU HAVE MADE YOUR CHOICE. THEREFORE, THE SHADOW OF THE AVENGER IS UPON YOU. FOR YOUR ARROGANCE YOU HAVE INVITED THE RAGE OF THE OLD MAN OF THE MOUNTAIN FOR WHICH THERE IS NO MERCY.

"So that's who she was working for."

Robert showed a deep furrowed frown of puzzlement with the introduction of this rogue action of the Old Man of the Mountain.

"That doesn't explain where she comes into this, or him, or us to that fact; this is an act against the Amman, why kill one of ours when we are not interfering in his private affairs? Unless the Old Man of the Mountain is attempting to take on us all," Robert posed. Doubt crept over him before he confidently stated, "No, there must be something else."

All, he hoped, would be resolved once this scroll was shown to the group to whom it was addressed, let us hope that this murderous act will be believed and that it was not staged by the Prince; who was presently taking the blame.

The scroll was immediately passed to the Captain who quickly read it then in turn handed it to the dead Emissary's aide.

As soon as the aide caught sight of the name of the sender, the Old Man of the Mountain, he wheezed deeply, his breath drawn in so sharply that he coughed with surprise, shocked by a momentary blockage in his windpipe. His complexion turned an ashen colour as the blood drained from his plump, pampered face, as a word spluttered with trembling terror from his quivering lips in a ghastly hollow whisper, "Hashashin."

"There seems little doubt about it," said the Captain, "his signature was written all over this tragic event."

The Old Man of the Mountain's reputation preceded him wherever his shadow was cast, so infamous was he that not a man woman or child could deny knowledge of his name. Robert knew that this black-hearted rogue took pleasure in subduing the countryside to mark the fulfilment of his exacting action. At this time, he was too far out of reach to make any moves against; if he could be seen he would probably be laughing now with the news of his latest success, though he cared nothing about what others thought of the outrages caused by him. In the room at that moment, only Robert was aware that there was a treaty between the Hashashin and the western knights; he also knew that the Old Man was not too keen on keeping his bargains and was quite prepared to push the patience of the western alliance to the limit. Because of their skills, they were useful in the game of espionage and that was a reason for tolerating them, though one day they would push too hard for their own good and, alas, that time might have come.

To compound his ability of power, the Old Man proceeded with finality in his murderous threats in public view and openness, so that there could be no mistake whatsoever as who was responsible for the killing. For it followed that those disciples that wielded the blade of retribution on his behalf, the Old Man always ordered them to end their own lives; their reward for their success meant they would be welcomed and accepted as martyrs into paradise.

When the Captain commented, the Emissary's aide buckled at the knees with the knowledge that the powerful and deathly arm of the Old Man of the Mountain had reached out and struck at them by taking their master. Their feelings of such hopeless insecurity caused them great consternation; some felt faint, others through of their insecurity with a need to run for cover, for there was little one could do to evade the threat once his intimidating shadow fell across an intended victim.

A heavy sweat had formed on the threatened Emissary's aide's brow; his hands were shaking as if in a nervous fit. It now seemed obvious that the aide believed himself to be the next in line for a fatal visit. With great design of thought, the assassin's purpose was always twofold, first the waiting of the event to attack the nerves so as to make the victim completely distraught before the final assault.

Robert turned away from the soft and timid aides; their life was too soft for him to bear; his only thoughts now were concentrating on who it was that jumped from the window. He nudged his companion du Bray, shifting his head to one side indicating that they were better off away out of the politics; it was time to leave the room and try to identify the body below. Robert's mind was in turmoil over the identity of the dead assassin; it struck him that she was not the type to be taking her own life, nor any path that was not of her own will; it made no sense to him. It came to him whilst making his way down the dimly-lit, spiralling stone staircase that that served as access to the garden, realising for the first time that he was unable to put a name to her. That was not all, her face had suddenly eluded him; only those dark penetrating eyes seemed to be the only true way of identifying her, coupled with her soft disarming voice which had recently been permanently silenced.

Suspended in nervous anticipation, Robert and du Bray made their way to the garden; the huge heavy entrance door that was the entrance to the greenery hung on enormous ornamental metal hinges which appeared strong enough to withhold an army. Du Bray in passing let his hand run across the surface of the heavy studs that held the iron hinges they were solid and he could not help but admire the workmanship. The builders and carpenters were men he thanked for their diligence and creativeness that he so many times in the past was left to rely on when in awkward positions, they may not have been fighting men like he, but together they made the country what it was, there was a knowing smile as he passed on his way into the hot open air that greeted him like a stifling wall denying him of fresh air. Jasmine was in bloom, its delicate blossom emitting its sweetness of fragrance; rosemary, roses and numerous other sweet smelling blooms combined with lavender to seize nasal sensitivities as the abounding confusion of their bouquets filled the small verdant oasis that was hidden within the huge stone structure that was the garden's wall. Du Bray slowed his pace taking in the mixed fragrances, admiring that the gardener's choice of planting was truly intoxicating.

Robert, oblivious to it all, had only business on his mind; approaching the broken and bent body of the assassin from across the sweet smelling garden, his mind's purpose was eager to clarify what his heart feared to discover.

The two knights stood over the crumpled body, staring down at the wasted life, its head embedded face down in the bed of green grass inhibiting its own identification. Du Bray mused in a discerning way that paradise comes in different ways to us all. He looked unemotionally upon the disfigured bent corpse. Robert, by this time was bending over the figure, carefully rolling the body over in anticipation and reluctance. He gingerly lifted the face veil revealing the smooth feminine features of a youth. Surprised, he looked up to his companion and back to the body; doubt was upon him, though he had never had a clear look at the woman's face, he could hardly bring himself to accept that it was the girl they were looking for; this one seemed hardly into puberty. His friend, being unemotional to that end, had thoughts otherwise; Robert endeavoured to turn the small lifeless head, placing his hand gently on the face; his mind more keenly taken with identification, he did not notice any unusual movement of the hair. Du Bray had keenly noted the movement, seeing the situation differently; placing his foot into the assassin's groin he began massaging it in a circular motion; it displeased Robert and he said as much, but bent down alongside. "Ha!" exclaimed du Bray, "This female is a boy." With curiosity running wild, he reached out forcefully pulling at the hair causing it to move; and as it slid away it revealed no hair on the head at all only a balding pate. Both men were taken aback, amazed as they viewed the exposed head of a male youth.

It all seemed unbelievable to the two men standing over the body; they could not avoid seeing that the hands still wore the cotton gloves that they witnessed held secreted razor sharp bloodied blades within them that were used to mutilate the Emissary. They were messy in their work but very effective; Robert fingered the fine blades that were ingeniously sewn into the gloves and secured along the length of the fingers by rings suited for that purpose, then when the fingers were flexed the knife ends were exposed like a wildcats claws ready to carry out their lethal task. "That's a further testament to the Old Man," said du Bray as he pointed at them.

"Well it's not her," said Robert turning to du Bray betraying a relieved look on his face, "it would seem that she was not open to this type of work, being too damn crafty to do it herself." There was no doubt in his mind that although it was not her, this dupe wore her clothes, which made her party to the crime, insisted du Bray.

Detecting the relief on his friends face, du Bray knelt by him; he sympathetically looked Robert in the eye, appealing with a gentle sensitive voice to forget her. He had guessed that his friend had been smitten by her and pleaded in his attempt to bring his friend to reality; though they both knew that the question begging was, where would the two of them be now?

With a shaking of his head, Robert stated that something was wrong in this whole affair. "If this was their purpose, then we have been misled in our expectations that they were involved in our mission," but he no longer saw it that way.

"Then why have they included us in their business by killing Godwin and abducting Hubert and Aldo?" Robert could not answer the question posed but somehow he believed they were confusing the theory he had originally had. "I know it is somehow wrong, but I also know that we cannot desert our friends and leave them to the mercy of their abductors." Anger disturbed him; they had proved their ability to outwit him and have now moved on freely to do more of their mischief after their success. "By God," said du Bray, "their cleverness pointed to their probable rank, I would wager that they are likely to be the Old

Man's fidawis in the field; they are as destructive as a regiment of cavalry; and as effective."

As the realisation of his friend's words sank in, Robert's face dropped, he knew du Bray was right.

"I swore an oath that I was going to catch up with her; believe me her day is coming, but there is much we have yet to do. If we can track her down, then we should be able to discover what all this is about and release our friends at the same time."

They stood a while before walking away, Robert admitted, "This land is both hostile and beautiful; there's a bewitching draw by its mystery and intrigue here; I have learnt to accept that fate can have a strange way of catching up to those that are unprepared and too cocky. She could be laughing at us this moment having the upper hand and probably believes that she had seen the last of us."

He spoke openly of the many puzzling events taking place in rapid succession, "It's hard to keep track of their fiendish trail of human debris, and it bothers me that we are being left behind each and every time."

It troubled him to accept why the Old Man was mixed up in a bid to oust the westerners; in his effort to rationalise, he stated that if the Old Man has a pact with the Temple, why would he need to carry out such an act of barbarity in Antioch?

Du Bray hesitantly interrupted Robert's thinking aloud by explaining that this act was not against us, but the Amman, who has religious differences against him.

"Hmm, we don't know that for sure, but yes you are probably right. But why act here? To hazard a guess I would say that we are not thinking this problem out correctly or seeing the true picture of events."

Meanwhile, alone in his chambers, the Prince sat alone pondering his dilemma, a goblet of rich red wine in his hand and a brimming golden carved ewer at his side. Should he need to replenish his goblet of thoughtful stimuli, it stood nearby on the floor at his feet within easy reach. He needed to think about the whole scheme of things, which in his present mood would mean drinking copious amounts of wine; strange, he thought, how the wine made things clearer; and with that he gulped down the contents of his goblet before refilling to lean back in his chair to assess the craft and cruelty shown to his person this day.

The Amman's aides were preparing to hurry back to Damascus and in fear of their lives, believing that the curse of death was hanging over their heads. It might not be very long before the accusations of incompetence and laxness of security for such high ranking visiting dignitaries to the Prince's household could be so easily overlooked. Worst of all, accusations of collusion with the Old Man of the Mountain had been levelled at the Franks. Due to the fervent religious differences that the Old Man of the Mountain had with the Damascans, they themselves knew that this weakness was enough to cause their own downfall should the Franks openly take up arms against them.

For those who did not wish for friendlier relations with the Franks, this event came as a gift to them; mumblings of discontent were already abroad with the Amman's belief that closer relations could be possible with the westerners. This thought had sickened the hard line faction and machinations for a vigorous form of rebuff to the Amman's plans, and now presented an opportunity to carry them through. It would be easy to turn the minds of the weak against the hated invading forces; by cleverly setting the stage for a future war, this dissenting group believed that once it was underway it would be hard to stop. It wouldn't take much to promote a conflict; they were already becoming an annual event in that part of the world.

Lounging into his cushioned chair, his feet now resting on an ornamental foot stool, it quickly became apparent to Prince Guy what to do for the best. Whatever was going to happen, it would most likely mean some kind of hostility; if it were to be a war, it would be bad for his plans. That would mean raising money for an army, which he could ill afford to find, especially after such a long period of unrest in the Principality. He had endured a lavish lifestyle that others had harped against; now because of it he was without the means to decide for himself the most temperate way securing his future. Unfortunately, there was only one establishment he could approach and that was the Holy See; but to have to suffer the embarrassment of approaching them would only mean that once in their clutches, the papal moneylenders would be demanding harsh conditions, and for him it would be too high a price to pay. It had not been so long ago that tentative but friendly propositions were put to him requiring certain favours to a request from Rome, which he declined out of hand, packing the representative off in the least ceremonial way. To make an approach to borrow money for the support of an army would give him little chance of surviving their endless lectures and to ensure a fulfilment of their excessive demands through possible land grabs. No, he dismissed that idea from his mind preferring to walk over hot coals rather than succumb to such demeaning demands. Although he had little time, he would wait and see what the immediate reactions of the Damascans would be.

If the outcome of this event resulted in a war, then so be it; fighting wouldn't scare him, though it bore costly burdens and he had fought too many long wars to be unsettled by such an outcome. His peaceful victory was his way out of the situation; who knows it would be quite a coup to secure a renewed peace pact with the Damascans, enabling his diplomacy to win the day against his real enemy, the clerics. He would be vindicated and able to reassert his position as contender to be the next leader of the Holy Land.

Guy the First, King of Jerusalem and the lands of Outremer, how the title fitted him, as would the crown; he thought a while on the sound and agreed through his clouded, intoxicated mind that it suited him well. It would not be easy to turn the tide of opinion back in his favour after the recent event, though he played no part in it and cursed its happening. In his cupped imagining, his head fell to his chest; the wine had taken effect on him, yet it had not stopped any of his machinations. Thinking further, he was convinced that there was just the slightest chance of his being successful; his brow furrowed trying to identify the priest that came by; he would give orders to his spies to be on the lookout for him with a rather large reward to safely bring him back and use as a lever against the clerics; that he felt would embarrass and expose them as movers in the affair. Then he could raise the money he required for mercenaries to swell his army and smash the pagan bastards that brought him to this end. Or if luck was with him, and why shouldn't it be as he had done no wrong to any man by bringing the crescent and the cross together, he knew his aristocratic standing would elevate him above all others throughout the Holy Land, leaving the path to the throne open.

The peace of the room was suddenly broken as his scheming mind drifted to the assassination. Like a spark igniting a brush fire, his cantankerous temper manifested, resulting in his ornate footstool, which had probably been the peak of some poor diligent craftsman's life's work, being violently kicked across the chamber in a fit of his royal pique, smashing against the wall and falling into a broken heap that was no longer any use save that of firewood. His hands clutched at his head; what on earth would happen, all because of some religious fanatic; in a state of disappointment, he suddenly felt that all had been swept aside into probable chaos once more. It's all as if it were planned, how the words sent a shudder down his spine at the thought.

Secretly, and unknown to this aspiring prince, there were others that played a game in the opposing side. Although they had no hand in the affair of the death of the emissary, some knew of the events to come; not all men had peace in mind with the Christian invader on that day. Meaning that some of those that had accompanied the emissary when the attack took place were horrified at the outcome, yet as soon as the shock of the event had subsided, they lost no time to use the convenience of the murder to their own active and evil ends. Though it meant that they too were under the shadow of assassination from the Old Man of the Mountain, the need to rid the land of the western invader took precedence over their own immediate safety. So when the scroll was made known to them, they had no case to use the murder of their leader as an immediate cause of provocation for war. No, it meant that to the world at large they would have to fabricate another reason to suit their purpose. For those aides in the pay of the dissenters it meant that they could twist the outcome into being seen as a collusion of the westerners and the Old Man of the Mountain to rid the land of their sworn enemy; and where in all of this was the child that they were supposed to collect?

When the chamber had been cleared by the Captain; the court was under no illusion that they had not heard the last of the dissention from the Damascans. Trust was difficult enough to come by other than through sincere contact; unfortunately peace clouds were rapidly turning into storm clouds of greater discontent. The lack of faith in their prospective friends was short lived; a guessing game of their intentions was about to be tested. On the departure of the Damascans from the citadel, orders had to be given to the keepers of the carrier pigeons to send a message to make ready and prepare for the worst. Prince Guy had a weakness; unlike his brothers before him who had proved themselves actively worthy in battle, Guy was a fighter but not a great leader of men, and in the main preferred the soft, easy life. The recent loss of his brothers, who had maintained the family honour, now left him exposed for all to see what he was made of. With Guy's weakness on display, he was not without intelligence, and was well aware that there were those around him more fitted for the battlefield. Satisfied in his mind that diplomacy would be his role, he settled on leaving the fighting and preparations thereof to his aides and his Marshal and looked towards clearer skies and his newly proposed fortune.

For the next few days, a presence of discontent and suspicion hung over the court waiting for news from Damascus. Fortunately for Guy, his granaries were full; all livestock from the surrounding region had been brought within the city walls to pasture. He always remembered the necessary warning words of advice from his grandfather when dealing with the Muslim fiend, 'Trust nobody and prepare for the worst'; Antioch, he always said, was impregnable to siege. It was pointless to play a waiting game, no matter how many men a general had or was prepared to throw at the walls of the city. With an army outside the walls to feed thousands, the truth was that once they had run out of food stocks, they would be required to hunt for their food "And answer me this," his grandfather said, "ten thousand men need a lot of feed and so how long would it be before they had killed all the game in the area?" It was a fair point and one the Prince believed was one that the enemy already knew; so how would they go about weakening their enemy to draw them from behind their walls? From now on, thought the Prince, they would be playing chess, and it gave him hope and some comfort to offset what he first thought was a weaker position.

It took the whole of the following day for du Bray and Robert to see the Captain whilst under the preparation for a possible siege. When they finally gained access to him, there was no greeting of cordiality like before, only a hand with the palm outstretched held in the air as if to firmly halt their progress further. His voice bellowed in renewed self-importance, "I could give you little time, gentlemen, it had better be important."

Blazing at the temerity of the ageing Captain, Robert could hardly preserve himself from striking him.

"What news of your investigation, Captain?" he enquired impatiently. The answer he received did little to dispel his anger. The Captain was astounded, he informed Robert that the matter of his friends now remained in the hands of the Prince himself; that, he snorted, was beyond even Robert's jurisdiction, irrespective of his rank; furthermore, adding insult to injury, he was ordered to be placed at the disposal of the Captain now that the citadel was on a war footing. Without allowing Robert to speak, du Bray snatched the scroll from Robert's hand and passed it to the Captain, who reached out and took it, reading its contents before looking at them.

"Why has it taken you so long to see me about this matter?" said the Captain evading what he already knew, by putting on a false air of authority and concern; by now the writer has moved on and cleared out of the region.

"Sir," spoke Robert attempting to control himself from bursting, "we have tried continually, but you have been absent and had little time for others being in deepest discussion with Prince Guy over the situation. Had we have been able to, we would have made our own investigation into the abduction of our friends, but you had the city closed."

"That is so; what would you have me do, ignore the situation and the orders of my Prince and give you whatever you wish? The situation could very well be dire; who knows if this time tomorrow or the next day the enemy will be at the gates." The Captain sighed, the excitement was catching up to him. "What do you want?" he snapped.

This was not the attitude that was expected. Where had the cooperation and new approach to friendly relations gone? Frustration and impatience swept over Robert like a cold wind.

"We need the ransom money and three fast horses," he said without thinking. The old Captain was taken aback at the issuing demand. "Do you indeed?" the Captain's blood pressure began steadily rising, "Is that all?" the words spilled out sarcastically. Knowing that he was now in control of the city and everyone within its walls, he was able to feel more than confident. Leaning back in his chair with an air of superiority settling on him, the Captain asked, "Let me pose you a question, who do you serve?"

The two looked at each other at such a silly question knowing very well whom they served.

"Well," bellowed the Captain impatiently.

Robert perplexed at the reason for such an obvious question and answered, "Our masters are the King and the Grand Prior of the Temple in Acre."

"So tell me," said the Captain, drawing the younger man onwards, "whom do you give your reports to when you're not in Acre?"

"If required out of courtesy, we always give our reports and liaise with the Captain of whichever area we are working in," replied Robert, his voice trailing off at the realisation of the words that were spoken. "But that does not mean that we are under your sole command," he retaliated. "It seems to me that you are forgetting that we have two of our friends out there and the fugitives that have kidnapped them will kill them if we do not do something positive to save them. Not only are these friends we seek," he continued, "but they are members of a service that is subject to the King's own council."

"Hah, not that again," the Captain roared as he prepared himself for a locking of horns in a mother of all arguments, he was not going to give way in his authority on someone that had duped him earlier. A knowing sardonic smile broke on his smug face feeling victorious to having his way. "There isn't any way I will allow you to play at riding around in search these women who are at the bottom of the recent trice.

You are now in the Principality of Antioch and under the jurisdiction of the said Prince; be careful that you do not stress your will against me. Horses I will give you, but, and this is a direct order, you will ride and be lookout along the southern ridges. If there is any intent or threats from the Damascans or any signs of invasion from their armies, then they will be camped somewhere on the plain and be easily seen from that point. If the enemy is to come, then they will likely skirt the mountains for cover." As his orders issued forth to the disappointment of the duo, du Bray gripped Robert's arm, expectant of how he was likely to react to the Captain's orders. Robert knew that his friend had acted for the best, but his rage had gone past the point of holding down; he shrugged off du Bray's grip in his anger, telling the Captain that he had no direct authority over them as they were free agents; they neither belonged to any army that could be seconded nor did they fall under his direct command; if anything they remained the Captain's superior. Du Bray closed his eyes and yielded to the inevitable; he knew there was no stopping Robert now.

Likewise there was a revengeful antagonism showing in the Captain's eyes. "Just who do you think you are?" he sneered contemptuously, and finally the Captain dealt his card that won the game of command for him by telling the arguable knight his intention, to which he had no way of wriggling out of. "We are initiating an attempted siege and you," he pointed at the two standing knights, "are going to submit to my command; that is the rule under any war footing. If you think that you are going to be riding around the countryside after your two women, then you had better forget it. I'm sorry about your friends," he admitted, "but casualties, you understand, will always occur in such circumstances, and no one should know that better than you." As if he was dismissing children, he concluded, "if you persist in blocking or disobeying my orders, you will be arrested and notice sent by myself of your actions of disloyalty to Acre, is that clear?"

"Sir, I protest," Robert intervened. "You could send a sergeant at arms to carry out such a task whilst we gather better intelligence."

"You mean like running after two tarts? Get yourself together and see sense." By this time, the Captain's patience had stretched to its limits, he was equally full of rage for his brothers in arms from Acre and ordered them in a raised voice to leave his office or be prepared for a stay in the cells.

Once outside, Robert let out his fury; he slammed the Captain's office door in anger, whilst the cleric working at his desk dropped his head closer to his work, knowing better than to look up to view the scene.

The mood was black and there wasn't any way that Robert was going to let the Captain restrain his efforts to rescue his friends.

"It is my guess that this Prince is playing all of them along, there isn't going to be any siege; we both know that if anything, it will amount to compensation. We need to do something positive."

"I'm with you there," said du Bray, "but we have no money and a threat hanging over us from our own people."

They made their way out of the barracks and into the crowded streets, and then towards the town and the apartments. Resigned to obeying the Captain's orders, du Bray could see by the look on Robert's defiant face that he had something else in mind; asking of his plans, the reply suggested that they had to look to their own. "Considering that the noble Captain probably hasn't seen any action for years, he's probably losing his nerve right now in the anticipation of a forthcoming battle that's not going to happen."

"Now then Robert, let's not get disrespectful and misjudge him because of the roasting he gave you," prompted du Bray. "He's a good man at heart."

"Good man, my arse, he is probably pissing himself right now and is too bone-headed to ask for assistance and advice from those that are more suited to battle conditions." As Robert's anger subsided, he gave way, "You're right, of course, he's alone and hanging on to all that is left of his office. We serve the same master, but we have to reach the snake if we are going to help the others."

Stopping mid stride, du Bray halted Robert's pace pulling on his arm, "What's got into you? We have just been given an order, which we are duty bound to respect."

"That Captain does not hold any authority over our movements. In the city, perhaps, but not once we are outside, don't you understand?" said Robert, "We are the arms of intelligence out here and more could be learnt seeking our friends."

The streets of the town were overflowing with people; the word was out that the castle was closed. Some gathering their valuables, others ran scared after the news of the assassination had leaked out and one thing was certain, they expected trouble to follow, but for them there was nowhere to run to. In his blind anger, he callously failed to be rational; the people who had the misfortune to be in his path were knocked aside as the force of his demeanour surged forward like some tidal wave of pique. None could be seen by Robert, who barged his way through the crowds allowing his anger and temperament to cloud his vision. The shouts of insult at Robert for his aggression from the crowd went completely over his head.

"As I was saying, it may be useful for you could scout the ridges whilst Edward and I seek out Aldo and Hubert, that way nobody is breaking any orders."

Du Bray thought over the proposition and felt at ease with the suggestion but was at a loss as to how they were going to raise the money; without it they had nothing to bargain with.

Robert had already made up his mind; purpose and intent had decided the outcome as he calmly stated "There is only one way open to us, it will have to be done the hard way."

Dusk was descending upon the city, bringing with it an uncertainty that held no prospect of security; and as further rumours of a siege circulated, those hemmed within the walls anxious to say the least. Those that had experienced such events previously offered little comfort to those now locked into the prepared citadel.

The Rescue

On their return to the apartments; Edward had prepared in anticipation of their leaving, he had three horses saddled and ready to ride. Provisions had been organised and a spare pack horse was loaded in readiness. In spite of the cloud of disappointment that Robert had laboured under after a refusal of help from the Captain; Robert showed his appreciation with a nod of approval. They lost little or no time reporting back for their passes to leave the barracks and the citadel.

Below in the streets; groups of people hung about in ferment arguing that the army's duty was to protect them whilst others felt that they should try to leave, but the gates were closed to most everyone. Robert had his own problems and would not stop for those people to allow himself to be drawn into their requests for information on the situation; for his refusal he was cursed and sworn at.

On reaching the city gate; the guards seemed in just as bad a temper as the street people; reluctance to address the passes or open the gates showed their fear for what they believed was to come. Encountering nothing from the guards but aggravated banter and slackness of their duty, they were threatened with being reported to the captain, with that they soon changing their attitude and with the passes being signed with approval, Robert was still having to stress that they were on a mission of the highest priority, only then did they believe that the group were off to gain help for the city. Once through the gates the trio then rode for their entire worth south on the road to Tripoli. Some miles further on the group came to a halt; this was where du Bray parted from their company to cover the mountain trails as ordered should the Captain's dread of an invasion occur, but before leaving they wished each other well; du Bray broke off eastwards whilst the others continued south.

They were over two days behind their appointed meeting with the captors of their friend's; and it would take almost another three or more days to reach their intended position at the canyon of the snake from where they were. With this knowledge Robert believed that to make up on the time; a dangerous but shorter route was the only one left open to them. Edward eyed his brother guessing his strategy; wincing at the thought of what he was about to suggest. With an appealing look in his eye he turned to his brother Edward. "It has to be the mountain path, it's our only chance to get there on time if we are to have any chance of saving them."

This was not an easy route, to cross the passes through the mountains and both were aware that they were taking a great risk. It was true that they would save much time but there could be dangers from any number of situations and the cold they knew could turn hard against them along the narrow paths they were choosing to take. In spite of the dangers that lay ahead of them they kicked their horses into action and headed off towards the trails that would lead them up to the high ground; many hazards would be encountered but Edward agreed there seemed no choice. They were his friends as much as Roberts and in such situations of their friendship it had never needed to be proved. To increase their risk the two would take little time for resting, it came down to a matter of the sooner they had crossed the high ground the sooner they would be able to take time to rest on the other side. They continued riding on into the gloom of anxiety that was descending, as well as evaluating in their minds the tricky trails that lay ahead there was a need for quietness to think on what lay ahead. It was unsafe to ride at speed as the darkness descended but they were driven men on a mission of rescue and were prepared to continue on horseback at a walking pace under the reduced light of the starry firmament.

The heavens were studded with more stars than they could count in a life time; or so it seemed, and as long as they were able they would continue their journey. So many thoughts passed through Edwards mind, many times he would look up to view the twinkling stars, he recalled in the past when they slept on the ground, how he gazed towards the heavens and talked of them, wondering if they were the eyes of the angels? Bewildered at that thought he shook his head; he needed to concentrate on where he was going, if only he could see what lay ahead? The two men were wearying; the cold was nipping at them as their trail drew them on even higher. Fortune was with them as they spied a dark outline of shelter, as they closed on it they felt it was their refuge for a place to eat and rest, though it was a dilapidated building they had seen through the glimmer of the twilight and recognised it as a shepherd's abode. Behind its ruined walls; it was enough to ward of the cold wind that was nipping at them from the peaks above. From his height in the saddle Edward viewed the wreckage, nothing survives in this land of turbulent upheaval, especially when a rampant army passes by bent on demonstrating the passions of war. There within the ruined walls they spent a little time; enough to squat down under the protection of a warm blanket to regenerate their tired and chilled bodies, it seemed barely sufficient time to rest the horses properly though there was luxury enough for the horses to feed and for them to enjoy a short nap.

Throughout the time of their stay they hardly spoke a word to each other, preferring the silence to any dispute of agreement, all that was on their minds was how they were to gain the safe return of their friends.

As soon as the sun exposed its awakening aura and life giving benefit to the horizon, the two brothers were once preparing to be in the saddle and riding through the early dawn and towards their destination to the canyon of the snake.

This place that the enemy had chosen for their rendezvous must have been of the woman's choosing; it showed that she was thinking all the time and had planned her scheme well. She was taking all necessary precautions; knowing that should her plans be faulted; she had a means of escape, which always served to her advantage.

The canyon of the snake was so named after a one time bandit who had built his stronghold there long ago. He was notorious in the region and was difficult to pin down whenever the attempts of destroying his stronghold occurred. The remains of his fortress lay deep towards the end of a deadly winding and twisting pass that had sheer walls to its side, once any unexpected visitor or enemy ventured into the winding trail; little hope of escape from cleverly positioned archers was impossible. There was however a crevasse at the rear of the fortress that offered safe passage to its far side by means of a rope bridge, and once across this bridge the escaping tenant was free of pursuit by cutting the ropes that secured the bridge.

The route that the two men travelled had changed dramatically, not only was it cold when the sun went down but it would grow colder during the time that they were at higher altitude. It was bleak where they were heading without any cover from the winds that could blow up out of nowhere. The ground was like iron and dangerous for the horses to cross, what soil there was had blown away centuries ago leaving sharpened edges that could injure their mounts. To be alone further on up without a horse left little chance of survival. They knew the risks and were prepared to continue; with luck the worst of their crossing would be over by sun down that evening. It was cold in the hills; yet they suffered it willingly because of its expedience; and even though at times they had cursed the heat of the sun in the valley, up in the high ground; it was sorely missed. Long ago they had left behind the green fertile fields and rich arable soils of the lower lands around Antioch; and soon they knew that they would no longer chance pushing their mounts across the unfriendly plateau they were heading for. They had reached the narrow paths that wound around the cliffs of the mountain, to one side there was a sheer drop. It was hard work having to pull and coax their mounts along and they knew it would get harder still. Their fears were more for the horse's survival than their own; for should the horses go lame; their hopes to rescue their friends would be lost. They reached a point where the climb to the plateau began. Christ Edward felt a shiver of the cold wind nip at him, here the hard exposed stony earth where deflation had occurred over many eons of passing time offered little comfort to their passage across this difficult terrain; it was the stark wilderness of the high mountains. At high altitude the earth had suffered dramatically by the severity of the elements, removing the surface soils and sediments leaving the earth stony, hard and exposed with their sharpened edges looking upwards as if waiting to inflict injury to those that crossed it carelessly. Only goats or sure-footed creatures survived here; and at this point for their own sakes they could not chance even to ride at speed for a short while for fear of damage to their mounts hooves.

When time seemed pressing and tension got the better of Robert, Edward had to remind his brother that there was no point in making such great haste. Many times the knight felt the need to remount and chance his luck when conditions falsely tempted him; but past knowledge of the seriousness of such a foolhardy decision and his brother's presence was always there as a quelling force to ensure their continued safe; but slow crossing.

Robert's mind was filled for his friend's safety, pictures of Godwin entered his head and in a silent prayed he entreated for his friends to remain unharmed. Robert had suffered and been in too many bloody battles to readily accept the teachings of turning the other cheek; even during the peace he saw the cynicism within his own ranks, enough to sicken his moral beliefs in his fellow man. But he could not prevent the words from forming; Lord he prayed let them not be sacrificed because of my late arrival. His eagerness was constantly pressing him; it was good that he chose Edward to be with him; for he was a buckler to calming his passion for action and speed. In frustration he gave out a loud groan as Edward spoke to ease his pace; Robert he knew he was right and slowed accordingly, passing over the stony ground and having to watch that each foot step was carefully taken over the rocky surface of the earth, and all the time they progressed the wind blew cold striking at their bones. Stopping momentarily with a feeling that all was hopeless, his brother did not need to question his reason, he too felt the same way, speed was what they both would have liked, but the balance of their mission was weighing too heavily to waste it on a senseless urge for speed.

They were wearing their blankets over their clothes against the winds bitterness; move on brother; Edward gently grunted we'll make it. Time became a reminder that they could not stop; not even when hunger snapped at their bellies; for each break was drawing a cost on the waiting time for their friends, and the hazards on the mountain was also a risk to their own survival. You don't need to remind me of that Robert retorted, if only we could get over this damned plateau to the passes. Patience brother; cried Edward shouting above the wind's whistle; at times the sound was like the wailing of women around their dead, it was not a pleasant thought . We will get there soon enough, let us not chance injuring the horses against any of these vicious stones, we will soon recover in due course when the wind drops. They walked slowly bent and huddled within their blankets, pulling their horses behind them, they too were affected by the winds, but the men had taken the precaution of blind folding the horses for their protection. The wind made the horses fearful catching flying grit as it blew at them, the horses were scared and the men had to wrap the reins around their hands firmly to prevent the horses running off and doing themselves a fatal injury. Edward shouted above the sound of the wind to reassure his brother that by staying close they had a better chance to calm the horses; though Robert wished for the entire world that God could open his hand and lift him to where they should be.

There was no quicker route, and on the plateau there was no protection when the wind blew, precarious as it was they had to keep going. Because of the their timing and ease the woman that they pursued would have been canny enough to have opted for the longer casual and safer lowland roadway, aware that her pursuers would have been unable to follow at any speed under the circumstances. Robert mused the bitch was confident of her position; that was plain enough; she could take her time knowing there was no need to hurry, aware of the mess that she had left behind, there would be a crisis and it would take days to sort out. He had been blinded at the reason for the direction she had taken; it was not what he had expected; once he had learnt that she was in the employ of The Old Man of the Mountain.

The open barren landscape was offering little ease, they would be deprived of the chance of finding water should they run out of their own supply; but thankfully there was always the snow up ahead to depend on. It galled him that their fate would be decided by their endurance and luck. They continued their upward course; the terrain became even sparser though it was some consolation that the wind had miraculously dropped. Their ascent to even higher ground became more exposed and the temperature dropped lower and conditions promised steadily to become worse. Their route led them alongside the upper reaches of the mountain and just below the ice field, when there they would have no choice but to move as fast as they could not wanting to be caught at that height when should they be forced to slow their pace and darkness fall to catch them out.

For now the bright daylight filled the deep clefts in the exposed mountainside, snow sparkled on the slopes in the bright daylight and at times they were forced to look away, fortunately they did not have to traverse those fields of snow. The coldness was noticeably fiercer, attacking their bodies mercilessly causing great shivers to taunt them; with everything they carried now for the cold nights being slung around them, they climbed onwards hoping that their meagre protection would be sufficient to protect them from the chills they had to endure. Stopping momentarily from time to time to examine their route, gave them adequate time to adjust their direction. There was a criss-cross of hard tracks; probably from wandering animals that grazed the area; it helped them a little to see better the shape of the terrain but wasn't making life any easier for the travellers. A confusing dilemma had confronted them on which way to walk, this was another reason why men had perished here; being lost and chilled it brought about weaknesses that could lead to death from starvation, madness and even death from wild creatures that knew these hills far better than any man. They viewed the winding criss-cross of hazardous trails ahead, with half closed hawkish eyes searching for the correct route that would eventually lead them in the direction of a downwards path and the Snake. The tree line had been left behind long past, apart from smatterings of snow only lichens and scrub were to be seen at this altitude. The slopes ahead showed they had to traverse loose falls of stone; they appeared to be their most dangerous points; with signs that frost was covering the stones they walked over; and that was no comfort.

At their present speed they had a slim chance of making time, their direction was becoming clearer but detail of the landscape was difficult for the riders to take in properly. The horses were no longer exhausted thanks to the sensible decisions made earlier, with the horses walking light it eased their previous exhaustion; but once clear of this terrain they would be once again called on to serve their riders determination. Endurance and patience for the knights became the test, they had to keep their bodies moving; pushing themselves exhaustively onwards almost to their limit. Following close behind, it was obvious to Edward that at times his brother's silence indicated that his mind was not where it should be, being most likely hatching a plan for the rescue. Their present purpose was too grave for them to lose their concentration at this time, one slip was enough to be injured; or worse sliding to their death on the scree slopes. Too many times Edward painfully bore witness to his brother's inattentiveness by his poor footing on the loose ground in his eagerness to press on. There was no doubt in Edward's mind; his brother was spoiling for a fight with the enemy to rid himself of his pent up tensions, if only for his own safety he would put it to one side.

They carefully meandered along the precarious winding pathways until they came across an open snowy area, Edward was quick to notice a quickening of Robert's intention as he made to mount his horse. We should walk a little longer brother he suggested, pointing out that with a kick of his toe into the snow against a stony lip in the rocks; we may not see their jagged edges but they remain waiting. One slip; that was enough said Robert there was an edge of aggressiveness in his voice contending Edward's suggestion. Cold was ever biting hard at them and they needed to move on quickly to lower ground, and across from this cold open space that was not too far away. They walked along gripping their clothing tightly to their bodies; clutching the blanket to give their thin clothing the extra protection from the chilling air that gnawed at them like baying hounds; but in spite of the short distance left to go Robert found difficulty in giving up his eagerness to be across this snow field ahead. "No wait" cried Edward, there was danger ahead; Edward felt it in his gut. Why throw away the gains we have made Robert when we are so close to the end of our crossing. The ground ahead was untouched and the snow appeared sound enough for them to make their way across it. Quickly Edward drew level; he grabbed at his brother's horses bridle and handed over the reins of his own mount, without a word being exchanged, Edward's caution was noted by his brother and the pace slowed to a careful stride. Drawing his sword; Edward began poking downwards into the snow before he would step forwards. Carefully testing the depth at each pace; the two men proceeded slowly onwards; until Edward stopped abruptly, get back, get back he cried in panic; fearful of what lay before them. His sword had entered the snow and gone uncommonly lower than he felt was safe to proceed. They had not realised the distance that they had advanced into the patch of snow until they stopped to look around; they were close to the middle of the snow field and looking back noted that they had steadily sunk deeper into the crisp snow layer with each step and were presently sinking almost past knee depth. Slowly so as not to disturb the ground Edward eased himself backwards from his place in the snow; it was easy for him but the horses needed to be calmly coaxed as not to create too much of a disturbance. Being safe and further back He turned to Robert whose face was grave with concern "I swear there was no ground beneath my feet other than pack ice" Edward said, "I suspect we were crossing a chasm of sorts, it would have been the end for us to proceed."

There was nothing else to do but to go upward and find another route to edge around this area and it was not too their liking to spend more time than was necessary with the coldness being as bitter as it was. They persevered in spite of the cold and finally reached a point where by taking an extended path reached the other side of the field. When they looked back they could see a small depression in the snow where Edward had stopped. My thanks to you brother, said Robert placing his hand on his brother's shoulder offering him praise for his forethought, admitting that his impatience could have gotten them both killed.

Eventually they were relieved to have passed the snow field; for a while they walked the horses along stony paths that still showed traces of thinly covered ice; it was not a comfortable walk in their thin leather boots

Signs of mountain wild flowers growing on the edges of the track indicated that their surroundings were slowly changing, they were descending to a lower altitude were they began to feel protected from the chill of the mountain air, relieved to be moving into less hazardous country which they suspected would lead them eventually to a dry arid plain.

Scrub and small windblown shrubs were beginning to abound in the rocky soils, with signs of colour welcoming the eye wherever they looked. With the land changing from the sizeable rocks they had to negotiate to lesser gravelly ground, and those treacherous stones behind them they could remount, giving them encouragement to make up their lost time. By late afternoon from the high ground of their route they were able to view in the far distance through the heat haze that shimmered across the horizon the outline of the rocks that were the canyon of the snake. They could go no further this day and the rock formation ahead was they knew a place where they would spend the night. They rested late the next morning knowing that they could only travel so far as the edge of the arid plain. To cross that they would have to wait until dark, and when ready they were in the saddle and on the road again. All the way down from the height of the mountain the heat haze remained in sight, they figured that it covered the wide endless plain that lay before them. Removing their blankets that had served them well Robert praised the sun for once, I never thought I would say it brother, but by God it's good to feel some heat on our backs Edward shrugged; I don't mind admitting it but I too wished for the sun to return. Robert Laughed; now that the tension of the crossing was behind them were both feeling more relaxed.

Edward standing in his stirrups commented that there was little wonder the bandit chose that place; it seems his men could see clearly across the plain from their high vantage point atop the canyon. This wasteland offered no succour to man or beast; other than betrayal of its approach.

Across the horizon there was no separating earth from sky, both merging in the heat haze that shimmered, distorting all that was beyond its view, only the darkened colour of the canyons rocks figured like a great harbinger of foreboding; without water the crossing to the canyon appeared to offer little other than a gamble to one's survival. Startled by a sound of pee-u above made Robert look skywards; he spotted a hawk circling and calling out, but he could not see a mate coming into view and wondered who it was calling to. At least there is life out here he declared to his brother; Edward smiled; it was a good sign and it cheered him.

Their pace began to quicken to a cantor; once again the restraining voice of Edward quietly reminded his brother to stay his enthusiasm; we can't cross the plain in daylight; the look outs will see us from a mile away.

"Once we are off the mountain," he continued; "it would be our best opportunity to give the horses a rest; as well as ourselves after the long uncomfortable journey. I think we may as well use the cover of the rocks below as protection until dusk before riding into open ground without cover. Let's make the most of our stay; they are expecting us so let's be ready in our own time," intimating nightfall to be the time to move.

With a silent nod it was agreed; it remained hot and by the time they had arrived at the end of the mountain trail; they were ready for their rest. The depression ahead at the end of the trail appeared to be all that was left of a boulder field with a wall of rock that rose and fell as if it had been carried along by a great weight at sometime past; they had arrived at the point where they could travel no further until nightfall. All day they had persevered the extreme coldness from early morning until noon before returning to having the sun soak their backs with the heat they were used to suffering and now sought the refuge of the shade for relief from the sun's rays. They walked their horses into the shade and let them feed on a handful of grain, it was time to relax and to eat a sparse meal, their departure was hurried and there was little time to think how long they would be riding for. What they had went some way to restoring their energy levels, their minds for the time being was focused of the job ahead. The meal was as good as it got whilst travelling; it was nothing less than a strip of a local delicacy of dried spiced meat that was smoked in the traders wooden buildings back in Antioch. They got used to such food and it was appreciated and accepted in silence. Chewing on the strips rejuvenated the juices that brought to life the flavours, considering that it was daybreak since their last repast they were well ready for what they ate. They knew not; how numerous their enemies were or what to expect on their arrival; no doubt they would work at reducing the numbers before concentrating on the rescue itself.

One thing was sure; the woman would not be taking any chances, it begged a question in Robert's mind if she was still present in the camp. They had discussed the likely hood that this whole escapade could amount to an elaborate trap, luring them this far away from any chance of possible assistance. Was she so mercenary that she was going to remain there to witness the capture and torture her new prisoners; Robert almost choked on his food at the thought. He didn't revel in the thought at her standing back watching him grunt his last sounds of repugnance to her demands, his stomach was churning at the thought of such an event. Or would they be taken alive to be sold as slaves or ransomed? The latter thought hurt more with embarrassment of such an outcome, no, he decided she would not be there being long gone. In order to capture her adversaries it may take more than her men alone, her people may be good at assassination but Robert and Edward might just be able to show them a few tricks of their own. She had proved her cunning and would not be easy to take; after previously witnessing Robert's skill in the field she would not allow herself to be lax. He would fight in any way he could believing she would have surmised this; or in any manner it would take to gain the release of his friends. This may have been her game, her ground but not her rules; and if she was to play at a warrior's game then she was open to the consequences.

For the present the two men had settled in the shade of a huge boulder rock making themselves comfortable, there were plans to discuss after they had rested, although the heat was burning like the coals of Hell and there was a discomfort within them from the chilling cold that had bitten deep into their bodies. Robert found it difficult to rest and was soon on his feet; looking to his brother he cleared his throat prompting to speak clearly.

"They may not be there," Robert offered with hesitance in his voice. "This could have been a ploy to lure us away whilst they escaped."

"Oh I think they will there," Edward replied, holding out his strip of spiced dried meat up in offering, "remember Robert, these people are expecting gold and whether we are a day late; doesn't matter to them. We should rest now a while," relax Edward told his brother, "the Lord knows we deserve a bit and he stressed it will put you in better form for what we have to do." Placing his supply bag behind his head Edward closed his eyes. "I've been watching you, on this journey brother," he added, keeping his restful eyes closed; "you are too much on edge, I too am aware what lies ahead of us, be patient you may be finding it hard to rest because your zeal is too great and your appetite for sport restless. Rest my boy, come over and stretch out a while and relax," he indicated by patting the ground beside him, "the woman is not going to come looking for us." Robert smiled at Edward, he was right of course; relaxation was needed and he wanted it but it was not so easy, the nerves were taught he wanted it over with.

Edward remained beneath the great rock where they had settled, he had found his refuge of coolness from the sun's overpowering rays. There he spread himself out full stretch on the ground in the coolness of the shade that the great ancient rock afforded him. Lying prostrate on his back musing over thoughts of the preparation he presupposing how best to understand what his enemies might have planned for their arrival. Meanwhile Robert in his restlessness was climbing the rocks above his brother, placing his hand outwards to hold his balance he soon recoiled, Christ he thought its hot here. He rested his back against the rock, it was good and gave into the heat as it penetrated deep into his back, after he was satisfied that the soothing heat had eased him, he slid down to rest on his haunches, in a raised voice Edward added that if understood them correctly they would probably anticipate a delay, especially after the chaos they left behind. Robert silently concurred nodding his head in approval; with a mumbling sound of concentration he screwed up his face viewing the open horizon and nodding in agreement. "You're probably right." Looking outwards he saw little through the glare, he decided to scout further along toward the end of the ridge to view the arid plain, perhaps it may look little better from a different angle. He climbed until he was in the cover of a high rock; where he could view the ground above the haze; although there remained unclear on the far horizon, in spite of it he could see at first glance that the rescue was not going to be easy.

Out across the open plain his eyes strained to settle on a dark black gash where he guessed the mouth of the canyon was situated; from where he sat he had to cup his hands to shield his view; his squinting eyes looked out once again for an unseen way into the canyon. From where he stood he was certain that they would not be seen when they rode out into open ground; as Edward had reminded him earlier it would have to be under the cloak of darkness; he was also aware that the crossing would be slow in the dark. The distance across the open plain was quite far; as his eye traversed the canyon he noted a number of small mounds which he suspected would serve as useful posts for any forward sentinels to surprise approaching riders. His evaluation of the plains terrain was filled with imagined shadows of depressions being dry river beds running across the mouth of the canyon hopefully anticipating that it was just that. If he was correct it could prove to be very useful to their approach, it was not as close as he would have liked it to be, but he fancied it might just give them a chance to move closer unseen. He sighed at the thought, it was an impossible breadth and openness of landscape, his eyes searched the barren view until his eyes grew tired with strain for an alternative route to approach the canyon from another direction.

His mind wandered back to his brother below in the shade, he too was feeling weary and knew it; his brother was right he did need to rest a little. Stretching himself once more he decided to seek the shade and join Edward where he could think on the approach for the evening's activity. He was barely standing upright and looking around when a shiver ran down his spine, glancing away from the canyon in the direction to where Edward lay; a distant rising dust cloud was stirring and it looked as though it was heading their way, appearing as though the rider or riders were travelling hard with intent. This could be trouble, there was no mistaking whoever it was they were travelling fast, he ran down to where his brother lay resting, nudging him awake with his foot to warn him of their unexpected company that they were about to encounter.

When a fight was in the making they did not waste any time in their preparations, Robert called to Edward for the horses, the deed was done almost before the asking. They were saddled and mounted in readiness behind rocks that covered their view from the approaching rider. With swords drawn they lay in wait listening for the rider's unsuspecting approach. It was their guess that it was probably a messenger; no one purposely took this route; if they were right it could be some use to them to gain their enemy's intelligence. With luck he may be carrying a dispatch or have news that they could extract to assist the success of their plan.

It seemed an age was passing as they patiently waited; then their ears were filled with the sound of the speeding horse's hooves. They came with a gentle thudding sound that grew louder as it neared the intended trap, oblivious to their position the rider was closing fast.

The ambush was set and the men were ready, suddenly they gagged at their surprise, there was no mistaking; it was their companion du Bray coming towards them as if he was being driven by demons. At the point of their planned interjection Robert rode across his path causing his mount to rear in fear by the surprise, du \bray was unsuspecting and was forced to struggle allowing his assailant to take the advantage, startled by the swiftness of the action he immediately went for his sword before Edward in a jovial mood called to him to sheath his weapon and stop acting so foolishly. Laughing heartily at their jest, the startled du Bray was filled with protestations and embarrassment, they greeted their friend happily despite his huffing and puffing and told him it lifted their hearts that he had joined them.

A whole new vocabulary issued forth the like that they had not heard before; when du Bray had settled down and became easy of temper, they sat together in the shade and conversed and resting for some considerable time together until the shadows began to lengthen and it was time for them to move on. They had talked over his leaving his lookout position; du Bray assured them that nothing stirred along the valley and all the time his thought were on what was happening during the crossing of the mountain. By the saints it was damned cold up there and almost lost his feeling, only for having to move so damn quickly could he maintain feeling in his body. It was a well I didn't need to piss, the listeners laughed at the implication and he went on to say that he wasn't in any mood to linger. He followed the tracks left by his friend which saved him much time, but man he told them it near gave him a terrible fear crossing where the snow field was. He relaxed telling them that had there been signs of an army's approach he would have noticed dust clouds from miles away; and you can guess how slow it would take for an army to reach his position; days he stated.

Robert had felt better now that there were three of them, it made all the difference and success now brewed in him. Mentioning a plan he pointed out weaknesses in their approach; and it was not long before they were watching the sun go down, it was then they saddled up to make their way to skirt the plain around to the canyon from a westward direction to avoid the enemy. In the absence of the woman they expected that look out and other guards would anticipate their approach would be from a northern route directly across the plain. Robert's idea was to disappoint that expectation whilst light of day was fading, as for those watching the plain the riders were out of view. They had passed half way from to the west of the canyon by that time; with darkness almost upon them they could see the flickering light of their enemy's campfire in the distance. They could not stop now needing to proceed onward as quickly as the light allowed them; this was their only chance to gain the element of surprise. With the cloak of darkness descending so quickly they were free in their approach, crossing the waste they required care not allow the horses to break into a gallop for fear of being heard or a dust cloud raised to alert the enemy of their approach. Through the gloom they could not see the canyon; only the beacons that the enemy had chosen to build which acted as their guiding light; guiding them inwards towards a possible trap. They had reached an area of undulating ground that brought curses all round; the drops in the land level caused them to lose the light of the fires, which had them losing their line of direction. Too many times for their liking they blindly had to make adjustments to their direction; there was not enough starlight to silhouette their true course. With a sigh of relief they reached the wall of the rocks, a good distance away down from the mouth of the canyon where the fires burnt brighter; time enough they guessed to allow the guards to believe they were in for another restful night. They left their horses in a recess at the base of the rock face; at this distance the horses could snort to their hearts content without being heard, whilst they moved ahead on foot until they had neared the tip of a rising mound.

Stealthily they dropped their nervous bodies closely to the ground and crawled forwards; with no idea what imminent danger they could be putting themselves in. It was too late to be worrying about that; only the need for success of their mission was firmly kept in mind; this was a time for care, the rescue was happening. Slowly and quietly they moved forwards until they reached the top of a hillock to peer beyond; the three huddled together and raised their heads to view the area. The light from the campfires immediately came into view; they were stacked high and burning brightly, inviting anyone out there to be drawn towards it. Above the fires at the mouth of the canyon they spied another burning on the plateau above; it seemed obvious that the larger fire at the base of the canyon was expected to draw any visitors to that place. It was there were they expected the knights to meet to pay the ransom; here also they were likely to be killed or taken by ambush. Edward was straining to count the soldiers camped in the canyon and claimed there to be about ten he could see; but he suspected a few odd ones must be posted here and there to close in should the rider's attempt escape. Sentinels were also posted high up above on the plateau, maybe five or six he guessed. Logic had him believing that they would most likely be archers placed there to secure the ambush.

With their heads barley peeking above the mound of the hill, all three continued looking out and talking in a whisper of what they were seeing; like hunting hawks they each avidly noted weaknesses in their enemy's defences. Robert saw something that he was unsure of, his finger projected forwards pointing towards the base camp. Look to the area of the fire he whispered; the large flickering flames illuminated the canyon entrance throwing out distorted shadows. Due to the unusual formation of rock structure that embraced the camp; it was difficult to see all in the recessed areas that were set back; making it impossible to count the true strength of the enemy stationed there.

There could be dozens of them whispered du Bray within twenty feet that we are unable to see, do you think that Hubert and Aldo are there asked Robert; I can't see any trace of them, but we will only find out if we move closer? In hushed voices they discussed various possibilities of approach but there was no point in attempting any kind of a plan until they discovered how many guards they were up against.

They settled for the further reconnoitre; agreeing to wait a little longer, perhaps they felt a change in the guard could take place. One thing was certain; they desperately needed to ascertain the reason for the two camps. Agreeing that they should split up and reconnoitre the area picking up on any forward guards; agreeing to meet later closer to the camp in what appeared another depression. This depression would take them closer to the enemy and around a rocky outcrop ahead; it was closer to the opposite side of the mouth of the canyon where a better view of the camp could be observed.

Robert and du Bray saw nothing untoward by the time they had reached the meeting point, they settled to wait for Edward to arrive. From here they could see more clearly, in the short time they had been in the hollow they had counted guards posted in the most awkward of places, making it clear that they could not be taking any foolish manoeuvres.

There was a movement behind them, scared; they tensed in readiness knowing that they could not afford to be discovered at this point. Through the darkness the form of an Arab soldier carelessly loomed before them. Two daggers were silently drawn as not to alert the sentry of their position and were immediately poised in readiness to silently strike; then they heard Edward's voice warning them of his approach, with a note of nervousness in the whispered message to stay their actions.

"Damn fool," retorted Robert, "what did you expect," the heat of the moment subsided and they enquired how it was that he was suddenly dressed differently. Edward dropped down into the depression to join them smiling and ready to tell his tale. As soon as he got around the hillock he told them, he came upon a careless sentry eating a morsel, probably his supper or a little extra he had probably saved for such a quiet time. "However," he continued; "I had to silence him by cutting his throat. I got the idea to steal his clothes for better cover," Robert interjected, "and then I suppose you thought to amuse yourself by scaring us."

"No," said Edward with a wry smile upon his face. "Let me finish, ten or fifteen feet below there was another guard and when he saw me he told me to get back to my post." Edward paused in his tale to show his new water bag, "I asked him for a drink from his water bag and when he bent down, it was my opportunity to strike."

"This probably means that there are other guards positioned along the mouth of the canyon."

"I wasn't able to see any others," said Edward shrugging his shoulders, trying to change the outlook on the gloomy news, Edward raised his arms; "I brought these along," holding up two full quivers of arrows and bows. "We could certainly use them; but a word of caution," said Edward, "those two guards could be missed should we tarry; so I think it would be prudent to act swiftly."

They surveyed the position once more through squinting eyes studying the now visible encampment, they began counting again and noting that there were no horses to be seen, which they agreed were either tethered somewhere further up into the far reaches of the canyon; or that the guards were foot soldiers left behind for this purpose.

The eyes of the knights scanned for every little clue to add to their strengths for the encounter, there was something that du Bray had noticed up above but could not quite make out. "Look up towards the top of the cliff," their eyes strained at the dark object which appeared to be lodged in partial shadow, he nudged Robert telling him there were two objects. Tethered on the plateau above, a rope was attached to the objects on the side off the overhang. With outrage in his voice Robert exclaimed, "Jesus Christ," thinking that he knew what it was. Recalling the ransom letter regarding how his friends may experience some discomfort being sewn into a camel skin.

"That's damned inhuman," Edward said dropping his head in disgust; the sounds of his voice echoed his exasperation. "That's the reason why there are two camps of guards, the one at the top will cut the ropes holding the bag if there's an attack at the bottom; while the ones at the bottom will use it as target practice if there is an attack at the top."

"Then that settles that," said Robert. "Our attack is to the upper smaller encampment; when the camp is quieter and in complete darkness; it could also be that we are probably going to have to risk passing by more guards on our way."

They remained where they were hatching their plan until it was well established in their minds. It was difficult and daring; but circumstances demanded such an outrageous plan. First Edward and du Bray would silence the sentries above and take their place and wait in case the watch was relieved. From this new vantage point it did not matter whether they were seen or not. They were dressed in black desert clothing and to the world they were tribesmen, except for Robert whose task it was to cross the face of the camp and keep low. From there he would seek out a route in which to scale the walls and meet them on the other side of the canyon. By this time their comrades would have been hauled up to a safe position and then they would shower a volley of arrows down into the sleeping guards

Before their attempt was to be made Robert advised that they would need to know the strength of the guards at the entrance of the canyon. When Robert had himself in position at the mouth of the canyon he would know for certain what he was up against. There was much excitement building from the tribesmen that sat around the campfire, they were clearly in high spirits; taunts were being delivered to one of their company; giving the impression to the watcher that some form of wager or just general gambling was being enjoyed. The group around the camp fire enjoyed their idle banter; laughing like young boys in their sense of security. One of their numbers was derided with jeers of his inability to reach a mark whatever that meant.

Suddenly an archer stood to his feet displaying an indignant air; replying to the taunt from his companion. Caught with a degree of embarrassment he took off his bow and placed a flight across his bow string, then drawing back the string in in spring like movements, he exercised his preparedness to shoot at a target. A challenge had been made and he was ready to prove his point. He was a loud mouth that couldn't stop talking which was followed by more laughing, and as Robert eyed the camp he could clearly hear another from around the fire remark that he would bring light to make sure. A second man from around the fire drew out a stout glowing log, agitating the fire as he did so. Glowing embers sent sparks skywards from his action creating a new temporary impetus to the flame that roared with the injection of air into it base. It gave off enough light to see what was going on; whilst the two standing men resumed their arguing to the others around the fire. The man with the drawn bow was definitely being urged on. Robert was drawn forward in anticipation of what was about to happen, raising himself dangerously almost calling out in horror at what he believed was about to happen. The laughing guard with the glowing wood let fly; tossing the blazing torch high into the air whilst the artful archer waited before letting loose his arrow up towards the blazing ember now in the canyon's shadow. Robert reeled and moaned as he heard the thud of the arrow piercing a target, the sound bedded itself into his brain, but what hurt him more was the scream that followed yielding what sounded like a last remaining sound as it echoed off into the night; before finally dying. The crowd below where joyous, and he could hear the man, who was holding the ember aloft in his hand confirming to the others that he had hit the target.

"You all heard it," argued the man establishing his point.

Another voice called, "That's 20 gold Bezants you owe us," and the encampment became lively again in riotous laughter filling the night's emptiness.

Robert was sickened to his stomach and grieved for his friend; swearing that this band of cut throats would suffer for the way they had made sport of his friend's life. In his place of dark concealment; Robert's eyes glistened, hatred filled his heart as he wiped away a concerned welling tear of compassion from his face with the sleeve of his robe, determined more than ever for his will to be iron hard and merciless to his enemy as they were to his friend.

After waiting some considerable time, the previous activity subsided, nothing further happened, the camp grew quieter settling back into idle chatter, he was encouraged that luck could be with them. Outside the canyon there was no change in the guard, and hopefully the camp would soon be settling down by the time the others were in position. It was difficult not to charge forward with the pressure of watching his friend die; Robert was a disciplined soldier and valued the advantage of surprise; knowing that it could mean everything to his mission and the rescue for his remaining friend.

When the time was right, he moved back to the others, and upon nearing them remained turned towards the shadow so as not to show any sign of wetness around his eyes should the moonlight catch his face. Robert decided he could not hold back what he had witnessed. Drawing on the need for urgency, it was suggested to save their remaining friend from being used as a target for further entertainment, they agreed that it would be to their advantage if they scaled the rear side of cliff leading to the plateau. Robert would make his way to the top of the opposite side of the canyon to meet them and give them cover should they need it.

They separated and painstakingly made their way to where they were to ascend to reach the top, Robert set off in the opposite direction to take up his position for the climb that lay ahead of him. Just past the entrance of the canyon Robert had stopped short to take stock of his position as best he could, in the twilight he scanned for any signs of any further presence of the enemy nearby. By this time he had reached what he had believed was a dried river bed between him and the cliff face, it was here that du Bray had previously mentioned somewhere ahead of him he expected guards. If they were here they were likely stationed and alert for riders; but not for any such foe as he, who was sneaking ever closer upon them. Adjusting the position of his bow to sit around to his back to give him a more comfortable position for crawling. He moved silently forwards across the flat ground snake like towards the gully. Sliding over the edge on his belly he eased himself quietly down the side of the embankment and onto the gully floor. Before making any forwards advance he raised himself onto one knee to collect his bearings now that he was concealed in the total shadow of the hollow. Below the level of the natural ground the depth of darkness cast from the sides of the gully proved difficult to see, anxiety grew within him as he feared he had to chance exposure by lifting himself up from the shadows to look around. With a fighting man's instincts he was ready to strike with the imminent danger heightening his fear. Preparing his readiness he drew out his dagger should he be discovered, and although there was not any stirring of sound he sensed that he was not alone. Unaware that over to his left not much more than an arm's length from him sat a sleeping guard, whose breathing was so shallow that Robert missed hearing him.

Looking hard with straining eyes down the length of the gully he could faintly make out the form of the sleeping man's companion looking outwards to the plain keeping watch whilst his friend stole a careless and what for him was to prove a lasting sleep. With stealth and swiftness he was standing over the sleeping man; shadowing his body in readiness to strike, in one action his hand firmly pressed across the man's mouth; at the same time forcing his body weight against his enemy with enough pressure to resist any sudden attempt of his rising, Robert slit the sentry's throat. Any dying sound emitted was lost into the clothing that smothered him; the sudden rush of warm blood from the victim was released onto Robert's body but he could do no more than hold him and receive the discomfort of the wetness that saturated his clothing. Wiping his blade; he adjusted the guard from his slumped position; safe in the knowledge that he wasn't going to raise an alarm. Without a sound of betrayal of his presence the silence of the evening remained unbroken, his watchful companion did not stir but remained looking out across the valley floor. Robert could do little about his discomfort; concentrating single minded and with equal purpose of intention turned to complete his objective. With his eyes set intentionally on the next target; he stealthily made his way towards the remaining guard. As before; Robert knew that his kill had to be as silent and efficient; the unsuspecting guard remained watchful and oblivious to the event that death was stalking him. The kill was in the same effective workmanlike manner as was his companion; with the deed done Robert quickly stripped the dead man of his clothes and changed into the dry dark clothing of the guard. Feeling better for the dry clothing; Robert was now able to scamper unimpeded across the open ground to the foot of the rocky edifice. Safely at the foot of the rock face, he became agitated at the difficulty in finding the indented fissure he had seen earlier; it was to be his planned route of ascent to the canyon's plateau. After much consternation he finally came upon it having proved to be further away from the where he had thought it to be.

The immediate anticipated dangers had passed; his next problem was to scale the steep fissure without being seen. Looking up; the height of the climb appeared impossible; it presented him with certain doubts as to his ability, but it was a bit too late for second thoughts with Edward and du Bray waiting for him to be where he wasn't. He was taking a hell of a risk even though he was under the cover of the darkness; his heart beat fast but he knew too much depended on him to delay. He undid the sash that was around his waist and quietly tore it into strips making a long rope. He took the bow and quiver and tied them together at one end; the other he tied around his waist, his route of ascent was not unlike an open chimney funnel leading all the way upwards to the plateau. He guessed its height to be about thirty or forty feet; he was not foolish enough to think that his climb would be easy; in fact he wondered why he had suggested the route in the first place. He looked at his weapons tied to the end of the cloth rope that he had fashioned; knowing that his efforts would be less hampered without them clinging to his body; his ascent was going to be difficult enough. Without the weapons there was to be no cover for his friends, and the plan would be doomed before it was under way. His means of ascent would be achieved by using all his strength and determination, keeping his back pressured against the wall of the fissure; whilst awkwardly drawing his body weight upwards, and at the same time maintaining his position with his feet locked against the fragmented sides of the rock. Giving one last look about and one up the fissure; he breathed a lasting breath and placed his back against the wall and proceeded to draw himself up. Supporting himself with his feet he slowly managed to ascend bringing along the dangling bow, quiver and sword below him. By the time he reached half way he had to stop to rest, he was sweating profusely, the climb was proving harder than expected causing his fatigued legs to shake nervously under the continued strain. There was difficulty in resting being half way up and shrouded in darkness; having solely to rely on his senses for his foot and hand holds, but knowing that he could not see out across the valley gave him comfort, that he likewise could not be seen by others.

By this time the other two knights were in position waiting and watching patiently for signs that Robert had made his assent and to show himself, the camp on the plateau was silent with its sleeping occupants unaware of the danger that they were falling into. Inside the walls of the fissure Robert continued struggling; slowly he gained further height; with each precarious movement he pressed on; encouraged that together they were going to free his remaining friend. Ten feet or more from the top Robert's legs almost gave way under the strain; fragments of weakened stone gave way falling with a clatter of sound. He had to wait for fear that he may have alerted a guard nearby; but the silence prevailed, there was no reaction. The muscles in his legs were shaking voluntarily whilst he strained to hold his position without any proper footholds to rest; with tortured muscles that screamed for release from the constant pressure; he feared that should he linger they would not hold him, threatening to drag him down to the canyon floor to his certain death; and at the same time raising the alarm.

His will was strong and he knew he was beyond any point within himself that calls for second thoughts; only the reminder of his waiting friends urged him on. Can't give up now he told himself; he was not going to allow his failure to become a haunting memory if he were to survive the fall; determined that he would not let his comrades down in their greatest time of need. His groping fingers scrambled blindly feeling for holds in the darkness; he fought to draw himself further, his breath was heavy from his effort and he longed to pause for a moments rest. Beads of sweat formed heavily on his brow and his clothes stuck to him further hampering his efforts to reach upwards. With all these concerns in reaching the top; his fear of falling was growing ever stronger, just at the time he was nearing his final moves. The remaining section of his climb was close to completion, he felt dust particles whirling around his face from the level surface of the plateau above; they increased his torment by adhering to the sweat that had gathered on his brow; irritating him with a temptation to wipe them away. Having resisted this far the need to give up, he knew he could succeed; if only he could outlast the new terror that beset him and the threat of his cramping muscles, each leg movement had him pressing ever harder to maintain his position, nothing now dear God he prayed could prevent him from overcoming his will to endure the task that he had aspired to complete. In his mind his leg muscles were becoming hard like iron, come on he goaded himself don't let them cramp on me now. Just as he was about to cry out from the agony that threatened to overtake him; his fingers felt the evenness of the plateau; indicating that finally he had completed his gruelling task and had made it to the top. There was a renewed rush of enthusiasm at the right time to save himself; he was half out and halfway remaining in the shaft almost breathless trying to heave himself upwards without realising where he found the extra energy to do so. His spent body; he agonisingly hauled onto the hard sandy surface of the plateau floor. Almost as if in panic; he scrambled clear of the gaping fissure; and for a short time he lay there as if stunned breathless and incapable of further movement. His lower body twitched spasmodically; lying flat on his back; he was without the energy he needed. His legs felt as though they did not belong to him; he tried to stand to ease his strained and cramped muscles; but he was not yet ready to move forwards "Christ's bones" he exclaimed failing to stand; vigorously he rubbed at the hardened muscles in his legs until the blood in his veins pulsated violently; near he believed to bursting point from the rigorous strain of the climb.

Once he had recovered sufficiently to move forwards he drew up the dangling bow and quiver that was still bound to his waist, then in spite of his weakened shaking legs made his way towards the edge of the canyon precipice opposite to where Edward and du Bray were positioned.

His progress forwards was slow in the darkness; it was much further away than he imagined and his heart was throbbing all the way to the rendezvous point.

Picking his way out of the darkness towards the light that illuminated his location he became clearly visible.

Edward nudged du Bray and sighed with relief at their sighting of Robert looming from the shadows after his prolonged delay, as soon as he too could see his friends he began signalling to them that he was ready.

Placing an arrow in the bow and drawing it fully back in readiness Robert signalled to his friends to begin the attack on the sleeping men around the fire. All was going well when one of the guards sat up disturbed by the scuffle of sound his attackers made whilst silencing his companions. He did not have time come out of his drowsy state to realise what was happening; instinctively he had to raise an alarm but froze like a statue; an arrow pierced his neck with such force it shattered his spinal column, killing him instantly; leaving the others free to finish their task. They pulled three of the dead bodies together, and propped them in front of the fire, their dead forms supporting each other to shield the light away from their activity.

If any of the guards at their lookout positions across the valley were still alive or awake; the less that could attract their attention the better. Silently they moved over to the stakes that held fast the ropes holding the camel skin bags that dangled over the edge of the cliff. With care and great effort they began hauling up the first bag that was free of any arrows, making sure that it did not snag and tear on the sharp edges of the rock face, endangering the life of their friend within. Slowly and quietly they drew up the bag to the plateau's surface hoping for silence from its occupant. Muffled noises began emitting from within and luckily they were not loud enough to alert the camp below. Once clear of the cliff face the big bag was dragged quickly far enough back as to be clear of danger from dropping back over the edge; with haste the two men began comforting it's occupant with whispered talk of his being rescued, at the same time prompting him to be silent. Edward drew his knife and carefully cut open the strong corded stitching that held the skin together to reveal Hubert looking out at them and gasped at the sudden intake of the fresh night air. Unfortunately the smell of trapped air from his confinement rushed out to the rescuers, the emitting smell was so strong it caused the two rescuers to turn their heads away in disgust. Hubert was naked and in a mess, his imprisonment in the darkness of the camel skin for so long had distorted his vision; making the welcome sight of his friends difficult for him as he groped about aimlessly to thank them.

"It's us," they exclaimed in a hushed voice, "Edward and du Bray, Robert is here too," Hubert entered into a continually babbling state and having a need to embrace his friends with relief, the state he was in would have turned many a man with a strong stomach away. Such was his joy of his freedom and his friends' fidelity, that tears of relief began welling in his eyes. With the need to silence him for the continued success and completion of their mission; they had to plead and pacify him for silence; reassuring the poor man that they were not going to abandon him.

The next sad act was that of pulling up their deceased friend in the arrow laden camel skin bag. It was stained heavily with patches of dripping and dried blood; and it was a dead weight, what little blood remained in the body seeped into runs that collected onto what appeared like a stalactite; growing from the remaining droplets clinging onto its tip, eventually dropping into the darkened space below on the canyon floor, they drew it up with equal care as when handling Hubert; drawing the body over the edge and onto the top. They stood silently almost not knowing what to do, their friend was before them in this bag and lord knows what mess they had made of him. Before they sliced the bag open they cursed his murderers; Edward grabbed at the deflated bag and cut at the stitching, it popped with each cut of the knife; all Edward could think of was the messy body of their other friend; Aldo. There was a surprise awaiting them; there was no body inside; only a carcass of a dead sow. Short for words, they gawped at each other speechless at the sight before them, their release from the expected grief came quickly. Though they remained puzzled at this exchange, both knew that their friend's life must still be in danger. This could now prove to have been a grave error of misjudgement on their behalf, alas they could not give the news to Robert, it was too dark for that kind of sign language.

Turning to Edward, du Bray stated that their work was not yet over, "Well there are plenty of bows around, let's arm ourselves," said Edward.

There were about ten sleeping in the mouth of the canyon below around the warmth of the glowing campfire; all were overlooked from above with clear lines of vision. The men walked along the plateau in the direction of the sleeping encampment; signalling to Robert to do likewise, with their bows already drawn back with deadly arrowheads pointing downwards. Once in position and ready; together they loosed their flight of lethal arrows, down towards the encampment below, each arrow finding its target and then another, until those below were all pierced and dead or seriously wounded, only the odd twitch of nervous reactions showed any indication of movement. It was over, ten or more men lay dead and silence of the night was only punctuated by the crackles of the blazing fire, the scene remained as if nothing had happened, Edward and du Bray moved back to Hubert who was still on the floor covered with one of the dead men's outer garments to ward off the cold. Offering their hand around Hubert's back they carefully pulled him to his weakened feet, it was difficult for him to stand after being in a sitting position for so long. Between them the two friends assisted Hubert down off the plateau to one of the enemy's horses that was resting nearby in the shadows.

Meanwhile Robert had to find a way down from his present position to join his friends; but in the darkness was away from any light to guide him. Leaving by way that he had arrived was not an acceptable option for him and so he walked the plateau's edge leading deeper into the canyon where he guessed the walls would be less steep. His hunch was correct; the plateau did decline in height but it was not going to be an easy walk off from the high ground. From where he stood to where he needed to be on solid ground below remained at least twenty or so feet for him to descend, his problem was that he could see very little and he could not remain up above until daybreak. Knowing that he would not have a better chance than the present he fumbled around the edge for hand and toe grips in his effort to descend. Part way down he believed that he could hear the sound of snorting nervous horses; and the lower down to the ground the sound became clearer. He could not see them, but being able to hear them clearly indicated that they were not far from him. Once again he was cast into a blind state unable to see any hand and foot holds; Robert wasn't going to give up at this stage and steadily progressed. The darkened slope was tricky, almost slipping at times making him scared for his safety, a fear rose in him, where there were horses; there would be guards. Noise could expose him and bring him to a swift end, half concerned for his safety and eager to re-join his friends he continued lowering himself carefully a little at a time down the darkened rock wall. A sudden tremor of fear caused him to freeze his actions; every hair stood erect bristling in anticipation of something about to happen.

There were voices that he could hear; Christ; he cursed; not now; Robert clung motionless to the rock face; beads of sweat formed on his brow in his helpless position anticipating guards searching the area. The horses that he heard earlier he realised were directly below him; acting restless and scared as his presence grew closer, whatever happened he did not want the animals to break into a panic. In his present exposed situation his mind raced calculating where he was; he could not tell what his approximate height from the ground was, if he was to chance a leap he preferred it not to be to his death.

The movement became more active and for the first time he could see the movement of horses though they were not very clear. Guessing that he was only feet above the horses meant that he was approximately about ten feet or so from the ground, so he questioned; could he jump? There was no doubt about the fact that he was the cause of the horses nervousness, could he climb down without being seen and above all scaring them? He heard voices again and they were approaching with the intention of trying to calm the excited steeds; it wasn't him they had heard but the restlessness of the horses. Sure as hell they weren't expecting him; no noise was made in the rescue of Hubert; so they couldn't be expecting trouble. They might suspect an animal prowling around in the darkness, their nearness of approach made their every word sound clearly; it wasn't what he had wanted; they had a better idea; returning to their camp to build up the fire.

Robert had not noticed any previous light; though the camp it seemed was tucked away around a corner; from where he was descending into the enclosure. He didn't like what he heard; they were making up the fire to return and their efforts sounded quite expeditious. Jesus, the light from the fire didn't take long to burst into a blaze of light; even though it was well away from him, he guessed that on their return with blazing torches they're going to see him. Clinging in his bat like stance to the rock; he listened to the endeavours of the concerned guards who were sounding eager to find this source of disturbance and roast its arse on a spit on the fire. When they did return; their glowing torches were not as bright as Robert had thought, he was relieved that they were unable to see him, but he was at about a horses height and could now see the ground beneath him, which was a little more than a man's height, guessing that it wouldn't be long before he was seen, he did something positive. Inching his way a little lower he decided in blind faith to jump the last few feet before they closed on him with the glowing flames betraying his position. In a last ditch chance he dropped to the ground landing quietly with the agility of a cat and quickly stood to his feet, a startled horse collided with him knocking him back to the ground, causing a little more excitement from the guards, "Something is out there," he heard them say worriedly; the guard ordered his companion to gather more brushwood for the fire.

Robert was quickly on his feet, drawing an arrow from his quiver, one of two arrows he had left; which he knew he could ill afford to waste. The wary guard moved a little further away in his search for wood but Robert could quite easily see him and let loose his arrow; it struck its target piercing the guard's chest. It sent him to his knees moaning and grasping at the flight, in a desperate attempt to suspend the pain inflicted upon him; he called out as he dropped to his knees. Robert quickly prepared himself for the other guard who had guessed the direction of the arrow from the way his friend was struck; advancing toward Robert with a drawn sword fiercely above his head ready to strike down his enemy. With the same intention of dropping the advancing guard Robert prepared to loose his remaining arrow when a frightened mare nudged him sending it slightly off his aim. Although the arrow struck its target, it caused little more than a flesh wound but managed to stop the man's rapid life threatening advance on Robert. The injured man wheezed with the shock of the arrow's striking force and gripped at his bloody shoulder wound in an attempt to stay his pain, calling out for help and the other guard.

Robert had no better weapon than his dagger, the sword he had remained tied to the cloth rope up above where he had left it on the plateau.

He unsheathed and held his dagger in readiness; strategically lingering behind the cover of the horses. A game of cat and mouse now pursued, the newly built fire denied affording Robert the cover he needed, and remaining as close to the shadows, he slowly traversed the line of horses searching for the position of the guard's legs through the gaps of the horse's movements. The guard was no fool; he had taken the same approach looking for his quarry; he too was squatting down in his search to flush out his enemy.

Looking about for means of advantage; Robert's attention was drawn to the shadowy rock face; detecting a ledge about shoulder height off the ground with sufficient clefts for hand and foot grips to haul himself up to it. It was a chance to take the guard unaware, providing that he would not stand up and look about himself. Edging his way towards the place of the ledge; he listened; whilst his eyes searched the darkness frantically like a preying cat. He could not hear the guard with any sureness that told him that his enemy was approaching. Only his battle wise senses and logic expected his adversary's movement to progress toward him, cunningly using the skittishness of the horses to cover his forwards sounds in whatever murderous attempt to annihilate his Frankish enemy. Fearing the fire might betray his position by casting a shadow; he held his body low and hoped his dark clothing afforded him to blend into the shadows convincingly.

It wasn't long before Robert could see the soldier; the wounded guard was approaching low down and getting nearer; pointing his sword before him in readiness for action. Five feet away from Robert he could hear deep broken breaths being slowly exhaled, the pain of the shoulder wound that the soldier was suffering was betraying him whenever he was bumped by the moving horses. Robert's senses and sharpness of vision had him watching the guards every move but he was not yet open to attack and until he was free of the protection of the animals he could do little to assail his advancing enemy with any effect. By the way that he cautiously hunted his quarry Robert believed that his adversary was no foolish foot soldier; wisely he covered the ground where he suspected his enemy to be hiding; cautiously keeping his nerve and waiting, for what was the right moment to strike.

The horses were urged around once more in his attempt to seek out Robert, there was nothing to be seen; which bothered the guard, in his inability to see little from his crouching position, the guard must have assumed that his enemy had fled and stood upright to look over the horses for a clearer view. This, it seemed, was Robert's chance to strike; the man was within his range and unprotected from his cover; it had to be now.

Launching his body outwards with force; he connected with the unsuspecting guard side on taking him down to the ground; his flying weight deposited itself on him like a crashing rock. He had gained the element of surprise and in the fall Robert had hurt the already injured guard further taking the advantage and enabling him to easily fulfil his task by burying the dagger between the guard's ribs. Panting with exhaustion he withdrew the dripping dagger and stood erect victorious, claiming his enemy's sword, tucking it into his belt; catching his breath; he paused to listen to his thumping heart with an excited knowledge of victory. His concern to safely leave the canyon and to be reunited with his friends was the only thought left in his mind.

While most of the horses were on their tethering lines which Robert gathered together, he held an idea that should there be any guards that where placed beyond the entrance and ready to give resistance on his exit then the body of the horses racing onwards in a wild stampede would be his cover. Robert mounted a loose horse and gathering holding the lines that held the leading horses, he screamed at the top of his voice sending the frightened animals stampeding forwards ahead of him. Riding wildly out of the canyon and passing the campfire at its mouth, in passing he surveyed the sight of the carnage that he was partially responsible for. Free of those doubts he had for his safety he rode into the space of the plain and when light broke across the valley with the sun rise, Robert could see the outline of three other riders ahead, he urged his steed onwards at a gallop to catch up to be re-united with his friends.

Their reunion was joyous; and it was certainly good to see Hubert again; they were jubilant in their success of the operation; being reunited, safe and from harm's way.

He did not enquire about Aldo believing that he already knew the consequence of his demise. As difficult as it was Robert ended his display of thanksgiving by throwing an arm around Hubert and he responded likewise in a comforting way; although it was quite distressing for Hubert whilst remaining in the appalling state after his terrible ordeal. They were together once more and it raised their hearts to have saved one other of their old company. Approaching cover on higher ground; Robert insisted that the group should stop as soon as they arrived at the scrub-lined escarpment above; near where they were approaching.

The previous night's activity had stimulated them to such a pitch that they were still riding on their nerves; victorious and jubilant though they were, rest was what their bodies cried out for; Robert could see it plainly in his own feelings as well as his friends' outward mannerisms. Edward and du Bray dismounted except for Hubert whose eyes had been faintly masked so as not to let the rising sunlight become a blinding hazard to him. Suffering his term bundled inside the camel skin for so long also had an adverse effect on his ability to maintain his balance. His friends; therefore had supported his sizeable body secured to his horse to prevent him falling off. Working together they quickly untied his bindings and lowered him gently onto his unsteady legs; assisting him as they manoeuvred his awkward form over to a comfortable spot where his back could be supported by a suitable projecting rock. They cared in such a way that they maintained a certain distance as they worked with Hubert; it was noticeable and necessary to escape the pungency of his condition. For too many days Hubert had been starved of conversation and company; it seemed that all he could do was constantly apologise for his predicament; begging them understand the reason for it.

"Care not old friend," whispered Edward "we do understand," and with their combined help, cared much for his needs before resting themselves.

Once they were all settled and relaxed Robert finally stated that Aldo would be missed, speaking of him as if deceased Robert prompted Hubert to remember anything he could that may help them catch up with this bitch of a wild cat that left him to be so devilishly killed by her uncivilised escort. In Robert's eagerness to learn as much as he could Edward realised that his brother was unaware that Aldo remained alive, at least he had no proof of this but he obviously did not see what was contained in the camel skin.

"I have news for you brother," he said catching Robert's attention, "the bag we hauled up from the cliff held inside the carcass of an old sow."

Stunned for speech Robert stuttered, "You, you mean that…"

"Quite so," answered Edward smiling, "he must be still alive."

"So where the hell is he?"

"A good question," retorted Edward, "and I wouldn't know where to start."

Turning to Hubert Robert asked for him to try and remember anything that could help them regain the safety of their missing friend Aldo.

Hubert; not quite ready for such examination faltered over what he believed were the immediate events after the abduction; explaining that he was in a bit of a state, feeling groggy and sickly and not knowing where he was or what was going on. It was about the effects of the hashish and that he was unable to recognise anybody; or anything; because by this time he was actively being confined in the smelly old camel skin, "I tell you Robert, you lose track of time; not knowing whether it's morning or night, nothing is as it should be." He emphasised how disgusting it was, sounding as though he had eaten something most distasteful.

Hubert's mind wandered; recalling his traumatic experience that sparked into a recollection "Ah," he said with startling surprise, "Come to think of it they did mention that one was sold, or a precious cargo, and that great care must be taken to preserve him from being damaged," he fell silent as if he had been struck dumb. Then with a slight jerk sprung back to life saying,

"That's all I can remember," and apologised, "I'm sorry." A pat on the shoulder and a kind word from Edward; reassured Hubert that all was now well.

With humility and all the sincerity he could muster; he announced to his friends that he was truly proud and pleased to be reunited back in their company again, with my very best friends he added with a sniffle. The effect of the release from his confinement was confirmed by his kindly remarks. The company was silent whilst they took in his sentiment; realising that this could have been any one of them. Contemplating on it; expecting that they too would feel no different had they been in Hubert's position. "Could I have a drink?" Hubert asked politely breaking the cogitative silence? A water flask was passed to him and he drank his fill, a fire was being made and Hubert could feel the warmth emanating from its youthful flames. When drawing a long swallow from the flask Hubert sounded his appreciation as he vented long trapped wind from his mouth, "ah that's more like it water and warmth" leaning forwards to gather as much of the flames heat as possible. He put down the flask and began rubbing his legs to generate the circulation. "In a few days I know I'll be as good as ever" he said cheerfully.

"That's most encouraging," remarked Robert, whilst chewing on his ration of dried meat. Robert thought aloud purposefully. "I wonder if we are meant to be here; away from Antioch?" he replied, "the woman has seen to that." Hubert sprung to life with Robert's remark,

"Woman, woman you say, I heard a woman's voice," chirped in Hubert restlessly as if contributing a useful piece of information to the conversation. "I could not see her you understand but from the sound of her voice and the alluring smells from her perfumed body I could not forget her. She must truly have been a beautiful woman, she spoke to me kindly, so much so that the memory of her voice has kept me sane all this time."

"What's that," Robert pricked up his ears, like an alert guard dog that's been roused from his rest. In his eagerness to find out more, Robert urged Hubert to think hard and try to give him more information so that he had something to work on, no matter how small. There was a note of dissent from his brother who begged that he give the poor fellow a chance to get over his ordeal, but Robert was having none of it; raising his hand in silent objection; insisting that Hubert carry on. "Hubert, did she speak to you? If so describe her voice for me," he asked anxiously.

"Is it important," he queried with a vacuous look upon his face; "I don't mind if it's going to help you," there was a silence that indicated to Hubert that nobody was being flippant; quickly he realised that the question would not have been posed with such a serious manner; an apologetic smile came to his face and Robert begged him carry on, urging him that he may hold the key to Aldo's release. I don't know about that, he paused thoughtfully continuing; her voice was soft and calm yet firm; she issued orders to somebody, I was angry yet somehow I remember the tone; it was as if she caressed me with her orders with the sternest yet gentlest of voices. He went on "it was as though", he paused searching for the words to express his feelings, the company around the little fire hung on waiting in anticipation for his next word. Courteously begging him to continue, "as if" he said "the soft sensuous voice could crawl all over me, smothering me you understand."

"It was very strange," he adjusted his position; and looked skywards from behind his blindfold. I recall now that she did not want me harmed; she was aware of my discomfort and told me so, she touched me gently through the skin that I had been sewn into; telling me it was not of her choosing to confine a brave man to such a fate, but she was bound to obey the orders of her mistress. The tentative group appeared to be waiting for more, they sat without saying a word; deep in thought imagining how any voice could possibly have such an effect on anyone. The words that Robert spit out were not kindly at all" she's nothing more than a black scorpion, and I am going to squash the life out of her scheming poisonous heart, that is if she has one, I swear by it," said Robert gazing downwards. Two of our company have been taken and I have sworn to settle with her.

"Two you say, I thought it was only Aldo that was missing." Robert screwed up his face with guilt at making such a blunder as to blurt out without thinking, poor fellow it was time to tell him for there was no way that he could ever have known. It's Guy, Hubert, they murdered him while he slept, it must have happened at the time when they abducted you and Aldo. There was another silence as the regrettable news sank in, it was not easily accepted. "Poor Guy" Hubert mumbled in a saddened tone we were good friends, "that was an unworthy and despicable way to do for such as he."

All around the camp fire were sullen at the sound of his words, Hubert began groping around to take a piece of the left over scraps that had been laid down for him, he looked towards Robert turning his head to one side as if seeing through his eye bandage. "Oh I do not wish to dishearten you further Robert, but she is well gone by now. Several days ago I think, apologising for his vagueness, I suspect that after I had been sewn into that bag, it was then that she left for the coast with Aldo. There was lots going on, so it seemed; though I was a prisoner to the darkness and blind to it all; it never affected my hearing, now that I come to think on it, I heard her threaten those who took charge of Aldo that their lives depended on the safe arrival of the goods at the coast; or something to that effect." Robert was now kneeling over Hubert, his hand gripping his shoulder; where on the coast he begged Hubert to recall, Robert's sudden pressure on him to remember such a vital piece of information set his mind racing, it confused him to come up with an answer at the flick of an eye, "I, I, am not sure," Hubert stammered.

"Think man," Robert's grip on Hubert tightened urging him to think very hard that it may still be possible to find Aldo.

Driven by Robert's insistence seemed only to make it difficult for Hubert to give Robert the information he desperately needed. "It's no good, I am sorry," Hubert cried, "you know that I would do anything for Aldo."

Robert leaned back and gave a long sigh of resignation. Bouncing back from defeat he turned facing his brother sharply asking Edward "What is the nearest port to us here from where we are."

Without having to think too hard he replied, "Lattakia, but it would most likely be Tripoli the assassins are known to have many friends there, then holding a hand forward in warning, to get there by the most direct route you will pass near Mas'yaf, I don't like it." Edward feared more than ever that they may be expecting us. Robert pondered on the warning before replying, "I think you are partly right, tell me if you had a prisoner that you wanted rid of quickly, would you not take the nearest port? Bearing in mind also that Latakia has many western and Egyptian vessels trading there, tell me said du Bray; what if they may be expecting us; or even a lone rider; they would be ready and I ask could we make it?"

"I don't like the sound of that," said Edward; who was well aware of Robert's impetuosity. "I am not going to Mas'yaf for goodness sake, if I have to go anywhere near it; I intend to skirt it."

"So you are planning to go, what if you get caught," barked Edward, "have you forgotten we are supposed to be on a mission for the Grand Prior."

"Give me time to think," Robert barked and recoiling back into his sitting position he grew quiet whilst thinking of a way to overcome his orders without actually breaking them. They sat in silence around the fire until Robert jerked forwards.

"All right this is what we will do."

Eddessa

The second Frankish state, the county of Eddessa, served as a buffer state to protect Antioch from Moslem attacks. It sprawled on either side of the Euphrates, and had an open border with hostile and unfriendly neighbours. Although it was occupied mostly by a populace of Christians, Armenians and Syrians under their protection; there were Moslem towns within striking distance. The Frankish armies ruled by garrisoning strategically sited castles from which they could enforce and levy taxes. In this sector of the Levant; it was also necessary to keep a tight control on the traffic that passed through the county; it wasn't unusual for certain Lords in defiance of their King to carry out profitable raiding parties against enemies their across the border.

This entire district containing a very fertile landscape and many prosperous towns endured a fractious peace; the Muslim likewise kept a belligerent eye with an opportunity to raid. The chief need for all border states; was manpower for the army, the Christians could not enlist locals because of the lack of trust, but they had as an ally of sorts; Armenian Christians. Some who could be persuaded to fight alongside the regulars as support to swell the numbers of men in the front line. Though their enlistment was always dubious, factions of the Armenians had proved themselves to be treacherous leaving commanders in a quandary whether it was sometimes apt to be better without them.

Geoffrey of Toulouse was a young and impetuous hothead; of all his traits; he had an inborn knack of irritating all around him at court with his petulant hot temper. His constant failure to behave in accordance with his position being the heir and next in line to inherit his father's dukedom of the House of Toulouse; it did little other than create dread for those that would depend on him for their daily bread for that day he finally succeeded to that high position. His manners were so appalling he had caused his family great embarrassment, he was also offensive to his betters; which was the fundamental reason for shipping him out to the Levant under the guardianship of the duke's brother Edward the Lord of the county of Eddessa. Out at the sharp end of affairs of state, it was hoped that his outlandish manners could be curtailed and his character brought into line. His arrogance of manner lacked respect for everything and anyone; including his uncle Edward.

In the House of Toulouse Geoffrey was somewhat of a non-entity during the first ten years of his life. Being a bastard son meant that he went through a difficult period during his early years; his pedigree or character should it be said; that of his dear beer swilling mother; did not fit into any position suitable within the Toulouse household. Though there was never any doubt regarding the qualities of young Geoffrey's manhood nor his sexual prowess; it gnawed at the master to prove that he was the best he had sired being without a legitimate heir. Living in a house devoid of the sound of children irked him; whilst his many bastards ran around the villages of the local countryside; but to everyone's surprise a new family member suddenly arrived without the obvious pregnancy.

It didn't require any speculation about Geoffrey's birth-right; the child held his father's image, all openly knew he was the child of his father's favourite mistress who resided in the near hamlet.

In spite that it was common knowledge that his wife was barren and unable to bear children; the father never the less brought in the bastard and had him raised within the household. To all intents he had become the son and heir; nobody dared say otherwise publicly, his father the Duke of Toulouse was not a man to turn the other cheek; nor overlook the foolish slip of a tongue from his contemporise, the boy was his and he would be damned if he was to submit to any belittling gossip.

In the years ahead; Geoffrey proved not too bright a son, brave and courageous, even calculating to some degree; but his intellect was sadly lacking and badly let him and his father down. His troublesome ways on occasion had been the reason for keeping him away from court, in fact as far away as possible.

Out in Eddessa, life had not changed him much at all, although he was billeted at his uncle's residence which was the sturdiest and strongest of castles in the whole county; he felt it was not good enough for him. It was located in northern Syria; on the edge of civilisation at the point where ones enemy regularly takes a daily eyeball view at their hated opponent's situation.

Geoffrey's natural aptitude for arrogance and rudeness made him many enemies; and he was very fortunate that he enjoyed the comfort of being under the protective wing of his uncle. It was not that Geoffrey was weak and feeble; far from it he was very much an oversized and handsome muscular ox of a man; with equal strength to support his size. As zealous a man there ever was to take up the sword in his own defence. No; Geoffrey's problem was that he never knew when he had gone too far, his manner was far from being gentlemanly with the opposite sex; and knowing no bounds with his rudeness towards his betters. Because of who he was; others often gave way and left his company; not for his sake; but more for the respect of their Lord, Edward; who was often seen to wince with embarrassment whenever the obstreperous nephew drew attention to himself. Too many times he was ushered to one side to be told his place, but it was like talking to a block of wood.

Due to the constant harrying from groups of insurgent Muslim tribesmen probing the security of Eddessa's defences, Geoffrey was unenviably appointed to carry out the dangerous missions of reconnoitring the landscape. To track down and destroy without mercy the irritating miscreants that hampered the profitable caravan trade that relied on the responsibility and the protection of the Lord of Eddessa. Any advance into the hills beyond beheld many hazards; yet it proved a useful opportunity to Geoffrey to gather first hand the geography of the enemy's territory, giving him an insight into his strengths and weaknesses both of the terrain and himself. This task it seemed continually fell into the hands of the ever impertinent knight; much to the glee of the older cautious members of the Court. His orders were always to bring back as much information of the enemy and their location as was possible, speculating nobles had deviously planted the idea in the mind of Edward that a need for this intelligence would aid the prospect of a lasting peace. At the same time hoping that during any of those dangerous trips into the hinterland the young upstart would to their relief come to his end in a heroic demise. For Geoffrey; the more dangerous the better; and it could not be denied that a certain respect mixed with loathing from his enemy; brought him credit and admiration manifested by certain amorous females of the court.

Geoffrey grew successful through his recklessness and revelled in the honour of his minor victories, small though most of them were; they were victories nevertheless, and many a knight shrank in stature whilst Geoffrey sustained a continuing good fortune. Unfortunately his arrogance off the field was similar to that on the field and once back in court should his lecherous eye fall upon any woman that took his fancy; well. Ceaselessly she would be chased and pestered until the news of his embarrassing activity grew so obvious that husbands had to step in to cease his nuisance and wanton harassment. Always laughing off any incident or nuisance; he chose to excuse his bad manners as the thrill of the chase, and when the chase proved fruitless there was always good wine to fall back on. Taunts against him were nought but amusing to him, and did much harm in uniting brother knights in their cause against him. When angered by his actions; jealous husbands; whoever they were complained bitterly to Edward resulting in Geoffrey's insufferable fits of wounded pique; which distressed him like a petulant child. Feeling assured that little could be done to threaten the nephew of their liege Lord; many an evening amongst his cronies he laughed knowingly; like a braggart he was. In return whether it be on the field or in the court; he denied to show any respect to the opposition, death was his sport; proving his enemies unworthy opponents who deserved little consideration at their end. Everything he did was initiated on a personal level, his only satisfaction being total victory. He was undoubtedly a warrior, brave, courageous, foolish, and savage with his foe and outstandingly oblivious to danger. His men loved him; believing him to be shielded by God; luck would follow those that went with God's man. In tight corners Geoffrey and his men had battled their way many times away from certain death, not because of any dastardly clever plan of Geoffrey's but merely because he was who he was.

Geoffrey's uncle, Edward the Lord of Eddessa, to whom he was supremely jealous of, began viewing his nephew as an untrustworthy deliberate needle in his side.

He was a problem he could well do without; his brother had done him no favour in sending him out to him and he was considering his brothers action as no more than a deliberate means of foisting this troublesome youth on him.

Edward felt insulted; it was not unusual to have a certain rivalry in families between the male heirs, and Toulouse was no different than any other. In his time, being the younger brother, Edward was second in line to inherit his father's title of the dukedom, so rather than wait for his brother's demise he grasped the initiative by taking up the sword and embarking on the crusade. His natural abilities to lead; and his valour on the field of battle won him many honours, among them being the eviction of his mortal enemies from the stronghold at Edessa; it was in turn occupied by himself with the blessing of his liege lord the King of Jerusalem. Within a year the entire county was free and a number of strongholds throughout the county were established under his banner, the creation of his own principality was underpinned. Although his brother was outwardly pleased for his achievement; it now meant that Edward had bettered his brother in rank and that somehow sent a message of displeasure back to him.

Edward was no innocent philanthropist; he was a man of his time and aware of his wayward nephew's reputation; never the less took up the request to be his nephew's guardian; providing he did not bring dishonour on the house and name of Toulouse.

The season for renewed fighting was upon them once more, this time with a serious intent, protected villages had been razed and there were serious threats to important towns where Geoffrey had previously established a small garrison, it had recently been raised to the ground and its soldiers brutally sacrificed.

Marauding bands of Seljuk bandits under the leadership of the Muslim chieftain named Malik began causing mayhem with much disruption in the areas between Eddessa and Manzikert. Roads were closed, travellers were divested of their belongings; sometimes slaughtered and the whole area held to ransom as Malik the Muslin chieftain tightened his grip on the populace at large. There were few major towns with garrisons giving the bandit group the run of the countryside. Edward's thinking led him to believe that should Geoffrey ever quell the activities of the Seljuk bandits; there could possibly be an opportunity for a further stronghold of influence establishing itself in that area.

For two years Geoffrey carried out his task with efficiency and finally caught up with Malik destroying his army of bandits and beheading the bandit leader in front of his own troops; before he in turn ordered his own men to put their prisoners to death. They were left where they were slaughtered as a mark of what could happen to others who felt they could take up where Malik left off.

When the news of Geoffrey's success was out; it travelled fast, his exploits and the news that he had named his garrison New Toulouse soon became known and he was swiftly recalled to Eddessa. Considering his abilities and his loathsome attitude in his pathetic attempt to be a gentleman at court, news of his success in the field spread, women swooned in his company. It was bad enough that he had an enlarged ego, and his green envious eyes turned filled with greed towards that which he coveted most. He covetously eyed the chair and its power that his uncle had fought hard to achieve. Geoffrey was not intelligent enough to allow his thoughts to be kept a guarded secret, he was known to be heard to run off at the mouth when he had over indulged in the excellent wine of the region. As a precautionary measure his uncle Edward had sternly cautioned him to still his tongue, his eyes and his ability to move copious amounts of ale and wine. The time for wagging fingers was over there was nowhere else to go as far as his uncle Edward was concerned. Should he disobey this command the consequences would be of his own making; having to suffer being packed off back to France or left to sell his sword as a mercenary; but not in Eddessa.

Disheartened by the rebuke and the impending threat from his uncle; he was aware that life could deliver a further harsh promise of penury should he be forced to explain away his return and failure to his father. Never had his uncle been so deadly serious; it shook him to realise that this was no longer a game. Without at least an estate or assets would be an embarrassment; he suddenly realised he could not live without the aid of his family. He therefore took the rebuke and promised to amend his ways; controlling his manners to become a more affable character; regrettably he displayed his manners like a restraining stallion.

Not all was bad for Geoffrey, he was rewarded for his services to his uncle with lands and the promise of a small fortune should he marry and settle down. A small stronghold that proved to be a glorified keep, together with a fair acreage of good arable land with running water through the estate; though some miles away down on the valley plain away from the life in court; it was a start to see what he could make of it.

Geoffrey's ambition and risk was more expectant of something grander; after the dangers he had undergone; this so called reward which would have thrilled most men was like rubbing salt into an old wound. As for Edward; he was pleasantly surprised of his nephew's acceptance and hopeful that this new responsibility of the land would make a lasting change to the tone of his character.

Geoffrey was fuelled with ambition; he was not cut out to be a glorified bailiff, sulking in the loneliness of his own company; he believed that he had been used, after all it was because of his efforts that had made the countryside safe and brought in prizes worth so much more in value to his ungrateful uncle. He liked being at Eddessa it was being at the nub of life where he felt he flourished as a battle scarred veteran; with the honours to show for it, down the valley was quiet and dreary; not Geoffrey's ideal, it lacked excitement there were no secret meetings of suitors or tired wives that fancied a change to a horny young warrior away from the tired husband. Disappointed and ungrateful; he now felt punished and ostracised; but he knew that a time would come when his services would be needed and perhaps then he would be in a position to improve his situation.

Sitting alone one evening whilst gorging on a lamb bone and drinking his fill as was his want whilst morbidly viewing his prospects in what had become a general disaffected state of mind, he pondered on how he had been unjustly treated by his uncle Edward. His mood was low and the cup at hand emptied quickly. Sourly; he viewed the emptiness of his sparsely furnished chambers; it irked him at what he saw; he had suspected that he had been managed away from life, women and the court, it hurt. The spell of his disgruntled inertia was broken by the announcement that a visitor was without awaiting to speak on urgent business. In his present state of mind; the young knight who was feeling a little worse for wear and sorry for himself was not good company. Wine soaked; his dejected sodden mood was about to give the order for the traveller to take himself off. The cautious servant; used to his master's fits of displeasure; was able to preconceive events that may unfold differently the following day. Sober in the daylight the master would have reason to stress his will for the servant shortcomings by boxing his ears for not making the business at hand clear to him. It was one thing to accept a lashing of the tongue; it was quite another to be on the receiving end of his masters fist when he was in a state of recovery of the night before.

If Geoffrey discovered that a visitor of importance had been turned away; irrespective of his condition; he knew he would have surely been in for a beating for not stressing the visitor's status. The servant whispered into Geoffrey's inebriated ear that the visitor had travelled far for need of this discourse, and that he was no less than a Papal envoy. Geoffrey gave a shocked grunt, he was never open to offering warm hospitality; nor was he at any time a convivial host; those that visited at night usually got short shrift; unless it was a female to share his bed; but a Papal envoy, now that was something else.

Perplexed by the reason for his caller to be here at this time was rank, he suspected no good, but he was up to their games and this could be sport. To him monks and their kind were devious; he hated pious priests; believing they were as evil as he; and when it came to doing any dirty work they were soon off the scene after leaving their mess behind. A sneer showed on his face, he gave a hmph they were loathe to soil their own hands; when there was shit to wade through and they quickly shrank away because they lacked the backbone and the stomach for such work. Looking downwards to his goblet of wine is his fruitless search for clarity, his fuddled mind suspected some form of collusion. He loved intrigue and was eager to learn why any envoy from Rome would have a need to seek an audience with him whilst skirting the importance of Eddessa. He promptly gave permission to allow him to be admitted. I'll see what he's after; then kick his Papal arse all the way off to Eddessa, he liked that idea and smirked into his wine with the idea of the sport. It was clear from the onset that Geoffrey did not take to this fellow, as soon as he clapped eyes on him he sniggered at the sight that he was an odd looking figure. Bent and wearing a rough woollen habit with its cowl pulled well over his head concealing his face in its shadow. The sparsely furnished room was illuminated by a log fire; crackling as it burnt furiously in the deep stone set hearth; sending sparks flying in all directions. The visitor who had sought its warmth felt threatened by the overactive fire and edged into the extremes of the shadows where he appeared to feel more at ease; whilst the flickering flames teased him spitting out their bright sparks pushing him out of the shadow towards the warmth he desired.

262

Geoffrey swilling down another mouthful of wine slammed his goblet onto the food-laden table and belched out his trapped wind loudly in his dislike for the visitor. He sat erect and stiff as he inhaled deeply the smoky air of the room into his lungs whilst his visitor lingered like a spectre on the edge of the shadows.

"From Rome I hear" roared Geoffrey in an intimidating loud voice, there was no reply as the visitor craftily played his role at seeking refuge.

Angered by the lack of response; the knight bellowed; that if he had travelled so far on Papal business he had better find his tongue soon and quickly; or he would rip it out. Another thing he added whilst the effects of the wine ran through his senses; was if he knew what was good for him he had better make use of the light where he could be seen, you look more like an assassin and I usually gut them; he growled. Patience or tact nor even the courtesy of good manners was a luxury that Geoffrey encompassed. Now what do you want he bellowed picking up his knife and stabbing the table. The small bent figure limped reluctantly forwards from the gloom into the open space of the room reluctant to leave the cover and relative safety of the shadows behind.

Catching his throat; Geoffrey almost choked gulping down his wine at the sight of the misshapen envoy that lamely limped awkwardly forwards.

The stranger in the hooded habit cautiously edged his way into the light, he was afraid of the company he was in; he hated men like Geoffrey who were violent. Most of his life he survived by pitting his wits against his adversary, but this fellow was a brute and had to be handled with care. Geoffrey sensed his fear like a hunting dog could smell the kill, he was not taken to tact or the sound of muted prayers that he thought he could hear. Christ he screamed; spare me the prayers; go on get out of here before I lose my patience and do you an injustice. It was obvious in Geoffrey's mind that this wretch of a monk was a weakling; not being used to standing before such strength of leaders; the man couldn't stop twiddling with his Rosary beads. Geoffrey drew in a great breath at the humorous sight he saw before him and with a loud laugh followed by a scowling huh; his usual lack of thought blurted out; by my uncles bollocks you must surely be the oddest choice he had witnessed as a Papal envoy.

Leaning back in his chair in his superior manner he pointed forwards a bone that he had previously been chewing on in the direction of the envoy, he stared at the meek looking character fidgeting before him. Geoffrey's bully boy voice filled the room; give me a reason for not slitting your throat priest; he threatened loudly. The envoy who was trying to be coy; was shaking with genuine fear; he had tasted Geoffrey's attitude and tried hard to avoid testing his temper. He didn't expect to confront him in this drunken state, and it was imperative that he get on the better side of him, but the wine was going to make his task here difficult to reach any form of reason. Geoffrey's voice filled the room once more cursing all priests and demanding to be shown proof of his claim. Ah yes, yes, the monk stammered apologetically at the demand; drawing forth from inside his habit a small rolled parchment with a huge seal attached. Stepping closer to the giant of a knight he gingerly passed the rolled scroll towards his direction across the table that was now awash with Geoffrey's spilt wine. With as much delicacy as he dared use, he prompted Geoffrey to observe the seal on the document, believing it to ensure his safety, he repeated himself regarding the seal assuring Geoffrey that it was authentic. The knight glanced at it with a distrustful and slightly out of focused eye; wondering if it was a forgery, he flicked his heavy eyes slyly upwards viewing the visitor once more, his mind could not truly tell what this seal was; he had never seen the likes of it or any Papal seal before; but if a game was to be played he feared nothing from this character before him. His mind pondered on both until he came to the conclusion that there was no doubt that it would be typical of Rome to send one such as he that now stands before him.

Having stood for some time waiting for Geoffrey's mood to change the monk felt that because he was still standing; the knight had accepted the monk to be as he purported. Geoffrey was leaning forwards in thought, the weight of his body on his forearms perusing the scroll which dripped from the tables wine dregs and held by both of Geoffrey's hands. The monk wondered if he was capable of reading it, he spoke first cautiously prompting Geoffrey to break the seal and read its contents, for what remained to be proposed he added could not get underway until he did so. Get back he roared at the monk; you're getting closer and you make me nervous, then drawing the knife from the table placed it in readiness for use.

The seal was duly broken clumsily in the knight's huge hands and he commenced to read; it said little other than that the representative's name was Bernard and that he was certified to be on Papal business.

Geoffrey leaned back staring, he didn't know what to make of this character and he didn't take to him; yet even in his present state he could not help admitting to himself that he was intrigued by the envoy's presence. He peered at the monk with hooded eyes, they must send him on these errands to put people off their guard or to feel sorry; he couldn't quite make up his mind which.

With a great sigh issuing forth he bellowed, "Very well little man what have you to propose;" Bernard was about to answer but the mood was altered, he was put off balance from his rehearsed speech as Geoffrey let rip with a fearsome fart and a belch that echoed round his sparsely furnished chamber.

Ignoring the uncouthness of the knight, Bernard began, "If it pleases my lord, it would be a little easier if I could be seated closer to you" he implored with a fawning unctuous appeal.

With an outstretched arm towards the benches near the hearth; Geoffrey pointed before rising. When he stood Geoffrey appeared huge in comparison to the priest, standing at almost six feet with wide shoulders to compliment his height; it was little wonder that women swooned at his size.

Bernard revelled in the closeness of the warmth, opening his arms welcoming the heat from the fire whose active flames had subsided in their intensity since he had entered the room. He absorbed the emanating warmth from the fire; looking across at Geoffrey he begged him come closer. Before Bernard could blink a dagger was held to his throat, Geoffrey drunkenly stated with a slight slurring tone that he didn't sit too close to monks; he couldn't trust them; what are you up to; his voice was accusing as well as threatening; quickly his oversized brutish hand searched him for hidden weapons. Fear showed; what little colour there was in his complexion drained rapidly from Bernard's face, Geoffrey satisfied that he was unarmed pushed him backwards onto his chair; telling him not to think of starting any funny business; he may have had a drink but he never trusted the clergy. Now get on with what you have to tell me he growled roughly.

Bernard's life in the cloisters had been sheltered; never had he experienced the like of this animal before, somewhere in his imagination he believed that knights were of a gentile spirit and nothing like he was encountering presently. But he too had surprises of his own kind and he had proved in the past that he was equally capable of felling men; but not in such a rough and rude manner as the one he was consorting with presently.

Bernard's head was still covered by his cowl; his voice emanated from within its shadowy darkness that covered his face. In an almost patronising manner he began, "Although you are not aware; there are those that have watched your accomplishments here with interest; you have impressed people that I represent; and they have a sense of sympathy with your regrettable meagre rewards," he paused looking around and adding cynicism to his remarks; that your lord has bestowed on you. Geoffrey sat silently and listened avidly. "The skills of Rome were not gained in a day, it had taken an age to overcome its troubles. Because of its ability to sustain those lean times and deal with difficult people; it survived and emerged into its greatness by learning to be wise and patient. But what has Rome got to do with my visit you ask yourself, admittedly it is far away; but its eyes and ears hardly miss anything that occurs; even in this stressful and dangerous land. We, he changed his words as though he had erred in his dialogue, those who view the events out here differently than that of the Lord Edward; who has not been as active as perhaps he could be in expanding the counties boundaries; and he paused; fulfilling his promises to the church." As he settled closer into a more comfortable position closer to the heat of the hearth he continued to spin his disparaging tales of Edward's recent failings.

Unfortunately for Bernard, Geoffrey was not as dim as he expected him to be and he had struggled in getting his message across.

"Get to the point," demanded Geoffrey impatiently "your beginning to be like a tickle in my arse that I can't get to." The envoy was taken aback by his bluntness and crudity towards him; he feared that he should tread carefully from then on if the conversation was to prove fruitful.

Father Bernard began probing Geoffrey for a way into his plan for somehow he had to have the hot headed knight on his side and under his influence, being the tool that he could use to render Edward free from Eddessa before he could leave.

Geoffrey grinned as Father Bernard went around increasingly in circles failing to get to his point,

"Christ in Heaven!" roared Geoffrey; Father Bernard almost fell off his seat with fright, Geoffrey's drunken eyes screwed up as he thought he perceived the plot that was being unveiled. He rose quickly grabbing at Bernard "Are you asking me to kill my own uncle so that you can take over at Eddessa?" He looked upon Bernard with contempt.

"Did a viper spawn you, devil's shit of a priest or whatever you are?" The words issued forth with disgust; "Know this before I throw you off the walls personally," his threat was followed by the action of his hand stretching for his blade. Bernard quivered with terror. "If you came here because you have heard of my discontent and disagreement with my uncle; I can tell you that he's a good man, and good for Eddessa. He has held that fortress for longer than most can remember making the county prosperous and expanded on his territory; now what more could you want."

With hands flapping about apologetically Geoffrey had come to the point a little late to avoid the worst possible outcome, "No, no, you misunderstand sir," the monk declared trying to free himself from the firm grip that held him, but Geoffrey was not letting go. "We do not want it," he spluttered, as if any dimwit could see, "but we recognise that Edward is ageing and his ambitions are not what they used to be, we do not want Eddessa; we want you to rule the city." Geoffrey's grip froze, the words did have effect; his grip slowly loosened on the coarse habit that Bernard was almost suspended in; bringing him to his feet almost running, Geoffrey's mind had instantly taken in the words of the monk before his bawdy laugh rang out long and loud, so loud was it that it filled the emptiness of his chamber with a madness almost frightening Bernard whose unsettled disposition sank further.

"Now we're at it ay priest; it's taken you long enough," dropping him back onto the wooden bench, Bernard rubbed the thin tissue of his rump that was smarting with the force of his drop. He looked at the giant with fear; but saw that in Geoffrey eyes there was a conundrum at work which the knight was finding quite perplexing. Geoffrey's concentration had him silent for a while; tell me what you propose; and make it good if you do not want to be flying off the battlements as you leave," and he continued to laugh heartily. Father Bernard suddenly lost his nervousness as he realised he had finally struck the chord that created unison between them, although it seemed that Geoffrey was feigning not to understand he knew he had him interested. As the night lengthened and Geoffrey's consumption of the wine grew, so he mellowed and his tongue loosened to reveal his true feelings.

Geoffrey did not know what time of the evening the monk left but he awoke as the cock crowed; slumped over his table, the stench of stale wine and burnt wax filled the air and the taste in his mouth little better. He wobbled somewhat as he stood on his feet unable to carry his own weight; but after a wobble or two he managed to stand steady. The heat of the fire had long died and Geoffrey shivered, but that was not all; he looked about him and there was no sign of his visitor. The thought of that funny looking character made him smile before it quickly turned into a scowl as Geoffrey remembered the topic of his visit. There was something that sent another shiver through Geoffrey, steadying himself he gripped at his head trying to remember what had been said and why his mind had slipped into obscurity. Did he; the bastard leave before or after he blanked out, Geoffrey was trembling; Jesus, he was afraid of what he may have said; or worse promised. He must get after the little brat if he can make the stairs and traverse them safely. His forward gait suddenly carried him onwards; bumping the walls; propelling him downwards and outwards to the courtyard where the horses should be.

Passing the kitchen he caught sight of his manservant preparing breakfast, stopping to support himself against the doorframe to regain his posture, he yelled at the servant; if he saw that little wretch of a monk that came calling last night leave. The manservant in fear of Geoffrey's mood answered quickly, replying that it was soon after he himself rose to start the day's chores, adding that he left in the direction of Eddessa.

A doubtful uneasiness befell Geoffrey; fearful at what the monk may have been up to came flooding back to him. Perhaps the wine loosened his tongue and got the better of him as he vented his feelings, a shiver ran down his back at his stupidity. The cunning twisted little bastard, his thoughts began to take shape; they horrified him, I could be done for if he goes to Edward and spills his spawny papal tongue to him. His mind raced; he had to solve his problem; his favourite cure for all his enemies was to kill them quickly; especially this one before he could blab what he knew to anyone.

A screaming panic stricken voice smashed the peace of the silent dawn's solitude "saddle up my horse" came the order whilst he was set himself to running back after finding his legs; a hysteria gripped him; taking three steps at a time up the spiral staircase to arm himself. Without standing to buckle up his belt he had turned and was sprinting back down the stairs towards the yard and his waiting horse. A young lad was about to throw a saddle over the horse when Geoffrey appeared. In his impatience he knocked the boy over and mounted the horse bareback before riding off out of the gate as if demons pursued him. Calculating the speed it would require to reach Eddessa; it would be easy for him to overtake a rider of the monk's stature; deliver him a silencing blow to relieve his future fears of anyone ever finding out what was said the night when the Papal envoy came visiting. He rode hard along the road until he spied the castle of Eddessa perched upon its high mount overlooking the valley, but there was no sign of any lone mounted monk. When he reached Eddessa's outer castle gate the sentry came out from the keep to challenge him; it was insulting that he was not recognised as the hero of Eddessa, his saddleless horse was rearing and turning in fright whilst Geoffrey struggled to remain mounted. He called to the sentry asking if a monk had passed by the gate this morning; to which the sentry replied that nobody had passed through the gate so far this day.

The monk had outwitted Geoffrey and he swore revenge upon him. Knowing that there was little else he could do he turned his horse and returned home in a foul mood.

When at court Geoffrey's noble links and heroism had always earned him certain favours with the females in attendance, and now there was a new face, a certain Spanish Lady Katherine was all he learnt of her name; she had caught his leering lecherous eyes and set his heart racing sparking a fancy to her.

Unfortunately for Geoffrey she was already married, however Katherine's husband was the ageing and feeble Walter Count de Navarre, cousin to the king and Brother in Law and Deputy to his Lord in the county of Eddessa. Harran became Walter's prize in his early years for his outstanding loyalty and service to the King. In his service he had held and maintained the city safely throughout many troublesome years; during his time the area had grown into being very prosperous. In later years his first wife fell ill and it became necessary to retire to Eddessa.

Marion, Walter's wife of many long years suffered a debilitating ailment of the skin brought on by the winds of the Kamsin. It was not a common complaint more that the climate dried the skin and reacted on its lack of moisture. Because her Jewish physician resided in the capital, when they retired they decided to move to Eddessa, it was the most sensible thing to do to be close to the physician; having the closer contact as her condition worsened. Walter knew that moving to the Court in Eddessa would hold no hardship as the Lord Edward, Prince of the region was his close friend, ally and brother in law. Sadly within the year of retiring Marion had died leaving Walter alone. Many times he planned on returning to Hurran; but Edward's concern for his old friend and brother in law thought it best to include him in as many court activities to reduce the lonesome void of Marion's passing. The great trust that Edward placed in Walter was well founded and it pleased his friend much, indeed Walter enjoyed his role, there was hardly a moment to spare when he was not in constant converse with the people of the court and helping out with the County's business. It was not until he was alone at night that he realised he missed a woman's companionship; he was past bedding females but desired the charm of their company; to talk and pass away the time now that Marion was no longer with him. During the daytime; he was far too busy to notice such a void, as people were rushing in and out of his life in the activities of overseeing his duties. He enjoyed being busy; it brought with it a sense of purpose. Being a military man he was used to everyday problems; the activity brought satisfaction and being with Edward he had settled into his new way of life; but wherever he seemed to be; so too was the young Lady Katherine nearby. He was not complaining; more he was flattered because she chose to spend much time lingering in his company; perhaps she felt safe? They had a platonic friendship and it grew out of trust that each respected the others position. She preferred not to be at court, away from the lustful and amorous men that were only after bedding a body for the night; as far as she was concerned kitchen maids were for that type of sport. She held herself above that kind of liaison; believing it was not for her, Walter was such a gentleman always courteous and charming. As time went by affection grew between them and eventually to everybody's surprise they were married. Although the marriage was never to be consummated; Katherine held her position loyally and proved herself a dutiful wife and companion. The marriage survived with some degree of success for two years or more until the duties he held became too much for him and slowly they were introduced back into the ways of the court.

Walter took on the habit of sleeping a lot; the truth was that he was ageing rapidly and his attention towards the young wife gradually diminished. The day held too many long periods of quietness which became a strain on her; leading to nervous tension which slowly resulted almost to a test of endurance. She was a woman alone; young and craving attention that was waning from her fading and retiring husband; soon she had no other choice but to look towards making new friends.

Walter was slowing down, he never noticed the change that was taking place in the marriage and unfortunately because of his inability to fulfil his wife's natural yearnings for company, age was dulling the spark in his life's interest.

Katherine was indeed a child bride, marrying Walter when she was little more than seventeen years. Flattered though he was; Walter was aware that his marriage was not made in heaven, but contented himself by possessing a beautiful young bride; considering himself more as her protector that an active husband. In truth, many doubted the genuineness of his physical ability; and after a time were surprised that the marriage lasted, but most at court were loyal to Walter and respected his charade.

As time drifted by a change that took place in Katherine that grew stronger by the turn of each day, like a metamorphosing caterpillar she became a woman. Her girlish beauty was transformed into that of a mature woman; inside she developed a yearning for excitement and a longing to feel alive. At court she began to glance discreetly at other men, not brazenly but with a very judicious eye for a quality that she couldn't recognise in most other men. That was until she became acquainted with Geoffrey who resembled that which was not refined but interesting in a different way. Curiosity stemmed from chatter; building into a fascination by his many successful pursuits on and off the field. He interested her, in spite of his brash and loud mouth but there was definitely something she admired about this man who was fearless in the face of his enemies. Most of all she sensed a danger of temptation in him; that excited her, after all he was such a fine figure and handsome to boot. Living the life of a lady in waiting, she had never encountered any form of danger in her life, but this impressionable brave and audacious knight who had fought the enemy many times and lived; received she noted an unrivalled respect from his elders; especially the ladies saying such things that made her blush.

Katherine felt daring enough to set out to have some impish sport with Geoffrey and to acquaint herself with an insight of the man himself, to see if he would be an adequate replacement for the one that she now was tiring of tucking up in bed. In order to do this; she first; very discreetly enquired through other various sources of the background of the man. How he used his day, was he wasteful, did he hunt what were his likes and dislikes; along with other questions; which appeared quite open and without purpose. Most of all in her calculating mind she really wanted to know how deep his pockets were and what wealth he had to inherit when his father died, after all she had to be realistic about what she was preparing to be tangled up with.

On one of those warm afternoons when Walter was taking his usual nap she sat in front of her upright tapestry frame and well upholstered chair in her drawing room looking out of the window across the plain. Below the lush fields spread out, they were part marsh and part arable farm land; insects at this time of year were thick on the air manifesting there mating purpose as they formed in dark clouds hovering above the marshes and often she watched the birds in a feeding frenzy swish backwards and forwards in flight fattening themselves while feasting on the midges. It was hot with a gentle breeze blowing to fortuitously refresh her; casually toying absent-mindedly with cotton and thread between her slender fingers she wondered what would become of her on her husband's demise. She pondered long on this subject, she would probably receive an allowance; whilst the bulk of his wealth she suspected would certainly be inherited by his son, who unfortunately preferred to be detached from her, being displeased by his father marrying one so young. He was the commander at the castle of Hurran, a soldier that on the one occasion she had seen him appeared stiff in character, it was then that he voiced his disapproval of their union. Holding a narrow idea of strict observances of the rules between man and woman, she paused from her tapestry, flushing with her image of him disturbed her and moved to be closer to the open window to take in the slight breeze that entered the aperture.

Adjusting her bodice to accommodate the coolness of the air she espied the simple folk toiling in the fields in the heat of the day. The sight of the peasants at their labours was not an end that she envisaged herself in. The daydream evoked a definite need to ensure her need for a secure financial position as paramount to her future aims, life out there appeared difficult, and she would have no part in accepting that particular end as her lot. Once more her eyes drifted over to the fields with the icy shudder of what poverty in life leaves open for simple folk; it filled her empty heart like a great tide rushing on to a barren sandy beach, dread washed over her encouraging her to leave the position of the window.

Once she had acquired an accumulation of information regarding the said gentleman she thought, the next approach was the man himself. To her amazement the thoughts that ran through her mind startled her ability to be so unscrupulous. She had never experienced a man before; yet she instinctively felt it not too difficult to send out a lure for the one she had in mind to trap. She giggled at the fun she was having; in her excited mind; a flush of ideas sprang forth almost making her dizzy at the choice of options open to her; for after all a lone woman has a duty to herself to secure her own future. She had heard of others who had taken lovers, but that was not her intention; she wanted something solid, though at the back of her mind she had played with such thoughts. In her immature mind it had all been a fantasy, there were times when she held such ideas but was scared by the outcome of being discovered. She was unresolved and like waves that came and went so too did her ideas, indeed she now brought them forward to form and support her hatching scheme. At ease in the comfort of her upholstered chair; she took the time to assess her designs on life that she realised she, through her own methods of manipulation could forge herself a future as well as a fortune.

A giddiness filled her head; it dawned on her that she had become quite a calculating young woman; smiling at her own intuitive artfulness, but she frowned as dark thoughts loomed at the chances she was about to take in her pursuance of her diversion from tedium. The depression soon lifted, though she calculated her future as bright; it would appear that most young fighting men have a short life span in this part of the world; which to her mind proved quite encouraging. With this thought in mind it offered a lucrative outcome to her scheme, though if they were to die young she would prefer to have husbands with fortunes to leave her. She began to picture herself more of a rich widow with suitors a plenty, as a plethora of schemes began forming very quickly with her dexterity of mind.

It was two days or more later at the castle when Geoffrey espied Katherine; she was walking the corridor, and immediately his ardour rose. How he fancied her; his mind filled with imaginings that he could feel his hands grasping her growing firm young breasts; supported by all the tight material draped around her. She was very stately he noticed in her posture, he liked that; her aloofness he sensed distanced her from the other women making him want her more. Christ he was hard for her; so much so he couldn't help himself from rubbing his hand across his growth. Innocently she did not realise that her style of movement gave rise to any man's hunger for her; she was voluptuous in the extreme and unskilled in her womanly lures; but time would awaken this beauty into a different creature all together. Watching her move; Geoffrey's lecherous eyes ached whilst his heart pounded with every covetous beat; he realised that he had best seat himself and look elsewhere for a while; or people would soon notice that bump in his lower regions; and laugh the rest of the day out.

It was later in the morning when the lustful Geoffrey; being so inflated with his own ego and keen to have her; did no more than stop her when she passed him by. He looked both ways; no one was to be seen; she was walking alone; towards a shadowy section of the corridor where there was an absence of windows to catch the light of day; stuttering he offered to make some form of silly dawdling small talk. His talk was frivolous; before she realised he began to crowd her causing her to edge backwards until she was against the walls of a niche and out of sight. In a low whisper he spoke proposing his desires in a most ungentlemanly fashion; daring lightly and insolently to rub himself against her like a dog would a bitch; displaying his desire for her. Her whole body became inflamed with surprised fear; it was a look of consternation that filled her face; it seemed to say it all. Her shocked reaction caused her to reel with embarrassment; making all the protestations a lady of her station could, with a need to dismissing his presence forthwith. He was coughing and choking on his own embarrassment as he came walking rather awkwardly away from her; and went on about his business. Because of his rashness in making such an indiscreet sexual manoeuvre towards a now distressed Lady Katherine, it concerned him deeply should this incident reach the ears of his uncle Edward. It seemed he had a knack for getting into trouble; such an outrageous action would take some explaining away. To face his uncle's wrath could evoke more shame on him than being defeated by an inferior enemy.

It was a little later when Geoffrey was seated in a chair in a friend's apartment within the castle; morosely he was quaffing a goblet of wine, when it suddenly came to him that in her protestations; she did not attempt to strike him as a shock reaction to his boldness. By now she would have had plenty of time to report this confrontation to his uncle Edward; why was no word sent out calling for him to report to his uncle; I wonder he mused; could this be that she may have other ideas in mind? Immediately a riot of ideas filled his lewd mind, with such an effect that it gave him an erection. Oblivious to his friend's conversation, the broadest of lecherous and hopeful smiles displayed itself; his eyes widened imagining the two of them engaging in sexual antics of abandon. Geoffrey's cunning face was trancelike and oblivious to the voice of his friend, which was lost to the walls that cooled the chamber from the outside heat of the afternoon. Friend that you are growled the ignored and offended speaker, it was obvious that Geoffrey's mind was elsewhere by the bulge growing between his legs. The voice in the other world was outraged; but Geoffrey was in paradise; you deserve what you get and Geoffrey nodded pleased with the words that drifted over him. His friend did no more than reach for a water ewer on the table, he filled a cup and spilt its cold contents across his lap. Shocked; the cold water caused Geoffrey to leap from the chair; so enraged at his friend's jest. Is that what I must do to have your attention, said the laughing Norris who could not control his mirth; Geoffrey's dream shattered; and he was not pleased. It was not received in good spirit; Geoffrey lunged out to strike his friend; fumbling over a stool that was positioned in front of him, causing him to look even more foolish when tumbling to the ground.

Geoffrey's friend sensed the embarrassment that was felt by his self-conscious friend and prepared to receive a repeated offensive swing as he scrambled to his feet. If you expect me to do you favours and all I get is you sitting, starring into oblivion with a silly smile on your face, you can forget it; said his friend Norris angrily. Geoffrey's anger quickly subsided as he realised his friend's reaction to his own rudeness. Straightening his displaced clothing, he apologised to his friend but declined to explain his reasons for his behaviour, they shook hands and Geoffrey left. No sooner had the door been closed around him he was running around the building in search of the lady Katherine like a dog on heat.

Back in her quarters, Katherine viewed the sleeping body of her husband slouched on the chaise. His face twisted in sleep leaving the corner of his mouth to drop, he seemed far from being the man she knew he had been. Walking into the adjoining room to escape the offensive sight of the man she once cared for, Katherine sat herself and prepared to work on her tapestry frame; at the same time reviewing the outcome of her encounter. Her mind settled on the very moment his body touched hers, he was a loathsome bullying hulk; the thoughts caused her heart to beat more rapidly and she drew long on her breath. Holding her hand to her brow; her thoughts raced, no man had been so close as to touch her that way. She began to rebuke herself for her folly allowing this incident to arise. She had no alternative but to admonish him for his impertinent undeserved action, what would he have thought of me had his advance gone unchecked? She pictured him as a strutting cock that would have been thinking it was another lucky day with a whore from the castle; it caused her to flush with embarrassment. She could not help having the repugnant impression hang on the minds of others, she would deny any such confrontation should it be raised from the mouths of men or hear of the gossiping women's stories such as she had heard in the past. Her breast heaved at that thought and refused to be connected to any scandalous whispers, her mind was disturbed while her spirit was thrown into confusion. Her mind meandered down many avenues of thought for some time before settling on the decision that her strutting cock would be tamed, then stretching she experienced a twitching sensuality in the region of her womanhood; hopelessly she was tantalised by the memory of it all. In the days that followed Katherine received gifts of rare perfume, golden trinkets, and an unsigned note pleading to rendezvous whilst out riding in the country.

The secrecy that followed became a source of great allure and excitement, which at long last raised her expectations of life from the ennui she had endured for so long.

In the ensuing days Katherine had remained distant yet courteous, giving no encouragement to Geoffrey's overtures whenever he presented himself. She was now certain that his continued boyish courting practice resembled a fish that had swallowed the bait and was ready for the reeling. His persistence in his efforts to court her was indeed very strong; when she was ready she casually let it be known that she would ride the following day offering her present company of friends to join her, knowing very well that they would decline her invitation. Being present as he so often was within earshot of Katherine's every word he heard thrilled him to his very being.

On the day that she was to ride, she furtively added a sleeping draft to her ageing husband's drinking water which he would drink each morning on waking as was his daily habit. With nobody left to offer explanations to for riding out, she left their apartment and made her way to the stables, there was no difficulty in having a horse saddled up or any prying and awkward questions about the expected route she was to take; now that the whole region was at peace. She was assisted into the saddle by a groom and she headed off down into the valley; turning out of sight into a partially wooded area where her planned rendezvous was to take place. Geoffrey was already waiting in anticipation; he rushed to her to assist her dismounting. Complementary words flowed in his greeting; unable to maintain his conduct, he grabbed at her and held her in an embrace smothering her with his kisses like some besotted boy. His hands cupped her heaving breasts. Allowing his weight to fall forwards; he pressed himself against her feeling the outline of her legs against his. In her effort to repel his over eager advance she shrewdly measured the amount of restraint required to cruelly torment her amorous assailant. She pushed and protested and in her turn responded by easing back her slender body sufficiently to set him erect. Geoffrey's impatience was his undoing; he was hot and ready, yet felt confused by her un-readiness to succumb to his amorous passes; resisting him after her willingness to meet. His mind suddenly became unsure; at first his reaction was of anger and refused to be toyed with.

"Do not play me like you would a fool, madam," he sternly warned, "for you will get more than you bargain for."

In reply she protested, "Sir, I play with you not, nor do I encourage you, have you not taken it upon yourself to make this outrageous advance on my person. How dare you treat me like a chattel of your own; or a scullery maid for your sporting entertainment? Have you not realised; I am lady in waiting to the princess and my husband is her brother."

That slowed his advance, she was cool and pushed him away whilst still protesting of his impertinence; proclaiming that that she was not a castle whore and would not be treated as such. He boldly held her once more; telling her how much he wanted her; that he loved her, but she was unaware of his true reasons for easing off with his lustful advance. Fearful that a word should find the ear to his uncle about his disgraceful conduct he knew his presence would no longer be tolerated, knowing there was no further slack in the line of forgiveness from his uncle.

Her head dropped as a word was about to form from her soft lips she paused then lifting her head holding her appealing eyes to his. He waited through her silence hoping that she was for him. As the morning sunlight shone around her he held her at arm's length, he spoke softly.

"Lady Katherine, since the day I saw you, your image has never left my eyes. I cannot sleep at night for the want of holding you, yet I fear like the goddess Venus; you spurn me and taunt me so for your own cruel pleasure."

Now she felt the time was upon her to snare him; she threw herself against his breast and feigned a sob, sufficient for detection, she continued that she too desired and wanted him equally as he did her, but she could not because of her marital standing.

Pushing her gently away he laughed mockingly at her statement of false loyalty, walking away from her. The gentle breeze that filled the trees now blew icy cold over her form; he was not a fool to be so easily duped she thought. He walked around her grinning unbelievingly,

"Hah, marital standing," he sneered degenerately, "you could have done better than that," the words came out as a disappointment to her as he turned his back on her once more and looked through the trees out across the valley to shield his anger.

Although Geoffrey felt cheated his anger did subside, he was aware of this woman's position and that her marriage to Sir Walter was a sham, she had much to lose over a wild affair. Resigned he thought to a respectable relationship, it did not hold with him, it was so much out of his character. He had been against her seductive, curvaceous and full bosomed body and found it ecstatically pleasing. So much so, he fought hard against his turbulent emotions to tear the clothes off her and take her where she stood, and he knew that he could have, but for her position at the castle. Instead; reluctantly he stayed his actions and crumpled in surrender against a leafy tree whose bent bough was as yielding as his will to succumb to her frolic of fancy.

"What is it you expect me to do?" he said reeling in submission.

Looking away, unable to hold the gaze of his piercing eyes upon her, her shaking voice coyly broke the awaiting knight's anticipation of being put off.

"I do not propose this with ease but before I am able," she stopped abruptly, faltering, then the words gushed forth alarmingly, "I have a husband who is past his best," she said.

With equal speed he broke the flow of her proposition.

"No madam," his voice filled the air with his displeasure, "do it yourself," his voice was filled with antagonism as his hand dropped to his dagger that hung at his waist. "As fine as you are; I should cut out your black heart madam for prompting such a request," he sneered. He knew very clearly what was being asked of him and he refused outright. His reddened furious face filled Katherine's heart with dread, regretting instantly at blurting out what so callously appeared to be a joint collaboration in the assassination of her husband. She had revealed her intentions and exposed herself in doing so.

"I am not a murderer!" he roared indignantly; then continued, admitting to have killed men in battle, which in a time of war was self-preservation. Still furious he was quick at confronting her, rebuking her for having the temerity and audacity to propose this plot to him.

With coldness in her countering reply, and half biting her tongue as she spoke, "Others could arrange it," she snapped. The air was humid but the atmosphere between the two was turning torrid with anger, catching a hold of his temper; he reeled at her persistence; turning his face to meet hers. To stop any reaction from him, she suddenly threw herself forwards clinging to him sobbing openly. "You must," she pleaded. With her sobbing face against his breast she appealed "I cannot lay with you until the deed is done." To add a little more temptation to the appeal the inside of her leg brushed ever so faintly against his as he drew her away from him; it caused sensuous ripples throughout his body. With clenched fists he controlled his ardour; but could not hold back his feelings.

"Sweet Jesus how you use your sexuality against me!" he exclaimed angrily. "Madam, in this country among the Jews there is a custom among the young infant males, as an offering to their God; the priests cuts away the excess skin from a boy's manhood. I swear at this moment I wish that I could have lost mine completely to be free from your tormenting touch; your pretence for an accidental brush is so deliberate. I can assure you; that you do it so expertly that I find difficulty in ridding you from my senses; I am trapped in your lure as a fly in a spider's web." Looking for a means to vent his frustration, raising his voice he bade Katherine to leave him before he takes her; and the devil with the consequences.

She softly apologised touching his hand, turned and walked towards her horse. She stood with her back to him, one hand on the saddle and calling to him for assistance to mount. Damn you; he cursed under his breath, she doesn't ask without twisting the plea. He walked towards her like an obedient dog, cupping his hands as a foothold she raised her foot into his stirrup whilst her hand reached out and cradled his nape, she was hoisted onto her saddle. She reined her horse round and made her way out of the wood, she had it in her to look back but prudence prevented her, she wondered should there be anyone about that may see her? On the road back to the castle; she thought how pathetic he was; and his whining about his wanting her. Had he have been a man he would have taken me she thought; I would have relished it and thought about my husband later, but I was wrong, he is not the man for me. Thinking deeper she knew that he was not afraid of anyone; but there was reluctance and it puzzled her.

Geoffrey stood watching her leave from the leafy place of their encounter; galled at her connivance; yet at the same time knew he would do the same himself should the tables be turned. Now he had her measure, and muttered aloud with a smile on his face we are birds of the same feather; he knew that one day soon he would take her, and the more he thought about it; in his heart the more it seemed likely.

Days passed before they encountered a further coincidental meeting. He was a paragon of politeness; Katherine could not give up the game and proceeded by complimenting him so on his improved gentlemanly manners. She felt deep within, that her fishing line had not been severed; just trapped and that her fish was struggling in vain. She parted with her company and left the room walking alone along the vaulted corridor towards her chambers. From behind her, a hand was thrust around her mouth; another hand was hauling her back into the shadows of the cloister from which there was no escape. Geoffrey's course firm hand did not release its grip from her mouth until she could recognise her assailant. This time there was no weakness of character shown; nor apologies offered for his conduct. With determination in his voice she was ordered to listen; carefully to what he had to say.

At first Katherine had visions of being killed, his eyes burned into her and for the first time she was truly unsure of herself and afraid of his intent. Alarmed and intimidated by his rough handling her heart throbbed uncontrollably and her breast heaved violently, unsure of his actions,

"We have a bargain you and I," he whispered eerily. "When this is done you will yield yourself to me," taken by surprise of his change of heart her frightened head nodded in approval, "swear it," he said, the words were forced through his teeth with great intensity and purpose.

He released his hand from her mouth to hear the fateful pledge; she uttered it firmly; "I swear it," she said panting breathlessly. Surprised he watched her take his open hand and kissed it as if to seal the dreaded bargain, and then his mouth, as her caress ceased; she muttered the question, when. Geoffrey did not reply but drew himself from her and walked away, he did not look back. This was indeed a different man she had encountered from that morning in the wood, a man with business on his mind. A man she preferred than the one she encountered in the copse.

Katherine dallied a little that morning, her mind not always concentrating on the wishes of her lady the princess. Observing Katherine's carefree attitude and lightness of heart intrigued her; she had recently been taken to low spirits and at times almost morose. The more she watched Katherine the more her inquisitiveness nature found difficulty in withholding the question. She called for Katherine to sit by her, and on taking her place; the princess explained to Katherine that she had been in low spirits that morning and was hoping to hear encouraging news to brighten up her dismal day. Katherine was quite shocked at the question, suspecting the Princess was being artful, thoughts flashed through her mind that she may have betrayed herself in some way, almost believing that her secret was no more. She felt exposed and flushed clutching at her neck she retaliated defensively with a note of haughtiness in her voice.

"If you must know; I have been deeply concerned for my husband's well being of late, he has not been altogether himself. I think he is unwell, he does not talk to me, but sleeps constantly and I fear for him."

"Then I take it that by your change of spirit; he has shown a recovery."

"Yes indeed it seems so," was Katherine's reply.

"There I was beginning to think you had a new man in your life," the princess nudging Katherine's arm and delivering a discreet smile at the same time.

Katherine was much older than her years and failed to fall for sympathetic cajoling. "How could you imagine I would do such a thing," her answer came hotly and with embarrassment.

It was the princess's turn now to feel uncomfortable, "Oh dear," she answered with a hint of apology in her voice; "I was only sporting with you, dear Katherine." The princess did her best to mask the note of cynicism in her voice. Something stirred within her; she was ever sure Katherine was up to something. It was one thing to hide an affair from a man; but not so easy to disguise it from another woman, there are too many little tell tale signs that betray guilt to a woman of the world. The words came out in a condescending manner, "Nothing surprises me my dear," she said chirpily, "I am much older than you dear Katherine, my eyes have seen much."

When the princess no longer needed company Katherine excused herself and made her way back hastily to her quarters where she felt safe; her nerves intensified and she needed to think. Safe; and seated at her tapestry frame; she was now regretting making the statement that her husband was unwell, when he's killed; questions will be asked and tongues will wag. What would she do, wiping her glowing brow, she rested it on the palm of her hand, slowly her hands dragged through her hair down to her nape where she clasped her hands and pulled ever tighter in the hope her problem would be relieved. Almost desperate with her thought; she rose and walked towards the window, gripping her palms she feared, could she stop the plan; believing it would be the safest thing to do. With desperation in her thoughts she decided that she didn't care even if I have to lay with him to stop it. A wave of panic flooded her as she desperately thought of how to get a message to Geoffrey; she knew that she could not ask anyone for fear of exposure. Her mind whirled in confusion but one thing was certain; she could not ride to his castle and resigned herself to seeing him before it had happened. Each day she searched for him franticly, but he was never anywhere to be seen.

One afternoon whilst Katherine was out riding as was her want of recent times Walter sat comfortably on his chair with his feet supported on a stool, he began to doze; heavy knocking at the chamber door brought him to his senses. Walter, startled by the unearthly din was spooked into ill temper, complaining loudly of the unnecessary need to rap so hard; "It's enough to wake the dead," he grumbled. Drawing himself out of his chair he approached the door; preparing to give off to whomsoever was on the other side, he moved himself quickly to match his heated mood; but on opening the door he discovered the corridor empty. An angry tirade resonated into the emptiness of the corridor; he turned frustrated by the event to re-enter his chamber when he noticed a piece of folded parchment on the cool stone floor. Must have been pushed under the door, he thought and eyed it suspiciously for a moment; stooping down he picked it up. He did not open it right away; but closed the door and walked towards the window where he would find it easier to read. "I don't like this sort of thing," he muttered to himself, he opened the folded parchment and began to read. It proved not to be enjoyable reading, Walter's anger suddenly turned to blackness at what he read, he was enraged and went to his wooden linen chest that was situated at the foot of the heavy four poster bed; he opened it and from beneath the piles of linen withdrew his sword. Buckling the on his belt and donning his cape he stormed out of his chambers making for the stables.

The princess sat in her private chambers relaxing before an open window waiting to witness the sunset; it was usually a spectacular sight; one that was never repeated on any one occasion that she viewed it. She was particularly fond of watching the array of colours that merged naturally to form the spectacle that had become a favourite ritual to her. When the sun dropped below the edge of the world at that time of the day and the curtain of light was finally drawn across the world bringing the darkness of night as its conclusion. She sat letting her mind fix on the child Katherine, though a woman the princess surmised that the girl may be feeling her feet, her mind drifted back to the first days of her seeing Katherine. Ah; she thought so young and lovely, quiet; yet full of energy, then as might; she thought of her brother Walter. A dear soul and loving brother, strange though, admittedly an odd mix she concurred with herself. What her brother Walter was thinking to wed her, she would never know. Probably infatuation, her lips pursed, this land she thought with its heat and confinement does much to change a person. There were many reasons why two people spend their life together, complicated as the marriage in question was, perhaps he needed the company of the young one to help him regain that something he lost along the way. She smiled and shook her head looking out of the window and out across the horizon, the sky now was beginning to lose its myriad of changing colours. Enjoying what was left of her favourite time of the day in her lofty room high above the plain below; an irritation was in her and she could not shake off her previous thoughts.

Of late she had watched this young girls mood swings changing her from one extreme to another, if she did not know better the princess sensed that something or someone was at the bottom of it all. The spectre of danger loomed and her fears and suspicion were aroused. That young woman had lacked the feeling when referring to her brother that she dearly loved; now the eyes of the princess began to tighten half closed; she perceived something more to her brother's state of health other than ageing. She decided to make preparation to have Katherine watched, being well aware that women out here suffer all kinds of privations away from their men. Loneliness is no companion; too many have fallen into that trap she mused.

In the late afternoon Katherine returned to her quarters and was surprised that her husband was not there. She thought it curious that she did not find him asleep in his chair. A chill ran over her body as she suddenly feared for Walter's well being, she had forgotten about the bargain with Geoffrey; then the shock wave happened, the blood drained away from her bringing a pallor to her cheeks making her feel quite ill. In her effort to dismiss any foul play she assumed he was out and about, but the seed of doubt was sown into her brain; thoughts began to flood into her confused mind and it disturbed her deeply. She did not have thoughts about his absence until dusk began to fall. Then genuinely concerned; she left her comfortable chamber and began a walk the corridors of the castle in search of her husband, raising her concerns audibly to all she met within the castle. Her sudden thoughts were the horses, her purpose of direction was toward the stables and making her way there ran down the spiral staircases with the nimbleness of a mountain goat; until she arrived breathless to find nought but empty stalls. Her mind raced grasping for sensible thought; she remembered at the rear of the building was a room above where the head groom resided.

With great urgency Katherine dashed around the building; ran up the timber staircase heavy footed in spite of her slightness of frame; up to the studded door of the room that housed the groom, wrapping on it hard as though she was wearing an armoured gauntlet, she panted with fear that her life may hang on the response. She was about to knock again when the door opened and the head groom presented himself, a rather dishevelled bearded character stood before her with dagger in hand. At the sight of the weapon she stepped back in fear; the groom explained apologetically that he was truly disturbed by the loud rapping on the door; thinking it was an enemy of his master and armed himself in anticipation for an affray. She knew him; he always assisted her whenever she took out a horse of her husband's.

In a pleading voice she enquired if her husband had taken out a horse. Placing the drawn dagger back safely in its scabbard, he continued by warning her of the dangers of knocking on the door in such a manner. Short of temper; she interrupted his flow repeating the question with urgency in her tone.

"He had indeed," came the reply from Silas the groom, "he went off this afternoon very strange like and disgruntled never seen him like that before."

"Do you have any idea where?" she asked curtly.

"I do not madam," Silas following up with his own question, "what's going on?" he asked straightening himself up, informing Katherine to seek the constable of the barracks.

She would not inform the groom of her thoughts but Katherine thanked Silas for his information and quickly turned and rushed off towards the barracks.

Half way there she decided on a different course of action deciding on reporting Walter's absence to the princess; knowing that she would move heaven and earth. Reaching the door of the princess's outer chamber she knocked slightly more politely than she did on the groom's door. Katherine explained to the handmaid of her urgency, leaving the now distressed lady anxiously standing at the door.

On the messenger's return she was permitted entry. The princess coolly accepted Katherine who began by making her apologies in her breathlessness and continued on with her account of her excited presentation. A day or two ago the princess would have warmly received the young woman, but now there was little or no warmth, but only a feeling of rejection shrouded her presence. The hard staring eyes of the princess befell Katherine, the gaze was long and icy; full of suspicion; the atmosphere within the chamber grew hostile, the now frightened young courtier explained her fears. "I was afraid of this," the words fell on Katherine like a thunderbolt; in her travail she was reduced to wordless utterances. Standing alone; without any one to reach out to, she began twitching and shaking in fear.

The princess had transformed herself from that of a gentile lady of rank and position to a fearful harridan, letting loose a tirade of questions that Katherine could not answer; for the harangue was so furiously fast. One question shook her to the root and should the ground beneath her have opened up it would have been a welcome escape from her now terrifying position that she found herself in. She was promptly asked "Who had she been consorting with, what is his name; how long has it been going on and so on?" came the accusing icy voice of the Princess. A thousand and one thoughts flashed across her muddled mind, but guilt is a difficult sin to disguise if you had never worn that mask before. She thought that she had been so careful; she had not entered into any kind of relationship even though, no, she stopped herself, it's too hard to bear thinking about. Katherine caught the acerbic tones of the princess's voice once more; as her order hissed through clenched teeth, "you will return to your quarters and remain there until I send for you tomorrow; for your sake; I hope that nought ill has fated your husband." Katherine curtsied and bid the princess a good night.

When Katherine neared the chamber door a caution rang in her ear from across the room, cold and piercing to the heart, threatening once more; that should anything untoward come of her brother, she may be receiving a change of quarters. This could mean one thing. How she managed to compose herself facing the princess she did not know, but there was a great sobbing of release that could be heard all the way down the corridor to her chamber.

When the constable arrived; Lord Edward had joined his wife who was looking very grave indeed. The Princess it seemed issued orders for a night search,

"But dear lady," pleaded Sir Giles Lampton the constable, "that could prove dangerous and a waste of time, besides my men," he pleaded. Before he could finish his plea the princess in a demonic mood rounded on the distraught and tired man, reminding him of his position and just whose life was in danger.

"Do I need to remind you that my brother had saved your life, and come to your aid when you most needed it, so many times in the past." There seemed to be no stopping the tirade of compulsion to redress his indebtedness. Giles had to stand there and suffer it; as the princess's anger rose to fever pitch. The Lord Edward remained silent for just so long as he though it necessary; allowing his wife to vent her anger, then discreetly reached to her, and squeezing her arm gently as a signal to abate her demands. He was quite prepared for her to have her say; his silence served as a measure of respect for her, after all, it was her kin. Easing her temper she approached the constable and confronted him; calmly beseeching him to find her brother.

"Giles, I want you to find him." Her eyes shut as she spoke in a more composed manner, so as not to allow any sign of a teardrop show in her eyes. To the wrong audience it might betray what could be observed as a woman's weakness, her state of mind, was certainly emotional. "Find him," the words came more now as a despairing plea, "I am asking you as a friend, find my brother for me."

Her repeated request seemed to soften Giles's attitude; he looked towards to his Lord; he knew well that she had weighted the demand in the reminder of the indebtedness; it's just the acerbic manner that was used to remind him of the duty owed. He smiled at Edward nodding his assent of her request; honour above any other reason made him comply. "Very well My Lady, it shall be done" he bowed and as he did so he bid his goodnight and retired. Away from the room he was relieved to be free from the swishing tongue of the princess, for a moment he felt sorry for them both. Searching in the darkness was not the best of ideas; if Sir Walter was out there he could so easily be missed. Back at the guardhouse Sir Giles was well aware when his orders were announced it would be like a rebellion, but he would cope with that; preferably the dissatisfaction of the men than the princess. Having given his word he would ensure the unpopular orders carried out.

When Katherine reached her quarters she partly hoped to find her husband back in his chair, but alas there was nothing but a chill within the chamber.

When the troop left, the searchers headed in the direction of the wood; where Katherine first met Geoffrey to propose the fatal demise of her husband, a place the searching soldiers felt held no merits being so close to the castle, but now that daylight was upon them they would leave nothing to chance. No trace of any man was to be found there and so they pushed on down across the valley. After visiting a number of villages they reached a third a little later than noon the following day. The sun was high and all were in need of a respite from its unwieldy rays, there was a well in this village offering a sensible place to stop to slake their thirst, the welcoming cool water would soothe their blistering dry throats. They looked about for signs of life; only the old women sat outside their houses; when asked for their help; they received only negative responses to their questions, and the order was given to mount up and press on with the search.

On the road out of the village the constable spied a group of peasants working in a field; caring for their crops. Venturing on a successful outcome he made his way towards them, it was a group of woman and a few young boys. The constable gave a courteous salutation and posed his question to one of the woman; who appeared to be the matriarch of the group. They had not seen anything, but a young boy chirped in and said he had spoken to an old man; he rode through the village in the late afternoon of yesterday. The boy spoke up when prompted by the matriarch; telling how sad he appeared thinking that he was ill. Fidgeting in his saddle with excitement the eager constable asked; what was his direction. The boy pointed south answering that the old man was looking for the wadi named as the place of the lost well, a water hole that long ago had suddenly dried. The answer at first was not received with belief; explaining to the boy that only the wastelands lay south. The boy agreed saying that was what he said.to him; but his sadness seemed to have overtaken him; I said I could fetch help; but he passed me by.

Now this was indeed bad news, he realised that Sir Walters command was at Hurran; but to cross the wasteland at that time of day was walking into the Devils smithy. He made his way back to his waiting party on the roadside and spurred them on in the direction of Hurran; but only as far as they could travel before nightfall. By late evening the tired and dusty search party arrived back at the castle, whilst the constable discharged his men he realised his duties were not over. There was one remaining reluctant task, which was to report the disappointing news to his Liege Lord. The tired constable wearily made his way up to the main chamber where it was his master's usual custom to be entertaining at this time of the day. Giles was ushered forwards before all within; being asked to present his report. He had no words to pacify the princess; but he tried to give her hope; adding that the troop would leave before dawn the next day; now that they believed they knew where he was going. When he mentioned Hurran; the news was not received warmly; whispered messages passed between husband and wife, the constable received half-hearted thanks for his efforts and was dismissed.

The weary constable left feeling that he had not satisfied his princess; no matter how useless it was to continue; it was in vain. .

Riding out of Eddessa before daybreak the following morning was a very tired constable leading his men down onto the valley road and then south directly towards the wastelands that led to Hurran. This time they were not blind to a positive direction, no more aimless meandering over hills and woodlands vainly seeking a possible thrown rider, the castle constable suspected that Sir Walter of Navarre was a dead man; waiting to be collected by this searching party.

Sometime later thought the constable he would be discovered, seldom being a pessimist; always a realist, his position relied on his intelligence and any thoughts of Sir Walter would be kept within himself, but time and perhaps circling scavengers would reveal the truth of the matter. There was urgency in this matter that he knew little of and that bothered him, but he knew something was afoot, the princess betrayed herself by her lack of control of her evil temper the previous evening.

Aware that Sir Walter was her brother; Giles's instincts leant towards something much more than an urgent appeal for his safe return, the princess was downright aggressive and giving no quarter, something he felt was burning her britches. His mind wandered in and out of this puzzle that he had set himself to solve as he jogged along in the saddle.

Reaching the area in mid-morning; the sun was climbing steadily to attain its noonday position; aiming its daily rays downwards, bringing with them the searing heat that he had grown accustomed to over the many years that he had been here in service. They were at the wasteland where a fine powdery earth rose from the earth with the least disturbance. Reluctant to stray from his intended direction, he was prompted to look around to check the men, his eyes widened in surprise at the sight, they sat erect in their saddles unknowingly coated in a white dust giving them a ghostly appearance. He almost smiled had it not been for the seriousness of their present task, the known water hole further on was where he decided to order his men to make for. Along the road to nowhere; no villages appeared in the emptiness of the horizon, strange he mused observing how the water holes where in the oddest of places.

Sometime in the past the well was the reason for travellers to pass this way, the water's importance marked the route for caravans to water their stock as well as the travellers thirst, it brought trade to the area; but that was a long time ago so he was told. Now with the water gone the deserts waste had reclaimed the area, not even a remnant of a hut marked the place of its passing. Pushing his tongue between his lips the constable guessed that they were about two miles from the water hole when a shudder ran down his back. Squinting through his dust caked eyelids causing the lines of his face to crack open the crusty layer of earth that had settled upon him, he peered hard through the haze that shimmered before him. What he had feared most was revealed in the blue distant sky ahead; there he could detected a circling of birds, not ordinary birds but those of a much larger kind; that gather when death hangs on the wind. He had seen them many times before in his time and his senses told him that there was most likely something or someone out there dying or dead. The order now was to spread out taking care to be ever alert for the body of Sir Walter and to be especially alert of quick sand, which this area was very well known for. The pace had changed into a cantor; the birds had indicated the urgency. Racing ahead; constantly alerted to the position of the birds; it was not long before they could see a dark outlined shape on the ground. It was too big to be a man and although the body appeared lifeless the waiting diners appeared patient in their feasting and had not yet commenced their banquet.

Vultures were nervous but not the killers; they were patient; for time was always on their side. Being carrion; they were flesh eaters of the dead; and in their way they were the undisputed cleaners of the land. With the speed; the distance between searchers and the waiting victim growing ever nearer; the lifeless shape in the sand became clearer, it was a horse. Giles could see that the scavengers had stationed themselves around the body waiting, only the odd bird that was brazen or hungry enough to venture forth in the hope to sample the awaiting dead flesh; moved closer. No more than a hundred yards or more away; the constable realised that a rider must be trapped beneath the dead mount; the few birds that ventured forwards were seen to be jumping away as quickly as their eagerness to begin their feasting. Driving his horses pace harder; Giles spurred onwards to prevent the birds from attacking their victim, at last he had reached the horse and the thrown rider. Dismounting almost at a jump he immediately rushed forward shouting to scare the waiting diners away; at the same time signalling to his men to make haste. There was no doubt that it was Sir Walter, he was in a poor state; with great care he leant over the injured knight who was barely alive and very weak. It was as he suspected; Sir Walter had been caught under his steed when it had fallen and was held fast by the weight of the horse on his leg, he could hardly say he was fortunate; though he had delayed the inevitable; being able to draw his sword and keep the birds of death at bay.

The constable emptied the last few remaining drops of water from his flask into a cloth and gently squeezed it onto his mouth before calling for more water. Dabbing the cloth over the cracked skin of Sir Walter's parched lips; then onto his face to cool him and make him conscious of the rescue. Within a short while Sir Walter was reviving but remained very weak and could hardly speak, his dried throat now partially eased from the painful state and need of water; he managed to whisper a weak thank you, concerned for his condition; it was imperative that Giles got the rescue quickly underway.

With constable's men standing around engaged in scarring away the waiting scavengers, those that stood waiting were ordered to help lift the weight of the horse carefully off the injured man. Two other men were ordered to ride like demons to the waterhole and fill as many of their leather flasks and return with fresh water for Sir Walter and the rest of the squad. Together in a concerted effort they managed to raise the bulk of the dead horse off Sir Walter; it was plain to see that his leg was broken and he was free of the pressing weight. How long this old soldier had endured his pain they could not tell, but the old knight was certainly able to retain possession of his will in not giving up his battle for survival against the waiting scavengers.

A man of the constable's company squat down besides his leader asking him quietly to view his findings; puzzled by the request the constable could clearly see that something had bothered the man. Take care of Sir Walter he ordered two of his men; turning to the soldier he inquired what this was all about; From inside his tunic he was surprised to see produced a bloodied crossbow bolt; it's this that the young soldier said, I have just taken this out of the horse's flank sir. On its discovery I guessed it must have come from that direction, pointing towards a hollow in the ground; Sir Giles was impressed with his skill and tact; saying as much; have you found anything else he asked? When the man answered no Giles told him "well lets go and find out" the two men walked away a distance and discovered a natural hollow in the sand. It didn't take long for them to discover where two sunken shapes were made; two men could have dug themselves into the sand. Sir Giles looked around for further signs but he was fired up with this discovery. This was loading his suspicions into this being a deliberate ambush. Further; he asked himself why; and who would do this was the next question. Sir Walter had no reason to travel to Hurran; it was too great a distance to travel; besides he carried no supplies. No he pondered; this was an arranged meeting; he thought long on the matter; concluding no other reason than the one he had already suspected. Killed or as good as where no one would find him. Nasty business; coming back to the present he sharply told the young soldier to keep that bolt out of sight and don't tell or show anyone of its discovery and don't lose it he warned; its evidence. There was a lot of thinking to do on his way back; he knew that the princess would have lots of questions for him and he didn't want to appear dumb and stupid. He winced as he thought back on her dark mood; he didn't want to have to take that again. Back with Sir Walter he wondered how best to move him with his leg in that state; and keep him comfortable. Riding a horse was out of the question. They would have make a cradle, with great effort they managed to construct a make do type of cradle out of tunics and surcoats; hopefully it would support its candidate until they were able to make something better and returned to Eddessa.

Sir Walter was very weak and the constable was most concerned of the possibility that he would not survive the journey back. Giles endeavoured to offer as much comfort to the weakened knight who he had admired and now felt sympathy to the injuries he bore; a break like that was enough to send most men out of their mind. More than anything; he wanted his curiosity satisfied for Sir Walter's present situation, but the ageing knight's weakness was such that communication was best left until he was ready. Carefully the troop of men transferred the injured knight with great care onto a make shift cradle made from clothing bound between the saddles of two horses having his splinted leg supported, there being no way of giving extra support until they could reach the next village where that particular problem could be overcome.

It was not an easy journey back to the village for Sir Walter; on reaching it they first made better splints for his leg and made up a more suitable stretcher, which sat between four horsemen before steadily making their way homeward. During the journey; the constable became deeply embroiled in the reasoning behind the killing of Sir Walter's horse; and why no direct attempt of murder of the knight was made. The deed was purposeful as was the place, they whoever they were; were not ordered to kill the man only disable him; and they certainly took care of that. Only those of the hashashin would be as devious he thought; lying in wait, he sucked in air as his thoughts led him to anyone that would gain from his death. What also bothered him; how was he motivated to leave the castle; it must have been something highly important to do that.

The constable's mind was agile when it came to difficult and unsavoury riddles; they were not so uncommon in the latter years. On face value; he thought Walter's passing would not have caused any suspicion; thrown from his horse to be left wandering to die in the desert.

In his thoughts the constable knew Sir Walter was a most liked man; so it was not likely for these people to be enemies from Eddessa, which left his suspicions to fall on family or wife. To tidy his mind he had to reason his way through the family, his son holds and possesses Hurran which is a successful outpost within the county; he holds no gain in this nasty game. So alas, he felt there was no other apparent candidate other than wife, lover or revengeful female. Knowing Sir Walter he presumed that he was too old for chasing wenches; leaving him suspecting the wife. She's young and pretty and in the bloom of her years; ready for the picking. His face became screwed; there was a small problem with his thinking, the girls not much more than a child and would know nothing of such people to contact. Shaking his head he could not believe that he was thinking right. Perhaps there could be someone with a fancy for her; if he was right then half the men in the castle would fall into that category for she was a fair one at that.

In the constable's thinking he believed he was without any definite proof; by suggesting the wife meant that she was bound up in a conspiracy to have her husband killed. If this was so, he must take great care in the way he presented his impressions to her ladyship; when completing his report; for he knew that he was not an accuser but a mere reporter of his findings.

The groundless shifting of guilt to an innocent person would weigh heavy on his shoulders, as mercy may be an unlikely attribute in the princess's judgement on hearing his report.

As dusk approached darkness the evening descended over the more fertile areas of the county as the constable altered his course. Heading towards the falling sun indicated that his return journey westward would soon be at an end, and rest would be the reward for the weary searching party. After a further lengthy period of sensing his route home in the dusk; he could barely see the distant rise of the mound where the great castle of Eddessa was situated; on high ground overlooking the plain.

Giles had sent riders forward to spread the news of Sir Walter's safe return, it set the castle into a buzz of activity, physicians were sent to his new chamber where the princess was to hold dominion over his recovery back to good health, but no news would be sent to his wife Katherine.

Throughout the night his sister had kept vigil at his bedside; longing for him be lucid long enough to utter a name to give cause to vent her revenge against the one she suspected most in the collaboration. No one could have nursed a brother more attentively, though; distressed and draped in empathy, she remained outraged by the event that gave her brother such unwarranted pain. Her heart ached, close to grief at the prospect of almost losing her brother in such an unworthy attack. She tended his sweating brow lovingly with cooling compresses and moistened his lips with regularity, whilst his wheezing breast gasped at breath for survival. Her thoughts were of an unselfish man that had given his all for the cause of the crusade and for the safety of those who put their trust in him. His career had been glorious, and his bravery indelibly stamped on the roles of honour by the exhortations of those nobles around the Levant and she loved him dearly.

When morning came the sun's rays flooded the chamber with brightness and warmth, the sleeping Princess was aroused by movement on the bed. Her brother's warm now enigmatic eyes stared open, his gaze fixed on her smiling loving form. Overcome with excitement to what appeared a recovery; her reaction was to lean across to give him reassurance that he was safe; that she was present to care for him. His once strong arms now weakly but gently held her and in his passing; his faint voice spoke barely breaking the silence within the room, it was a brief and transient awakening of his confused imagination; there came a distant calling for his previous beloved wife, Marion. Smiling as his sister caught hold of his limp weakened hand he turned and smiled as if he was reunited, Sir Walter slipped away from life unable to sustain his last great fight for survival, the grieving sister by his side wept silently over his now aged and frail body, free from the turmoil's of his latter years. Her joy was short lived and punctuated with a tear that rolled down her face, not one born of joy; but a distressing sadness of her brother losing the battle of life. Being the last remaining sibling of that name; it now remained for her to delve to the bottom of this mystery, which brought her loving brother to his dreadful demise. She believed in her constable's report that her brother had been duped in some way to leave the castle and lured into an assassins trap. How, when and why she could not tell, but one thing; suspicion certainly fell on one female within her court. Wounded to the core, sadly alone she bore her sorrow and tears, for she was sure the world outside would not witness any fragility in her proud and stately character; as it was at present, even though at such a trying time her grief was an understandable reducer of her fortitude.

When the news came to Katherine it was received with mixed emotions, she was mystified as to how her husband fared; the event leading up to Walter's demise was kept from her. She showed anger at the prospect of being kept from her husband in his hour of greatest need, but she was helpless to act. The guards on her door were under strict orders to restrain her should she try to leave her chamber. Only the need for news was all she begged of the guard; denied of that; she was confronted by a wall of hardened silence on the matter. Fear of the princess's anger grew within her; could she be connected and would the secret of the liaison be kept hidden.

Unknown to her there was a great service held in the chapel in Sir Walters memory, dignitaries from all over the County were present to pay their last respects and of course his son was present; fuelled with anger; he had his own questions to be answered. Katherine was still confined to her room despite the note she sent to the princess beseeching her to allow her to see her husband.

Throughout the period of the passing of Walter of Navarre, certain changes began to take place within the county.

To add to the upset whispers and rumour were abroad that the Seljuk Sultan had made a pact with the Mamlukes in the south. At first there was no acceptance of any such an agreement possibly taking place because of the deep divisions from previous pacts. A call for a Jihad was abroad but the knights of Eddessa thought little of it; refusing to accept any basis of the rumour. Believing that without a leader to cement the factions together into one unified force; action would amount to an empty gesture. War was an unprofitable period for most men; it cost lives and money.

Never the less; further rumours began to ferment, reports of armed forces passing through Cilicea were repeated. Assessing the strategy of an enemy it made no sense at that time that they would be threatened; rumours they believed were only rumours. If anything, from the news that had come to them; it would be more likely that there may be a more concentrated push in the making, which was believed to be Antioch. Where any invading army was to strike first; was a question that needed an answer, there was no definite news and until the force presented itself on the horizon; that force remained non-existent. The defending strongholds of Antioch were on alert and in full readiness for siege, granaries were full and there was plenty of livestock within the walled pasture areas. Antioch had proved to be almost impregnable against an attack; for those that maintained its strong position were at ease and very confident of incurring many losses on those that attempted any such attempts of siege.

As for Katherine; the furnishing of her chamber that once afforded her comfort now seemed worthless, emitting no warmth in their fine workings or feelings of security. Instead they became reminders of her own stupid folly; in her diversion from boredom and the uninteresting people within her sphere. Now there was very little comfort for her present situation, Katherine's fear of exposure was greater than life itself; for fear of discovery consumed her. At the window she could saw flaming torches carried by the sentry's embarking on their night duty; listening as their voices drifted up towards her window; she detected a pessimistic voice ring out regarding the uselessness of it all. As a terrified and sorrowful tear graced her rose coloured cheeks, it came to rest before surging forwards under the weight of the deluge that followed it.

The Trail of the Scorpion

Within the short time of leaving his friends behind to make their way back to Antioch and safety, unknown to Robert and his fellow scouts, a great army of Islam had already began to amass and were travelling along the far eastern plain in contingents, spaced and manoeuvring in wide circular routes to avoid discovery. The Muslim leaders had used the events in Antioch for the calling together of the people. The emirs worked swiftly, the Amman was slaughtered in a plan that was in motion before the event in Antioch took place, but that was only known to the few who had hatched their own plan and with events turning as they did, it proved a convenience for their rising against the foreign enemy. They had suffered the yolk of oppression and uncertainty for too long; the time had come to cement a union of purpose to the people to rid themselves of the barbarian and annihilate their enemy once and for all. To do this they called for a Holy Jihad; so determined was the intent of their mission that they sacrificed regard for their family ties or anything that they held valuable towards that end. Such was the intensity of their purpose, they acted carefully in advance, thinking nothing to the rape of their valuable forests for their war machines, which were bigger than ever before and more numerous to help fulfil their purpose in smashing their enemy's fortifications. Their plans were a united project with other great families and leaders across the land in this concerted outcome. First, they planned to surround the outlying Crusader castles of the north with a fist of men laying siege to hold each fortress firmly in place until their main armies arrived to relentlessly bombard them into dust. They intended to descend on their enemy in their thousands, giving the armies of the Red Cross no option but to cede their fortresses or be destroyed; when they viewed the size of the armies number they would be sure that would be their final epitaph was being written. In their terms, they were prepared to tell the Franj that there would be no hope of relief, as all other fortresses nearby were likewise under the same threat. The hand that held them fast would be closed into a steel grip; the defender's only chance for life was an impossible choice of changing their faith to save themselves or to perish in the sand they stood in, and there would be no quarter given. Such was the intention and immensity of the besieging army that they planned to form a defensive line against any advance across the country for relief from the south, at the same time denying any news of events to filter either one way or the other between their strongholds. Once the Crusader fortresses in the strategic Northern outposts were slowly crushed, the road would be open for even more men to flood across the plains. This time the Mussulmen were an unstoppable force; their eyes, like their army, would keep looking south to the next stronghold until eventually they would take Jerusalem. Likewise, the armies of their Egyptian brothers from the south advanced northwards adopting similar tactics; they would slowly strangulate any movement of would be confrontation; slowly bit by bit, they would destroy their enemy's army once and for all.

Robert's prime concern now had two purposes; first, the safe return of his friend Aldo, and secondly, the bringing to heel of the female who arranged the murder and further abduction and abominable treatment given to his friends. Hopefully, he believed, he would smash her and her cohorts that held the key to all the present disturbances., Although he was unaware of any of her plans, he suspected that somehow she had it in her fiendish ability to somehow usurp the King of Jerusalem's power, and that strengthened his purpose to stop this dangerous character and bring her to justice.

He had never met anyone like her; it seemed she had a penchant for cruelty and chaos, a barbaric streak that had remained hidden when they met. Although she was alluring and he had shown weakness by allowing her image to gnaw into his very innards, the fragility of his character, where she was concerned, proved a revelation and shocked him to the core. He could not alter what had happened, but the realisation of this fact honed his determination to destroy that which almost destroyed him. He was on her trail and would resist and refuse to yield to any hardship in his goal; yet somehow his emotions remained confusingly mixed. She was a cog that was set in motion in a madman's machine of destruction that was set to cost us all dearly, so he was told, and he felt that he was alone in his effort to restore the security of their existence in Outremer that was at stake.

The road he travelled to the coast was mostly through torturously rough hill country, high forested peaks and deep ravines, and care had to be taken not to carelessly push his mount to a point of exhaustion or injury should it be forced to stumble and throw him. Diligent in pursuit, his enemy was days ahead; there seemed little chance to rescue Aldo, yet he believed that her eventual capture would yield the explanation of what was going on.

Tactfully, whilst he picked his way along the dark sun starved rugged trail; his mind was filled with wild ideas of the future events of when he caught up with the woman. Hubert's ransom never sat right in his mind, reasoning that it was a lot more money than would be usually asked for a hostage of an ordinary knight's rank, a Duke, maybe yes, but not a knight; why didn't they just kill him? She would not act without calculated reason. No, there was much more to this ransom, it must have been planned to draw them to the canyon and their fateful demise; because a trap was suspected, they were steadfast in their willingness to chance the cost as men of Robert's ilk would prove a different value. The more he thought, the wilder were his imaginings and further away from the facts he became; best that he clear his mind of this enigma and await his arrival in Latakia, or he would end up losing his logic and sanity. Low branches brushed against him, yielding the pungency of the pines; it filled his senses, though it was a distraction that he welcomed and took in with a favourable heart. Care was his watchword; he constantly scanned the trail closely for signs of ambush and could not relax to a peaceful state of mind. The forest was thick with growth; shadows constantly had him reaching for his sword. This was no ordinary trail, but there were obvious signs that riders had travelled that way before and not so very long ago. The thicket gave way to the odd open areas of green patches where grasses grew high and the wildlife came to graze; in these openings, Robert could see the route of the hills ahead of him and thankful of it he was for it gave him the ability to judge the way ahead. Out of the thickness of the Pines, he could smell the sea on the breeze; he lifted his nose to catch its saltiness. A smile formed, for it told him that the following day he would be at the port where he hoped matters would clarify the mystery that he had pursued for so long. She was in his head; he struggled to prevent images of the annoying female from his thoughts; thinking more on how his friends were fairing. Thoughts stirred in him of how long it would be before Hubert would gain his sight after being in total darkness; the bastards that thought that idea made him angry firing him to promise that whoever thought of that idea he would make suffer when he found out who was responsible. Christ in his wisdom set some twisted minds to evil ways to taunt his fellow man. He had seen much since he had been in this land and he knew he had seen a lot worse; though when friends are hurt, it rebounds somehow on those around them. He wished that life would not be so cruel and hurtful, though he calculated that his enemy was saying something similar about his kind. Mmm, he fancied being back home hunting in his own forest instead of in this one, where there was far more dangerous sport to be had.

During the time he passed through the last clearing, he fancied that the forest stretched out before him to the sea or where he suspected the sea to be; travelling was slow; soon he hoped he would be looking for a suitable patch to rest. Night out here, he thought, could be dangerous; though he had seen not seen or heard any sounds or smelt any trace of an enemy, but he knew it didn't say that he wasn't around. In his mind, he gambled that she knew he was on her track or suspected it; of that he was certain. A woman like her wouldn't take any chances; if he had escaped her men at the canyon then he guessed he would be touching a nerve and probably closing on to something that she could not allow him to know of. It was interesting that Aldo was nobody of rank, so why take him to a port to be sold and shipped out. If he was a noble and he could see that he was, who would want to buy a knight of the Crusade? It did beg the question that somebody, perhaps in Europe, was the reason he was separated; could Aldo have had a rich lover? "Jesus," he exclaimed, "I've been at his side for three years, who is he?" As a knight his value was little, he had no knowledge of the future designs or events. His ability to fight was admirable, but nowhere near as able as Hubert or any of the others. He realised that his theatre of movements was being controlled by a stranger to him; Aldo was a true friend whom he had broken bread with for the past three years; then suddenly this woman had popped into his life from nowhere creating mayhem.

It told him nothing, only that through her devious trickery she had spun a web into which he was presently tangled and twisting in all directions to no avail. In the midst of his rambling thoughts, a sudden belief began to settle on Robert; Aldo could have had connections at court that he was unaware of; otherwise who was it that would pay a worthwhile ransom for the likes of him? The strength of friendship was founded on reliability and honesty, the past was left dormant and unspoken of, unless it be from the freedom of a man's own volition of friendship that prompted them to talk on such matters.

Following the track, a shiver caught his spine; soliciting his fears, he wondered if he was being used yet again to bait another trap, this time for himself. Jesus in Heaven, I wish I knew more?

The day had been long and light was beginning to fade as late afternoon came on; for some time now, Robert knew that he would soon have to rest up for the evening. This high ground he was travelling did not offer much in the way of resting places, but fortunately it wasn't long after when the trail he was travelling led him past an old shallow cave beyond a clearing. Luck was with him, seeing it to be a good dry place for shelter to make camp for the night; he believed it a good place to stop but first, his task would be to ascertain that it was not the refuge of any wild creature. Fierce cats were known to roam these hills and he did not fancy being tangled up with their kind, especially if this turned out to be the lair of a female cat with young cubs.

Closing on the cave, at first glance he could see that it did not go back very far, but deep enough to be suitable for shelter for a one night's stay. He dismounted and set about tending to his horse for the night's rest; being his only company he talked to his horse, as he often did, rubbing it down and generally tending the animal's needs. As he did so, he blew into its nostrils causing it to respond with a snort in reply; it amused him and sensed the horse's response touching heads in a gesture of companionship. "You're a good friend," he told the horse, whose head reared up as if in acknowledgement; it was a way for him to think out loud, and he believed understanding between the two achieved a companionship and bond. He left his horse feeding on the sparse grass around the open space, knowing that he would not roam. Once his chore of grooming and feeding was complete, he set about caring for himself. The earth all around was a carpet of dried pine needles and small windblown twigs strewn about after probable storms blew through the trees and the hills, which was quite expected at this elevation. After gathering his tinder he set about sparking the flints that he carried with him, easily he created a spark before it caught into a flame within a small pile of dried grass and small twigs. Although it was not an immediate worry, the ground cover was excessively dry and he noticed that the sparks that flew from the crackling flames continued to glow when they came into contact with the dried carpet of kindling around him, thinking that might be a danger when he slept. Though his thoughts idled he thought only on the fire, the warming flames were welcome as the evening chill descended and began to bite, the coldness descended quickly and he was soon gathering the heat in his hands to rub extra warmth into his body. To fulfil his comfort, he built up the fire and wrapped himself in a blanket, settling down he began to chew on a strip of dried meat whilst his mind thought further on the possibilities for the following day.

Though his supplies were basic and sparse, he chewed away appreciatively, In the course of his chewing he considered whether to move his fire into the cave for extra comfort. He dismissed that idea believing that a good sized flame in the open and the smell of it would keep any unfriendly wild visitors at bay; thinking no more of it, he settled down in expectation of a good night's sleep.

The evening lapsed into darkness; Robert had earlier collected sufficient wood to maintain his fire for the night and had it stacked nearby; all around, the moonlit, wooded slopes were filled with the relaxing sounds of nature and the star-studded sky that he gazed up, the night was clear to offered no threat of bad weather. Whilst the heavenly sky twinkled like diamonds from the myriad of stars, the moon's glow filtered the darkness; Robert remained huddled by the fire to catch its warmth. It was not too long before he was asleep after his long day's ride.

The night passed quietly and the fire's spirited flame soon subsided; its crackling voice had given way to a reduced glow and the sounds of the night had taken Robert into his slumber. An active soldier never sleeps to a depth of total unconsciousness, but learns to train his senses at times of rest in a guarded and light manner. He was not expecting to be aroused by wild creatures or to be taken off guard by the uncertainty of the fires flame, though his attention was suddenly induced to the sound of breaking twigs that lay all about. His sensitivity caused his eyes to open wide, his body stiffened and his hearing grew ever alert for further sounds. His hand cautiously made its way onto the hilt of his khatar alongside his resting body, waiting patiently for the next sound to tell whether the approaching foe was man or beast. It happened again; as he suspected, the breaking of the twigs was far too heavy to be an animal; the sounds he heard came from careless and reckless footsteps; Robert's body tingled with an alertness that puts the body into a mixed state of readiness and fear. Somebody, he believed, had been watching him, carefully studying his every move and waited, perhaps even trailed him from the canyon. Quietly and without any suspicion to reveal his wakening to his would be assailant, he moved himself into a position of readiness should he be rushed. He remained to all appearances sleepy and restless to give the impression that he was unaware of their approach and of no threat to them. All ears, he listened intently gauging sounds of the oncoming noises that signalled their approach; more snapping twigs alerted him to their number; they were two; any time now, he guessed they were about to rush. His senses were sharpened by fear, even though he was ready for action; though he instinctively knew their eagerness to kill him would also betray their direction.

When they came, they were clumsy showing themselves as hirelings; he threw back his blanket unleashing his khataar from its scabbard and swiftly blocked an oncoming sword that would have most certainly split his skull open wide had he not been ready for them. Quickly lifting his foot, he managed to send his speeding oncoming assailant hurling over his laying position giving him the chance to rise quickly to his feet. No sooner was he standing when another attacker rushed at him, yelling blood-curdling threats of death, but his attack was recklessly thought out, he surged forwards with sword arm flailing wildly in a cross slashing motion. To an expert swordsman such as Robert, fear of such a mad onslaught held no threat for one trained in the disciplines of sword play; feinting weakness, he encouraged his assailant on. Ducking to one side, his opponent was unable to counter Robert's deceptive move. Ignorance of the art proved too late for him as he felt the cold steel of Robert's khataar slicing through his thin clothing and across his abdomen releasing a sudden rush of warm blood from a gaping wound. With the surprise of unexpected contact, he stumbled forwards in shock and amazement, sending him to his knees. The warmth of his body left him as a mouth gaped in his gut area, causing his innards to erupt forwards to be held back by his clothing which had him immediately grasping at to prevent any further loss. All thoughts of his foe were suddenly forgotten, for him his mission was over; all he could do was to concentrate on sealing the open gash that had liberated his guts. Meanwhile, the other attacker had caught his second wind, determined he was returning to overpower Robert to fulfil his mission. With his sword in one hand and a dagger in the other, the assailant was this time cautious in his attack; jabbing at Robert and probing for a weakness, the two men fought, circling each other in the shadow of the failing light of the fire. Robert knew that if total darkness befell them, it could present dangers for him from a lucky wild, flailing action of this other undisciplined madman.

Whoever these men were, Robert instinctively knew they were not trained soldiers but thugs out to rob or just hired for an assassination; no matter, any man with a sword is dangerous. However, that did not stop Robert's caution, ducking from the fast wild slicing actions of the villain, then alas what he feared most happened, the light of the fire suddenly fizzled out leaving them both in total darkness. The glow of the ashes had died, but air around it remained warm when Robert accidentally closed on it; the residual heat allowed him to orient himself in the camp at that moment, but nothing more in regard to where his enemy was coming from. For those darkened moments, every move depended on sound; both men slashed out wildly, their blades whooshing as they wildly slashed through the night air, each missing their appointed targets. Robert's ear felt the waft of the blade as it closely whistled by, indicating that it came from his left; to engage his opponent he had to turn full circle. If nothing else, he realised that this fellow was light on his feet. Crouching close to the ground, stock-still Robert waited and listened carefully for any sound that may betray his opponent's position and give him an advantage. Motionless and alert for any clue, he remained in his position as the sound of another slashing sword action cut through the darkened air with a purposeful whoosh just above his head. That was what he had waited for; guessing that the attacker was somewhere close and approaching his right, standing somewhere almost directly in front of him. Rolling forwards close to the ground, Robert swung out his sword arm in a wide arc violently, contacting with his opponent's lower leg as he passed. Warm blood squirted across him; with yells of agonising pain filling the air, the assailant went down screaming with the contact of Robert's sword with such a blow Robert knew it had cut deep to the bone. The fight was almost over, but he could not afford to be over confident and lax. All he had to do was wait quietly for a while, waiting for further agonising sounds, and then a whimper came. As he expected his attacker could not withhold his pain in silence. An injured, hollow sounding crying voice issued from out of the darkness, pleading for mercy, moaning like a stuck pig that he was. A trace of echo in the sound of his voice indicated to Robert that he had managed to find the sanctuary of the cave; it offered him somewhere to fix his back to and spring at Robert should he be so foolish as to approach without vigilance.

Robert had also sensed the position of cave and the sounds of his enemy, but could see nothing through the darkness; he stood beyond the caves mouth deliberating whether to enter, but he was not so foolish. Calling out to the wounded man to surrender and throw forward his weapons towards the sound of his voice. It didn't take the wounded man long to cede to Robert's call; the sword was thrown out obediently; he had used two weapons but there was no sound of the dagger hitting the ground. Robert was not new to these tricks, guessing that this man was going to put up a fight like a wounded animal. Outside the cave, he remembered he had a pile of brushwood to rekindle the fire in the morning; feeling around blindly, he soon found sufficient for his needs. Blindly and with haste, Robert traced the position of the dying fire by feeling for the warmth of the fires remains; it proved easy to locate. Although it had diminished somewhat, the ashes held a residual heat. Once more, he called to the cave, telling the man to surrender peacefully whilst he quickly grabbed at dry pine needles to spark a flame from the dying embers for what was urgently needed to create a blazing light.

The remnants of the old embers had just about enough warmth in them to allow Robert time to lightly sprinkle on dead pine needles to rekindle a flame. He worked with the greatest of speed, blowing hard to energise the little glow that was beginning to give hope to his frantic efforts. With great relief, his actions began showing signs of reward; the smoking brush began to manifest the quickening of a spark to ignite the first flickers of a weakly flame. With his eyes flicking continually towards the cave for any indication of movement and with one ear cocked in that direction, all his efforts were given to building small twigs onto the struggling flame. Satisfied that his quarry remained put, he relaxed to await the fire to begin to build for the light that was so desperately needed.

Once more, he repeated his call into the darkened cave, ordering that should his assailant refuse to surrender, he would wait until morning until he was sufficiently weakened through loss of blood before killing him like the worthless dog he was.

There was a huffing and puffing and sounds of general dissent, even appeals in the name of Allah that his weapon was dropped somewhere; he did not know where. He was cunning; Robert heard neither truth nor word of surrender, but nothing would encourage him until there was enough strength of flame in the fire to enable him to finish the task. The light from the glowing embers sprung from the once pitiful and struggling flame to a blazing frenzy; he quickly grabbed for more substantial wood to sustain the fire's hungry insatiable appetite. When he was ready and the flames were busy with a crackle of attack at the added fuel, the blazing wood spit and sang out into the silence of the night like a hundred harbingers heralding the would be assassins waiting doom. In the light of the invigorated fire, Robert could see his assailant's wounded shadow cowering low at the end of the cave; he craved for mercy as the brightness of the fire grew, showing the miserable form of the assassin holding onto his injured ankle in a desperate effort to stem the flow of blood from his messy wound. He was not in poor shape, yet it was apparent that he was not about to run anywhere; Robert was aware that the wound was severe by the amount of blood that had spilled forth onto his clothing.

Assessing him, Robert suspected that he would fight like a mad dog to survive; hope could only be his wounded opponents' chance of freedom. In Robert's thoughts, he weighed the chances that an act of kindness not to kill the man; should he yield some vital information might prove to be of some benefit to his quest for the woman. It was a failed assassination; better live wounded than die for pride. Nearby, the assassin's companion remained weakly moaning where he had fallen; he was no threat, being fearful to move in case his wound opened further and his innards threatened to feverishly spill onto the spiny laden earth of the camp. Sensibly, the wounded man remained as still as could be; he presented no danger and was safe for the moment; perhaps this Franj was not quite the bad demon he thought he was, though he could fight well. Approaching in his direction, Robert bent over the man and tore cloth from his clothing, then returned to the cringing attacker within the cave, who could do nothing, only beg for mercy. He tossed the rags forward to the man in the cave to use as a strapping to wrap around the bleeding leg wound. "You see," Robert told the wounded man, "I can help. I am a reasonable man; it is not my wish to injure you further; you have my promise on that, will you help me? All I ask is that in return, you will tell me what I need to know about the woman." Although the injured man did not raise his head fully, Robert could see the lips curl into a snarl. He was reluctant to submit; it prompted Robert to wonder what kind of hold she had over these people. Scared and hurt, the wounded man's dark gimlet eyes darted around the cave looking for where the wrapping had dropped; quickly he scrambled for them in a desperate bid to stem the flow of blood from his oozing wound. Robert watched as his enemy's bloodied hands worked quickly to tie the bindings tightly around his wound giving him back the use of his free hand. Walking back towards the fire, Robert wondered if this man in the cave was going to prove awkward; he would need to replenish the flame; a bright flame that was enough to continue illuminating the cave. Robert was confident that he was in no danger, so he worked with the fire; the wounded assassin he noticed could hardly hobble; he was not going to rush him. Tossing more of the gathered kindling onto the fire, he waited for the blaze to increase, his mind more at ease and aware that he had the advantage of fitness over the pain and injury of the wounded assassin. He fed the fire, casually pushing the wood with his foot forwards piling the surrounding brush and pine needles onto the flames before returning to the cave and the wounded man. He could see him clearly as the fire flared up into activity; from the look of his appearance, Robert could tell that the beaten adversary feigned a cowering submissive stance; he was not yet ready to surrender and to a soldier's eye, had positioned himself in readiness to lurch forward when ready. He needed this man for information and would go to lengths to spare him, but, alas, he could tell that it was not to be. Nearing the man, he could sense death was near; being triumphant in this affray, he needed to give out the impression that he was oblivious to any further attempt of attack, and showed an air of superiority as the victor of the fight, at the same time offering the impression that his guard had dropped.

Like a jungle cat wary of its prey, he paced before his enemy from side to side whilst feigning a careless aloofness to the wounded individual. Once again, he offered terms for his life, carefully at the same time he judged that there was enough space between them as a caution to make it difficult for the man to spring onto him.

"Well," he demanded, "who sent you?" he pointed with his khataar at his leg wound and told him that he could have further assistance with his wound if he required it. Instead, the wounded man remained insolently silent; he was stubborn and not the type to surrender, and the look in his fearful and watchful eyes told Robert that he was cornered and waiting for his chance, measuring every step that was made before him.

In order to entice him to make his move, Robert had to offer him encouragement, entering into a harangue of threats, finishing finally with one of death; at the same time, stepping that extra pace forwards enticing him to spring. That was the opportunity that the wounded man had waited for; he suddenly lunged outwards with the dagger, which flashed in the light of the blazing fire committing a curse on Robert as he endeavoured to fulfil his mission. He did not see the khataar, it rained down on him with such speed and terrifying force that the wounded man did not even feel his death as the steel of the sword split his head apart down to his neck.

He fell abruptly at Robert's feet without a sound being uttered. It was over; remaining on guard and alert to any sudden rush, he looked around for any others, but there were none to be seen or heard; all hostile sounds had abated, the fire crackled and the silence of the night returned. Robert walked across to the wounded man and rolled him over with his foot, he was clutching his stomach, quietly moaning in his effort to prevent any loss of his innards spilling out between his clutching hands. His hands and arms were bloody from the bleeding wound. Robert stooped over the wounded man to inspect the severity of the cut; he had seen worse, and there was little chance that he would die, but declined to give that information up.

"Tell me who sent you," he commanded, but there was no reply. The man stared back blankly with fear in his eyes and fearful of the blade that Robert had so expertly wielded. Repeating his question once more, he promised this time to spare his life and put him on a horse.

Dubious about how genuine his enemy's words were, he remained silent for a while.

Robert bent over the squealing man and spoke calmly, pointing out that death from a stomach wound was a very painful and a lingering way of dying.

The silence remained; the would be assailant, considering his options, began to slowly to speak, panting nervously before breaking into an uncontrollable babble, which Robert had to stop, telling him to speak much slower if he was to make any sense of his words. Now was the time for truth, he was helpless to resist and knew that Robert had power over him to further harm him or keep his word. When the words came, they were reluctant utterances; before a flowing frankness of his orders followed. "We only had to wait three nights to see if anybody was following before we picked up your trail." He became at ease as he spoke; Robert carefully viewed the wound more closely, at the same time listened intently. "We were to kill whosoever followed."

As Robert tore back the layers of cut clothing to further clean the wound, he enquired, "Who gave the orders?" He admitted that he knew of no names but it was a woman; of that he was definite. "There were two of them with a giant murderous villain, they cared not for mercy or understanding that we had families. It was a vile hag that spat her orders from behind a veil," he was quick to admit that he had never looked upon her face, but he feared her greatly. "We long ago pledged our loyalty to the Old Man of the Mountain; the hag threatened to kill all in the village should they decline her order."

It was as Robert suspected, and the knowledge of her sealed her identity. "And the name of the other?" inquired Robert. A further negative answer caused the man to fear a reprisal pleading as he spoke.

"Believe me, I beg you, I do not know her name, unlike the evil villain that is the curse of Allah that walks with her, the young one is calm and cold as any winters night and talks sweetly, but her words play tricks with men's minds."

As Robert worked, he listened, although he could not help feeling that he had weakly fallen to her voice like other men.

The wounded man by this time had become talkative, he was receiving aid to his wound; and was terrified as he cautiously watched Robert.

"She is not one to idle or to mix words with, we are afraid of her and only a fool thinks about disobeying her. She too is a she-devil and cunning. She walks with death that one; she has no fear of any man; we of our village know that she looks deep into the hearts knowing of men, you are a fool to think that you can lie to her for she knows all that is told. I tell you, it is foolish to try to hide your feelings, for she, above all, knows the weaknesses of men and women alike." His words struck deep into Robert's conscience, causing him to screw his face up as the truth was laid before him. There was a reckoning coming to her, he had sworn it, and it was well that she did not know that it was he that was going to bring her down to heel; for Robert had made his mind up to the task.

It was not uncommon for a beaten enemy to deliver up information, after all, the two fighting men recognised the need to overcome one's foe, but when

Allah guides the heart of the victor to be merciful and attend to the deed of healing his enemy's wounds, it is only honourable to give up a warning of the dangers to his future cause.

"We fear her powers more than the cruelty of the hag that walks with her; she is known among us as the Scorpion." His tone emphasised her name as if it were some deadly disease; she has the powers of the devil. "So great are they that those foolish enough to go against her suffer death; believe me, it does not follow quickly. I have seen her vengeance, beware of her," he warned, "as she is the right hand of the mad dog Hassan of the hashashin." The words came out almost as a regret of the mention of the name.

Robert's head nodded in agreement, "That sounds like her alright," said Robert under his breath.

The man on the ground moaned and tugged at Robert's arm. "Please," he begged, "save me, I do not want to die."

"Tell me, are there any others with you?"

"There were many men in our village, I swear to you. Please save me, do not leave me here in this empty place to die away from my family."

Robert had considered leaving him, then decided against it after giving his word. He looked into the man's eyes and spoke. "You have done as I have asked and it is not my intention to make you suffer more, but if you are to live, that wound," he said, nodding to his stomach, "the wound has to be sealed." The man's eyes opened with fear, "You said you were going to help me."

"If I am to save you, you must be brave for what is to follow." Robert explained that he had to seal his wound and to do that it meant that pain would follow. "You must trust me." He rose and went where the dead man was laying and set about ripping his clothes into long shreds for bindings. Picking up his dagger, Robert walked to the fire and placed the blade into the hot ashes. There was disbelief in the wounded man's eyes as he watched knowing what was to follow. Robert bound the man's torso and lower abdomen and looked back to the fire. The blade was glowing red hot and ready; looking at the wounded man, he told him that there was no other way to help him. "When this is done, you will sleep for a day and you should rest for another. If you move too soon, you must do it with the greatest of care, or all the pain you have suffered will be for nothing. Alas," he said, "I cannot stay, at sunrise I will have to move on to find this she-devil you have told me about."

He thanked Robert for keeping his word adding, "If you want to catch up to the woman you should make for Lattakia."

"Then Lattakia it shall be."

"May Allah smile upon you and bring your task to a victorious end," were his last words. Robert reached for the blade, telling the man to prepare himself for his ordeal and may Allah deliver you back to health to live a long life. He stooped over the man and placed a thickened stick into his mouth; he asked if he was ready. Sweating with fear, the man nodded his head in anticipation for the hot knife to sear his wound. The sizzling flesh and the muted screams of the sealing blade put the man into a state of unconsciousness; it was done, and Robert had kept his word. With the wound treated and bound, Robert retired;

he suddenly felt tired and lay close to the fire catching its warmth whilst tiredness crept upon him.

The coverings on the sleeping man were drawn up around his head so that he could not be recognised, then, for safety sake, he reluctantly retreated to the shadows where he spent the rest of the night, cold and huddled against a rock.

The night passed without further event, at sunrise he had found where the assassin's horses had been tethered and searched them for anything that may help in his efforts to easier locate the woman. After the previous night's event, Robert's spirit was higher, feeling confident of closing the gap on the woman and Aldo. It would be afternoon when he reached his destination, and hoped that it was not too late for him, after all, he was two days behind.

Fortunately, thought Robert, the shipping in this part of the world never ran to an exact schedule; although he had lost two days, ships also lost time at sea, as he had previously experienced on his earlier journey out to Simeon. Perhaps it was too much to hope that her ship could also be delayed.

As the smell of the sea grew stronger, he began to question his own ability as to how to find his quarry and his friend Aldo.

Lattakia

Lattakia was a large port; not knowing where to start his search knocked Robert's confidence askew at the size of his daunting task. His approach along the hilltops overlooking Lattakia gave his pessimistic outlook a more deep-seated sense, causing any attempt at being positive to wane further. His tree top view enabled him to survey all below. The harbour was full of diverse types of shipping, over twenty or more of the type that could sail across the great sea he guessed, as well as the many small craft that crammed the harbour. Arriving at the port town, he made his way through the bustling streets; they bore the usual heavy smells of wood smoke, body odours, human waste and the cooking that filled his nostrils and caused his eyes to smart. His task, he feared, was too much for him; the cause being how he was to know that his enquiry would be truthfully answered. Unless paid handsomely enough, no mariner or merchant on the quayside would admit that they were carrying a Latin soldier; and if his friend was nearby, he probably wasn't going to be in a state to be able to attract Robert's attention to where he was. He reasoned that he could only enquire initially if any ship was bound for the western ports carrying a stricken passenger; or if luck was with him, catch sight of the woman. He had decided that he would view them first and eliminate those ships that would not be taking on passengers, as most busy traders filled their decks and hulls with cargo being not too eager to take on awkward passengers with problems, especially those that may be whining once at sea.

Men and slaves were jostling carrying their loads and their wares on their shoulders, making passing difficult. He could have ridden on through them and carelessly pushed the crowds aside, but for fear of attracting attention or causing no end of trouble for himself, drawing the attention of his presence was something he wished to avoid. People looked sneeringly at Robert from eyes that were partially cast downwards, muttering disrespectful curses loud enough to be heard; here there was no respect for his kind, only rancour in their words from harboured animosity and aggravation that was stored in their eyes as he passed by. The crowd's hostility provoked them to acting stupidly by trying to block his path; he could see what they were up to and he wasn't having any of their game. With determined persistence, he urged his mount to force a pathway through the crowds in the main street and onto the dockside where he was confronted by yet another horrifying ordeal. Cargoes of all shapes and sizes blocked any open passageway along the length of the quayside; it was the same wherever he looked. Disheartened, he was lost to a way of finding his friend. He feared that time would not allow him chance enough to complete his task; some ships could leave on the changing tide and by the sounds that came from aboard the ships it wouldn't be too long before that was to happen. After trying two or three ships without any luck, he stumbled across a group of dockside urchins. It gave him an idea; with the aid of these scrawny filthy boys he thought he may achieve a way to reduce the effort of his daunting task in part of the time. This called for tact and a little wit to get them working for him. He dismounted and called over the one who appeared to be the leader. Bending down to meet his size, he tantalised him with a gold piece that he held in his hand. "Do you want to earn it?" he asked, knowing that it would be worth more than a dream just to hold it never mind possess it. Moving the coin from side to side across his line of vision, the boy's eyes enlarged beguiled by the shining coin; his eyes were so transfixed to it that he was almost salivating. Holding forth the gold piece tightly in his hand, knowing how these urchins would snatch at such a prize and run, Robert let it sparkle in the sunlight for all around to see. They had never before seen one so close and as chance would have it, it could be theirs.

Oh, this westerner was not so clever, thought the boy; working for him was not a hard task, but he doubted that their efforts would be wasted when he chose to deny them the reward of their bargain. The prize was so much money; was he toying with us for we boys were defenceless against him? The boy's mind was filled with all manner of thoughts. It was so close and shining, held tightly before the fingers of this man before him, its golden hue waiting for him to have.

"Your words and your money are painfully tempting," said the boy, "and it offers us great need for that which you hold, look around and you will see that we have no shelter to sleep under and no parents to look out for us. I ask you openly, sir, is this some trickery that you are playing on us just to use us for your sport?"

The sight and allure of the gold piece had not gone unseen; it attracted the rest of the group to gather around and listen to Robert's offer. He commended the lad for speaking plainly, stating his position as head of the urchins.

"Are you are all eager to win this piece?"

"Yes," they keenly replied.

"What I will ask of you is a simple task," and placing his hand on his heart, he swore on all that was holy in his faith that he had meant every word that he had spoken. "I have a need for certain information and my time is running out; now listen carefully and this will surely be yours." Once he had their attention, he spoke slowly, describing the women and one other who may appear to be sick along with an escort of armed men. There was a sudden eagerness and instant babble of seeing soldiers two days previous, but to them they were soldiers of a different kind; mercenaries, they told him, and of the type of company no honest man would want to keep; for they were cruel and heartless, calling the boys gutter rats and vermin, so they paid no attention to them.

Before sending them off, Robert decided to give an added incentive of a further gold piece to the one that came back with the information he required. They became willing servants to the promised prize; they were working for a fortune, a chance such as this they believed passed their way once in a lifetime. He had won them to him. "Mind now, I want news before the tide was to change," and he warned them sternly that he would not put up with trickery. To emphasise his meaning, he drew the blood stained khataar from its scabbard as a token of his word. The gazing onlookers swallowed with the sight of the blood stained blade, promising that they would be loyal to their word and their task. They looked to their leader, who broke up the group into sections for allotted areas of the dock, telling them to check out all ships before scattering them into the convergence of crowds.

One by one, they returned after exhausted enquiries, but none with the news that Robert wanted to hear, until one came to report that he might have something, adding with temerity a question that if the news was not good, would the gold piece still be his. Robert leant forwards eagerly to hear the news, startling the bearer. His hand reached out and pulled the startled boy closer to him.

"What is it, lad?" asked the man, assuring him that if it were the correct type of news, the coin would surely be his, but not to dally with his information. The boy was hesitant; Robert somehow suspected a different reaction from him, having a hunch that something was not quite right. Not so long ago these boys went crazy with the chance of earning his gold piece, yet this lad was slow to reveal what he had learnt; was he making something up to appease the enquiring knight? Robert's eyes were fixed hard on him, searching for the truth.

"Come on, boy, out with it," coaxed Robert, "do not waste my time, tell me what you have found out."

He suddenly came to life as if he had made his decision. "Well, sir, a ship sailed on the morning tide across the sea, I do not know where," said the boy. "Can I have the gold piece now?" he cheekily asked.

"Lots of ships left on the morning tide. There's more, what about the woman and the sick man?"

"There was a woman, I am told, but she did not leave. The sick man was handed over to another who has taken care of him."

"Where did they sail for?" Robert asked enthusiastically.

"I do not know and neither did he who helped load the ship." The gold piece sparkled as it was exposed in Robert's open hand, which now extended generously towards the boy to be taken. As his dirty hands seized upon it greedily, Robert's hand closed locking onto the boys dirty outstretched fingers.

"Sir," said the ragged dressed boy, "you promised two gold pieces."

"That I did, and you will receive it when you take me to the one that helped load the ship."

At the end of the quay, it had become less crowded and Robert was able to keep up to the running boy who was eager to earn the second gold piece. Pushing his way along towards the end of the quayside, he saw that he was heading towards an alley, which raised his suspicion against the devious little urchin; he could have sold knowledge of his own presence for further remuneration. The boy remained at the end of the alley, pointing downwards for Robert to proceed on his own.

"What now, boy?" said Robert, bending low and grabbing the urchin around the neck to avoid his struggling free. The boy, unable to escape his tight grip, cast his eyes to the ground; Robert drew the boy's face to his; there was guilt in his hungry eyes. This was a trap if ever he saw one; the boy seemed less confident and nervous with the thought of his exposure.

The other boys gathered and were waiting to see that Robert's debt to them was paid and began to doubt that they were not going to see this gold piece as was suspected. "Hold," called Robert, "I am a man of my word and I have no intention of deceiving you." One gold piece he handed to his leader, "You will trust him, won't you? But first, there are questions I must put in order to know that I am not being tricked. Is that not fair?" The faces on the urchins spoke of their expectation, but in their hearts they knew this westerner was no fool.

Suspicion filled Roberts studious eyes as he held the struggling boy, his intuition was working to overcome the situation; he had to turn events to his advantage. This boy was no more than eight or nine, yet Robert sensed that on these streets the boy grew up very quickly to survive, understanding fully what money was all about. He was also sure that he had been brought to this point to be snared like a rabbit, but he was not such a fool to put his head into any snare for something so glaringly obvious.

With a smile on his face and his head held to one side in question, "Have you betrayed me boy for more gold?" the question was put angrily. There was a gasp from the boys at Robert's searching question.

"I would not do such a thing, sir, I swear it," lying as best he could. Robert did no more than quickly put his hand into the boy's shirt and felt around, pulling out a pouch of three gold pieces.

"My, you're windblown rich all of a sudden." He felt like slapping the boy for what appeared an obvious and careless betrayal. There was a prompting of disapproval from the leader of the boys, more to do with the fear that one of his own gang betrayed them and that his dream of owning a gold piece was lost forever.

"I'm going to teach you a lesson that you are not going to forget in a hurry," he threw the pouch to the leader of the boys, "keep this and watch what happens when a man is betrayed." There were objections that seemed he was about to die with the knowledge that he had been found out.

"And now I need you to tell me what I want to know." The steel of the khataar sang as it was drawn from its scabbard, the boys stepped back and their eyes widened in fear.

"Oh no, my little friend, I am not going to hurt you." He spun the boy around, dropping his arm between the boy's legs and lifting him up supported on his forearm and held tightly to his chest that the boy's light weight was tight against his body, and it was useless to try to wriggle free. Replacing his khataar, Robert's hand covered the boy's mouth.

"We are going to walk this alley, and you, my little friend, are going to be my shield, so that should any unexpected friend of yours try to cut me down, it will be you that will receive the cutting blow. Death will be quick with very little pain to worry about."

He turned the boy's head to catch his eye to tell him of his impending fate. "Now, that's the fate of betrayers; don't you think that's clever of me, yes," he mused, "life is very cruel and you never know when misfortunate will be near to call on you. Now which way did you say that I was to go?" It was a monstrous, cruel trick to have the fate of the young lad believe that his life was about to end so horribly; the boy was truly horror struck. He looked to his friends for support, but having let them down and shamed them at his act of betrayal, they looked down or away to his pleas. His life was in the hands of Allah and this barbarian westerner had found him out; unable to flee from his fate and the grip of his captor, he gasped helplessly. As youthful as the boy was, he realised the error of his greed that gold had in luring him into the dark side of life, for which was regrettable. If only he could be spared, but he knew that an assassin was waiting to strike a knife into him by mistake; his expected doom almost made him faint. Tears filled his eyes and as hard as he wriggled in sheer panic he was unable to escape the grip in which he was held. His screams where wasted as they reached no further that the suffocating hand that covered his mouth. Robert knew that he had suffered enough in his game and turning the horror stricken face towards his, he asked the demented boy if he had anything to tell him, warning him first, that the time for lies was over. He had a choice, to suffer the fate of his khataar, the assassin's blade, or gain his freedom. He placed the boy down on his feet but refused to let go. The boy was so overcome with his fear that Robert's arm was wet from the boy's urine, and so weakened had he become that he had difficulty in standing. In his stricken state, he held Robert's leg and begged forgiveness and mercy before continuing to make his explanation.

Once again, Robert was certainly learning the ways of his cautious and canny enemy; she left nothing to chance and it appeared she certainly did not underestimate Robert's tenacity or his ability to survive her rear guard measures. In the coolness of his battle-ready mind, he congratulated the mysterious lady's tactics in covering herself on her damnable cunning, and although he did not approve of her nickname, he fully recognised the meaning of it, adopting the greatest of care and respect in her pursuit.

When the boy had made his enquiries, it had alerted the assassin that his questions were obviously on somebody else's behalf. This was the assassin's reason for being here and succeeding in his task would greatly boost his desires for personal reward from his own master. At his request to aid him, the boy refused, telling him that he was going to receive two gold pieces for this information. Taken by the boy's temerity, the killer was about to slice the boy from ear to ear when he realised that he could use the boy to lure the Franj to him, and so the payment of three gold pieces was handed over and the boy swore that he would bring the stranger to him.

The tables had turned now he had three gold pieces in his pouch; it was better than a share of one or two later. Seizing on the opportunity, the little urchin was enticed into a traitorous act, one that he would do willingly for the greater reward of gold by delivering Robert to a quiet place where he would be eliminated once and for all. For this small thing had elated him by his sudden change of fortune, his heart set beating faster at the thought of the day's good fortune. It was as though people were raining money down on him and he became thoughtlessly intoxicated by it all. But chance had caught up to him, and he was to be taught a lesson on the severe consequences of trying to serve more than one master for his own avaricious reasons.

Looking down the narrow alley that offered little room for evasive action, Robert could detect a dark shadow, indicating a recess in the wall of the adjacent building; it was, he suspected, the obvious place for an assassin to hide.

Speaking sternly to the youth but with a somewhat milder tone, "There is one more thing you must do for me," pointing towards the recess. He told the boy, "Wait until you see me above that place," pointing to the roof top on the building opposite, "before calling out for me to enter the alley as you would have before." The boy was quite helpless and was not yet over his shock of the terrifying ordeal he had been through; still unable to walk let alone run away, he nodded in abeyance of Robert's command and to his surprise a gold coin dropped into his lap and the boy looked up to see Robert winking at him in approval.

"I always keep my promises."

Robert words stayed with the lad until he turned and walked out of sight around the building, where soon after he reappeared on the roof. Having scaled the wall of the house to the height of the timber projections that served to support a heavily laden vine, his task became easier; balancing like a fakir, he walked the open rafters until he reached the flatness of the roof, where he positioned himself to view his waiting enemy below. It was as he expected and he could see the assassin had tucked himself into the shadows and was casually waiting, unaware that the man he waited to slay was looking down on him. He was unseen from view of the alley but not from above from the roof of a building. He was casually eating a piece of fruit whilst waiting to deliver the death blow to his would-be victim. Robert waved to the boy, who on seeing his signal began to call out aloud

"The man you seek lives at the end of the alley, down there, sir." At the sound of the boy's voice, the skulking assassin became alert to his task and crouched, coiled in readiness to pounce on his would-be unwary victim.

Up above and inching closer, Robert was careful not to allow his shadow or any clue to his whereabouts be known until he was ready to leap down from the low-roofed building behind the awaiting assassin. The assassin had crouched, ready to spring as if he were a cat ready to pounce on its victim. Robert could see that this assassin knew what he was about; it was as though he could sense his victim's approach being slow and careful; his arm raised in readiness to strike with the fierce-looking dagger, poised in readiness to strike at his victim. Robert was not waiting and took the advantage of the element of surprise, launching himself downwards, not giving his victim a chance to realise that his plot had been foiled. He took the awaiting assassin by surprise, colliding into him and forcefully knocking him in contact with the building; he did not spare the murderer any quarter and brought his sword down smartly across the man's back, seriously wounding him, causing the black clothed assassin to slump helplessly forwards but not dead. The knight stepped across him, pulled back his victims head so he recognised the man that was to end his life in this world before slitting his throat without an effort or second thought, with similar intent that he would have received from his assailant.

He walked out of the alley and on reaching the boy that had attempted to betray him, offered him his hand to aid his walking; he looked down to the boy, who showed a certain reluctance to do so after witnessing such an abject lessen. With a beckoning of the movement of the fingers, the undecided, pensive look on the face of the lad thought better of refusing and took the knight's hand to assist his rising. Meanwhile, the older boys rushed down the alley to relieve the body of any gold the dead man may have had on his person, it was hard for these boys to exist on the street - life taught them to survive the only way they could and this was one such example.

Robert caught the young lads questioning looks, stating, "By the look on your face, you appear to be unsure." The boy remained silent and deep in thought, and obviously his question was about the money. "I shouldn't ask about that," said Robert anticipating his obvious thoughts; the perplexed surprised look on the boy's face seemed to reflect his dismal thoughts.

"Your blood money is with your leader; do not ask me but the one that has looked out for you this long while." The message was understood by the boy; hanging his head with a certain shame, no more was said. He returned the boy to the others and gave them the rest of their money as promised without saying much about the past event; as for the boy, he was once more dependent on the group and it was up to them as to whether he would be branded an outcast for his action.

Disappointed by missing his friend's departure, there was no more that Robert could do; he had lost the chance for any rescue and saving his friend, who, according to the boy's message, was on course for a destination that he knew not about. Mounting his horse, Robert bade the gang of urchins goodbye, promising them that should he ever need their assistance again in the future, he would know where to find them.

In his need to locate his friend Aldo, Robert had deprived himself of a need to eat; the juices in his stomach were gurgling away and calling for attention. He could handle fasting, he did it all the time; more than anything else he was ready for rest after his long, eventful day. Tiredness clouded his mind; a moment's rest would give him chance to gather his thoughts to anticipate a strategy that might offer another way to the woman. With the meagre rations left in his bag, he would stop somewhere further along the road; but for now, like a leaf on water, he was drifting aimlessly out of the port town with no idea where or what to do. It was late in the afternoon and the sun was showing signs of dipping towards the horizon, leaving the sky a myriad of flaming colour; it was so stunning it almost begged him to stop and take it in. Arriving at an isolated barn he had passed by earlier in the day, he stopped to view it; it would be warm and dry place to stop and safer, away from peering eyes that may spy on him. Entering the barn, he dismounted and tended his horse before collapsing his tired and exhausted body onto a heap of loosely stacked hay; in the main, he knew well why his mood was dispirited and crestfallen. If only he had been earlier; this, he admitted, was nothing less than a failure, leaving him heavy in heart. Two friends lost in days; ah, it was a loss that weighed heavily on him, but that was the nature of his work. But most of all, what nagged at him was his wounded pride, and he had to admit, it was all down to that female, the scorpion as he now knew her, she had out witted him once again.

Spent of energy, he lay back on his bed of straw; his body soon heated bringing on tiredness that led to sleep. Relaxed, he gazed skywards through the open loft doors, taking little notice of the beauty that was filling a star filled evening sky. His jumbled mind was filled with perplexing thoughts of what he could do next and what she would be doing at this moment. Going over the possible events, he accepted that Aldo had been shipped out to who knows where and that he may never see him again; but the woman remained here, her task complete, being most likely on her way to Hassan in his mountain stronghold near Mas'yaf. He was beaten and he did not take to it easily, his hand tightened into a ball at the thought of catching up to her. He cursed the woman; it left him feeling unsure of what to do, but she was the key and it was imperative to find her before she reached the fortress.

He pondered on the problem for quite some time; there was little real knowledge to direct him, but should he err now, all would be lost. Aldo had gone, which could be considered her task fulfilled, leaving her only to report to Hassan, but where she had to go was not best travelled in darkness. In his mind, he guessed if she was to stop off somewhere it would probably be the port; no, he corrected himself, it could not be there; he would have encountered more than one of her guards had she been in Latakia. So she had definitely left and decided not to continue her journey, then did she have other business and if so, where would she stay? The thoughts whirled around his head, eventually settling on a likely place out of town, say, a caravanserai on route to Mas'yaf. Robert was no stranger to this area and would say he knew it reasonably well, but it escaped him as to where there was a caravanserai on the road leading to Hassan.

Enveloped in his straw bed, he grew more comfortable and relaxed, his body warmed and began to feel heavy; his eyes grew tired for the want of rest, and soon he was asleep.

Somehow, within his drowsiness, his brain continued to operate, attempting to solve his dilemma regarding the woman. Suddenly, as if jolted from a nightmare, he sat erect, his eyes bright and alert, rebuking his dullness of mind for his foolishness speaking aloud as if to an audience.

"You fool, she would not return to Mas'yaf until she was sure that those she sent to eliminate me had reported back. But they couldn't, so now she knows that I am still with her; and arrangements would surely be made to see that her task was completed; that's what probably delayed her. So while she is waiting yet again, where would she be? There is no other place to stay other than this town." With the realisation of his words, he was on his feet drawing his clothing around himself as he walked hurriedly towards his horse to saddle up once more for the road, muttering curses to himself.

As far as he knew, there was no other place suitable for the one he sought; it was only natural that she would wait there, away from spying eyes; as powerful as she was, she would not advertise her presence, knowing that word could just as easily reach her enemy of her whereabouts.

In the silent darkness, he sat aloft his horse on a rise that delivered a distant and unimpaired view; the caravanserai he sought sat nestled below; the place seemed restful, though he knew not for how long once he had arrived there. It was a clear night yielding brightness in the moonlight's glow, the path downwards to his destination was clear. He did not linger, for the period of darkness had become his ally; time was not his to waste; quietly, he urged his horse onwards until he reached the walls of the caravanserai. A light wind had risen from nowhere, shunting the clouds across the heavens; the starlit sky winked as the moon became veiled by a cloud to alter the degree of illumination; with his vision temporarily impaired, he could do no more than listen. Fortune was at his side it seemed, for nothing above the sound of the breeze could be heard of his arrival. The walls of the caravanserai were built tall to ward off all would-be thieves, obscuring any attempt at viewing the compound from without its walls. Had there been dogs about, they most surely would have announced his arrival; for that he was relieved. He stopped close up to the high wall, spoke in his mare's ear and patted her neck and effortlessly moving himself to a standing position on his saddle to see within the compound. His fingers groped to grip the top of the wall; with little effort he drew his body up to shoulder height to afford a better view of the other side. It was not as easy as he first thought, for his scrabbling was noisier than he expected, but once up and precariously perched, he could see into the yard. Like a cautious cat with straining eyes, he probed the distance across the open compound; the moving clouds continued to shroud the light of the moon, restricting his need to see all. There was a movement, a rustle that possibly indicated horses off to his right; he could smell manure but could not determine their number. His hand slipped over a loose section of the top of the wall; as he strained to draw himself further up for a better view, heavy flakes of spalled baked clay fell noisily to the ground on the other side. If that didn't arouse somebody, he would be surprised. "Damn," he cursed under his breath as the clay fragmented; all he could do was hug the wall and remain where he was, like a statue. Christ in Heaven, he cursed his fortune; there was not a stir. The clouds lazily took their time in drifting across the illuminated disc of the moon, bringing sufficient new light across the compound to reveal the once darkened void. Now he could see the coral and the horses; he counted over a dozen or more. If they were her escort, then she didn't move around without being short of help; he had better be careful for what he was about to do.

As far as he could tell there were no burning oil lamps in the house that he could detect; every window was shuttered and dark. It could be, and he dearly hoped that it indicated, that all within were soundly asleep.

With the return of the moonlight, Robert had an opportunity to discern the true layout of the area. Taking a chance before moving, he grabbed at a few loose, friable pieces of clay walling that had not fallen and hurled them over towards the direction of where the horses where corralled. Sure enough, they moved themselves nervously, snorting loud enough to be heard; should there be any guards dozing nearby, he would detect them also. It was a risk he felt he needed to take; better that he moved knowingly than be carelessly taken in an action he had accidentally stumbled into. The horse count was enough to tell him that the odds were too high to risk being stupidly caught, but revenge compelled him onwards. Getting the answers he required made it paramount to either reach her or kill her in his attempt. He also noted that there was no door visible into the building, though the position of the barn with its doors ajar indicated that it was likely located within.

He was many things, but never meek; determined he had no other choice than make his move. After a strenuous effort, he was standing atop the wall and resting momentarily to catch his breath, taking another look around to see if the compound was safe before dropping down into the yard. He swiftly approached the barn, gaining sanctuary in the deep recessed shadows of the building, relieved so far that his progress had not been impeded by any nervous and loose animals; it would surely have been the end with the guards alerted; the only thing he could hear was his own heart thumping. So far, events had gone with him; now was time to enter the barn and within he would push his luck to the limit, in the hope of gaining access to the main building. Quietly with the stealth of a thief, he slid between the doors of the barn, his khataar drawn ready for action should anything go awry. His nose twitched with the smell of unwashed bodies and animals; the sounds of the soldiers in their deep repose guided him through the maze of sleeping men. Robert moved carefully through them, praying for hope of safe passage in the direction of the house wall where he had figured that the main door would best be located. His guess was that it would be positioned somewhere at the end of the barn where the two buildings were joined. The hand that held the khataar was nervously sweating; the deeper into the barn, the stronger his grip became on the weapon. The nerves of his whole being were on edge; his body sweat ran uncomfortably and beads formed on his brow as he ventured passed the sleeping men en-route to seek the door.

The depth of the snores gave him heart to advance; he had managed to reach the house wall at the end of the barn, but there was no door to be found. He hugged the shadow for fear of discovery; inching along the length of the wall he desperately hoped to discover the illusive door. With his arm extended, he groped through the darkness feeling for the opening and he silently prayed for a door's latch that he dearly hoped would soon be within his grip. Goats in their stall nervously sensed him and edged away, but fortunately they kept silent in their nervousness. Though they gave out no sounds of alarm, they remained frighteningly nervous enough to keep moving; if there was to be an alarm it would be the animals that would betray him. Standing rigid, many ideas went through his mind; he was no predator but he knew not how to prove that his presence was only fleeting. Slowly, he turned his back to them in the hope that they could not meet his eyes; taking a deep breath, Robert moved onwards away from the animals with the hope that they would settle. His hand travelled along the length of the wall catching on all the darkened edges until he was rewarded and relieved that his assumptions of the door's position were somewhat correct. At last, he had arrived at the door and, to his relief, found the frame and the latch which his hand was quickly onto. He froze as there was a further rustling noise; the animals in the pen were growing restless, causing him to pause in a semi-panic; again, he had to allow them settle, but it was plain that they had not been pacified. The weight of his hand quickly and silently moved the wooden latch upwards, allowing him to carefully push the door open; he was through the opening quickly and deftly closed the door silently behind him. His heart was thumping and his mouth was dry from the ordeal; that he felt was too close for comfort, breathing as though he had run miles; resting his tensed body against the coolness of the wall on the inside of the room, he waited to bring his heart to beat at a much steadier rate. Should anyone wake by the restlessness of the animals, he would no longer be in the midst of the enemy or in jeopardy of being openly discovered.

From the culinary smells that filled his nostrils, he assumed that he was in some kind of preparation room or kitchen. He sheathed his sword, hoping that from here on he would have no use of it. The Kitchen having no windows for moonlight to guide a pathway, the room was pitch black; if he was to move forwards, it had to be like a blind man and that could be disastrous. There was only one way to move safely and that was on his hands and knees; at least, he thought, there would be less chance of noisily falling or knocking over any obstacles. And so it was, he steadily moved safely forwards. The floor was laid with flags of thickly cut stone and cold, which helped tone down the heat of his anxious nerve-racked body; a great heavy table loomed before him but it was too late to avoid, bumping his head on its hefty square leg, he was relieved that there was no movement of the table to give notice of his presence. The sound resonated around the silence of the vacant room and caused his teeth to snap at the shock; in reaction he wanted to cry out, but he controlled himself, settling to rub his bruised head. Fixed to his position, there was nowhere to run and hide and so he remained motionless, hoping that no one heard the sound of his collision on the other side of the door. The need to move on urged him to forget the throbbing bump that was beginning to form on his sweaty forehead; with no idea where to go, he could only navigate his way blindly around the table that he guessed held a central position on the floor. At last, in his blind movements, his groping hand brought him upon a step that led to another door. Its flat surface felt good suspecting that he was across the darkened space, especially when his hand carefully proceeded upwards in search of the latch. It was a relief to be off his knees to escape the coldness that struck through from the heavy stone slabs underfoot. The latch was carefully and quietly raised, allowing him to pass through its opening, where he immediately stopped noticing a glint of light escaping from underneath an adjacent door to his right. It was enough to make him freeze in his movement; one careless slip could bring all his care to a finish, and for good. Still as the night, he stood motionless, sensing through the darkness the direction he needed to be going in.

After closing the door, Robert's curiosity drove him towards another door; his hand hovered on the latch in uncertainty to see who and what lay on the other side. Before attempting to enter the room, he unsheathed his sword noiselessly from its scabbard; placing his head to the door, he listened for any sound while his free hand lifted the wooden latch opening the door with silent dexterity, pushing forwards sufficiently enough to see into the room. It was untidy with accumulated wares; at the far end in the dimness of the shadow, a man was slumped sideways over a chair. He would not be any threat, the tie of the wine bag still wrapped around his wrist pulled him to one side of his chair as it fell to the floor, where he had lost his grip on it before drifting off into a drinker's oblivion. His assuming eyes guessed that it was most likely the proprietor; for a moment, it was in him to advance towards the man and silence him for good, but considered the disadvantages of possibly arousing the drunken man before reaching him. He hesitated, thinking better of the move, before quietly retreating and quietly closing the door and moving on along the corridor. He tried two other doors without success before accidentally stumbling silently forwards in the darkness on a badly laid stone floor slab, only to land onto the lower tread of the wooden staircase. Christ, curses silently spilt from his mouth; again he was stilled, then his eyes followed the treads upwards, sensing it right to believe that the woman's presence must be above. Instinctively, he rose to climb each riser in silence; with the hopes and trepidation of his conviction, he was quickly up to the gallery where more rooms were to be located. In the time that he had taken to act, he had convinced himself that there were no other places left for the woman to be.

The light on the next floor appeared to be better; the windows of the landing were not shuttered, allowing shafts of moonlight to penetrate the upper floor and illuminate its darkened corners. Thankfully, with the aid of the moonlight, he ascertained that there were three rooms on this landing and two were open, indicating there were no occupants in them. Along to the end of the corridor remained a third and the door was closed, which, he believed, behind it lay the one he sought, and with a free conscience she was probably sleeping soundly. His teeth ground in anticipation of his success; a revengeful temper grew in him with thoughts of the woman at his mercy, sending his heart beating at a quicker pace. Too many times her womanly ways had so easily seduced him into dropping his guard by her strong impressions and her femininity and beauty. It was she who had wantonly stole his affections because of her behaviour and guile; now it was different, he had learnt through those difficulties that she had become no more to him than a dangerous opponent who was a rarity of her kind, and yet he was reluctantly anxious of the probability of having to kill her.

Outside the door, his hand rested on the latch and silently moved it upwards; carefully and quietly, he inched the door forwards, no more than a squeak to allow him to listen for the sound of the breathing of her deep repose. His head pressed close into the slight opening; his thumping heart proved difficult to hear anything about its nervous beat and so he proceeded to gently push ever so lightly against the door for better detection of her. There was a sudden resistance that caused him alarm and beads of sweat to suddenly form on his brow; his guard was sharpened to her ways and suddenly feared that he was about to cause all within the building to know of his presence. His forward actions froze; every hair on his sweating body stood on end and his hands began shaking waiting for something to happen. Guessing from the minor resistance of the door, some kind of warning device had been carefully contrived to warn her of unwanted visitors. Within the distance of the opening gap, there was a space for his fingers to venture carefully around the door, blindly feeling into the darkness of the other side. His tactile fingers found what he feared he almost disturbed; it seemed like a solid object, perhaps a bench, which, fortunately for him, she must have been casual in her preparations at retirement after fulfilling her fiendish duty of handing over his friend to whoever they had met.

With Robert's cautious inching of the door forwards, the obstacle behind must have trapped itself in the doors cross bracer; instead of falling to raise the alarm, it instigated the caution that he had observed. How clever, he admired her thinking witnessing a further demonstration of her ingenuity; she was good, but the crafty witch had faltered this time, allowing him a second chance which he was not going to waste by moving imprudently. So, she had thought no man would enter her bedroom uninvited; he smiled at his luck; it served him well with a chance to be upon her before allowing her time to be armed or raise an alarm. This is her room and no mistaking; he could not forget the fragrance she wore which caused his nose to twitch; chills ran the length of his spine. Her tricky manoeuvres were certainly proving her mark to the last; awkward though his task was, he had managed to support the bench in his fingers, and once within his grip, he gained enough space to safely open the door further and gain silent entry into the room.

Like a lengthening shadow, he was swiftly and silently by her bedside; his body loomed over her in indecision and his form blocked out what the little light there was coming from the window, yet there was still enough light to see an outline of her small head against its supporting headrest. Her pretty head being uncovered and even in the dimness of the room she presented a favourable likeness with her hair loose and flowing on her pillow, showing a sweet innocence of her features at repose. From his boot, he drew a small dagger, whilst his other hand clamped down hard across her mouth. The shock of his action startled her and it surprised him that her will to escape was so vigorously staged, creating a tremendous wrestle for freedom that surprised him, but he would not yield his grip. With the feel of sharpened steel pressed against her cheek, he whispered in her ear an earnest warning not to struggle or cry out for help; now her life lay in his hands and only she could foolishly forfeit it by crying out and raising the alarm.

"As I have held you once before like this, you know that I will not let you go." Immediately realising his words, the identity of her captor was revealed;

she ceased her struggle and easily gave in, which somehow puzzled Robert, suspecting more possible trickery. Well, pity or weakness was not in him for her; his first task was to have her silent; he did that by stuffing a silken garment into her mouth. Next was the task of securing her; he drew her arms to her side to enable him to concentrate on what lay ahead. Robert awkwardly and quickly tore strips off the bed coverings with one hand while he set about binding her mouth to prevent any screaming; escaping from the building was going to be difficult; it was his only way of questioning her. Working with a speed that surprised her watching eyes, he flipped her over and over until she was tightly bound in the covering that she was previously sleeping in. In this cocoon of cotton, she was held fast and incapable of movement, being rigid and unable to wriggle or become a nuisance to her abductor. To ensure the point, he tied her wrappings off to keep the loose ends in place with a further torn strip of the bed linen. She lay there on the bed quietly like a chrysalis, quite unable to move; Robert looked upon her tightly-wrapped form, she appeared quite alluring. With no time for idle imaginings and without any plan of escape other than his spontaneous reactions, he stopped to think as the success of her abduction had been so rapidly completed without any forethought.

Walking briskly to the window, he opened the shutters quietly, allowing the moon light to flood the room; the yard was clear but there was an uncertainty within his heart. He had achieved most of his objective and strangely he was suddenly lost for what to do for the best. He couldn't stand here scratching himself, he had to get away; knowing whatever he had planned he had to be doubly careful of his actions from hereon. Opening the window, he leant forwards and peered along the length of the roof; there was no movement from the yard below, only the night sounds. He was safe so far, but did not care for what he could now see; he didn't bargain for being on another side of the compound, away from where he started. He had to make this moment his chance; the roof sloped and was tiled, it was only a step down and easy for him to reach with the woman on his shoulder. He knew he could travel its length but at its end, a tree grew between the building and the wall; he needed to be able to access the wall as that was his means of quick escape. It could be a problem to escape by this route, meaning he would have to traverse the branches of the tree to reach the wall; from where he stood, he could not judge the distance of the gap to the wall. Having to carry the woman it might prove awkward; he was not too bothered about crossing the roof, only how he was going to manage the tree at the end of the roof. There was no other way; if he dawdled any longer the guards may be waking up, then he could be up to his neck in sharpened steel. No, he didn't need that; he was back at the bed and grabbing at his package that was his hostage. He pulled her closely to him; she was light in weight, smelling good as a woman should, so good that his mind was dallying, wandering from his reason for his being here. He spoke to her in a whisper, clearly enough for her to understand how she was to be transported away from the caravanserai. His strong yet gentle hands gripped her, and in one lift she was around his shoulders like a rolled carpet making their way to the window. He had bound her tighter than he realised or she was doing her best to remain rigid for safer transportation. Quietly, they made their way along the roof towards the tree, mindful of a fear that he could step on a loose tile and cause it to slip; should that happen it would be the end. Robert took his time along the ribbed surface of the roof; when nearing its end he froze; a shadow moved below, a guard had woken from his sleep and gone outside to relieve himself. He seemed to be enjoying the experience, lazily taking his time to piss; the noise seemed loud enough to wake the others, but he finished and returned to complete his sleep. The woman was held firmly and as comfortably as was possible whilst he remained static, and did so for a while until the guard had returned to his bed of straw and was off to sleep again. Although she was small and of little weight, his muscles began to ache with the prolonged strain of his position, but once he was able to continue moving he overlooked the discomfort.

The tree at the end of the roof was going to be a little trickier; its branches did not reach as near to the wall as he would have liked them to be, requiring a short leap to gain its use for descent wasn't going to be comfortable for the woman. To make his task easier, he had to let her know what he was about to do; he whispered his intention watching her reaction; given the nod of understanding, he traversed the branches that held out their limbs for him until he crossed as far as the main the trunk. He was well aware that she could have made his task very difficult and even caused him to fall, but then it could have resulted in extreme injuries to herself, so perhaps she was being sensible and biding her time. From this point on, life was going to be difficult; he pulled her down and around to face him, but she didn't escape without a slight knock to the side of her head on a projecting branch that Robert had desperately reached out to grip. The knock did not go unannounced, there was a whimper as her head made contact; Robert tried to apologise but all he received was a foul look from behind the bindings; it spoke sufficiently of her shock and her discomfort. Once he was stable and steady of balance, he was able to bring both their bodies around the trunk and onto the other branch. He was smiling to himself at her misfortune, though she could see no trace of his amusement. With his head so close to hers and her bandaged body against his, it did not prevent her perfume rolling up his nostrils like a fog that began to envelop and captivate his feelings. This was not the time or place for such distraction; ignoring her, his next step was to reach the narrow width of the wall and concentration was his priority. With his arms full, he could see that he was unable to reach the wall safely, but dropping down to a lower longer branch held out a better chance to reach the wall; struggling with his hostage, he found it difficult to make the lower branch with her body around his. He took off his sash and looped it around the trunk to enable him to maintain his balance, next came the walk along the branch that would take him to the wall. This too held its problems, for the branch above he was to rely on for balance, failed to reach the distance. Above, there was a stronger branch that would fulfil his purpose; his idea now was when he had reached the limit of the shorter branch, he would loop his sash over the higher branch to maintain his balance for the short distance he had to swing across to reach the wall. This he did, and in one successful swing, he was across his main obstacle and hesitantly gripping the wall, though he unfortunately arrived with another bump, the impact of which was taken up by the body of the woman. There was another groan of disquiet and an apology; here there was no other way to gain the top of the wall but to place her on it like he would a package, telling her first of his action. Finely balanced, he told her that once in place, she should not make any move or she may drop to the ground, which she may not survive; her eyes said everything as she looked at him, such as, one day I will get you back for this. Once free of his hands, he was up onto the top of the wall and taking her back into the position close to him; until he was confident of his position, he would remain holding onto his support. He was pleased with himself, believing that the task was not as difficult as he first thought, though he did have second thoughts for the final drop to the ground. He could not spare her any illusion as to that part of his plan; preparing her for what was to come next, he whispered a warning to her of the imminent and plummeting descent yet to come and his escape to the other side of the wall.

"There is going to be a bit of a fall now," he whispered to her, "I will try to make your landing as soft as I can." Looking at her with a smile breaking on his face; her eyes were starring hard at him in amazement at his statement and her fear of his outrageous handling of her.

"There is no need to be afraid," he assured her calmly, as though he was talking to a child; the wildness in her eyes told him that her temper was up.

Tying her to the back of his body and at his mercy to do with her as he would, being helpless in her rolled up mummy-like state, his thoughts were how best to overcome the drop before them. Clutching the wall, he allowed his body to slowly slide down the wall until it stopped abruptly a man's height from the ground; he desperately clung firmly to the top of the wall until he was sure of his readiness to drop. His shoulder muscles strained under the weight, causing him real pain. "Oh," he cried quietly at the strain; this woman doesn't know what I'm going through to save her from further discomfort. With a slight swing of his body to and fro, he gauged his fall carefully. Giving up his grip, he fell like a stone; when he touched the ground, he did so on his feet before falling backwards with the woman under him; almost dutifully as though her concern mattered, he rolled away to save her further discomfort. The impact was taken by his backwards fall, but that did not stop her from making sounds of protest to him through her bindings. He released her and stood her up, telling her that the fall wasn't that bad after all; through her protestations, he drew her head to his chest in an attempt to quieten her; there was something in the closeness that rather appealed to him.

Robert knew that when daybreak came, all hell would break loose, and it was of great concern to him that two people on one mount could not outpace her guards, no matter how few they were. Any attempt to lose the searchers in the hills would eventually be overcome; he knew eventually they would be caught and he tried not to think of that eventuality. Perhaps, he thought, a better way to lose them would be in amongst the milling hordes of Lattakia. First he would have to make a false trail and lead his pursuers into thinking he had made his way back into the mountains, heading north to join his young companions.

The guards suspecting that their mistress would not be taken so easily, Robert decided to lay a false trail from a string of beads that hung around her neck; by doing this, he felt they would recognise the trinket and hopefully throw them off the trail. They rode quietly through the late night slowly not making any sound until they were well away from the caravanserai, before speedily riding away. Pausing in a shallow stream, he tethered his horse to an overhanging branch of a tree; the woman was going nowhere in the security of her cocoon and unable to escape remaining perched over his saddle. Here was a good place to start his ruse; the ground was quite stony where no signs of his horse's shoes would show any imprint. Dismounting, he scattered a few beads to serve as his false trail in a direction that appeared he was making for hill country and from the direction he came. Aware that his captive was still unable to move, he quickly ran up the hill to a rocky outcrop and dropped his last few beads; from here on, his hopes for success may serve him long enough to confuse the riders of her troop.

When Robert reached the streets of Lattakia, he was relieved to find them deserted; there was nobody about to witness his bringing in a prisoner bent over his mount. It was a risk to venture openly here with his prisoner, but for him there was no alternative. His idea was to reach the urchins down at the dock area; with their help, all his hopes rested.

It would not be difficult to spy them curled up like night creatures into the oddest of resting places between stored cargoes. Once he had found one, it did not take long before he had found them all. When the first boy had recognised him, he soon became awake believing that a possibility of more coins would be coming their way. Robert dismounted, leaving his stiffened, struggling bundle tied awkwardly across his saddle. Tired though they were, they instantly recognised the stranger with the gold pieces and were soon milling around him, eager to please the beneficent stranger. He walked through them as if he were passing through a field of high corn stalks, stroking their heads gently with the palm of his hand, venturing forwards until he reached the centre of them; there he squatted to meet the eye of their leader and discuss his business. In the dimness of early dawn and in a hushed voice, he reminded them of their offer that should he return, they would be ready to offer their help.

When he spoke he did so looking about their inquisitive faces for signs of dissention; they seemed not wholly to pay much attention to his words for the curiosity was diverted towards his horse and the female strung over it. It amused them to see the parcel of linen with a struggling female showing nought other than the top of her head. Young as the boys were, they did not gather around her for fear of being disrespectful to their friend, but they could not contain the inquisitiveness as to why she had been bundled up in such a fashion. The woman's predicament could do nothing about the staring faces, not even a curse could pass her lips. Strangely for them, they were quick to see that their friend was a true man of the world that would have no nonsense from a woman that had tested his patience. Somehow, there was a natural understanding for the situation she had landed herself in; in their eyes, there was no doubt at the suggestion that the warrior knight had unfinished business with her; though tantalised by the untold story, they felt they had guessed what was on Robert's mind. Robert did not say too much about her, only that there was much between them and her family.

The leader of the group who must have been no more than thirteen spoke up, "Welcome back, my friend, are you in need of our help again?" he enquired with an eager smile and a knowing laugh about the business of men. "Tell us, how can we help you?"

Preparing a place to sit, he entered into his request and intimated that he had unfinished business with the struggling woman, who upon over hearing Robert's disgusting remark about family matters made sounds of protests from behind her bindings.

"Is there any way a small boat can take me and my friend to a place away from here, unseen to others, where we can rest for a while, perhaps a few days?"

The boy instinctively nudged him and smiled mischievously. "I trust you have still some gold left in your purse," said the boy, "remember, we have many mouths to feed."

"Aye that I do, but I will not be robbed of it by your youthful guile."

"Then follow me," hailed the boy, knowing that he had the answer to the request, adding that he knew just the person to ask, and with a glint in the eye knew that his recompense would also come easy. Following him towards the end of the quay Robert was taken to a small ramshackle fishing hut made of scraps of driftwood and clay. Robert was told to wait for a while until the boy returned; when he reappeared, he could be seen eagerly pulling an aged, reluctant fisherman from his hut, still correcting his clothing in expectation of being introduced to the impatient knight.

Robert greeted him respectfully in the early dawn, asking if he could take him and his friend to a quiet place. The crude fisherman said something quickly in jest and all around laughed, save Robert, who simply snapped his request once more demanding abruptly, "Well can you?" He did not need frivolous talk just to get onto the right side of a fisherman's humour. The man remained smiling and took no offence at Robert's snappy remark, concurring to his request, showing Robert his boat. "I can take you for a gold piece to my place around the bay," and pointing with a gnarled, cut finger in the direction of a far off distant point, adding, "Nobody will bother you there."

Robert stroked his mount's nose, easing him as the crowd of youthful urchins drew closer in anticipation of some offer that Robert was about to make to them; at the same time, his silent reluctance gave him the opportunity to balance his plan quickly in his mind. He turned to a boy and asked him if he could ride.

"Sir," replied the scruffy urchin, "I was born in a saddle."

Handing him the reins, he ordered the boy, "Get this horse to me within the next two days at the fisherman's house and your reward will be a gold piece, treat him badly and you will receive a beating for your laxness."

The boy smiled and assured the knight that he would never harm any animal that was entrusted to his care. Happy with the response, Robert patted the boy's shoulder as a sign of trust and turned to the mariner, who was patiently waiting on him to complete his business.

Once the agreement to ferry them to his hut was assured, the ageing mariner made his way to the boat. Robert followed behind carrying the woman in his arms; he laid her in the prow sitting almost opposite to her whilst the old man busied himself before attending to the shabby looking sail. The boat rocked from their awkward embarkation, whilst the old man jabbered incoherently from one dialect to another pointing to a headland they would be heading for, explaining that they should reach his fishing hut in the early afternoon.

Robert began to feel better, more at ease now that they were aboard the small sailing craft. As the tidal waters lapped noisily on the hull of the small wooden craft, the oncoming sea breeze refreshed Robert's upturned head to lift him from his tiredness. He dropped his eyes and viewed his captive, propped awkwardly in the boat, encased tightly in her linen wrappings. Apart from her petitness, the tightness of the bindings erotically displayed the outline of her feminine form. It struck him as odd that she seemed to accept her captivity, offering no resistance as if she had completely resigned herself to the fate of her situation. Her eyes though had quite another meaning, as did they when she was helplessly taken and transported from the caravanserai to the port. She caught his ogling gaze, whilst hers never changed from a hateful and revengeful look that transfixed him. Yet, for him, a curiosity filled with questions for his friend's recovery; she sensed they likewise oozed with hatred for her and her kind for what had happened back in Antioch. Revenge, it seemed, would serve one or the other; that, she thought, was down to Robert's ability to stay ahead of her men. Thinking on that matter, it was eventually most likely to be a bloody conflict when they met up, for she was too important a person to leave as captive to the westerners. She had guessed the moment she opened her eyes what he had in mind for her, why should she care of the outcome? She had followed her orders and more than once tried to avoid contact with this man, he had proved resourceful and there was something about him that she held in regard. She was long passed playing frivolous games for her own amusement, he had shown his colours showing that he was determined to track her down and he had eliminated those that she placed as rear guards. This man was worthy of respect able to think and act for himself; somehow all that appealed to her sense of independent thought, presently measuring him to be more dangerous than she first imagined. But his future downfall was written, as sure as grains of sand, in the desert; and it was regrettable, for her guards were not known for their wit and understanding. Their minds would be concerned only on her rescue and to help overcome their embarrassment of failing their master's command to guard their mistress, who was too important being their master's right hand in the field. That was only part of what was to come; she could see how he would be humiliated and it was a shame that this daring warrior would meet his destiny by such an unfitting end.

For the moment, reality must rule, she was under no illusion that it was she that was his prisoner; there was an anxiety to her unawareness as to how this franj would react once they had arrived to their destination. In the depth of the darkness of her eyes, she could not betray a certain fear, a fear that she had not experienced before. It was one thing being a captive, but it was the waiting for the way that barbarian warriors acted when bored, she feared he may be driven to pouncing on her like an animal in an instant. Mercilessly, she had seen they had taken their pleasure on helpless female captives, unprepared for the coup that they as victors regarded as their right of victory to the pleasure of their prisoner's expected future defilement.

Robert sensed her emotions and the fear of her awaiting end of one sort or another on reaching the other side of the bay and instead of allaying her fears, he informed her not to look so downcast. He was a man of honour and he would not trouble himself to carry out any such action that she seemed to fear; he finished by telling her that she would tell him what he needed to know. His words did not appear to make her situation any easier; looking on to her stern face, he decided to let her stew in her own juices, giving her the chance to undergo similar treatment as she would have inflicted on others. There she sat in the prow of the boat, solitary and shivering like an injured creature waiting for the end, preparing herself for her eventual fate.

Beneath the wrappings, she was near naked; the coldness of the night had not yet given way to receive the blessing of the sun's warmth that she was used to, and even whilst held in her tight bindings, she awkwardly attempted to draw them tighter around her to ward off the early morning chill. He viewed her, perceiving in his study a certain fatalistic resignation; her normal stature appeared to relax, seeing her resistance against the world wane as she looked fatalistically blankly seawards to the ever receding horizon.

Standing over her, checking the security of her wrappings, he half-heartedly apologised, expressing his regret that he was unable to offer her more comfort. "But I believe we will soon arrive at our destination where I will surely attend to you further." She could not help but wonder if that a veiled threat the franj was making; is he sporting with me, she thought the Frankish knight a devil as he withdrew to his own position in the boat.

There was no sport in this capture for Robert, but an urgent need to find the answers to the disappearance of his friend and reasons that lay behind the death of another; he worried little of the concern about any warped ideas that beset her and her fate. Her body was worthy of that of a princess and she was fair to the bargain but he had to put any such ideas aside until those answers he required were forthcoming

They had sailed for most of the morning and rounded the distant headland, as the old man had indicated, just as the sun was beginning to rise to a greater height; shortly after, Robert was wading ashore carrying his bundled captive with him. He stopped and looked around to survey his refuge before walking up onto the deserted sandy beach that had a backdrop of hills around as shelter; he nodded his approval at the sight and was content with their location. The human package that rested in his arms was now wriggling like a worm for her independence; he did not have the patience to allow her to make her own way, deciding that progress was more positive carrying her. Had he have wanted, he could have caused her much belittlement, watching her waddling awkwardly like a duck in her attempt to struggle through the watery runnels that ran across areas of the long beach into the sea. There was no reason for such an action; for, contrary to rumours of the barbarity and cruelty of the Franj, he remained calm and gentle like and refrained from demeaning her situation. The tide was out; the cabin seemed further away than he had imagined; walking through puddles and shallow runnels, their approach took quite some time to reach the small but decrepit looking fisherman's wooden shack; from this distance it was hardly much better than the wreck of a house he had back in Lattakia, it was disappointing and in his opinion that it appeared to have seen better days. She began to wriggle again, this time with more forceful action in his arms; protesting in the only way she could through her gagged bindings in a series of loud intermittent noises through her clenched teeth. So vigorous was her struggle to make herself understood that she could walk ably on her own to maintain her independence and pride in an effort to manage to walk unassisted. He felt her hands ball into fists within the wrappings; Robert half looked at her in her cocoon state as he walked on, at the same time telling her to be still and that she was trying his patience. The face from behind her wrappings could only growl its disapproval and glare in disgust and hatred for her captor, who appeared not to be taking the least bit of notice to her struggling resistance.

Robert hadn't cared about the woman's protest; he should slap her and teach her a lesson, but that might only create more opposition in her unwillingness to cooperate. Time was not on his side, for he knew that her people would be combing the countryside at this moment looking for her. No, more important to him was the information that she secretly held, as a hundred questions he needed answers to filtered through his mind. The weight in his arms felt little more than that of a young child securely cradled in the solid muscled arms; to jolt him from the concentration of his thoughts, she required a little more effort to hold his attention. A further loud shout of cursing protest from the woman brought his mind back from his thoughts, giving reason for him to pause and stare down at the helpless bundle he carried. His head dropped towards her, fixing a penetrating stare into her deep brown eyes. Their eyes became fixed in their searching gaze; it became embarrassing to her and she yelled at him again in her own way for freedom to walk.

A vacuous look settled on Robert's face as he was aware of the outcome of her foolish protestations and demands; on second thoughts, he decided after all that it might not be such a bad idea to do as she bid. Carefully, he set her standing and waited for the expected result; she stood wobbling and looked ungraceful. With restricted co-ordination, she moved forwards clumsily; he smiled at her effort to display her independence, an independence he could not wait around to view and prodded her. Cruelly she was sent to the ground helpless unable to prevent her fall, he watched as she keeled over helplessly into a bundle onto the damp sand. Assuming that his message had been conveyed, he picked her up and continued walking on smartly towards the shack. She did not speak again.

In the meantime, the old, smelling fisherman had walked at speed beside them, offering jibes and lewd gestures to the woman of what she was about to receive when her master got her inside the shack. His balled fist and forearm were gesturing the outcome of her futile protestations. He had a hollow and pathetic mocking laugh and Robert was quickly tiring of him; then fortunately, he had the mind to run on before he received a cuffing from the heavy hand of the knight.

The door was opened for them and they were ushered into the darkened room; the smell that greeted them was rank and overpowering, causing their heads to turn away in distaste. Apart from accommodation, the look on their faces indicated their disbelief, guessing the old fisherman must have used the shack as his smoke house. The sing song whines of the old man were not slow in holding out his hand; he had completed his part of the agreement and waited to receive his gold piece as was promised. When it dropped into his palm, his fingers closed on the coin as if a trap had been sprung. Exhibiting a toothless smile, his face lit up as if he had been touched by the sun. Before leaving, he told them that they could use the house for as long as they liked, then, like a paid jongleur, manically rejoiced and laughed as he made his way merrily skipping along the beach to his boat, a happy man.

Standing amidst the darkened shambles of the cabin, Robert's searching eyes caught sight of the old man's bed; that was where he decided to deposit his troublesome bundle. Dropping her like an unwanted package onto the crumpled dishevelled covers on the straw paillasse, great plumes of motes surged outwards seeking out a new place of settlement. The cloud that billowed upwards was captured by the sun's shafts of light that pierced through the holes and cracks in the walls. In the gloom of the darkened room, the piercing rays sucked the floating dust from wherever they made contact, drawing a spiralling of dirt and flotsam upwards into eventual oblivion through the badly spaced gaps in the roof timbers.

The woman came to rest, coughing through her coverings in the heap of dirty covers causing a further mumbled protest, which Robert decided to ignore. Her mind was filled with anger, it was an insult to be treated so; she continued with her tirade of useless sounds such as they were. His patience was short at his upset with the filthy hut and he sternly warned her against speaking, warning her that complete silence was the required order. His annoyance took over whilst he posed on what to do next; as for her, there would be plenty of time in the future to say what she felt to others.

She was driven to enragement with his treatment towards her, and her eyes were searing as if thunderbolts were to be aimed his way and her quizzical eyes followed his every movement around the scruffy room of the shack.

Unconcerned with her discomfort, he purposely ignored her endeavours of ranting; his first task was to open the shutters to release gloom and bring in some light and air into this place; the stench that had been contained within was near overpowering. He looked around and found a water butt in the corner half full, which, after smelling it, surprisingly considered it fit for drinking. There was a ladle hanging on the wall nearby, which he wiped over with his shirt before scooping it into the water to fill before tasting. That's not bad, he thought, and dipping it once more turned and looked over to his captive, who was still helplessly confined within her bindings. He looked away, amused at the sight; the hurried way in which he had bound her covered most of her face allowing only her eyes and the top of her head to be visible. She must be almost gagging on the rag he poked into her mouth; realising that she, like him, had not had anything to drink since they fled the sarai. Dipping the ladle into the cask, he filled its cup and sipped some more to gesture his approval. "You must be in need of this," indicating the water, hoping that she was not too stubborn to accept it when he walked over to share it with his captive. Poking a finger inside her bindings, he pulled at the mouth plug and drew it out; he could see the relief, though she was not about to thank him for the deed. He next pulled at the sheet from side to side until they loosened sufficiently to allow movement of them to move freely away from her face exposing her mouth. The ladle was gently offered to her rosebud lips; she drank delicately from the brimming ladle until she had drained it of its refreshing contents. She was about to give thanks for his consideration, but Robert cut her off, reminding her that he ordered silence until he was ready for answers to his questions. Her eyes fell obediently, giving up any effort of argument; instead, like an untrusting slave, continued observing his every move as he went about his preparations for their stay, not giving her a second glance, which irked her somewhat.

Although bound by the bed linen that she once slept in, she remained subdued; her mind was ever active and she was well aware that if she was unable to make contact with her enemy, she would not be able to probe his weaknesses and her sharp and agile mind was never slow to locate one. Looking around again, he found a wooden cup, rinsing it before pouring in any water which he placed on the table returning the ladle back beside the barrel. He walked across the room towards her, his face stern and without any gesture of his intention; she shrunk back defensively, unable to prevent any attack whilst fear grew in her eyes as he neared her. Instead of a suspected beating, he spoke quietly and calmly with an appealing note in the sound of his voice. He looked directly into her fearful eyes and spoke.

"I'm going to free you, do not disappoint me as there is nowhere to run to." It would be pointless, he offered casually; and she knew it. If there was nowhere to run, she rationalised, then it would be more productive to watch and learn about her captor's intentions whilst he was at ease. She did not fear what she could not overcome, knowing that it was her only opportunity of studying him and his ways. Gently pulling on her bindings to ease the tightness, his efforts were slightly clumsy, not wanting his actions to appear as though he was about to molest her. Each time he tugged to loosen the bindings, she pulled away in a resisting motion; drawing the covering back to her body though, he eventually managed to achieve some slackness before she began to fight defensively against his attempts, finally abruptly stopping him. He was unable to fathom her reasoning for doing so, but she would not yield to his help as he protested.

"Whatever is the matter with you?" he blustered. Had he gone too far? Robert became ill-tempered with her and protested that he was only trying to ease her discomfort, but instead he turned his back on her and threw up his arms as if he had lost patience with her

As though berating her captor, she issued strongly that she would not yield or be touched by his hands for she was not properly covered; sarcastically she added that she was snatched from her sleep. Changing her tone, she spoke softly and hesitantly and with subdued defiance; Robert, for the first time, looked upon the face that had remained partly shrouded from his view before.

He stared quite rudely, unable to alter his gaze; he had only imagined her features when they were hidden by her veil, but now in the shabby hut with its splintered wooden walls he looked upon her through the piercing rays of sunshine. By God, he uttered; frightened though she was, her beauty was holding him in a spell bound gaze. She was so beautiful; his dried lips found difficulty in parting and his throat was strangely hoarse when he spoke.

When he had realised that his mouth was gaping he asked, "Tell me, how is it that one so fair, with so much beauty, could mete out such cruelty; it is indeed beyond my understanding?"

Her complexion was honeyed and her skin soft almost polished yet delicate in contrast against a mantle of shining silken black hair that crowned her beauty; it set his mind to wander in search for comparisons to match her fairness. Flashing images crossed his mind; he was suddenly home, it was a warm sunrise, the light autumn haze was rising from the earth drawn skywards to meet the sun's warmth against natures natural tapestry, the sound of a 'hmm' barely broke through his lips in agreement to his minds projection, and her deep red soft pouting lips humbled the depth of colour of any garden rose.

The image seemed wasted as reality returned, prompting him to ask the question, why she took on such a role in life as The Old Man of the Mountain's assassin.

Clumsily, she had managed to shuffle across to the little wooden table, which was situated nearby. By this time, her arm was free to move inside the loosened wrappings but she was only able to bring her hand to her neck of the bindings and modesty of exposure prevented her from drawing her bare arm openly free to expose any nakedness to the western barbarian. Robert watched her with interest until eventually she carefully and awkwardly wriggled her arm free until she was able to pick up the cup from the table without any exposure of her flesh to her captor's eyes. Awkwardly, she held it inside an outer covering of her wrappings, thus allowing herself sufficient freedom to work her hand with some dexterity. The watchful eyes of her enemy had made her suspect of his every move; he assessed her ability to manipulate the cup with mindful thoughts. With raised eyebrows, he watched as she bent forwards, awkwardly reaching the cup with her mouth to artlessly drink without worrying about any silly and futile effort, but her attempt at showing off to drink without spilling it proved harder when taking the water down. This only presented herself in a vexatious mood; she sat awkwardly on the wooden stool near the table, clutching the unwound bindings close to her. She was clever; he observed, more so than he at such a trick; it was a show, as far as he was concerned, at being artful with a warning that she needed to be watched. Once she had drained the wooden cup, she thanked him in her soft mellow voice, but now noticeably without her usual confidence. Her nervousness showed, and for the first time she uttered that there was much that he was not aware of, "Remember these words, Franj, all is never what it appears to be."

What was she trying to say? Was it a trick? She was intelligent enough to persuade him only to see her as she was, to weaken her enemy and take advantage of his foolishness. All this time he was watching her, and whilst pacing the floor behind her, listening to the mellow sound of her voice; there was a noticeable apprehension entering the confidence that she was used to having; suddenly he felt that she was afraid of him. And there was no doubt that whilst she was uneasy at Robert's position of being behind her; it did nothing to make her feel any easier. Her words fell on Robert's uncaring ears with icy coldness; he would not abuse her, yet he wanted the information that she held. Being the victor today gave him an advantage in position, he wanted to learn of her abilities and more; he knew that she was clever and capable and that she was the Old Man's emissary and no doubt she had talents that he could never have imagined. There was no doubt she could not match him in any fighting circumstances, but he could tell she had a hidden strength that he felt could more than match his. Apart from the fact that she was a woman and could use her body to gain many favours, he knew her to be canny. Too many times he had learnt that much himself; not only from other men that had failed her orders and lived, and she had a name that unnerved him a little. Now his suspicions indicated that if he were to confront her, could she try to work the same magic on him to bend his will? He had to admit that was why he preferred, for a while anyway, to remain behind her.

After a while of his pacing silence, she asked him what he was doing; she could have turned to see for herself but for her aloofness. It seemed that her confidence was returning, for she asked Robert to face her as she was afraid he was going to beat her unexpectedly; like any man with backbone, she preferred to see what was coming, but he did not believe that was her real reason for the request.

After recognising that all this so-called ability was just being artful, it became his opinion that she was just a woman, though a very clever one. Drawing up a stool so that he sat facing her across the rickety table, he stared at her, bringing his deep set brown eyes level with hers and in a coaxing tone stated that, "Yes, we have much to discuss, you and I."

With gentleness in his voice, he posed his first question, "What did you do with my friend, the one you sent away on the ship'?"

Her eyes fell away from his stare, knowing that this question was coming. In her present situation, she was unable to answer fully to his satisfaction, at the same time she could not betray the master of the mountain whom she served by answering what she felt to be the truth. For a short time there was a silence, but it was not within her to lie. Robert was keeping a close watch on her every movement for a clue to whether she was going to feed him the shit that he was used to at court. He was familiar with that line of answer and felt that he would know in an instant if she was trying it on. She breathed a long sigh before answering, "Alas, you must understand franj that I am merely a tool and I am not at liberty to tell you what I do not know. I am here not only as the servant of my master, but also acting as the voice and eyes of my master, and it would be unthinkable of me of to be aware of what is in his mind, nor could I be so bold as to question my orders for the reasons to any commands that he makes on me." Her reply told him little, though he believed her; it wasn't the whole truth but just a way of leading him away from what he wanted to know, and although Robert was aware of who she served, he had to ask the question to hear the answer from her own lips.

"You, franj, ask unusual questions when you know well whom I serve, and I dare say that he is no stranger to you in particular, for I believe that you have met him."

Jesus, he thought, how does she know that? He had met with the old fox and always believed that they were truly alone when they met. It was true he had dealings with the Hashashin, but he had never confronted this new mad man, Hassan himself. Now she was trying to turn his mind away from his friend Aldo, but Robert presented his question once again. She yawned, "I am tired, it has been a long night and day." She said it as if she were speaking to her lover as she appealed for rest.

Evasiveness was not what he expected; it irked him to think that she would attempt to toy with him. "I will ask the question once more, then you can rest. I mean only to help you. Just tell me what I need to know."

She came back at him with spirit in her voice, "You will set me free, no doubt," tilting her head to one side with insolence, scoffing at his appealing soft approach. Then her tone changed, "I am not a fool, franj, and I think less of you for treating me so."

Rising to his feet and raising his voice somewhat he sneered, "That's the last thing I would do to a little viper like you. You have treated my comrades abominably, on your command your assassins murdered my friend whilst he slept, another you had sewn into a camel skin and you abducted another and sent him across the sea for some kind of reward, no doubt. How do you suppose I feel?" he huffed. His temper rose with the thoughts of how relaxed she appeared. He gripped the ends of the small table forcefully and wanted to tear it apart with his iron fast grip whilst she watched his action.

With the most severe threatening tone he could muster he told her, "If you refuse to tell me," the glint of a dagger flashed as it was drawn partly from its scabbard, "you realise that I will have to extract the information that you feel so loathe to give up freely." His eyes burnt with anger at the depth of hopelessness in his efforts to regain his missing friend; showing how the loss of his friend tormented his thoughts, pointing him into a path of anger that he tried not to yield to.

She perceived his loss and feeling for his companions in his demands and said as much, but she somehow secretly felt that he would not harm her, and although her thoughts became detached from his voice, they quickly returned to reality as his strength of voice threatened her once more.

"I will not allow you to leave here without telling me what I need to know."

Resigned to her fate, she looked him directly into his eyes replying in a fatalistic tone of defenceless resignation, "That again is something I cannot do, she watched his reaction and before he could respond she continued stating that she was only a servant. I fear that you must do what you have to do and I have to submit to my fate. Franj, you have no idea what it is to be bound to another like a dog in obedience forever without any means of disapproval."

Robert wheeled around, infuriated by her stubbornness, wanting to strike her for her lack of co-operation, then she continued.

"Franj," she appealed, "listen to my words, for as true as Allah, I will not lie to you. It is as I told you earlier, all is not what it appears and I can assure you if by dying by your avenging hand gives you satisfaction, then so be it. It will satisfy me to know that I did not fail and will die content knowing that the one whom I care for most of all for will be spared the sadness of my passing. So strike hard, Franj, and strike deep. Should you wish to kill me, I am ready." She was cold and uncaring for her demise and almost welcoming her end.

Perplexed by her response, Robert was passed being confused and angered; she had somehow turned the tables again. Completely confounding him with her diversion of words, that she loves another whom she was willing to die for, it did not sound as though it was he that she served, or any religious reason, and he considered her strange reply for some moments in search for her reason. He was amazed at her coolness. "Do I have to stoop to torture, to prize this information out of you?" he said, in an almost pleading manner.

"If it is your will to do so, I have no alternative but to suffer it. I am your prisoner and helpless," she sounded resigned and ready for it. "But before you partake in the pleasures of my pain," she said, "I tell you here and now, I do not know all what you need to know."

He was truly perplexed; he could see now that there was somebody somewhere that had a tremendous hold over her. He had never tortured a woman before or even hurt one physically and it was not in him to start now.

After a short silence she spoke once more, "It is my belief that you do not wish to cause me any harm, but you do require what you think is in my head. Whilst what you want is something that I cannot yield up to you because I know not fully all the details that you require. In this event I am merely a link in a chain, and I am only allowed to know enough as is necessary, for it was my task to complete only a portion of a plan before handing over to my successor." Robert flew into a terrible rage provoked by her coolness and audacity as she sat there under the threat of death; saying the things she did made him feel quite foolish and he was not used to being taken so.

The petite package before him appeared to have the upper hand in this affair.

"The blood in you boils hot, because I show no fear of you?" With a slight shrug of her shoulder, she admitted that she did not wish to die or equally feel the pain of his torture. "I am sure that I will succumb to the pain, and the answers will not be to your liking though they be true." Hopelessly, she was trapped and fatalistically knew she was in no position to alter what she could not control. "But I can tell you this of your friend; that he is in no danger and he suffers not, for where he goes there is no other who can care for him better."

Another riddle to further confuse him. "What is this nonsense that you talk of?" he demanded.

His mind hung on her words, she was giving him clues, yet his anger failed to pick them up.

"There is something in what you say irks me. Care, what do you mean care? My friend is fit and young he does not require to be cared for." As he spoke he became angered that they may have inflicted some terrible debilitating injury on him. Robert's mind raced for some form of clarity, until he sat almost shocked with the horrifying thought of some outrageous state of mind they had inflicted upon him.

"What in God's name have you done to him?" a tear of anger almost welled in his eyes as he appealed for further knowledge of his friends wellbeing.

"He remains as fit as you or I, unharmed in all ways, but," with hesitance in her voice she continued, "he sleeps much. It was the instructions of my master that a potion be prepared so that he will become dependent on it, yet remain in a tranquil state so long as it is administered".

"By whom?" Robert demanded as his throat filled with a lump in disgust by the ensuing statement.

"One I believe that loves him more dearly than all his friends, and that is all that I can tell you on that matter." She spoke casually and openly, indicating that she was telling the truth.

Robert's words that followed did little to give her hope, "I fear your silence on this matter will return to haunt you forever. I have no choice but to take you back, you do understand."

There was a pause before speaking, once more in her resigned commitment she spoke, "Think not too far into the future; you and I, Franj, are of little consequence in this game and it is very doubtful if we shall ever see freedom again. My master is too powerful a man to allow us to escape his grasp." Silence fell upon them and not a word was spoken for some time, Robert thought long on her words. "You know more than I of what is going on. Am I right?" he asked. "It is as you state, she answered and there is little that I truly know and little that I am allowed to know, and, furthermore, it does not profit me to know. I merely serve a demanding master."

Robert could not stand for this type of talk that made no sense to him; anger crept back into his manner. "I tell you this, you are not helping your situation with your reluctance. You deserve a thrashing for your insolence. Why do you protect your master so? You have stated he cares little for you."

She exhaled long in resignation. "Why is it that when a woman remains silent she is insolent? I know that I have the better of you, and you do not like it." she spoke with antagonistic authority not caring how Robert would take it. Pushing him further she blurted on, "Who are you that says you will thrash me? I am not an animal or a slave to you; truly you can bully me when you feel fit to, but I will never be your animal. You that has dared to look upon me and removed me in the dead of night from my sleep, leaving me unfit to be considered respectable, and look at me, I remain improperly clothed. Franj, you are uncouth and uncivilised, you enter our land like savages, rape our women and kill all before you, plundering our beautiful cities of their wealth and desecrating our holy places," and before running out of breath she asked stingingly, "how are we supposed to accept you?" Robert retorted, "This is a war and it is the nature of war that causes men to commit such atrocities. Have I as much as struck you or harmed you?" he implored. "I have had provocation, by God, have I had provocation! Your tongue is too sharp and you know not when to hold it," a warning finger shot from out of nowhere as he wagged it furiously at her, "and your insolence knows no bounds," the words came spilling out without thought. By this time, he was pacing the floor inflamed by anger; his agitation grew intensely and the need to retaliate by placing her across his knee and slapping her hide so hard she would have difficulty in sitting down almost overwhelmed him into action.

It was not normally in him to go on so, or threaten a female with violence; it gave him no satisfaction, rather it embarrassed him to do so. He respected her intelligence and was in awe by the ease in which she perceived any man's character; she was indeed a rarity among any of the women he had known, but he would have none of this talk. He was irrational and his guilt in the matter changed, causing him to become apologetic about the state of her dress in some ways to amend his outlandish behaviour, but it was necessary to abduct her in order to get the information about Aldo.

He viewed her appearance from across the room and could not help but admit that liked what he saw, before idling across the creaking boards of the make shift dwelling towards her.

"I must confess," he said sitting down facing her, "you are easy and pleasing on the eye and by no means a disappointment, even in your disagreeable state."

Pulling her coverings closer to her body as if threatened she retorted, "Am I to take solace from your words?" She cautioned herself for speaking out so quickly as she realised that he had cast his eye over her body, and should he wish to defile her she was unable to defend herself from any forceful advances. Robert's mood changed; he was on his feet again pacing the room of the little house trying to control his temper.

"By heavens, I was only paying you a compliment," he was confused by his attempt to smooth the roughened ground between them. "It appears I'd be better replace that gag to curb your tongue from running off so." He was angered because of his inadequacy to make rational contact with her.

She uttered a loud, "Ha," in defiance of him; at the same time knowing that he could have reacted angrily. So, she thought, he has a conscience; not all the Franj are barbarians then, she thought, but this man she perceived had other qualities. Once more he looked upon her, realising that she had prompted a means of contact. He didn't want a confrontation, knowing that nothing positive would come from it; better, he thought, to ease back and try again later. He searched through the bag of supplies that he had carried in on arrival and produced a handful of soft silken robes that seemed to fit within his hand. Filled with embarrassment that there was no reason for withholding her clothes filled him with anger with the knowledge that her being caught up in the wrappings wasn't helping matters. It came to him that a gesture may help; simply by giving her back her clothing to enjoy a respectful appearance could be a start. He pushed them to her across the table and made his way towards the door, making the excuse of wanting fresh water while she dressed. In an effort not to appear soft, he angrily grabbed at the water bucket spilling most of its contents exposing the excuse he had devised.

It was a positive move, one that raised a smile and a nod of approval of his manners. Whilst dressing alone in the cabin, she thought of her master, Hassan. When news of this event reaches him, his anger would be such that the whole countryside would come alive with men scouring every nook and bush for them. If it took all his men a month, he would not rest until they were found, and on that she was confident. Though she dreaded the thought of long the days ahead when she would have to undergo unending questioning by Hassan, he would have to be sure that she had not betrayed him by giving up any of his secrets; no one could hide the truth from him.

It was a little later when Robert returned with a fish, sufficient for both of them. It had been the previous day when they ate last, so it was a welcome sight. He noticed that she was dressed, sitting at the table and her face was uncovered. Immediately he set about preparing a fire to cook the fish when a voice from behind broke the silence between them.

"It would be better if there were spices to rub into the flesh before it meets the heat, the fish is bland and tasteless without it. Does the fisherman have anything in his larder?" she asked enquiringly.

With his back to her, a faint smile broke on his face; she had broken her silence for no known reason appearing friendly, now what was she up to. At least he was thankful that she could not see the look on his face.

Hoping for a further reaction, he posed the question, "Do you think perhaps you could do this chore, as I am not used to preparing food in any other way but plainly?" A small white lie, for he had looked after himself for so many years and had become quite proficient at supporting his own needs. His request was taken up with an added statement that, "The franj do not seem to be good for much." Although her response riled him, it was his belief that he may possibly get more from her if he was to let his defensive guard fall; all appeared to be going well as she crossed the floor passing where he stood holding the fish and made her way towards a niche in the wall. She sighed as she looked searching through some wooden containers; with a sound of a successful find, she walked back taking the fish off him, then returned to the niche and began rubbing the spices into the fish skin.

"Lend me your knife whilst I prepare this fish, I need to cut it," Robert looked at her, adding that he thought it better that he cut the fish as his throat felt better the way it was. They were working together; the dissatisfied rage Robert had earlier shown had long subsided; meanwhile his fire was underway and with the prepared fish fixed onto a skewer, it was placed across the fire.

Later, they ate well and Robert complimented her on her culinary expertise with spices, which raised a small smile of appreciation. They both grew tired from their long day and eventful flight from the serai in the early hours of the day. They yawned together; they both had ideas of the sleeping arrangements; Robert broached the subject, telling her that she should lie on the fisherman's bed and rest. Seeing suspicion in her eyes, he assured her that he would sleep on the floor and she should try not to be afraid; he would not attempt to endanger her maidenhood.

"I would kill you if you tried," she muttered.

Robert positioned himself across the door as a means of securing it from her escape and the tired duo slept peacefully that night. The following morning, as light and sound entered through the cracked walls of the hut, Robert was uncomfortable with a feeling of unease that all was not as it should be.

With his head on the boards of the floor he felt a tremor; fear grew in him believing it to be the sounds of distant thundering hooves; riders!? He was up and staring through the shutters but there was nothing to be seen from his viewpoint. He moved quickly over to the woman and shook her, warning her to rouse herself. In a scared state, which he had never observed in her before, she enquired in a frightened manner, "What is happening?"

Robert peering look through the cracks of the shuttered window offered the word, "Visitors." In the distance, across the expanse of sand, twenty or more riders came into view, approaching the house quickly from the cover of the hillside. Robert suggested that they make a run for it, but it was not to be. Alarmed by her reply, it was now obviously the woman's turn to dictate her orders telling him, "I expected this. Now, Franj, if you want me to save your life, you will do as I say and perhaps both our lives will be spared." It was a gamble that he decided to take when he looked again to view the riders approaching the hut.

They were being surrounded and from the dust cloud that marked their arrival, a voice cried out for Robert to give himself up and bring out the woman within to show herself unharmed.

Robert called back that he would show himself and talk with their leader, warning that the woman was with him and if fighting started, he could not guarantee her safety. The door opened slowly and cautiously he pushed out the female sufficiently to let them see her serving as a shield to him. She had been rebound, but differently than the night that Robert had taken her, and her face was covered.

This was the result of her instructions to Robert when he had seen the band of men approaching. Had any man looked upon her face, her acceptance by the Amman Hassan would no longer have been of less value to him believing that she had been defiled. At the sight of her appearance, there was a notable gasping from some of the front riders.

"Is there one among you named Kasim?" he called. As he repeated his call, through the haze of the rising dust, there was a disturbance of parting horses in their ranks to allow their leader through what was a close grouping of the wall of horsemen, all dressed in their black galabias and looking menacing.

When he came into view, he was riding tall and aloof in his saddle atop a black mount; slowly in his own time he progressed forwards as if time mattered not to him. He too was dressed in black like his men; Robert noticed a larger than usual formidable looking sabre hanging from his belt. The black scarf from his turban was draped across his face, projecting forwards as it hung loosely over the man's large hawkish nose. Robert looked directly at him with a soldiers gaze, assessing his enemy from behind his mask of black silk that continued to wrap around his neck. Robert could see the rider's dark satanic eyes, they were filled with venom, cruelty oozed from within their abysmal depths and he imagined that there was a knowing grin of victory beneath his mask; and with all means of escape cut off, he looked down victoriously upon his prisoner to be.

"So you wish to speak with me, Franj," the captain said, "well then," he said cheerily, "first you must release my master's aide."

Robert spoke out, "We have no quarrel, you and I, and our masters are at peace, if you give me a horse when I am clear of you, I will release her". He didn't really think that they would swallow that line, but he had to try.

"Ah yes, I have your horse," and giving a sign by raising his arm to one of his company beckoned a rider come forwards with Robert's own horse; seated atop of it was the little ragged urchin from the dockside, scared witless, bound, gagged and terrified.

"I will ask you once again to release the woman."

There was a silence as Robert tried to think out a plan on the spur of the moment; a sound of steel being freed from its scabbard issuing a warning to those around, Kasim had drawn his huge sabre from its scabbard. The unmistakable whistle as it cut through the air followed by a thud as the head of the innocent boy hit the ground. Kasim was not waiting, he knew what Robert was about and delivered his graphic warning.

Robert was numbed by the effect of his coolness of callously slaughtering the boy. While Robert's attention had been distracted by Kasim's ploy; another of his group had sneaked around the hut unknown to him as he was backing away from the main body, only to fall into the path of the awaiting ambush. It came from a near lethal blow that came savagely from behind striking Robert's head when the young boy was ruthlessly murdered, rendering him unconscious.

Captured

When the blackness lifted from his numbed aching head, Robert was lying at the feet of Kasim; instinctively, Robert rubbed at the source of his throbbing pain in an effort to ease the pounding pulsation that had taken effect. Kasim's sword dropped down to Robert's throat, the blood of the boy remained sticky on the blade; the pressure applied to the blade was sufficient to cause him to raise his head upwards to view his captor's smiling face.

He spoke in a high whining note to match his victorious spirit.

"That was a foolish move you made, I am surprised that a man of your experience thought of his prize before saving his own life." He continued by tapping his sword tip on Robert's chest as if to goad him into action. "Nor was it the act of a good soldier," he sniggered, "or was there another reason to your action perhaps?" he asked curiously. His attempt to probe Robert's emotions was feeble and unskilled; force was what he was used to, unlike the woman whose wit was far greater than his could ever be.

Through a haze of his double vision that produced the shape of his swaying captor, Robert spoke up without showing any nervousness for one in his predicament.

"The woman meant nothing to me, other than bringing her to justice. She was responsible for the death of my friend and the imprisonment of two others."

With a half-smile on his face Kasim sneered tauntingly, "Your justice is weak, Franj, you should have killed the woman." It was what he would have hoped for, as there was much disliking between the two. Robert was about to tell Kasim what he was thinking, but the provocation may have caused him to retaliate in spite of the woman's words of warning to him earlier. By showing his anger, the big man had made an error and exposed the knowledge that there was some kind of power struggle between him and the woman; it was information that may serve Robert well on a future occasion. Through the thumping fuzziness of his mind, Robert was doing his best to be sharp enough to outwit his captors as soon as he was able. Before he could focus properly, a soft-footed boot pushed his face towards the speaker bringing him back to the present. Kasim was confident with his prisoner bound at his feet; his sneering voice once more broke the silence, "Tell me truthfully, franj," said the big man, "why did you not deliver your justice with the same swiftness as I demonstrated with your little unwashed messenger?"

Robert ignored the question, he felt it unworthy to answer to one such as he who was less than his equal; being little more than a common cut throat, he was neither a trained soldier nor an efficient servant, only a rough lackey who sought to serve himself. There came a half laugh as Kasim carried on with his attempted belittling criticism.

Kasim's face was filled by a cajoling smirk on telling his prisoner, "I had admiration for you, franj, the way that you entered into the caravanserai as you did, passing my men whilst they slept; it required much nerve; it has now become the source of much embarrassment to me. Abducting my charge as you did puts you in a different class of men, I will have to watch you carefully." With a chuckle, he added, "Perhaps I should kill you after all." Robert stared at Kasim with disgust; if he thought he was going to get the answers that he wanted, he was going to wait a long time. The face that taunted him took on a gruesome change and the hand of the big man gripped Robert around the neck and began slowly pressing on his windpipe, and in a snarling tone proffered the words that no man makes a fool of Kasim and lives. With the pressure increasing, Robert believed that this was no longer a game of words; the man was deadly serious as he felt his life's breath slowly leaving him; he was being choked and could do nothing to save himself as more pressure was exerted. Robert gagged for air; he could see the delight derived in the black eyes of the torturer; at the power he held over his unarmed and helpless prisoner. "I ask you again, why did you restrain yourself from delivering our kind of justice when the woman was sleeping? It would have been merciful."

Robert was helpless, he felt his eyes begin to bulge as the pressure on his windpipe was squeezed almost shut causing a fire in his lungs beginning to burn; then Kasim began to laugh out loud as he released his grip on his prisoner's throat, watching as Robert helplessly choke for air. "We will have much sport on our way, you and I," said Kasim, "on our journey to Mas'yaf. I will not kill you, though I think you will wish for your death to come." Moved to the need to kill his tormentor, Robert swore that he would not yield to his games, nor would he bend in the face of death. This was not the end, and promising himself that if he were free, he would swiftly deal with his tormentor and teach him a lesson. Robert's breath was fast; Kasim watched him; cunning as a fox, Kasim was able to tell how he had hurt and provoked his prisoner; now that Robert knew he would not die, he liked it less to feel that he was to become the focus of his captor's amusement. Controlling his temper, he spoke up with hardly a voice that could be heard because of the hurt in his throat; in a disapproving tone, he told Kasim that he was a brave man that took his pleasure from attacking defenceless prisoners.

"Justice," Robert added, was not his to deliver. I know your purpose and it is to take us back and present us to your master to clear your rotten name for disobeying his orders. I will tell him how easy it was at the serai, how I strode boldly passed you and your men. Had I have had the time, I would have pissed on your men in passing, I am sure they would not have noticed being so soundly asleep before, taking your charge under your very noses." Robert wasn't allowed to say anything further as a back-handed slap knocked him back to the ground. The look of hatred in Kasim's eyes burned, he wanted to finish the franj there and then; Robert felt that he was never going to reach Mas'yaf. With a bloodied mouth, Robert picked himself up; he was weak and stunned, no match for his enemy. The sound of the sabre being drawn from its sheaf filled the air and the hairs on Robert's neck stood prickling as he waited for the end. With defiance in him, Robert urged Kasim on stating that the name of Kasim may be written in history with the blood of those men and boys who were bound and defenceless when he slew them. He tried to continue goading Kasim, pushing until he was about to draw back for the killing blow; it was then that the woman spoke out sternly, ordering Kasim to sheath his sword or she would report him to the master for his arrogant show of defiance to Hassan's wishes. He wanted to slice Robert in half, and would have, but it was more than he dare do than show an open disregard for the Master. Robert's eyes opened wider as he realised the sword was being sheathed; it was not through loyalty but obviously through a fear of the threat of what could eventually happen to him should he defy the mad man Hassan. Approaching Robert, she warned that it was most unwise to push this man to the limit of his tolerance, "This time, Franj, you came close and failed in the effort to find death at the tip of Kasim's sword." That was not the way she expected a brave man to die. She continued, "Unlike you, he does not have the capacity to judge honour over how death is delivered, being nothing less than a foolhardy bully. You will understand now that our roles have changed. Regrettably, I must deliver you to our Master." Now you have it; she spoke to Robert in his own language so that she could make it plain that she could help him but not save him.

Kasim's face turned into a scowl, Robert was saved from the wrath of his sword, but the hate in his eyes told him that if he could have his way, revenge would eventually be his to have. Robert thought deeply on what had been said, and realised that if Kasim was absent for his own reasons when he was meant to be present the night of the abduction, then had disobeyed his orders and gone missing with the intention of seeking his own pleasures. Yes, he thought, he certainly was in deep trouble; how the devil was he going to wriggle out of that when he faced Hassan? She was right about Kasim, his anger did not die; his sword arm was raised as if frozen in defiance with a challenge to the authority of the woman to whom he was there to protect. Though Robert was unable to see his face, he could plainly see in his searing eyes the contempt that drove his defiance to the edge of his tolerance. His hatred was great; Robert was learning watching Kasim's insubordination wondering that should he defy her, what would be the consequences? A thought of murder passed through his mind with the knowledge that he would have been the likely candidate to have caused this event. Robert further surmised that not all the men under Kasim's command admired him and would support whatever he ordered over the woman's orders, realising that he did not have their respect to take that step of fate. She was right when she spoke of his stupidity; her voice spoke firmly, reminding him to think carefully for his own future. She told him that he was not such a warrior that could slay all the men in the camp; for if he did not obey her, he would spend a lifetime as one of Hassan's zombies to consider the consequences of his disobedience. This pint-sized woman showed no fear to the giant that she berated; it was certain that he feared any threat of what she spoke of. He shuddered at the thought and he reacted very quickly and became humble, making excuses that she was driving him beyond the limits of his anger. She dismissed him like a child, making him appear small in stature before the men. Foolishly, he could not leave the scene without a threat to Robert about his revenge, but when she spoke next, she gave him little chance but to leave quicker than he wanted.

"When our master has finished with him, he will still fetch a handsome price, but Kasim, if you wish to defy me as well as Hassan, then so be it."

Kasim stayed his hand knowing that the woman would bear witness to his action; she was far from being his favourite person and hated the fact that he was duty bound to obey her. Should fortune one day smile on him just briefly, perhaps a little accident would befall this beauty and be rid of her and then Kasim would rise to command; thinking he was just as clever as her, one day he swore, one day he have his way, perhaps it would come sooner than later.

From Kasim's reaction, it seemed that he was unsure of himself when she was around; he was no leader, though it was apparent that whilst the men feared Kasim, they showed respect but only obeyed the woman, acknowledging her as the true arm of Hassan. Robert had briefly seen for himself that Kasim had ambition and showed his loathing to obey her; a man his size taking orders from her, yet he did, and it gave Robert an idea that he may be able to use that situation to his advantage in the future.

It was not uncommon to ransom valued prisoners, and Robert suspected that he would become one of those that would fetch such a price; therefore, it would be very difficult to excuse such a waste of a valuable prize. Hassan did not give way to indulgences from his captains; they were there to obey his word. Kasim's failure at the serai was a bad error, leaving him in fear that his pleasure could be at the cost of his forfeiting his own life in return. An order was snapped out and two guards lifted Robert to his feet, but his liberty remained restricted. The woman stood before him thoughtfully looking at him, how the situation had changed, viewing him with scant emotion before she strode off she remarked in passing to Kasim, "If you have finished with him, we should make haste." Kasim, with insolence in his eyes, stared hard before nodding; he would have taunted his prisoner more had he have had a chance. One day, he thought, she would go too far and his master would see for himself how she deceived him, then he would have his chance to even up the score but for now, he turned to give an order, waved his hand and the entire band began to decamp.

Robert was roughly manhandled and his bonds brought to his front, his bonds were tethered to a long lead; he would be walking to Mas'yef and was to be drawn along in tow behind two riders, for what promised to be a long, hot and rugged day. Kasim took delight in warning him before setting off that they would not be stopping; should he foolishly stumble, it would be his decision whether to be dragged the rest of the way.

Mas'yaf lay some distance away and it would not be reached before noon the following day. Escape was all Robert could think of; fearing the confrontation with the religious fanatic Hassan, it was a thought he preferred not to dwell on. From stories he had heard, once inside his stronghold, he feared that his self-will would, and could easily be taken from him by devious means, and worse of all, the woman would be watching to gloat over his reduced demeanour.

By midday his feet were aching and really hot in his short leather boots, but he was glad for them over the stony mountain paths that he was being drawn forcibly along by his cantankerous captors. His wrists were raw from the chaffing from his leather bonds and no matter how hard his efforts to loosen them, the constant tugging on the line ensured that situation never arose. By late afternoon he had suffered enough; how long he could maintain this pace he did not know. His legs felt as if they did not belong to him, being numb from the feet up. He was only too well aware that should he stumble, he would be as good as dead and that would please Kasim. He couldn't allow that, for he knew from his earlier threat that by the time they had made camp, he would not have a shred of skin on his body. He had to endure all, in spite of his agony and without a rest; his mouth and throat were raw for the taste of water; it was freely passed around and spilt purposely to torment him by the riders that set the pace for him to follow. Kasim obviously was making sure that he would not be fit in any way to slip his bonds to allow his prisoner the opportunity to make him appear foolish once again. For his part, Robert had resigned himself to becoming the captive that he was, but refused to give up hope of escape.

As dusk approached, the riders finally dismounted and prepared to make camp for the evening. Robert was dragged roughly to a place away from the warmth of the campfire near to where the horses were tethered for the night and left to rest with his hands bound at his back. He did not have to be pushed around by any guard towards his place of resting; his body was spent of energy and was willingly ready to collapse after the long arduous walk over the gruelling broken terrain. His feet throbbed like hell, he was sure that blisters had formed and burst and his skin was severely chaffed and sore, but more than ever, he longed to take off his boots to let the air get his swollen feet. Later, a guard came to him leaving him a fair sized piece of khubz and a goat's skin of water at his side but in his restrained situation with his arms secured behind him he was tantalisingly unable to either eat or drink.

Robert suspected that it was Kasim's doing to exercise his sadistic power over him; in his present mood, he was unsure through his fatigued state whether he was hungry or just too tired to bother. It was not too long before he had another visitor, the woman. The cold air of dusk brought with it a fragrance that awakened and tricked his numbed senses. Robert's eyes slowly flickered open to reveal a new situation; it pained him to realise that there was now a role reversal and she was his new tormentor. He lay in a pained, exhausted state and in no shape to react; and as much as he wanted to, the spirit that was his manliness willingly yielded to her presence, but to show some spark of defiance, he struck out with his angry tongue to vent his anger on her.

"I suppose this is your way of entertaining yourself, wanting to see me grovel, well you will have a dull evening if you waiting for me to make a fool of myself over my torment. Well go ahead and laugh," he blurted out, trying to rise, "don't stand there staring at me."

She drew the attention of the guard that was posted near the horses to come to her side. Stooping low to meet Robert's eyes, she asked for a truce, adding that she had heard when men like him join in battle and were defeated; to escape certain death they could claim a cessation of hostility by yielding and giving their word that they would agree to being taken as prisoner. Furthermore, on their word of honour, they also agreed not to escape. This was what was put to him; Robert laughed as if taunted; he was in no fit state to escape and agreed; she looked at him as if she were testing the truth in his eyes, then she nodded, saying that she never took him for a fool. For a short while only she told him she would free him and hold him to his word, then she spoke quietly to the guard to do as she ordered.

He was dumfounded and rather taken aback by her action; though it was done and the guard dismissed, Robert mumbled some form of apology for his rudeness before thanking her for her consideration and misjudgement on his treatment.

She stared back with deep honest eyes as she took his arm to inspect the extent of his wrist burns,

"I am not as cold, nor as difficult as you may imagine, franj," she whispered, "you are like so many others that mistrust me." When she spoke, his hungry eyes stared hard at the bread lying before him; being unable to resist its temptation, he snatched at it and greedily stuffed it into his mouth while she watched him, knowing it was expected. She placed a small silver box by him, telling him that within was a salve for his weary feet; she stood back and left, but not before telling him that he should not be slow in caring for his injuries. He stopped his eating as she rose and humbly thanked her again; at the same time he could not but help but ask the question, why her change of heart?

"Alas, I do not see this world quite your way, though we remain with the similar masters with opposing beliefs who also have not changed their ways or their points of view. I will say that back at the fisherman's hut, you could have treated me differently; in that short time, I learnt much about you and your way."

"Oh," exclaimed Robert. "How is that?"

She did not reply at first. "You are not like the others that I have met, I detected what some such as Kasim would call it a weakness, let us say; for myself I could see a gentility, a humanity in you that struck me as rare and pleasing. A warring barbarian undoubtedly you remain, but different. I believe that in your own way you showed me respect, therefore I am only returning the courtesy for your kindness. But be warned, franj, I am afraid you must prepare yourself spiritually to meet my master."

A shiver passed over him as she made that remark, a smirk showed on his tired face that was transparent to her.

"There I was thinking more into it," he jibed teasingly.

After being dismissed, the guard had reported back to his captain Kasim to inform him of the woman's orders, and now with the knowledge of her actions, Kasim came storming into their presence demanding by what authority had she to interfere with his prisoner. She stood her ground and warned Kasim that not only were his previous actions unacceptable, she might yet have words to fall on angry ears when she was through giving her account to Hassan of the last few days. Hassan would not look favourably upon an underling that put personal pleasures before that of his own master. The words stopped Kasim like a bolt; he had no answer for her. Once more he was robbed of having his way, she had also made him appear foolish in arguing with her and that was always his undoing. His yearning to strike her for her resistance in denying him the right to command as he saw fit grew like a boiling pot almost to overflowing; in time, his temper was stilled, as his brain again worked out the consequences. To strike her would have been tantamount to striking his Master, he knew it, and because of it he hated her more; it showed in his contorted face and blazing eyes; he did no more than turn and leave.

When Robert was alone, he was able to remove his worn boots; carefully he rubbed in the welcoming salve that she had brought to him to treat his tender skin. The salve was cooling, it soaked into his skin almost instantly, feeling the throb of pain ease slightly when he massaged the salve onto his blistered and bleeding feet; he had no idea how the salve was put together but thankfully relief came almost instantaneously to the bloodied tissue with each coating. If the salve was good for the feet, it must be good for the wrists he thought and he set about lavishly smearing the ointment on the worn and cut skin of his raw and tender wrists. In the process of massaging the ointment around his tender wounds, he had unconsciously also smeared his leather bonds and in doing so, realised that the salve had given a slickness for the bonds to move with ease towards the thick of his hand. With the chance of freedom now made possible, he would continue to work on the leather thongs that bound him until he had succeeded in removing them. Unfortunately for him, orders were hailed to make him fast to the tree that was supporting his tired body, which immediately put paid to his ideas of escape. Burly guards that were not chosen for their brains approached him, almost cursing him for the trouble that he had caused them because of Kasim's embarrassment. Reaching out, one grabbed his hand and tied a further thong to the existing wrist bindings, then hauled his arms above his head and tied them off on an overhanging branch. He was roughly handled by the guards, who must have been under some threat by Kassim should he escape in the night, so they dutifully ensured that Robert was bound fast and could not make any attempt of escape.

The night passed uncomfortably for the knight, but because of the previous day's exhaustion, he slept deeply only waking when the numbness of the bindings caused him discomfort.

The camp was roused as soon as the sun raised, its glowing corona above the darkened horizon; orders were sharply snapped loudly to prepare their prisoner for the road ahead. Being trussed so tightly against the tree, when the guards cut his bonds he fell forwards and was unable to save himself for the lack of feeling in his arms. His whole body ached and he feared that he would not make it to Mas'yaf. There was laughter as he careered forwards onto his face; all Robert could do was gather himself and try to bring some life back into his aching arms, which had turned white with the sparse flow of blood through his veins. They pulled him back to the tree and left him still bound around the wrists, knowing there was nowhere to go now that the camp was actively preparing to move out. The crumbs of bread lay around the tree that the night creatures had not eaten; he avidly scooped up and ate hungrily, even a piece that the ants were busily trying to make the most of, for he knew that he would not receive any succour from Kassim that day, nor when he would eat again when they reached Mas'yaf. There were loud voices; he could hear shouting at the camp regarding him and he frantically made efforts to hurriedly put on his boots. Fearful that Kasim would notice them off, aware that his wicked sense of cruelty may tempt him to take them away from him for good, and he didn't fancy the thought of walking the rest of the way to Mas'yaf for Kasim's twisted pleasure.

In spite of his rough handling and difficult night of sleep, he had been grateful for the salve. His bleeding and cut feet from the previous day's walk had been given much relief and his sleep, such as it was, was rewarding to his injuries.

The small container of the healing salve remained by his feet, neither the guards or Kasim had removed it, if the coming march was to be anything like the previous day then he had better keep it close to him. He did no more than reach out for the salve and, before he could be seen, quickly placed it within the sash of his clothing. It may even come in for more useful purposes, he thought, at a time when it would serve him well.

Fearful of the future and suspicious of every move around him, he shrunk back as a burly guard had been sent to prepare him for the march. Roughly, he was pulled this way and that; he was a puppet for the making of laughter; it suited Kasim that he had an object of derision to maintain the appearance that he was in command and also to keep his men's spirits high. Being hauled to his feet made him aware of the stiffness in his aching legs, and whilst he stood under the support of the strong arm that held him fast, he tried to stretch his aching limbs without notice and relax for a brief moment. Then, as the men mounted up to continue their journey, he was once more harnessed to the riders immediately in front of him to take up the same position he held the previous day.

It was not long before he was reminded of his weakened state, as pain of his contused feet and the stiffened limbs bore witness to his painful injuries and the torment of another journey on foot. The morning's trek was promising to be a rough one for Robert, for he was familiar to the geography of that area. The troop was making for higher ground; it was rougher terrain and he knew that the going would get tougher as the day wore on. A long time ago he remembered scouting out Hassan's hideaway fortress when the King's army was considering an attack on him some time earlier a year or more ago after Hassan refused to pay his agreed dues. His memory of the terrain was that it was hard and rugged and the fortress protected by the surrounding mountainous terrain made it almost impregnable. Alas, his situation did not offer much to be thankful for as a tug on the straps jerked him forwards and pain brought his mind sharply back to the present, reminding him that he was wandering off course.

Confusion

The huge Muslim army had travelled northwards along the corridor of the deep valley to Eddessa and veered away almost secretively in a wide circular route so as not to give their enemy notice of their presence. It would not be usual for any advancing army in its past to have manoeuvred as such, as their habit was to strike as hard and as relentlessly as possible at their nearest target in an effort to throw the enemy into a state of confused terror. Differently, this time there was no obvious forward thrust and the army quietly and purposely avoided Eddessa, targeting small towns within a twenty-mile range of the capital that the Christians depended on for supplies and reserves. Stories normally spread like wild fire following any conflict of horrendous brutality and suffering, but on this occasion there were no reports from the incursion. Whoever was leading this army was eradicating all contact and closing a fist around major targets in the line of attack.

Not a man, woman or child was spared from the sword; it suited the assailants to be so ruthless that they made a clean sweep to secure the area so that no communications would leak out, this the commanders believed would add weight to the silent terror that awaited those in the citadel.

Armies could spend days, even weeks, to reach the point of readiness for siege; but this army became like a phantom, forever changing its direction and splitting into smaller forces making it harder to keep track of.

The great army's vanguard came and disappeared swiftly like a changing wind until news of its advancing presence reached Antioch, but by then the enemy had closed its iron grip, leaving it impossible to call on others for aid and support against the unstoppable force that threatened them. Rumours were abroad of another army from the north circulating the court and now there was credibility forming in the anticipation of its arrival. The two great armies together would make their attack on Antioch more decisive, laying out the whole of the northern sector of the Levant, like a mouse nibbling away at cheese until only crumbs of resistance to the invading armies remained. All supplies of men and military would be made easy for swift support to their advancing army's needs. With the advancing horde, a new leader was present; he was adept with a masterful approach to understanding the problems that had held back the unity of his people and dogged the Muslim people for too long. This indeed could be the beginning of the end for the Franks in the Levant; it appeared little could be done to prevent it; the armies of the holy sea, it was believed, were to be once and for all decisively defeated and banished from the land of the faithful.

Father Bernard hastily made his way northwards in the direction of the pass of the Cilicean gate in the Taurus Mountains en route for Constantinople. He travelled the dangerous pass, whose great chasms with their sheer dark arched walls threatened menacingly over all that passed through. Such had been the case on many occasions in the past that his worried fingers fervently played across the polished surface of the wooden beads of his rosary in his prayers for a safe passage. His mind was consumed half in prayer, the other half in fear of the thought of ambush or surprise attack from high above, which had been frequent and often the surest way to impose devastating casualties on those strangers that dared advance the forbidden road.

Father Bernard was returning home, but, to achieve the course to his destination, had first to traverse these long lonely avenues of dark crags. Though he had in his possession a means that would see him safely through this dangerous route, he nervously continued passing their intimidating fissures always with his head crooked upwards to stay the arrows that he imagined would rain down to kill him, causing the hair on his neck to stand rigid. To say that he was afraid was an understatement after undergoing a successful mission, believing that should he fall by a stray arrow, it would be an injustice to his efforts on behalf of the cause he had set out to achieve. His imagination tortured his contorted mind into supporting his fears that somewhere above, somebody might be concealed and waiting for him to come by. He was not a warrior that fought men with a sword; he was a simple priest that usually spent his time in prayer and among others of the same ilk. The road offered nothing of comfort to the lone travelling monk; even the light of day was denied a place to rest within these forbidding crags. Here there seemed that there was no protection for him in the mountain pass, only the chance stares from those that shepherded herds of goats as he passed by. Given the chance from a reasonable distance, he could assure that he could explain to any foe that he was of high rank and that he was on a joint mission for their leaders as well as his own. As soon as he felt that there was no likelihood of meeting any other western traveller, he was keen to display the pennant given to him from the Nicean Sultan. This was his protection, being told that it symbolised from whom he was sent. Being his supposed guarantee for a safe passage as soon as he entered the pass, he had soon decided that if nothing else it would give him comfort in its display, expecting recognition from those above giving him a degree of consolation and safety. The safe conduct pennant that was flapping in a haphazard manner was fixed behind him, attached somewhat dubiously to his saddle, which bared the colours of the Seljuk chieftain of that province. He was running a calculated risk in this display, hoping that it would not be seen by the militia journeying the opposite way; the discovery could mean that he could be arrested to return for questioning to an official in the north of the county, and that meant Antioch. It was not a place he wanted to visit, especially under arrest, knowing that events had got very hot after he had left. The success of his mission was never guaranteed and should it be the case that it fail, he would no doubt, have to think quickly of some plausible explanation should that eventuality ever arise. He shuddered with fear that it would not befall him and bring all his efforts to a collapse, as anxiety built within him, making great efforts to divert his mind away from his inner insecurity.

To overcome the sensations of agitation, he examined in his mind the new structure that he had inaugurated for the rebuilding of his mother church's wealth and esteem to its former glory. Should he succeed, he would most certainly be greatly rewarded; his mind wandered, sinful flashes of vanity flared in and out of his egotistical imaginings. The trappings and adulation that came with rank made his mind magnify the rewards for his success; perhaps he would at last be recognised with an advisory position closer to the Holy Father himself.

Overcoming his jubilant thought, somewhere in the back of his mind he felt concern; there were trivial wrinkles in his master plan; nothing that he could place a finger on, but suspicions ran riot. He believed that he would not be harmed when he reached the palace at Nicea, believing that he was safeguarded with the papers he carried of their agreement; no matter how events turned, the sultans, he believed, would not dare refute what they had signed up for. Chasing away any inkling that events may deviate from the true direction, regrettably there were rumours, growing signs of unease as the time of action grew nearer. Though there had always been an element of doubt regarding the reliability of the factions in the Seljuk camp, it niggled him that there was an apprehension to go along with the conditions put forward by other eastern council leaders. It was all too late now, it had been a risk but he remained hopeful that he would be able to collect those documents of the truce and the agreement to the tithe that he honestly believed awaited him.

So far his plan was on course for the final agreement.

Unknown to him, there was aggravation; in his absence, a dire upset had transpired; an idea had sparked the hot-headed emirs and certain ruling families to secretly usurp the agreement and attempt to institute their own opportunity for a war, especially after Father Bernard's own manipulative efforts to shackle them into a willing peace. Unknown to him, this was to be his greatest error of judgement. In his belief that all men would follow their leaders and uphold the honour of the treaty, he did not bargain for those chief rulers that were soured to the western beliefs, containing warlike aspirations of their own agenda that saw an opportunity in his plan for total retribution.

His visit and payment to Hassan of the Assassins had been accepted extremely well, although he had no idea what he too was planning, only that he had a decisive scheme to enable him to put a substitute plan to use within the shortest of time. Antioch, it seemed, had become the melting pot of all the discontent for the neighbouring states; serves them right, father Bernard thought, for they were self-serving and covetous; he chortled, no man could do better. It did not appear that any of his plans had openly failed; indeed, events, he believed, had turned quite fortuitously in his favour, knowing that the politics would soon move into a fine balance of unease after the brutal death of an emissary from Damascus.

Considering the Eddessa point, father Bernard pondered over his words with the foolish and dangerous upstart Geoffrey, a pompous and crude ass if ever he had met one. If anything was ever written in the sand, it was Geoffrey's eventual downfall. Sniggering almost knowingly that Geoffrey would have been in quite a confused state of mind not knowing of what he had said and signed up to on the night of his visit. He was arrogant and dangerous company to be in especially for one such as he that had no experience of knightly combat, but easy to overcome when it came to brains; my, my how these so-called aristocrats believed in themselves. Bernard puffed out air from his lips in his disbelief of the fool Geoffrey and his expectations and greedy avaricious convictions in the belief that he was worthy to rule Eddessa; if nothing else, he was another ideal means to de-stabilise the country. As to whether he would take the bait and seek out the inducement that had been dangled before him was another matter, but Father Bernard was sure of his assessment of him and had no doubt in awarding himself a self-congratulatory smirk to settle on his smug facade at the satisfactory progress so far of his plan.

The yeast of discontent was well on the way to rising; the recipe for a satisfactory split was forming between those ingrates of the Holy Father at Eddessa as well as in Antioch.

His passage through the long and hazardous mountain passes took two full days, and passed without event. It was only when he reached open country did he begin to relax from the awful tension that had built up within him from his trial of passage through that foreboding pass.

It was a further four days journey to reach his destination, the great walled city of Nicea, whose white walls were more than a farsahk in length and topped with two hundred and forty turrets being the capital of the Seljuk Sultan. Set out on the green hills on the edge of the placid Ascanian Lake, it appeared quite a formidable sight to travellers, with its huge encircling walls which no doubt offered great comfort to those who sojourned within them.

Feelings of anticipation grew ever stronger in him; he sensed that it would be here that he would secure his plan's final success or failure. A faint shudder passed over him as he almost gagged on the thought of failure; it was not a word he had ever felt comfortable with.

There was a slight breeze building, which would be welcomed to relieve the heat of the searing sun later in the day, giving Father Bernard a sense of added comfort. Daydreaming as he rode along of the new life to come, a troop of horseman appeared on to have gathered on the horizon from beyond the distant ridge; they must have seen him, for he was expected. The good father reached into his baggage behind his saddle and quickly rummaged through its contents to produce another silken banner which he immediately raised in a flourish at arm's length above his unfortunate misshapen head. On its identification, the riders came galloping forwards. Father Bernard swallowed uncomfortably; they were palace guards and their approach was fast and intimidating; he hoped that he had done the right thing in drawing their attention. When they reached him they shouted their orders; because Bernard was not understanding of their tongue, he became rather confused and scared. Although he was not harmed in any way, he felt uneasy and that they had been sent to find him to escort him to their master's domain. When Bernard had disappeared over the horizon, rumour had it that he was never heard of again.

The Fall of the Northern Territory

The army that was approaching Antioch was lost in the darkness, leaving the eyes of those that had viewed the dust cloud earlier in the day confused. Though not yet seen, the marching hoard on its forward advance bewildered those spotters as to its intended purpose and its disappearance. This was by far the largest army that had ever been amassed and seen by western eyes, causing such an effect to the onlookers that they believed that it would be unstoppable.

There was no doubt in their minds that it was from Damascus, a prearranged plan must have been hatched to coincide with the visit of the Emissary and his spies. Such a force must have been in the making throughout the period of the peace treaty and kept highly secret. The horsemen that sat atop their distant hill viewed its size and discussed the military situation, with a need to get word out to every stronghold in the region; this confrontation was going to get much hotter than the noonday sun. Du Bray and Edward agreed that the unfortunate episode with the Emissary may not just have been a simple political act to remove a man who wanted to support a peaceful settlement with the franj. The butchery of such a popular man at home would have had his supporters baying for Jihad, with most men wanting to offer themselves for service in revenge of their Emir's man.

Rather than waste any further time for discovery of its direction, it was more purposeful to report back to the captain at Antioch also to deliver their handicapped companion to a place of safety and recovery within that sanctuary. Du Bray and Edmond, with Hubert in tow, rode day and night without rest for fear that their news may go unheralded should the approaching army have sent out a forward party to cut the access of the roads ahead to keep all news of the imminent approach secret until the moment of their confrontation.

It was early dawn when Antioch came into view to the riders; fatigue and thirst was their enemy now, leaving them limp and drained of energy to make that last concerted spurt to deliver their news of the impending attack. By the time that they had reached the gate, they were ready to drop, bent in the saddle and wavering with exhaustion driven by their duty to deliver their dire news. The knowledge that they carried was unable to be communicated audibly; their throats swollen with thirst caused their voices to become hoarse. Coated with dust and unable to reply to the sentry on watch, who feared a reprimand should he allow them through; instead, he refused to let them pass, holding them there suffering their pain until the officer of the guard had made a decision of letting them enter through the great gate of the citadel.

The captain was aroused by the noise coming through his open window and rose to see for himself the cause of it. Once the riders were through the gate, they were within the captain's view. Surprised at their dishevelled appearance, he did not recognise them at first, but then he remembered sending out the scouts. Believing his action to have been correct, that something was in the air, he guessed it would not be welcome news to the ear. He could not help but momentarily stare as he realised that there was one of their number that was unknown to him and another of their number missing. Rubbing his furry chin in thought at the disabled rider, it heightened his curiosity as to why he was blindfolded. He shouted from his second storey window that they were known to him and to care for them. For his age, the old Captain was quite active, as it did not take long for him to be standing before the scouts and asking numerous questions. Water was being given to them sparingly, but they were too weak and tired to talk; they were helped to the captain's chamber and sat propped up in chairs by those around them who were interested in the news of what the scouts held concealed in the weakened heads. The wives of fallen knights that had dedicated themselves to tending those that were sick had been summoned from the hospital and were dutifully washing the caked dust from the faces and caring to revive the new arrivals.

The Captain looked on and as the women tended to Hubert; when it came to removing his wrappings from his eyes, Edward silently stopped them, gesturing for them to leave his dressing on yet a while longer and continue with the refreshing washing of the face. The Captain soon realised that this was not their leader as he had previously thought; for one thing he was not the right shape, although he had been so actively busy the past days he was alarmed by this discovery. He bent down to Edward and spoke, asking about Simmonwood, their leader, but there was only an undistinguished whisper croaking from Edward. Guessing that it would be the same with his silent companion du Bray, he ordered his men to take the arrivals into the hospital where they would receive fuller treatment, announcing that he would be along later after giving the disturbing news of their arrival to his liege. Before he left, he ordered a small detachment of men to ride out to discover if there was an impending emergency, with orders to report to him immediately on their return with their findings.

The three tired scouts slept on the uncomfortable wooden hospital beds for a short while before the captain, who was in urgent need for information, roughly awakened them. His own scouts had returned and reported no signs of an advancing army anywhere; in fact, they reported that there was not a stirring and that the plain was free of all signs of life.

Du Bray took the brunt of the captain's impetuous handling, almost pushing him off the pallet that he lay on, and although he was unable to call out loudly in protest, he retaliated the only way he could, by brandishing a dagger that he had concealed within the bed linen. The Captain was startled with du Bray's instinctive reaction of a sleeping leopard. Reacting as he was unsympathetically disturbed as he slept, his dagger was drawn and with such purposeful intent as to render serious harm to his assailant. In so doing, he nicked the weak flesh of the older man's wrinkled throat, causing him to yelp as he managed in time to step back in fear of the blade plunging deeper into his aging wrinkled flesh. Guards were all around with drawn swords, with du Bray's instant reaction ready to pin the knight down, awaiting the Captain's orders. The hand of the Captain slipped from the wound exposing a red dribble of scarlet running towards his vestment; he was livid, filled more with acute embarrassment for his discourtesy and thoughtlessness as he stood holding his hand over the nick in his neck which was trickling blood from beneath his hand. The guards were ordered to sheath their weapons; at least the captain had the presence of mind to realise that the attack was of his own careless making. Du Bray realised his error, though he did not apologise but berated the Captain in a horse whisper for his stupidity of awakening a fighting man that way, especially one that lives on the edge of his nerve each awakening day. What could he expect from this hostile country; it was not a nursery for belligerent men to have their way. The Captain held his tongue and decided that there was much more going on around him that made him feel on edge. "We need to talk," said the Captain, "all of us," indicating with his hand flowing around the two others sleeping soundly. "Wake your friends, eat and then come to my chamber," he ordered. "We have much to discuss," he then turned smartly and retreated from the hospital room holding his neck.

When the three later arrived at the captain's chamber and in a better mood being refreshed after eating and sleeping off their tiredness, they were guiding Hubert as they went. The wrappings around Hubert's eyes had been changed and one less layer had been left off, leaving sufficient light now to penetrate his veiled vision in the hope that he may within another day be able to endure the full light of day. Presenting themselves before the Captain, whose attitude had time to cool since their last meeting, he did not invite them to be seated, except for Hubert; he watched as he was aided into the place of the chair waiting to start his interrogation. The explanation of their condition was to shock the Captain into disbelief and anger when he began probing their reason for their early return from their mission from the field.

Du Bray and Edmund looked at each other with disbelief at his question. It was du Bray that offered the information, for he could see the rankled look in Edward's eyes at the Captain's attitude of scepticism. Their report amounted to discovering three days earlier of seeing a rising dust cloud that indicated an army of such enormity as perhaps ten thousand men on the move along the central valley and it was approaching in our direction towards Antioch. "What else were we to do? We rode continuously without rest being in the saddle all that time without supplies."

"How," the Captain barked abruptly, breaking in to du brays report and asking searchingly, "do you explain that my men could not find any trace of your army?"

"That I do not understand," replied the puzzled du Bray; there was a silence of troubled minds set to solving the riddle presented to them.

Edward listened before offering the explanation by slowly easing out a thoughtful and lengthy, "Unless..." hardly above an absent-minded thought which attracted all heads to turn towards him.

"Yes, unless what?" demanded the Captain, leaning out of his chair with interest.

"Unless," Edward repeated, "they have swung off to unite with another company, in which case they may be..." Looking around the chamber, he caught sight of a map of northern Syria, he walked over towards it and stood pensively thinking out a rational explanation. The Captain grew restless in anticipation of what he Edward was thinking; his impatience offered nothing of consequence to Edward's concentration on the matter. When he stopped his impatient chatter, Edward continued making thoughtful noises, moving his fingers around the map tracing out a theory of his enemy's possible movements. His mumbling ceased, building to a realisation of their planned movement; this time he confidently blurted out; turning to face the Captain as he spoke, stating, "They are not heading for Antioch, and my guess is they will make for Hurran and then Eddessa." Realising in an instant what Edward had suggested, his other two companions listened attentively as he spoke. There was a nod of agreement. They seemed to agree that this mad-sounding scheme suddenly made sense, whilst the captain sat blank faced in his chair.

A loud guffaw of laughter filled the chamber; the Captain was almost bent in two shaking his head as he laughed in amusement. When his laughter ceased, he became quite serious; a scowl showed very plainly, asking however had they become intelligence officers? He had expected better than that from them.

Du Bray did not take to that kind of language off anyone and became quite angry at the Captain's arrogant behaviour, accusing him of being a fool if he could not see what could possibly be unfolding before him. To stress his point even more so, he walked over to where the map hung; in temper he ripped it from its secure fixing and walked back to the desk where the Captain sat. "How dare you take such a liberty with my furnishing!" roared the Captain, who was dearly upset at du Bray's indifference to his impolite action.

Du Bray could have slapped the aging Captain, who had stupidly thought more of his property than his duty. "If you had read our orders properly and listened to Robert Simmonwood." He spoke down to the Captain, who had become quieter and solemn, withholding respect for his position when he spoke. The annoyance in du Bray's voice became more authoritative, explaining that if another army of equal size united, there was no reason to attack Antioch. Using his finger to outline Edward's theory, he pointed out that the real line of the Frank's defence were the castles of Alleppo, Hurran and Eddessa, which stood facing the enemy looking eastwards. "Once they were taken or occupied under siege," he added, "and if there has been a pact with the Seljuks, they could easily take care of Antioch whilst the northern border is opened up with nobody to arrest any advance, the enemy will pour into this area sweeping all before it." It was obvious the Captain did not want to acknowledge the explanation, as defeat was already written across his paling face after listening to du Bray.

As if grasping for a way out of acceptance, the Captain drawled out a disbelieving, "Yes, but when you have been out here as long as I have, you will realise that the Muslims have fought longer and harder among themselves,"

"Not if somebody has united them," broke in Hubert.

"That's most unlikely," said the Captain, fighting off the not so unbelievable hypothesis that was beginning to swamp him. Taking an opportunity to avoid further embarrassment, he veered away from the present subject. Drawing down on Hubert, he asked, "And you, sir, I have never met you, yet you sit before me."

Du Bray broke in, "There is much more to do here. After we have rested, we will ride east and find your army and send out warnings to all around us if it's not too late."

"How dare you usurp my authority!" bawled the Captain. "I give the orders here, you will do no such thing. Furthermore, I want an explanation for this man here," pointing to Hubert.

The air was getting tense; du Bray could not suffer the disinterested Captain, who for whatever reason failed to want to grasp what was going on. "Might I advise you, Captain," said du Bray, "we do not come under your direct command and that has already been pointed out to you once before. If you have a mind to hold us against our will, then you will answer to the Grand Prior in Acre and the King, which is a punishable offence and one that would bring your family name into disrepute."

Feeling that matters where getting out of hand, du Bray decided not to put too much emphasis on the matter, hoping that the Captain would see sense. "That is, if you continue to be so foolishly blind to prevent us from doing what we have been sent out here to do," without time to take a breath, du bray continued, "endangering the populace of Antioch and those of the other principalities in this sector for your own self vanity is tantamount to treason."

That was it, the air almost crackled with tension. All held their breath as they waited for the Captain to make his response, which came immediately. "Consider yourselves confined to the hospital until I think of other ways of dealing with you," and he yelled at the top of his superior military voice for a guard to escort them away.

They sat in the hospital and were silent looking at each other, knowing that the Captain was going to sit tight and do nothing. Inactivity and the knowledge that catastrophic events were going on out in the country when it was their business and duty to be about it, they set about discussing a plan to escape. Hubert was not yet ready to go with them and he suggested that he be left behind, if not for the sake of the people of this city. They decided not to move until darkness, then they would use Hubert's condition as a ploy to bring in the guard; the rest would be easy. In the subdued quietness that followed their plotting, they rested, while the heat was choking the oxygen from the air making their waiting more uncomfortable.

High in the hospital wing, Edward gazed out of the window across the quiet plain; in his calculating mind, he guessed that if the march northwards by the advancing army goes accordingly, the enemy could surround Eddessa within two weeks. This would leave the whole of the north-eastern sector trapped in their strongholds and unable to relieve anyone in need. The question begged to be answered, and Edward held onto it like a dog with a bone. By holding the north-eastern sector in a stranglehold, he knew the enemy could afford to leave this area remaining free, whilst they reduced their enemy selectively and with effect. Pacing the floor of the room, he attempted to try to grasp the problem from a different point of view and to do this he repeated his intelligence over and over through his perambulations of the room.

In truth, if news of the sieges were contained, the rest of the country would have no inkling of any disturbances to the north. It could be months before the Muslim armies would be free to turn themselves onto Antioch and by that time the rains would be upon us and the campaign would have to start all over again the following year. It did not quite make good military sense, but Edward could not yield the problem as his indolent gaze reached the horizons of the rich pasturelands against the hazy distant Blue Mountains in the west. It was a rare and beautiful sight and he looked long upon it enjoying its pleasurable scenery. The air was filled with a choking sweetness and birds busily sang as they flitted two and fro making their preparations for nest building in the open crevices of the fortresses sturdy stonewalling.

With an easy mind, he watched with interest as each bird returned to weave its intricate thread of straw or grass into the framework of the nest construction, noting that there was no one place that the birds gathered their material from but came confusingly from all directions always leaving the watcher to shift his concentrated gaze from one place to the other. In doing so, it confused the eye completely as to which direction they were coming from with the next piece of nest material. He smiled at the antics of the carefree, winged builders and wished that life for him could have been as straightforward. Looking back over his shoulder, he saw his sightless friend stretched out uncomfortably on the hospital pallet; calling to him, Edward asked if he would prefer a seat at the window to receive the comfort of what little breeze there was on his face. Hubert thanked Edward for his thoughtful gesture and agreed to sit there as was suggested. Edward helped him while du Bray took advantage of the opportunity to catch up on his lost sleep. Edward placed Hubert in the most advantageous place to receive the gentle balmy breeze; it blew intermittently in gusts up from the valley while they chatted for some time. During that period, Edward asked Hubert if he thought it possible for the Muslim to unite under one leader.

"Why not?" answered Hubert, "It's been done before with devastating consequences and you know when the cry for a Jihad goes out and catches the imagination of those embittered people that have lost sons in previous wars; it takes some stopping once they come into a united purpose."

The converse continued and to break the stagnant military theme, Edward talked about the busy antics of the nest builders on the ledges of the wall outside.

"Yes," Hubert replied with a chuckle in his voice, "you watch them flying out one way and they seem to return from another, always having you guessing from which direction there coming from next." Edward smiled at Hubert's reply and as though stricken by some debilitating shock he let out a cry of announcement. "By God!" Edward cried out, almost falling off his stool and leaning over to grip Hubert in his revelation.

"The answer was here before me. I could see it, but until you repeated it, it never dawned upon me." Hubert was left wondering what Edward had stumbled upon and sat there with a baffled silly smile upon his face.

"Don't you see?" said Edward, "We are all looking eastwards whilst there could be a spearhead heading from the north to take us by surprise."

"Do you think that could be the case?" he asked quizzically "That would mean an introduction of the Seljuks and they are not always in agreement from their Mameluk brethren."

"Yes, but if, as you rightly suggested, that there was a new leader who had cemented the families giving purpose to his call whilst forming all men into one unified army to once and for all rid the land of us. We could not stop such a number coming together.

He stopped before asking what he thought of his suggestion, to which he replied, "Devastating."

Storm Clouds Over Eddessa

In Eddessa, there remained a nut to crack and a score to settle; but without the proof of a witness to verify or accuse, only one person was kept under very close scrutiny by order of the Princess Leanora. Now that the burial of her brother was behind her, she became obsessive in her will to track down the murderers of her beloved brother, and firmly believed that Katherine was at the bottom of it all. For the sake of justice and the sureness that she would not taint her soul against having her quietly and efficiently murdered as she could so easily do. Instead, she preferred to keep her at distance and confined to the castle of Eddessa watching her until such time as Katherine would betray herself and her accomplice, then, and not before, would she strike. Cunningly, she felt her patience would be rewarded; once she had compounded her guilt, Katherine would suffer the punishment of quartering, which was not the usual end for a lady but such was the bitterness of the princess, she would insist upon it and not settle for anything less; she would be revengeful to the last and she meant to have her way.

It was a number of weeks later that Geoffrey had occasion to be at the castle after staying away for so long; it had not gone unnoticed by many of his female admirers who first thought that he had been taken by an illness. Many husbands too had gained from his respite, enjoying the sanctity of their bed; without harbouring suspicion that their wives were not missing at various times of the day when this notorious character Geoffrey was about. He in turn ached for his bargain to be sealed with Katherine, so much so that his mind was set to call on her, but at the last moment thought better of it. On the day before visiting her, he was fortunate enough to accidently discover a person posted nearby acting as a spotter for those that may be drawn to visiting Katherine. Avoiding committing himself to a watching eye, he turned and waited to see what developed. He would not fail a second time to reap his reward; he ached to lay with Katherine and had to be sure, for he was aware that the princess suspected Katherine, even though she had no direct hand in the affair. To be exposed and given up to his aunt or found sharing a bed with Katherine would have been the end for him. There was also no love lost between him and his aunt; indeed, if it had not been for his uncle's unending patience and his need to use him in the field, he was certain that he would have been packed off home in disgrace some time ago. Thoughts of his uncle's use of him brought an anger swelling within him.

He would prize this watcher from the place of their hiding; to do this he walked quietly and covertly along the stone passageway of the cloistered balcony until he neared the place he suspected the sneak to be harboured. A smile broke on to his face as he was alerted by a creaking door hinge as his footsteps neared the door next to Katherine's room. He watched it close quickly as not to betray the watcher on its other side, but it was too late; he had discovered the lair of the spy. Walking on, not giving any clue to where he was going or who he was, as soon as he reached the stairwell he took to the stairs three at a time up to the battlements and along the upper balcony running back towards the staircase that would lead him back down to the opposite side to the point where he suspected the artful watcher was secreted. Noises outside created an inquisitive eye to be at the door to discover the origin of the sounds emanating from the corridor, Geoffrey saw a face but he was unable to discover the true identity of the surreptitious observer; he coughed loudly, hoping that the sound would travel across the open quadrangle to alert the watcher. Curiosity was always the best bait known to encourage a spy from their furtive hiding place. The door squeaked open again, but there was nobody to see, and not to lose an opportunity, the impulsive watcher exposed herself opening the door that bit further for her to poke her inquisitive head around to see who was about; it was her undoing and she would never have an opportunity to report further to her suspecting employer, Geoffrey's aunt Eleanor. It was a maid, he could see her clearly; by opening the door to get a better look and in doing so she had sealed her own death warrant.

There was a leering smile on Geoffrey's face being successful in his ruse; the door was closed and before making his next move, he had a good look around to ensure there were no other accomplices or witnesses to his next lethal and vicious move. All appeared clear for Geoffrey to entice the watcher further to expose herself without alerting her of anything amiss; he began talking to himself quietly with varying levels of tone as to imitate two different voices. Sure enough, there was an announcement of the watcher's curiosity as the creaking door opened sufficiently giving Geoffrey the opportunity he had planned for.

Viciously and with great force, he pounced with hostility against the door where the unwary occupant had crouched for her tentative ear to pick up on the sounds outside. A low sounding whimper could be heard as the door impacted causing the maid to be sent flying against the opposite wall. Dazed and injured, she lay crumpled on the stone slabs of the cold floor; Geoffrey slid into the room quietly. He stood over her moaning crumpled body before delivering her a heavy and fatal blow with the edge of his hard, calloused hand to break her frail, aging neck with the ease of snapping a dead twig. In order to dispose of her body and not wanting to alert any guards that anything was amiss, he cradled her in his arms. Before entering the corridor, he looked about before making his way quickly to the staircase where he lay her body as awkwardly as possible near the bottom of the spiral staircase, leaving all to suspect that the woman accidentally lost her feet breaking her neck as she fell.

He was up the stairs and tapping conspiratorially on Katherine's door, just so loud as not to avert anyone's attention to his presence. He waited impatiently looking around, exposed to all as he stood outside the door; he did not like the exposure, cursing her slowness in answering the door, knowing that it would certainly raise too many questions should he be seen.

At last and not before time, relief came to him as he heard the latch on the door being raised; before the door could open properly, he had pushed his way impatiently in to confront the one that he could not keep himself from. Before she could berate him for his brash stupidity for coming to her, he longingly held her in his strong arms almost crushing her as in his covetous embrace. She responded more out of her nervous insecurity than her love for Geoffrey, fearing that surely he had not come to seal their bargain at this time. As soon as she had struggled free of his arms, a barrage of questions began to befall him like rain from heaven; it took quite some time to reassure her that he had not been seen and he begged her not to think of leaving her room unless he came for her. Her resolve crumbled; she began to break down, crying into his padded colourful tunic with her arms tightly around his, she begged him to take her away from this place. Oh Mother of God, he thought, do I have to suffer this; the situation became confusing for him; he was not used to females sobbing on him and for a first time felt softened by her weeping pleas. He began to wish that he had not visited her; the sensations of her uncontrollable heaving breasts against his were causing him some erotic sensations.

Afraid that she may be heard by a passer-by, he warned her to cease her wailing unless she wanted to draw attention to others. Holding her, he gave her instructions; he told her bluntly that he would have to stay away longer than intended but pleaded with her to be patient. He had to leave her now before being discovered, but would return at night by way of the window. He kissed her softly on the lips betraying his deep affection for her, which afterwards she thought was out of character for Geoffrey, being such a brute of a man she believed he was.

It was not long before Geoffrey was back in the main hall without a trace of suspicion and discussing with his uncle plans to expand the county and carve out a place of his own without showing disrespect to him. He had a need for a larger estate and if he were in the future planning to be wed, his own existing home would be inadequate for his needs.

The news took his uncle by surprise, almost leaving him aghast at his nephew's approach to settle down. When he finally got over the shock, he congratulated him, asking him all manner of questions, particularly who it was that he had in mind that he intended to wed. Preferring to be vague, he had no definite idea, stringing his baited uncle along intimated a possibility of somebody in mind, and that he would rather keep that answer to himself until he had made the right approach to the one of his choice. His uncle's smile faded with thoughts of a married women whom he suspected he had consorted with entered his head; abruptly, the uncle inquired that he hoped there would not be any embarrassment over the wedding. "Not at all," assured Geoffrey as he sat fermenting his plan to have his will with Katherine, allowing the smile to return to his uncle's face; the news seemed to fill Edward with a child's excitement as he rose from his chair.

"I will go and tell your aunt immediately, she will be so pleased that you have decided to settle down." The thought of his aunt knowing almost drained the blood from Geoffrey's face; he jumped up to stop his uncle from racing off, begging him to hold on to his secret.

Reminding him of his earlier words, it was his intention not to let anybody know, "After all, it was my intention only to ask your advice on the matter in order so as to secure a plan for my intended and our future children." His uncle, taken in by Geoffrey's empty words of marriage, showed a certain secret pride that his nephew had consulted him and not his usual drinking friends. Assuring him that he would stand by him and on the day of his marriage and that he would not be disappointed at his wedding gift. "What about the dowry?" the uncle asked.

"Well," replied Geoffrey, "it could be that there will not be a dowry."

"What! No dowry, well, my boy," replied the uncle, "I hope she is worth it," as visions of the girl being a local passed through his mind. Edward was not bothered by that fact, but no dowry to bring forward meant that he would have to work hard for his start and perhaps he thought that might not be such a bad thing for him.

"So be it," cried his uncle, "it has pleased me that we have had this discussion, man to man. I will admit I am glad that you are showing signs of maturity at last, Geoffrey."

Edward was genuinely excited and elated by his nephew's intentions and left him with a positive spring in his step. Geoffrey's feelings were surprisingly more buoyant as he laughingly congratulated himself that his move to mention marriage may have done him some good. Uncle Edward is a bigger fool than he thought to swallow that one, but his aunt she was another matter. He thought her an evil-minded bitch that would be up to him, which set him fearing that she might have to suffer the same consequences as her brother for him to soften the old boy up and get his hands on his money and lands. The more he thought of it, the more he considered murder to be the best course of action. With the Princess's spies here and there, he may just be taken unawares, then everything would be lost.

It would take him a full day to ride eastwards to Mardin and seek the help of his assassin contacts. There should be no problem as he had done business with them before; and paid them handsomely for it. Yet it seemed to wound him somewhat as the avaricious side of his character painfully thought of putting all that money out for a fruit that he had not yet tasted, but then it only made his dark, lecherous yearnings burn all the more hotter. His first concern would be to leisurely find a way to taste those forbidden expensive fruits that he had not received in return for the removal of old Walter. The thoughts of Katherine incited his passion, urging him to hatch a further plan to make good his visit, perhaps tomorrow evening; how he almost frothed at the mouth with insidious gusto.

The following day, he had made plans to stay at the castle all evening, making an excuse about being too drunk to ride home, and before riding from his own residence, he excitedly wrapped around his body sufficient rope to reach from the battlements to the Lady Katherine's window below. He had carefully calculated its required length and added a little more for security. Bulking his already large size even larger, and with the help of his cape, he hoped it would secrete his size and pass by the guard unnoticed. He rode the five uncomfortable miles to Eddessa trussed like a chicken, but knowing its cause he did not care a jot. His every moment was filled with the thoughts of the Lady Katherine urging him on and drawing out the waiting moments to his long awaited expected coupling.

Dusk was passing into the evening and the light faded quickly; his approach through the gate went unchallenged as most of the sentries knew him well, being a popular and colourful character with the men at arms. Safely through the castle gate without a question about his size, he rode onwards reaching the inner gate where he passed through easily, sharing a laughing remark with the inner sentry. His first need was to climb the staircase unseen and plant the rope ready for his midnight rendezvous, which he immediately set about doing. Taking the steps to the battlements three at a time, he reached the top unseen; sweating profusely, he leant back against the wall to catch his breath and looked about; there was only one sentry on duty, making his task that much easier. Keeping to the shadows, he passed along the parapet to a convenient place to where he was to scale down to Katherine's window. In this time of peace, guard duty was limited mainly to the outer walls only, hallways and including the lord's personal bodyguards. Remaining where he was out of sight of the sentry, he began unwinding the rope from his body; in his haste to remove it from his muscular form, he forgot just how long it was as he was almost becoming entangled in its unwinding. Thankfully the task was soon complete, Geoffrey was beginning to become impatient and ill tempered; next he had to find a place to hide it in a suitable place away from the sentry, who really would not be alert for much more of the evening. He watched the sentry walking away from his position before taking a chance to step out into the open and throwing one end of the rope over the wall, allowing it to dangle loosely out of sight. He tied the rope off securely around the crenellation of the battlements that were hidden in shadow before disappearing down the staircase to be with the other guests as if he had just arrived.

The main hall was full of visitors of importance; banners were strewn around the great room giving it an air of welcome reunion with old friends. They banqueted lavishly and, for once, Geoffrey's mind was on other things as he dined and listened attentively to what was going on around him. He was in good spirits all evening and his charade of drunkenness went by unnoticed by the others, accepting his conduct as nothing unusual from Geoffrey's obnoxious self. When the hour was right, he sloped up to his uncle Edward slurring his apologies for his having to leave, using the excuse that he felt that something he ate had not agreed with him; it made him want to vomit the whole mess up. His uncle, used to such behaviour, was angry and disappointed and expressed it so in the face he pulled. He said as much, expressing that when they had their talk the other day, he expected to see a change in him from then on. He sincerely hoped that the one that he intended to wed was not here this evening to witness the disgusting state that he had gotten himself into. "Really, Geoffrey, will you never learn?" Edward retorted, hoping that the censure would go some way to stem his degenerate ways. It was just like being scolded as a naughty child, but he did not care so long as he could be with her; he apologised profusely for his pathetic behaviour and shrugged it off as the last of his flings. He excused himself to his uncle, who could not be rid of him soon enough and watched as he reeled through the doorway bumping into a guest as he went by; his uncle could do no more than roll his eyes and look away in disbelief. No sooner was Geoffrey clear of the other visitors and staff, he was off running up to the battlements where he cautiously checked for the sentry before stepping out into the open moonlit battlement; there were tar lights burning every twenty feet, enabling him to detect if anyone was present. The guard must have been off duty earlier as he hoped, giving him plenty of time to make his preparations to scale down the wall to his Katherine. The wind blew cold and helped clear his head of the strong effects of the wine; clouds were in the sky, which he hoped would shield any shadow of his presence from guards that patrolled the outer wall.

Katherine's window was about fifteen feet below and he could easily see it from where he stood. There was ample rope; his plan was for him to sling the rope around himself and climb down to the window of Katrine's room and release it when he had entered the room and gather it in for the time when he left so that no one would be any the wiser to his engagement with her. Holding the rope in both hands, he stepped over the battlement wall and onto the face of the rough, stone wall where the wind buffeted him from side to side as he descended the sheer heights. All was well until he came to the window, which he discovered to be closed; he tried to prize it open with his fingertips but there was a fastener on it barring his planned entry. He cursed at her stupid actions at barring the window and remained swinging, suspended above the ground, cursing as he foolishly had to knock on the shutter to get her attention. The knocking seemed to last forever and his grip seemed to be failing as he swung freely backwards and forwards in his suspended limbo whilst waiting in anticipation for her to open the blasted window. Eventually she arrived and opened it out of curiosity, not expecting him to be swinging on a rope outside.

"What are you doing out there?" she cried stupidly. It was well that his cursing was lost, unheard in the blustery winds that blew past him and into her fine featured face. The force of the incoming rush of wind blew her fine straight hair upwards forcing it to fly wildly as she stood in the opening. There he was, clutching onto the rope agog; he could not help it as the wind whipped at her night shift drawing it back against her lean body causing her breasts to appear waiting for him, begging to be caressed. Only for the weakening of his arms hanging on to the rope, he would have remained there. Survival and the waiting outline of her curvaceous body spurred him on and in through the window, opening into the waiting warm room.

He was freezing cold and the muscles in his arms were agonisingly painful, but he was in; his leering eyes fell upon her like a hungry animal, drooling for the feast of her body. Stepping forwards to embrace her, she recognised the look in his eyes and she became fearful of his size and rough handling.

Katherine raised her arm to stop him, warning him that if she was to scream it would be the end for both of them and before he could utter a word of protest, she continued that she had no intention to breaking their agreement but she would not be taken roughly like a whore in a brothel. First, she insisted that he do something with that rope which was flailing around in the wind begging to catch somebody's attention and secondly, to close the window and keep the cold out of the room. "Then, and not before, you will warm your hands and body against the bright embers of the fire whilst I retire and wait for you to warm yourself before coming to my bed, but mind," she retorted disapprovingly, "think well before you handle me coarsely." Geoffrey's meek obedience was out of character; he stayed his appetite becoming completely obedient to her wishes, carrying out her sensible requests without complaint. There was enough flame left in the fire after he had attended to her demands for warming himself; looking about, he set about raising a flame by collecting all the small pieces of unburnt kindling from the side of the hearth, which when alight placed on the last of her wood to build up a lasting fire.

It was not long before he was out of his clothes and holding his naked body before the flames for warmth; he was anxious to be at the pleasure of Katherine's body but would not move from the fire until he was sure to deliver a warm contact before eagerly turning to the bed and her waiting form. She lay motionless, waiting as his shadow loomed near to her; against the dimness of the room the silhouette of his manhood was depicted in the flickering light of the fire. He slipped beneath the sheet that covered them both and with the touching of flesh, she warned him once more to be gentle, explaining that she had never endured this experience before. Geoffrey did not reply, but held her smooth voluptuous body in his strong arms before exploring her rising breast. It was a long ecstatic night for both as they lustfully enjoyed the pleasure of their bodies. Katherine was racked between pain and joy as she for the first time experienced the pleasure of his sex, longing for him to be remaining within her always.

Light was breaking and Geoffrey had much to lose if he were to wait and be caught; pulling her clinging arms away from him, he drew himself from the warmth of her bed and her demanding sensuous body. She thought that he had suddenly become cold by his interest to leave her as he feverishly donned his clothing and walked to the window.

The open window brought a draught with it and she quickly put on her shift to see him safely out into the open, whilst Geoffrey tied the rope to the sturdy table and jammed it across the open doorway. He was up on a chair as Katherine was begging him to stay, but this time it was Geoffrey's turn to berate her for acting so stupidly and allowing sex to blur her mind; he kissed her passionately before climbing out of the window and telling her that he would return tomorrow evening and this time she was to leave the window ajar so that she could hear his call; he then slid down the rope and watched whilst she pulled it up. She sat alone by the window feeling lonely after he had gone. Her time of confinement seemed long and lonely but this rough and ready knight had been her source of release; she had discovered a different side to him that she felt would become a happy experience she could accustom herself to. Her consolation for the rest of the day was her memory of the past night's passion and the sensations and feelings that filled her waiting body until his return.

Geoffrey was alive and feeling very potent, his feelings of the previous night would not leave him; she was nothing like the rest of the whores that he had served and bore no liking to her manner of seduction. She was as ready as he to couple and had it in her to satisfy him for the first time ever and it had dawned on him that together they could stand the test of time. His mind was made up; tomorrow night he would discuss his plan to rid her of the threat of his aunt Leanore and with her gone, his uncle Edward would give way easily. All day long he longed to be with her; his empty hall was noticeable for the first time and his chamber was untidy and all his servants suffered the raw end of his tongue for the general condition of the place.

For the first time, he viewed his home as a hovel; such was her influence after lying with her for a short time, what would she do for him after a year? His mind was filled with all manner of grasping ideas and ways of making his uncle totally reliant on him once that cow of a woman, his aunt was removed. His day was moody and long; all he wanted was to just slip in and visit her but it could never be that easy, his waiting was painfully endless and restless. How could this be that a female could bring such misery to him, the valiant hero of Eddessa? He was up and in his stables saddling his horse long before dawn broke and riding the countryside to clear his confused mind.

By dawn, he had come across his friend Norris, who had been out early to hunt with friends; loudly he was hailed and invited to join them when Geoffrey entered his camp, inviting him to join in the sport but first to sit and share breakfast with them. Geoffrey dismounted and walked over to join his friends, Norris apologised for not inviting him on the hunt the previous night. Excusing the need to apologise for his drunken condition, Norris continued; he knew it was his way of slipping off to his whore's quarters and before Geoffrey could utter a word of protest, Norris loudly declared for him not to deny it because he was always disappearing with the kitchen maids.

"By God, I swear if half the children in the castle don't sport your looks." Geoffrey could have easily killed him for that remark. How dare he call Katherine a whore? All he could do was feint a smile, rather than risk the chance of betraying himself. Geoffrey stood motionless and deep in thought; it dawned on him that they were not aware with whom he was seeing; deciding it was better to let all their stupid snide remarks directed at him go by over his head.

"By God, Geoffrey, you're morose today, what ails you?" scoffed Norris.

"I ate something last night that did not agree with me, that's why I am up so early this morning riding and now I feel worse for seeing you," he jested.

With a hearty slap on the back, Norris announced, "That's more like the Geoffrey I know, always jesting, not a serious bone in his body"

It was not what Geoffrey wanted to hear this morning and barked back, "Shut up, Norris, and hand me a cup and that wine." His friend filled the cup to overflowing and as it was handed to him, he drank it down before refilling the cup; picking up a meat bone, he began chewing heartily on it. In a way, he was grateful when he was called to the hunt, giving him a chance to discard the unwanted bone and to throw away the wine that he had no desire for. He mounted up with the others and went along with them as he had nothing better to do; it would, he thought pensively, keep him out of everybody's way for the best part of the morning or even the day.

Geoffrey was more open than others, as well as being offensively rude; that, it seemed, was a natural attribute of his character, but falseness of feelings was difficult for him to portray; he didn't mind lying, he did that all the time, but today somehow he was not overjoyed with the idea of spending the whole day pretending to be in idle converse with his noisy friend Norris and his loose acquaintances. Something in him wanted to shout out his love for Katherine; he was bored with hunting, wanting to be with her, so half way through the morning he retired from the hunt and found himself casually meandering along hidden pathways in the brush that eventually brought him onto the road leading to the castle of Eddessa. When he realised where he was, he grew irritable for his inadvertency and questioned his reason for going there so early; but Eddessa drew him in as if he was helplessly trapped in a whirlpool of his own desire and he could not shrug it off.

He entered the cool shadows of the main hall of the castle expecting it to be empty; a cry went out for him to present himself, it was his uncle Edward and he dutifully sauntered over like a petulant boy that was in for a scolding. He thought it wise to promote an apology for the previous night and then begged to sit, which he did without permission whilst his uncle continued to give him a dressing down over that very subject. It was as he expected, first his condition the previous night and then it was onto a different subject that made Geoffrey surprisingly take note; another maid had given birth to one of his bastards. Norris's words filled his ears as he sat denying everything and thinking how silly women were for lifting their skirts so readily. After he had said his peace, his uncle appealed to him pleading to change his ways. Taking on a more solemn tone, he addressed the weary and troubled younger man that was slumped sluggishly in his chair.

"I am speaking in the strictest confidence with what I am about to say to you," Geoffrey looked up at him and noticed his expression of reluctance to say anything further, he began hovering, finally gripping his shoulder drawing him upright,

"Look my boy, you must change. I cannot give you the responsibility to high office if you do not." Geoffrey's mouth opened in disbelief; at last, he thought.

"When?" asked Geoffrey, eager to learn more.

"Not so fast," his uncle broke in. "I have used you and your right arm to make certain gains and secure this county from our enemies. I am appreciative for that; when you marry and settle down and prove your worth, you will inherit my chair and eventually all that goes with it. You are going to be one of the richest men in the Levant." Geoffrey, for once, was silent; it was what he had deserved but found it hard to take in; when the news filtered into his brain, he asked his uncle what he would have to do to fulfil his role.

"We, your aunt and I, have chosen a bride for you that would bring you further wealth and standing and a union of two old families." He was about to protest the arrangement but stopped before he let out his secret; he had chosen the one he wanted and would have no other. His head was buzzing with conflicting thoughts, whilst his uncle's words passed over him as if distant and inaudible. "Who is she?" Geoffrey demanded, breaking into his uncles flowing proposition.

Taken unawares, Edward stammered before answering, "It is the daughter of Joscelin de Le Puiset."

"What!" Geoffrey exclaimed. "That little minx? No, uncle," he protested, "she prefers female company, I know for I have already tried," he decided to go no further because of the appalling look of disappointment on his uncle's face. "Uncle," he protested, "I have one in mind and I do believe she would give me many off springs, but I cannot just come out and reveal her name when I am, if you permit the usage, working on her."

In a bid to hang onto the proposal, Edward offered a chance that perhaps prudence and understanding could eventually endear them both to grow fond of each other, it was a suggestion put forward with his usual sagacity on delicate matters.

"Not for all the money in Eddessa," Geoffrey yelled crabbily.

"Well," prompted Edward, "it might come to that unless you have a solution and a better idea than your aunt." Geoffrey was deeply hurt by his aunt's interference in his personal matters and he said so, adding that when he mentioned the idea of marriage he stressed that he held his uncle to his confidence. That was embarrassing for Edward, but as he explained to Geoffrey, his marrying or thoughts of that nature, which came as an overwhelming surprise, found it too difficult to keep the news from his wife and his greatest confidant.

"Well," blubbed Geoffrey," and look what has happened, we are now at this difficult impasse because of it."

"All right," Edward yielded, unhappily and frustrated by his reaction; becoming annoyed, more so that it was his fault, he agreed that he would soothe the waters between his wife over the matter of refusal and not compel him to any other choice they make.

Edward turned to Geoffrey, "Be warned, do not take too long, as by broaching this subject, you realise that you have set yourself a difficult task in pleasing your aunt Leonore." Agreeing with his uncle, Geoffrey calmed Edward's impatience and he begged to be excused. He had to get away from his family and get some air; the upset of the suggested marriage had made him feel as though he was choking through lack of air from the strangle hold that his uncle was tempting him into.

Geoffrey made his way outside to the courtyard to sit quietly to develop a new strategy and to clear his mind. The day was hot with little of the freshness of air in and for further comfort, he sought to be in the shadow and slumped into a slouching position as his long body sat stretched out to the ground as if exhausted. This approach from his aunt was going to turn into a demand that he could not avail himself to, it was as plain as the nose on his face. He sat toying with his problem; if he were to admit that he was in love with Katherine, she would see old Walters's death as a collusion of the two to bring about his downfall and that could be very embarrassing; it would only be an admission and he would be jailed, what could he do? With a spark of an idea, he decided that tomorrow he will ride to Mardin and make with his contact a contract to remove that tinkering cow of a woman from his life once and for all; as for his uncle, he would be easy to deal with later. The thought of his proposed deed brought other matters to mind, such as the night he was visited by the Papal envoy, causing him to wonder how he would fare in their eyes. If it was true that they wanted him to control Eddessa, then they would have to deal directly with me; the thought of that outcome made Geoffrey feel quite important. He lay in total recline viewing the sky, his head dropped backwards bringing the castle walls looming into view, turning his mind to other events. He longed for nightfall and its ensuing darkness, which would spread its cloak of invisibility across him as he scaled the wall to be with his waiting lover.

Images of Katherine ran through his mind like ripples on serene water tickling his imaginative thoughts; he smiled a secret smile of a lover knowing that no one else knew their cherished secret. Those thoughts made him impatient; he rose to his feet to escape the boredom of inactivity and ambled around the grounds before coming to a halt were he had climbed down the sheer wall face on the early morning of yesterday and stood boldly across from her window in the hope that she may see him. Katherine did see him but she was not about to play the same dangerous game as he, she longed to call down to him but to do such a foolish thing may incur her premature demise; since the previous evening, she had found much to live for. The day seemed to drag and it was a relief to watch the sun go down when she opened her window in anticipation for Geoffrey's signal to drop the rope to give him entry and to rekindle the flame of life that was barely burning in her lonely heart.

When Geoffrey eventually arrived, he did so noisily, gasping with shortened breath and complaining about the energy he had expended from the rigorous climb up to the window. She ran to his waiting arms and caressed him tightly, nuzzling her soft cheeks into the roughness of his cool unshaven neck as she moaned about his absence; she had missed him and to remind him, she drew him closer towards the waiting bed. Their passions instantly flared like a kindled flame that gave ecstatic life into a long and joyous evening whilst entangled in their act of loving courtship. Later, he put it to her if she would marry another, trying to be coy and clever as he sounded out what her latent intentions could be. To his surprise, her reply insisted that he was to look no further for anyone to share his bed, as they were now joined forever; she would stop at nothing to hold him obediently at her side. He was touched with her honesty and for once in his chaotic life, found a partner who was his equal; and as he lay besides her, his thoughts wandered into deeper and darker events that were on his mind regarding his aunt Leanore.

Katherine being the subject of her vengeance, she offered little resistance to Geoffrey's intended plot, but Katherine warned him that his aunt was no fool and to take the greatest care. The next morning, Geoffrey had left the castle well before sunrise and was riding hard for Mardin. It was his intention to attempt the round trip before night fall that day so as not to raise any suspicion should he be sent for only to find that he was not there to offer a reply.

It was early hours of the following morning when Geoffrey returned. It was noted, but there was little reason to wonder where he had been as it was not unusual for him to have been consorting with a woman in Eddessa. Except for the fact that his horse was sweating from his hard ride, so to avoid gossip he walked the horse into the stables and brushed him down and covered him to make it appear normal.

At his meeting with the assassin contact, he had stressed that it was necessary to move quickly as time and events were not in his favour; making his way to his bed chamber he could think of little else.

Two mornings later, the princess Leanore was being assisted in her dressing, as was her usual habit at that time of the early morning. It was unusual that her handmaid of many years who had not missed a day in her employment thus far had failed to be present this morning. Instead of being at her side, there was a replacement, a slightly over attentive, middle aged woman whose features were expressionless and walked with a limp. The princess was taken by her ability as she soothingly combed the princess's long, fine burnished strands of her hair, following up each brushing action with a gentle touching of her head with her slender fingers. It delivered sensuous feelings within and it pleased the princess to allow her to continue. The woman was polite and well-spoken and was quick to respond whenever she thought the princess may have been testing her as she judged her abilities; she wore an especially fetching fragrance that the princess could not help but admire; the attentive maid weaved and bobbed about around her, almost drowning the princess with the power of her fragrance. She could not help but feel envious at the strength and purity of its vapours, which far superseded anything that she possessed herself; it raised the princess's curiosity. It also aroused a certain suspicion and envy as to how a handmaid could afford such an exotic fragrance having been intoxicated by its alluring perfume; casually, the princess asked how she came by it.

"Come by it my lady, no," she smiled, explaining that she had not come by it; she had been helping in its manufacture since she was a little child in her father's business.

"That is amazing," replied the inquisitive princess smiling, continuing her inquiry asking all manner of questions about its manufacture. The maid, with her lure, had by this time entrapped the princess's curiosity. With great craft, she teased the princess with the need for wanting it, telling her all manner of lies about its secret properties. When the maid had finished her boastful monologue, surprisingly, she offered the princess a gift of it to sample. Reaching down into a secret pocket within her dress, she produced a miniature phial and like a sly jackal offered it on her in her outstretched hand. At first, the princess was of a mind to snatch it from her outstretched open hand; trying hard to show restraint, the maid watched her detecting the hesitance, but there was an unwary glow in the covetous eyes of the princess as the handmaid urged the princess on that she may freely take it without the need to offer any reward in return. The soft, pale skin on the hand of the princess reached out her rapacious fingers and picked up the phial. She studied it, unsure of its way of opening it until the handmaid took it from her. The princess's face showed disappointment like a child at its temporary loss of something of value; with reassurance in her face and eyes that reflected honesty, the crafty maid assured her princess that she would endeavour to open it for her; bringing back the smile to the disappointed face. The head of the container was turned screw-like and she held the open phial at length close to the princess's nose.

"Take in its seductive and pleasurable vapours," she urged. The princess inhaled deeply as she took in the sweet noxious vapours of the balmy fragrance, uttering sounds of exquisite delight from its intoxicating bouquet. Its enchanting fragrance drifted deep into her lungs filling her senses and making her feel light-headed and giddy as she was urged to take in each greedy perfunctory breath. The princess's aimless mumblings secured the maids success; a lethargy overcame her, slumping forwards into a helpless heap onto the assassin's lap unconscious from the perfumes mysterious effect. The limp body was dragged over to the bed were the woman struggled to sit her victim upright before attending to matters of dress and completing the brushing of her hair. From inside her jacket, she produced another phial which she opened and placed to one side, then fitting what appeared no more than a harmless thimble on her finger she dipped it into the phial then applied it to the veins on her neck holding it there momentarily. Three times she repeated this process before replacing all the phials into her pockets and tidying up any traces of disturbance before cautiously leaving the chamber.

Later that morning, the absence of the princess caused concern, provoking those that normally attended on her to enquire of her general health. In due course, concerns grew for her attendance; a lady in waiting was sent to her chamber to seek the reason for depriving her friends and courtiers of her presence. There was a rush of people as the news went about in search of Edward. When the knowledge was broken to him, he became distraught and unwell with the news of his loss being announced. For a day or more he locked himself into his wife's room mourning her, where she sat casually on the bed as the female assassin had left her, whilst Geoffrey and Katherine cavorted in enthusiastic euphoria of sexual abandon free of the only threat for their prolonged relationship.

During the day, Geoffrey was most attentive to the wellbeing of his uncle, aiding him in all manner of chores and proving to be invaluable to the running of the everyday business of Eddessa. This was a new experience for Geoffrey, he was in his element in his new role; in his discovery of his uncle's lordship, he was fascinated with the careful considerations his uncle must have balanced to achieve this standard of business that passed through his territory. The lengths Edward went to achieve the balance of the faiths to live in harmony throughout the province was something that Geoffrey had overlooked. Whilst he would have tackled some problems with sword in hand, he began to realise that government was a little more complicated than he had at first imagined. Peace and unity had always been in the forefront of Edwards's aims of ruling, amazed at the time that he must have spent in promoting laws and rights of all that encompassed his county. Tired and lost in a crashing world, Edward grew to lean on Geoffrey in the short period of time of Leanore's passing. Geoffrey had noticed a demise in Edward's stature; no longer was he so confident in his judgements nor was he quick to defend those that were unable to stand up to others who were guilty of taking advantage of the noticeable weakness now emanating from the base of power.

Even Geoffrey had grown a little careless as he strolled to Katherine's quarters and without showing himself until dawn. Soon tongues began to wag; rumour circulated which eventually reached Edward's ears of the disappointing news of his nephew's action; depressed and disillusioned he sent for Geoffrey. Before his uncle in the great hall, Geoffrey was forced to give an account for his visits to Lady Katherine. Geoffrey lied very convincingly deluding Edward, who in his weakness of the loss of his Eleanore had found it difficult to concentrate on anything much of importance. Edward had become half a man, who had lost his sharpness of mind since that fateful day of his beloved wife's demise; she would have easily proved Geoffrey the liar that he was and Geoffrey knew it. Instead of a stern warning to cease his visits, he asked Geoffrey to curb his manners and show respect to his dead aunt's memory. Geoffrey could have laughed in his uncle's drawn, sad face, but he had too much to lose and he was not yet ready to snatch from his uncle what he considered rightfully his, earned by his exhaustive efforts of the past.

It was not long before Katherine's name was raised again; the spies that had been employed by the princess had dutifully reported to Edward, who, needing to believe their words, furiously marched with an armed guard to her chambers to confront them both. Approaching the door, he could hear the raised voices of their laughing; angered by Geoffrey's decision to go back on his word and curb his behaviour, Edward forced the door and marched in to be confronted by two naked bodies at the height of their frolic. The high spirits sank at the sight of Edward, who immediately ordered Geoffrey to leave the castle without argument; his eyes settled on Katherine with disgust, not from her actions but from the memory of his late wife's suspicions that he cared not to listen to. When her anger was provoked by her brother's death, her words of accusation were frowned upon. Katherine shrunk back covering her nakedness with guilt and shame; he ordered the guards to escort her to other quarters where she may cogitate on her shortcomings for come the morrow she will have many questions to answer.

Geoffrey's mind raced with ruinous thoughts of the impending consequences of his being found out; in his panic he thought of running. It would solve nothing; he knew that in his heart he would eventually have to answer either to his father or his uncle. He prepared himself for the confrontation that awaited him. Aware that to save his own neck, his only way out would be to lie about his relationship with Katherine. There was no word from his uncle for days, which relaxed Geoffrey into a state of false security, making him feel safe and free, but he needed to know what information had spilt from Katherine's tongue as he had visions of her being torturously stretched on the rack. Unknown to him, she was still imprisoned in the depths of Edward's dungeon and undergoing a tremendous battle in her nervous state of the terror that she anticipated.

From the edges of the county, news arrived of an army on the march, which bore no rational sense to Edward; he was at peace with his neighbours and had been for some time. He knew no reason to the contrary to promote any reasons why an army should move against them at this time. Nevertheless, he dispatched riders to verify the sightings and in turn ordered all knights and fighting men in the surrounding areas to report with their families to the castle at Eddessa. The scouts never returned, and when the approaching army was sighted, it came from the northeast after travelling from its destination in the south. There was no time to calculate its strength, but from the signs of the endless horde it was by all means a mighty force. What knights drifted in were few; the oncoming army's plan to sever all links to the surrounding villagers had lost no time fulfilling their orders. Eddessa stood alone, the usual stream of people that would have raised the alarm never appeared. Missing also was their added livestock; usually it was driven into the castle in times of siege. The enemy had used initiative and guile on this occasion, pointing to its purposeful intent.

Edward stood on the battlements of the great fortress; he feared that this time there was a difference. He dithered as what to do; he had no plan and stood alone. For the time being, he was safe behind the walls of this great castle. Aware that he was unprepared for siege or able to lead his small army of knights out to meet the advancing army, his time of fighting sieges was passed and he knew it. Hollow words resonated in his head; if only he was a younger man he would know what to do; yet his world was dark and he was balancing on its edge, his troubled mind fragile. Ideas flashed through his experienced aging mind, finally settling on the idea that perhaps Geoffrey could once again do some good for the name of his family and vindicate himself from the slur and disbelief that hung over him.

Geoffrey answered the call and presented himself as cocky as ever, giving his uncle assurances that with the right men under his command, he believed that the day was as good as won; they had faced these odds before, he told his uncle fearlessly. Edward was uncertain, but the confidence and past record of his young nephew swayed him to believe otherwise. Geoffrey's rashness, coupled with his uncle's poor judgement regarding the safeguarding of Eddessa, was chancing everything on the word of a liar and fool; the good life was at a halt, being punctuated by their imminent doom and the sealing of their bloody fate; the army that pursued them had no intentions to show mercy.

When Geoffrey rode out from the fort, taking the best of men with him, he looked a splendid sight but before the sun had climbed to its height not one of those defiant souls were left standing. Within two days, the stronghold that had withstood a dozen attacks previously did not last long, thanks to the foolhardiness of Geoffrey's tongue that convinced his uncle to confront the enemy. If history was to tell its own tale, it probably would say that a long drawn out siege may have had a different outcome in the shape of events in the Holy Land. Geoffrey's foolhardy attempt to win the day was like a starving man receiving a punch to the solar plexus, causing the whole defensive front of a well-fortified position to collapse to the might of the oncoming enemy. Filled with the taste of victory, the attacking hoard scaled the walls like mad ants on a honeycomb and in two days they had taken their revenge on the Christians, and with Eddessa being no more, the Muslim Hoard had begun to slowly smash each stronghold that stood before them.

It was a bloody wind that blew across the land and it lusted for vengeance after such an oppressive history it had endured under the rule of the Franj and their kind. Now it was their turn, and they were not in any mood to take prisoners for ransom as they had done so in the past; theirs was a last chance battle to rid the lands of the faithful, of the intruding, Christian pigs. It was a united front with all the other Muslim families sending out a decisive message to any other outside influences whose trespassing and colonising eyes may be turned towards the lands of the east, and that the fertile valleys that were once the home of the sacred prophet himself, were not for the taking, nor would they tolerate or subjugate themselves to any other foreign prophets alongside their own. The land was destined to a conflagration, the like that was never witnessed before; as the bloodlust of the avenging army grew, sweeping itself across the land like an unrepentant wind, causing all before it to suffer its dreadful crushing force as it victoriously grew in its intensity. It refused to cease until the shores of the eastern Mediterranean were free of its Christian yoke.

Mas'yaf

A little past midday, the band of black robed hashashins neared their final destination; the great natural rock walled edifice of their master's abode manifested its haunting image of foreboding. To Hassan and the entire group, it was their place of safe refuge in that area, and once within the walls of the high craggy rocks that towered skywards, those within were certain of their advantage over any ensuing hostiles.

Great black shadows spread across the rough tracks that meandered along the edges of the towering precipices, cloaking the riders' obvious presence in an intimidating shadowy darkness. The walls of the fortress being the mountain itself made it all the more difficult for advancing armies to overcome it. It was not unlike many a crusader castle where entry to its inner walls had to be gained through singular entrance tunnels which were guarded by sinister murder holes along its entire length.

Being built into the rock face, it rose up from a base deep below the rocky hills a hundred feet or more skywards; welcoming them like a great protective shroud.

This was Robert's closest view of the stronghold; he admired the choice of site, and feared it; being very carefully chosen he knew that it was almost impregnable. Along the canyon were sentinels ready to raise an alarm should there be unwelcome visitors; as for the entrance and its approach, there were no guards, but there was at its end a great heavy port-cullis that closed off the tunnel to trap any advancing soldiers where they stood to be cut down from those protected from above behind the cover of the murder holes. Seeing this depressed Robert's willingness of any attempt to escape, for it seemed an idea that was almost impossible. Robert's troubled mind was filled with Hassan's future plans for him; he had doubts of how in God's name he was to be strong enough to resist the mad man within, and how he would withstand his torturous stay until such a time for his believed escape.

They entered the keep at the base of the mountain beyond the port-cullis along further dark tunnels that were illuminated with tar-doused lit torches fixed on wall brackets that gave off a smoking black flame that filled the air in places with an unusual smell.

Robert endured the pain of the bonds that pulled him along like a mule, having no choice but to follow and was exhausted by the walk. Realising he had entered the point from which there was no return, Robert's heartbeat dropped to its lowest ebb. He viewed it for the first time with pained crushed hopes; the true difficulty of his task lay before him, for any chance of escape was all in his imagination. Beyond a small closed courtyard, the group entered a series of tunnels, where at varying levels the main group of men departed by other passages.

Alone with the woman and Kasim, he was pulled along like an unwilling dog, too tired and too weak to resist. A flight of roughly hewn stairs appeared; there they stopped for a reason that he knew not; the woman left for a moment and shortly reappeared before proceeding to climb upwards.

Up and up the stairs spiralled making the climb seem endless; Robert's legs felt as though they didn't belong to him; he had tried to count the steps to divert his attention from the climb but his weariness made him lose count with only his determination carrying onwards. He could not show weakness here, for to fall would have brought joy to the giant's heart to purposely drag him for what was left of the rest of the way. At last, light suddenly shone brightly, almost dazzling his eyes as they approached an opening that served as a lookout point; it was situated near what he believed was the top of the staircase, its spacious window looking down the length of the ravine and across the landscape, no advancing army or even a lone rider could avoid being seen in their approach. Two guards were in place; only a small wall of rock lay between him and infinity; his spirit was diminishing, life, he feared, held only the terrors of the madman and for a moment he chanced the thought if he could face death by jumping into the sunlit space where he would avoid that which awaited him. By the time he thought on his fate, he was being pulled onwards passing that point which offered freedom from further pain, alas, even that was denied him. This section of the staircase was a stroke of genius of the designer's mind; no one could reach the upper level, only by way of this exposed section. It was boldly carved out of the cliff face making it completely exposed to a sheer drop; outside, a balcony that appeared to travel along the ravine, where he believed other balconies also projected for the times of siege; there, archers guarding the way made it impossible for any enemy to advance further without heavy fatalities.

Most steps he half climbed, others, he unfortunately was drawn stumbling along; when that happened it caused a searing pain to his wrists, his legs were only working on reflex and his determination to reveal he was of stronger stock than the bullying Kasim who must have been surprised at the knights resistance to reach this far. His weary legs almost cramped under the strain of the arduous upward rise. There was no need for guards, for escape from this point was, it seemed, impossible; hopelessly, he was towed along to his fated audience. In his resolve to continue Robert did not stop but avidly took in all that was around him like a caged cat, should he ever at some time make his break, the knowledge at least may be useful. He needed rest; his feet were again bloody and swelling, he felt the pressure in his boots. Sooner or later, he expected, even longed, to be in a cell, only then he believed peace would come upon him, and his limbs could recover.

He was weary and getting worse and he knew that he was helpless to flee, even if he were able it would only make life more difficult for him.

Eventually, they came to the summit of the wide, winding staircase, where it opened out into a further great cavern; in this place, Robert suddenly fell in awe of what his eyes beheld. They had arrived; the rough-hewn work of the passageways that had taken slaves years to create had led to an unbelievable palatial setting. The chamber they had entered into was filled with such light that it dazzled, which left Robert shading his eyes whilst his open-mouthed expression at its brightness of splendour awed him. His vision momentarily blurred with the light caused his eyes to ache; instinctively, to rest them, he looked downwards into a deep dense black marbled floor, its highly polished surface almost made him feel he was in water and his reflected image did little to boost his ego. Slowly raising his head, he was overcome at the beauty around him; in the splendour of his place of enclosure, somewhere here was his prison, yet he did not expect his place of rest to match this. His eyes followed a path upwards along the marbled walls that rose within the chamber to the domed ceiling. Multi coloured veined marbles, with cleverly positioned hollowed secret shafts allowed sunlight to burst into the great chamber, causing the light to seek out the tightest of corners to further illuminate the great hall. The colour arrangement created images of confused designs as the sunlight climaxed their flowing patterns of strata that had been cut by the hundreds of skilled craftsmen. The effects were of a cascading river of colour that fell sharply into the floor's blackness, swallowing up all the images around and above and yet held them in its reflection through time. He was aghast at its intense beauty, finding the sight before him incredible and unbelieving; how could such beauty exude from the imagination of such a murderous character that was no more than a bandit priest? The room was also bedecked by multifarious silks, rugs and scatter cushions lying about the central position of the floor where he supposed the guests of Hassan ate their fill before having to discharge some form of service in payment for the hospitality extended to them.

Robert was so taken by his inquisitiveness; his disbelieving and marvelling eyes travelled everywhere taking in the surroundings; such were his instincts of admiration, his inquisitive eyes were drawn towards open doors. Where beyond he witnessed verdant lush gardens; bewildered by sight of the oasis beyond the doors, he could not take in how this could be the same place he viewed from below. His eyes were everywhere, partly in viewing his surroundings and partly for assessing his captors. There was no doubt that his host was a man of culture and taste, learned and having a certain penchant for comfort, beauty and good living. They stood waiting for their master to eventually enter to speak with them, but for Robert his curiosity urged him to explore further, a natural reaction perhaps, but not for a prisoner as he was soon to find out; not only was he forcibly restrained, but struck with a cudgel rendering him unconscious. When he came to, his efforts to raise himself from the marbled floor were prevented by the weight of a heavy foot pushing against his head; his face seemed to be sucked into the dense reflection of the black marbled floor ever closer into his own reflection, and guessing whose foot it was, he couldn't help but wonder when it was going to release its downward pressure. A strong hand suddenly gripped his nape forcing him like a dog to move in unison wherever the grasping grip chose to move him. With his consciousness returning from the pain of his tormentor, his throbbing head reeled from the earlier blow that had rendered him numb, and between the pulsating throb, a distant voice could be heard. He began to recognise the sound of Kasim's voice and longed for a sword for a chance to teach this bully a lesson. His head hurt and did not feel that it was a part of him, though his mind gradually became lucid, regaining his senses and the situation at hand.

Through the chaos that raged around him, strains of another voice could be heard.

"This is the man that caused you so much trouble." The voice that spoke was high pitched and older; it struck Robert that whoever it was, the speaker seemed to measure his words as if he wanted him to understand fully the conversation about him.

"Remarkable," the voice continued, "He does not look such a threat." The speaker obviously studied him, although Robert was helpless.

Kasim was ordered to bring his prisoner closer to allow Hassan to view Robert more closely. Robert's head convulsed as the Kasim's rigid grip enclosed his neck; Christ, his grip was strong like iron, causing Robert to wince as he was painfully and forcefully moved forwards again. To ease the excruciating pain, Robert fought to turn his contorted face sideways to ease the pressure of a grip that restricted what little movement he had. Kasim's sadistic streak must have heightened; he knew that he was hurting his prisoner, relishing every moment he held control. He showed his mastery by squeezing ever tighter in its effort to force him forwards to the base of the dais and to the foot where the aged man sat.

Hassan sat before him on a great carved high backed chair more suitably likened to a throne, clothed in black with a long fluffy curly beard, as white as any mountain snow Robert had seen. Hassan suddenly snapped at Kasim, "Release him." He could plainly see Kasim's pleasure. "Do not treat my orders as an excuse to gain your own means of pleasure, or you will find yourself on the wrong side of my will, do you understand?" Kasim tried to mutter an excuse but the master was having none of it. "You have displeased me enough with your defiance of my orders and that I will not tolerate," Hassan growled, "I will deal with you later." Kasim grew almost childlike, terrified at what Hassan could so easily subject him to.

Robert peered upwards to view his captor, his neck hurt as he straightened his neck, the ageing Hassan smiled in return in a condescending manner. Almost frail and gentle looking, the voice almost sounded welcoming and with a warm tone; the elderly man bent forwards to observe Robert's pained face.

"You have caused our guest much discomfort. I fear he will get the wrong impression of our show of hospitality." Hassan spoke gently and slowly in soothing tones so that Robert could understand him, but he was not taken in by the gentle sound of the resonant tones. "We have met before." he said surprised. "Then, you showed intelligence, but now I see you are no different than all the others of your kind. Here you are at my feet, look at you, you look more like a savage. Well, I can't allow an intelligent man such an injustice. Perhaps," he said mockingly, "when we have one of our talks you will be suitably attired and refreshed."

He had his fill of this man and his deeds; he had witnessed harsh and brutal events by his hashashin, such as the treatment meted out to his friends, and now he was having to suffer his mockery.

When the shadow of Hassan's powerful hand fell across the unfortunates to be named as an enemy, it was not simply destiny that was visiting, but sheer terror at its utmost.

Robert felt that he was experiencing such treatment; a nod from Hassan and he was dragged back and made to be seated in a sitting position below the dais; he found it difficult to remove his inquisitive gaze from his host. Hassan's returning stare from his dark beady eyes was terrifying to the point of making Robert feel unclean and unsafe. Although Robert was defiant, his bravado was only a bluff and not a very good one; he felt fearful of this gentle-looking man whose frail hands twiddled with his worry beads whilst he spoke; whilst his examining stare was unending, burning into his prisoner's very soul. Hassan began to speak from his small tight mouth; it presented itself as a small orifice from within the fluffy white beard shrouding his face. Icy shivers filled Robert's body, hi gaze fixed on the speaker's words that held no encouragement for his future sojourn within these very walls.

"I see by your stare that you are a curious man, and I suspect a very dangerous one," coldness now crept into his tone yet his demeanour remained cool.

"I do not like men such as yourself, you cause me to worry, therefore I will not waste my time with you. But be warned, Christian, I will snuff out your miserable life like I would extinguish the flame of a candle should you give me a good enough reason." His words were purposely filled with threatening intent, and they flowed from him calmly; there was no doubt that he meant every word. Then the shape of the bearded mat of hair on his face changed into what looked like a smirk, "I am sure you will have much to tell me when we speak tomorrow after you are rested."

"Take him away," he said demonstrating the tiredness of Robert's company, with a nonchalant gesture of the hand as if swatting a fly. Robert felt the tight grip of Kasim's hand draw him away from his master. "Kasim," came the call from Hassan, "mark this man and I swear as Allah is my judge, you will change places with him tomorrow. Think well on my words and report back to me when you have delivered him to his place of keeping."

From the palatial court of Hassan, Robert was taken into a darkened cavernous quarter of the stronghold, away from the splendour of Hassan's chamber where the walls filled a man's mind with awe; they were back into areas of crudely worked rock walls. During his passage to what was to be his last refuge, Kasim taunted him with the detailed events of what was waiting for him on the morrow; how, and when his master would turn his strength of will into sand.

"I hope you're there too so I can tell him how easy it was for me to take the woman while you were away playing with the whores in Lattakia." With those remarks, Kasim stopped and almost felled Robert. Kasim's eyes were filled with rage and his fist was almost crashing down on Robert, his rage had crumpled his control. Robert laughed in a goading manner urging his torment into open provocation.

"Remember tomorrow," he spat back, and Kasim ceased immediately, remembering his master's words.

He was pushed forcefully onwards along darkened rough stone corridors illuminated by flickering torches in iron brackets and past open heavy wooden doors towards where he expected the cells were placed, wondering which one he would he eventually arrive at as being the one reserved for him. There was no comfort waiting for him; when they finally halted it was in a dark and dank place. Water dripped from the permeable stone ceiling, promising nought but a night of broken sleep from the monotonous and agonising sounds of seeping water dripping from the ceiling into the pools that lay on the floor. An iron door was opened and Robert was forcefully thrust into the darkness ahead of him and before he was able to turn around, the squealing door slammed hard against its metal keeper and the sound of the turning of a metallic locking device penned him securely into the abysmal cell from which he felt there was no escape. Cast into the darkness on all fours, Kasim laughed at Robert's misfortune, his face twisted into a scowl, you have wanted water during your journey here and now you can drink your fill from the cistern above you. Kasim walked away, the sound of his laughter echoing in Robert's ears. It must have been the have been the most uncomfortable place in the fortress. Robert was soaked from the wetness of the pools of water that he had landed in; dripping and exhausted he fought against fear of the trial that awaited him on the morrow. The salve that had been smeared on the previously tightened bonds that had held his bloodied wrists for so long had begun to slacken a little since he had been released from the rider's constant tugging at his restraints. A little more effort and determination might give him enough room to slide his hands through the greasy loops. Robert was tired and desperate and fought against his fatigue; he would not give in to the idea that Hassan could have him turned into a zombie.

Groping in the darkness for something that represented a sharpened edge of prominent stone, he frantically searched for anything which he may chafe the bonds that held him. His disappointment was desperately disheartening when none were to be found. Alas, his jailor had thought of everything, the cell that contained him had been hewn from solid rock, and the walls dressed correctly so that such an event to find an aid of escape would never be possible. In desperation and one final act of defiance, he screamed into the darkness cursing his captor. Wet and tired with no one to resist his gestures that were hopeless; though it was so, it was his only act of contempt for his jailer. The shouting of his refusal to co-operate before he faced the next day's trial sapped his strength; dejected, he fell against the cold, iron gate that imprisoned him, his will to further react was slowly waning. His hands slowly slid down the cold metal bars turning the dewy droplets of condensation that clung to the cold iron door to wet streaks; forming minute rivulets running down onto his sleeve as he sank lower. Futility stifled him as his tired knees slid slowly to the sodden floor. At that position, kneeling in despair on the floor, he had finally reached his nadir.

It was unlike Robert to suffer any form of self-inflicted misery; he was tired and the lack of ideas to escape became futile; convinced that all was lost, his mind began to weaken. Beaten by the hopelessness of his situation, unexpectedly he jumped as his hand was pricked and bloodied on the sharpness of a barb of metal, immediately sending his mind and heart racing, this must be his opportunity to free himself from his bonds. Avidly, for some time, he worked the leather thongs that bound him against the small barb until he was able to slowly tear through to achieve his freedom.

During the period of Robert's confinement, it was essential that Hassan's jailer check on the prisoners from time to time; this was something Robert had depended on and waited for. As soon as he heard his presence in the corridor, Robert moved into the shadows of his cell and feigned a vomiting fit. The jailer paused outside Robert's cell and jeered at him, not expecting to hear anything other than perhaps a prayer from a desperate man, he listened to the noises of illness that emanated from out of the darkness.

The jesting and laughter from the mocking jailer began to change to concern as he watched the retching body of his charge fall lifeless. It was more than his life was worth should a prisoner expire whilst in the cells before the master had the opportunity to enjoy the interrogation of its occupant. For such carelessness he might be punished; many times he had watched Hassan at work; he called it scientific research. Allowing a lapse of vigilance was inexcusable, and for his denial of his pleasure, Hassan may turn his attention to the jailer, for he was not a forgiving man.

Robert's act of sickness worked; he listened to the jangle of the keys as the jailer fumbled to his belt to obtain the right key that would unlock the gate that threatened his liberty. A torch and a club were held at the ready before the jailor proceeded towards the hulk doubled up on the sodden floor of the cell. At the moment the guard bent over Robert to turn him, he was furiously struck with the hardened fist of the fighting man, knocking the jailor senseless back against the wall of the cell. Robert wasted no time and was quickly up on his feet. He bludgeoned the guard with his own club and once more with his avenging fist, rendering the guard completely senseless. Stripping the man of his dry tunic and shirt, he took the knife that was held in his waistband and tucked it into his own; then locking the cell door behind him so that the jailor could not raise the alarm, he made his way as quickly as he could up to the end of the corridor where the gaoler had been stationed. He looked around and spied food on a table that had likely been the jailer's sustenance for the day; crumbs and a crust with figs. Meagre though it was, he decided to eat it knowing that he could never tell when he was next going to eat. Attacking the food, he stuffed it into his mouth greedily and failed to chew because of his mouth's fullness, having to remove most of its mass to swallow. He drank water from a wooden cup and steadied his greed realising that it would be consumed quicker if he was to take time and be seated. His watchful eyes darted everywhere and his ears where alert to every sound. He realised that the place where he now sat was well out of earshot should any sound be emitted, and not a place where others would congregate in their spare time. Still tired and pained but nourished by the gaoler's meal, he was at least free of his captor. Freedom gave his tired body a new impetus and he made for the stone staircase to where he guessed Hassan's chamber would be. Eagerly, he ascended the stone steps to be sharply reminded that he had walked for some miles without rest; he may have eaten and felt better for it, but the strain of his aching legs needed more time to restore the energy that he had lost to his aching muscles. The pain told him that he would not be travelling far that night, but this was his only chance and knew that he would need to draw on extra reserves of energy if he were going to succeed. That was the problem to him now, how to get off and away from this mountain; he had to try even if it meant that it would cost him his life doing so. The passageways did not look familiar, but he guessed he must be right; he recalled the strange shaped brackets with the bright burning torches and the side tunnels off the one he was in were dimly lit; another thing, the ground was increasing its slope, assuring him that he was going the right way.

Robert's cold, shivering body gradually became warmer as he moved further away from the darkened and wet cavern that had threatened his liberty for all time. Tired and scared by the thoughts of any prolonged stay, he progressed trying to restrain such thoughts from entering his head. The corridor remained travelling upwards and there were steps he remembered, and the tunnels appeared drier and the air somehow sweeter; it gave him heart believing it was the direction he sought. His nervous tension dismissed; tiredness that had once dogged him gave way to a heightening of his mind that grew alert in the anticipation of his venture into renewed danger and every fibre of his tired body bristled in preparation for action. He had reached the stairs where he was almost pushed down and struck by Kasim earlier; it's a pity, he thought and hoped that he might not be around to witness Kasim take his place. He knew that he had to be ready for action; his hand moved towards the dagger that he had taken from the jailer. Proceeding onwards, he saw the dimly-lit corridors illuminated by brighter flaming tarred reed lights; he recalled them as he left the chamber on his way to the cell; now it was as if they were beckoning him onwards, towards the moment sooner or later where some form of confrontation was to grow. Fortunately, there were no guards to be seen; his progress went unhindered through any of the junctions in the corridors, then it struck him; in this establishment there was no need for such a posting; nobody had ever achieved outsmarting the Old Man of the Mountain's deputy, not yet. He sensed that he was nearing his objective; Hassan. There was no doubt in his mind that he was going to kill him if he refused to impart the whereabouts of Aldo; if not, it would be better to rid of his threat than being turned into a zombie for Hassan's purposes.

There was light up ahead and it was not long before the sound of muted voices drifted on the still air of the passages as he neared its end. His approach to what he gathered must have been the main hall brought with it louder sounds of what he believed were raised voices; somebody, he gathered, was not as popular as they ought to be. Drawn closer towards the sound of the rising voices, Robert found himself positioned in the cover of the chamber's archway at the opposite end of the great magnificent marbled room that he had first been brought to when he entered this place.

The voices that were raised were those of Kasim and the female, unusual as it seemed there was a heated argument in progress, which the eavesdropper could hardly believe he was listening to, regarding, of all people, Aldo. Robert's ears pricked up, careful not to let anything escape him, this was most likely to be an informative squabble. The black-hearted Kasim was on the defensive as the woman was giving her report; Kasim sat back chortling, breaking in with heated words that the task should have been allotted to him. Hassan rebuked Kasim for leaving his post, allowing the girl to be kidnapped. It surprised Robert to see how weak Kasim was when the Master spoke and aggressive when remarks flowed between him and the woman, who tried hard to deriding her ability and authority, at the same time stating that he would have done things differently had he been in charge. The female sounded to be able to fight her own case, showing no fear of the bullying giant Kasim, who was unable to remain cool and thoughtful. His temper was getting the better of him into what was developing into a very heated argument.

Kasim was being made to look a fool; his failure to be dominant betrayed any authority he may have believed he had. He was physically moving towards the female in a threatening stance but she displayed nothing but coolness in the face of adversity. Acting as though he had had enough, Kasim was close to exploding into violence; Robert had witnessed that lack of control earlier in the passageways. When the ageing Hassan intervened, he dismissed Kasim, calling him a thoughtless fool and denouncing his ability to lead men; why he even lacked of wit in such a small quarrel.

"You are a fool that has taught me a lesson," barked Hassan, "in the morning you will answer to the lash; now leave us unless you wish to anger me further." It must have been Hassan's way, allowing these mini quarrels to develop so that he could stand back and assesses each of his entertainer's strengths and weaknesses. On this occasion, he detected Kasim's weakness to overpower the small female that confronted and bettered him. She had wit and guile on her side whilst the giant, the dull headed Kasim, had only his strength. His remaining defence would have been to reach out to his aggressor where she stood, but the clever and wicked Hassan was not in the mood to lose such a valuable servant as she just yet.

The dismissal was not taken easily, but he knew better than to argue with his master, as old and frail looking as he was. Kasim walked away a crossed man, contemptuously muttering and cursing this day and the day that would come when he would revenge himself on the accursed woman, for the one thing he despised most of all was losing an argument and being told that he was an incompetent fool.

Robert's attention had been held by the events of the argument and almost carelessly allowed himself to be seen as Kasim exited the chamber, but in his rage Kasim was blind to all. Robert fell back quickly in time into the shadow and his hand defensively gripped the dagger at his side. Secreted and standing well into the shadows for greater surprise, he reluctantly had second thoughts about attacking the giant Kasim. It may be better to withhold the slaying of his enemy in case it was not so clean and swift and an alarm raised during the struggle. If that was to happen, he had gained nothing in his efforts of escape thus far, and the hope of finding the whereabouts of his friend would be lost forever. Although his presence was overlooked when the burly Kasim approached, Robert's heart pounded fearfully in anticipation. There was a draught as the hulk of Kasim passed by still in contention and muttering his discontent from his dismissal. Robert breathed a little easier as his main threat left the chamber, but he would wait a little longer to be safe and think out a strategy.

Waiting for Kasim to be well clear before moving further, he peered again into Hassan's chamber; it was illuminated by numerous candles and they gave out a strange light making the affair before him appear like actors playing at theatre. Warm air touched him as he poked his head forwards watching the old man pacing the marbled dais. Hassan was beset with anger and showing it as he chastised his aide for allowing herself to be so easily kidnapped by a spying foreigner; who would suffer the next day for his meddling. Had he defiled her in any way demanded the ranting Hassan, the ageing voice continued, it was unworthy of her, and came as a disappointment to him; his harangue was about to enter into full flow when it slowly curtailed and finally lost for words at the sight of Robert walking toward them prepared for action with a dagger in his hand. The girl spun around to see what had caught her master's eye and had distracted him from the sudden cessation in her chastisement. Dumbfounded by the sight of the prisoner approaching, Hassan was lost for words allowing the woman to take over.

"You are rash and foolish, Franj, for entering this chamber without care. If you were resourceful enough to escape why did you not run?" she asked.

"Because there is unfinished business between us," Robert's hoarse words were delivered in little more than a whisper.

She was perplexed at his statement. Collecting her thoughts, she fleetingly glanced across towards her master and enquired, "Do you mean your young friend?"

He looked at her directly in the eyes and stressed that; that was exactly what he meant, "And I will not leave until I have that information or your death."

There was a nervous laughter in the air as the old Hassan commended Robert on his ingenuity to escape incarceration from his dungeon. He had been the first ever to do that; I must have a word with the fool of a jailer in the morning to teach him a lesson in obedience. Angered by laxness of his man in the cells, he seriously warned his visitor to make the best of his freedom whilst he could, and not to waste his precious time pressing him for information about matters that were not of his concern. His bearded face no longer displayed laughter being serious and displaying a disdainful glower. Robert was in no mood for evasions, he was tired and very aware of his insecurity within this evil place; ready to stop any and all that may threaten his purposeful intent.

"Now tell me," said the ageing Hassan mockingly, "before you kill me, how do you plan to get by all my loyal guards?" with arms stretched towards the on-looking female, "and of course my dear loyal and faithful aide," he added.

There was no doubt about the imbalance of numbers; when Robert was about to answer he spied a khataar hanging on the wall across the room and ran to remove it from its decorative scabbard with the intention that it would better aid his chances of escape.

Then with a smirk on his face that told others that he did not care much for threats; when directing the point of the blade forwards, he replied almost scoffing.

"She was careless once and allowed herself to be taken as my prisoner and that clown of a right hand you call Kasim made it that much easier for me." Before he finished his sentence, he noticed that the smiling open face of Hassan had dropped into a dark vexatious scowl; anger was seen as the tyrant sucked air through the orifice in his bearded face; it was quite so, but he did not need to be reminded of it from the interfering Christian.

It was offensive and challenging for the Christian knight to mock him so, Hassan face turned to thunder. Her carelessness brought him here; she would pay for her mistakes, indeed that was the very subject that she was being berated for and he was cruelly deciding on building her punishment now.

With a disdainful tone in his voice, Robert turned towards the ageing Hassan almost mocking him at the way he used the term, "Loyal," which was shouted out with disgust, causing Robert to almost choke on the word.

"What do you know about loyalty? You rule through fear and terror. I can tell you, loyalty is what comes freely from within; born from duty and honour and a willingness to serve. "There was nothing but emptiness in your kind of loyalty; save the need to indulge in the mire of poison and confusion that you," pointing his sword at Hassan, "have tricked and hooked your dependants into, through their need to rely on you for the continuance of their dependency for the need of hashish." He was wound up by adding his anger and hatred for Hassan's evil methods, which reviled and nauseated him so much that his anger urged his temper on to cut the ageing leader down where he stood.

A sardonic twisted smile settled over Hassan's face; the old man was angered by Robert's taunting, but tried hard not to show his feelings; to his mind the westerner's words proved quite perplexing, he needed to be enlightened.

"You have much to learn about loyalty, my young friend. It comes, as you rightly say, from a need to serve and do ones duty, perhaps a demonstration would best serve." Before Hassan was able to complete his sentence, Robert was at his side, his dagger pressing into Hassan's scrawny ageing rib cage whilst his sword arm was ready to defend his stand against any guards that entered. Protesting at the eagerness of his enemy's intent to pierce his ageing body with his weapon that was presently pressing a little too hard against Hassan's body for comfort, Hassan tried to abate Robert's heated temper by using his soothing tone of voice. Pointing out that he had acted hastily and merely wanted to demonstrate an exhibition of his subject's steadfast devotion towards their master, and that he would give his word that he would not summon any guards, because he had nothing to fear.

"A small display of loyalty is all I ask of you to witness," said the old man, his dark searching eyes met with Robert's. "I promise that you will be free to continue your escape," he said sardonically. Robert was silent which acted as an indication for Hassan to proceed.

"Ali, Ali ben Fahide, my great friend," he called clapping his hands impatiently. There was fear suddenly across the face of the woman and she moved towards Hassan as the name of Ali was called out. Taken unawares by the swiftness of her advance towards Hassan, caused Robert to step aside raising the khataar for action as there came a frightened appeal from the woman, throwing herself to Hassan's feet pleading for his reconsideration.

"Master, no," the girl, exclaimed fearfully, she begged; anything but to use this person for his demonstration.

Clearly shocked, Robert noticed the look of genuine fearful anticipation on the girl's face, she became rigid and tense as she lay spread appealingly and clutching at her master's feet reaching out, clenching both hands together, pleading against her master's action. Hassan's hand was raised to cease her objections, the other to assist her to her feet to stand beside him, his soft gentle voice told her that, "This is only a test of loyalty, my dear." Then his voice changed from one of softness to the sharpness of a rebuke to get up, as a thin bearded and aged gentleman appeared shuffling happily and obediently towards his master. He appeared shy and quite gentle as he approached the two men, smiling. He was aged and small, almost gentle from his appearance. He did not look to belong here; he was not a soldier of any kind, and out of place, thought Robert. As he neared, it did not take Robert long to notice that this man was influenced by one of Hassan's narcotics, a tool he presumed that this devil used excessively to the full on all his house guests. He stopped short of the two men held in his indelibly happy state.

Hassan greeted him softly as a friend, then beckoned him to walk into the garden where he could better inform his master about the stars in the heavens. As the elderly man happily acceded to his master's wishes, they turned and walked through open doors into the illuminated garden, where the smell of scented flowers filled the night air with their heady mixed perfumes. What sinister mood was Hassan in, and what was he planning to turn this harmless, happy smiling individual into? The audience followed closely behind, unaware of what was to be further asked of him.

They paused in a marbled area of an extensive patio on the edge of the garden, the sight of the twinkling stars set above in the moonlit night sky were caught and reflected in the polished marbled floor. The aged gentleman began telling the audience about the moons relationship with the souls of mankind.

Hassan broke in, thanking the old man, but then he ordered him to walk nearer towards the parapet that bordered the high garden's walls.

Fearful of her master's desire for wicked amusement, the woman threw herself once more prostrate in supplication for his mercy at his feet and begged him to take this test no further.

"Punish me in any way you feel, but I beg you, do not hurt my father. He has served you far more worthily than I, and does not deserve to be repaid this way."

Robert was a speechless onlooker in the theatre that he found himself in; he was still unaware of what was going on and felt helpless to avert Hassan's exhibition. Unaware of what he was about to do as his head turned in concert, from master to servant and back again. He certainly never expected to see this hard-hearted woman, begging and cringing in deep concern for another on her bended knees.

Her pleading words fell on the deaf ears of Hassan; he ignored her plea and continued his punishment in the vilest of ways.

Addressing the old man once more with jocularity in his tone, he asked, "Do you remember how we used to talk long about the wonders of flight, Ali?"

Ali, in his intoxication, moved waving his arms and trying to lift his body from the marbled floor and smiled with a look of wonderment in his eyes while the wicked smiling Hassan teased the elderly gentleman further. His words tantalised the old man who continued in his act of flight in circular motions. Ali became excited, exclaiming that one day perhaps it would be possible and that perhaps, who knows, man may even be able to touch the stars themselves.

Concerned for the old man's safety, Robert pushed closer to Hassan warning him to stop the charade.

The girl was speechless, sounds of her endless sobbing filled the night while her tears streamed down her rose coloured cheeks, and her beautiful youthful facial features were transformed into that of a hag. Her facial preparation began to form rivulet-like tracks down a rain sodden hillside, and was uncontrollably sobbing over this frail ageing man. Once fated to be the tool of a scheming villain of the world, she was now reduced to little more than a blubbering, helpless child.

The old man was at the edge of the parapet flapping his arms and talking of his machines that would fly. The floor of the canyon was hidden by the night's darkness, giving no sign of the dangers below. All eyes were turned on Hassan. Robert poked his dagger menacingly into his side telling him once more to stop this folly, but Hassan would have none of it. Arrogant and conceited with his own greatness, urged on by the desire to show his power, he laughed long and loudly as he ordered the old man to demonstrate to all how easy it was to fly. "Fly, Ali fly! And spread your wings." Laughing and carefree, the old man walked the carpet of darkness; the girl ran forwards in an attempt to stop her father from falling to his death, but all she caught momentarily was the draught of his jacket as it slipped passed her outstretched hands, sailing downwards after her father had plummeted into the depths of darkness of the canyon floor below. He disappeared; he was gone; there was no sound of a crashing frail body on the rocks below but only the wails of an orphaned girl who witnessed the wanton death of the only person she ever loved. She gave a final howl of loss into the night where her beloved father disappeared, before collapsing onto her knees like a wild creature giving in to death, her heart heavy and broken. Her loss of the parent that loved her like no other, ceased and faded into the night, she grieved and wailed lifelessly on the floor at Hassan's feet. Oblivious to the shock and severity of the despicable event, the great Hassan, aloof and arrogant as ever, now called on her to come to the aid of her master.

"Show me your loyalty, my dear," he commanded. "Forget what has just happened here, he was a man that served; you and I are greater beings, come now I call on you, your master is in need of your help." He spoke impatiently as the tone of his manic voice raised in pitch. She was fixed in her bereavement, howling into the night; the scene dumbfounded Robert as he watched her motionless in her loss. "Come girl," hastened Hassan impatiently, "I need your aid." Robert noticed her movement; he had thoughts of rendering her unconscious; he did not wish to kill her unless he needed to should she attack him whilst he made good his escape with Hassan as his hostage. That idea crossed his mind and was put aside. Whilst he stood fixated to the spot, he watched and waited, sensing that this game was not yet over. Hassan stood erect and aloof, defiant against Robert. In his arrogance, he believed that he was not in any danger and suspected what Robert had in mind.

"How far do you think you will get?" he jibed. "This little wild cat at my feet will not let you get beyond the limits of this garden." Scoffing now with confidence, he viewed the girl awkwardly. Rising slowly to her feet, disappointed at her dilatory speed, he snapped his fingers at her to move herself along as the night air was turning chilly. Robert swung Hassan in front of the girl to act as a shield before he proposed to render her unconscious, and at the same time allowed the point of his dagger to pierce the surface of Hassan's side threateningly.

Wincing and deeply offended as the dagger cut through his clothing and nicked his soft flesh, he could not take his eyes off the girl who was standing starring into the eyes of Hassan with burning tearful eyes.

"He was a kindly man," she sobbed, "the balance of his fate was always in your hands whilst you used me all these years." Tears of grief were flowing from her soft brown eyes while the words came out accusingly.

There was something different about her. The power within her soft foreboding voice channelled itself critically against her master, who became antagonised by her defiance to act without reluctance. Hassan jerked himself into anger at the thought that she, a subject, was anticipating disobeying him. He yelled at her, threatening to allow Kasim to abuse her before his troops if she did not act now to protect him. Robert was mystified as the argument developed before him and became somewhat unsure as what to do for the best. His plan began to crumble as the girl bowed gently before her master, a submissive gesture that delighted Hassan. He was impatient and unused to being subjected to delay; his short term of unease was due to come to an end and, delighted, he smiled triumphantly at Robert at the thought of being freed from his captor. Once more, she looked upon the smiling and smug face of her master and into his empty, crazed eyes for the last time.

The air became filled with the revengeful wails of a half-mad creature, as she began savagely and unceasingly slashing at his throat, blood spattered everywhere, her hands moved so fast that Robert could hardly keep sight of the speed of movement. Both victim and Robert were transfixed; Hassan's torso became a fountain of blood, he was far from dead; she was extremely skilful not to cut too deeply into any vital points. For once, Hassan had lost the use of his voice and became a wobbling, useless statue for her revenge. Standing quite still with her head tilted to one side, she studied him silently, gone was the power that he once wielded, and gone was any fear of him.

Her father was dead; he could not be brought back; but how she wanted to grieve for him. She could have handled his death so much easier if he had met with a fatal accident, but by the persuasive orders of her master's cruel and sadistic bent to punish her for some exhibition of her loyalty was too much.

Whilst Hassan stood motionless, it was as though she wanted him to test what power he possessed, but there was nothing he was capable of and no danger to man or beast any further. It was she that held the power over him, and now for his folly, life would come to an end when she was ready. With wide, terrified, unbelieving eyes, he waited for the end. Leaning forwards, she whispered audibly, in her old language of the mountains of her birth that was unknown to Robert, which had an effect on Hassan. The nerves she so expertly severed to hold the assassin's mastermind between life and death had him tottering; her whispering cursing words took its effect, causing Hassan to tremble whilst held in his paralysis, and death did not come on swift wings for him.

It was quite obvious to Robert that when so moved, this female was no better than her master; as his end was delivered, he watched coldly as the Master of Mas'yaf drowned painfully in his own blood. Coughing and gasping for air as the last of his blood bubbled from his lacerated throat and out through his once snowy white beard that was now a bright red colour. Her action was so swift, Robert could not tell what she had done but the result was testament to her efficiency of action. Hassan finally collapsed to the floor into his own evil blood that pooled around him. In her misery and suffering, she was finished; it was over. Two small blades were seen to drop from her bloodied hands as she turned and slowly walked away; void of any remaining life towards the parapet.

For one worrying moment, Robert thought that she was about to join her father, and quickly ran to her side urging her not to contemplate any thoughtless action, but now they had to leave and she had become the only hope he had.

"Leave me," she said trying her best to hold back her sobs, "to grieve. Go find your friend." Robert was not having any of this remorseful self-pity, he cajoled her and used all his powers of persuasion for her to unite with him, but she was right, it was more than obvious that Robert was more concerned for his friend than her personal grief. He would not yield to her forlorn state, he could not, for he knew that she was his true chance of escape. She was a logical person and used to thinking; he felt that in her situation she really needed comfort, but he also was aware that she was not an ordinary woman that would break down meekly. He had to reach out somehow to appeal to her sense of survival, "You have no place now," and further added if Kasim were leader, he would take great pleasure in carrying out Hassan's threat of abuse.

Tired at trying to move the immovable distraught woman that she was, he was taken aback when she suddenly agreed, on the understanding that together they would assist each other in overcoming their dire situation and escape this terrible and foreboding stronghold.

Standing motionless and silent at the wall of the parapet, she suddenly acknowledged the sense of his argument, giving instruction to him to wait for her for just a brief moment. Robert didn't care much for that idea; she caught his sideways look at her as she turned to face him, as if she was about to betray him, but she was quick to remind him that trust had to be the key to their union. She left the chamber and returned after a brief moment of absence bearing a small lamp, and a small filled satchel across her shoulder, which had little significance to him.

The tear stained face that was had been wiped clean, leaving faint tell-tale smears across both her cheeks; he was gladdened to hear her sharply order him to follow her and be silent. Her commanding air set him at ease, yet he failed to understand how she was able to put aside her grief and return to becoming her old self. Confident that she would somehow deliver him to the freedom that he was once been used to, he never commented on the change of her character. Neither did he mention how his feet pained him, or how the aches in his legs bothered him; he was in flight with the woman who was giving him more than a slender chance of survival.

Their direction of flight was outward across the garden; he doubted her direction, believing that the way of their entrance would have been more direct by the way they entered, but he followed obediently. Robert was confused as they penetrated the shadows and an abundant flowering growth of heavy shrubbery; once within, he was to discover that it was little more than a deceptive curtain across the mouth of a cavern. There before them was a crude downwards winding stone stairway that had been roughly cut from the rock that led into a darkened abyss, and hopefully their freedom. Carefully, they picked their way downwards into the bowels of the cavern with little more than a flickering oil lamp that hardly gave any light out to point their way through the slippery and threatening darkness. Dripping water filtered through the rock face high above, causing the steps to grow mossy and extremely dangerous underfoot. Tarred torches in metal brackets fixed to the wall waited to be lit for the fleeing couple whose senses now had heightened to the business of flight. Robert placed his hand on her shoulder, and pointing out the torches, he endeavoured to reach upwards to unhook one. Because of his ignorance of their safety, she screeched a warning of danger.

"My master is a very cunning man and has set many traps here for those foolish enough to try to steal away from him." She suddenly realised what she had said and stopped speaking, only to look up at him with her corrective eyes as if to announce his error.

"Look!" she pointed knowingly to a fine cord that led up to the roof, "Above us is a net of stones ready to fall when that torch is taken from its holder. If you escape the falling rocks, the walls of this passage have holes big enough to show the glow of a flaming torch to those few that know of this escape route, see here." And as Robert caught up to her, he felt the draught of wind nudge him as he passed an opening in the rock face.

"I see what you mean," he admitted with embarrassment.

"That is why we have the small oil lamp to avoid that happening. We are safe while our light is poor, Franj, you must learn to apply your patience and concentration, and above all, trust in me. The light is sufficient for us; tell me why we should point the way that we travel for others to see, for I am certain, Kasim and the others are not aware of this escape route." He was impressed by her guile, under his breath he called her all the artful mothers ever created. It was an understatement, and somehow he was glad that they were fleeing together.

They descended the steep stone staircase quickly. She proved to be more agile than he as the gap between them began widening; thinking little of it, he put an extra effort into his strides to close the gap between them and remain within the faint glow of the lantern. As his speed increased, so did his momentum; he suddenly realised he was catching up to her without realising that she had stopped. Try as he did, he found it difficult in stopping, but just in time; as he jolted to a stop, he caught hold onto the rough edges of the cavern walls.

"Fool that you are, Franj," she began berating him again for not realising what he had almost done; until she finally came to a cessation of her harangue. "I warned you to take care, you are like others that have perished," she went on at him, "only a fool rushes head on into danger without thought when he is threatened by the chase." She held her little dim lantern out but Robert found it difficult to see what it was she was showing him. "Come onto the step with me," she beckoned. There was a sharp rush of air from below, where he soon realised that the next step was one to oblivion.

"Franj, I am aware that you suffer fatigue, if you cannot keep up with me then you must say so and I will slow to remain with you. Hold on to my shoulder while we carry on down the last remaining stairs."

There was wounded pique at that remark; it had caused Robert to blink his eyes at the sound of her remark. That was a liberty, 'if I can't keep up to her,' he could have laughed if it wasn't true, but only for that moment. When the steps came abruptly to an end, he felt cold air blowing in all around them, and confronted by what appeared no more than a narrow fissure in the rock face. Turning to Robert, she explained the danger ahead, as if she was his mother talking to her young son. "This is where we must take the greatest of care, for once beyond this opening, we will be on little more than a foothold, and in total darkness. There are grips which we will have to feel for." She began to unwind a silken sash that girdled the slimmest of feminine waists, but in the dimness of the lamplight, though he felt the draught, he could not yet see any opening.

Handing him the end of her sash, she prompted him, "Tie this to your body so that we can remain close to each other." She spoke to him reassuringly, firmly reminding of the dangers that lay ahead. Now that they were bound together so would their fate be united, she told him, "It could be your hell or our freedom." From now on, there would be no light to guide them. "You must take great care, for once out there, we will walk a ledge no wider than a child's hand and there will be no second chance if either of us slips. It is from this point on," she told him, "that I put the greatest trust in your ability, for this will be our test of unity, fortitude and courage. Do not feel ashamed to pray to your god to be with you, as I will plead to mine to see us safely through our trial."

Robert smiled knowing what she meant before she doused the flickering flame of the lamp; then in total darkness and with little room between them, they felt their way towards the wind and freedom.

The two squeezed through the narrowest of openings before emerging into the night, and it was as she predicted they were to balance on the narrowest of ledges. The wind whipped at their faces, indicating that they were still very high from the canyon floor. Their clothes suddenly inflated with the wind as it rushed at them with a purpose of carrying them off before they had a chance of making an effort to traverse the precarious cliff face. Step by step, they edged forwards into the darkness, precariously inching along the narrow ledge blindly as she had previously described. They moved very slowly keeping together; groping for hand and foot holds that they hoped would lead them to freedom along the course of the ledge, she talked calmly above the sound of the wind indicating every hold there was to guide him safely. The silken sash that held them closely together caused them to touch each other occasionally in their progress along their perilous route, but this was not the time or the place for wistful fancies. The steel of this woman amazed Robert, she was little more than a waif in size, yet she feared nothing, a stalwart, worthy of a command in any army that he knew of, and was quite prepared to give her the respect that she warranted. He also was not forgetting her abilities that he had recently witnessed, and with that, he would think twice before taking any such liberties with her, should they ever reach safety.

"We are across, Franj," she shouted once he was clear, and motioned for them to rest a moment where the path became much wider. "How do you feel?"

"My legs are tired," he replied, "but I can go on, it's just crossing such a narrow ledge."

"We have no more like this, but there is still much danger." She had no sooner stopped talking when she declared that they should continue.

"But I thought we were going to rest," said Robert.

"So we have," she replied, "now it is time to press onwards." In the gusting wind she pulled him closer to her to hear her voice above the wind. "You have done well, Franj," she commented, "but now I must further warn you not to reach out to the rocks we pass by to maintain your balance. This trail is not a natural one, but one constructed on Hassan's instructions, danger will be constantly with us. These rocks," she explained, "are finely placed to give way if touched and set off balance. It will only be a short but hazardous climb down until we reach a sheer path that should lead us out at the rear of the canyon. There, if we are not careful, we will come upon the soldiers of Hassan, and all could be lost. We need horses. Without them," she observed, "we would be picked up before noon. It is at that place that I speak of, where they knowingly guard this single exit; that is where we must take great care. There could be many sentries, I do not know, but we will do what we must because that is the only place where we can furnish our needs. If we are successful, we will have a chance, but be warned, it will be the making of our discovery and we must not fail in stealing all the horses if we are to escape."

"Well," sighed Robert and with some relief of their escape so far, "she tells it how it is."

They made their way carefully through the darkness, fearful of the least slip in their footing, and down to a place overlooking where sentries stood posted and fires burned brightly. He could not see around the outer perimeter of the encampment, only where the fires burned. This was a place where the soldiers relaxed and spent some of their leisure time. It was a small encampment where the women came to visit and entertain those that required their services, and there was plenty of evidence that their services were being used. Robert glanced down at the woman, but she was not interested in the cavorting antics of the soldiers, her hawkish eyes, he guessed, were scanning other areas, looking for the positions of the sentries. In such a place where danger never lurked for them, most of the soldiers appeared content relaxing, except for those that were athletically occupied proving their manhood. There was only one guard to be seen; he was perched high on a small out crop of rock nearby, and where their path to freedom would fall into his line of vision, whilst he overlooked the ravine's approach. He would not expect any threat from the rear, so it was easy for Robert to come up behind him and physically toss him over the edge before he could realise what was happening to him. With the gusting wind, nobody in the camp heard the sound of his scream as he plummeted downwards to his inevitable death. Meanwhile, they covertly made their way down to the horses; whilst Robert became a rear guard to the woman's active plans. She silently gathered the horses together and walked them wide of the camp so that hardly a sound was made.

Few people could move that many horses without a sound; how she did it Robert could not say, and to ask her would cause embarrassment to his inability to equal her. Before the sun had risen, the two fugitives were well on their way to Lattakia, aware that the body of Hassan by this time should have been found. All the camps in the area would by now have been alerted, ensuring the certainty that the hunt would be under way. After what he was further told, Robert's main concern was to catch a ship before the tide turned; only then would his escape be assured and only then would he breathe easily, knowing that his pursuers no longer were able to follow his trail, he also hoped that his new associate would give him some advantage to their escape.

They rode without stopping; the line of horses that they had in tow would ensure a swift arrival as they changed their mounts whilst on the move. Their guarded route across the high plateau avoided the deep, defensive mountain passes that were in need for their escape; the woman had to be congratulated for her skill and knowledge of the area. Soon they were out of the ranges and racing across the valley floor that would lead them on to Lattakia and the sea. It was shortly before noon when they arrived in the Port town and much was to be done before they would be on their way.

The Crossing

When the boat left the harbour, a fair wind gave impetus to the ship's sails; Robert had gasped when he heard the woman ask for passage to Venice, but anywhere was better than having the murderous Kasim follow them. Robert eyed the captain curiously; he appeared familiar but had difficulty in focusing his troubled mind on where it was from, he could not place his face due to his tiredness and the extreme pressure that he had been under during his frenzied flight to freedom, and neither could he care at that moment. He presently felt quite safe and relaxed with the knowledge that his pursuers were no more. Other thoughts now troubled his mind; his appearance was shabby, his clothes were not fitting for one such as he, making him appear as if he had been picked up from the gutter. Though he would not be recognised, his appearance would raise many questions, awkward ones, he suspected, for which he had no story suitable to back up any prying suspicions.

To add to his troubles, the course of recent events had diverted him from his true objective, and no excuse imaginable would normally support such actions of disobeying his orders by leaving a mission for personal reasons. In the loneliness of his present situation, he wrestled with his mind over his appointed duty, but it was hard for him to break faith and be disloyal to his young friend Aldo, and hoped that his colleagues in his absence would cover or speak up for him.

Turning over the recent unravelling of events in his mind, he was certain that the trail he was following would certainly give fruitful answers to finding the source of the all the troubles that sent him on this mission.

There had been little conversation between the two during their flight to freedom, and now his tiredness and her need to be engaged in averting those awkward questions away from her unkempt travelling companion gave him a space to think.

Strange, he thought, a few days ago we were enemies, now they were on the same side; he hoped that she would be readily willing to give him the many answers that he sought, but then on second thoughts, perhaps it would be better that he display his patience and wait rather than rush onward thrusting too many questions upon her too soon. This venture of working with his enemy was a new experience for him, and he was wary of having to completely trust her, though she had proved herself back at Mas'yaf. Those thoughts were troubling! There was no question that this was a plot to get on his side, for he knew that she too was being hunted, and that the killing of Hassan was no friendly squabble among friends. No, what she did back there was a definite step across the line of whose side she was on, or should he say which side would she choose from this point on; one thing was certain to him and that was that the Old Man of the Mountain would not spare either of them. The word must surely have got back by now and their time was truly running out, it was only a matter of when or how, until the vengeful killing of her master Hassan would be avenged. Where would he be now, he asked himself ,had she not agreed to their odd pact enabling them both to get him away from that wretched place Mas'yaf? Well, that was a topic that he was not too keen to dwell on; he closed his eyes and shivered at the thought of being a guest of Hassan's. That black-hearted fiend would probably have turned him into an informer or, worse still, an assassin under his dark influence to be used like some puppet, however and whenever he willed it.

The rise and fall of the ship, the sound of the bow parting the waves with the sun overhead comforted his mood, somehow provoking the tiredness that began to overtake him. He looked for a place to relax out of the way of the busy crewmen to enjoy the chance for his tired and aching body to recover whilst lazing in the sun.

A place near the bowsprit was ideal, and it was there that he settled down and made himself comfortable and in no time at all, relaxed into a deep sleep; he did not know for how long; but his mind was thrown into a haphazard jumble of thoughts when he was later awakened by being roughly shaken.

"Wake up," a voice said angrily, there was anxiety and sharpness in the voice.

He was being pushed roughly sideways, at first his instinctive reaction was to lash out, luckily, she had the perception to shake him by his right arm suspecting his obvious reaction.

When he came to his senses, his annoyance subsided in recognition of her; he smiled boyishly as he saw her standing before him.

Her face showed no trace of good humour, nor was her manner carefree; her eyes pierced into his with a damning disapproval for his disregard of caution.

"Only a fool sleeps on one of Hassan's vessels," she angrily whispered her annoyance, scolding him again for his laxity, and the look on Robert's face manifested the ignorance and negligence of the fact.

"Did you not know?" she asked surprisingly.

He grimaced with guilt as he took in the news admitting that he could not stop himself being so exhausted. "You did not mention it before, how was I to know?" he blustered.

"Did you not think about how easy it was for us to get aboard? I am known and respected in Lattakia."

"You mean feared, don't you?" he sarcastically replied like a petulant child.

She did not like his remark, it showed in her dark troublesome eyes, "Remember, Franj, I was the arm of Hassan."

That statement he would not forget. "Do you suspect anything?" Robert asked, concerned that he may once again be called to defend himself.

She intimated her uncertainty to Robert that she had only suspicion, a feeling you understand. He understood that kind of gut feeling, it comes from experience of the danger of being in tight corners, and unaware of a certainty of knowledge, which had brought him through many a scrape on the very same intuition. His thoughts were jarred as he added, with a ponderous look on his face. "I vaguely recall seeing this captain before, where, just escapes me"

She eased and shocked his memory with her answer, telling him that this was the same man that gave him and his companions passage to Simeon. "It was no mistake, for we knew of your interests in Antioch; and where we also had business of our own to fulfil at that time, which would not stand to failure." He was quite prepared to take her word for it, but could not help asking, where on earth did she receive her information?

She remained silent, realising it was pointless to pursue his question; he changed his tack and suggested that if the captain were to make a move against them, it would not be until nightfall, when they expect them to be asleep.

The words were no sooner from his mouth when the rotund captain cast his shadow across them, presenting himself whilst they were in deep discussion; against the sunlight, the captain appeared little more than a dark image. Robert's eye followed the moving figure, although he was static with the deck, the captain appeared to be bobbing about, caused by the swelling action of the waves.

He bid them the courtesy of the day and found it difficult to remove his questioning eyes off Robert, at the same time attempting to delve into their business. He could not help but observe Robert's unkempt dress; he spoke, questioning that they appeared to be in somewhat of a hurry when they boarded, also that they were without provision for the voyage, indicating to him that their passage on this vessel was not planned.

She took the inquisitive captain aside holding his arm in the kindest of ways, lulling him into a state of relaxation, asking of him to be kind enough to furnish her travelling associate with some clean clothing. Forgetting himself, the captain replied in a disingenuous tone that he needed to be better informed into the westerner's origins; with a stern and menacing tone, she reminded him that it was not a healthy occupation to question the business of those in the employ of the brotherhood. In the gentlest manner, her previous warning was reinforcing the hint that he chanced the dangers of an early demise by interfering into Hassan's business. The captain swallowed hard and the colour drained from his uncertain face at the prospects of falling foul of the madman Hassan.

He knew that he had taken a liberty in questioning the most feared and potentially dangerous person within the organisation. Her firm and pleasant manner in determining his position reminded him that he was no more than a lowly cog on the lowliest wheel of a great machine. His apology came swiftly as he felt the shadow of death closing ever nearer on him; backing away from further questions, and by changing the subject, he cordially invited them to share a glass of wine and some bread after their hard ride. She looked at him again, as if this stupid captain did not know when to give in, but excused his whimsical foolishness having extended the hand of hospitality towards them.

Robert never ceased to learn from this petite female, who was able to move mountains and strike the fear of death into those who opposed her will, and she did it with a meaningful pressure by implanting doubt and fear without ever raising her voice. Their situation was perilous and trust was far from Robert's mind as a thousand suspicious thoughts ran through his head. He had now added cowardice to the captain's attributes, which to him meant he was definitely not to be trusted. Robert's eyes closed allowing his mind gently to move towards the evening; his suspicions on how they may be jumped on by way to the captain's quarters was quite probable, or perhaps their food could be drugged, he was not sure, but he feared something dubious was in the wind.

As the moment heightened for him, so did the hairs on his neck fairly bristle for action; watching the look on the woman's face, he immediately replied that he would gladly and thankfully take advantage of the kind offer made to them. Rising to his feet, he caught the piercing eye of the woman who appeared to have suspected something similar in the untrustworthy captain's offer of hospitality.

It was when he had gone that she quietly admitted to Robert that the voyage was, she believed, to promise some threat to their liberty, admitting that although she had been distracted, she thought that a message by flashing mirrors had warned the captain of their flight from Mas'yaf.

Looking more like a mariner than a mercenary in his newly acquired clothes and washed appearance seemed satisfactory to Robert. At the appointed time of day, the two made their way along the darkening deck towards the after section, stopping at the staircase leading down to the captain's cabin. The light was subdued along the corridor even with the door ajar there were shadows cast along the passageway, it was an ideal place to be set upon, With suspicions running high for their safety Robert had second thoughts of it, being restricted for manoeuvre and offering little chance for any action. No, this was no place for men to be fighting; he reasoned that his judgement was correct, fighting men would need more space if there were to be a scuffle. With his hand held up to his lips to signify silence, they crept down the staircase and along the passageway. The captain's door was a little way further along and in deeper shadow; at the door he listened and heard the sound of muffled voices. Robert also suspected that more than he was expected to be sharing the captain's bread and wine. He was intuitive of their game and silently gestured to the woman that it was time to knock on the door. They listened to the footsteps within as they stood discerning the goings on within; in spite of their bodged efforts to be concealed, Robert counted three in total within. With a loud knock, Robert made it known that the invitation was being honoured. There was a hush within, which made Robert grow more suspicious when the captain's footsteps could loudly be heard making his way towards the door and opening the cabin door to greet them cordially, at the same time stepping aside away from the door, inviting his guests to enter. The captain appeared in a good mood inviting them to move forwards, Robert had made his entrance quickly and the two men came together, gripping the clothing of his host, he pulled the waiting captain around into the position where he would have been standing in the open doorway. Aware that his plan had gone askew, the captain screamed for his life as the expectation of his boson's actions were about to follow through.

From behind the door, a club landed squarely on the captain's head exposing the dastardly plan, the club's contact with the captain left the boson exposed and stunned as his error became obvious to all. Completely dazed by the blow, the captain suddenly lost the ability to stand; his legs crumpled under him as he sank to the floor half-conscious. By the look on the boson's face, he was left in shock at his error; he remembered seeing only a hand raining down on him as the hilt of Robert's khataar struck his forehead, rendering him unconscious. Cringing and whining holding his head, the captain lay sprawled on the bare deck of the cabin; with one of their number had thought better to Robert instantly and forcefully kicked against the door, causing a sudden yell of surprised pain to emanate from behind it. The khataar was at the ready, its steely point hungry for action as he drew back the door to find another miserable sea dog holding a bloodied nose, and at the sight of the threatening khataar above his head, he fell to his knees begging for mercy. One good blow from Robert's fist sent him keeling over to the floor and in no way spoiling for any more punishment.

Standing over the captain, Robert guided his sword to nestle under the prostrate man's fat sweating double chin, urging him to scramble to his knees where he was made to remain. Trembling, beads of sweat formed over his twitching eye brow and gathered into a larger droplet until the liquid fear dripped onto his cheek before running down over his fat, quivering lips.

"I don't think much of your hospitality, captain," remarked Robert, his tone changed demanding to know what this action was all about.

The kneeling man did not know how to answer Robert and made up a story that he thought the woman was in danger and it was his duty to save her, hoping to be rewarded by Hassan.

It was true that he knew the woman, and the one that she served, but this fellow was lying, and Robert knew it, but how could he prove it?

She stepped in front of the captain who dropped his head at the sight of her. "Look at me, captain," she demanded; her soft, dulcet tones fell upon him like the weight of a fallen mast head. "It is true that you know me," She put the question to him watching him nod his assent. "I have a name amongst those who fear me," she said softly, "perhaps you will tell, my friend, what it is?"

He did not wish to bandy words knowing well her reputation, nor did he intend to rouse her to anger, but he feared that he had somehow passed the point of mercy. He was racked with fear at her bequest, showing the sweat to ooze from his flesh to soak his thin shirt with darkened patches that indicated his fear. His voice was lost somewhere deep within, all he could do was to shake his head in his hesitance to speak.

"Come, speak up, captain," she goaded him once more in a more severe tone, but the captain was truly terrified. Devoid of any words, he placed his hands together as if offering a prayer for mercy, afraid to say what he had said quite freely when she had not been around. "Do you think I do not hear you when my back is turned? Come now, the name." The captain's tongue worked feverishly to promote enough saliva in his mouth to speak; in a hoarse voice, he whispered only half a name 'scorp...' before drying up with his fear; as much as he dared say it fully.

"I do not hear you." She bent her head closer to listen to the movement of the captain's timorous mouthing. She straightened up with a look of lost patience upon her face. "Oh, so all of a sudden you fail to speak to me, very well, if you cannot use the tongue that God gave you, it is most likely that you have no use for it."

She looked to Robert who guessed her bluff on the captain and immediately took up a position behind him pulling his head roughly back and placing his two fingers in the captain's nostrils causing his mouth to open. In the light of the cabin, there was a glint of steel as a small blade appeared in her hand from nowhere; she made no secret of its presence, expecting that the captain had already seen it. With her nails embedded in the captain's face, she squeezed at his chubby mouth causing him to shout in pain; at the same time it instinctively opened wide enough to allow her to take a grip his tongue with the sharpened nails of her delicate fingers. He had fallen for her ruse and now she had a hold of his tongue, gripping it with her nails and holding it fast. He could see that his time had run out, and that she was no longer in a mood for games as she raised the glinting blade before his eyes. His scream filled the cabin causing crewmen to come running to their captain's aide.

The cabin door was swinging open freely; in a short time half a dozen men were soon stood frozen watching, filling the gap, horrified at the sight before them seeing two men down and their captain held in the clutches of the woman's grip. Robert warned them sternly to withhold any action they may foolishly contemplate, for they too could suffer the same fate if they refused. "Return aloft," he called, "and continue your duties." The audience remained, fearfully frozen by the events that were happening by the scene that was being played out before their eyes. To add to the terror, she turned and spoke to the audience that remained in the doorway, asking if any of them had witnessed a tongue being cut out. In a most wicked and nonchalant manner that was almost laughing, she told the horrified and staring crew that a tongue was only soft flesh and held little resistance to a sharpened blade, but she added its severing was inclined to be a very messy operation.

By now the trembling captain, who was left kneeling helplessly before his inquisitor was losing his water and making audible noises showing a willingness to speak. Releasing his tongue, the captain demonstrated a squeaking sound of liberation, exhaling audibly the sound of his relief; with free will the information she required came tumbling forth without further constraint.

He told them that a signal had been sent from the shore by a flashing glass, telling him of a great reward for the capture and return of the woman.

The news made her breathe deeply, "So that's their game," she said. "Well now we understand each other," she fell silent thinking on what to do. For the time being, she needed the captain's navigational skills to enable them to reach their destination, with that in mind she decided to spare him, but he was not going to be let off without something to think about. She held the knife closely to his nose, almost ready to cut deep into his flesh.

"This will be the last time that I will warn or threaten you, my captain, the next time you lie to me you will lost this nose and you ears. I will display your dishonesty to the world for all to see. Now cease your simpering.

"Shut up," she ordered, "and show me your loyalty by striking a bargain to preserve your miserable life, in return for a continued journey without further attempts on our lives."

"Yes, yes daughter of Hassan, you have my word," he grovelled, kissing her feet. She watched the coward completing his act of submission, with as much sincerity as a cunning fox. She was not taken in by his word nor did she expect him to be true, but noted that he would be out for revenge and in a mutinous mood for quite some time to come. She understood those feelings and knew how to deal with such a situation. She had been trained by professionals in the ways of her enemy for most of her life; dealing with people like this worthless captain would not be a problem.

Releasing her grip on him, she watched how he slumped and instinctively ran an exploring hand over his face discovering his features intact with some relief, and then into his mouth; he remained bent double in his kneeling position thankfully clutching his uncut face. Allowing enough time for the shock to subside from the captain's ordeal, she began issuing orders, causing the captain to scramble to his feet in panic.

"You will start by offering us the food you promised, and don't think of playing with it, for if you do, I will soon find you wherever you may be hiding. Do you understand?" she snapped.

"Right away," the obedient captain almost fell over himself issuing orders to accommodate his guests.

When the two were left alone, Robert began to feel uneasy; it was not mistrust, but oddly enough he felt a little sheepish alone with her. She had changed from a deeply hurt woman into an ogre, and wondered if he could ever get close to her fearing that she may end up consuming him.

Together they had achieved much, but as he looked at her he could not help but notice that she had lapsed back into a figure of a sullen girl, with her eyes fixed outwards to sea.

Foolishly, he offered a weak gambit into conversation wanting to ask about her father, but when he began to probe, she turned away as though anticipating his question and cut him short, almost forbidding any further discussion on the subject; how her perceptiveness irritated him and he retaliated cursing aloud.

"By the good God above, I was not meaning to pry."

"Franj," she answered in a superior way, "I was instructed by the best and believe me I knew that your intentions were for the best." She spoke truthfully telling him that from an early age she had expert tuition in the ways of the world and in the cunning ways of mankind in particular. There were certain teachings that he would never understand, particularly those of hers.

"I will not break down with my thoughts of the past," she said, adding almost arrogantly, "you must learn that I draw my strength from within. At this moment I do not wish to explain further, but I ask you to leave me in my silence to repair myself."

That was plain enough; he felt like a child that had been told not to speak and hoped that it was not going to be this way for the rest of the voyage.

The heavy wooden chair in which she sat and supported her small frame seemed to dwarf her as it was made to suit the rotund body of the captain, who was a much more robust character than she. Cradled in the chair like some pontiff, she haughtily began laying down rules whilst on board,

"I will tell you now, Franj, I respect you and admire your proficiency with weapons of war, but do not try to get close to me. In your countrymen's eyes, I am not considered as a good person to know. My past is littered with misdeeds, and I know you will never be sure whether to trust me. Certain things you have learnt bear that out from your short experience of being with me, but there is much more that you are not aware of." She spoke straight and convincingly, with no shame attached to herself, and before Robert could speak, she held her up her hand, stopping him from offering any explanation or reply before continuing. Speaking at great length she stressed her need to be left free to mourn her loss in her own way and to plan for what lay ahead, but not before giving Robert an opportunity to sit and ponder on her abilities, which he needed no lessons after witnessing her recent display.

"You look at me, Franj, and see a monster, am I right? Whatever I am may be so in your eyes, that change took place a long time ago. But I tell you this, and I say it with an open heart, I am no liar. When I give my word, I keep it. I have been moulded and shaped in many ways for a specific purpose in life, and I know only survival and the serving of my master." As she uttered those last few words her voice broke somewhat and tailed off. "So do not be afraid, sleep not with your hand on your sword, for you have no need to fear me."

A silence fell upon them, Robert knew not what to say in reply, he was not used to such arrogance from a woman, but then she was like no other woman he had ever met before.

How was he to survive the voyage without conversation and the need to know what was in her head. It struck him that this woman was totally insular, and full of inner strength, and her silence galled him to be led blindly. Did she not realise that her protection was in his strong right arm? And he was further put out when he was encouraged to remain silent when asking why they were going to Venice or anything personal.

Robert sat back comparing his education, which in comparison to hers must have been meagre. He had been taught to hunt and had received lessons in reading and everyday mathematics from the scholars at the nearby abbey. He grew with a balanced mind, judgement in matters for the ruling of his property and the governance of his people, which was derived from his father or his own experiences. When he became of age, he learnt to stand and fight for whatever he could take and retain. Although he knew right from wrong, he was raised to be fair; there were certain lessons that would never leave him.

The workings of his mind constantly had him assessing this partner he had chosen to side with. Unlike him; there was an emphasis, so it seemed, towards her scholastic past; she was canny, he would give her that, but when it came to a fight, he could not see what her ability in battle would have been. She reminded him in some ways like a certain Father Denis from long ago; he was a scribe, he never lifted a hand against his fellow man, yet had an ability to move mountains with a stroke of his pen. He viewed her slyly as she sat in the oversized chair of the captain; she was looking out into the great sea and nowhere in particular, probably filled with thoughts of her father. He knew she was no warrior, yet oddly enough he was astonished by her calculation and clarity of reasoning. She was not afraid to speak out and be truthful when she had told him of her early development and education. In her many ways, she was teaching him that something learned is something less secret, and nothing given up keeps the book of knowledge firmly closed; he could not help but wonder what this partnership was all about.

A rapping on the cabin door brought them both back to the present; the muffled voice of a crew member from the passage way nervously and hesitantly announced the arrival of their food. The door opened slowly; he was afraid to enter until the door had travelled fully, allowing him to be seen by the occupants. For his own security, he feared he may be cut down if he were to approach without warning. With a smile on his rough lean face, he entered carrying a plate of bread, salted beef and fresh fruit. Being just out of port, the fresh food would last for just a short period before having to rely to ship's general rations. The crewman did not look at the woman when he spoke up; pointing out that the food would not always be so good and plentiful; rations he told them always reduce in quality towards the end of the voyage. There was no reply; the staring eyes and silence that met him caused him to be nervous and apprehensive; he had seen enough when he stood earlier at the door viewing the impending fate of his unfortunate captain. Placing the food upon the table top come desk that was used for the captain's chart plotting and place of business transactions, he prepared to leave without a word, knowing that he was being carefully watched by both the guests. Feeling relieved that his duty was completed without penalty from the woman, he nervously retraced his steps back towards the cabin door. His hand had just reached out to lift the door latch when a voice hailed him causing him to halt in apprehension in his tracks, causing a condition of stress to ripple through his body like a shock wave, suffering a thousand fearful thoughts as he stopped dead in his shoes. His sudden anguish caused him to quake, finding it difficult to reply; she had called him back to the table, both onlookers considered his speed of step as dilatory and reluctant, raising suspicion until finally he was standing before them. In that brief lull of time, the crewman stood shaking and pondering on his fate. He could not control his fear and blurted out that all he did was to deliver this food; he swore that he had not touched it nor did he know anything about the captain or his plans. A slice of meat was cut with the knife that lay on the side of the plate. "Did you prepare this food?" she asked of the trembling mariner that stood before her.

"Oh no," he replied hoping that no blame could be attached for any inferiority of the food, "as I said, I was only ordered to serve you with it."

"Good," she said, "eat this," and tossed a slice of the meat over to the man who then presumed that perhaps it was not what it should be. He declined, stammering, why, he was only a poor servant; there was fear in his heart and only suspicion from the diners. Robert's sword was drawn and threatened the sailor with its use.

"If you refuse to eat you will taste the steel in its stead, which is it to be? Are we to believe that this food is tainted or worse?" provoked Robert. The mariner, caught between the two, timidly stretched out for the food and with closed eyes and a prayer in his heart, hoped that all would be well with the food before inserting the meat into his mouth. His pocket would not normally extend to the cost of such food, but he chewed the meat for what seemed an eternity, extracting its flavoursome juices before hesitantly swallowing it waiting for the expected result, next came the bread and a glass of wine, which he ate without hesitation, finishing with the wine testing. The proof of the food being edible resulted in a smiling upright mariner.

"Which would you like me to try next?" he asked. It became obvious that he was enjoying his task and that he was truthful in his knowledge of its preparation. Cheekily, he offered to sample the wine further, but Robert dismissed him; but not before being told that he could be called on again at any time. Once gone, the hungry diners began ravenously eating without a word passing between them as they ate.

The rest of the voyage went along painfully silent and without event; as for the woman, the crew got used to her, and after a few days had passed, they began extending her the usual courtesy of the day. The captain remained distant and as far away from his passengers as was possible. He did not know what was happening between her master and her, nor did he now wish to become entangled in any way that could harm his living or wellbeing. As for her mercenary friend, he would get what was coming; patience would be the key to his revenge.

Robert tried so many times to get closer to the woman to indulge in small talk but she was too insular for him, giving him no opportunity to open or continue any conversation.

The winds were favourable; the captain remained silent and careful not to make any approach to the woman making the voyage most acceptable, then one day whilst on deck the two stood together and noticed a new coastline.

"Where you do suppose we are now?" enquired Robert to one of the crew working nearby.

At the sight of the coast, the mariner gave a smile, offering a finger in the direction. "Over there," he said smiling, pointing to the distant headland, "that is what is left of the old town of Otranto, that is the first sign that we are almost home."

"So about two or three more days sailing?" enquired Robert, with a thoughtful look on his face with the knowledge of the voyage coming to a close; he turned to the female who had come closer to him to listen to the crewman's conversation. Feeling that this was an opportunity to converse with her, he casually began to speak.

"I know that you do not want me to pry or talk, but I must admit you are a difficult person to get on with, you have not even told me your name."

In a relaxed and quiet voice that could hardly be heard above the breeze she uttered, "It is the way I want it, Franj, believe me it is for the best. We made an agreement, you and I, to help each other, we made no agreement to be intimate. Have trust in me, Franj, for I have faith in you. Learn to enjoy your own company, then you will be less reliant on that of others." With that said, she turned and walked further along the deck.

Damn, damn that woman, he knew that there was to be no intimacy but a little conversation, he was lost to do right. Although it was not what Robert expected to hear, it did go some way towards putting him at ease, knowing he was not being completely shut out. Following the surprise at the opportunity to speak, he decided to follow her, prompting,

"If it is not too much to ask, what plans do you have when we get to Venice?"

She stopped and turned looking around; there was nobody around in ear shot. "It is not Venice that I think about, but the end of our voyage."

Slightly perplexed by her remark he replied, "I'm afraid I don't follow you," said Robert looking quite blank.

"Franj, you are an excellent soldier and keen on the ways of war. You are one that I will say I have most confidence within the field, but I was raised among the hashashin and I know the intricate ways of the mind and of those that are weak, especially when it comes to revenge." Robert rolled his eyes, a compliment followed by a rebuttal; he would appreciate a straight forward answer instead of the jam and honey. As the two rested against the rail of the ship, letting the wind wash over their faces, her hand gently slipped onto his arm. Turning and looking at him, "I say to you, be prepared and be ready. Before this voyage is over, I will be looking to you once again to protect me from these sea wolves." It was a silly thing to do but he bowed mockingly, telling her that he would wait, being ever ready for her order. It hurt his feelings to think that he had missed a vital clue to danger and almost felt like sulking that the woman had pointed it out, but when her hand touched him, he suddenly felt alive, but it was her words that sent the blood racing as if his heart could burst with her sentiment to him. He had hoped that the gesture was not just one of empty encouragement, but one that offered a little more. In truth, he realised that as bad as she had been, he could not help but admire her ever since he first laid eyes on her across the moonlight deck of this very ship in what seemed such a long time past.

Throughout the following day, Robert was on edge with everything and everybody ready to draw his sword whenever he felt there was a hint of a threat, and having the woman tell him many times to relax made matters worse. The ship sailed on northwards along the Latin coast, and the crew were in better spirits and eager to be ashore; nearing port gave the crew something to look forwards to, such as drunkenness and lying with base women. The day before they were to dock, when the two were alone on deck and out of earshot of any crewmen that could overhear their conversation, she turned to Robert and whispered.

"I feel what is coming will be soon." Robert immediately grasped the opportunity for conversation, but she held up her hand and walked on leaving him to believe that she did not want others to overhear what they were talking about.

As the day passed without event, they talked casually with the crew and walked the deck for air as if they had no idea of any plan for their removal, and all appeared as normal. There was bright sunshine and a gentle breeze for the sail, enough to make any mariner happy knowing that his home port was near.

When the sun dropped below the horizon, the two sat below decks in their dimly-lit cabin in silence and in anticipation. The cabin's lamp swung and squeaked in monotonous harmony with the creaking of the ship; it was not long before there was a gentle tap on the door. Surprisingly, the boson, a well-made stocky man that had passed his better years of fitness, entered with a flask of fine wine from the captain, one he was saving for a special occasion the company was told, a celebration for the completion of a safe and profitable journey. He placed the bottle on the small unpolished and scarred table, which was anchored to the deck. He waited momentarily, hovering as if waiting to witness something, and as there was no communication to be had with him, a sudden half smile appeared on his grizzled unshaven face, and managing to utter a guttural word or two such as, 'right then,' he excused himself and left the cabin. It could not be more obvious that their moment of betrayal had arrived.

Primed with the warning from the female of what could happen, Robert turned to her saying, "I find it insulting to being taken for a fool, I suggest we throw this away and feign sleep, it shouldn't be too long before our visitors return."

She smiled, "It pleases me to hear your warning, Franj, perhaps I am not wasting my time on your education as I thought." Robert smiled and could not contest her remark.

As the evening progressed, silence fell upon the ship; Robert placed himself close to the door with his ear as close to the jamb as was comfortable, without having to suffer the draught that occasionally whistled in. Somewhere nearby muffled voices could be heard, and then the steady creaking of weight carefully stepping down the staircase, indicating that two or more men paused in their movement as they weighed heavily upon the treads of the stairs making their way down and along the corridor leading to the cabin. Before they reached the door, Robert was back in the position where he sat when the wine was delivered. There seemed a long pause of inactivity as the would-be assailants made lengthy their plan of attack, which was obvious to Robert; that he would be rushed and butchered whilst the woman would be taken for the previous promise of a reward. The door latch moved slowly followed by the door quietly inching its way open. Out of a squinting eye, Robert spied three silhouettes in the dimly-lit passageway. All appeared as though the wine had been drunk and its purpose fulfilled; a glass rolled aimlessly to and fro across the table with the gentle rolling rhythm to the rise and fall of the ship as the wind gently filled the canvas sails driving her serenely through the calmer waters of the coastal approach. The other glass spilt on the floor, as if overcome whilst drinking in its potent contents. They were the signs of dormancy that manifested itself to the cowardly eyes of the would-be murdering crewmen entering the cabin, putting them at ease.

The two passengers whom the crew feared appeared to be rendered as two harmless lambs ready for the slaughter. Cautiously, the boson and his would-be fellow assassins entered the cabin creeping forwards with daggers and clubs at the ready, their cowardly leader paused half-way across the floor to assure himself that he could proceed with his most violent intention before taking another step closer to his victim. Robert timed their mood perfectly; he had waited until they were really sure of themselves and then at the point of deciding their readiness to rush the final few feet onto him, he moved like lightning. The oncoming crew men were completely taken by surprise with his sudden movement; the shock of which had them transfixed to the deck whilst he slashed out with his khataar at their leader across his upper legs. The sword sliced cutting deeply, blood spouted everywhere as the slicing action severed his main arteries causing an out-flowing of copious amounts of blood to spill onto the cabin deck. Then, before returning with a backwards slash causing little suffering for the second assailant, the bloodied Khataar sliced deeply across his neck through his jugular. The third, the boson as brave as his captain, fell to his feet as the two supporting shipmates lay in their own blood dead and unconscious, crippled for their part in the act. The weasel words of the boson did not account for much as Robert coldly ran his sword deep into the boson's innards leaving him there writhing in agony.

"There will be another in this act, probably above waiting patiently for the sweetness of the result," said the woman. Robert stepped across the writhing body of the boson and began stripping the clothes from his body and changing into them. Raising up the near dead boson over his shoulder, who was still gasping in the final throws of death, he made his way out of the cabin; turning to the woman, he suggested that what he did next may bring the other one out of his rat hole. He climbed up the stairs awkwardly carrying the weight of the moaning boson on his shoulder, banging purposely from side to side as he went out onto the darkened deck. It was a relief to be out of the half-light of the passageway, knowing that it would be difficult for anyone to recognise him. He entered the darkness of the deck lumbering with the boson over his shoulder; he was disappointed not to be met by the captain, but quickly deduced that he was more likely to be waiting in the shadows concealing himself from view. The hulk of moaning baggage that he carried across his strong shoulder indicated his location; struggling, he made his way along the side of the ships gunwale to a place clear of the rigging. He made it look as though his task of carrying his enemy was very difficult, when a voice from the shadows called.

"It is good that he suffers that one." The moment he had heard the voice, Robert alerted himself for action, giving a crude laugh of satisfaction in reply and at the same time mimicked the boson's voice as best as he could and called for a lift to toss him over the side. The load suddenly became lighter as the body was eased from him; the strong squat, heavy hands of the captain took a grip on the weighty carcase of the boson. Robert could see the captain's form, but was unable to recognise him in the darkness; making his task that much easier for him. Catching hold of the shoulders of the dying man, together they laboriously drew him up onto the rail of the ship. Robert gave a deep sigh of relief to have the boson off his shoulder; pausing to take a breath, with one last concerted effort, they pushed him off the rail and heaved him over the side. There was a sizeable splash with the boson's heavy impact on contact with a surge of passing water that took him silently away to be lost in the night. Robert bent over, appearing to be out of breath, and mimicked another laugh of completion, not wanting to be seen at close quarters by the captain, who thought his action to be quite normal under the circumstances.

"He will be fish food soon," mocked the captain cynically, "what about the woman?" the captain enquired.

"She's below with the others," Robert said gruffly. He gave him an amicable slap on his shoulder and with eagerness in his voice said, "Then let's get down there and give that devil's bitch a good slapping and teach her who is master here."

Robert could hardly hold back the laughter as he followed the captain below decks; he was a different man now that the tables appeared to have been turned, and made off with a positive spring to his step and a chuckle in his confidence. Turning to enter the cabin, the captain stiffened, numbed and stationary within the frame of the door as he viewed in disbelief the sight before him that he least expected; Robert heard him utter the word "demonio." Confused and unsure, he panicked and attempted to bolt for it as he viewed the bloody mess of his other crew men.

"I had nothing to do with this," he foolishly declared, seeing the sight of the woman sitting upright and in no mood for him by the evil look on her face. It all came upon him in the flick of an eye, and he knew he had lost the battle. In his effort to dash away, he got no further than Robert's solid chest standing directly behind him, making any attempt of his escape impossible. There was a puzzled and disbelieving look on the captain's face as he viewed that of Robert's.

"If I'm here, then where is the boson?" Robert laughed mockingly, gesturing to the captain that the two of them pushed him over the side. There was no way out for him, he realised the truth of his situation and this time he knew he could not lie his way out of it. The little toady captain was pushed forwards and onto a chair were he resigned with his head in his hands.

The tables had now turned as she stood before the repenting captain; antipathy showed in her glaring eyes from behind her facial covering, signalling to Robert she placed her index finger towards her lips as a sign for silence, after all, there was no rush to interrogate him. A deathly silence befell the cabin, enlarging the whimpering sounds of the captain who became aware that his enemy was patiently watching as they allowed him to take on his pathetic miserable sobbing of his guilt; he was truly confused with their waiting inaction. Eventually, what seemed a sentence to the distressed captain came with the sound of her sickening velvet voice, breaking the silence and causing his hair to bristle and a rapid pulsating to increase his troubled erratic heartbeat.

"Now then, my captain," she addressed the worried mariner with a sneer in her voice, "I am going to give you a better chance than you offered us." The captain raised his head showing a certain mystification on his face at her remark, almost smiling at the thought of getting away with the heinousness of his attempted crime; perhaps, he thought, she still needs me. A feeling of great relief made him easier now, almost cocky at what appeared an unsuspected and very welcome last minute reprieve; he suspected that she still needed him to moor the boat safely into a very tricky harbour. With her back to him, she asked curiously about the message that was flashed to him after he had left Lattakia. He delayed with his answer but she was having none of it, "I warn you, captain, we are passed playing at games, if you are thinking of an answer to satisfy me, don't," she said with a sharpness in her voice. The change and purpose of warning in her voice irked him, making him feel more uncomfortable as he twitched nervously.

"I said that I would offer you a better chance to save yourself, well, if you desist from letting me hear the truth, then that option will be lost."

The ship creaked homeward like a tired lady towards the safety of the lagoons harbour, as did the captain feel that his time for telling his truth would deliver him from the terrors of death by her hand, which he feared above all other things at this moment in time. Before she could snap at him once more, he willingly offered up the full message and after he delivered the information, she inquired who the sender was.

"Why, Hassan of course," answered the captain. The faintest of smiles showed on her face indicating that Kasim assumed control.

"Very well, captain, you have co-operated and told me what I wanted to know, now I will give you your chance." Turning towards him she offered a glass of wine in each of her outstretch hands. "One of these will send you into a sound sleep before you are thrown over the side; the other will give you freedom from the knowledge of the terrors awaiting you. "The captain looked bemused and challenged the woman for breaking her word.

"I only said I would give you a better chance than you gave to us." She wore that superior look on her face; it told in her eyes as they almost glistened with delight in the dimness of the cabin. As the unpleasantness of the correction was brought home to the trembling captain, who now seriously reviewed his possible fate; fearfully, he began to twitch nervously on his chair.

"No, no I refuse to take part in this sick game for your enjoyment," she laughed mockingly in the captain's face. The voice bristled with anger as she asked, "Who dares defy me when I offer terms? Especially to one who is no more than a backstabber. Look about you, these are your men that lay here, and through your own foolishness and your assistance, another member of this company has already been sent to rest in the deep waters."

The reminder of the foul deed caused the blood to drain from the captain's stricken face, turning him a paler shade of grey.

Once more, he was ordered to drink and once more he refused. The whistling sound of the Khataar from Robert's sheaf broke through the silence and the sword rested on the flesh of the pulsating nerve in the captain's neck. Her sickly tones returned to him, vile and wicked that he thought she was. "If you refuse once more, my friend will cut your throat as he would a pig," raising a finger to catch his attention, she proceeded explaining, "the cut would be only half-way, causing you to die in the most appalling of deaths whilst we watch you with the knowledge that you grope for your last breath."

The already terrified captain's eyes widened, with her words settling on him with the weight of the decision he had to take. His time of argument was long passed and his choices limited; if it was to be the drink, then he believed that he held a fifty-fifty chance. His trembling hand reluctantly reached out hovering over one glass and then the other until he had almost burst into tears under the strain. Finally, he settled on one and sniffed at it suspiciously before drinking it down, and then handed the empty glass back to the woman. He felt well and began to smile at the thought of out manoeuvring her, when suddenly he began to weaken and tremble violently and waver; he grabbed at his throat to assist in his breathing as he gagged for breath before finally collapsing in death.

She stood over him, uttering the words, "You chose freedom."

All this time, Robert remained silent throughout the captain's ordeal. Whilst agreeing that he got his due sentence for his dastardly plot, it shook him to stand back and study the woman as perhaps she truly was. There was no doubt in his mind that she was truly calculating and without mercy or compassion to her enemies. It disturbed Robert somewhat; he liked this woman, and yet with all her intelligence it appeared that she cared not a fig about mercy. How was it that she was trained to be so far removed from humanity and grow up with such a tainted heart? But that was not of her choosing, for he recalled her words of how she had been raised. She did not pretend to be anything other than an envoy for her master, and had previously admitted to him that she had been shaped as a tool and that he would not always like what he saw; how right she was.

Venice

Relieved to be on dry land and away from the tensions of living aboard ship, the two left the ship and the hopeless crew behind, who after docking, were undecided on whether they were in an awkward situation or had fallen into good fortune.

There was nothing hereabouts familiar to Robert, leaving the two lone seekers of truth to bumble their way along the Venetian quayside looking for some indication of the one that they sought.

Robert had managed to discharge the need for his old cloths and exchanged them for those that the boson used for his best; the fit was far from perfect but they did give him an air of some respectability, whilst his female companion preferred to remain in her own clothes.

Robert certainly felt out of character from what he was used to wearing, though he appeared more suitably dressed and inconspicuous, unlike the female who wore her dark eastern garb and a face veil. It was at her that people stared, their curiosity rose wherever she went.

Venice was host to many races, but the like of her was rare, especially as half of Europe were away fighting her kinsmen. Not all people were curious, some who had fought overseas recognised the dress she wore and spit at her feet as a sign of disrespect or jeered at her as they walked by. Robert was about to beset about one fellow but was instantly pulled back; their mission was more important than correcting a labourer's manners.

It was afternoon and although they had caught and docked on the noontide, it was much later when they disembarked to make their way into great city. Lost as to where they should start their mission, it was suggested by Robert that they make their way to an inn and put the word out from there; it seemed the most likely place to find a willing tongue to give them the answers they sought in exchange for the price of a drink. In agreement with that suggestion, it was decided as their best course of action, and after walking the streets they finally found a suitable inn, where, once inside its doors, they edged their way through a convivial bustling crowd cheerfully drinking and having their fill of the daily fare.

The air within the inn was heavy, filled with tantalising aromas that drifted across the room to meet its customers, promising a fare that would satisfy all. Robert was certainly taken by the sight of a spit, loaded with two sides of lamb being basted in oil with tufts of Rosemary sprouting from its sizzling carcass;

the greasy roasting lamb freely emitted its mouth-watering fragrance. The hot fat that exuded from its carcass glistened and when it dripped onto the fire, the flames reacted by exploding and spitting back hot jets of colourful fusion with heady roasting aromas that they had recognised the moment they had entered the establishment.

Being a busy establishment with plenty of people moving around tables was a good sign that the fare would be well acceptable. Robert had to raise his voice to attract the one man in the centre of the room and was the living hub of his ministration. The inquisitive eyes of the newcomers locked onto this man until he had noticed them in need of his attention, he gestured with a smile and a wave of his hand before making his way towards them. He was popular by the way that he held people's confidence, having an ability to skilfully console his waiting patrons whilst graciously receiving the compliments for the fare that was being served. Wearing an apron that was large enough to cover a table around his larger than life form, this rosy-faced man could be no other than the landlord and the man they waited to approach them. He arrived in a hot sweat and smiling a broad grin of welcome to his establishment. They took to him right away, with his big fat open face that only reflected a warmth of his intention. Rooms were what they had to secure, but first, after their weeks on ships rations, they required food to eat.

At a guess, he was a entering into his late middle-aged period, he was as generous with his comments as he was jolly in character, his oversized proportions were most certainly a testament to the standard of food that was served and that in itself made Robert feel that he had chosen well. Whilst busying himself attending to the attention of his patrons' needs, the landlord was like any good businessman, making sure that all his customers were well satisfied with the fare and spending well, which was obviously the cause for the landlord's high spirits. Approaching him, Robert held her close when they enquired if it was possible to stay; the jolly man responded favourably at the additional business, telling them that he had plenty of room for them; a reply that pleased the newcomers to feel accommodated. It was then that after securing their lodgings, Robert had followed the landlord towards the kitchen with the woman on his heels enjoying amiable conversation as they went. Who better, thought Robert whilst he had the landlord's ear, than to explain their plight of being in an unfamiliar port, seeking a man that also was a known trader.

"I know many people," he told them, "most of the traders use his establishment when doing business at the harbour. Does this individual have a name?" Robert was eager to answer, believing that he was to receive a positive reply.

"He is a friend from the Holy Land and his name is Aldo Rici," he described the young man as recently been abroad in the Holy wars and had been brought home in sickly condition. With the sound of the name, Robert was surprised at the reaction and response of the big man. He had noticed the changing effect that the name had on the landlord; it was as though he had been struck down with an instant ague that turned his bowels to water. It didn't go unnoticed from the woman either; the man was shaken to the core and although they could not argue with the landlord, they knew they could not pursue the enquiry further. The landlord feigned not having any knowledge of such a name, adding that the name was unlikely to be from his part of town. His wife, who had overheard their conversation, interceded on hearing the name; she held onto her husband's arm as if to prompt him from saying anything further; instead she, with reticence, also denied any knowledge of the name and implied that perhaps it was another name of a like sound.

Robert suspected that they knew well who his enquiries were directed to and believed his luck may hold if he were to try again than to leave the matter standing. Persisting, he stated that the name was not Aldo but Luca Rici, "he is the one we seek." A further wave of fright hit the landlord's chubby face as if he had caught a chill and been hit from behind. Shaking his head furiously as if it were going to fall off at any moment, he immediately forced his most sincere apologies on the two, further declining their money and telling them that he had been mistaken about the room they had earlier agreed on. This was most unexpected; they were truly shook at the landlord's reaction; they looked at each other searching for an answer, their state of dumb silence was cut short as the landlord continued.

"No, I am sorry, sir and madam," he said firmly, "but you cannot stay, here I must have been wrong when I said we had rooms." The innkeeper was blushing red and was agitated as he spoke, making every effort to usher them from his establishment and free himself from that name which suddenly hung about him like a disease-ridden jacket. There was a mystery here; the landlord and his wife were clearly scared; they could both tell the signs and instinctively knew that this Luca Rici was a most disliked character.

"Please reconsider, man," pleaded Robert, "is it not obvious that we are in need of food and shelter? And we pay the asking price." But his appeal fell on deaf ears; something terrible had unsettled the landlord.

Quizzing the two strangers, the landlord asked brusquely if they were friends of that person, to which Robert replied that he had never met the man, "Why does it bother you so?"

Short on words for the moment, the landlord only gestured with a raised hand before catching his breath. "Alas, I am unable to say, and I dare not, now that you have mentioned his name." Bending low and speaking in a whisper for none other to hear than those facing him, he began to explain.

"I'll admit to you, sir, you do not look like a friend of his, but no matter what your business is, think again before you go through with it." The landlord was really worked up, but it did not appear that he was to have a change of heart in regard to their boarding.

"If you know what's good for you, be on the next vessel out of here, that's the best advice I can offer you. I'm warning you, sir, for the best, if you get caught up with the likes of him and he finds out that you're staying under my roof, he will use his power to have the two of you removed, and I mean permanently," indicating drawing his finger across his throat, "and destroy me and mine into the bargain. It is well known to us that he doesn't like witnesses you understand, and yes it is true that I am in dread, for who he is and what he can do. My knowing that you seek him out puts me in equal danger, he would not rest until my name and my family has been removed from the face of the earth; he is the most evil and feared man I know."

His words spilt out as if the name tormented him, and still speaking in a whisper he added, "I beg you once more, sir," searching for the right words that would carry more weight of meaning, "a young man like yourself, sir, and your wife, well..." he exclaimed. He stood shaking his head dizzily and without explanation. For those that looked upon him could plainly see the fear that welled within him, afraid to say what was in his heart; he just kept uttering to just forget him as it could bring you both to great harm. He did not stop there but went on to say that, "This port has a reputation of losing people and no one will dare ask questions of his business."

Grabbing Robert by the hand, he pleaded, "Give up your search, sir, and you may stay but," he stopped abruptly, his message was well understood. They knew they could not give up on Aldo and said as much, though the landlord's comments were taken in and they regretfully turned to leave the inn to find another further on.

They entered the street feeling hopelessly set back, but amazed at the news that Aldo's grandfather was such a tyrant. Even the woman noted the effect on the landlord's fear; it was like that of her old master, Hassan. Robert did not comment, only held the object of her old master in his mind, and come to think of it, what he had seen of her in action wasn't exactly motherly.

Set back and slightly dejected, they moved on along the way only to hear a call for their attention, the hasty landlord came running after them.

"Sir," came the panting call, "a moment, please!" the innkeeper shouted, moving quickly towards them with his arm raised beckoning them to wait. The sight of him waddling his enormous form swaying duck like along the cobbled street cheered them up, thinking there was a change of heart.

"I had to call you when I saw you heading the wrong way," said the landlord. "If not merely to warn you not to travel in the direction you are headed, for that way," he spluttered, "that way will lead you into the lions' den." Robert appealed once more to the man, telling him that he and his wife had travelled far and it was late afternoon and that all this travelling could upset his wife's condition and as he said it he wrapped his arm around his supposed bride pulling her into him. Caught by the sympathetic appeal, the compassionate landlord hovered on his earlier decision, "Oh dear I" catching the appealing look from the eyes of the woman had him screwing up his face as in great indecision of his earlier judgement of the couple. Finally giving in with a humming and haring, his earlier stance of the stony-willed landlord subsided back to the soft-natured man that he truly was, agreeing to let them stay the night. Robert embraced the man joyfully for his kindness, but not to be overcome, the landlord stepped back, his face changed from that of a lovable, rotund man to one who seriously stressed and sternly warned them that there must be a condition; they must remain indoors and not to speak to anybody of the man that they seek.

The woman knew this man's fear and then thanked the landlord and congratulated him for showing such caution. She bent forwards, bringing his hand to her jashmak and kissed it. "You have the goodness of your God with his understanding and beneficence," she proffered. It was quite obvious that the landlord took it in, his chest rose from his stomach as he straightened his back in a self-satisfying style; it seemed to go some way to smoothing out the earlier misunderstanding.

Nobody was more surprised than Robert at her action, causing him to nearly laugh in her face and it did not go unnoticed. Instead of being silent, she stood straight, looking up into his eyes, she told him that he had been a warrior for too long and that he had lost the ability to recognise the simple honest men of the world from the secretive and manipulative ones. The landlord was taken aback and quite flustered by her flattering remarks and quickly came back to reality, standing between the two of them he hurried them back with his arms around their backs as if he were chaperoning back his own to the safety of the inn.

Inside the inn, they were ushered into a side room that the landlord kept reserved for various select merchants who favoured his establishment and his wife's cooking whenever they had business to complete in the area.

They could dine and rest in peace and at the same time; the landlord ensured that he was keeping them separate from his regular patrons and their enquiring general inquisitiveness. Once alone and seated at a table awaiting food to be brought to them, Robert mentioned the event outside with the landlord. He was poking fun at her and she did not show amusement, but took his comments well.

"Franj," she said relaxing back in her chair, "you have no humility, you must be arrogant to the last and I fear it is a great failing in you."

Oh, she knew how to criticise with purposeful intent; his admiration of her and her abilities was so great it knew no bounds, but she was always able to bring him to earth with a bump by making him feel self-conscious. Now that he was reduced, she had noticed how it affected him by his sullen expression; it was not her intention to be so stern and nudged him telling him she was jesting. Immediately, he perked up, as if given an elixir that worked magically on him. His smile was a demonstration that he was redeemed from the aside as well as not damaging the relationship that was growing between them. He replied, saying that he was not used to such taunts and asked her not to jest in such a serious manner as it disturbed him.

There was a message in his remark and although she kept the meaning to herself, she refrained from replying to his comment, but added, "I tell you, Franj, I am beginning to feel more at ease with you of late."

Well this was extraordinary, could he believe his ears, was that a compliment he wondered; before he could continue, in came the landlord with the much-needed food to sustain their now ravenous hungry appetites. The meals were placed before them on the heavy wooden table that separated them before returning to his duties elsewhere, leaving them alone to themselves. The steaming meal had its effect on Robert, begging to be consumed with gusto whilst her hungry eyes gazed apprehensively with a reservation to eating the soup-like food that she was unused to eating. Go ahead urged Robert and eat, its good, a stew was not what she was used to; then, watching her companion spooning it with avidness into his mouth, it gave her some assurance of its content. Now, for the first time when they were alone, she dropped her yashmak to eat, noticing the look of surprise upon Robert's face. To dismiss her action, she simply admitted that she was honouring him, as he was the first man that she had allowed to see her face unveiled. He was surprised and said so, and leaning forwards towards her, retorted quite frankly that he had already looked upon her face.

"Before," she said in a reprimanding tone, "you stole that look brazenly like a thief." After a pause she added with a half-smile on her face, "I sit here now and freely allow you to see me as my God made me, which in my country is a reward only for a husband to see, so you must understand, Franj, as an ordinary man, you should accept what you behold is a great honour that I bestow on you."

A huge smile broke across his face, before it dropped flat self-consciously when she let it be known that it was not an invitation for him to think it meant other than something that it was not. All the time, different aspects of her make-up unfolded, showing an array of different attributes, and to him they were improving and not quite as bad as he began to think of them. In spite of her hunger, she ate her food slowly and in silence without a word being spoken except for the sounds of their food being so heartily enjoyed. Robert finished first and ate a further two pieces of fruit before she had finished her meal, then he mentioned that he should perhaps talk to the landlord once more about his young friend. With that, she began to replace her veil; Robert commented that she did not have to do that now that she was in Italy, it was not the custom for women to cover their beauty. His sudden slip of the tongue made him blush with embarrassment having blurted out what he thought without realising what he had said before he had said it. Her smile showed a slight embarrassment as she dropped her head but she replaced her veil nonetheless. Not long after the landlord returned to fulfil his duty of clearing away their dishes and see if they required further nourishment. Robert asked to pass his compliments to his wife for the meal; that pleased the landlord enough swell his chest and plant a huge smile of pride on his face.

"She has a special talent in the kitchen, does my wife," and he patted his sizeable middle; then with his deft hands filled the huge tray he carried and whisked away their empty platters.

It had been a long time since wholesome food had been enjoyed so; even the woman agreed on the acceptance of the food. When the landlord returned, he was in a garrulous mood, being all smiles eager to tell them that he had passed on their comments onto his wife. Robert asked if he would stay for just a moment to listen to the story of the youth that they sought named Aldo.

The landlord's smile dropped, wondering whether he should be willing to learn anything at all regarding the grandson. His apprehension was quickly noted and Robert assured him that it was as much about him as the young grandson. Sitting down, the Landlord agreed as long as he didn't learn anything that could be detrimental to him and his wife; they could see a nervousness showing but, despite his reservation, he wore a most interested look on his face, prompting Robert to begin.

Robert's story started some three years previously, of how the youth had once saved his life whilst in the jaws of an impending and certain death. A detachment of men he told the landlord that he had led were engaged in battle and were outnumbered after being ambushed; the fighting was vicious and bloody.

"We were screaming and shouting all sorts of insinuations at the enemy to keep our spirits high whilst fighting for our lives, it's partly to do with a madness that takes over men's souls in battle. It's as though we become somebody else, it happens to us all, on both sides; it's as if the gates of Hell have been opened and we become consumed by the breath of the evil one, but we are all driven to gain victory." The landlord was being absorbed into the story, even open-mouthed at the effects of a soldier's demeanour. "However," Robert continued, "we were surrounded by the oncoming enemy and fighting like demons for our survival when he had been bumped by a stray horse. Things like that happen also; if horses are not slaughtered they end up going wild with the amount of barbed weapons aimed at them. The ground quickly grows slick from the blood of men and dying animals; battle is a sorry mess that you're better off avoiding. Well," he added, "I stumbled off balance; it was as much as I could do to keep swinging my sword wildly trying to cover myself from further harm. If it's not the enemy in front of you that are after blood, it's the surge of men that comes from behind trying to kill or cover you. "As I was saying, I felt that I was done for and before a sword could bury itself in me, a shield deflected its point to give me the time needed to recover and stand again to continue the fight. Only for the intervention and at great peril to his own life, Aldo had moved to protect me, for those fleeting moments he forced himself forwards before me and taking my place to hold the line, it was an action that saved my life. Within a short time after, a horn blew, signalling the advance of a relief, the supporting militia from our left flank had moved forwards to add to our support. That action saved us and won the day, but not before many good men had fallen on both sides; the reaper you know cares not from which side he strikes with his scythe of death and by the amount of dead and dying that day, he worked with much effort. If it wasn't for that young man Aldo, I believe that I would not be talking to you this day."

"It is as you say," interjected the woman, "good men perish in battle, wasted by the wills of their arrogant leaders."

"I suppose your right," the landlord said, "you are indeed a brave man sir and I would not want to go to war; there is enough turmoil here and in the streets outside for my liking. Though I respect your reasons now that I understand your story; a man should always stand by his friends no matter how difficult the going is, the landlord proffered."

In return for such gallantry and rashness of action, Robert added, "I made a pledge to defend and befriend this young man and watch over him as much as was healthy, so long as he was under my command and breathing in God's fresh air." Robert snorted "Though I have a habit of calling him 'the boy,' I know that he is a man in his years and spirit. I recall that he was reckless almost beyond help; to my older eyes, almost inviting death on any day that we would bear arms, as if he had something to prove and without care of thought for himself. There were those loose of mouth that goaded him on; but to my mind they too were infected with the same battle fever as he, many times I did all I could do to hold him back and keep him safe."

"What exactly is this sickness that you refer to?" asked the landlord.

"Have you ever seen a mad dog?" interjected the woman. "It is a mixture of the humours that involve the nervous disorder and a feeling that you must kill everything in sight until then you are not safe; is that not right, husband?" With her hand she indicated on the surface of the table, "You see," she explained, "the line that separates madness from bravery is very fine indeed when in battle."

"My, madam, you almost sound as if you are a physician and have been in battle yourself. She smiled a knowing smile, listen to her interjected Robert for she has much knowledge, does my lady, it would serve you well to heed her for I have never known her to be wrong."

With an air of understanding, the landlord agreed, "Women are a little like that in their own world, I suppose. I would never argue with my wife about kitchen matters. But about your friend..."

"As you say, I think he must have been affected with the battle madness that takes fighting men into the darker places of their soul. It is, I fear, an evil sickness that eats away the soul," said Robert.

The woman was silent; she knew well what Robert was talking about and she was surprised by his depth of feeling towards his friend. Not wanting to give any indication of this, she held her head down; while the landlord patted Robert's shoulder and told him that he was a good man. There was a brief silence; it was the landlord that spoke first.

"Well, I must say, that does not sound like any kin of Luca's to me, but pray tell me, Sir Knight," asked the landlord, "how come he fell so ill for his grandfather to have to go and fetch him?"

"Ah, well," stammered Robert, looking over towards the woman, "that is a different story."

"Now that I come to think about it," said the landlord, "Luca was recently away from Venice but no one witnessed his return in the recent weeks gone by," and he added, "it would have not gone unnoticed, not in a place like this if you know what I mean. Not a thing in Venice happens without being talked about; that does not eventually drift through this place.

"Guessing aloud," said the landlord, "I would say he came into the lagoon at low tide and ashore by a small craft. Nobody has seen him out and about, but everybody knows he is back. Believe me, he is like a creeping sickness over this city and we all know it by his squeeze on the guilds." Sitting back in his chair he added with a faraway look occupied with his thoughts, "Yes, it's hard to believe. He is not like all boiled eggs when it comes to his grandson, rumour had it that he adored him, the word is that he was about to retire giving over everything to the young man. He was not known personally by any of us your young friend, and no one would have believed it when the young man joined the cause to fight against those pagans overseas."

He had no sooner said the words when he looked across to the woman; it was an embarrassing slip that he regretted as he noticed the woman's head drop forwards to hide her disappointment. Robert also felt a little self-conscious over the landlord's last phrase and quickly added, "Not all of them."

The landlord, taking the hint, apologised for his generality of condemnation and excused himself to the woman before repeating Robert's words, "No not all of them," and added, "just some of them." Although it pleased her that the landlord begged pardon for his slip, she knew deep down they both had much to excuse for their own peoples characters, but that was humanity.

The day passed by so quickly and into the early evening. In their privacy, they discussed of what to do as well as how to go about their gathering of intelligence from the unsuspecting landlord. He had been in and out of the room checking on them most of what was left of the day, probably more for the sake of making sure that they were not in contact with any other person. When their conversations were drawn to a silence, the landlord noticed it and thought it best that they would be willing to retire, and without giving them a chance to speak, told them to follow him whilst he escorted them to their room for the night.

Once the door of privacy was closed and they were alone in their room, she turned to him and suggested that he find a place to sleep other than the large bed that yearned to be filled with its invitation of crisp clean sheets.

"I will sleep beyond under the window," he offered, "don't you go worrying yourself about me.

"Furthermore let's make a truce about this room - no arguing," before he took it upon himself to jest with her by mentioning for her not to forget that he had also seen her in bed, remember, hoping that she would see the amusement in his remark. She was about to insinuate allegations but thought better of it; it seemed that she was beginning to understand his humour. He leaned towards the window drawing the curtain aside peering out through its crudely formed glass panels, which seemed to distort all manner of shapes he viewed beyond.

"We will have to make contact with Aldo's grandfather tomorrow," he turned his head towards her in time to see her hopping into bed exposing the bare flesh of her lower leg and thought it better that he turned away as quickly as not to cause her any undue embarrassment.

"How did you view the old man when you saw him in Lattakia?"

"It was merely a transaction, though it is true what the landlord said, he was a difficult man to deal with. For what it is worth, I had read this man and did not like what I believed I encountered. But you must remember, I was not there to have dealings with him, other than handing over his grandson, your friend," she added.

Like a pig in a market place, Robert thought. He hated the thought of Aldo kept in a sleep like the dead, he was so full of energy. It was his friend she was talking about and his mind went back picking up the image of the camel skin bag full of arrows that had been draped over the cliff at the canyon of the snake.

"Are you thinking bad thoughts of me now, Franj?"

"How do you do that?" With a noticeable tone of incredulity in his reply.

"What?" she asked casually.

"Read my mind," he was getting quite worked up over it.

"Rest is what you need, Franj. Take advantage of the fact that tonight, rest is safe, a luxury you have not enjoyed for a long time."

He thought on it for a while and then piped up saying, "You have the bed."

"Go to sleep," was the sharp reply.

When they rose the following morning, it was late; the two had slept late purposely so that they would be free from any contact with other boarders. Their morning repast was more of a structured approach to how they set about finding and talking to the dreaded villain Luca, long enough to locate the whereabouts of Robert's friend Aldo. The location of Luca's office they got from the reluctant landlord, who made Robert swear that he would only pass such information over if he gave his oath of silence should they be unfortunate enough to be interrogated by Luca at some later stage. When it was time for them to leave, the landlord wished them luck as they left the safety of the inn to confront the wealthy ship owner, Luca Ricci.

Before finally parting, the woman asked of the landlord a boon, if in case they did not return to hold for her certain items of property. If, as expected, the eventuality that countrymen of hers may possibly come looking for her, she would appreciate that he give them the satchel. She suggested that descriptions were not necessary and that he would know them when they made contact with him. "There would be no danger to you or your family, indeed," she added, "there could even be some kind of reward," she said, smiling.

The landlord looked perplexed, saying that it all sounded very mysterious to him, and so did Robert, he never knew that she carried anything of value.

"There is one more thing," she interrupted the worried innkeeper who was about to ask a question. Handing him a money pouch, she inferred once more that if they were not heard of again, the contents of the pouch would be his for the keeping, in thanks for his understanding, but if they were to return she may be grateful herself of its need. The landlord was keen to perform the favour, though reluctant to see them leave and seek out the one person half the city dreaded. He repeatedly stressed his deep concern for their safety with that Ricci fellow, and he spoke the name as if he had a bad taste in his mouth. He could not help but look about himself warily as he said it, regretting instantly as the words fell from his undisciplined tongue, knowing that should any word of it get back to Luca of his comment, he could very well be seeking a new accommodation of his own. The jolly features of the landlord dropped into the guilty frown of his changed features, but recovered quickly in wishing them safe passage wherever they may be, and to especially take care of you know who before he bade them farewell.

Robert was full of questions and in a chatty mood as they walked along the busy street from the tavern. Following the instructions from the landlord, the two soon found themselves in a thronging piazza where a market was in full attendance. The surrounding buildings on three sides were large and old and slightly dilapidated and a small row of buildings on the other side took pride of place with its unusual classical design. At the edge of the canal, a larger building took pride of place. It was as described to them, a tall, three-storey terraced building with an appearance of gracing better times and now looking somewhat jaded, though not neglected. They watched and waited to see who passed through its doorway but alas never the one that they expected to see. Finally, they decided to enter the portal themselves and speak with the keeper of Luca's empire, to which, on entering, were surprised when they faced the keeper therein. A weakly lame clerk, bent and showing a white mantle of tussled hair, probably come about through years of being harassed by the notorious employer. His lined and thin features showed him probably to be undernourished or perhaps just worn by the strain of his work. Not yet into his middle years, those facial lines indicated hardship; he made his way towards them displayed a severe limp, together with show of great pain in his effort. In Robert's eyes, the man must have had grit to maintain the agony that such a debilitating injury had for him. The pain he bore was reflected in his lack lustre sad eyes, he could not hide its being a constant companion through his everyday life, when he reached them he was courteous and spoke softly and yet, for some unknown reason, it seemed agitation was in his voice, most probably owing to the strenuous effort and discomfort of his situation.

Robert enquired after his master, the clerk's eyes quickly scanned the two before him, they were not like others of Luca's type; but many different types came and went from these offices, all of a mixed bag of people, certainly never a woman, unless she was base, but these two in his estimation were definitely different. He enquired into the nature of their business but he was declined an answer, for that reason, he told them he was unable to assist them in any way.

"Would there be another way to see him perhaps at his private residence?" Robert probed. A whistle from the clerk of a sudden intake of air as Robert asked such a bold question; the reply that came was that he never had known his master carry out personal business from his home. Drawing a blank from their enquiries, the two thought it better to leave without further probing; they were watched by the clerk, who remained at the small window of the office taking note on their direction. They went as far as the inn across the square from Luca's office; the wily clerk suspected that that was where they could watch those that frequented the office. He was correct in his assumption, Robert and the woman stayed beyond the time of the morning making lengthy enquiries as to where Luca's residence could be located, but on every occasion they were shunned out of fear.

It was not until mid-afternoon when they were finishing off their refreshment that a stranger did confront them. A ragged, shabby individual, no more than a thin effigy of a man who served as a runner for the office; he had untrustworthy eyes and stood before them in a reluctant manner, not too sure of himself his lip trembled as he blurted out a message that the man that they seek was now in his office. He was about to dash off, considering his task completed when Robert caught a hold of his jacket.

"Not so fast, my friend," Robert's smiling face assured the messenger that he was not in any danger as he wriggled to escape, it seemed that Luca kept his servants in fear for he plainly showed that he was not comfortable having to answer any questions put to him. The messenger begged to be freed as Robert's grip tightened on his already worn tunic.

"Just a question or two," Robert proposed, "now who sent you and how did you know where to find us?"

The messenger was caught in a fork of destiny, afraid of the consequences of replying to the stranger and afraid of his master should he find out that he had blabbed an answer.

"The clerk at Master Ricci's sent me, he watched you come in here and word had got back that you were asking too many questions for your own good."

A smirk of knowing showed on Robert's face, he released his grip on the messenger and watched as he speeded away as if a demon was on his heels, out of the door and into the street to be lost in the crowds. Robert looked across the table and spoke his thoughts out loud.

"This could be our undoing, you know that from now on danger trails us, it would be safer if you stayed behind and watched for me."

"Franj, are you thinking of my safety?" she purred.

"I cannot see what you have to offer this man, Rici," she added candidly, "I am the only one who can give him something to believe in." There was an incredulous look on Robert's face as if he was wondering what she was up to now.

"What have you in mind?"

"If I can persuade him that the potion that I handed him in Lattakia was hurriedly made and that I have been sent to produce one of less potency, perhaps he will take me to his grandson."

"What about me?" said Robert.

"Oh, don't worry, Franj, you will be watching my every move, and be ready to rescue me if you feel that I am in any danger."

He thought some while on the matter, then said decisively, "If you are alone with him I will never know if you are in danger. I'll just have to be your body-guard and stay with you at all times."

Agreed on their plan, they approached the offices of Luca Ricci once again, this time it was with the knowledge that danger lay ahead and they had to be on their guard as their lives would probably be threatened. Walking through the office door, the noise from the street rushed in behind them to fill up all its silence. Being in line with the door, the incoming draught caught the fine strands of the clerk's hair, causing them to lift and fall to the opposite side of his parting. Without bothering over his appearance, he continued working, bent double over his bookwork; he hardly took the time to look up, but spoke telling them that he would attend to them shortly. His entry completed, he placed down his feather quill and looked across in their direction.

"Good, you received my message then. You have been persistent in your enquiries," a knowing smile crept into the corner of his mouth, "the master will see you soon," he assured them.

They waited for some time. Robert paced the office impatiently in the anticipation of trouble looking this way and that fearing that something would happen. There was nothing but silence within; the only noise that could be detected was the scratching of the quill that indicated the clerk was diligently kept to his work. The waiting was not what Robert was used to, which disturbed him, yet appeared to have the opposite effect on the clerk. Eventually, the sound of a muted bell tinkled, hardly audible to their ears but the clerk was alert to it and was up limping his way towards the darkened void at the end of the room where the stairway led up to his employer's office. The sound of his foot being dragged up the stairs recorded the clerk's inability to lift his injured foot; his boot bumped on every tread of the stair, like a loose appendage being towed along. When he finally returned, he told the waiting couple that they would be seen, and turning away to lead the way, the woman held him back and spoke, telling him not to trouble himself as they could find their way to his master's office at the top of the staircase. The clerk was reluctant not to carry out his duty but grateful for the consideration, aware that his condition was not normally mentioned sympathetically so. He hated people to sympathise without a second thought for his suffering; only his master delighted in seeing his pain and weakness, and he had learned to cope with that over the years.

The top of the stairs was almost total darkness except for a squint of light that peered through the edge of the loose fitting door. She lightly knocked on the darkened oak door that was hardly visible in the dark shadow of the windowless passage; an aged but strong voice called from the other side beckoning them to enter. Robert held the door open for her to enter like the servant he was supposed to be, passing into the dimly lit room, Luca sat silhouetted behind his desk with a numerous amount of burning candles around him, creating his form as the focal point within the room. The ageing face of the seated man appeared a kindly one to any that were unacquainted with him; although the lines on his face were heavy for his years, they were softened by the silver threads of hair that caught the light. He was immaculately though plainly dressed in his pure white silken shirt and showing a deep collar and a heavy red velvet jacket hung loosely open all the way beneath the desk. It hung in neat folds from the shoulder with its loose baggy sleeves that must almost covered his knees; it didn't take much to see that Luca was a man that liked to dress and show himself off. He was sitting upright in his huge wooden chair with his arms folded across himself as if in some form of anticipation of their visit. He did not rise but remained seated, an outstretched hand welcomed them into the room, and his voice quite mellow and warm appealed to them to come closer to the light so that his old tired eyes could view them clearly.

"So, you are not what I expected to see. It is not often that people make such persistent enquiries after my person, have we business to discuss?" When the woman was seated, she dropped the hood from her dark cloak letting him see as much of her face as he had seen before. In the bright candle glow, his face shrunk back contorted, the eyes of his pallid face narrowed as he felt he half recognised her. As if discovered in an evil act, he had become alarmed at her presence and his tone changed, wondering where she had come from and why. The face now took on a quizzing and purposeful mood with his eyes peering through half open lids, as she sat before him like someone accused.

"I know you, don't I?" he posed, spitting out the question in a challenging sort of manner.

"We met in Lattakia when I consigned a cargo to you."

"We did indeed." That confirmed it, leaning back in his chair surveying her as his eyes went from her to Robert who remained by the half open door.

"You have a strange companion," he said sharply observing Robert, "he's not one of yours."

"He is a mercenary, I brought him with me, as I am a stranger here and he of your kind it was decided that he accompany me and I can rely on him."

"Oh, that's wise," he said thoughtfully. "Yes, very wise," he repeated; he came forwards off the back of his chair with a slightly threatening tone in his voice.

"So now, tell me, why have you been asking around the city for me?"

She was very cool and quite unmoved by his probing and almost hostile change in tone.

"In Lattakia, we had to move very quickly, everything was carried out hurriedly and the same applies to the potion that I handed to you."

His face screwed quizzically and alarm set in with the unpleasant news, as he demanded, "Are you telling me that there is something wrong with the potion that I have been giving my grandson?"

"Only that it could be a slightly stronger potion."

"This potion," Luca asked with a certain concern in his tone, "is there any danger that it could harm my grandson?"

"I must admit it could, yes," she said, "but only if it is continued to be administered in its present strength, there is a slight danger. The boy," she sighed pausing before speaking, "he may become addicted to it and may never regain his consciousness, leaving him suspended in a place between life and death."

Luca became livid and was suddenly standing, leaning across his desk, pointing his finger over towards her. "We made a bargain, you are supposed to be experts in your science, I entrusted you with the life of my grandson and you were paid well." In his flustered state he searched momentarily for words to strike her with, "You have reneged on the bargain. If you have cheated me, you will never leave Venice."

He became almost demented and found it hard to find the words to speak until he regained his composure; he kept looking at Robert and the khataar that hung from his sash. There was no one to call on that could handle a professional guard, especially one of hers, but it was clear to her that his fear for his grandson would not leave him. Whilst she calmly sat there ignoring his ranting, she waited for calm to re-enter the meeting and he took his seat. Looking at him coolly and without emotion, she waited, watching; he was in a state of panicked confusion, making the situation edge towards danger. Then in a soothing tone, she asked Luca again if he wanted his grandson to die.

Without thinking, Luca was on his feet once more demanding what kind of question was that to ask him, insisting that she do something about his condition. The paper that had lain on his desk had been instantly screwed into a ball in Luca's sudden rage. Waiting for calm once more before she spoke, she advised Luca that the boy was in no danger at present and that she would bring him back to health. Quite sternly and without raising her voice, warned Luca about any attempts to stop them leaving Venice should he foolishly consider injuring an emissary of the Old Man of the Mountain, it would serve him well to remember that her master's arm could reach far.

"My master's power is all encompassing; should you consider harming his emissary, the shadow of death will be forever over those that treat him lightly." She told Luca plainly that her master would not yield until Luca himself and all that bore his name were wiped from the face of the earth. Luca did not enjoy being threatened and hesitantly gave way to the woman; she was strong and it reminded Robert of Hassan's power. Luca may have been master in Venice, but he knew the reputation of The Old Man of the Mountain and willingly, for the moment, succumbed.

"Heed my words carefully, old man, we do not renege on bargains, we seal them with our word and our deeds; why do you think that I am here before you? Besides, you have nought to fear," she said arrogantly, "my master was well pleased with you and your gift," and waving her hand as to dismiss the subject, "now let there be no more of this talk of treachery."

Luca was without an answer, being slightly embarrassed; she was right and he sighed as if to give in, but she caught his sly, foxy, flicking eyes as he looked twice at her.

"Of course, you are right," acting as if a player on the stage; the old man act in Luca came back, but it fooled no one. He must have used the ploy countless times on the unsuspecting, only to turn on them when it suited him best. There had to be a change of atmosphere to reduce the tension and she suggested that the sooner she could be shown to his grandson the sooner their work could be underway.

"I'll call my clerk to make the necessary arrangements to stay at my house and to escort you there."

"Surely we could do that downstairs."

"Yes, I suppose," not wanting to make an exhibition of the clerk's pain, he conceded, though he was deprived of his daily sadistic treat against the clerk that he despised. "Very well," he submitted tersely not wanting to display his fit of pique, "see that it is done."

It was a relief to escape the smells of the burnt candle grease in the confinement of the office that had filled every crevice of the dark dingy room. The air in the passageway may not have been fresh but it was like a breath of clean air to be away from Luca. They walked out of the door and stood momentarily out on the small landing before their descent; she felt a rush of air from above indicating that there were empty rooms beyond and that something above was in need of repair. As for the steep darkened staircase, she also noted how difficult they would be to ascend in silence. All these things she stored in her memory, for somehow she felt she would return to this place.

The clerk was informed of his master's wishes from the woman for which he questioned, unable to take in at first. He did not know what to say, for never since the time that he had been engaged in Luca's slavish employment did he ever have anyone to relay his master's orders at his desk. Only someone of equal temper or someone that would be of extremely good use to his employer, for the wicked Luca to lose out on the joy of watching another such as he to painfully drag himself up the stairs to indulge his cruel master's warped sense of dominance.

Time flashed through his weary head of when he was foolishly taken in by Luca. He was in the employ of another then and rising in status, being so trusted, he became innocently mixed up in one of Luca's schemes to cheat on his employers; by the time he had realised what was going on, matters had developed and it was far too late for change. Luca had snared the young man into fulfilling his role in his innocuous scheme. He met Luca in the street and tried to beg him to do the honourable thing and speak up admitting all; but when Luca refused, a scuffle of sorts broke out and Luca pushed him against a temporary scaffold that was supporting a load of unsecured masonry. The supports moved sufficiently to dislodge the load causing it to fall on him. His leg was so severely crushed that it was impossible for him to walk properly again. If it had been left to Luca, he would have let him lay there until he died; but he remained a threat and there were people about who could be witnesses; he could not afford publicly to be accused of such a crime. Not wanting his scheme to be discovered, he called for help making out there had been a terrible accident. Though he could have had him discretely removed, Luca feared that his sudden disappearance may have led to many questions being asked. Caught in a tenuous situation, Luca was unsure what to do for the best; remarkably, he pointed out to him whilst on a visit to view his condition that he would be useless in his previous work so why not he suggested work for him. It was an offer that was not arrived at with guilt and charity in mind; to keep him close was Luca's intention to keep him from opening his mouth and ruining his little money making scheme.

For this act of compassion by this woman, the clerk recognised her reasoning and thanked her without expanding on his situation; but intimated that it had been too many long years since such an act of kindness was shown to him whilst serving under this roof. Shaking his head with the knowledge of what he had seen go on in this establishment without ever a kind word toward him, he wished her well and advised her to take particular care for the future. Then, turning to a shabbily dressed young man sitting on the far side of the room, he raised his hand to beckon him into service; he was another of Luca's runners of errands for the clerk; his orders were to guide the two strangers to the house of the master Signor Luca.

The streets were not as full as they were earlier when dusk began to fall but it struck Robert that instead of heading inland, they were keeping to the direction that headed adjacently along a route that ran along the edge of the lagoon. It would be expected that a wealthy man such as Luca would live somewhere on high ground where it would be easy to survey all below, but now they were travelling on the dockside and heading towards a large house at the end of the quay. The property was walled on three sides, it had a frontage which stood out against the other houses and there was an outer gate with railings around it. There stood a small untidy patch of garden, which could hardly be seen now that the sun was setting. The house, like the office building, looked as though it had seen better days, it was or had been a grand house in its day, but somehow the present appearance did not do it justice. They expected a large house and were not disappointed in its size, although it was not expected to be on the edge of the lagoon where the mists would shroud the house in its haunting unhealthy cover of mists that spread its dampness throughout any open windows, giving rise to chesty coughs for its occupants.

There was somebody waiting to give them entry into the house; word had got there before them, as the outer Iron Gate was unlocked so the main door of the house opened and on their entry they were shown to a waiting room just off the hall entrance and there they were told to wait until the master arrived.

Their wait was a chilly one; the big house was without warmth as the evening drew in and it was quite sometime later when Luca arrived home. On his entry, he sighted the two strangers sitting in his waiting room, immediately he spoke up, inquiring if they had seen to his grandson. They replied that they were ordered to remain where they were and to wait for his return; that was precisely what was done. Luca's face grew deep red with anger and immediately called for his manservant; being certain that he had done exactly what was expected of him, the servant arrived obediently before the master with the belief that all was well. It was not to be as he expected; Luca confronted the foolish servant and ranted; the man became cowered, expectant it seemed of punishment. Showing a different side of his character, Luca expecting that the servant should have known better than to keep his guests waiting, especially those that were to help the young master Aldo. Knowing that no servant of Luca's would dare look his master in the eye, the watchers looked on as the servant tensed himself in readiness to take an immediate thrashing from Luca's walking stick.

The poor servant had taken more punishment than was necessary for laxness. Robert could not stand by and watch the punishment as the wheels on the man's back burst and grew wet with his blood, it was sickening to watch the display and was about to act to move and stop Luca's action, when the woman caught his sleeve in time to warn him not to interfere. The ageing despot did not cease the punishment until his arm grew weary.

The onlookers watched and were silent; though Robert's blood was boiling for such an undeserved action and merely took in the scene in disgust. Luca appeared to take pleasure in his display of power over the unfortunates that were in his service; it also showed those watching that Luca could be a most dangerous and sadistic adversary. Ignoring the crumpled whinging heap that lay on the floor, Luca then without a second thought, walked around the cringing mass that was the bloodied servant as if he were no more than a piece of dirt to be avoided in an alley. Stretching out an arm as he walked to a small polished rectangular table that stood against the wall, he picked up a glowing candle housed in a small, cheap candleholder and gestured for the company to follow him. The stairs were steep and dark, not unlike those inside his office, but they did not seem to bother him as he nimbly picked his way up them. It was only when he neared the top of the stairs that he broke his silence, he stopped and turned holding up the light, and almost apologised for his action, adding that he could not stand a laxity in servants overlooking his orders. The woman spoke agreeing fully with his actions saying that her master may not have been as lenient as he. When Luca replied, Robert almost choked on his words, "Yes, I have heard he is very hard on those that he chooses to place in positions of trust."

Before stepping off onto the second flight, he impatiently bid the two to keep close where they could be seen as they climbed the darkened staircase to the landing above where there was not even a trace of light anywhere along the sparsely furnished landing and corridor to be seen. There was a pause and the company came together before the door of a room; they waited while Luca took his time fumbling through a mass of jingling keys looking for one to fit the lock. As a second thought, it struck him that the key was elsewhere and fumbled through his pockets where he eventually withdrew a key which he then struggled in the darkness to locate the key hole. At last, the key entered noisily into the lock, indicating that there was no concern of disturbing the person within. It turned easily and the door was opened, and by the time that Luca had withdrawn the key from the door, he experienced a feeling of draft sweep by him causing him to arch backwards in surprise. Satisfied that the key was safely back in his pocket, he stooped to lift the candle to light his way to the bedside of his comatose grandson; from the light of the candle, he was shocked to see the woman bending over his grandson. With a disgruntled tone in his voice he called to the woman to step away from the boy, at the same time asking how she arrived at the bedside before him. She gave Luca a disinterested look and he began chastising her for rushing into the room without his permission to do so. She stood her ground as Luca tried to bully her into a sorrowful submission; but he had not bargained for her strength of character.

The woman was not interested in Luca's pettiness and retaliated with the importance of her patient's health at heart and could not wait whilst he dallied around his pockets to put away a key that was taking him an eternity. Seeing that she had caused Luca to stop and think, she retorted how futile it was to underestimate her abilities.

"You know where I have come from and who sent me, I am hashashin," she told him. He gulped with that knowledge; he knew what she was, but to be reminded sent a shiver of fear down his spine. She chided him on his silly attempt to keep the house in darkness so to prevent others from finding a doorway that led to his grandson; how she knew his motives scared Luca.

"Do you not realise that my master would not send to you a novice in the esoteric arts? You underestimate me and I am surprised to see such a weakness of this kind in such a powerful man." She had Luca examining his actions, he was taken aback, did she not witness the demonstration below, how could she think that was a weak? She walked towards him, calmly telling him that she had the ability to see through the darkness and walk through closed doors. "You westerners can only hide and fear the dark, while we scientifically understand and use it to our advantage." She continued to berate the ageing man blinding him with the mysteries that he could not comprehend, "Use your head for once and see the gift that my master had sent to your aide in this situation."

She almost smiled with her speech of abilities that truly confounded Luca; he had never met anyone like her and he was beginning to see her as some kind of witch. Through the dim flickering flame of the candlelight, Luca's face distorted, half in anger, half in doubt and uncertainty, coupled with a certain fearful respect of her; he dare not challenge her ability, having for years heard of the stories and the mysteries related to the hashashin. What worried him most was her witch-like powers, she may turn against him and place him under a spell that could be used to strike him into a withering fool, he could not allow that. Who was this female that could do such things, true she was at his grandson's side before him, a shiver passed down his back, she must have flown to be at the bedside long before he had picked up the candle off the floor. In her black robes he did not detect her in the darkness. In his circumspect mind, it caused him great concern; a passing thought flashed across his mind, from now on he would treat her as a threat, for he realised she appeared everything that she said she was.

Meanwhile, she looked over the young man, lifting his eyelids to peer into his dead eyes; what was it she could see that was any different from his viewing, her actions baffled him. She continued to view the depth of his sleep making silly sounds of so-called understanding and ordering Luca to raise the light so that she could look deeper into the boy's eyes, but it was poor and shadows impaired her view. It was useless, the old man bobbed in and out of the light hoping to see whatever it was that she was hoping to find. He was a nuisance alongside her; losing her patience, she demanded that she wanted the room filled with light so that she could see deep into his eyes to better ascertain the young man's condition. The old man's worried and agitated face grimaced with apprehension for his grandson's recovery. He snapped out orders but there was no one within hearing distance to obey his commands. It made him more annoyed to have to fetch the candles himself and to have to leave the room to the two strangers, but his concern for his grandson was paramount in his mind and he would do anything she asked, though he loathed it and her. He acted so cantankerously and audibly cursed as he went off, and she lifted her head to Robert and winked as he breathed a sigh of relief picking up on her knowing that she must have been smiling under her yashmak.

Robert's look of anticipation left him; she had played her ruse out dangerously to the end by pushing the irascible Luca to the limit. Robert sensed the old man's vehemence at her disregard for him, leading him to suspect that in the back of his mind she could have alerted the crafty old dog into taking some kind of precautions against them. The untrusting Luca was back into the room in no time at all; and just in time to catch the woman leaning across to inform Robert that she had done what was necessary. The old man's ears twitched almost as he tried to pick up on what was said between the two; but because of the distance between them he was unable to understand what was said between them.

"We are finished until the morrow," she spoke in a hushed voice in the hope to prevent Luca from raising any loud objections. Suspicion had filled his ageing face as he gave her a thunderous look of angered disgust, guessing that he had been conveniently and easily managed out of the room. This time it was he that ushered them out of the room, not forgetting to lock the door behind him and ensuring their passage into the darkness of the landing. They were to stay the night as his guests and would not hear any argument against his wishes, nor would he hear of talk of alternative accommodation. They would eat at his table this evening and discuss their plans before they were to be shown their room.

A dark thought ran through Robert's mind of the last time he was kept as a guest against his will, only this time the insistence was a little more subtle.

They were escorted along the passage and onto the darkened stairway, a sudden draught raced up towards them from the opening of the front door. The vestibule door below was open sufficiently to allow those on the stair to see the newcomers entering. Peering over the rail there stood two burly characters having entered discreetly in their way but were clumsily so as to betray their presence; and they detected the maid carelessly beckoning them not to speak whilst being shown through into the small waiting room adjacent to the hall.

Luca moved ahead quickly to the bottom of the stairs and closed the door of the vestibule by slamming it to announce his anger with the maid for her carelessness in leaving it ajar. The exercise had not been overlooked by either of the two descending the staircase; this was a new development and a probable threat in preparation for them. Luca attempted to divert their seeking eyes and their minds away from anything that may warn them for what was about to come. They were led along another dingy passageway devoid of bright light until they stopped outside another door. This time, when Luca placed his hand on the knob he cautiously paused before entering; turning, he looked at his female guest as if to block her entry and telling her to wait. It was an empty, childish thing to do, but to Luca it served to put her in her place. They entered into a room of brightness together where a fire was burning and a table was laid ready for dining.

Luca proved himself a genial host whilst at the table; the woman sat apart, facing the wall as not to show her face whilst eating, it created an opportunity for Luca to mock her situation in retaliation for showing an inordinate lack of respect to him earlier.

Later, as they sat around talking by the fireside, the woman broached the subject of need the following day to be taken to the nearest apothecary where she would purchase her various powders for a potion that she would need to make up to her own recipe.

Luca frowned noticeably at the request, insisting that it would be far simpler to write down the recipe so that it could be sent for this evening in readiness for her to administer it the following day. This she would not hear of. The potion that she required was known only to her and her father and that was the way she intended to keep it. Caught by the mention of the loving memory of her father, her words hung on her lips. Robert detected a sudden quavering in her voice. Afraid that her subdued emotions may betray her, Robert quickly changed his tack on the conversation, alerting Luca that should the potion be weighed out incorrectly it could possibly lead to terrible consequences. He noticed Luca's quizzing expression when he voiced his opinion; Luca retorted angrily that he was suddenly talkative for a hired man. At the same time reminding them both that should anything happen to his grandson, it would lead them to a very grave situation, which could have terrible consequences for them both.

Robert challenged the old man, telling him that the woman's safety was in his charge; should he continue with his taunts, then he would finish his task by slitting Luca's throat before he had time to call out. Luca was not normally moved by threats but he swallowed hard, a sweat instantly formed on his brow; holding up his hand he begged to be forgiven; the threat was only a reaction, he apologetically added, as he only wanted to preserve that which he loved so dearly.

"Then let there be no more empty banter of threats, for you are not aware of the dangers you place yourself in when you make such remarks." Luca became a different man now that he had discovered he had two vipers under his roof; and dangerous ones at that. It would take much planning to have his way; time would aid him to collect around him enough bodyguards as he required for his safety. This deviation from the subject of Aldo's wellbeing had given him enough time to hold Luca's attention as he noticed the woman's hand reach upwards to her face as if to stroke a premature teardrop from her deep, dark brown eyes. The source of her sudden sorrow stayed with her as she turned and starred into the glowing logs upon the burning fire trying to imagine the simple and gentle face of her loving, departed father. Once her momentary glimpse of the past have lifted, without turning to face Luca, she asked him coldly if he was to perpetually continue with his silly threats of the dangers they were exposing themselves into should they fail.

She had had enough of his nonsensical bullying and told him so, which did not go down very well at all, leaving Luca to have the final word that he would not stand failure.

"I will repeat to you once again what you have difficulty in understanding. My master," she said, "has sent me to you to ensure that all is well and will remain so. Do not make the error of vexing or making an enemy of him. He commands powers that you do not comprehend and if he had the mind to for his own pleasure, would watch you whilst you prayed to your God for death to take you."

A shudder went down Luca's back with her words; he noticed her transfixed gaze into the fire, fearing she was about to work some spell; speaking twice to her before she sensed that attention had fallen on her. Realising her slip, she raised her head towards Luca and apologised for not responding.

"The fire called to me telling me of a death," she said.

"I don't believe you," Luca laughed, but he could not tell if she were telling the truth; it scared him and he edged a little away from her.

"You think not," and she stared hard into his eyes, further unsettling Luca; he didn't know what to think, but his mouth had gone suddenly dry. Reverting into her ever pleasant voice, she asked him had he not ever daydreamed or thought of a place where he would much rather be at any moment in time. Robert looked at her in awe how she dragged herself from the edge of exposure back to a light-hearted conversation as if nothing else was on her mind. Robert's gaze was fixed on her; his thoughts examined that she was not the stone that she portrayed herself to be, more a very disciplined young woman. He felt the more time he spent with her being away from those who were used to control her in their wicked ways, it left alone the softness of her sensitivities which began to show through the hard shell that she had grown accustomed to wearing.

The evening grew wearisome; the talk was empty and meaningless, urging the couple to retire to their respective rooms, Luca remained behind propped in his comfortable chair close to the fireside. The role of Luca's play acting, the part of the lonely old man, was not accepted by Robert; he knew that once they were considered out of the way, this person's intellect would sharpen back to lightning fast. The waiting henchmen would receive their orders for whatever skulduggery lay ahead for them to carry out, and Robert would be waiting. In the darkness of the bedroom that was on the first floor, Robert was suspicious of the two who were waiting in the room below at the bottom of the stairs; he listened carefully with the door ajar waiting until there was good reason to move forwards along the passageway closer to the balcony where it would enable him to eavesdrop on what he suspected was to be their intended fate.

Robert's room lay towards the middle of the passageway, and in total darkness, which meant that he had to grope his way along towards the balcony overlooking the stairs. The monotony of waiting grew until he heard a door open below and the light of flickering candles illuminating the well at the lower end of the staircase at the end of the passageway. He hurried forwards as silently as he was able, but did not expect to encounter an obstacle that he overlooked on his way from the room. On colliding into it, he reached out and grabbed whatever it was to stop it from exposing his presence when a squeak of protest brought the realisation that he had bumped into a living object, that of his companion who had the same idea as he.

"Franj, could you not see me?" It was to be another whispered rebuke. He held her for what seemed an eternity, and became oblivious to her cursing him. He felt the warmth of her body against his and a longing to stay that way swept over him. She brought him back to reality by pinching his ear but without such severity as to make him shout.

"Don't be a fool," She chastised him for his oafishness before making their way together towards the stairwell.

The two shabbily dressed ruffians of Luca's acquaintance found it difficult to talk in a whisper when they were making their report to Luca; the eavesdroppers heard them informing him that the strangers had docked in the harbour on a ship from Lattakia, which was minus the captain and several crewmembers on its arrival.

"We spoke to most of the crew, one was scared stiff of the woman who was afraid of saying much, he told me that she was a she-devil who could make you feel all warm one moment then roast you the next. Others just spoke of her just as fearful and all agreed that she was an ill omen. As for her bodyguard, he was handy with the sword, took ten of them out at once, so they said." It irritated Luca that the woman could be considered any more than she was, and in a fit of rage clenched his fists ranting and cursing as quietly as he could, telling them that he had enough of this nonsense. Before he dismissed the two ruffians, he told them to stay within close calling, as he would most likely have need for them again tomorrow. Before closing the door on them, he pressed the necessary silver coins into their awaiting hand as they disappeared into the night and likely to the nearest tavern. The two left Luca somewhat relieved, and the listeners made their way back to the safety of the woman's bedroom where they began to plot the next move in their struggle against Luca and the rescue of Aldo from his grandfather's clutches.

The following day Robert was up early, he dressed hastily as the words of his host came rushing back to remind him that this was to be their last day. It seemed unreal that he should want to terminate the presence of those who were about to save his grandson before their act of revival was complete. He stood outside the heavy eight panelled walnut door of her bedroom unsure of her being awake, gently he tapped once as not to startle her from her sleep. His back was to the door as he preferred to keep an eye on the passageway for any lurking service staff of Luca's, after all, there was much he anticipated this day. He was about to knock again but his concern against waking her proved unnecessary as the door silently opened before his second knock contacted with the panel of the door. She reached out and pulled him into the room almost pulling him off balance in the act of bringing him quickly into the room from view, there was much to discuss and they were soon busy exchanging opinions of the various thoughts that transpired during the previous night's events.

Secretly, they made their plan for the day, deciding to stay together at all times, agreeing that where one went the other would follow, making it difficult for either of them to fall prey to the deceitful ways of Luca.

Downstairs there was movement, and both were aware that it would best be safer amongst the company than be outside and blindly waiting for something to happen. Leaving the confinement of their bedroom, they ventured downstairs to find the master of the house in the dining room where they had spent the previous evening. Luca was seated at the long refractory table barking out his orders to one of his quaking minions regarding cargoes of incoming ships. He curtailed his business as the two entered, dismissing a servant who showed some relief to escape his master as he churlishly slipped passed the two strangers entering the room. The woman looked about and congratulated Luca on his rising so early to attend his considerable affairs of his business.

Although Luca sat smug, he was aware that the compliment was false and that she only played to his vanity, but it served his ego well that others were aware of the fact that his trading empire was far reaching and worthy of such admiration. He replied sharply that he had carved out his wealth from nothing and only diligence and hard work would maintain its successful continuance. His manner changed and looking her squarely in the eye, stated he disliked losing control, but unfortunately some events were beyond his guidance. "That is why I now have to rely on you," pointing his bony finger towards her.

His shifty eyes screwed up to present a calculating pose and the pointing finger once more wavered like a divining rod at her; almost in a threatening manner, his hollow croaking voice began to upbraid her.

"After you have reassured me that my grandson's health is as it should be," he broke off in silence, but his empty stare was still fixed on her, sensing that he may have gone too far to break the tension; a smile broke out across his wizened deceitful face.

Anger erupted from the woman who responded forcefully, "I thought we had overcome the childish approach to our being here, I am not a child or a lackey that you can beat with a stick such as you did with your servant." Without letting Luca speak she continued "I should send a message to my master, Hassan, telling of our difficulty with you. Perhaps you will change your mind if others take our place and leave your grandson as he is."

Luca's frown turned into a scowl, he did not like being pushed into a corner or spoken to this way and told her so. A silence fell upon him with the thought of others taking her place; these confounded pagans, he thought, had powers that made his skin creep with an uncertainty of turning on him. Only for his need of her talents did he hold back.

"I have great plans for my grandson," he said, easing himself back into a comfortable position in the chair, a lighter tone fell into the conversation. "All of this, all the rewards of my efforts are his; I willingly give it all up so that we can share it together. So that is why your presence here has become so important and vital to me," and with a sterner tone warned her again that he was not a man who could swallow disappointment.

She became flippant in response to Luca, she was playing her game with some alacrity; he was becoming tiresome with his diatribe and knew that should she wish to rid herself of him, it would be a simple task.

"If that is all you require, consider my task done," was her reply to the old autocrat that sat at his table now with his mouth open to her casual response. His elbow became planted to the table and his hand came to his face; his skinny fingers ran across his mouth in awe at her dismissal of his words. He could not quite take in her sureness of the task that lay before her, his eyes were searching for weakness but there was none to be found. She stood before him as a statue, aloof and indifferent, with a complete change of heart expressed rousing approval. Apologising for his bad manners in allowing them to stand before him, he invited them to be seated whilst food was brought to sustain their appetites. Once more, she sat away from them behind a screen to eat her food rather than expose her face to the monstrous ogre at the main table.

There was no more unpleasantness at the table during their breakfast and it did not come as a surprise when Luca offered that one of his servants should escort her to the apothecary, whilst indicating that Robert should stay behind. Aware of his game, she insisted that it would be just as easy for the servant to escort both of them. Disappointed, but not wanting to disclose that he was against her decision, he did not press his insistence and agreed without displaying any trace of the anger that was rising within him.

Later, when they returned from their visit to the apothecary, they hurriedly made their way to the bedroom where young Aldo was resting. When they entered the darkened room, she ordered Robert to open the shutters of the window as to let the long-awaited light fill the room that was large and could be airy if only Luca would allow it to be so. Hot on their heels, Luca entered the room and the sight of light streaming into the room sent him into a hysterical outburst attempting to close them after Robert had opened them.

When Luca made an effort to sidestep Robert, he stepped in front of him blocking his every move in his efforts to close the shutters.

"For what reason do you want the darkness to return?" she snapped. Before Luca was able to reply, she informed him that this was a place for the living and not the dead. She strode over to a small table near the window and from within her dress she produced several wraps, which upon opening presented an assortment of coloured powders. Luca bent over the table in an attempt to ascertain what the powders were and how they were combined to be so potent a mixture. She was angered by his interference and admonished him in the kindest of ways, at the same time ordering him to fetch water and a glass for the potion. Once again, her disrespect for Luca's position was shown openly, he was filled with such contempt for her; he angrily shouted for a servant to do her bidding. His rage became like a bursting dam that could no longer hold back the weight of its water; once the servant had left, he confronted the woman for her attitude towards him berating her for her disrespect in his own house.

Robert watched Luca carefully and moved a step closer as if he considered her in danger of attack from the angered Luca. She stayed her hand to Robert and turning to Luca, she questioned him as to why he was so concerned with her business when she had not interfered in his. She continued to reduce the man, pushing the wraps towards him provoking him to administer his own dosage should he wish. With an overwhelming urge to slap the woman, yet fearful of her guard, Luca could do no more than throw his arms in the air in frustration and shout threats as he stormed out of the room. Robert asked why she did that, fearing that provoking him that way was unwise.

Soon after, the servant arrived with the water and placed it before her, leaving the room very surprised with a smirk of admiration, having been able to witness her master being reduced in stature by a woman.

With her little finger extended to the heap of powder she carefully scooped the required quantities with the extended growth of the nail of her little finger into one pile to form the mixture before tipping it into the glass that was to be the dose that made up her elixir. Robert noticed that only four of the powders were used and he respectfully enquired why she purchased so many if she did not need all of them?

"Franj, if that man had half a brain and I returned with four powders it would not be long before I was of no use to him at all." Robert's silence was his acknowledgement of her skill and wit in confounding Luca and getting him out of the way.

As each of the little piles of powder were emptied onto the surface of the still liquid in the glass, they watched and observed the powder float momentarily before eventually drifting downwards towards the bottom of the glass to disappear and change the translucence of the water into a cloudy mass. She stirred the mixture and raised the glass to the light, watching its colour change as the swirling water turned from a dirty colour back to pale. Rather than ask why and what she was about, he was content to watch silently wondering just what she could see in the murky mass of the greyish water. When ready, she turned towards the bed prompting Robert, who dutifully followed her towards his young friend. Robert on one side to raise the weakened body and to lift the head of his friend, and she the other to pour the relieving potion into his open dried and parched looking mouth. With Robert supporting Aldo's unconscious head, he watched as the potion was gently poured with care into his friend's mouth, at the same time asking how long it would be before his friend regained his consciousness. Patience was all that was indicated, whilst he was still supporting his friends head. Watching her pour the remains of the potion into Aldo's mouth, he reminded her of the last time they tended to a friend of his together.

There was a 'hmm' sound from behind her veil as she looked across, reminding him that it happened a long time ago, she drew out the word 'long' as if to make it sound forgotten. He questioned her memory and stated his surprise that she made it feel like a lifetime; disputing that she had not forgotten anything of that occasion, and prodded at him for being foolish and off his guard. He reddened at her reply; it embarrassed him to make him feel as though he had foolishly fallen for her trickery, he became irked at her reply and it showed as it entered his tone at the feeling that he had allowed himself to be used.

Once more, she detected how it affected him and replied that she was only teasing, but she went on to teach him that much can be learnt by provoking anger in an adversary. He knew that, but subtlety was not how he went about his business; a soldier, he felt, gets answers far speedier if cold steel was held at a prisoner's throat.

In her own thoughts, she must have known that Robert had softened to her a long time ago, yet there was so much growing between them. She also had grown to understand him and likewise warm to his company; they seemed to make a good partnership. The thought of getting closer worried her; they were two different people and in her land were enemies.

The potion by this time had been gently administered and Robert lay Aldo's comatose head gently back onto the soft, downy pillow. At this moment, she flipped the tie on her veil allowing it to drop from her face, Robert caught his breath as the light caught her face and highlighted her beauty. Seeing Robert's reaction, she responded by shrugging her shoulders explaining that she needed air and that he had seen her face before so there seemed little to concern oneself about. He tried not to stare, and took fleeting glances to make sure that she had not covered up again whilst looking away.

The waiting seemed endless as the time dragged by; curious as to how the drug worked, Robert was filled with questions relating to just how the next dose would affect his young friend. The concern for his friend's well-being manifested itself conspicuously, which prompted the woman into telling him that his fate presently lay in the hands of his maker; only time would tell.

"Are you saying that this is a bit dangerous? I thought you said it would save him." She looked at him with that familiar stare he was used to receiving these days that told him that he lacked faith.

"Well, I don't expect any problems if that what you are asking. I admit that I have not used this potion before."

"I ask you," Robert persisted, "what chance do you think he has to lay in a place between here and his maker for eternity? Christ's Blood, Robert exclaimed, I thought you..."

She cut him off, telling him that she said nothing of the kind only that she had induced his condition as she had done many times before. "Before you make rash judgements, consider that I would not make up any potion or poison without being aware of its antidote. Franj, do you take me for a fool that blindly stumbles along the road of science; I am proud of what I can achieve and confident of this outcome. Now settle yourself and have faith in me."

Robert considered himself well and truly informed; he did trust her but he wished to God that she had told him that there might be some risk as to warn him.

He pointed towards his sleeping friend, "I owe him so much, you know what I told you, it just makes my guts turn to water at the thought that I may have let him down."

"Franj, you are a strange man. Do you mean that his life is in your hands? This is not so, for you have followed your friend into the lair of danger to be beside him in his time of need. Are you not by his side and doing all you can to help him through his trial of sleep? No, no, my friend," she added calmly, "you are doing all you can putting yourself at risk in his service; now let me hear no more of this talk of guilt." She had a way with words, convincing him that he was wrong about himself and what was happening.

"Yes, I suppose you are right in what you say, perhaps it is foolish. I will leave it to fate and pray."

Her head lifted and her brow furrowed with an inquisitive sudden desire to understand this man who spoke showing that he was some way to be resigning himself to fate and it interested her to pose a question to him.

"Do you believe in fate, franj? Could you admit that your future was previously written?" He walked away not knowing how to answer; questions such as those had crossed his mind many times as he continued to tell her that certain events relating to that very question had strangely made its effect on him also. He began to pace the worn almost threadbare rug upon the timber floor, as was his manner when he was unsure. That's a question he had often asked when he was alone; here he was sharing his thoughts with a woman that he had once called his enemy, discussing of all things philosophy of life. Reason was never in his mind when his life was in the balance; life in battle demanded its own set of rules. He pointed out that his warring life travelling from battlefield to battlefield coloured his eyes and littered his mind with such varied experiences that on occasion they had learnt to see their enemy with a different view. His pacing came to a stop as he gazed out of the window, her voice broke his contemplation.

"Perhaps, franj, you have a heart after all," she smiled as she spoke.

He supposed that she was poking fun at him again, turning to look to see if her face betrayed a smile; but, alas, she sat there quite passively her loveliness shining out at him.

"I understand you better as a warrior, franj, your secret emotions appear to be tearing themselves apart and I am somehow finding it quite refreshing," she said. There was an arousing murmur from the bed, bringing them both to Aldo's bedside to investigate. Robert was speaking to him but in his dazed state little sense penetrated the numbed mind of the young man. Robert looked across the bed with appealing eyes; in her perception she felt for his helplessness as she explained the effects of the soporific and concern, she added, that it had been stronger than she anticipated, but at least he was reacting favourably to the potion. The tension on Robert's concerned faced marked his disturbed state of mind; a comfort to the anxious knight, she suggested that there be a further wait before administering another dose.

"We are winning the battle," she said, "like all battles, patience is required to study the enemy and combat it for a successful result. So be patient, franj, if the way is clear, we will administer another dose which would surely bring him from his torpid condition." For some time they waited in pensive silence, cogitating when he would wrench himself from his dream state back to some vestige of reality.

With a reassuring restlessness, he moved from his static deathlike position and began once more to moan.

"What is happening?" asked Robert as Aldo whimpered.

Her face revealed little of her concerns, "It is well, be patient, he is freeing himself from the bonds that hold him." Another movement gave Robert hope; he spoke to his friend letting him know that he was here, but his voice showed no effect to the sleeping man. Like the rise and fall of the tide, Aldo was beginning to show erratic signs that he was winning his battle, and it seemed that for those moments they too were riding a tide of expectation. When he uttered any sounds, they remained those of a comatose man, being slurred and thick; optimistically, their expectations of his recovery that he was coming out of his numbed state were positive. To assist his wakening, she ordered water for Aldo which Robert did not need to be asked for a second time. In the blink of an eye, he was eagerly back at the edge of the large bed and handing the refreshing water to her. Before she offered the glass to his mouth, she dipped her fingers into the water, running them over his parched and thirsty, waiting lips with tender gentleness. Considering him ready for drinking, she allowed him only small amounts so that there would be little reaction to any remaining potion that may be re activated in his system. There was little more to do but wait and the two sat patiently listening to Aldo's delirium as he rambled on, in and out of consciousness whilst trying to tell his tale of gibberish until her soothing voice convinced him to relax and rest.

"He will sleep again and when he awakes he will be aware of his surroundings but for our safety, I do not know how to convince his grandfather that he must dream for a little longer."

It was mid evening when Aldo stirred again. This time when he awakened, he easily recognised his close friend that was by his side. There was great surprise and joy as Robert greeted his friend and he the other. Although it must be said that young Aldo was not quite as full of zest and vigour as he may have liked to be, he was for the first time reasonably lucid yet remained groggy after his long rest in the cradle of no man's land. Encouraged by the sight of his friend, Aldo was full of questions as may well be expected, but most of all an uncertainty fell over him when he viewed the woman for the first time. Somewhere from the depths of his muddled mind, Aldo struggled to understand why she was present; he couldn't remember her. Though she was a stranger to him, he could not take his eyes from her, as if through his confusion he was beginning to recognise something of her; his reasoning began to change into one of uncertainty and fear. Childlike, he struggled to ease himself closer to Robert for his own premature security; though it was partial, his mind was emerging from its nightmare.

It was all Robert could do to work hard on him to convince him that she was the force of good in all of this mystery that enveloped him his clouded memory, for without her, he would surely still have one foot in the nether world, where his life hung precariously in the balance of eternal sleep.

What he would find very difficult to explain was that the cause of this affair lay at the door of his own doting grandfather, who for his own selfish and twisted reasons had much to answer for having caused great harm to one, and death to another of their company.

Trying not to over-burden the young man too much, they decided to let him slip back into a regular sleep, leaving the rest of their story to be told the following morning.

It seemed odd that Luca had not only omitted his presence but withdrawn the hand of hospitality banning anyone, so it seemed, to attend on their needs. Robert decided to descend to the rooms below where he could hear the movement of the servants. Submission by starvation could well have been in Luca's mind but it only served to last until there was to be a confrontation, which is what inevitably was to come about.

The stairs and hall had become shadowy but without the need for light to assist to guide one's way through the gloom that was descending into the less lit areas of the house.

Alert for lurking shadows, Robert braced himself for action as he made his way down towards the kitchen in the hope that Luca had not previously ordered the servants to be hostile towards him. At the kitchen door, he reached out tentatively raising the latch he hoped would bring him into an empty room where he could help himself unhindered by any concerned staff. Quietly, he pushed the door open so that it moved under its own weight; he was surprised to see a kitchen maid standing across the room, and she was humming a tune in low tones to herself as she performed her duties. This was most unexpected to hear the sweet sounds of a melody in such a place, being far from a happy house. Not wanting to startle the singing maid, he quickly looked about to see if there were any other staff about before proceeding to cross the room.

Robert coughed aloud as to draw the attention of the maid without scaring her and spoke after he did so; she stopped what she was doing with a start and turned swiftly in shock. She had recognised the silent intruder who shattered her daydreaming stance the moment she turned, he was one of the guests that had given her master a difficult time. Robert's smile allaying her fears that almost caused her to jump with the sound of his coughing, she had remembered him from the previous evening; he smiled many times at her when she was serving at the table. He had also spoken kindly to her as she fumbled with the crockery and Luca berated her for her clumsiness at the table; Robert was thoughtful enough to pass her a compliment on her efficiency, which was unusual in that house. She smiled back and curtsied all in the same action, she was not used to guests entering the kitchen and was unsure of how to greet or address them. To reduce any tension, Robert winked at her, causing her to blush, then posed his question if there was any food for them. Having taken a liking to his pleasant approach, it wasn't long before he was leaving the pantry with a tray of food sufficient for their needs after sweet-talking the young girl into opening the larder.

Back in their room, the two munched on their illicit meal laughing at the thought that Luca would be furious when he hears that they had eaten without having to beg him to be fed. With guilt in his heart, Robert realised that somebody may also have to take a beating for their good fortune and it rather took the shine off his victory. The night was long and once more without a visit to the room from their absent host, this absence only indicated that he was most likely concentrating his efforts in preparation for the elimination of all witnesses once their purpose of their immediate task had been completed, and not before would he deem it suitable to show himself. The tension could not be escaped as the hopes of the pair who remained by the bedside; waiting in anticipation of a successful outcome of their assiduous endeavours would, they dearly hoped, bear the fruit of accomplishment when morning came upon them.

Speculating that time was limited, the two knew they had to get their version of the grandfather's escapade and his machinations over to the sickly Aldo to become apparent if they were to stand any chance of success. The revelation that they had schemed for during those long waiting pauses had to unfold before Aldo could be exposed to his cunning grandfather and at the same time imperil their own position.

Expectations

The eyes flickered and the mouth moved in anticipation for needy sustenance; the body restlessly edged out across the expanse of the large comfortable bed like a babe in a new world. As the two caring companions inadvertently dozed due to their own lack of comfort, the young patient began to stir into consciousness as the light of day began agitating his flickering eye lids. He gave a drawn out long awaited yawn of awakening from the depth of his sleep; the noise propelled both dozing carers to their feet staring across at each other through the sleepiness that had almost glued their eye lids together from their long vigil. With great joy at his awakening, Robert held the young Aldo, greeting him back to consciousness.

The reality of Robert's welcoming words did not bring any added clarity to what he was being told; he was staggered with the young man's eventual great flow of questions for him to answer to give some clarity to his confused state of mind.

By the time that the dawn had given way to daybreak, Robert had given Aldo the complete account of the events that had led from his abduction to the transportation back to Venice and his imprisoned subconscious state thus far. Robert had spoken continuously but he could not help noticing Aldo constantly flicking his eyes over towards the darkly dressed outline of the woman that was unrecognisable stationed across the room.

As of yet, Robert had not introduced her for his own reasons, waiting for the right time when he considered it to be appropriate. No matter how much Robert talked of events, it became obvious that the distant figure that stood away from Aldo's immediate focus had become something of a disturbance to him. Confused with how Robert was to present her as a force of good and working with him for his friend's benefit, he began to expand on his reasons for the boy's condition and how she was the only one to be able to bring him to a state of recovery. Robert's explanation was not as clear as he would have liked it to have been; Aldo's distorted sense of reception, which was vague and half hearted, caused him to break out into a sudden sweat as if something had been deeply troubling him.

The story seemed not to convince Aldo; his jumbled mind had him in dark blind alleys as the knot of confusion tightened on him. Light was suddenly blocked out, allowing a hazy curtain to fall across his reality. It seemed too much for the once delirious mind to absorb the explanation in one attempt; he grew silent as he pondered over the story. When he did react, he found it difficult to accept his grandfather could submit one such as he, his beloved grandson, to such an ordeal and took a stand of denial in accepting such a story. Clutching only to his own convictions rather than be convinced of other wilder twisted interpretations, his dissolved logic fought to come to terms with such an outlandish story that he was told.

As his friend attempted to clarify and reason through the mystery, Aldo became agitated and spoke hurtful words to Robert that were quite unnecessary, accusing him of wild things such as trying to steal his inheritance. In the grasping ramblings in the illogical dark of Aldo's confusion, the potion's workings had disturbed him so that tirelessly he clutched for anything to believe in, anything other than what he had been told of his grandfather. The truth of past events would not likely be recognisable in his soup like memory with all his information being without a start or finish.

Lost for a way to clearly explain anything further, Robert wished that the boy would find sleep again to give his mind another chance to sift through the past events that had been placed before him; probably it would not make any difference to him, but it was quite clear enough that the woman had carried out her orders diligently. She had stood near the window without speaking or watching with her back to the two men as if divorced from the whole proceeding, but listening intently all the time. She too feared the difficulty that her companion had shared in convincing Aldo of the past events and wondered what to do to help. With her specialised talents, she was aware she could have put the young man into a trance without his knowledge to convince him more easily, but weighed the consequences of the dangers that could lay in wait for him. If Robert was to be convinced that she had done everything she could for his safety, then she would only act whilst Aldo was awake and was as rational as could be expected, which concerned her equally, for the strength of her potions needed great care in their use along with her understanding of the recipient's condition. At present, she could not tell if this young man was strong enough in his inner self to delve into the depths of his own mind to remember the haunting voices of his past. Whilst his body was strong, she feared that his past existence in the comfort of his grandfather's house had weakened his spirit with his easy living. Aldo lay silently, his eyes warily watching for any movement about him; the man at his side he had recognised and accepted as a friend but somehow he presently felt unsure. A new fear welled within him as he watched the movement of what had remained a dark ghostly shadow that loomed close to the window begin to make its way towards him like an avenging crow. It came to a stop at the bedside and stooped level to his ear. Apprehension fell across the young man, sweat bubbled on his fevered brow, unable to move from his weakened state his fear of the stranger grew as her face came close to touching his. Something in the depths of his frightened senses touched him, causing the extremities of his body to come alive with anxiety. She was quite still and purposeful in not making any attempt to move or speak. He breathed erratically as her face almost touched his before easing his tension; recognition is what she wanted, not the visual kind but more of the sensual. His nose twitched as he caught the fragrance of her perfume, and as a key unlocked a closed door, so did her fragrance unlock his closed mind, bringing with a certain order that opened his sleepy eyes with a searching recognition.

Robert watched in disbelief at how silently and effectively she worked; he would never have thought of a similar approach, nor would he have anything of the sort to apply to create such an alarming result. He noticed Aldo's reactions; his dull sleepy eyes rolling as if he was affected by a shock that sent messages of interest to his mind to probe deeper into its darkened corners seeking for a clue to when he had first taken in that fragrance. Reactions began to take place, his hands and feet became irritated as if something had triggered this motionless young mind back into life. Turning his head slightly to one side, his lungs rose and fell as he took in a fuller draught of the hypnotic fragrance. His eyes closed in concentration; where was I? He was asking himself.

He recalled the alluring fragrance and tried desperately to seek its origin as he fell back into the depths of his past. Her mouth moved to his ear where she began to repeat in a whisper her past conversations with him whilst he was her prisoner.

With words that were not overheard, she spoke into his ear; the hairs on the receiving orifice began to stand on end, great beads of sweat formed on his brow and he instinctively reached out and grabbed at Robert's arm for support. Panic fell upon him, his breathing became disrupted and his manner was agitated. His mind had been aroused; the past had flooded back like a terrifying nightmare, and sickeningly he sensed the atmosphere of his brief imprisonment of sleep caught in the heady narcotic that sickened him for reasons that he was unable to recall. It frightened him that he may not have truly escaped from it and may have to return to its haunting darkness, causing his breath to become abnormal and rapid. Through the haze of his confused memory, it was her voice that had condemned the act and had ordered that he be released from its hold; then, only through the kindness and sweetness of her mellifluous voice did he recall the hold of his confinement. She had spoken only briefly to him, telling him that he was to enter into a deep sleep and that he would soon be walking in paradise where his beloved grandfather would awaken him and take him home and to safety.

There was no doubt that to the unknowing onlooker; her healing talents were extremely effective, and whilst evoking his nightmare which culminated into the fearful torrent of torment. To return him to tranquillity, her hand slipped into her garment and produced a small vial which she offered to his face. Whatever it was the escaping vapours calmed Aldo's torment; she picked up her silken robe end and dried the sweat from his brow. Aldo's grip began to relax on Robert's arm and the eyes that before viewed him with confused suspicion now were disarmed and apologetic. He turned to the woman with questioning eyes where fear was no longer present, the hand that held his other arm was his assurance that his friend beside him was his protector and he was no longer in any imminent danger. It brought a smile to her face when he turned back and thanked her for bringing him back to reality, and almost reluctantly asked where they had met. When she truthfully informed him that she had been his jailer, he shrank somewhat causing Robert to intercede quickly with an explanation that she was now helping us. In a better position to clearly explain the dangers and that both parties were acting in Aldo's assistance, it was required once more to enter into the charade that could free them from the grips of the doting and dangerous grandfather.

When Luca entered the room, he was not the testy character he usually showed himself to be, which was a little disconcerting to the two. Suspicion entered the air as he showed himself now to be smarmy, although his interest still lay with his grandson, who now appeared at rest. He sought the boy's condition with concern and needed to know if he was now free from the unstable sleep that he previously suffered. Holding out her outstretched arm, the woman offered the new potion to Luca. Her instructions were implicit as to how and when Aldo was to receive it in order for him to maintain his quiet repose. Warning him that when it was finished, he would awaken from his sleep naturally and must not seek to prolong his rest further, only patience, attentive nursing and faith in their God would see him through.

An exclamation of protest went out from Luca; he was not willing to accept anything from the almighty; left to Him anything could have happened to his grandson. It was he that took matters into his own hands to bring his grandson back from that land of certain death and pestilence; it was he who had to deal with the villainous assassins and he that would protect the boy. Once more, he asserted that he would have walked through the gates of Hell to rescue him; there was no doubt that the old man was genuine in his affections for his grandson. Due to his loving outburst of loyalty and affection for Aldo and unknown that his grandson was only feigning sleep, he had inadvertently moved the young man's emotions, causing tears to form in his closed eyes and welling onto his quiet face. The voice that spoke was not of a soldier but a sobbing boy crying out for his grandfather; quite plainly Luca had been duped and he did not take to it kindly as his secret was out in the open. Luca raged while the young man sat up his face wet with tears of sadness and disappointment for his loving grandfather.

"Leave us, leave us," he shouted at the two, who realised that their plan had suddenly gone awry.

Now had to be their time of escape from the man that was threatening their future liberty, and to linger would be foolish of them.

They hurriedly made their way down the stairs towards the great door of the house and they neared the point of liberty when a hurting blackness descended on them both.

Robert woke up with a throbbing headache and in darkness; he was securely tethered, unable to touch the source of his pain, but he knew there was a lump on his head and it hurt with meaning. He was bound with his hands behind his back, and then he realised that in their flight he had dropped his guard, guessing that the two ruffians must have been lying in wait for them in the shadows at the bottom of the stairs. He could not tell where he was; apart from being in the dark, it was smelly and damp, and the air was earthy to the smell indicating that it was a cellar that they were in and it was possibly below the water level of the lagoon.

A woman's voice called out weakly as if in pain from across the darkened cellar but he was unable to see where she was. They spoke consolingly towards each other before trying to seek out each other's form and position. As their eyes became familiar with the darkness and with the aid of her voice to guide him, he shuffled across the damp floor until at last he had found her. They spent a long time in the darkness trying desperately to free themselves; it was much later before anyone came to see them, and when they did it was not for friendly converse.

Being below ground and without means of light to give them some sense of time of their imprisonment was a torture in itself, and it meant that they could not regulate day or night, being like lost souls in a nether land without any sense of time.

Carrying flaming torch-lights before them to show their way through the maze of low dark passages, they were noisy and full of their victory and bent over as they walked. When they entered the place of the captives, their voices were carried on dank, smelly air, sounding hollow as they approached them. There was a high sharp tone to one of the voices that Robert imagined was Luca and the others were rough and gravel-like. There was a sound of keys jangling on a ring, which was noisily inserted into a lock and eventually turned. The noise echoed hauntingly, it seemed so loud in the quietness of their confinement, and the lights they carried flickered wildly showing their shadows to be like avenging evil demons ready to mete out their revengeful will.

When they entered the cell to look upon their captives, they saw Luca who was accompanied by his two rough henchmen. Robert recalled secretly seeing them on the evening they first attended Aldo. He received a welcome kick in the groin to ascertain whether he was awake; when it proved that he was, Robert cursed the ugly brute who delivered it. Luca laughed and sneered at their efforts to fool him, but now it seemed it cheered him to feel that they were to give him his long awaited revenge. In an attempt to make Luca have second thoughts of whatever it was he intended to do with them, she warned him that others would come looking for her and that he was making a foolish mistake if he thought that he would escape the Old Man of the Mountain. Luca's haunting, hollow laugh resonated around the empty cellar; it had a crazed ring in it and was eerie to listen to the echoing sounds of a mad man's voice bouncing hollowly off the cellar walls. He stood over the woman, who was unable to retaliate whilst fastened in her bonds. Stooping to catch a handful of her hair in his hand, he pulled her head toward him and gave her the kiss of death, sneering as he stood upright and pushing her helplessly away. He relished in his sadistic pleasure the act of telling her that he hoped that she would enjoy her swim in the lagoon later at high tide. He was particularly acerbic towards her as she had previously treated him with disdain and lacked respect towards him in his own house. As he left, he turned, telling them brusquely, "Nobody gets the better of il pescacani and lives to tell of it." The cellar door slammed behind them, echoing around them with a positive completion to his threat. The bound duo listened to the sounds of the victors laughing when the door slammed loudly behind them; the voices faded but the high feelings that had inflated their jailers' conviction of success resonated in the walls to haunt the prisoners. The threat of death, it seemed, had changed from their being instigator of provocation, to one of victim.

Despite their endeavours to free themselves, the ropes that bound them were too tight to make any rapid headway on loosening them. The total darkness made it very difficult to distinguish anything that could possibly assist in their escape from the fate that awaited them. Robert moved around the wall awkwardly feeling like a blind man for anything that was sharp to his touch. At last, his perseverance found a rough ashlar on a corner that allowed him to begin feverishly rubbing against the bonds that bound him secured on the keen edge of the masonry in a desperate effort to abrade the coarse rope fibre. It seemed an age of rubbing tirelessly; in the time he worked on the rope, he felt wetness and a stinging; blood began to flow from abrasions of his wrist but he was undeterred and continued to feverishly saw away at his bonds, up and down against the rough stonework of the wall.

Despite the cuts stinging effect from his ham-fisted efforts, he had to continue slavishly to divert his attention away from his wounds. Again, he cursed himself for allowing his guard to drop so easily and be captured; Luca was not so easily overcome as he had discovered to his regret. It was too late for recriminations; because of its ease, he considered his confinement an insult to his worthiness as a soldier; taking it badly as a slight upon his ability in avoiding his enemy. He had known more devious and dangerous characters than Luca that had held him and would not give in to suffer any state of hopelessness without a fight. The mutterings that came through the silence and darkness of their place of captivity were familiar, though unexpected from a woman; he was learning that she too could curse as well as any man. Was there any way, he asked her, if she was able to escape; her answer made him wish that he had never asked the question. He wanted to reassure her, but because of her past demonstrations of ability in the arcane arts, she was secured to such a degree that it was almost impossible for her to move. She cursed and cursed her confinement, so much so that he had felt he should ask her to give it all a rest; he understood her situation of helplessness, but he felt that her efforts were best directed elsewhere.

As each strand of the rope fibres weakened and broke, it encouraged him to pursue that end, in spite of his stinging injuries he was inflicting on himself. Disappointingly, all too soon, the flickering light of the coal tar torches warned him of the ruffians return, and as the light grew brighter, their closeness filled the outside area of the door with the light of the burning flame; he quickly stopped and lay on the floor quite still. The two men entered the room noisily and making straight for the woman, standing over her, they delivered two or three good kicks to her defenceless body, delighting in the experience to ensure that she would be cooperative; they were scared of her, yet one dared to touch her telling his companion that her titties were not so big; they laughed and picked up her limp body between them and carried her away.

442

Wherever they had taken her, it did not seem far, as they soon returned for Robert before he could complete his efforts of chaffing the last few strands of the bonds that held him. Expecting similar treatment on their return, he was surprised that they preferred not to render him unconscious for fear that he would prove an awkward weight to carry. The look of hate for them on his face was so plain to see that it made them wary of a threatening capability that only cowards detected in their foe. Although bound and harmless to them, they still felt unsure; with cudgels in hand, they warily circled him, falsely laughing at their chance of sport. In trying to dodge their actions, he was promptly kicked hard; fortunately, he was not attacked further as they ordered him to get to his knees. Robert gave out a cry of pain as their blows made contact with him; they were laughing, secure in their freedom to do as they pleased. His fear was not for their pleasures that they took of his disadvantaged state, but that the frayed ropes that barely held him might be noticed to the eye of his would-be assassins. They were impatient as Robert awkwardly got to his feet; and Robert action to secure his secret had him edging his back to the wall; his eyes glared at them like a frightened cornered animal.

They were aware that he knew his life was over, but they were not going to hang around for any last stand; the smaller of the two bullies drew a long poniard sticking it close to his neck threatening him to move or die where he stood. Robert played along moving away, always with his back to the wall, dexterously gathering the loose frayed strands of rope together so that they would not be seen. He continued walking backwards, watching them like a trapped creature that he was, being pushed back until he was outside the room that had confined him. Onwards he was goaded along the passageway at the point of a dagger, but as long as he could keep his back to the wall he was willing to do their bidding until he was certain his opportunity showed itself. Water dripped from the stone ceiling overhead, plopping rhythmically onto the water below; rivulets of green stained the walls being wet with algae indicating that the sea was not far away from them. This passageway undoubtedly led to the lagoon; along this tunnel he was to witness the means of his intended fate; fear was a part of Luca's plan in his design to terrify his victim. He was almost free, and hope grew in him as long as he could maintain the display of fear to keep his aggressors from seeing that he was about to give his guards a surprise they were not expecting.

Along the passageway, he could hear more clearly the sounds of rushing water, as if water was drawing the river he was doomed to journey; it came to him that it was the sound of the tide ebbing, it grew cold and smelling stronger of salt, he realised that he was in some kind of underground sewer with another smell that filled his nostrils. Momentarily looking away in the direction he was heading, he received a glancing blow from one of his captors rendering him semi-unconscious and causing him to stumble to his knees. They had had enough of this baiting and wanted to get their job over with; there was ale in the tavern and silver pieces in their pockets for them to enjoy instead of playing games with foreign individuals. They dragged Robert along the rest of the corridor onto what appeared to be a loading bay where a crude raft lay tied up.

It was dropping with the tide and he saw the woman laying helplessly tied up with a net of rocks tied to her ankles; there was no mistaking its purpose was to weight her down and send her quickly to her waiting fate. Robert was dropped down onto the deck of the raft opposite the woman and instead of attaching the similar net of rocks to him, their concern was about getting the job done and impatiently cast off into the long dark dripping wet tunnel that lead to the sea.

The waterway they travelled was not too long; in his recovering moments, Robert had suspected that this tunnel must have been used many times in the past, proving very convenient for Luca to be secretly rid of his unwanted guests, such as the likes of himself. He also noticed that there were no sides to the tunnel to walk along and he wondered just how long he had left before they reached the lagoon. The raft came to a bumping halt as the skiff banged awkwardly against a huge wooden portcullis and began turning on its own with the pull of the current as if it would make its own way out to sea.

One of the villains jumped off the raft onto a parapet and hauled on the ropes that controlled the wooden portcullis; had the raft not been secure when the barrier was raised, it would have been quickly drawn seawards, where it would have drifted away aimlessly into the waiting lagoon without its other occupant.

With the port-cullis up the man joined his villainous friend once more, they set course drifting to the will of the current out into the darkness of the lagoon to what must have been their designated spot. Robert worked for all his worth on the last few strands of the ropes whilst the woman continued to draw their attention with rebellious insults. One by one, the remaining strands of Robert's bonds began to break free, but still the final strand held him fast, whilst the woman had held their attention to enable Robert to wriggle and squirm, unseen in his efforts to free himself. The smaller of the two unwashed thugs had had enough of the backchat and of the female's insults and grabbed at her, his unwashed face met hers closely as he laughed uncontrollably at what was to befall her, calling for his friend with him to help toss her over the side now. An argument broke out that they were not out into deep enough water for their bodies to be lost completely from sight. A push from the woman secured her fate as she tried to make contact with one of the ruffians; her action was reciprocated with an even harder kick to her stomach. The raft rocked unsteadily as tempers ran high and the moans of pain filled the night air around them. Her action had secured her own fate; the two, insecure on the rocking skiff, wobbled about with their uncontrolled movement and grew uneasy for their own safety on the unsteady raft.

"Let's get rid now," came the shout, "or else I'll do for her now."

But the other thug cried, "No," repeating their master's wishes of having them know and feel every dreading moment of their impending doom. If in the future Luca found out that their bodies had been dredged up in fishing nets to discover that they had been knifed, he would surely repay his disloyal employees with the fate that they should have delivered to his other prisoners.

Fear of being overturned and suffering the same fate in the water had taken over their thoughts; struggling on the unstable raft, they wrestled to get a grip of her.

As soon as he was able to stand, Robert did so, but it came late as he heard the splash of the woman hit the water.

Robert broke free of his bonds a little too late to save her from the sea and hurled himself at both the men pushing them off the raft as he plunged into the water after her, leaving the others helplessly struggling for their own survival. He swam deep down into the inky black water where they had dropped her, searching blindly hoping to touch her, but without any luck. The stone weights had carried her down quickly, leaving him to feel about without any hope. He had to find her, but his lungs were at bursting and had to surface for air. The draft of water was only about ten feet, but it gave no clues to her location. Being deep enough for the sea to do its work, he gulped air as he surfaced and went down a second time. The water was as black as the night above, all he could do was feel about blindly; as he groped about, there was hope as something caught in his grip, something silk and it was being drawn away from him. The changing tide was pulling them both out of the lagoon and out towards the sea. His aching lungs grew hot, bursting for the need of air and screaming for relief, but in a desperate and tenacious effort to bring her to the surface he gave one more blind outwards lunge, to grasp her evasive body. Once the soft flesh was in his grip, he tirelessly hauled her, including the weights which threatened to drag them both down further. With all his inner power, he swam upwards kicking the water up to the surface with the woman tightly in his grasp; he was gasping and struggling as he broke the surface, honking for his need of air; but she was not, time was against him if he was to save her. They were in a channel and the rushing tide was being drawn swiftly outwards to the sea. In the light of the moon, Robert detected outlines silhouetted above the water line which he was sure must have been sandbanks.

The pull of the weights that threatened their survival had to be neutralised as he could not sustain the energy required to carry them in the current much further. The nets must have been hurriedly and poorly made and with all his strength, he pulled drastically at the stringy mesh, pulling it apart until he had torn them sufficiently to release most of the stony load that was threatening to drag them both down into the depths. With what strength remained in him, he swam onwards, holding her head above the water. Exhausted and with his failing strength, he made for the sandbank, towing the woman laboriously along with him as he went.

It was a relief when his feet began to tread sand, indicating the firm feel of the sandbank, safety was all that mattered. The sand beneath his feet yielded to his weight and making his progress difficult; part way out of its depth, he had to make the rest of his way on his knees to maintain his balance. In this manner, he had a chance to fight the tide and a chance to draw the woman ashore to revive her; and he dearly hoped it would not be too late for her. Even though he was on firm ground at the edge of the water, the force of the running tide continued to pull at his sodden clothes. His tired body refused to yield its efforts to pull the woman to safety in his struggle against the pull of the sea and though his safety gave him encouragement to be aware that he was safe, he continued to draw her to the highest point of the bank. His struggle was exhausting as though the sea was fighting to claim that which was offered up to it. He was not yielding; he knelt breathlessly over her, fighting for what he first needed to do, catch his breath. At last, the draw and force of the sea was no longer a threat, but he was truly spent, tired but still staunch-minded in his zeal to save her. He was aware that if she was to be given any chance of being saved in his breathless state, he had no alternative but to press on, even though there were no signs of life in her to give him encouragement. His efforts seemed endless but he would not yield in the fight to rekindle the life that appeared dormant. In a further desperate attempt, he hauled her over towards rocks that formed a breakwater against the rising tides and positioned her onto them with her body hanging limply over them. His resolve in dispelling the seawater from her swamped lungs would not desist and he shouted at her in his frustration to help herself.

No matter what manner of names he called her in his effort to intimidate her anger for a responsive awakening, he hoped beyond hope that she would recover from the fading life that appeared to be ebbing like the tide.

Robert began to feel himself lapsing into total exhaustion when she coughed and desperately gasped air; at the same time, water trickled like a stream out of her mouth from her swamped lungs. She remained stationary in her position, slumped over the rocks coughing and spluttering whilst Robert remained spent on all fours unable to promote any further effort. Finally the coughing subsided; there was no more water to exude from within her but her throat burned like hell and she could do little more than roll off the rocks onto the sand exhausted and into a state of unconsciousness.

With the success of his efforts being manifested, he also collapsed, freely giving way to his exhausted body.

The beach was soft beneath him and he could do no more than to give in to its calling, where he lay until daybreak.

The rising sun offered warmth to his back, but it was his aching limbs that awoke him. He opened his eyes slowly and saw the light of day. Though he remained feint of energy, he was alive and free of his nightmare. When he moved, it was not without its effect; his body told him bluntly that it was in no mood for any repeat of the previous night's ordeal. Peering about through salt-encrusted eyes, he saw the faint shape of the crumpled body of the woman lying next to him and quite still; he remembered her coughing so he believed her to be alive also; she must have crawled close to him before finally collapsing.

Fearful for her condition after what had passed the previous night, he was not about to let her life slip by again. It took a little time to rouse himself but when he was active he was moving a little loosely and as quickly as he could. He felt old, as if a weight was pressing down on him, and it took some moments to realise that he had been caked in sand and salt. He shook his clothing as best as he could and watched the dried sand fall from him; surprised to see the amount that he had discharged to the beach, he moved over to the woman.

Shaking her roughly in anticipation of his worst thought, he went about shaking out her clothing as best as he could. She awoke with a sudden sharpness in her voice, berating him for his treatment, which relieved him and raised a smile of cheerfulness, for he had dreaded that his previous attempt at revival was only half-hearted under the strain of his emergence from the swirling sea. Still holding her, she paused in her outburst, recalling the situation from the night before, remembering her fall into the sea and her dramatic demise into the cold deep water's embrace. She responded differently now, surprising Robert with her action, she held herself to him, her head to his breast as a child might silently grip its mother for security. How odd, he thought of her reaction as she rested for one who acted as a go between for death, and now he cradled her in his arms like one that's missed out on affection all her life. She murmured something in a whisper; he could not understand the dialect, but gathered that she had thanked him as she clung to him. Moving moments never last as long as one would wish them to as the reality of their position dawned on Robert. Sunrise and awareness brought more important issues to mind, taking precedence over the niceties; such was life's survival pattern and the removal of the remnants of the empty nets that clung to her ankles like the weed from the lagoon. With their awakening to the dawn, their most immediate and important issue was getting off this little sandbank in the middle of nowhere and surrounded by a threatening sea. Helping her to stand, he told her that the tide must soon turn and probably cover this place that had become their refuge. Now it appeared the opposite, and knowing that the tide might take them back to shore, it also may catch them in a harmful current that could just as easily swallow them. Alone with nought but the great sea behind them and the lagoon before them, they somehow hoped that sooner or later somebody must pass by. As time dragged, they watched for fishing boats and signs of the tide turning; their anxiety was fast turning to trepidation for the two marooned individuals that held each other on the lonely, sun-baked sandbank. They were finally relieved to see sails of fishing boats entering the deeper waters of the lagoon; it was just in time that they were spotted by the fishermen who waved back to acknowledging their plight. The turning tide began running inwards to the lagoon, and it was notoriously running fast, advancing on their refuge reducing the sandbanks dimensions ever smaller while they anxiously watched its progress and waited to be rescued. Time has a way of chilling the blood on the hottest of days; for the two, they could only scream out their pleas to the fishermen to hurry as the waters lapped around their feet.

They stood together, supporting each other; waiting in excited anticipation, they clung to each other with a different understanding, and although they were not lovers, they were united with a bond that made them stronger. They waited, and it must be said it was not with patience, but they could not go anywhere, being prisoners to the will of the incoming tide, but in their hearts they believed that they would be saved. It was a great relief to them when the fishermen waved back and finally arrived not a moment too soon; they were unable to understand their rapid chatter, but that didn't seem to worry them; only that they were so grateful for being rescued.

The Game Continues

Safely ashore and back on the mainland, they had no other choice but to make their way covertly to the place they had been previously offered safety and shelter. It was fortunate the fishermen who rescued them were on their return from the sea to put them safely ashore at the quayside where they unloaded their catch and lucky it was for them that there were not many people about to take notice of them. In the state that they were, laden heavily in salt and sand, only workers were about on the quay and they showed no interested in them, being too busy to get their load ready for market. No matter how much they kept to the shadows for fear of being in the minds of others, someone, they feared, would sooner or later be called on to be forcefully reminded of the two people saved from the sea. It took them some time to locate the inn; it had proved difficult from the outset, having not approached the inn from this side of town where they had spent their first night, and they dared not ask for any help in locating its position. Trailing the weight of their mud and sand-clogged clothing, which was most uncomfortable, they overwhelmingly needed to change out of them. They recognised certain buildings before seeing the inn and with that they hurried along to reach its protection; they knew they could not be seen entering and waited in the cover of a nearby doorway until the few people that were about in the street where either passed or otherwise engaged in other business to not notice them sneaking like rats off a waiting ship into the side entrance of the inn.

When the landlord first saw them, he was sweeping out the main room; glancing through a glass panel of a door, he was taken aback with shock, hardly believing his eyes at the sight of the two standing in the rear doorway of the empty tavern, save for a small number of his early local regulars who were too busy talking to notice their entry. With the speed of a much younger man and in such a manner as not to attract attention, he ushered the bedraggled pair into the small room adjacent to his pantry for privacy and further knowledge of their situation.

With an appalling look of surprise, he was filled with a mouthful of numerous questions, and telling them that when they failed to return, he and his wife feared the worst.

"You do look desperate, what on earth happened to you the landlord asked as he examined them?" Without a breath, the big man was in a reprimanding tone told them that he had warned them about you-know-who. "Don't tell me I didn't warn you; but you were wilful and had to go, oh yes" he went on as the words came tumbling out without a chance of not letting anyone have a chance to speak. They had to stand like children whilst he ranted; if they hadn't realised his concern, they would had burst out laughing. His fleshy jowls wobbled as he had laid into them like a deranged and concerned mother whose children had stayed out all night and learnt what trouble really was. The continued questions tumbled out before answers could be given, leaving Robert and the woman to sit on a barrel and wait until the troubled landlord's display of concern subsided. The innkeeper noticed Robert's bruised hands and cut wrists with congealed blood that had hardened by this time into lumpy puss-filled masses.

"Those hands need attention," he said in a serious tone. "Momma," he called loudly, forgetting his purpose for ushering his friends into the side room. Then, before leaving the room to seek for his absent wife, he sternly warned them to stay where they were, as if they were naughty children who should remain in hiding and not disobey him again. They smiled to each other with the innkeeper's concern as he left the room, when in no time at all both returned in his fussing manner; they made a fine pair, both as round and jolly as each other.

When the eyes of the landlord's wife befell the sight of the two, she became quite horrified and before anything could be said, she took the woman by her hand and led her out of the room. The landlord's mood, meanwhile, had subsided and was in a lesser agitated mood to scold; all he wanted now was an interesting story to listen to and in his eagerness to hear the account, he told Robert to rid himself of the gritty clothes that he guessed must have irritated him.

When, finally, he was able to step into his bath it was much later. In the room up above, water carriers trailed in one by one to fill his tub which diverted his attention from the woman. The salt-encrusted mud that had dried on him proved really difficult to remove; in the early days of his soldiering, water was never something to become familiar with, but in his time, under the heat of the desert, it gave him a liking for bathing. His time in the heat for his own comfort made him adopt the local custom of washing and bathing each day, not only did he get used to the habit but looked forwards to his refreshing early morning splash. Fair to say that whenever he was out scouting, habits sometimes reverted back to the old ways; as for the present, if he really wanted to remove the grime, there was nothing left but to give himself a good ducking. Staying under the hot water, he rubbed at the grit that adhered to his skin; the refreshing water raised his spirits making him feel better for it. After he had bathed and rid himself of the grime of the sea, the clean feeling he had was like a glowing mantle about him; he was ready to be dressed but lacked clothes to wear, he wondered what to do knowing that he could not walk about in his nakedness. The thought of displaying his masculine form to the maids made him secretly smile; he was so refreshed the idea was growing on him. Saved from his dilemma, the landlord at the right time arrived with a bundle of his clothes for Robert to put on until his own were dry from washing. He looked at the landlord and declined his offer, for he did not wish to present himself before others in clothes so many sizes larger than his own to be laughed at as a fool. Choosing was not an option if he was to be dressed; left to refusing the offer he told the landlord that nakedness suited him better. The landlord, not satisfied with his choice, shrugged his shoulders and left, leaving Robert unsure not knowing if it had been caused by the man's injured pride. But he returned to drop bed linen in his lap.

"You may have a soldier's body," the inn keeper told him, "but you must cover yourself whilst under my roof." Being left with nothing else to do, Robert sat waiting for his clean clothes with nought else but a sheet wrapped around his person. He had seen nothing of the woman, which evoked some concern in him for they had not been apart for such a considerable time since their leaving the Levant.

He remained miserably confined, alone in the emptiness of the room pondering on his next move, when she walked through the doorway, presenting herself fully dressed and looking absolutely splendid in her washed robes. He looked at her with critical eyes and told her that she was a fine sight to behold; another thing struck him; she wore no yashmak, displaying her beauty to all for the first time. His finger pointed towards her face; she answered him before he could end his statement saying that perhaps he was right; it was better and would prove less noticeable for her to adopt the western custom. She said it as though it had little consequence, but he felt that for some reason it was for him, he hoped it was for he secretly smiled within at the idea of its being so.

"You're dressed," he exclaimed, then went on to ask why his clothes were not ready; she called him an ass with little sense if he did not realise that his heavier material would take much longer to dry than her silk robes. He was peeved because he lacked freedom to move about; the thought of him having to hold a sheet around himself to prevent his dignity from being exposed embarrassed him, which he told her was not easy to swallow. Now that they were alone, there were things she had to say to him that she preferred not to put off any longer; moving across the room to the window looking out to the street with her back to him, her words did not come easily. She did not falter, but anticipated that what she was about to say was not kindly, especially to him that had saved her from the deep waters of the lagoon. Being that she would not duck what had to be said, her confidence was a little wavering. Robert sat half turned, viewing her slim petite figure not taking in a word that she was saying when she also turned to him and caught him watching her. His eyes slowly met hers and remained fixed; it seemed for some time before she came to him. She had seen such looks before, but from this man she no longer allowed it to bother her; she smiled faintly, wondering, realising her speech had broken before she continued.

"Since I awoke on that sand bank this very morning, I have been haunted by the events of the last night. Being dropped into the waters of the lagoon and weighted down to sink to its endless depths was indeed an experience I would not wish to undergo again, indeed I have thought of little else," she spoke softly and with sincerity. "It was you that brought me back from the edge of death, Franj, when you didn't have to. I can say now that in our short time of knowing

450

each other, much has passed between us both that has been good and bad." Robert was about to interrupt but she stayed her hand. You could have easily perished, for you too were in that boat of death, but you risked all when there was no need and carried on to save me. Why did you do that?" she asked. Robert was short of words. He started saying one thing, then said another; he gestured with his hand in search of a word, feeling embarrassed by the candidness of her question; then lost to express what he genuinely thought, he shrugged showing an open mouth, not knowing what to say.

"What does it matter," he blurted. She looked at him and read his rosy face's admission of affection; for once it was not easy for him to speak out so plainly about. It was true indeed, his face reddened and it wasn't embarrassment but a fear to admit the truth; there was so much he wanted to say but any admission of his feelings might have appeared that he had spoken foolishly and out of turn. After all, she was different and a wanted woman, but she had an influence on him despite having a price on her head; what could he say, 'I've fallen for you and want you to live with me'? In this situation, he loathed the truth but could not find it in him to fight it. Besides, there were customs and a difference of worlds between, them, apart from being an enemy.

"Franj," she called and poked his arm; he had drifted away in his thoughts which created deep embarrassment for him, enough to have him lie about it.

"Listen to me, Franj, I have much that I have to say to you, it is a time for complete honesty now. Now that we are sharing this undertaking and working together, I must be completely honest and open to bare what I have hidden from you." Robert looked at her surprised; he was glad that he had not spoken out and made a fool of himself. "Do you recall that time aboard ship when we sailed to Simeon? When we met, I must confess that it was my orders to attempt to illicitly hold your affection for a while. It was a method of clinging to you, should I need to make use of you in the future."

"Anything else?" Robert asked, being taken aback by what he thought of her plan; his mind was racing. Honesty, she called it, more like her audacity; his blood was caught between hot and cold and he could not help it but look very down-hearted, her words showed so plainly in his face.

"You must understand that I would have used you, it was the nature of my life then. I lived only to serve and survive for there were those who could pressurise me in the most despicable of ways. You saw the way I was tormented and begged, yes begged, that my father would be spared, he did not deserve that end. It was Hassan that held me in this grip, though I make no excuses for the way I was shaped, I did all because of the fear of Hassan's will. I am aware that I impressed myself on you a little deeper than expected, you could not hide that from me, and inside, it pleased me, for there was a difference in you and you were a warrior that I admired. What happened at the Palace in Antioch was already a plan in motion before I ever saw you. The Amman and the Old Man had been mortal enemies for a long time caused by the deep religious differences between them, there was indeed a great rift." Once again, she looked him in the eye telling him that she was the tool to merely see Hassan's plan through.

451

"What about my friend at the house?" Robert's voice had changed to one of disgust, "Was there a need to kill him?"

"Alas," she replied, "that was not of my doing. On this I wish that you will take my word and as I have told you many times, I am not a liar, it was Kassim, the captain of Hassan, it was his strange way of leaving his mark. Within his heart lies a cruel streak whose only show of strength is to cause pain, you yourself discovered that. It was his way, inflicting pain and suffering on others, not unlike my master. It was a weakness that served the master's purpose to allow him certain indulgencies," she corrected herself, "then master. By allowing him his weakness, Hassan saw into his soul and stupid as Kassim was, he thought that Hassan favoured him. It was my part that to see that all of Hassan's plans were carried out."

"And the other woman," Robert asked, "what of her?"

"Uma too was wicked when it came to pain, but her powers were spent, Hassan believed that she could spend her days teaching other students the ways of misery and how best to gain the rewards from seeing others suffer. As for the prisoners in the camel skin, that also was Kassim's doing, as I have said, he was the captain of his men and suffering served as an example of making prisoners bend to his will. It probably satisfied him to know there was little chance of escape once inside the skin and less for him to worry about."

"The whole lot of you are no good," he said angrily.

"No, Franj, search your own conscience, that is not quite so, for have not your own people set about such atrocities that you could not bring yourself to admit? Franj, before you condemn me you must look into yourself to judge fairly."

He clutched at straws by offering the argument that war is different; offering a weak argument was not worthy of him and it shamed him to splutter out such a statement.

"Is it so different that your people can walk across battlefields defiling and slitting open the bodies of the innocent. Delving into their innards for valuables that they may have swallowed, or the hundreds of men and women that were left hanging from the walls of a city after its conquest? No, my franj, it is not right, it is inhuman." He could not argue with her, as it was one of the reasons why he left the field so quickly after battle; it sickened him to see his countrymen in such acts. The sights often haunted him; it was true that there were unnecessary actions of barbarity on both sides, he had truly witnessed it. He did not want to talk further and asked her if this conversation could be continued another time.

"As you wish."

Her honesty did not stand alongside his; realising that her openness had upset him disappointed her; perhaps it was not the right time, she stood and quietly and left the room. The day passed by and Robert had worn his coat of despondency for long enough; much had passed through his mind, especially the bloodshed and pain of his time here. The wanton and wasted lives of friends and other good men he had known, but what could he have done being a man alone? He had not seen her during the day, expecting that she, like him, had given up their folly of ever thinking that they could make a life together. Sitting close to the window, he suddenly realised how time had passed him by; people, he guessed, that were passing by outside were now doing so with the idea that their day's toil was almost at an end. The tide had turned and some ships had left their place of birthing and he hadn't even noticed their sailing; he pushed his hands through his hair as if wondering where had his mind been all that day. Now, when he gazed out, clouds were racing across the sky and the sun was dropping towards the horizon to set. Though he was stiff, he guessed that there were moments that he must have dropped into sleep and not realised his tiredness; there was still a lethargy in his body and it was not yet in him to move himself to anything. Stretching to relax, Robert sat alone surrounded by his melancholia of the past, pondering over their conversation, clinging onto past events and recalling certain horrors of days gone by; there was no excuse for him to seek out mistakes of those he served. My God, his eyes had been opened long ago and he would not use them to seek out a reason or an excuse for anything that he had done to cause him embarrassment. War is war, he was raised for it and he had been educated about it by those he presently served; events became facts of life that he could not change. It was useless wrapping himself in guilt for the whole of creation for all the wrongs that are carried out, why do men get so eaten up with excitement for survival for the oddest of reasons? It's just a state of mind, he supposed, an extension of the way you feel and unfortunately it continues to consume men like a canker deep within, long after the battle. He had always examined his actions in an attempt to maintain his honour, though he would not wholly condemn his own, knowing that the enemy also engaged in their own cruel ways.

He could not keep this mood up; instead of calling the landlord, he slunk away quietly; suspecting that he would be billeted in the same room as he had previously been, he did not feel so cordial any more.

In the room she appeared asleep; his bed on the floor welcomed his tired body and he buried himself beneath the sheets and it was not long before he had entered into a deep sleep in the knowledge that this evening there were no villains waiting for him.

As stars twinkled and the moon looked down peacefully upon the city throughout the stillness of the night, the moon's glow lengthened its brightness across the floor of the bedroom. A slender figure stealthily moved into the shadow and remained there. It stayed motionless as if it neither wanted to move one way or the other. As if geared by some mechanism, it moved forwards in stages to the bed where it divested itself of its apparel and slipped serenely under the covers without disturbing the sleeping occupant. Robert later woke with a start, discovering the warm softness of the body that lay next to him. A voice whispered sweetly to him not to make a sound or he may awaken others.

"Take me in your embrace and be kindly," she whispered, "tell me of your bidding, for tonight I will offer myself to you willingly."

He did not have to worry about the interloper into his bed, for he instantly knew who she was and for an age he longed to do just as she bid him.

The next morning they lay together entwined like ivy branches clinging to a host. "Are you awake, Franj?" she nudged him gently in his bruised muscular side and he concurred with a grunt of a sound for yes. There was a long pause before she spoke.

"We have to go back."

"To where?" Came the half awakened reply. "To the house of our enemy, the evil one, Rici, we have unfinished business; and besides, it was true what I said to the landlord some time ago, that my people will come in search for me. For me the score is of a personal nature, but his office is the place I need to plant something that will finalise my plan and secure the demise of that wicked man. And do not forget Aldo, your friend, he also has to be freed from the grip of his vicious grandfather."

In his half-awakened state, Robert hummed in a low disinclined state of agreement, admitting similar thoughts have been in his mind also.

"But what and why do you have to put into the office? It's a bit dangerous, you could be caught; his thugs could be waiting for you." Questions rolled off his tongue; he did not like the idea and it irritated him, the very thought of it was totally disagreeable.

There, alone in that room, the two discussed their plan as if nothing had happened between them.

Robert was all of a fidget, "there could be too much danger and besides we have only just made our future known to be together," he embraced and drew her lissom body to his, telling her that a fleeting arrangement is not what he had in mind, and that she meant too much to him now.

They lay together in silence, Robert was stroking her hair absent-minded when he realised she had never told him her name.

"Tell me about yourself, where do you come from and why did you never tell me your name?"

"Franj," she exclaimed, becoming coy trying to evade the question,

"Robert," he interjected. From where they lay, her eyes travelled to the window almost becoming distant.

"It has been so long since I have heard my name that I feel that I can't remember it, my real name..." she said wavering on the subject before her words evaporated, declining to give up that which she was not yet ready to impart and changed the subject. Strangely, as if she was still bound by the bonds of the hashashin, she desisted. Robert tried to reason the reluctance but would not press her, knowing that in time she would yield it when she was good and ready. Hassan, somewhere from the depths of eternity, must have been calling to her for secrecy. Instead, she began to describe the place of her long past existence.

"I come from a place in the valley of Allamut in the mountains of the Elburz. To me it is a most beautiful place," though, she admitted that she had not been there for a long time. She knew the reason for that, but it was kept hidden, knowing that should Hasan Ibn al Sabbah learn of her visit, he would know to use the lives of the villagers against her should he ever wish to do so, similarly the way Hassan had used her father as a cat would under its paw. She rambled dreamlike through her childlike memory.

"If you were to follow the road that winds into the mountains out of the plain like a rope that has been thrown to the ground, it will take you into a most lonely region of forests and mountains. There the pines are tall and the air is clear and fresh held within a strong smell of pines resins. The people there are of a happy disposition and hardworking and, would you believe it, known for their handsome appearance. My father's brother was the village leader, my father, I was told later, was a serious boy, naturally gifted with a knowledge of herbal medicines; as he grew he became widely known in the region as a healer, and when his name became known to the Old Man of the Mountain he was taken by men with a promise of greater scientific rewards. The Old Man placed him under the tutelage of his own scientists who educated my father into their ways sharing their knowledge and over the years he became the Old Man's physician and I, in turn, was taken as a hostage to keep my father loyal. In the meantime, because I was of the right age, I was trained in many pursuits, which had proved to be a valuable asset to him over the years.

"On the seldom occasions when my father and I were united, love and happiness entered my life like a ray of sunshine that unlocked my passionless heart." She paused slightly, as if to catch a glimpse of a memory past, before her eyes turned glassy and tearful. "When we were together he made me laugh and reminded me that I was still a young girl." Her knees crept up to her chin to catch the sheet that she held and, still in a pensive mood, smiled as she momentarily caught an amusing thought, which remained inside of her. Robert lay and silently watched this she-devil transform into an ordinary woman, a woman that he had recently held and was revealing images to him of her inner most self. What he had once imagined of her to be nothing other than hard rock had suddenly come to life with a heart that was as soft and tender as any that he had known. She had earned her name, the people that knew of her could bear witness to that, committing foul deeds that to his kind was inexcusable and here she was sitting alongside him and talking dreamily like a young girl.

"How I treasured those moments together, they were all my secret moments safely stored in a secret cupboard and only I held the key." She held her hand to her heart indicating her safe repository, "But, should I dare to tell of that treasure then I would have been severely beaten and made to forgo food for showing such a weakness. My life, it would appear, has been coloured only darkness and shade and fashioned to serve only one master. It seems as though I have lived in shadows of another world all my life." Her hand went to her forehead as though there were recriminations of regret, but there were no tears. "I have knowledge of potions and have been trained as a thief of possessions as well as the manipulator of the hearts of men, but until this evening past," she turned and looked directly into Robert's eyes, "I vow that I have never shared the bed of any other man than you my franj. She looked away for a moment and began her to recite her list of talents. I have abilities to scale walls, walk through darkness and to be fearless in the face of my enemy." Without a pause for breath she rattled on, "I have been instructed into reading the words and the mind of others, my voice is lower in tone, which carries an unknown quality when used dispassionately or otherwise. I have been instructed in the art of negotiation, to instil fear by implication and stress the need to be obeyed without using force. Punishment and death have also been within my sphere of influence. I can speak the dialects of the mountains and the lowlands and your own tongue, Robert, and that of the people of the Syria and beyond into the land of Egypt and Greece a land that I have never visited." He had smiled at the sound of his name; in it was an inaccuracy peculiar to her people. Then she paused, "There are also things that I have been taught that I do not wish to talk on," she changed from talking of her role of abilities and looked at Robert. "So you see that what you can have as a friend is no innocent young woman. I tell you this, franj because of my trust and belief in you, and in many ways I perceive your protectiveness towards me, which I like, and for the first time ever, I have come to rely on another." Then once more she spoke further, holding her open hand on his face and gazing into his dark, searching eyes. "You must excuse my openness but it is the way of my teaching; you and I have come far and, if I am not mistaken, are destined to be together for some time."

Robert beamed, his grin filling his face as she said those last words, thinking that it would be expectant of him to have made that sort of gesture towards a lady. Her confidence and forthright attitude staggered him as she had reeled off her talents, which Robert thought were more fitting for one of his own band. He reached out, throwing his arm around her and drawing her towards him, hugging her, telling her she was probably right, then hugging her again they both burst out laughing.

He tensed a little before broaching a question that had bothered him for some time, as to who the band of men belonged to that they defeated so easily on the road to Antioch.

"Oh," she replied, "well at that time you did us a great service, for they were probably sent by the Amman of Damascus to eliminate us. Somehow, he must have partly learnt of our presence and feared the interference to his plans and possibly a dangerous outcome that we would have created. Perhaps they feared that we were about to assassinate his daughter to reach for him, for as you may be aware, the Old Man and he were mortal enemies and the plan that was enacted so successfully was what he got wrong."

"So in part we had a hand in the assassination without realising it." Robert almost lost breath with surprise as he spoke.

"Had it not been for your curiosity at the boat and your persistence on the road we possibly could have been ambushed and slaughtered along that same trail."

"Then I would not have lost my companions, nor would I have been here."

"It is as you say, Franj, I consider it fate, whatever is written is so."

"Well, what about your mistress, what happened to her?"

"You are a most inquisitive man, franj," she teased, "but I will tell you now, it was only her function to oversee the intended kill and once it was done, she returned to Alamut were she had other business."

"And what was that?"

"I told you once before that I was not informed of reasons or anything other than my task, for that information you will have to ask her yourself. I beg you, Franj, do not seek her out, for she has more venom than the lonely cobra."

There was genuine concern in her answer as she looked away as if to ponder on the dangerous task that Robert unwittingly may have been thinking of.

That day was spent rather lazily, they did not venture out of doors, as they did not wish to be recognised and hazard the chance of giving away any knowledge of their survival to Luca.

As nightfall came upon them, they waited until all was quiet before making their way to the house of Luca Ricci at the far end of town on the edge of the lagoon. Although oil lights still flickered in windows and threw up haunting shadows across alleys, their progress was unimpeded as they made their way through the long shadows of empty streets. The cobbled streets that echoed to the sound of footsteps during the daytime where quiet, and only the sounds that echoed from darkened passages were hollow and of no threat; it was long past that time respectable people busied themselves out if doors. All had now retired indoors to the safety of their own dwellings, leaving the darkness to others that sought its incongruity and certain advantages of such a late hour. Occasionally, the presence of stumbling drunks and whores were to be witnessed, causing them no resistance as they stepped over their intoxicated hulks as they manoeuvred their passage through the back alleys to conceal their recognition to those that would be alarmed by their presence.

Towards the water front, the moonlit reflections on the sea's lapping waves reflected a light that gave rise to the image of Luca's three storey house; it loomed from the darkness as they neared the outer walls around its foreboding and ghostly façade. With fresh memories of their last sojourn within its walls still holding vivid memories, apprehension to return to its interior was growing within Robert. His fear was not for himself, but for the one that was by his side. Her presence had become something other than a working partnership; they had become reluctant lovers out of the events of their recent experiences, which gave rise to Robert's apprehension of her being injured or worse. Whilst she was driven with a passion to enter the house and make their way to Aldo's room, wake him and try to persuade him to leave and flee with her and Robert away from the clutches of his grandfather.

They approached the gateway and suddenly stopped, noticing an unobtrusive shadow and outline of a large plump figure leaning alongside one of the two stone gateposts that stood like stalwarts before the short pathway to the house that supported two great iron gates that barred their way. Robert suspected that by his shadowy outline, he was the one that had delivered him a swift kick to his groin when he first laid eyes on him when bound defencelessly in Luca's cellar. By the vengeful look on Robert's face, she sensed the thoughts that ran through his mind.

"Put away those thoughts of revenge," she told him, "this is not the moment for such action. Let us make contact with Aldo and ascertain his needs to aid in his escape. That alone would be sweet enough, to think that the monster that lives within would have lost his most prized possession, taken from under his nose while he slept." He knew she was right, but one day he would have his moment with that oaf at the gate; as for now, he had to concentrate his thoughts of a way into the house. Silently, they backed away into the shadows leaving the lone sentinel to the front of the house undisturbed, moving off around towards a safer aspect where they could scale the boundary wall unnoticed. Peering over the wall Robert could see the presence of guards placed around the house meaning that Luca suspected that they were alive and would somehow foolishly seek their revenge, but he was ready for them to make a slip and fall foolishly into his hands once again. With the guards being so many in number, it meant that their place to scale the boundary wall would be the first obstacle and clearly there was no place they could try without being seen. To show themselves or leave behind any trace was to lose their objective and give all away; they had to seek another way.

"We will find another place where we can gain entry," Robert suggested.

"We cannot do this," she told him, "Luca is too well guarded."

Robert questioned her statement, asking how they were going to get in.

"Only I can do it alone," she answered, "there is a way, but it will mean scaling the walls up to one of those balconies."

"That's impossible, besides," he told her, "I can't let you endanger yourself now that we are together."

"Fear not, my Robert, this is what I was schooled in, remember?" There were protests, but he knew that she was probably right. In his heart, but he could not help in showing her that he was afraid of her being taken; she held him, reminding him that she needed him on the outside to come to her rescue should their plan go wrong. He could cope with that, and with that in mind she told him to assist her by cupping his hands to give her a safe foothold. Without a sound, she placed her small foot into his hands and with a sudden effortless upwards jerk from him she was on top of the wall and over without a sound. He could not watch her progress, but instinctively knew that she was more competent than he to scale the walls of the house, after all, as she had told him, it was not her first time in such a task. She dropped silently to the ground on the other side without a sound from the high wall, remaining in a crouched position in the shadow so as not to reveal herself. In her black silken clothes, she blended into the darkness, making her form difficult to detect, but she was alert, and immediately moved around the perimeter of the house picking out the position of the guards. About the house there were three guards, one front and rear and one to the side, proving that Luca was not taking any chances with his security. No bodies had been washed up, his worthless ruffians had argued that if they didn't sink they could have been drawn out by the tide to be lost at sea; because they could not positively account with any certainty of their demise from the task that was previously set for them to carry out, they had to be prepared. She made her way silently to the side of the house that stood free of guards facing onto the canal; at the corner of the main wall of the building, she set about nimbly scaling its quoins and rough brick facing. It was difficult for Robert to clearly follow her progress, and in those fleeting worrying moments when the clouds moved by giving way to the moons glow, he did gasp at her ability. There, on the corner of the stone quoins of the building, he could detect faintly the movement of her dark outline; he was amazed at her agility and daring to scale the sheer heights of the house without falling off. The more he watched, the more he wanted to cheer her on; in his eyes, she was truly remarkable.

Incredibly, she progressed across the spalled brick face of the building with the ease of a reptile on a sheer rock face until she reached an overhanging balcony, which she guessed would be the room of Aldo. The spectre gained position onto the balcony and rested; a small thin blade was produced from within her clothing and prized between the joint of the casement windows.

Her experience in such matters was as artful as ever; using the finely shaped tool, she silently slid it into the small gap between the opening edges of the casement windows to make contact and raise the metal latch that kept the windows closed and secure from inside the room. Once within, she drew back the curtains to less than a hands breadth to allow in sufficient light to illuminate the room without causing any disturbance to the sleeping occupant. Taking up a position in the shadows that concealed her form against the wall, she waited for her eyes to accustom themselves to the darkness of the room before moving forwards to inspect the sleeping occupant.

Carefully, she made her way to the bedside and found its occupant rolled over and soundly asleep, the sleeper was partially hidden by the bed covers that were pulled high over his head. Her hand slid inside the covers and sought out an area on the back of the body, her arcane esoteric knowledge instinctively sought out a location where she began to softly stroking the sleepers back. Moving her hand across the tired flesh of the sleeper, she began to work with her fingers until she realised with a chilling dread that it was not that of the one she sought; now it was too late, for her adept finger work caused the figure to turn restlessly, exposing his grunting and disturbed unshaven face, it was Luca. The moonlight that sparsely entered from the gap in the drawn curtain highlighted the stubble of silver bristles on his ageing face; her manipulations had not placed her in any danger of discovery as he was sleeping soundly.

Silently and quickly, she rose and made her way over to the door and into the dark passageway. Unsure of the corridor, she took stock of her position before venturing to her right which, if her memory would serve her correctly, would lead her to two other rooms, of which one was used as a store room. Her eyes, now familiar with the darkness, drew her attention to the shadowy outline of a vacant chair placed outside one of the doorways. It was obvious to her that a member of the household had sat there attentively during the day to alert the master should any sound or disturbance emanate from its occupant within. The question now was, where were they now? The large walnut-panelled door she faced had to be the one; as the pressure of her outstretched hand squeezed on the handle, her senses prompted her towards caution; there was no explanation why, only instinct cautioned her advance. A glancing back-wards look at the vacant chair alongside her caused hesitation, it was probable that the occupant of the chair was now within.

There were four more doors along the passageway, which required checking to be certain that her reluctance to enter this room was born out of justifiable doubt. She applied due caution, opening each door only to view a stark emptiness within to be revealed. As she moved with great stealth and confidence through the darkness of the passageway, she arrived back at the door which posed her reluctance. Stooping to one knee, she levelled her eye to the keyhole, only to reveal a solid darkness beyond the closed door, the key was in the lock and she had to view the room to know the number that guarded Aldo. There was only one way open to that end, it meant that she had to get on to the balcony outside the window to ascertain their number, should they be secretly positioned to raise an alarm. By way of the adjacent storage room was her only chance, she saw that there was a small window that would enable her to pass through with relative ease.

Quietly, she opened the window and perched herself into a comfortable position across the open casement; it came easy to her; she then drew her legs up and pivoted her body to pointing outward where she sat very precariously for her next movement. Dangling precariously in an attempt to reach across to the other balcony became problematic. The distance of the balcony she had to reach was not as near as she had hoped it would be. From her position on the small open window, she soon realised that to launch herself forwards onto the next balcony would prove difficult for her. She was calm and her heartbeat was steady; she felt good in herself. With a calculating confidence and with silent agility, she allowed herself to slide down the outside wall until she was suspended by one hand from the window sill, searching for a safe foothold on the joints of the brick course before she came to rest. She could see one of Luca's henchmen below but it did not bother her. She was silent in her movements and besides Luca's men were apt to be lax and inattentive. In her suspended spread position, she was still short of the balcony and her arm soon began aching from her suspended weight as she persevered to stretch forth that extra distance. Searching with her foot along the jointed brickwork, she edged it searchingly along the jointed brickwork, her foot through the softness of her soles felt for a decent grip until she found a new footing. A brick that had been poorly racked at the time of its manufacture had been damaged and remained improperly pointed when it was set into the wall. This gave her the opportunity she required to free her straining hand from the window and at the same time launch herself forwards from her foothold of the damaged brickwork when she released her grip on the window. The action was precisely timed and she launched herself forwards, barely catching onto the ironwork of the balcony and left swinging in mid-air. Something had stirred the guard making him move around beneath her while she hung there momentarily, once passed her she swung her body through the darkness until she had wind enough to draw herself upwards and over the balcony top to safety. Crouching into a dropped position, she paused to concentrate her mind to the work at hand, standing askance of the slightly drawn curtain, she surreptitiously peered through the gap of the curtains that had been carelessly drawn.

It was some relief to her and justification that she curbed her enthusiasm in refraining in her eagerness to enter the room enthusiastically, discovering that her suspicions were justified when she pressed her face to the window noticing a sleeping figure sprawled in a chair alongside the bed. She released the catch on the window by jiggling the slender blade the way as she had managed once before. Unknown to her, when the window was eased open, the handle of the latch was previously damaged and loosely fitted, causing it to fall to the ground with sufficient noise to wake the sleeping guard at Aldo's bedside. Recoiling quickly into the shadows, she waited for an alarm from within. Surprisingly, the guard did not flinch from the noise; as caution was her guardian, she stayed her eagerness to enter, pausing further, making sure that no other person had been alerted in the house. With a gentle push, the window opened with ease and without creating any unnecessary sound to arouse the sleeper at the bedside. Stepping through the opening, she made her way silently towards the bed by way of the back of the chair, the blade she used for entry was firmly held in her grasp should it be necessary to use it on the awakening sentinel. An empty jug on the floor at his feet measured the depth of the guard's dormancy; his finger on his open hand was still remained caught in the stone jug handle from the moment that he lapsed into his stupor.

It was obvious in her mind that Luca did not pick his thugs for their fervency and loyalty to him when this was how they exhibited their devotion to duty. Despite the fearlessness of their warriors, it disgusted her to view westerners as weak and corrupt; greed and with a thirst for strong liquor, she surmised, it must be their reason for living that spurned them on. Able to ignore the guard, she leant forwards and gently shook the sleeping Aldo, but alas he was not stirring. It was obvious that he had been given another soporific to deaden his strength that they had previously endeavoured to rebuild earlier. Luca was a fool not to heed her warning, though she had used the threat as a means to frighten him there was a grain of truth in her words for an over use of the drug. There was a glass standing adjacent to what appeared a ewer of stale water, a small amount was poured into the awaiting glass.

Her slender index finger sported a large amber gemstone on a ring, flicking it open it revealed a secret reservoir of a white powder held within its cavity. Holding the glass high towards the meagre shaft of light entering through the curtained window, she carefully measured out a portion of the contents into the murky water within the glass. With the powder floating on the surface she swirled the water in a circular motion as she had done earlier until it formed a whirling vortex, she watched it carefully until she was satisfied that the powder had dissolved.

Placing an arm around the limp body of Aldo, her light frame struggled with the awkwardness of his dead weight until he was propped up into a near-sitting position and able to take the fluid that she began slowly offering between his parched lips. Breathing heavy from her strenuous effort to maintain his position, with great care she made sure that the potion was accepted without a drop of it being wasted. All she could do now was wait until the body had accepted the potion to work its magic.

The waiting and the slowness for his body to react disappointed and unsettled her, she anxiously began to coax Aldo into consciousness by shaking him and gently slapping his face in her effort to urge him into awareness. Her inner self wanted to shout to him but restraint was uppermost, knowing too well the dangers of alerting the household. At last, after an impatient wait, she began to relax as signs of consciousness began to manifest; he was stirring, and with this positive act brought hope of getting him up and quitting this dreadful house, which was encouraging. The effects of the powder would make him obey her without argument and hopefully endeavour to speed his movement when he found the strength to stand. Unfortunately, he was sloth like; any movement activated impatience with him; her efforts proved arduous, drawing his legs around to the edge of the bed for a standing position proved quite difficult. Once walking, she expected that he would become less awkward, but so far her attempts to make him stand upright failed. His weakness showed in his inability to find his balance, after all, he had been asleep for an age it seemed, and without added support, it caused him to buckle at the knees almost pulling her over on the bed with him.

The sleeping sentinel remained slumped in the chair and oblivious to any noise, allowing the pair to freely struggle in their efforts to escape confinement. It was obvious to her that there wasn't any value in her expectations of leaving the house, but there was a chance that was worth taking to evade their discovery. When his absence was made known, there was a possibility that they may overlook scouring the house and search for Aldo around the town, where Luca was known to have many enemies. It would be quite clearly expected that others might have lent a hand in his escape and that they would not risk remaining within the grounds of the house with a need to whisk him away to a place of safety and isolation from Luca. The more she persuaded herself of this possibility, the more she believed there was a definite chance to succeed.

Heaving him up onto his feet, she used all her ability in supporting him; slowly, she walked her weak ally out of the room and into the darkness of the corridor and into the start of a life of awareness for the young man once she was secreted in a safe hiding place. She had time during her recent sojourn to reconnoitre the house and was aware of the upper floor and the emptiness of the rooms above.

If she could find a safe place within the roof space, there was a chance that they could secrete themselves and wait until the next day before they made good their escape. Her present task was to achieve co-ordination of Aldo's brain and limbs. Climbing up the narrow staircase to the attic was not proving to be an easy single-handed operation. Between the awkward body that she had to support and the extreme effort of remaining silent, it was no mean feat. However, with difficulty and fortitude, somehow, the task was achieved and a suitable place close to the eaves in the roof space was found adequate for them to rest. The first objective being attained and, before leaving him to rest naturally without the aid of potions, it now left only the notice of her intentions to be made known. She had to leave Aldo for a short while to seek her waiting partner outside, who by now must be thinking the worst may have happened.

It was easy, she thought, locating Robert, most likely he would be the one bobbing up and down in the shadows with impatience mixed with genuine concern for his long delayed friend. He had not seen her or heard her silent approach but almost jumped out of his skin as she dropped down off the wall above him to land equally silent alongside him. He was angry at her delay and inquired with a note of irritation in his voice of Aldo's welfare. He relaxed when she told him that all was well with him but almost exploded with fury as her plan of returning was unveiled. To be truthful, he was not used to being on the outside of events; also irking him was the awareness that her ability of stealth was far better than his. Sensing his disparity with the situation, she leaned on his arm telling him that all would be reliant on his strong arm at this time on the morrow, when Aldo would be fitter in mind and body to endeavour to make their chance of escape. She reached up and pulled his head down to hers kissing him softly before disappearing into the night shadow to return to Aldo in the attic.

The Road to Hell

The following day, there was uproar in the house. Luca was livid with the loss of his grandson, so much so that that he had the guard beaten within an inch of his life for his laxity. The screams of pain reached out to the two fugitives; to Aldo it was an awakening of a different kind. To the woman, it was as she expected; it came as a measure of the hurt and incredulity that Luca's house could be plundered in spite of his guards whilst he lay sleeping. If only he was aware that she entered into his room and massaged his back to see his face without his knowing, what would his thoughts be then?

People were running everywhere; the hiding duo shrunk back into the shadows hidden within the darkness of the roof space, they shrank in apprehension when heavy frenzied footsteps were heard approaching the loft area. The careless seekers missed them, they were too interested in keeping out of the way to miss a beating, hoping to escape from the house later with the other search parties to search the back streets. Mumbled voices were heard to say that their interests should be outside where it would most likely that those who had him were to be found. Aldo did not help matters much with his pleas for sustenance after his protracted fast; unable to help, she mused how it would benefit westerners to live under different conditions for them to toughen up a little; but that thought was no solution to her situation and she knew it. Hunger did gnaw at them and she knew too well that while they could endure the fasting, it would have its consequences later when she tried to move out with his strength sapped to almost nothing. The day dragged by mainly in silence, apart for the loud expectant rumbling from Aldo's inconsolable stomach appealing for food, and night could not come soon enough to escape their confinement.

When the house grew silent, sounds of any internal searching were no longer audible, indicating that the search had now extended to the external surroundings of the streets. Luca would not yield until some clue of his grandson's whereabouts was made known to the band of searchers under Luca's vicious employ. Although it was tempting to seek further knowledge of the situation, it was unwise to endanger their place of hiding within the house; therefore, it was wiser to remain silent and safe.

Night eventually fell upon the city, bringing the usual sounds to herald its arrival; it was not the familiar sounds from the street, more the seditious sounds from around the interior of the great house. It had now been one whole day and almost a complete night silently spent in the dingy, draughty corners of the roof space. It did little to help their stiffened limbs being unable to move about for fear of giving away their place of refuge to the domestic staff who would have willingly given away their secret out of fear that there master who would have eventually found out their error. The need for food and drink almost urged her to seek out the sustenance Aldo required, she would not yield to the impulse, but it took all her will power from the need to survive to resist that gnawing, foolish temptation. The sound of footsteps coming and going could be heard at regular intervals; doors slammed in temper behind Luca's aggravated henchmen, who were not allowed to rest until they had found their quarry. It was obvious that movement from their refuge would not come about until the early hours when, most of the guards were seeking to close their tired eyes for a brief respite from the day's long search.

Unknown to the two transients of the attic, there were others that had reached the shores of this great city during this time. Two visitors from far away, dark skinned strangers to this part of the world, their pigmentation and dress caused others to stop and stare at the like of them; they were not a regular sight on the street. Their purpose was to recover an item, given as a gift to their master as a gesture of good faith in return for a service rendered. It had been snatched back from them like a petulant child's weariness of sharing its possessions; the donor of the gift was Luca and the recipient the murdered Hassan, who had been the second in command to the Old Man of the Mountain. Whilst he had lain dead by the hand of one of their own, the news was carried to him of the appalling event. Needless to say he was furious; as for Hassan, he had been a loyal servant, but what was missing from The Old Man's possession was worth a thousand Hassans. The very name of The Old Man of the Mountain sent a chill down the spines of ordinary men, indeed his name was carried only on a whisper or a mime for fear that another should eavesdrop. Therefore, any overture or understanding with such a notorious person was deemed to be placing oneself into the most precarious of situations. Only the gravest of penalties would be levied should one withdraw or break one's word with the Old Man of the Mountain.

On this occasion, the gift was an ancient Muslim scroll written by the revered prophet's own hand, which to any holy man was priceless beyond expectation and had been left in the safe keeping of Hassan, for the Old Man of The Mountain would be loath to give it up easily. To steal or attempt to steal property from Alamut was stupid and invited death. Now that this sacred scroll was gone, the Old Man could only guess that its true value had been realised by the man that had bartered with it for his help; and his eyes looked vengefully westward for its recovery.

In an age gone by, when Luca was in need of sustenance and warmth, he himself slew the bearer of this treasure and held onto it all those years without knowing its true worth, until chance and circumstance gave him the idea to trade with it.

Though Luca had snatched it from a lone merchant on his desert crossing, he had kept it safe and he too was loathe to give anything up; after all those years, its useful purpose turned out to be used in exchange for the abduction and safe return of his grandson. Considering the prize, this simple act was carried out with the utmost of efficiency and alacrity by the adherents of the Old Man proving the gift well earned.

Wasting no time after their landing, the two new strangers paid handsomely to raise the question of Luca's whereabouts. They paid well to seek out the location of his residence in preparation to call on him during the moonlight hours in the dead of night. Unknown to Luca, whose preying eyes were usually alerted to newcomers, especially those wanting to seek him out, their presence had escaped his attention whilst his mind and time was pre-occupied by the disappearance of his grandson. Oblivious to their presence and their reasons for seeking him out, he was quite unaware of the significance of these two particular mysterious strangers in Venice; Luca's distractions were to prove a very serious mistake for his future.

When night fell, the two left the comfort of their lodgings and did what they were most used to doing; sliding into the shadows of the night and becoming invisible to make a house call to the home of Luca Ricci.

Seeing the guards it must have been obvious to their minds that they were expected, condemning Luca's actions more so. It seemed that there was no other explanation; discovering the numbers of guards positioned around the building ensured that this house was his, the one they sought, they saw it as a pathetic effort to protect himself from them, they were also surprised of his advanced intelligence in preparation of their coming.

Their onward approach went unnoticed as they passed by the gates almost laughingly; ignoring the two ruffians guarding them, their ineptitude at being alert caused the intruders no problem in their passing. Invisibility was their stock in trade and they passed easily, as had one other recent visitor that they were unaware of.

Their choice of entry was the most convenient window at ground level; with ease and stealth, they had managed to gain entry unseen before disappearing into the darkened room. They passed through the house efficiently as though they had once lived there; without fear of being discovered, making their way up the grand staircase they headed towards the bedrooms, checking each room as they passed down the corridor until they eventually came to Luca's room. The unsuspecting Luca slept undisturbed and deeply as if he had not a care, whilst the two noiseless intruders set about leaving the evidence of their visit behind. This visit was not meant to harm or threaten him, merely to leave notice of their being present and to demonstrate the insecurity in his own presumed safety, even though he had executed his own cautionary attempts of protection.

They left the room as silently as they entered and without disturbing anything, disappearing back into the night as if nothing had happened. Unknown to the two emissaries of the Old Man of the Mountain, other eyes had witnessed their approach and departure knowing fully their agenda. Only the experienced eyes of one of their own kind would have the learning to pass through the darkness with the same comfort of the other intruders, one who had been trained in those same arcane talents. It happened as the fleeing duo made their way downstairs from the loft spaces in their own bid for freedom. Aldo, whose body was weak from his confinement and lack of sustenance, realised that his body would not carry him much further, and to underpin what strength he had left, she rested him in an alcove at the bottom of the stairs leading from the attic. It was then that she sensed her countrymen entering the building from below. Quietly, she placed her hand over Aldo's mouth telling him that there were others making their way up the main staircase. Through the darkness, she saw their shapes before they sensed her, and covering Aldo with her black coat concealed him further into the shadows to escape detection until they had moved on. If Luca had awakened, it could have been all over, but they were more subtle than that; she knew what they were about and that Luca would be jumping scared the following day if he had any sense. So, for her, the duel had turned from a sport to a deadly serious affair. If she was to win, this turn of events of her countrymen entering the equation meant that she had to finesse all she had in her possession to overcome any suspicion of falsity in her future plan. Once knowing that the others had left and they were secure, she coaxed Aldo to his feet and proceeded with difficulty to descend the next staircase to the kitchen and freedom.

By the time they had reached the side entrance from the servants' quarters, Aldo collapsed; he had buckled at the knees from his week state of health. He was finished and told her he could go no further, no matter how kindly she talked him into standing it had no effect; this had to be expected, knowing that the young man had not been sufficiently fed for long enough to give him the strength for such a purpose of a deceptive escape. Worse, it seemed, was the effort to stand him upright in order to walk into the shadows where he could not be seen. She looked around, her eyes searching through the dark void of the small garden in the hope of seeing something or someone to help her out of the predicament that she had now found herself in. Aldo's condition had become almost hopeless, and she was unable to manage him further on her own. Her thoughts raced for a solution to her predicament; to remain here was certain to be discovered, her options were difficult; to leave him behind and chance his discovery or leave before she herself be detected and possibly taken prisoner once more. It was unacceptable to leave, believing all her efforts to have amounted to nothing; if only Robert was here, though she could attach no blame to him. She must look for him but first she would have to hide Aldo. Above all things, she feared discovery and the thought of being tossed into the lagoon again by Luca's henchmen.

No sooner had she tried to move Aldo, the sound of heavy feet on gravel alerted her of somebody approaching her position; she feared that the guard would surely come across them in the darkness. There was no other option than to leave Aldo as a decoy whilst she stepped back into the shadows and prepared herself for action. A large, oafish picket was visible by the sheer size of his outline, his hulk came lazily lumbering towards them but not too idle to see the slumped body of Aldo supported by the house wall. On seeing the missing grandson he chuckled convinced that luck was on his side.

"In the name of the Madonna, what have we here?" Talking down with a sardonic giggle in his voice as he spoke, he reached out to arrest the tired and weak body of Aldo. Fortunately, Aldo had the sense to divert the oaf's attention so that he would not suspect another was with him, he appealed for help to the guard promising a reward for getting him to back safely to his grandfather. This ploy certainly slowed the fellow down in his action to render Aldo senseless; the thought of a reward diverted his sense of reason from suspicion as to whether he was alone.

From out of the shadows lunged a slender hand with deathly intent brandishing a stiletto burying itself to the hilt in the guard's side. He stood motionless, wheezing for a moment with the shock of the blade entering his muscular body before reacting; then, as if he gained a second wind, his hand gripped the knife and the arm of its bearer. With his wild reaction, he summoned his strength and with monstrous force flung the woman out from the shadows like a toy into the open where he could finish her off. He was strong and built like an ox, and she was in his grasp; dazed by the force of her awkward fall, she waited for him to complete his deathly act.

Numbed as she was, it truly perplexed her that she had not stunned the man more effectively, hoping to withdraw the blade and try again. Now she was the one that was helpless and it was plain that there was not going to be a second chance, she had to act quickly for there was no doubt she was no match for this huge fellow. He lumbered towards her and stood over her, dwarfing her small frame as he towered over her, she watched as his arm reached out to finally to grip her and crush her in an act of revengeful supremacy. Her terrified eyes transfixed on the giant of a man as he suddenly became statuesque, she heard him wheezing once more for breath before he swayed forwards then back one last time. She was caught up in her own fear, but she was not too slow to move away from him before he toppled to the ground with a thud where she had lain, like a gargantuan tree in the forest that had finally met its end. Watching him fall, she noticed the hilt of deadly poniard had pierced his neck in a lethal downward strike stopping him instantly. Dumbfounded by the sight of the hulk by her side and knowing that she had no hand in the event, she dared slowly to look upwards to another shadowy figure that stood directly behind the fallen guard. Her trance-like state was broken as a voice asked her if it was her intention to lie on the garden all night; realising who her saviour had been, she gasped with relief as he bent forwards to assist her rising.

She was swiftly to her feet altering her manner and began berating Robert for taking so long, at the same time she gratefully complimented him by calling him her strong right arm. The task now was to hurriedly move Aldo across the short space of open ground and into the shadow of the wall where they could have some chance to view the sentries better and finalise their escape. With ease, Robert picked up his weakened friend and made his way cautiously across to the wall and into cover. Aldo, being helpless, was carried in his friend's strong supportive arms; he thanked Robert for what he was doing for him and almost broke out into conversation. Weak as Aldo was, Robert could not help telling his friend in a brusque manner to shut up as there were guards everywhere.

Cautiously, they made their way back winding their way through dark alleys, always keeping to the safety of the shadows and to the refuge of the inn. For their own safety, they had to make many detours to evade Luca's searching parties, and had been alarmed at the size of his private army. His villainous thugs were not afraid to bully and cudgel the answers they wanted out of anybody that they suspected were being evasive or withholding information in their task to find the missing grandson. At one turn, they were alerted by smashing sounds of glass and screaming as men tore into a family and their property; it seemed as though they had the run of the city and law was immaterial.

When they returned to the inn, the old proprietor was confused at what do for the best, fearful for his and his wife's safety and unsure of the danger to his livelihood. Extending the hand of help to Luca's enemies was one thing, but to be caught harbouring the grandson of such a hated and dangerous man was quite another. The fear of extreme reprisals that Luca was able to inflict on anyone that dared to scheme against him loomed in the back of his mind; he was far from young and unable to start again and also lacked the strength of his warrior boarders. After much careful thought, he regretfully asked them to leave, apologising all the way to the rear exit.

"You must understand," he told them that he could not resist the will of Luca's killers. Robert appealed with sympathetic eyes at the landlord whilst cradling his sick friend in his arms, pleading once more to stay long enough for his friend to eat a meal as it was clear to see by his ashen face that he was in dire need of nourishment and could possibly die left in his present state. The good-natured innkeeper fell foul of the appeal; he took a long look at the sickly friend, whose drawn appearance and dull eyes appealed to him like those of a forlorn begging dog when in great need, and with a conceding sigh of defeat from his gentle heart agreed to yield his argument against them. Resigning himself to his foolhardy decision to stay, he brought them back to the kitchen, but turning on them, he sharply added that as soon as it was safe to leave, they must go.

The landlord closed the half-opened door quickly so not to draw further attention to the lighted exit with his unreasonable though friendly guests standing at the side door. He greatly feared that this deed of generosity may hold terrible repercussions for him but at the same time he felt he was secretly striking a blow against the most hated man in Venice. Obviously, the only thought on the minds of his friends was that they were safe and could not wait to relish the wholesome vitals that the innkeeper's wife so proudly served. The innkeeper served bowls of nutritious thick hot stew to them; Robert helped his friend Aldo to take his food whilst the nervous landlord watched them anticipating the worst, pacing the floor with agitated steps and eyes that urged them to hurry. From time to time, he would leave the kitchen to attend to his legitimate late guests and return eagerly to see what progress had been made at the table. He muttered all the time of the unforgiving vengeance that Luca would meat out should he know that he harboured his grandson; the female caught a hold on his words and pulled the innkeeper's apron as he passed by. She whispered in his ear that Luca may no longer be a threat to anybody within a few days; this very evening he had received a very special visit that he would learn about when he awoke later this morning. Not realising her full meaning, he blubbered on but felt there was no need to repeat himself.

Meanwhile, Aldo had taken part of his stew and Robert was near finished his when noises from the other room broke the atmosphere of calm within the kitchen. It was Luca's henchmen, they had finally entered the portal of their sanctuary and were bullying the innkeeper's customers in the other room; amazingly, when the innkeeper's trade was threatened, he showed a pluckier front and quickly left the kitchen to sort out the disturbance. Robert viewed the scene through a crack in the door, laughing to himself at the antics of the innkeeper, who in his own hot way was clever enough to side track the two ruffians. He recognised them and had enough practice each day with awkward customers that ate the fare and tried to avoid payment. Calming Luca's louts in their offending and officious bullying manner, he offered them a drink or two; it reduced their overzealous attitude and disruption of the landlord's trade. At first they showed their nasty side, threatening the landlord should he withhold any knowledge of these villains that stole away Luca's grandson. The landlord kept filling their glasses telling them that he wanted no trouble, after all, he reminded them, hadn't he always looked after them? Giving them the bottle to finish, he quietly eased them out of the inn and on their way.

After the ruffians left, the innkeeper could do little more than wipe the perspiration from his slightly balding pate and breathe a sigh of relief that they did not force their way into looking around the kitchen. He came through the doorway returning to the trio who greeted him with applause and congratulations for his resolve in removing Luca's villains from the premises so expertly that his ego got the better of him, and in the inflated state, he simply forgot to ask them to leave.

After a good night's rest, Luca woke to another bright morning; the smell of salt air drifted through the open window from the lagoon. The taste in his mouth was raw and he passed his tongue around his mouth in the hope that it would wipe all traces of the taste away, but it remained; a glass of water sat on a small cupboard at the side of his bed; he yawned long and decided to rise. Drawing back his covers, he swung his scrawny ageing legs to the side of his bed, arching his still tired body forwards and scratching his finely layered silvery hair. Once more he yawned and, wiping the sleep from his eyes, he nonchalantly reached towards the cupboard top for his glass of water. With his vision bleary, his hand weakly sought his bedside drink and clasped hold of the glass, as he did so, his hand pushed up against something that was so light that he hardly noticed its presence.

Without a second thought, he drank a long swallow on the needed refreshment to relieve the sour taste in his mouth and replaced the glass to its position on top of the cupboard. His tongue smacked around his mouth making the most of the refreshing taste of the water, he felt better and opened his eyes to reality; suddenly, he noticed what he had inadvertently brushed against when reaching for the water. His face became stern and filled with thought; filling his lungs with air his body came alive; every nerve tingled, even the hairs on his neck seemed to stand on end at the sight before him. He had heard of such things before and known their meaning; this was not an easy event to take in. That bitch had said that others would follow; now it seemed that they were here. He picked up one of the gifts and smelt it; there was no mistaking that they were cakes of Hashish. Luca was not a man to be spooked easily, but in this case he knew and feared death was close at hand unless he did something about it quickly. He stared down in horror at the two little cakes before him and his brain began to hurt; so many thoughts were racing through his hurting mind that he broke out into a screaming rage; his guards must have slept to allow an intruder through and into his bedroom. Panic was within him, he ran first to the door then over to the window; impatiently dragging back the curtains, he stared out expecting to see dead bodies all around his house but there were none, the guards were in their position as if nothing had happened. Without dressing, he ran in his nightshirt down the staircase calling for all help in a frenzied panic. Before he could reach the lower half of the stairs, a dozen or more guards were in the entrance and facing Luca at the foot of the staircase in his terrified panic. He berated them all and cursed them for allowing an assassin to enter the house. He had paid good money for their service and this was how they repaid him.

The guards were mystified at his claims, had Luca lost his mind, after all, he was standing in front of them healthy and untouched. They disagreed and argued that they were at their post without moving throughout the night; Luca became more aggravated with their lack of understanding, stamping his feet in his tantrum, he cursed savagely ordering them to follow him upstairs to his bedroom. Up they came and stood gathered at the door of his room, still unaware for any reason for Luca's temper. Wound up, Luca beckoned them forwards ordering them around his bed. He waited until they were in full view of his cupboard, but the imbeciles could not know what to look for until he pointed to the two small cakes, some even dared to snort at their appearance as if Luca was entering into some sort of ageing fantasy. It aggrieved him more at their refusal to accept the evidence lying before them.

In his frustration, Luca was drawn to shouting, grabbing a cudgel from his bedside to beat the next idiot that dared ignore his master's alarm. Explaining about the cakes being a warning of his impending death, he went on to lecture them sarcastically whilst cradling his cudgel affectionately in his hands telling them at length about the hashashin and their pernicious use of the narcotic hashish to deprive men of their wills and turn them into murder slaves.

"In that distant part of the world where they come from, they went unopposed because of idiots like you," he waved the menacing cudgel at them as he spoke, "who do not have the brain or the spine for such things. In that land far away, they remain feared and respected but now they are here and have been in this room sometime in the night." His cudgel thumped the floor to emphasise the point and almost turning hysterical as he spoke with a tear of temper welling in his eye. "It is their living, and too many people, to their regret, have received this threat and dismissed it," he pointed to the two little innocent looking cakes that were innocuously placed on the cupboard, adding, "in the same way that you have, and those ignorant idiots for their folly perished a terrible, terrible death." He gave them all a new directive, to find these people and above all not to threaten or harass them in any way, but to cordially invite them to visit him at their convenience to put right whatever wrong he could possibly have done them.

A voice from the group spoke out about the usual way of disposing of them in the lagoon. This infuriated Luca so much that he swung at him with the cudgel in great anger missing because of his ill temper, screaming at the loutish idiot that he had not taken in what he tried to make so painfully clear. After dismissing them, he was in no mood to carry out business at his office; his heart was racing and it made him feel exhausted and ill; instead, he secreted himself in the safety of his home for the rest of the day.

The news that Luca was seeking strangers from the Levant soon reached the ears of his adversaries in the inn. It was to the girl that all eyes were directed, as she was the only one intimate with the ways of the Old Man of the Mountain. By the activity around about, she knew Luca had received his direct message from her recent confrere, and soon she planned her own message to be delivered. It was late afternoon when the news of the whereabouts of the strangers was made known; the girl began discussing her plan with Robert, requiring his assistance to break into Luca's office to plant what the strangers have come to retrieve.

Robert looked puzzled; he didn't quite follow until the she produced from within her bag a roll of leather, which, on seeing it, he first inquired its use, then its worth. He was told that to him it would prove to be of no consequence, but to such a man as the Old Man of the Mountain it was beyond value. She began unrolling it to reveal a text of golden letters carved upon its leather surface and a decorative edging highlighted in coloured inks; she continued her explanation, telling him that the scroll before them was believed to have been written by the hand of the prophet himself. Robert let out a whistle of air from his lips, it was then he realised that to any Muslim holy man it was a sacred relic and beyond value; to an assassin holy man who had earned it by mutual agreement, he had correctly guessed that it was his by right and would want it returned. In a quizzical way, he told her that he was sure he had seen it before, she agreed; it was this very scroll that Hassan was studying when you were brought to Masyaf. Before leaving, she stole it, and when they reached Lattakia, she had sent off a carrier pigeon to Allamut, the mountain stronghold of the Old Man of the Mountain to report that Kasim had made a bargain with the westerner to steal the scroll from his master for money. Unknown to her, he had discovered her plan and escaped the Old Man of the Mountain's revenge; Kasim had sworn to kill her but her note told of her loyalty and was in pursuit to retrieve it from the double-dealing westerner that had offered it up for the return of his grandson.

The message was designed to wipe out the enemy she had left behind and also help in her own legitimate disappearance. What she now needed was to hide the scroll within Luca's offices, and at the same time send a messenger to the strangers telling of Luca's plan to delude the Old Man and retain the scroll.

The strangers had not made any attempt to hide themselves away and it wasn't long before they were tracked down and a meeting for a dialogue between them and Luca had been arranged, but they refused outright such foolishness to visit Luca in his house. As an act of good faith, Luca agreed to meet them on their own ground to ascertain their reasons for seeking him out, and, if possible, point them in the direction of the person most likely to have a hand in the design of this mistaken venture. The meeting was agreed, Luca turned up with two bodyguards as a precaution, at the same time offering an explanation for their need. They did not extend him any courtesy, only demanded the return of the scroll. Luca's mind immediately became aware of their reason for their presence but denied any knowledge of the scroll, telling them he had handed it over in Lattakia and had not laid eyes on it since that day. Excitedly, he asked for time to explain to them the events of the recent week and how the female and he had become acquainted, and how she stole into his home and abducted his grandson under his very nose and was still missing to this day.

As the time of his interview drew out, Luca sensed their interest in the woman and, knowing that he had their ear was very convincing, when he left them the two were debating an alternative and eventual outcome of a further search. At first they found it difficult to accept that the female they were acquainted with could have no reason to secrete the scroll for herself; after all, she was one of them. Perplexing as it was, Luca's introduction of the female confused them, and it had showed distinctively in their expression. Luca could not unfold the other part of his story, leaving the travellers slightly confused at the news and were equally thrown off course by this change of information as all reports indicated that she was dead. Due to this turn of story, they postponed their intended actions against Luca and decided on a new course of action, to ascertain the truth of Luca's diverse explanation. With this turn of events, they felt that it would cost them little to search for the woman, to discover for themselves if they had been told the truth.

When the news of a search reached the ears of the fugitives in the inn, and that the strangers were paying urchins to seek out certain individuals, it created great concern and a need to act faster. The strangers from across the sea had different methods, knowing this presented a new problem of time, meaning she had to plant the scroll in Luca's office before Robert could continue in his role and she was detected.

As soon as the evening came, she was ready to make her move. Darkness now would be her only cover, the streets were too dangerous to walk and the chance of discovery was too great. The only way, she mused, would be across the rooftops; she could do it quite easily and be safely back before morning. At the right time of lateness when all was quiet, she stood at the high attic window gazing out across the city of twinkling lights, waiting for each one to be finally extinguished before setting off. When she was ready and sure that she enjoyed the freedom of total darkness, she flipped the lock on the high window and looked back to Robert and smiled. It was pointless to try to change her mind and go with her; besides, he did not have the same agility as she on the roof tops, and he may end up injuring himself and worse draw attention to them both. Discovery would be the end and he knew it.

Comfortably she made her way out on to the rooftops soon to be enveloped in the darkness of the night; only the movement of the passing clouds gave occasional outline of her silhouette until she was finally gone and lost to the darkness. Her passage across the town did not go quite as smoothly as she had expected, there were points along her route that caused her to make detours as some streets where too wide for her to cross by rooftops.

Finally, she reached the piazza where Luca's office building was located to her right; there, she stopped to survey her position; seeing that there was no easy approach to it but from the street level, she began to make her way down from the high point that she had occupied. Two guards were posted outside the office entrance, causing her to take an alternative and more difficult approach to gain entry via the adjacent building. Avoiding the guards was easy, they never suspected her presence as she scaled the timberwork of the next building and gained entry through a rickety window.

Once inside, she passed through the building searching as she went unseen for another route into Luca's main office. She climbed a rickety staircase; moonlight drew her attention upward to a skylight window triggering a question, was the adjacent building of the same design offering a duplicate window? It was tricky to reach up to raise the heavy window and open it safely on the rusted hinges she detected, but once open, she was up like a cat and onto the roof of Luca's building where she discovered her assumptions to be correct; and as luck would have it, there was a duplicate window for her to gain access.

The window opened easily into a vacant room posing her no problems, she dropped down into the darkness making contact with the floor with the lightness and agility of a bird. In her quietness, she detected muted sounds in the building emanating from below, others were present perhaps, she feared, in Luca's office.

Her eyes had grown used to the darkness, but she remained still, taking in as much as she could of her surroundings and the sounds below. Slowly, she made for the door; the boards beneath her feet began to loudly squeak even though she was light of body. This was unexpected, the moment the noise had been emitted she had stopped, now she had to look beyond her footsteps and take in as much as she could of this dilapidated building. It was clever of Luca not to repair the floor, through the gloom she was able to see that boards were missing. Carefully, she plotted her way towards the door, easing it open sufficiently to ease her ear into the void of the corridor to receive better the sounds from below of those individuals that that she could hear talking. Below, the distant voices continued to engage in idle conversation, it sounded that they were on the ground floor. Once again, fortunately for her, Luca's guards were not carrying out their duties properly. From her earlier visit here, she remembered that the stairs leading to Luca's office housed the creakiest of treads; any attempt to gain access to the office via them would surely alert the guards, which could also be to her dis-advantage. She took her time to recall Luca's room and the window; it was fitted with bars ruling out entry from the outside. Looking ahead at the narrow passageway once more, she thoughtfully discovered another way open to her.

Not without an element of risk, she decided to embark on the final stage of her task. The floor of the corridor was no different than within the small room having missing boards, she suspected that on the occasions that Luca must have ventured up here, probably to store some of his many documents, he had a rail fitted to the wall to assist his balance in case he should lose his footing over the rotten woodwork. Leaning her weight on the handrail, it appeared sound enough to support her body's feather weight; wedging her back into the corner of the wall she eased herself up onto the rail, steadying herself by placing the flat of her hand against the surface of the ceiling to maintain her balance before she began traversing the hand rail along the length of the wall to the stairs. At the staircase, it became easier as she was able to lean across to the adjacent wall, sliding carefully down the rail until she arrived at Luca's office door. With stealth and ease, she was entering the office whilst the idle chatter continued below, only louder now. As quietly as was possible, she opened the office door; the nauseous smell of burnt candle grease greeted her with its unwelcome waxy stench, it hung within the very fabric of the room causing her to raise her hand to her nostrils. How this man languished here day after day was beyond her.

The task at hand was to secrete the leather scroll in such a way that would not be so easily detected; an item of value would be kept within easy access and near to hand, she thought, to the one seated nearby. At the right of Luca's desk stood a number of shelves stacked with rolled documents, which one would never suspect a valuable scroll to be secreted amongst such mundane contracts. Removing one at random, she unrolled it, placing the leather scroll within before rolling it back up, tying it off and placing it back within the mass of the other papers taking note of its position and shelf. Satisfied at her completed task, her nerves suddenly crackled, jolting her into action as the stairs began creaking as someone climbed them heading towards the office, it had to be one of the guards checking that all was well, ensuring that their duty was being thoroughly carried out. When the door opened, a dim light was proffered into the smelly room followed by a scruffy poking head that scanned the suspected emptiness. The light faded as the door slowly closed and the weighty body trundled downwards to a serenade of the creaking stairs.

She arrived back at the inn with the same degree of silence that she left, surprising all as she entered the room. Lying awake in their beds, waiting for her return and news of her achievement. Robert spoke, asking if her venture was successful, a nod of assent was her response and a slight self-satisfied smile. The bait was in the trap; all Robert had to do was tell his story indicating roughly just where to look.

The following day, Robert made his way briskly to the accommodations of the visiting strangers; he was not eager in his duty and knew that everything depended on getting his story right. Access was not automatically allowed until he mentioned to the servant that he had information of a certain scroll that was being sought; he was told to wait as the door was closed in his face. When it opened again, he was invited forwards and searched before being ushered forwards to confront the two young dark-skinned characters, whose faces bore great smiles on his meeting them.

Unlike Luca's reception, refreshment was offered which Robert respectfully declined; they buzzed about him like a long lost brother, interested in his comfort before they eventually came to the nub of his being present. Robert quickly came to the point, telling them that news of their presence in the city was much talked of and that they had seen Luca. It was true, he admitted, that he did not like Luca at all and he carried news which he felt would not be to their liking. Part of his reason for being here, he told the two, was to warn them of the many deceits of Luca Rici. He continued to tell them, that not so many days previously he had experienced Luca's hospitality by being beaten up, to verify the fact the bruises on his face and body bore out his words. After suffering the beating, he was tossed into the lagoon with a weight attached to his ankle, which, fortunately for him, had been carelessly tied. The story did not seem to be going too well as they probed into the reasons for offering this goodwill towards them; perhaps, he suggested, to start at the beginning. A perplexed look appeared on their faces followed by a smile as an indicator for him to commence.

The tale commenced at the fortress of Hassan, recounting his escape and Kassim's involvement with Luca. Only that he had overheard of the scrolls value had he decided to recover the scroll, using it to bargain for the release of his drugged friend, the grandson of Luca Rici. His lengthy story purposely had gaps relating to the role played by the female associate of theirs, which after much questioning, they eventually prized out of him. Unsure so far of their belief in him, he had no measure of their acceptance thus far; a pensive look coupled with a silence was his only hope that they would show their interest. He was disappointed when they spoke; it was not with eagerness but without feeling and a desire to have the story told to be rid of him; well, that was how he received it. He was sure that he had lost the cause or could it be, he mused, that they were much better at this sort of thing than he?

Desperately he needed some hint, knowing that he had kept to the planned story and felt himself go a little shaky by his lengthy pause. It was as if they had all day to listen and patiently waited, teasing him to give them something really interesting to think about. His silence had been long; he apologised for his hesitation in continuing which was met with a gesturing wave of the hand as if to say in his own time. He straightened himself in the hard chair that had been offered to him and, clearing his throat, began to inform them that he had withheld an important piece of information, which was not going to be to their liking. No response; again, there was a pause for them to hang on; it seemed like a lifetime until a serious sounding note in the voice insisted he continue.

Encouraged by the tone, he hoped that in their waiting their guise of nonchalance only masked their interest. He stumbled to get the words out in such a way as to ease the news of the loss of their brave and tortured friend that was thrown into the lagoon before him. The two came alive from their pretence of disinterest; leaning forward, one asked with a searing look in his eyes for Robert not to stop. With a great sigh, his body dropped to a slumped position as if he were reliving his ordeal. Alas, he offered, that she had lost consciousness from the brutal beating and foul treatment that she had received from the villains belonging to Luca.

"They defiled her before they killed her, then, when they had transported us to as close a spot to catch the tide, they tipped her over into the murky waters, she could not escape the sea as she was heavily chained and sank quickly." The tide was running fast and when he was sent overboard there was little time for him to free himself to look for the girl, survival was uppermost in his mind, which took every ounce of his energy.

The two now were charged, actively agitated by the appalling treatment to one of their own; murder was in their eyes and they could not conceal it as they asked question after question about the diabolical treatment that had been meted out to their associate. They spoke now rapidly in their own tongue; Robert suspected that their outrage as much as anything was due to their blindness of being taken in by Luca. One spoke out probing for the information of the scroll; Robert told them he knew not its actual location but at the time they were in Luca's office. He paused at that point in his story to catch his breath and was urged to continue. Picking up the tale, he told them that whilst in his office, Luca became very agitated when the female began to peer into the shelf of rolled contracts that were stored nearby his seated position, which she suspected held great significance in the search for her master's property.

He was surprised he told them when Luca jumped to his feet, he was clearly angered. Impatiently, he drew her away from where she stood. Thinking back, it was obvious he was afraid that she might discover something of value and who knows, perhaps somewhere nearby was the hidden the scroll you seek. Changing the subject, he invited us to his house to dine. It later became an invitation that we came to dread accepting, due to the fatal conclusion of the visit."

After further questioning that Robert had undergone, the two men seemed satisfied with his tale and thanked him for coming forwards with the information. Before departing, he begged one favour having undergone the recent torments with Luca's men; he was divested of funds to pay his host for his and their associate's accommodations. There was a pause, then, one reached inside his clothing and drew out a small purse of coins, which he threw onto the floor at Robert's feet. As the purse hit the ground, the sound of the coins rang around the quietness of the room, making him feel conscious and slightly embarrassed at the lies he had just told. His body bent forwards and came to a sudden stop as the point of a short sword caught his hand as he was about to take possession of the small pouch. The eyes travelled along the line of the steel blade and up the arm to the bearer who looked Robert in the eye as he asked him if the reason for coming forwards was for the money. Robert drew himself upright and explained that he was an honourable man, and that so far in his life he had never had to beg or ask for money. Being aware of their business and the need to bring the truth to their notice, it was an opportunity to gain a means to pay his way and rid himself of the shame of being something that he was not, a fraud. Before they could pick up on his choice of words with the phrase opportunity, he offered his explanation.

"Revenge was first in my heart, but knowing of your skills and abilities it will keep my hands clean of the blood of the scum that tried to do for me. The money keeps me from becoming nothing more than a thief in the night." He further added that should their paths cross in future times, it may be he in the position to befriend them for their courtesy shown to him this day. There were smiles all around as the sword was lifted; he was free to go as he pleased with a warning that should they feel duped, he too would pay dearly for his misdemeanour.

Back at the inn, they sat around whilst Robert related on the saga he had just endured, telling of the trials he felt he encountered waiting for some clue of acceptance of his story. At one stage, he almost felt like leaving but failure was not in him so he stuck it out; in the end he believed that they too accepted his tale as the truth. He confessed to his friends the difficulty in lying, he hated it; sitting before them he sweated, but was aware that their future depended on its outcome. When Robert had finished, the woman told him that they had tested him, watching his every reaction although he would not be aware of it. She congratulated him, for it was true, as he had suspected they were much better at the game than he. The request for money was also good, she told him, securing their belief that western soldiers were in the main mercenaries and money was tantamount in their everyday life.

"As for me," she said, "by this evening they will be here to check on your story to make sure that you are alone and I likely dead. They will then visit the premises of Luca where they will find the scroll before paying a final farewell visit to him and by morning I swear he will be dead."

She turned and looked at Aldo who was much stronger after almost recovering from his state of prolonged narcosis; he was so much thinner than when Robert last rode with him. Sadly, with his head hung low, he admitted that he feared for his grandfather for all his evil ways. He dreaded the entire mess and the knowledge of what was about to befall him; yet, alas, he realised he was powerless to stop it; after all, he was to be the harbinger of his own fatal demise. He sat quietly saddened by it all, almost shedding a tear for the good times that he had remembered of his grandfather, whilst the other two, on viewing his dejected posture, decided to leave him to his self-consolation. Once outside the room, Robert sympathised the young man's plight but there was none from the woman. She prompted Robert to recall the night on the skiff when they were tossed into the waters of the lagoon without any chance of survival. She now stated that they would work all day clearing away all trace of her being present. Airing the room was another task she had completed, also, she added to Robert they would be apart this night in another room. When the two friends from Allamut arrive, they will soon be checking out Robert's story looking for any sign of her and they will be diligent and silent in their work. She noted the quizzing expression on his face and sharply told him that he had better believe her. There was no argument, the ways of her people were best known to herself; besides, she somehow knew he would lose any wager he would care to make with her.

It was a cloudy evening; when the night sky was at its darkest and the moon had dipped behind the clouds, all was quiet, allowing a blackness to encompass the inn. Aldo slept soundly while Robert laid awake waiting unable to sleep, after what the woman had told him he was expectant for something to happen. Outside there was a slightest sound of a scratching when the window opened, it hardly broke through the silence of the darkened room before an incoming draught blew in, announcing the strangers' arrival. Prepared for their entrance, Robert allowed the entry to take place; there was not a sound at first but he felt a presence of their being close to him. He listened very intently for sounds and could not quite make out what he could faintly detect. His ears strained as he realised what it was he could hear, sniffing, they were trying to pick up traces of the woman's perfume or fragrant body smells as they passed around the room of the sleeping duo. Fortunately, she had not worn any fragrance on her, save her natural one, and the afternoon was well spent in preparation washing out the attic rooms where they had been billeted for which reason had now become apparent to him. His arm hung over the side of the bed close to the wall, a dagger concealed in his hand. Although they were no threat to him, he was not taking any chances should they get to close for his comfort.

The intruders exposed themselves as they passed through the door, catching the light from the moon that had been partially illuminated by a passing cloud. They did not stay long and returned leaving the door slightly ajar in their passing; there was no sound in the room or at the window; they disappeared into the night as quietly as they came. He lay awake, stunned by their efficiency and remembered somebody prompting him of their expected arrival later that evening. Damn her, he thought, she was right again, as much as he wanted to, there would be little sleep for him that night with the thoughts of what was to follow.

The skylight on Luca's office building roof opened without a sound and a dark shadowy figure slipped into the darkness of the interior being immediately consumed by the darkness below. The men from Allamut worried not about darkness; to them they were quite at home within it. They dropped into the emptiness of the room as quiet as cats landing from a tree. Like her, they encountered the sounds from below and cautioned to the sound. The board sang out for them as they did for her, warning them that ahead lay other problems to overcome. They were unaware of the condition of the fabric of the building and the creaking boards continued to mar their progress, but not for long, as they soon spied the means to overcome the dangers that lay ahead. They remained still when they heard a guard at the bottom of the stairs checking out the noise above; the glow of a lamplight showed itself below and a guard who had inquisitively climbed the stairs as far as Luca's office called out to his associate that all was clear. He opened the door, pushed the lamp forwards and peering inside saw nothing but an unoccupied room.

"Rats more likely," came the shout, informing his companion below for what he considered the noise to have emanated from. Closing the door, he made his way down the creaking stairs back to his wine and card game, muttering the words 'rats, rats,' being more concerned that his cards had been exposed during his absence.

Warned by the sound of the creaking boards, the intruders availed themselves to the handrail in the same way as their predecessor, silently traversing down the stairs to the office door.

Inside the room they surveyed the many shelves of scrolls for what they were looking for, there were so many they had to laboriously work their way around the room before standing on another creaking board. It wasn't long before the straining boards sounded the approach of the guard making his way up the stairs again. This time, when the door opened, the hidden intruder could see the silhouette of the guard against the glow of the lamplight. In his outstretched hand, the watchman held a flickering oil lamp and a cudgel in the other; as he walked forwards into the room, a curved blade sliced through his jugular vein and across the throat quietly killing the unsuspecting guard. He stood stunned in a motionless state, copious amounts of blood spewed over his corpulent greasy façade. Numbed and dazed, his deathly stance held in balance, the intruder's skill was precise and wise. Before his victim finally dropped to his knees, his overweight mass was being supported by the hand of both intruders as his collapsing body was lowered to the floor, being shrewd and careful to the end, the lamp had first been taken from the dying man's hand, which was willingly given up, whilst the assassin watched him carefully as he became a corpse.

There was little time now. Aided by the use of the lamp's illumination, he quickly spun around to see quite clearly the last shelf of scrolls as described by the westerner earlier that day. One by one they were tossed out onto the floor until a littered mound had soon built itself up into an untidy heap. There appeared to be hundreds, before one betrayed an extraordinary weight, proving to be worthy of investigation. Once again, they were alerted to the sound of the creaking stairs; they knew the dead man shared the responsibility with a friend; they must allow him enter and take cover once again. Certain that there were no more men below, the intruders had very little time left to waste, when the guard entered the room, the silent blade was thrust into him causing him to immediately to fall, but the kill was unclean. The guard tried as he could to send out an alarm before a returning blade was dispatched to finish the job. A sound of joyous expectation heralded the finding of item of interest; on drawing forth the heavy rolled contract, the leather scroll they were searching for fell to the ground with a bump. His hand grabbed the prize and whispering a prayer to his God, inserted it into his dark tunic; picking it up, they made their way quickly from the building.

Luca lay sleeping deeply in his large comfortable bed, his mouth half open allowing free passage to his snoring sounds to dissipate into the darkened openness of the room. Suddenly, he began to choke unknowingly; linen was being stuffed into his mouth and he could not move; in his half awakened state he realised he had been pinned down. A lamp was lit and faces showed themselves through his sleepy haze, Arab demons were upon him, they propped up the terrified Luca. Their accusations of heinous deeds of double dealing issued forth, the words hissed through their vengeful teeth of his insidious lies and foul murder of their associate. His head shook so hard in denial and temper that an abundance of tears fell rolling over the thin tissue of skin that covered his wizened and mortified face. The face that was once crazed with fine veins beneath the tissue paper surface of skin giving an impression of a healthy bloom was no more, all blood had now drained away to white, ashen with the horror that he knew faced him.

The leather scroll was waved before him; his recognition of it caused his wet red eyes to bulge in astonishment. Wailing in panic through his linen gag, he finally recognised that he had been outsmarted and his head dropped as he conceded his defeat, it appeared to his assassins an admission of his guilt and the blades of vengeance fell heavily upon him many times leaving his blood-soaked body lying prostrate across the bed.

The news of Luca's death spread like a plague throughout the city; when the event was made known to Robert via the landlord of the inn, it was retold in a most graphic form by an excited innkeeper. Robert knew that he could not withhold the news to his young friend of the outcome of the previous evening's events but hardly knew how to spare him the pain, nor could he shield him from seeing his mutilated grandfather in his present state.

Within three days, Luca had been quietly buried and Aldo had been notified that he was his grandfather's sole beneficiary. He had inherited a vast fortune but had no stomach for the business interests of which there were a great many. Instead, he appointed Enrico, the long-suffering crippled clerk as the new overseer, managing all transactions with a salary fitting to the position. In return, he pledged his loyalty to the young master, ensuring that from that moment on the name of Rici would lend itself to honest trading, a name to be proud of and honoured.

One evening after the party had eaten, when they were relaxing around the innkeeper's little snug room, Aldo broke the news that he was making plans to return to the Levant; there was much that needed to be put to rights. Robert broke in lending his agreement to the suggestion but he was not sure how it would be for him, having broken off from a mission to chase across the world after a friend. He turned and looked at the woman whose face held straight against her disappointment now that they were about to disband. He was about to ask what her plans were, but he sensed her feelings and thought better of posing the question. Free from the need to be in hiding, and relaxed from tensions, they talked freely that evening and late.

Aldo retired, leaving the others alone; he sensed that there were things that the two had to speak about, especially now that they spoken of leaving. For a short while after Aldo had left the room, the two chatted endlessly but always skirted the topic of parting. Robert, desperate to discuss the future, did everything but come to his point. Eventually, and tired of waiting, she suggested that she retire, hoping that he may finally have the courage to bring up the subject that they may talk of their future plans together. It was not that he was without courage, but apprehensive that his own ideas of the future together may cause her embarrassment or worse still that she should turn against him, causing him equal embarrassment.

His hesitancy was almost his downfall; she rose, crossed the room almost reaching the door; he blurted out part of his intended question of staying with him when they reached the Levant. Toying with him but without any purpose to fluster or make him feel any discomfort, she walked back, sitting close to him to reaffirm that she had already agreed to return with him. In her answer, she intimated that there was more, but firmly believed that it was for him to broach the subject as to what it was that he actually wanted. When it came to matters of the heart, his head became rather clouded and embarrassment or confusion numbed his judgement. Her thoughts were more practical; she had more to lose staying with Robert; it would be for only a short time before she could be arrested for her earlier crimes. Knowing that he would be unable to do anything to help her, she suggested that they both think about it and not make any hasty decisions before the time comes. She left the room, leaving Robert to ponder on a plan to solve their dilemma.

Aldo had taken a new house for himself; the old house of his grandfather's had too many memories and the city wanted to meet this young rich man who was only home for a short time from the Crusading wars.

The following afternoon, whilst on the terrace overlooking the tranquil lagoon, the gentle breeze blew across from the open sea causing ripples in the sea's rhythmic swell. The gentle movement caught up in the bright afternoon sun sent shimmering spangled flashes dancing across the broken surface of the lagoon to dazzle the eyes; out there was another world. Enjoying the serenity of their respite, life seemed not to hold a trouble.

They were well-rested after their ordeal of Luca and it was Robert who, after a long pensive mood, broke into the soft gentle composure that nature offered them. He broke the news that there was a ship leaving on the evening tide for Tyre the following day and it was his intention to be on it, besides, it was high time that he returned. His departure was long overdue; Lord knows, he said, what is going to happen when he reported back. He knew that those that waited on his news would expect more of him when his explanation came out. If the others failed to notify Acre of events, he could find himself on a charge of treason; he dared not imagine what that could lead to. Being an honourable man, he had to go back and speak truthfully of his actions and the reasons for them. Being truthful, he was a little apprehensive to grasp the nettle of action; he had a woman that he wanted by his side; but his time had come, he did not know what was happening abroad nor could he know what to expect when he stepped ashore. Duty was one thing, but he had to know what became of his brother and friends, a unit of such men does not break up so easily; the questions that had passed through his mind whilst his head rested upon his pillow were countless and repetitive.

There was a silence in the company as others thought of his intention to leave; their own thoughts withheld until the woman acknowledged that his thinking was correct and that it may be better if she accompanied him, should he agree. Of that there was no question; he reached out for her, touching her hand as a sign of his acceptance. The thought of her at his side was not only comforting but reassuring; he hoped she had been considering staying with him. He had a second chance to make another attempt to talk of their future and there was a faint smile on his face, which did not go undetected as she flicked her eyes across in his direction in time to conceive it. Aldo had said that he too was eager to go, but his grandfather's affairs had been complicated and difficult to unravel; besides, he had seen the Duke over his abduction and was required to spend some time at his side for a forthcoming event. Robert suspected the Duke's daughter might have had a hand in persuading him from leaving; she was young and quite a beauty. Aldo was her match, after all, he had overnight become an extremely wealthy man worthy of supporting a young woman of such noble birth, giving the assurance that the Duke's daughter would be well cared for and able to continue her life in the style that she was accustomed to.

They spent the rest of the warm afternoon simply enjoying their own company, happily remembering their old friends and acquaintances that they genuinely had the pleasure of meeting up with again.

It was not quite the same for her, as then they were on opposing sides and from time to time in their arguments she teased them over their own military blunders for her own pleasure for not giving their opponents the respect that they deserved.

By noon the following day, they had assembled at the quayside and ready to board the ship for Tyre stopping off at Cyprus to replenish supplies and discharge their cargoes.

At the dockside, Aldo embraced his good friend Robert and wished him God speed, reassuring him that it would not be too long before he would join them wherever they may be. They were warm sentiments, though Robert knew that his friend's life was changing and he would not return to the fighting; now that a female was involved with him, she would make sure that his young friend's future was a safe one. If she loved him, and he was sure of that, he knew she was intelligent enough to ensure that she would not be his widow; besides, the Duke was too powerful for him to go against the wishes of his beloved daughter. He wished Aldo the very best for his future and he expected that it would not be too long a wait before the wedding bells of St Marks were ringing out a wedding announcement, but seriously believed that it was not goodbye. When it came to the female, she too succumbed to Aldo's long embrace and in a whispering voice he thanked her for all her efforts to bring him back from his fated sleep. He had never mentioned anything of the abduction, though they held themselves together closely in a warm embrace; whispering in her ear sincerely that he absolved her of any part in it all and hoped also that they would meet again soon. She smiled as she stepped back, telling him that she also would miss his friendship; to escape the embarrassment of showing any weakness or sadness at their parting, she suggested they had better leave before the captain pulled up the plank and left them behind for Aldo to care for.

All three came together for one final parting embrace before Robert and the girl broke free and walked the plank to board the ship. They stood on deck waving to Aldo with their own thoughts in their minds of leaving. When the plank was drawn up, it was a sign to them that the parting was final; it is painful to leave friends and they all felt it deeply. The ropes were untied from their moorings and orders given to let go of all lines; Aldo shouted his last goodbye to Robert and suddenly fell silent as if he had forgotten something. He shouted up to the girl that he never got to know her name and he now asked for it. She smiled and replied that it was not known to any man yet, but hoped that it would soon be revealed when asked properly, tilting her head to one side slightly as if indicating that it would be made known to Robert first. Unfortunately, because he was standing alongside her, he was unable to pick up on her gesture and wondered why Aldo was knowingly grinning so broadly at her response.

The ship began to edge away from the quay in a bobbing motion.

"Set half sail," shouted the captain as mariners moved to their stations. The outgoing tide pulled the ship away from the wall whilst Aldo stood watching the ship begin to turn seawards. Once, a long time ago it seemed, it was he that was leaving and it was his grandfather that was standing in a place just as he was filled with a similar sadness in his breast. Clear of the dock and in deeper water, the sails caught the wind and they waved their last goodbye to their friend. With the ship in full sail, their speed increased with the wind, filled the hungry billowing main canvas to speed them into the far reaches of the lagoon and the open sea. Aldo had patiently waited on the quay, watching the ship clear the harbour and sail out to the horizon; so much had happened in his life, good and bad events came and went just as did his good friends.

There was only the two of them now; she turned to Robert, looking long into his open manly face, stating that now that we have parted from his friend what were they to do? She was serious, declaring for the first time that she could not go back or ever contemplate being in any stronghold that Robert would reside for fear of her past catching up to her.

"You understand, Robert, that I would be unwelcome; my history conflicts with everything that your people are. How long will it be before your people learned of my identity and what terrors are held in the dungeons of your castles? No, we both know they are far worse than those of Luca Rici. Like the Old Man of the Mountain, your holy men enjoy their pastime with the hot irons and the contraption they call the rack. Once in their grip, they have a way of extracting the words they want to hear from those that come under their power. It is not for me; your superiors, those men in high office, would not think to spare me. To keep their hands clean they may even give notice of my being alive to Allamut. There are many ways of dying; believe me, death would be certain and it would not come swiftly. You know that don't you, Robert?" She spoke knowledgeably, for she was not naïve; he did not know how to answer her, his head dropped as though he knew that she was right once again. He had evaded the subject for so long that she had him backed up against a wall with nowhere to go. He had foolishly believed that he could protect her from all evils, but she had seen through his day dreams into reality. Only when she voiced the truth did he realise the future; it told him he had to let her go or seal her death as sure as they stood on the deck together. Living without her was not in his plans, though at this moment in time he had no alternative ideas. Her and her kind, he admitted, were not all bad; he thought that he could convince himself but he had seen her in action and knew that his good intentions were not enough to save her from any of the assassin's sent after her, or even those of his own people or anyone that could place her in danger once he was returned to service.

The ship ploughed its course lazily southwards through a calm sea and into the late sunny afternoon; together they remained quiet standing facing out to sea, letting the breeze wash over them and the salt spray flick at them as they harboured their secret thoughts to themselves.

It was a peaceful and harmonious voyage for the couple; they were always at each other's side throughout their time aboard, but their time together was solemn and without the light-hearted air they had begun to share in Venice. It had struck him that he did not have to return to Acre to make a report; to do that would be an indication that nothing was known of his existence. They could leave the ship in Cyprus and start a new life; it all seemed to fall into place as a solution to his dilemma. That was until he told her of his plan.

It hurt her to have to say the things that had to be said to make him see sense. "Do you think that I would stay with you, an honourable man, Robert, to wait for the day when you heart died because of me? Realising that you had turned to being a traitor to everything you knew was right. Do you think that happiness is made of argument and distrust; our love and everything that holds us close will shrivel and die becoming worthless, for that is what it will amount to."

"No," he whispered, afraid to say anything further. He held her close with a tear welling in his eye; he knew he was losing her and she was the only one that was brave enough to release him from the torment in his heart.

"You will face your superiors and take their punishment. What happened to us is no one's fault, we have taken a wrong course on the road of life, it is fate. I tell you this," she said, looking Robert in the eyes where he traced sadness in hers, "we have nothing to feel guilty for, but you will never know any happiness until you have suffered your fate, and when that happens, Robert, I will once again be there to heal your pain. As for me, I am not the rock you think I am; I too am made of flesh and blood. I admit to you that once I was hardened and cold, forged like steel into serving those that I swore service to; that is until I met you. You have changed me and given me a reason to live like a normal person. I cannot deny that I learnt to carry my pain a long time ago in Allamut, knowing that you cannot always have what you want. Believe me, my love, it pains me as much as it hurts you. I may have to live in the shadows and hidden places, but I will never be far away from you. I will survive for the time that is to come. Concealed and waiting; though I long to be with you, I cannot risk foolish thoughts of revealing myself for fear for my own safety but I promise that we will be together again." He held her tightly, knowing that she had the strength of heart to see them through; shamed though he was, it gave him strength knowing that. Standing, listening to her spoken thoughts made his bravery seem half-hearted compared to hers. She was right; he would stand before his judges believing his course of action to leave when he did was right; how was he to know otherwise.

In the coming days, land was sighted; the waters grew busy, seeing more ships than was normal, all heading westwards. It took another two and a half days to reach the port of Kyrenia at the northern side of the island of Cyprus. There, they witnessed broken ships that had limped home as though they had been in a sea battle. The harbour and surrounding area was choked with shipping, so much so that they could not see any navigable way into the port. All aboard ship were puzzled at the sight; the captain needed to be ashore having business there; it seemed that getting through these ships was going to be a trial in itself. The two watched with interest as the captain was lowered to a boat awaiting him to reach his agent ashore; there was business of the Rici line to be transacted and he was keen to see it completed. Something told Robert that he had to be on that boat; he looked at her and in an instant she sensed his need; both hastened towards the captain as he was about to be lowered to the waiting boat. At their call, the captain turned, stopping the men from lowering him.

"We are coming with you," called Robert. The captain was not a man to be taking orders from strangers and brusquely told them he had no time to take his passengers on a pleasure trip ashore. New to his position, he was not aware to whom he was talking to; he cared not to waste his time, telling the men to continue lowering him. Robert felt that he had better retaliate in a gentle way rather than to attack him verbally.

"You know that I was seen off by your employer, Senior Rici, the man whose life I travelled from the east to save, and did so. He is one of my closest friends. I ask you captain, think how will he receive such news that you withheld me from carrying out my sworn duty and made me swim ashore?" The captain stared hard at Robert thinking fast; the man before him was a stranger, why should he accept such a story? He was loathe to believe in Robert and demanded proof that he was who he purported to be; after a deep breath, Robert drew out a paper that Aldo had handed to him before leaving. He was in two minds whether to grab him for his insinuation that he was a liar, but he knew it was better for Aldo's sake that the captain should complete his journey. Once the captain read the note, he was soon apologising; the dilemma he had been caught up in was cleared. Quickly, his decision was reversed and the men instructed to prepare to accommodate other places to be taken ashore. He was not foolish enough to lose his first ship for the sake of injuring the friends of his employer; it was nothing to him to drop two passengers off that may turn out to be a problem later.

The harbour was large in size with a capacity to take in many ships, so many that Robert could hardly count them. It was indeed a maze to manoeuvre between the ships at anchor and a danger for those in such a small boat to attempt; they had to take extra care that they were not caught up in the swaying huddle of ships as they navigated their way through on their way forwards to the quay wall. All the time, Robert was asking what was the cause of this gathering armada? Nearing the quay, they could clearly see crewmen leaving their ships carrying many sick people ashore on pallets. At first, thoughts of plague ran through his mind; eager to discover the truth, he waited patiently as they neared the steps up to the quay. Ashore, he was stopped in his tracks as he realised that they were not sick individuals but wounded soldiers and civilians. The last words he heard from the young captain were to be back at the boat before the tide changed or he would have to leave without them. By the amount of casualties, it was clear that these people had been under siege and fled from an army. Many of them being military men were being sought out and taken to the castle where they would hopefully find care and attention to their injuries. He stopped the first person he could, asking them what had happened for the cause of such flight; the answer shook him rigid.

"We are the survivors of Antioch," he told Robert, "the greatest Muslim army we have ever seen besieged us; they covered the hills around us like ants on a shit heap; they battered the fortress night and day for a week with siege engines the like that we had never seen before. When the walls were nought but rubble they gave us the opportunity to flee. The road was open to us and we fled whilst the soldiers chose death by remaining to stand trying to hold the walls. I'm afraid," the man said, "I fear not a man will survive that onslaught; I hope sir that you have no kin back there; for it was said that there would be no quarter given."

At that moment, Robert winced and his face creased, thinking of his brother and friends. Could they have been on the walls, he asked himself; the news shook him and he looked to the woman for an answer. Reading his thoughts, she held on to him adding that if they were there, they would do what brave men do; duty was always with them. The quayside was lined with the wounded being tended; there were hundreds it seemed, some blood soaked, others just wounded, old people exhausted and too old to sustain the torment they were put through. Those that were wounded received make shift dressings until a physician made his way around to them; some, Robert knew, would die before he came; it was a wonder they had survived the sea crossing. Men they passed lay almost delirious, calling for water or loved ones that were long dead; they probably tried to hang on to their possessions back there, but the truth was obvious, they would never see those loved ones again. For their valour, those that were no threat must have been offered the chance of freedom along with the walking wounded; with some generals mercy was often in their heart for those that had fought well. His eyes closed in sympathy for those that remained; they, especially women and children, once the soldiers had satisfied their needs, no matter what mental state they were in, would be destined for the slave markets. What a mess, what a loss. He dearly hoped that Edward was alive; he walked on blindly thinking that he should have been there; his mind was filled with confused thoughts of guilt. There were wounded soldiers lying around hanging on to life; he was about to help one when he recognised the old captain nearby from Antioch calling for water. Strange for a soldier of his rank to be here, Robert thought, bending forwards he spoke to him; but the man was only half way alive.

"Can you help him?" he appealed to the woman, but there was a blank look on her face; the man was dying, what was it that she was expected to do? He pulled her close, "I need to talk to him," I need to know that Edward..." she broke away in a disturbed state.

"Robert he is dying, I know that it is painful for you."

"Please," he implored her, "help me."

"I have no tricks, only the powder to use to jolt his mind and he may not be strong enough to survive it."

"Please," he begged once more, his pleading eyes stared helplessly. She would not deny him anything, only warned hesitantly that it may finish him, and to do that she needed water to dilute the mixture. There was no shortage of that; he had noticed enough pitchers nearby for those in need. He returned with a crude-shaped cup with enough water to fulfil his need. She was hesitant and looked to him again asking if he was certain of his decision. A nod was all she needed; asking him to cover her from view, she opened the ring to spill enough powder into the water to do its work. The old man took the potion and was peaceful for a while; when the powder began working he spoke only of ramblings, of the end of the world and of the falling rocks from the loaded trebuchets. They both bent close to him as she ordered that he remember the men sent from Acre. There was much going on in the confusion of his mind between pain and memory, but the powder would bind him to the attention of the speaking voice that soothe his pain. He suddenly grew restless; fearing that his agitation may be bringing on some kind of seizure. There was a rattle in his throat; through his garbled utterance they heard that the blind man was dead.

"Were there others?" she urged.

"Gone," he said, "gone." His eyes flickered as if some clarity came to him; he saw Robert and asked for more water. This was bad news indeed; Robert did no more than place the refreshing water cup to his lips; he had not recognised Robert; all his attention was in struggling to drink the water, thanking him for his kindness.

"Do you remember me?" Robert urged. "We met some time ago and argued in your office. I had come from Acre with other men, are they alive?" All he received was a glazed look from the captain. "It's me, Robert Simmonwood, do you remember me?" He wanted to shake the captain but for his weakness. He tried as much as he could to appeal to his memory but the old captain was quiet.

With a sudden haunting outburst of accusation, he cried out, "You left us, you left us. Traitor!" he screamed, "Traitor!" It seemed that everybody on the quay had stopped at the sound of the accusation; a silence descended and all eyes fixed towards this man accompanied by an eastern woman being called a traitor. This was a bad turn of events; people were so shocked; they were beginning to gather in disbelief that one of their own could be responsible for all this suffering. Robert had to leave; there was no point in arguing with this man or a mob. Then approaching towards him, he saw soldiers and knew that he would never explain anything to them rationally with so many dead and dying lying around.

"Come," he said, drawing the woman with him, "come quickly or else we will be torn apart by the mob." Walking away, there was agitation in the voices of the mob that was growing, they were angered and began calling after him; to enlarge the lie, the old captain continued in his ramblings calling him a spy. Up into a maze of streets, he was driven to escape the eyes and attention of those back at the quay; rounding a corner of the street he urged her to hurry.

"It seems that it was not such a good idea to arouse the captain and if I'm not mistaken there will be some kind of reward out for me before nightfall. Christ's blood," he cursed, "this has turned out to be a real mess." Away from the crowd, they entered a small empty square. Here they stopped to gather their thoughts, only to see three soldiers emerge from an alley. They were hunting him like an animal and recognised him as their man; three against one seemed good odds to them as they worked out a plan of capture walking towards him.

"Lay down your sword, traitor," their leader said. He was a small round man; a sergeant with a big mouth with a thugs way about him that should have known better than not to assess an enemy. Worse still, Robert could smell the sweat off him and it appeared as though he was in need of a wash. The other two were no better; there was no lawful opposition on this island to challenge their ability. Robert could see that they were only brave among simple folk that presented no threat. One of the men asked if he was responsible for all these people dying.

"The old man called you a spy, it is our duty to bring you before our leader to serve trial."

"I won't be going anywhere with you," Robert told them, "but I will bring myself to your master when the heat of the crowd has subsided, I give you my word on that."

"You give us your word, did you hear that boys?" the sergeant said laughing. "And while you're giving us your word, I suppose you will be aboard some ship bound for home. No, I don't think so. Take him, boys." Swords were drawn and Robert reacted as he would.

"I don't wish to injure any of you, but think again, I beg you."

There was a charge and the clashing of steel, a scream issued forth as Robert side stepped an oncoming sword and quickly slashed down onto an opponent's arm, cutting him deep. He would be out of action for a time; the others tried to take advantage of Robert's action but they were too slow to be a danger; meanwhile, Robert parried another sword and followed through, while the woman had stuck a small blade into the thigh of another. That made three wounded men that had nowhere to go or be in a fit state to take anyone anywhere. Moaning, they were left helpless on the ground nursing their wounds.

Robert knelt telling them that he didn't want to fight with his own people, but he added sneeringly, "You are poor excuses for soldiers that can't think of nought but your own favours. Come," he said to the woman, "we must leave this place."

"Leave!" exclaimed the sergeant, "You won't get far, spy. We'll have you on a bonfire yet, and I'll be there to spit in your eye as you fry." Robert was about to go back and finish the loud mouth but she held him.

"We must go. We are in this together now." They left hurriedly and made for a way cross country to be lost in the greenery and out of sight. A little further on he stopped; he held her, thanking her for her action in the fight.

"I am a wanted man now. That means if you stay with me you also will be branded as a criminal and subject to the same punishment. This I cannot allow, for I love you too much to bring you to such an end." For once he had admitted what he had not been able to say all this time; it confused her a little, though she had already made that step in declaring her thoughts and having stood alongside him in the fight. Once again, she had to explain what he failed to see in their relationship, pulling away, she asked him; if he did not see her taking part in his defence and the crime of wounding a king's officer.

"As for being a criminal, I have been one all my life. I too do not want to give up on you now that we are branded as one of the same. Robert, every moment now is precious. Let us be together, it is our only chance to outlive this dilemma, so let us not waste it and be rid of indecision once and for all. We may be hunted but we will be together trying to unravel the dilemma that has fallen upon us." Robert held her to him, his eyes searched the hills and the streets leading to them, there were people in them and he could not tell if they were coming for him.

"You're right," he admitted, "that's what we will do," and hastily hurried her along with him to the cover of the roadside shrubbery, there they scrambled along the edges of the ditches until they were free of the buildings and able to make their way up into the hills, but before he left the cover of the trees he kissed her and told her he loved her.